Two i... ...featuring the Lester family

Mr Harry Lester
rescues a beautiful, provocative widow
but faces
An Unwilling Conquest

Miss Antonia Mannering
could dwindle into becoming an old
maid or make
A Comfortable Wife

Author Note

The two books in this volume, AN UNWILLING CONQUEST and A COMFORTABLE WIFE, continue the stories of characters met in the earlier two volumes of the Lester family books, namely Harry Lester, and his rakish friend Philip, Lord Ruthven. The Lesters were the first family I created where successive books dealt with the romances of siblings and friends, and as such the Lester books were the conceptual precursors for many of my subsequent works. Readers everywhere now flock to such works, happily 'tuning in' for the next 'episode' to see who next falls victim to love, and with whom, and how.

In AN UNWILLING CONQUEST, Harry, the second Lester brother, flees London for Newmarket, determined to escape any leg-shackle fate might have waiting for him in the ballrooms. Fate, however, proves rather more far-sighted, having arranged for a distraction in the person of Mrs Lucinda Babbacombe – who, to Harry's irritation, he finds he cannot ignore – to be waiting along the Newmarket road.

Subsequently, in A COMFORTABLE WIFE, Philip, Lord Ruthven, having seen Harry married, reluctantly turns his attention to his own lack of a wife. In this, he discovers his stepmother's niece, Antonia Mannering, very ready to assist him. But Antonia has her own agenda, which leads them both to re-evaluate what they truly need for a comfortable life.

I hope you enjoy these final two volumes about the Lester family.

Happy Reading!

Stephanie Laurens

STEPHANIE LAURENS

A Suitable Marriage

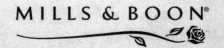

MILLS & BOON®

*MILLS & BOON and MILLS & BOON with the Rose Device
are registered trademarks of the publisher.*

*First published in Great Britain 2004 by
Harlequin Mills & Boon Limited,
Eton House, 18-24 Paradise Road,
Richmond, Surrey, TW9 1SR*

A SUITABLE MARRIAGE © Harlequin Books S.A. 2004

The publisher acknowledges the copyright holder of the
individual works as follows:

An Unwilling Conquest © Stephanie Laurens 1996
A Comfortable Wife © Stephanie Laurens 1997

ISBN 0 263 84095 6

062-0504

*Printed and bound in Spain
by Litografia Rosés S.A., Barcelona*

CONTENTS

The first romances **Stephanie Laurens** ever read were those of Georgette Heyer, and romances set in Regency times continue to be her favourites. After escaping from the dry world of professional science, Stephanie took up writing such romances for her own pleasure. Now residing in a leafy suburb of Melbourne, Australia, she divides her free time between her husband, two teenage daughters and two cats – Shakespeare and Marlowe. The cats, needless to say, are the most demanding.

Readers are invited to visit Stephanie at her website: www.stephanielaurens.com

Already available from Stephanie Laurens:

A Season for Marriage
combining
The Reason for Marriage
and
A Lady of Expectations

An Unwilling Conquest

Chapter One

"Is it the devil we're running from, then?"

The question, uttered in the mildest of tones, made Harry Lester wince. "Worse," he threw over his shoulder at his groom and general henchman, Dawlish. "The matchmaking mamas—in league with the dragons of the *ton*." Harry edged back on the reins, feathering a curve at speed. He saw no reason to ease the wicked pace. His match greys, sleek and powerful, were quite content to keep the bits between their teeth. His curricle rushed along in their wake; New-market lay ahead. "And we're not running—it's called a strategic retreat."

"Is that so? Well, can't say I blame you," came in Dawlish's dour accents. "Who'd ever have thought to see Master Jack landed—and without much of a fight, if Pinkerton's on the up. Right taken aback, is Pinkerton." When this information elicited no response, Dawlish added, "Considering his position, he is."

Harry snorted. "Nothing will part Pinkerton from Jack—not even a wife. He'll swallow the pill when the time comes."

"Aye—p'raps. Still, can't say I'd relish the prospect of answering to a missus—not after all these years."

Harry's lips quirked. Realising that Dawlish, riding on the

box behind him, couldn't see it, he gave into the urge to smile. Dawlish had been with him forever, having, as a fifteen-year-old groom, attached himself to the second son of the Lester household the instant said son had been put atop a pony. Their old cook had maintained it was a clear case of like to like; Dawlish's life was horses—he had recognised a master in the making and had followed doggedly in his wake. "You needn't worry, you old curmudgeon. I can assure you I've no intention, willingly or otherwise, of succumbing to any siren's lures."

"All very well to say so," Dawlish grumbled. "But when these things happen, seems like there's no gainsaying them. Just look at Master Jack."

"I'd rather not," Harry curtly replied. Dwelling on his elder brother's rapid descent into matrimony was an exercise guaranteed to shake his confidence. With only two years separating them, he and Jack had led much the same lives. They'd come on the town together more than ten years ago. Admittedly, Jack had less reason than he to question love's worth, nevertheless, his brother had been, as Dawlish had observed, a most willing conquest. The fact made him edgy.

"You planning on keeping from London for the rest of yore life?"

"I sincerely hope it won't come to that." Harry checked the greys for a slight descent. The heath lay before them, a haven free of matchmakers and dragons alike. "Doubtless my uninterest will be duly noted. With any luck, if I lay low, they'll have forgotten me by next Season."

"Wouldn't have thought, with all the energy you've put into raising a reputation like you have, that they'd be so keen."

Harry's lip curled. "Money, Dawlish, will serve to excuse any number of sins."

He waited, expecting Dawlish to cap the comment with some gloomy pronouncement to the effect that if the madams of society could overlook his transgressions then no one was safe. But no comment came; his gaze fixed unseeing on his leader's ears, Harry grudgingly reflected that the wealth with which he and his brothers, Gerald as well as Jack, had recently been blessed, was indeed sufficient to excuse a lifetime of social sins.

His illusions were few—he knew who and what he was—a rake, one of the wolves of the *ton,* a hellion, a Corinthian, a superlative rider and exceptional breeder of quality horseflesh, an amateur boxer of note, an excellent shot, a keen and successful huntsman on the field and off. For the past ten and more years, Society had been his playing field. Capitalising on natural talents, and the position his birth had bestowed, he had spent the years in hedonistic pleasure, sampling women much as he had the wines. There'd been none to gainsay him, none to stand in his path and challenge his profligate ways.

Now, of course, with a positively disgusting fortune at his back, they'd be lining up to do so.

Harry snorted and refocused on the road. The sweet damsels of the *ton* could offer until they were blue in the face—he wasn't about to buy.

The junction with the road to Cambridge loomed ahead. Harry checked his team, still sprightly despite their dash from London. He'd nursed them along the main road, only letting them have their heads once they'd passed Great Chesterford and picked up the less-frequented Newmarket road. They'd passed a few slower-moving carriages; most of the gentlemen intent on the week's racing would already be in Newmarket.

About them, the heath lay flat and largely featureless, with only a few stands of trees, windbreaks and the odd coppice to lend relief. There were no carriages approaching on the Cambridge road; Harry swung his team onto the hard surface and flicked the leader's ear. Newmarket—and the comfort of his regular rooms at the Barbican Arms—lay but a few miles on.

"To y'r left."

Dawlish's warning growl came over his shoulder in the same instant Harry glimpsed movement in the stand of trees bordering the road ahead. He flicked both horses' withers; as the lash softly swooshed back up the whip-handle, he slackened the reins, transferring them to his left hand. With his right, he reached for the loaded pistol he kept under the seat, just behind his right boot.

As his fingers closed about the chased butt, he registered the incongruity of the scene.

Dawlish put it into words, a heavy horse pistol in his hands. "On the king's highway in broad daylight—never-you-mind! What's the world a-coming to, I asks you?"

The curricle sped on.

Harry wasn't entirely surprised when the men milling in the trees made no attempt to halt them. They were mounted but, even so, would have had the devil of a time hauling in the flying greys. He counted at least five as they flashed past, all in frieze and heavily muffled. The sound of stifled cursing dwindled behind them.

Dawlish muttered darkly, rummaging about re-stowing his pistols. "Stap me, but they even had a wagon backed up in them trees. Right confident of their haul they must be."

Harry frowned.

The road curved ahead; he regathered the slack reins and checked the greys fractionally.

They rounded the curve—Harry's eyes flew wide.

He hauled back on the reins with all his strength, slewing the greys across the road. They came to a snorting, stamping halt, their noses all but in the low hedge. The curricle rocked perilously, then settled back on its springs.

Curses turned the air about his ears blue.

Harry paid no attention; Dawlish was still up behind him, not in the ditch. Before him, on the other hand, was a scene of disaster.

A travelling carriage lay on its side, not in the ditch but blocking most of the road. It looked as if one of the back wheels had disintegrated; the ponderous contraption, top-heavy with luggage, had toppled sideways. The accident had only just occurred—the upper wheels of the carriage were still slowly rotating. Harry blinked. A young lad, a groom presumably, was struggling to haul a hysterical girl from the ditch. An older man, the coachman from his attire, was hovering anxiously over a thin grey-haired woman, laid out on the ground.

The coach team was in a flat panic.

Without a word, Harry and Dawlish leapt to the ground and ran to calm the horses.

It took a good five minutes to soothe the brutes, good, strong coach horses with the full stubbornness and dim wits of their breed. With the traces finally untangled, Harry left the team in Dawlish's hands; the young groom was still helplessly pleading with the tearful girl while the coachman dithered over the older woman, clearly caught between duty and a wish to lend succour, if he only knew how.

The woman groaned as Harry walked up. Her eyes were closed; she lay straight and rigid on the ground, her hands crossed over her flat chest.

"My ankle—!" A spasm of pain twisted her angular features, tight under an iron-grey bun. "Damn you, Joshua—when I get back on my feet I'll have your hide for a footstool, I will." She drew her breath in in a painful hiss. "*If* I ever get back on my feet."

Harry blinked; the woman's tones were startlingly reminiscent of Dawlish in complaining mode. He raised his brows as the coachman lumbered to his feet and touched his forehead. "Is there anyone in the carriage?"

The coachman's face blanked in shock.

"*Oh my God!*" Her eyes snapping open, the woman sat bolt upright. "The mistress and Miss Heather!" Her startled gaze fell on the carriage. "Damn you, Joshua—what are you *doing,* mooning over me when the mistress is likely lying in a heap?'' Frantically, she hit at the coachman's legs, pushing him towards the carriage.

''Don't panic.''

The injunction floated up out of the carriage, calm and assured.

''We're perfectly all right—just a bit shaken.'' The clear, very feminine voice paused before adding, a touch hesitantly, ''But we can't get out.''

With a muttered curse, Harry strode to the carriage, pausing only to shrug out of his greatcoat and fling it into the curricle. Reaching up to the back wheel, he hauled himself onto the body. Standing on the coach's now horizontal side, he bent and, grasping the handle, hauled the door open.

Planting one booted foot on either side of the coach step, he looked down into the dimness within.

And blinked.

The sight that met his eyes was momentarily dazzling. A woman stood in the shaft of sunshine pouring through the doorway. Her face, upturned, was heart-shaped; a broad forehead was set beneath dark hair pulled severely back. Her features were well defined; a straight nose and full, well-curved lips above a delicate but determined chin.

Her skin was the palest ivory, the colour of priceless pearls; beyond his control, Harry's gaze skimmed her cheeks and the graceful curve of her slender neck before coming to rest on the ripe swell of her breasts. Standing over her as he was, they were amply exposed to his sight even though her modish carriage dress was in no way indecorous.

Harry's palms tingled.

Large blue eyes fringed with long black lashes blinked up at him.

For an instant, Lucinda Babbacombe was not entirely sure she hadn't sustained a blow on the head—what else could excuse this vision, conjured from her deepest dreams?

Tall and lean, broad-shouldered, slim-hipped, he towered above her, long, sleekly muscled legs braced on either side of the door. Sunlight haloed his golden locks; with the light behind him she could not make out his features yet she sensed the tension that held him.

Lucinda blinked rapidly. A light blush tinged her cheeks; she looked away—but not before she registered the subdued elegance of his garments—the tightly-fitting grey coat, superbly cut, style in every line, worn over clinging ivory inexpressibles, which clearly revealed the long muscles of his thighs. His calves were encased in gleaming Hessians; his linen was crisp and white. There were, she noted, no fobs or seals hanging at his waist, only a single gold pin in his cravat.

Prevailing opinion suggested such severe attire should render a gentleman uninteresting. Unremarkable. Prevailing opinion was wrong.

He shifted—and a large, long-fingered, extremely elegant hand reached down to her.

''Take my hand—I'll pull you up. One of the wheels is shattered—it's impossible to right the carriage.''

His voice was deep, drawling, an undercurrent Lucinda couldn't identify sliding beneath the silken tones. She glanced up through her lashes. He had moved to the side of the door and had gone down on one knee. The light now reached his face, illuminating features that seemed to harden as her gaze touched them. His hand moved impatiently; a black sapphire set in a gold signet glimmered darkly. He would need to be very strong to lift her out with one arm. Subduing the thought that her rescue might well prove a greater threat than her plight, Lucinda reached for his hand.

Their palms met; long fingers curled about her wrist. Lucinda brought her other hand up and clasped it about his—and she was airborne.

She drew in a swift breath—an arm of steel wrapped about her waist; her diaphragm seized. She blinked—and found herself on her knees, held fast in his embrace, locked breast to chest with her unnerving rescuer.

Her eyes were on a level with his lips. They were as severe as his clothes, chiselled and firm. His jaw was distinctly squared, the patrician line of his nose a testimony to his antecedents. The planes of his face were hard, as hard as the body steadying hers, holding her balanced on the edge of the carriage doorframe. He had released her hands; they had fallen to lie against his chest. One of her hips was pressed against his, the other against his muscled thigh. Lucinda forgot about breathing.

Cautiously, she lifted her eyes to his—and saw the sea, calm and clear, a cool, crystalline pale green.

Their gazes locked.

Mesmerised, Lucinda drowned in the green sea, her skin lapped by waves of warmth, her mind suborned to sensation. She felt her lips soften, felt herself lean into him—and blinked wildly.

A tremor shook her. The muscles surrounding her twitched, then stilled.

She felt him draw breath.

''Careful,'' was all he said as he slowly rose, drawing her up with him, holding her steady until her feet could find purchase on the carriage.

Lucinda wondered just what danger he was warning her against.

Forcing his arms from her, Harry struggled to shackle his impulses, straining at their leash. ''I'll have to lower you to the ground.''

Peering over the carriage side, Lucinda could only nod. The drop was six feet and more. She felt him shift behind her; she jumped as his hands slipped beneath her arms.

''Don't wriggle or try to jump. I'll let go when your coachman has hold of you.''

Joshua was waiting below. Lucinda nodded; speech was beyond her.

Harry gripped her firmly and swung her over the edge. The coachman quickly grasped her legs; Harry let go—but could not prevent his fingers from brushing the soft sides of her breasts. He clenched his jaw and tried to eradicate the memory but his fingertips burned.

Once on *terra firma,* Lucinda was pleased to discover her wits once more at her command. Whatever curious influence had befuddled her faculties was, thank Heaven, purely transitory.

A quick glance upwards confirmed that her rescuer had turned back to render a like service to her stepdaughter. Reflecting that at barely seventeen Heather's susceptibility to his particular brand of wizardry was probably a good deal less than her own, Lucinda left him to it.

After one comprehensive glance about the scene, she marched across to the ditch, leaned over and dealt Amy, the tweeny, a sharp slap. "Enough," she declared, as if she was speaking of nothing more than kneading dough. "Now come and help with Agatha."

Amy's tear-drenched eyes opened wide, then blinked. "Yes, mum." She sniffed—then shot a watery smile at Sim, the groom, and struggled up out of the thankfully dry ditch.

Lucinda was already on her way to Agatha, prone in the road. "Sim—help with the horses. Oh—and do get these stones out of the road." She pointed a toe at the collection of large, jagged rocks littering the highway. "I dare say it was one of these that caused our wheel to break. And I expect you'd better start unloading the carriage."

"Aye, mum."

Halting by Agatha's side, Lucinda bent to look down at her. "What is it and how bad?"

Lips compressed, Agatha opened iron-grey eyes and squinted up at her. "It's just my ankle—it'll be better directly."

"Indeed," Lucinda remarked, getting down on her knees

to examine the injured limb. "That's no doubt why you're white as a sheet."

"Nonsense—oooh!" Agatha sucked in a quick breath and closed her eyes.

"Stop fussing and let me bind it."

Lucinda bade Amy tear strips from her petticoat, then proceeded to bind Agatha's ankle, ignoring the maid's grumbles. All the while, Agatha shot suspicious glances past her.

"You'd best stay by me, mistress. And keep the young miss by you. That gentleman may be a gentleman, but he's a one to watch, I don't doubt."

Lucinda didn't doubt either but she refused to hide behind her maid's skirts. "Nonsense. He rescued us in a positively gentlemanly manner—I'll thank him appropriately. Stop fussing."

"Fussing!" Agatha hissed as Lucinda drew her skirts down to her ankles. "You didn't see him move."

"Move?" Frowning, Lucinda stood and dusted her hands, then her gown. She turned to discover Heather hurrying up, hazel eyes bright with excitement, clearly none the worse for their ordeal.

Behind her came their rescuer. All six feet and more of him, with a lean and graceful stride that conjured the immediate image of a hunting cat.

A big, powerful predator.

Agatha's comment was instantly explained. Lucinda concentrated on resisting the urge to flee. He reached for her hand—she must have extended it—and bowed elegantly.

"Permit me to introduce myself, ma'am. Harry Lester—at your service."

He straightened, a polite smile softening his features.

Fascinated, Lucinda noted how his lips curved upwards just at the ends. Then her eyes met his. She blinked and glanced away. "I most sincerely thank you, Mr Lester, for your assistance—yours and your groom's." She beamed a grateful smile at his groom, unhitching the horses from the coach with Sim's help. "It was immensely lucky you happened by."

Harry frowned, the memory of the footpads lurking in the trees beyond the curve intruding. He shook the thought aside. "I beg you'll permit me to drive you and your..." Brows lifting, he glanced from the younger girl's bright face to that of his siren's.

She smiled. "Allow me to introduce my stepdaughter, Miss Heather Babbacombe."

Heather bobbed a quick curtsy; Harry responded with a slight bow.

"As I was saying, Mrs Babbacombe." Smoothly Harry turned back and captured the lady's wide gaze with his. Her eyes were a soft blue, partly grey—a misty colour. Her carriage gown of lavender blue served to emphasise the shade. "I hope you'll permit me to drive you to your destination. You were headed for...?"

"Newmarket," Lucinda supplied. "Thank you—but I must make arrangements for my people."

Harry wasn't sure which statement more surprised him. "Naturally," he conceded, wondering how many other ladies of his acquaintance, in like circumstances, would so concern themselves over their servants. "But my groom can handle the details for you. He's familiar with these parts."

"He is? How fortunate."

Before he could blink, the soft blue gaze had left him for Dawlish—his siren followed, descending upon his servitor like a galleon in full sail. Intrigued, Harry followed. She summoned her coachman with an imperious gesture. By the time Harry joined them, she was busily issuing the orders he had thought to give.

Dawlish shot him a startled, distinctly reproachful glance.

"Will that be any trouble, do you think?" Lucinda asked, sensing the groom's distraction.

"Oh—no, ma'am." Dawlish bobbed his head respectfully. "No trouble at all. I knows the folks at the Barbican right well. We'll get all seen to."

"Good." Harry made a determined bid to regain control of the situation. "If that's settled, I suspect we should get on, Mrs Babbacombe." At the back of his mind lurked a vision of five frieze-coated men. He offered her his arm; an intent little frown wrinkling her brows, she placed her hand upon it.

"I do hope Agatha will be all right."

"Your maid?" When she nodded, Harry offered, "If she'd broken her ankle she would, I think, be in far greater pain."

The blue eyes came his way, along with a grateful smile.

Lucinda glanced away—and caught Agatha's warning glare. Her smile turned into a grimace. "Perhaps I should wait here until the cart comes for her?"

"No." Harry's response was immediate. She shot him a startled glance; he covered his lapse with a charming but rueful smile. "I hesitate to alarm you but footpads have been seen in the vicinity." His smile deepened. "And New-market's *only* two miles on."

"Oh." Lucinda met his gaze; she made no effort to hide the consideration in hers. "Two miles?"

"If that." Harry met her eyes, faint challenge in his.

"Well…" Lucinda turned to view his curricle.

Harry waited for no more. He beckoned Sim and pointed to the curricle. "Put your mistresses' luggage in the boot."

He turned back to be met by a cool, distinctly haughty blue glance. Equally cool, he allowed one brow to rise.

Lucinda suddenly felt warm, despite the cool breeze that heralded the approaching evening. She looked away, to where Heather was talking animatedly to Agatha.

"If you'll forgive the advice, Mrs Babbacombe, I would not consider it wise for either you or your stepdaughter to be upon the road, unescorted, at night."

The soft drawl focused Lucinda's mind on her options.

Both appeared dangerous. With a gentle inclination of her head, she chose the more exciting. ''Indeed, Mr Lester. Doubtless you're right.'' Sim had finished stowing their baggage in the curricle's boot, strapping bandboxes to the flaps. ''Heather?''

While his siren fussed, delivering a string of last-minute instructions, Harry lifted her stepdaughter to the curricle's seat. Heather Babbacombe smiled sunnily and thanked him prettily, too young to be flustered by his innate charms.

Doubtless, Harry thought, as he turned to view her stepmother, Heather viewed him much as an uncle. His lips quirked, then relaxed into a smile as he watched Mrs Babbacombe glide towards him, casting last, measuring glances about her.

She was slender and tall—there was something about her graceful carriage that evoked the adjective ''matriarchal.'' A confidence, an assurance, that showed in her frank gaze and open expression. Her dark hair, richly brown with the suspicion of red glinting in the sun, was, he could now see, fixed in a tight bun at the nape of her neck. For his money, the style was too severe—his fingers itched to run through the silken tresses, laying them free.

As for her figure, he was having great difficulty disguising his interest. She was, indeed, one of the more alluring visions he had beheld in many a long year.

She drew near and he lifted a brow. ''Ready, Mrs Babbacombe?''

Lucinda turned to meet his gaze, wondering how such a soft drawl could so easily sound steely. ''Thank you, Mr Lester.'' She gave him her hand; he took it, drawing her to the side of the carriage. Lucinda blinked at the high step— the next instant, she felt his hands firm about her waist and she was lifted, effortlessly, to the seat.

Stifling her gasp, Lucinda met Heather's gaze, filled with innocent anticipation. Sternly suppressing her fluster, Lucinda settled herself on the seat next to her stepdaughter.

She had not, indeed, had much experience interacting with gentlemen of Mr Lester's standing; perhaps such gestures were commonplace?

Despite her inexperience, she could not delude herself that her position, as it transpired, could ever be dismissed as commonplace. Her rescuer paused only to swing his greatcoat—adorned, she noted, with a great many capes— about his broad shoulders before following her into the curricle, the reins in his hands. Naturally, he sat beside her.

A bright smile firmly fixed on her lips, Lucinda waved Agatha goodbye, steadfastly ignoring the hard thigh pressed against her much softer limb, and the way her shoulder perforce had to nestle against his back.

Harry himself had not foreseen the tight squeeze—and found its results equally disturbing. Pleasant—but definitely disturbing. Backing his team, he asked, "Were you coming from Cambridge, Mrs Babbacombe?" He desperately needed distraction.

Lucinda was only too ready to oblige. "Yes—we spent a week there. We intended to leave directly after lunch but spent an hour or so in the gardens. They're very fine, we discovered."

Her accents were refined and untraceable, her stepdaughter's less so, while those of her servants were definitely north country. The greys settled into their stride; Harry comforted himself that two miles meant less than fifteen minutes, even allowing for picking their way through the town. "But you're not from hereabouts?"

"No—we're from Yorkshire." After a moment, Lucinda added, a smile tweaking her lips, "At the moment, however, I suspect we could more rightly claim to be gypsies."

"Gypsies?"

Lucinda exchanged a smile with Heather. "My husband died just over a year ago. His estate passed into his cousin's hands, so Heather and I decided to while away our year of mourning in travelling the country. Neither of us had seen much of it before.''

Harry stifled a groan. She was a widow—a beautiful widow newly out of mourning, unfixed, unattached, bar the minor encumbrance of a stepdaughter. In an effort to deny his mounting interest, to block out his awareness of her soft curves pressed, courtesy of Heather Babbacombe's more robust figure, firmly against his side, he concentrated on her words. And frowned. ''Where do you plan to stay in Newmarket?''

''The Barbican Arms,'' Lucinda replied. ''I believe it's in the High Street.''

''It is.'' Harry's lips thinned; the Barbican Arms was directly opposite the Jockey Club. ''Ah—have you reservations?'' He slanted a glance at her face and saw surprise register. ''It's a race week, you know.''

''Is it?'' Lucinda frowned. ''Does that mean it'll be crowded?''

''Very.'' With every rakehell and womaniser who could make the journey from London. Harry suppressed the thought. Mrs Babbacombe was, he told himself, none of his business. Very definitely none of his business—she might be a widow and, to his experienced eye, ripe for seduction, but she was a *virtuous* widow—therein lay the rub. He was too experienced not to know such existed—indeed, the fleeting thought occurred that if he was to plot his own downfall, then a virtuous widow would be first choice as Cupid's pawn. But he had recognised the trap—and had no intention of falling into it. Mrs Babbacombe was one beautiful widow he would do well to leave untouched—unsampled. Desire bucked, unexpectedly strong; with a mental curse, Harry shackled it—in iron!

The first straggling cottages appeared ahead. He grimaced. ''Is there no acquaintance you have in the district with whom you might stay?''

''No—but I'm sure we'll be able to find accommodation

somewhere.'' Lucinda gestured airly, struggling to keep her mind on her words and her senses on the late afternoon landscape. ''If not at the Barbican Arms, then perhaps the Green Goose.''

She sensed the start that shot through him. Turning, she met an openly incredulous, almost horrified stare.

''*Not* the Green Goose.'' Harry made no attempt to mute the decree.

It was received with a frown. ''Why not?''

Harry opened his mouth—but couldn't find the words. ''Never mind why—just get it into your head that you cannot reside at the Green Goose.''

Intransigence flowed into her expression, then she put her pretty nose in the air and looked ahead. ''If you will just set us down at the Barbican Arms, Mr Lester, I'm sure we'll sort things out.''

Her words conjured a vision of the yard at the Barbican Arms—of the main hall of the inn as it would be at this moment—as Harry had experienced it at such times before. Jam-packed with males, broad-shouldered, elegant *ton*nish gentlemen, the vast majority of whom he would know by name. He certainly knew them by nature; he could just imagine their smiles when Mrs Babbacombe walked in.

''No.''

The cobbles of the High Street rang beneath the greys' hooves.

Lucinda turned to stare at him. ''What on earth do you mean?''

Harry gritted his teeth. Even with his attention on his horses as he negotiated the press of traffic in the main street of the horse capital of England, he was still aware of the surprised glances thrown their way—and of the lingering, considering looks bent on the woman by his side. Arriving with him, being seen with him, had already focused attention on her.

It was none of his business.

Harry felt his face harden. "Even if the Barbican Arms has rooms to spare—which they will not—it's not suitable for you to stay in town while a race meeting's on."

"I beg your pardon?" After a moment of astonished surprise, Lucinda drew herself up. "Mr Lester—you have most ably rescued us—we owe you our gratitude. However, I am more than capable of organising our accommodation and stay in this town."

"Gammon."

"What?"

"You don't know anything about staying in a town during a race-meet or you wouldn't be here now." Lips set in a thin line, Harry shot her an irritated glare. "Devil take it—look around you, woman!"

Lucinda had already noticed the large number of men strolling the narrow pavements. As her gaze swept the scene, she noted that there were many more on horseback and in the sporting carriages of every description thronging the thoroughfare. Gentlemen everywhere. Only gentlemen.

Heather was leaning close, shrinking against her, not used to being stared at and ogled. She raised hazel eyes filled with uncertainty to Lucinda's face. "Lucinda…?"

Lucinda patted her hand. As she raised her head, she encountered a boldly appraising stare from a gentleman in a high-perch phaeton. Lucinda returned his scrutiny with a frosty glance. "Nevertheless," she maintained. "If you will set us down at…"

Her words trailed away as she glimpsed, hanging above a broad archway just ahead, a signboard depicting a castle gateway. In that instant, the traffic parted; Harry clicked his reins and the curricle shot forward—straight past the archway.

Lucinda swivelled to peer at the sign as they moved steadily down the street. "That's it—the Barbican Arms!" She turned to look at Harry. "You've passed it."

Grim-faced, Harry nodded.

Lucinda glared at him. "Stop," she ordered.

"You can't stay in town."

"I can!"

"Over my dead body!" Harry heard his snarl and inwardly groaned. He closed his eyes. What was happening to him? Opening his eyes, he glared at the woman beside him. Her cheeks were becomingly flushed—with temper. A fleeting thought of how she would look flushed with desire shot through his unwilling mind.

Something of his thoughts must have shown in his face—her blue eyes narrowed. "Are you proposing to kidnap us?" Her voice held the promise of a long and painful death.

The end of the High Street appeared; the traffic thinned. Harry flicked his leader's ear and the greys surged. As the sound of hooves on cobbles died behind them, he glanced down at her and growled, "Consider it forcible repatriation."

Chapter Two

"*Forcible repatriation?*"

Harry shot her a narrow-eyed glare. "You don't *belong* in a race-town."

Lucinda glared back. "I belong wherever *I* choose to stay, Mr Lester."

His face set in uncompromising lines, Harry looked back at his team. Lucinda looked ahead, frowning direfully.

"Where are you taking us?" she eventually demanded.

"To stay with my aunt, Lady Hallows." Harry glanced at her. "She lives a little way out of town."

It had been many years since she'd allowed anyone to order her life. Nose in the air, Lucinda held to dignified disapproval. "How do you know she won't already have visitors?"

"She's a widow of long standing and lives quietly." Harry checked his team and turned onto a side road. "She has a whole Hall to spare—and she'll be delighted to make your acquaintance."

Lucinda sniffed. "You can't know that."

The smile he bent on her was infinitely superior.

Resisting the urge to gnash her teeth, Lucinda pointedly looked away.

Heather had perked up the instant they'd quit town; she

smiled when Lucinda glanced her way, clearly restored to her usual sunny humour and unperturbed by the unexpected alteration to their plans.

Feeling distinctly huffy, Lucinda looked ahead. It was, she suspected, pointless to protest—at least, not until she'd met Lady Hallows. Until then, there was nothing she could do to regain the ascendancy. The infuriating gentleman beside her had the upper hand—and the reins. Her gaze flicked sideways, to where his hands, covered by soft doeskin gloves, dextrously managed the ribbons. Long slim fingers and slender palms. She'd noted that earlier. To her horror, the memory evoked a shiver—she had to fight to quell it. With him so close, he would very likely feel it—and, she suspected, would unhesitatingly guess its cause.

Which would leave her feeling embarrassed—and even more deeply disturbed. He evoked a most peculiar response in her—it had yet to fade, despite her irritation at his autocratic interference. It was a distinctly novel feeling—one she wasn't at all sure she appreciated.

"Hallows Hall."

She looked up to discover a pair of imposing gateposts which gave onto a shady avenue lined with elms. The gravelled drive wound gently along a slight ridge, then dipped to reveal a pleasant vista of rolling lawns surrounding a reed-fringed lake, the whole enclosed by large trees.

"How pretty!" Heather looked about in delight.

The Hall, a relatively recent structure in honey-coloured stone, sat on a rise above the drive, which wound past the front steps before curving around the corner of the house. A vine stretched green fingers over the stone. There were roses in abundance; ducks clacked from the lake.

An ancient retainer came ambling up as Harry drew his team to a halt.

"Thought as we'd see you this week, young master."

Harry grinned. "Good evening, Grimms. Is my aunt at home?"

"Aye—that she is—and right pleased she'll be to see you. Evening, miss. Miss." Grimms doffed his cap to Lucinda and Heather.

Lucinda's answering smile was distant. Hallows Hall stirred long-forgotten memories of life before her parents had died.

Harry descended and helped her down. After helping Heather to the ground, he turned to see Lucinda looking about her, a wistful expression on her face. "Mrs Babbacombe?"

Lucinda started. Then, with a half-grimace and a frosty glance, she placed her hand on his arm and allowed him to lead her up the steps.

The door was flung open—not by a butler, although a stately personage of that persuasion hovered in the shadows—but by a gaunt, angular-featured woman a good two inches taller than Lucinda and decidedly thinner.

"Harry, m'boy! Thought you'd be here. And who's this you've brought?"

Lucinda found herself blinking into dark blue eyes, shrewd and intelligent.

"But what am I about? Come in, come in." Ermyntrude, Lady Hallows, waved her guests into the hall.

Lucinda stepped over the threshold—and was immediately enveloped in the warm, elegant yet homey atmosphere.

Harry took his aunt's hand and bowed over it, then kissed her cheek. "As elegant as ever, Em," he said, scanning her topaz gown.

Em's eyes opened wide. "Flummery? From you?"

Harry pressed her hand warningly as he released it. "Allow me to present Mrs Babbacombe, Aunt. Her carriage broke a wheel just outside town. I had the honour of driving her in. She had some idea of staying in town but I prevailed upon her to change her mind and give you the benefit of her company."

The words tripped glibly from his tongue. Rising from her curtsy, Lucinda shot him a chilly glance.

"Capital!" Em beamed and took Lucinda's hand. "My dear, you don't know how bored I sometimes get, stuck out here in the country. And Harry's quite right—you can't possibly stay in town during a meet—not at all the thing." Her blue eyes switched to Heather. "And who's this?"

Lucinda made the introduction and Heather, smiling brightly, bobbed a curtsy.

Em put out a hand and tipped Heather's chin up the better to view her face. "Hmm—quite lovely. You'll do well in a year or two." Releasing her, Em frowned. "Babbacombe, Babbacombe…" She glanced at Lucinda. "Not the Staffordshire Babbacombes?"

Lucinda smiled. "Yorkshire." When her hostess only frowned harder, she felt compelled to add, "I was a Gifford before my marriage."

"Gifford?" Em's eyes slowly widened as she studied Lucinda. "*Great heavens!* You must be Melrose Gifford's daughter—Celia Parkes was your mother?"

Surprised, Lucinda nodded—and was promptly enveloped in a scented embrace.

"Good gracious, child—I knew your father!" Em was in transports. "Well—I was a bosom-bow of his elder sister, but I knew all the family. Naturally, after the scandal, we heard very little of Celia and Melrose, but they did send word of your birth." Em wrinkled her nose. "Not that it did much good—stiff-necked lot, your grandparents. On both sides."

Harry blinked, endeavouring to absorb this rush of information. Lucinda noticed, and wondered how he felt about rescuing the outcome of an old scandal.

"Just fancy!" Em was still in alt. "I never thought to set eyes on you, m'dear. Mind you, there's not many left but me who'd remember. You'll have to tell me the whole story." Em paused to draw breath. "Now then! Fergus will get your luggage and I'll show you up to your rooms—after a dish of tea—you *must* be in need of refreshment. Dinner's at six so there's no need to hurry.''

Together with Heather, Lucinda found herself hustled towards an open doorway—a drawing-room lay ahead. On the threshold she hesitated and glanced back, as did Em behind her.

''You're not staying, are you, Harry?'' Em asked.

He was tempted—sorely tempted. His gaze not on his aunt but on the woman beside her, Harry forced himself to shake his head. ''No.'' With an effort he shifted his gaze to his aunt's face. ''I'll call sometime during the week.''

Em nodded.

Prompted by she knew not what, Lucinda turned and recrossed the hall. Their rescuer stood silently and watched her approach; she steadfastly ignored the odd tripping of her heart. She halted before him, calmly meeting his green gaze. ''I don't know how to thank you for your help, Mr Lester. You've been more than kind.''

His lips slowly curved; again, she found herself fascinated by the movement.

Harry took the hand she held out to him and, his eyes on hers, raised it to his lips. ''Your rescue was indeed my pleasure, Mrs Babbacombe.'' The sudden widening of her eyes as his lips touched her skin was payment enough for the consequent hardships. ''I'll ensure that your people know where to find you—your maids will arrive before nightfall, I'm sure.''

Lucinda inclined her head; she made no effort to retrieve her fingers from his warm grasp. ''Again, you have my thanks, sir.''

''It was nothing, my dear.'' His eyes on hers, Harry allowed one brow to rise. ''Perhaps we'll meet again—in a ballroom, maybe? Dare I hope you'll favour me with a waltz if we do?''

Graciously, Lucinda acquiesced. "I would be honoured, sir—should we meet."

Belatedly reminding himself that she was a snare he was determined to avoid, Harry took a firm grip on his wayward impulses. He bowed. Releasing Lucinda's hand, he nodded to Em. With one last glance at Lucinda, he strolled gracefully out of the door.

Lucinda watched the door shut behind him, a distant frown in her eyes.

Em studied her unexpected guest, a speculative glint in hers.

"AGATHA'S BEEN WITH ME forever," Lucinda explained. "She was my mother's maid when I was born. Amy was an under-maid at the Grange—my husband's house. We took her with us so that Agatha could train her to act as maid for Heather."

"Just as well," Heather put in.

They were in the dining-room, partaking of a delicious meal prepared, so Em had informed them, in honour of their arrival. Agatha, Amy and Sim had arrived an hour ago, conveyed by Joshua in a trap borrowed from the Barbican Arms. Joshua had returned to Newmarket to pursue the repairs of the carriage. Agatha, taken under the wing of the portly housekeeper, Mrs Simmons, was resting in a cheery room below the eaves, her ankle pronounced unbroken but badly sprained. Amy had thus had to assist both Lucinda and Heather to dress, a task at which she had acquitted herself with honours.

Or so Em thought as she looked down the table. "So," she said, patting her lips with her napkin then waving Fergus and the soup tureen away. "You may start at the beginning. I want to know all about you since your parents died."

The sheer openness of the request robbed it of any rudeness. Lucinda smiled and laid aside her spoon; Heather was dipping into the tureen for the third time, much to Fergus's delight. "As you know, what with both families disowning my parents, I hadn't had any contact with my grandparents. I was fourteen at the time of the accident. Luckily, our old solicitor hunted up my mother's sister's address—she agreed to take me in."

"Now let's see." Em's eyes narrowed as she surveyed the past. "That would be Cora Parkes that was?"

Lucinda nodded. "If you recall, the Parkes family fortunes had taken a downturn sometime after my parents married. They'd retired from Society and Cora had married a mill-owner in the north—a Mr Ridley."

"*Never* say so!" Em was enthralled. "Well, well—how the mighty did fall. Your aunt Cora was one of the most intransigent when it came to any question of reconciliation with your parents." Em lifted her thin shoulders. "Fate's revenge, I dare say. So you lived with them until your marriage?"

Lucinda hesitated, then nodded.

Em noticed; her eyes sharpened, then flicked to Heather. Lucinda saw—and hastened to explain. "The Ridleys weren't exactly happy to have me. They only agreed to house me, thinking to use my talents as governess to their two daughters and then to broker my marriage as soon as maybe."

For a moment, Em stared. Then she snorted. "Doesn't surprise me. That Cora was ever out for her own gain."

"When I was sixteen, they arranged a marriage with another mill-owner, a Mr Ogleby."

"Ugh!" Heather looked up from her soup to shudder artistically. "He was a horrible old toad," she blithely informed Em. "Luckily, my father heard about it—Lucinda used to come and give me lessons. So *he* married Lucinda instead." Having done her bit for the conversation, Heather returned to her soup.

Lucinda smiled affectionately. "Indeed, Charles was my

saviour. I only recently learned that he bought off my relatives in order to marry me—he never told me.''

Em snorted approvingly. ''Glad to hear they've *some* gentlemen in those parts. So you became Mrs Babbacombe and
lived at…the Grange, was it?''

''That's right.'' Heather had finally relinquished the soup;
Lucinda paused to serve herself from the platter of turbot
Fergus offered. ''To all appearances Charles was a well-to-
do gentleman of moderate estate. In reality, however, he
owned a considerable collection of inns up and down the
country. He was really very wealthy but preferred a quiet
existence. He was close to fifty when we married. As I grew
older, he taught me all about his investments and how to
manage them. He was ill for some years—the end was a
relief when it came—but because of his foresight, I was able
to handle most of the work for him.''

Lucinda looked up to find her hostess staring at her.

''Who owns the inns now?'' Em asked.

Lucinda smiled. ''We do—Heather and I. The Grange, of
course, went to Charles's nephew, Mortimer Babbacombe,
but Charles's private fortune wasn't part of the entail.''

Em sat back and regarded her with frank approval. ''And
that's why you're here—you own an inn in Newmarket?''

Lucinda nodded. ''After the will was read, Mortimer
asked us to vacate the Grange within the week.''

''The blackguard!'' Em glared. ''What sort of a way is
that to treat a grieving widow?''

''Well,'' Lucinda held up a hand. ''I did offer to leave
as soon as he wished—although I hadn't thought he'd be in
such a hurry. He'd never even visited before—not really.''

''So you found yourselves out on your ears in the snow?''
Em was incensed.

Heather giggled. ''It really turned out most fortuitously
in the end.''

''Indeed.'' Lucinda nodded, pushing her plate away.
''With nothing organised, we decided to remove to one of

our inns—one a little way away from the Grange, a place we weren't known. Once there, I realised the inn was far more prosperous than I would have guessed from the accounts our agent had recently presented. Mr Scrugthorpe was a new man—Charles had been forced to appoint a new agent a few months before he died when our old Mr Matthews passed on.'' Lucinda frowned at the trifle Fergus placed before her. ''Unfortunately, Charles interviewed Scrugthorpe on a day he was in great pain and I had to be in town with Heather. To cut a long story short, Scrugthorpe had falsified the accounts. I called him in and dismissed him.''

Lifting her gaze to her hostess's face, Lucinda smiled. ''After that, Heather and I decided that travelling the country getting to know our inns was an excellent way to see out our year of mourning. It was exactly the sort of enterprise of which Charles would have approved.''

Em snorted—this snort clearly signified her appreciation of Charles's good sense. ''Seems to have been a very able man—your father, miss.''

''He was a dear.'' Heather's open face clouded and she blinked rapidly, then looked down.

''I've appointed a new agent—a Mr Mabberly.'' Lucinda smoothly covered the awkward moment. ''He's young but extremely efficient.''

''And goes in awe of Lucinda,'' Heather offered, looking up to help herself to a second scoop of trifle.

''As he should,'' Em replied. ''Well, Miss Gifford as was—you've certainly done your parents proud thus far. A capable lady of independent means at what—twenty-six?''

''Twenty-eight.'' Lucinda's smile was crooked. There were times, such as today, when she suddenly wondered if life had passed her by.

''A very fair achievement,'' Em declared. ''I don't hold with women being helpless.'' She eyed Heather's at last empty plate. ''And if you've finally finished, miss, I suggest we retire to the drawing-room. Do either of you play the pianoforte?''

They both did and gladly entertained their hostess with various airs and sonatas, until Heather fell to yawning. At Lucinda's suggestion she retired, passing the tea trolley in the doorway.

''Indeed, we've had an adventuresome day.'' Lucinda sat back in an armchair by the fire and sipped the tea Em had dispensed. Lifting her gaze, she smiled at Em. ''I can't thank you enough, Lady Hallows, for taking us in.''

''Nonsense,'' Em replied with one of her snorts. ''And you could please me by dropping all the ladyships and just calling me Em, like everyone else in the family. You're Melrose's daughter and that's close enough for me.''

Lucinda smiled, a trifle wearily. ''Em, then. What's it a contraction for? Emma?''

Em wrinkled her nose. ''Ermyntrude.''

Lucinda managed to keep her lips straight. ''Oh?'' she said weakly.

''Indeed. My brothers delighted in calling me all the contractions you might imagine. When my nephews came along, I declared it was Em and nothing else.''

''Very wise.'' A companionable silence settled as they savoured their tea. Lucinda broke it to ask, ''Do you have many nephews?''

From under heavy lids, Em's eyes glinted. ''Quite a few. But it was Harry and his brothers I had to guard against. A rapscallion lot.''

Lucinda shifted. ''He has a lot of brothers?''

''Only two—but that's quite enough. Jack's the eldest,'' Em blithely rattled on. ''He's—let me see—thirty-six now. Then comes Harry, two years younger. Then there's quite a gap to their sister Lenore—she married Eversleigh some years back—she must be twenty-six now, which makes Gerald twenty-four. Their mother died years ago but my brother still hangs on.'' Em grinned. ''Dare say he'll manage to cling to life long enough to see a grandson to carry on the name, the cantankerous old fool.'' The last was said affectionately. ''But it was the boys I had most to do with—and Harry was always my favourite. Blessed by the angels and the devil both, of course, but such a good boy.'' Em blinked, then amended, ''Well—a good boy *at heart*. They all were—are. I see most of Harry and Gerald these days—what with Newmarket so close. Harry runs the Lester stud which, even if 'tis I who say so—and Heaven knows I know next to nothing about horses—such a boring subject—is hailed as one of the premier studs in the land.''

''Really?'' There was not the slightest trace of boredom in Lucinda's face.

''Indeed.'' Em nodded. ''Harry usually comes to watch his runners perform. Dare say I'll see Gerald this week, too. Doubtless he'll want to show off his new phaeton. Told me when last he was up that he was going to buy one, now the family coffers are full and overflowing.''

Lucinda blinked.

Em didn't wait for her to find a subtle way to ask. One hand waving, she airily explained, ''The Lesters have traditionally been strapped for cash—good estates, good breeding, but no money. The present generation, however, invested in some shipping venture last year and now the whole family's rolling in an abundance of the ready.''

''Oh.'' Lucinda readily recalled Harry Lester's expensive elegance. She couldn't imagine him any other way. Indeed, his image seemed to have fixed in her mind, oddly vivid, strangely enthralling. Shaking her head to dispel it, she delicately smothered a yawn. ''I'm afraid I'm not very good company, Lady—Em.'' She smiled. ''I suspect I'd better follow Heather.''

Em merely nodded. ''I'll see you in the morning, m'dear.''

Lucinda left her hostess staring into the fire.

Ten minutes later, her head pillowed in down, Lucinda

closed her eyes—only to find Harry Lester on her mind. Tired, adrift, her memories of the day replayed, her inter-actions with him claiming centre stage. Until she came to their parting—which left one question to plague her. How would it feel to waltz with Harry Lester?

A MILE AWAY, in the tap of the Barbican Arms, Harry sat elegantly sprawled behind a corner table, moodily surveying the room. A smoky haze wreathed a forest of shoulders; gentlemen mingled freely with grooms and stablemen, tip-sters wrangled with bookmakers. The tap was all business this evening; the first races, those for non-bloodstock, would commence the next day.

A barmaid came up, hips swaying. She set a tankard of the inn's finest on the table, smiling coyly, one brow rising as Harry flipped a coin onto her tray.

Harry caught her eye; his lips curved but he shook his head. Disappointed, the girl turned away. Harry lifted the foaming tankard and took a long sip. He'd abandoned the snug, his habitual refuge, where only the cognescenti were permitted, driven forth by the all-but-incessant questioning as to his delectable companion of the afternoon.

It seemed as if all in Newmarket had seen them.

Certainly all his friends and acquaintances were keen to learn her name. And her direction.

He'd given them neither, steadfastly returning their bright-eyed enquiries with a blank look and the information that the lady was an acquaintance of his aunt's he'd simply been escorting to her door.

Those facts proved sufficient to dampen the interest of most; the majority who frequented Newmarket knew of his aunt.

But he was definitely tired of covering the lovely Mrs Babbacombe's tracks, particularly as he was trying his damnedest to forget her. And her loveliness.

With an inward growl, Harry immersed himself in his

tankard and tried to focus his mind on his horses—usually an enthralling subject.

"There you are! Been looking all over. What're you doing out here?" Dawlish slumped into the chair beside him.

"Don't ask," Harry advised. He waited while the barmaid, with a fine show of indifference, served Dawlish before asking, "What's the verdict?"

Dawlish shot him a glance over the rim of his tankard. "Odd," came mumbling from behind it.

Brows lifting, Harry turned his head to stare at his henchman. "Odd?" Dawlish had gone with the coachman, Joshua, to fetch the wainwright to the carriage.

"Me, Joshua and the wainwright all thinks the same." Dawlish set down his tankard and wiped the froth from his lip. "Thought as how you should know."

"Know what?"

"That the cotter-pin on that wheel was tampered with—half-sawed through, it was—*before* the accident. And the spokes had been got at, too."

Harry frowned. "Why?"

"Don't know as how you noticed, but there were a curious lot of rocks strewn about that stretch of road where the carriage went over. None before—and none after. Just along that stretch. No way a coachman could miss all of 'em. And they were just round a corner so he couldn't see them in time to pull up."

Harry's frown was intense. "I remember the rocks. The boy cleared them away so I didn't have to drive over them."

Dawlish nodded. "Aye—but the carriage couldn't avoid them—and as soon as that wheel hit, the cotter would have snapped and the spokes after that."

A chill swept Harry's nape. Five mounted men in frieze, with a wagon, hiding in the trees, moving towards the road just after the carriage went down. And if it hadn't been a race-week, that particular stretch of road would almost certainly have been deserted at that time of day.

Harry lifted his gaze to Dawlish's face.

Dawlish looked back at him. "Makes you think, don't it?"

Grim-faced, Harry slowly nodded. "It does indeed." And he didn't like what he thought at all.

Chapter Three

"I'll have Y'r team out in a jiffy, sir."

Harry nodded absentmindedly as the head-ostler of the Barbican Arms hurried off towards the stables. Pulling on his driving gloves, he strolled away from the inn's main door to await his curricle in a vacant patch of sunshine by the wall.

Before him, the courtyard was busy, many of the inn's guests departing for a day at the track, hoping to pick a few winners to start the week off on the right note.

Harry grimaced. He wouldn't be joining them. Not, at least, until he'd satisfied himself on the score of one Mrs Babbacombe. He had given up telling himself she was none of his business; after the revelations of yesterday, he felt compelled to brave her dangers—long enough to assure himself of her safety. She was, after all, his aunt's guest—at his insistence. Two facts which undoubtedly excused his interest.

"I'll get along and see Hamish then, shall I?"

Harry turned as Dawlish came up. Hamish, his head-stableman, should have arrived yesterday with his string of thoroughbred racers; the horses would be settling into their stables beyond the racetrack. Harry nodded. "Make sure

Thistledown's fetlock's sufficiently healed—I don't want her entered unless it is.''

Dawlish nodded sagely. ''Aye. Shall I tell Hamish you'll be along shortly to see it?''

''No.'' Harry studied the fit of his gloves. ''I'll have to rely on your combined wisdom this time. I've pressing matters elsewhere.''

He felt Dawlish's suspicious glance.

''More pressing than a prime mare with a strained fetlock?'' Dawlish snorted. ''I'd like to know what's higher on y'r list than that.''

Harry made no effort to enlighten him. ''I'll probably look in about lunchtime.'' His imaginings were very likely groundless. It could be no more than coincidence, and two likely females travelling without major escort, that had focused the attention of the men in frieze on the Babbacombe coach. ''Just make sure Hamish gets the message in time.''

''Aye,'' Dawlish grumbled. With a last keen glance, he headed off.

Harry turned as his curricle appeared, the head-ostler leading the greys with a reverence that bespoke a full appreciation of their qualities.

''Right prime 'uns, they be,'' he averred as Harry climbed to the box.

''Indeed.'' Harry took up the reins. The greys were restive, sensing the chance of freedom. With a nod for the ostler, he backed the curricle preparatory to making a stylish exit from the yard.

''Harry!''

Harry paused, then, with a sigh, drew in his impatient steeds. ''Good morning, Gerald. And since when do you arise at this ungodly hour?''

He had spied his younger brother amongst the crowds in the tap the night before but had made no effort to advertise his presence. He turned to watch as Gerald, blue-eyed and dark-haired as was his elder brother Jack, strode up, grinning broadly, to place a familiar hand on the curricle's front board.

"Ever since I heard the story of you escorting two excessively likely looking females who, according to you, are connections of Em's."

"Not connections, dear brother—*acquaintances.*"

Faced with Harry's languidly bored mask, Gerald lost a little of his assurance. "You mean they really are? Acquaintances of Em's, I mean?"

"So I discovered."

Gerald's face fell. "Oh." Then Dawlish's absence registered. Gerald shot a keen glance at his brother. "You're going to Em's now. Mind if I hitch a ride? Should say hello to the old girl—and perhaps to that dark-haired delight you had up beside you yesterday."

For an instant, Harry was shaken by the most absurd impulse—Gerald was his younger brother after all, of whom he was, beneath his dismissive exterior, distinctly fond. He concealed the unexpected emotion behind his ineffable charm—and sighed. "I fear, dear brother, that I must puncture your delusions—the lady's too old for you."

"Oh? How old is she?"

Harry raised his brows. "Older than you."

"Well—perhaps I'll try for the other one then—the blonde."

Harry looked down on his brother's eager countenance—and inwardly shook his head. "She, if anything, is probably too young. Just out of the schoolroom, I suspect."

"No harm in that," Gerald blithely countered. "They have to start sometime."

Feeling distinctly put-upon, Harry heaved a disgusted sigh. "Gerald…"

"Dash it all, Harry—don't be such a dog-in-the-manger. You're not interested in the younger chit—let me take her off your hands."

Harry blinked at his brother. It was undoubtedly true that

any discussion of Mrs Babbacombe's situation would proceed a great deal more openly in the absence of her stepdaughter. "Very well—if you insist." Within Em's purlieu, Gerald could be relied on to keep within acceptable bounds. "But don't say I didn't warn you."

Almost gleefully, Gerald swung up to the curricle's seat. The instant he was aboard, Harry clicked his reins. The greys shot forward; he had to exert all his skills to thread them through the traffic thronging the High Street. He let them stretch their legs once free of the town; Em's leafy drive was reached in record time.

A stableboy came hurrying to take charge of the curricle. Together, Harry and Gerald mounted the steps to Em's door. The oak door was set wide open, not an uncommon occurrence. The brothers wandered in. Harry tossed his gloves onto the ormolu table. "Looks like we'll have to go hunt. I expect my business with Mrs Babbacombe will take no more than half an hour. If you can keep Miss Babbacombe occupied until then, I'll be grateful."

Gerald cocked an eyebrow. "Grateful enough to let me tool your greys back to town?"

Harry looked doubtful. "Possibly—but I wouldn't count on it."

Gerald grinned and looked about him. "So where do we start?"

"You take the gardens—I'll take the house. I'll call if I need help." With a languid wave, Harry set off down one corridor. Whistling, Gerald turned and went out of the main door.

Harry drew a blank in the morning room and the parlour. Then he heard humming, punctuated by the click of shears, and remembered the small garden room at the end of the house. There he found Em, arranging flowers in a huge urn.

At his languid best, he strolled in. "Good morning, Aunt."

Em turned her head—and stared in stunned surprise. "Devil take it—what are you doing *here?*"

Harry blinked. "Where else should I be?"

"In town. I was sure you'd be there."

After a moment's hesitation, Harry conceded with the obvious. "Why?"

"Because Lucinda—Mrs Babbacombe—went into town half an hour ago. Never been there before—wanted to get her bearings."

A chill caressed Harry's nape. "You let her go alone?"

Turning back to her blooms, Em waved her shears. "Heavens, no—her groom accompanied her."

"Her groom?" Harry's voice was soft, urbane, its tone enough to send chills down the most insensitive spine. "The young tow-headed lad who arrived with her?"

He watched as a tell-tale blush spread over his aunt's high cheekbones.

Disconcerted, Em shrugged. "She's an independent woman—it doesn't do to argue overmuch." She knew perfectly well she should not have let Lucinda go into Newmarket this week without more tangible escort, but there was a definite purpose to her ploy. Turning, she surveyed her nephew. "*You* could try, of course."

For an instant, Harry couldn't believe his ears—surely not *Em?* His eyes narrowed as he took in her bland expression; this was the last thing he needed—a traitor in his own camp. His lips thinned; with a terse nod, he countered, "Rest assured I will."

Turning on his heel, he strode out of the room, down the corridor, out of the door and around to the stables. The stableboy was startled to see him; Harry was merely glad the horses were still harnessed.

He grabbed the reins and leapt up to the seat. His whip cracked and the horses took off. The drive back to town established a new record.

Only when he was forced to slow by the press of traffic

in the High Street did Harry remember Gerald. He cursed, regretting the loss of another to aid in his search. Taking advantage of the crawling pace, he carefully studied the crowded pavements from behind his habitually unruffled mien. But no dark head could he see.

He did, however, discover a large number of his peers— friends, acquaintances—who, like himself, were too experienced to waste time at the track today. He entertained not the slightest doubt that each and every one would be only too willing to spend that time by the side of a certain delectable dark-haired widow—not one would consider it time wasted.

Reaching the end of the street, Harry swore. Disregarding all hazards, he turned the curricle, missing the gleaming panels of a new phaeton by less than an inch, leaving the slow-top in charge of the reins in the grip of an apoplectic fit.

Ignoring the fuss, Harry drove quickly back to the Barbican Arms and turned the greys into the loving hands of the head-ostler. The man confirmed that Em's gig was in residence. Harry surreptitiously checked the private parlour and was relieved to find it empty; the Arms was the favourite watering-hole of his set. Striding back to the street, he paused to take stock. And to wonder what ''getting her bearings'' meant.

There was no lending library. He settled on the church, some way along the street. But no likely looking widow haunted its hallowed precincts, nor trod the paths between the graves. The town's gardens were a joke—no one came to Newmarket to admire floral borders. Mrs Dobson's Tea Rooms were doing a brisk trade but no darkly elegant widow graced any of the small tables.

Returning to the pavement, Harry paused, hands on hips, and stared across the street. Where the devil was she?

A glimmer of blue at the edge of his vision had him turning his head. Just in time to identify the dark-haired

figure who sailed through the street door of the Green
Goose, a tow-headed boy at her back.

PAUSING JUST INSIDE the inn's door, Lucinda found herself
engulfed in dimness. Musty dimness. As her eyes adjusted
to the gloom, she discovered she was in a hall, with the
entrance to the tap on her left, two doors which presumably
led to private parlours on her right and a counter, an extension of the tap's bar, directly ahead, a tarnished bell on its
scratched surface.

Suppressing the urge to wrinkle her nose, she swept forward. She had spent the last twenty minutes examining the
inn from outside, taking due note of the faded and flaking
whitewash, the clutter in the yard and the down-at-heel appearance of the two customers who had crossed its threshold. Extending one gloved hand, she picked up the bell and
rang it imperiously. At least, that was her intention. But the
bell emitted no more than a dull clack. Upending it, Lucinda
discovered the clapper had broken.

With a disgusted grimace, she replaced the bell. She was
wondering whether to tell Sim, waiting by the door, to raise
his voice in summons when a large shadow blocked out
what little light penetrated from the inn's nether regions. A
man entered, burly, brawny—very big. His face was heavy-
featured but his eyes, sunk in folds of fat, appeared merely
uninterested.

"Aye?"

Lucinda blinked. "Are you Mr Blount?"

"Aye."

Her heart sank. "You're the innkeeper?"

"Nay."

When no more was forthcoming, she prompted, "You're
Mr Blount, but you're not the innkeeper." There was hope
yet. "Where is the Mr Blount who *is* the innkeeper?"

For a long moment, the burly individual regarded her sto-
ically as if his brain was having difficulty digesting her

question. "You want Jake—m'brother," he eventually offered.

Lucinda heaved an inward sigh of relief. "Precisely—I wish to see Mr Blount, the innkeeper."

"Wha'for?"

Lucinda opened her eyes wide. "That, my good man, is a matter for your brother and myself."

The hulking brute eyed her measuringly, then humphed. "Wait 'ere—I'll fetch 'im." With that, he lumbered off.

Leaving Lucinda praying that his brother took after the other side of the family. Her prayers were not answered. The man who replaced the first was equally burly, equally overweight and, apparently, only fractionally less dimwitted.

"Mr Jake Blount—the keeper of this inn?" Lucinda asked, with no real hope of contradiction.

"Aye." The man nodded. His small eyes swept her, not insolently but with weary assessment. "But the likes of you don't want to take rooms 'ere—try the Barbican or the Rutland up the road."

He turned away, leaving Lucinda somewhat stunned. "Just a minute, my good man!"

Jake Blount shuffled back to face her but shook his head. "Yer not the sort for this inn, see?"

Lucinda felt the breeze as the inn door opened. She saw Mr Blount's eyes lift to the newcomer but was determined to retain his attention. "No—I do not see. What on earth do you mean—'not the sort for this inn'?"

Jake Blount heard her but was more concerned with the gentleman who now stood behind her, hard green eyes on him. Gold hair, gently waved at the ends, cut in the latest style, a well-cut coat of light brown worn over buckskin breeches and Hessians so highly polished you could see your face in them, all added up to a persona Blount recognised very well. He didn't need the many-caped greatcoat that swung from the gentleman's broad shoulders, nor the patrician features and hooded eyes nor yet the tall, lean and well-muscled frame, to tell him that one of the bloods of the *ton* had deigned to enter his humble inn. The fact made him instantly nervous. ''Aaah…'' He blinked and looked back at Lucinda. ''Not the sort who takes rooms 'ere.''

Lucinda stared. ''What *sort* of lady takes rooms here?''

Blount's features contorted. ''*That's* wha' I mean—*no* ladies. Just *that* sort.''

Increasingly certain she had wandered into a madhouse, Lucinda stubbornly clung to her question. ''What sort is that?''

For an instant, Jake Blount simply stared at her. Then, defeated, he waved a pudgy hand. ''Lady—I don't knows wha' you want wi' me but I got business to see to.''

He lifted his gaze pointedly over her shoulder; Lucinda drew in a portentious breath.

And nearly swallowed it when she heard a drawling voice languidly inform the recalcitrant Blount, ''You mistake, Blount. My business here is merely to ensure you deal adequately with whatever the lady desires of you.''

Harry let his eyes meet the innkeeper's fully. ''And you're perfectly correct—she is not *that* sort.''

The particular emphasis, delivered in that sensual voice, immediately made clear to Lucinda just what ''sort had been the subject of her discussion. Torn between unaccustomed fluster, mortification and outrage, she hesitated, a light blush tinging her cheeks.

Harry noticed. ''And now,'' he suavely suggested, ''if we could leave that loaded topic, perhaps we might proceed to the lady's business? I'm sure you're breathlessly waiting to discover what it is—as am I.''

Over her shoulder, Lucinda shot him a haughty glance. ''Good morning, Mr Lester.'' She gifted him with a restrained nod; he stood behind her right shoulder, large and reassuring in the dingy dimness. He inclined his head gracefully, his features hard-edged and severe, suggesting an impatience to have her business aired.

Inwardly grimacing, Lucinda turned back to the innkeeper. "I believe you were visited recently by a Mr Mabberly, acting for the owners of this inn?"

Jake Blount shifted. "Aye."

"I believe Mr Mabberly warned you that an inspection of your premises would shortly take place?"

The big man nodded.

Lucinda nodded decisively back. "Very well—you may conduct me over the inn. We'll start with the public rooms." Without pause, she swept about. "I take it this is the tap." She glided towards the door, her skirts stirring up dust eddies.

From the corner of her eye, she saw Blount stare, open-mouthed, then come hurrying around the counter. Harry Lester simply stood and watched her, an inscrutable expression on his face.

Lucinda swept on—into the gloomy, heavily shuttered room. "Perhaps, Blount, if we were to have those shutters wide I might be able to see well enough to form an opinion?"

Blount cast her a flustered glance, then lumbered to the windows. Seconds later, sunshine flooded the room, apparently to the discomfort of its two patrons, one an old codger wrapped in a rumpled cloak, hugging the inglenook, the other a younger man in the rough clothes of a traveller. They both seemed to shrink inwards, away from the light.

Lucinda cast a shrewd glance around the room. The interior of the inn matched its exterior, at least in the matter of neglect. The Green Goose was fast living up to Anthony Mabberly's description as the very worst of the Babbacombe inns. Grimy walls and a ceiling that had seen neither brush nor mop for years combined with a general aura of dust and slow decay to render the tap a most unwelcoming place. "Hmm." Lucinda grimaced. "So much for the tap."

She slanted a glance at Harry, who had followed her in. "Thank you for your assistance, Mr Lester—but I'm perfectly capable of dealing with Mr Blount."

The green gaze, which had been engaged in a survey of the unwholesome room, switched to her face. His eyes were less unreadable than his features, but other than distinct disapproval and a species of irritation, Lucinda couldn't be sure what their expression portended.

"Indeed?" His brows lifted fractionally; his languid tone was barely polite. "But perhaps I should remain—just in case you and the good Blount run into any further… communication difficulties?"

Lucinda suppressed the urge to glare. Short of ordering him out of her inn, hardly supportive of her ploy to conceal her ownership, she could think of no way to dispense with his attentive presence. His green gaze was acute, perceptive; his tongue, as she already knew, could be decidedly sharp.

Accepting fate's decree with a small shrug, Lucinda returned her attention to Blount, hovering uncertainly by the bar. "What's through that door?"

"The kitchens."

Blount looked shocked when she waved him on. "I'll need to see those, too."

The kitchen was not as bad as she had feared, a fact she attributed to the buxom but worn-down woman who bobbed respectfully when introduced as "the missus". The Blounts' private quarters gave off the large, square room; Lucinda disavowed any desire to inspect them. After closely examining the large open fireplace and engaging in a detailed discussion with Mrs Blount on the technicalities of the draw and the overall capacity of the kitchen, which, by their impatient expressions, passed over both Blount's and Harry Lester's heads, she consented to be shown the parlours.

Both parlours were shabby and dusty but, when the shutters were opened, proved to have pleasant aspects. Both contained old but serviceable furniture.

"Hmm, mmm," was Lucinda's verdict. Blount looked glum.

In the back parlour, which looked out over a wilderness that had once been a garden, she eyed a sturdy oak table and its attendant chairs. "Please ask Mrs Blount to dust in here immediately. Meanwhile, I'll see the rooms above stairs."

With a resigned shrug, Blount went to the door of the kitchen to deliver the order, then returned to lead the way up the stairs. Halfway up, Lucinda paused to test the rickety balustrade. Leaning against it, she was startled to hear it crack—and even more startled to feel an arm of steel wrap about her waist and haul her back to the centre of the treads. She was released immediately but heard the muttered comment, "Damned nosy woman!"

Lucinda grinned, then schooled her features to impassivity as they reached the upper corridor.

"All the rooms be the same." Blount swung open the nearest door. Without waiting to be asked, he crossed to open the shutters.

The sunlight played on a dreary scene. Yellowing whitewash flaked from the walls; the ewer and basin were both cracked. The bedclothes Lucinda mentally consigned to the flames without further thought. The furniture, however, was solid—oak as far as she could tell. Both the bed and the chest of drawers could, with a little care, be restored to acceptable state.

Pursing her lips, Lucinda nodded. She turned and swept out of the door, past Harry Lester, lounging against the frame. He straightened and followed her along the corridor. Behind them, Blount shot out of the room and hurried to interpose himself between Lucinda and the next door.

"This room's currently taken, ma'am."

"Indeed?" Lucinda wondered what sort of patron would make do with the sad amenities of the Green Goose.

As if in answer, a distinctly feminine giggle percolated through the door.

Lucinda's expression grew coldly severe. "I see." She shot an accusing glance at Blount, then, head high, moved along the corridor. "I'll see the room at the end, then we'll return downstairs."

There were no further revelations; it was as Mr Mabberly had said—the Green Goose was sound enough in structure but its management needed a complete overhaul.

Descending once more to the hall, Lucinda beckoned Sim forward and relieved the lad of the bound ledgers he'd been carrying. Leading the way into the back parlour, she was pleased to discover the table and chairs dusted and wiped. Setting her ledgers on the table before the chair at its head, she placed her reticule beside them and sat. "Now, Blount, I would like to examine the books."

Blount blinked. "The books?"

Her gaze steady, Lucinda nodded. "The blue one for incomings and the red one for expenditures."

Blount stared, then muttered something Lucinda chose to interpret as an assent and departed.

Harry, who had maintained his role of silent protector throughout, strolled across to shut the door after him. Then he turned to his aunt's unexpected acquaintance. "And now, my dear Mrs Babbacombe, perhaps you would enlighten me as to what you're about?"

Lucinda resisted the urge to wrinkle her nose at him—he was, she could tell, going to be difficult. "I am doing as I said—inspecting this inn."

"Ah, yes." The steely note was back in his voice. "And I'm to believe that some proprietor has seen fit to engage you—employ you, no less—in such a capacity?"

Lucinda met his gaze, her own lucidly candid. "Yes."

The look he turned on her severely strained her composure.

With a wave, she put an end to his inquisition; Blount

would soon be back. "If you must know, this inn is owned by Babbacombe and Company."

The information arrested him in mid-prowl. He turned a fascinated green gaze upon her. "Whose principals are?"

Folding her hands on her ledgers, Lucinda smiled at him. "Myself and Heather."

She did not have time to savour his reaction; Blount entered with a pile of ledgers in his arms. Lucinda waved him to a seat beside her. While he sorted through his dog-eared tomes, she reached for her reticule. Withdrawing a pair of gold-rimmed half-glasses, she perched them on her nose. "Now then!"

Beneath Harry's fascinated gaze, she proceeded to put Blount through his financial paces.

Appropriating a chair from the table—one that had been dusted—Harry sat by the window and studied Lucinda Babbacombe. She was, undoubtedly, the most unexpected, most surprising, most altogether intriguing woman he'd ever met.

He watched as she checked entry after entry, adding figures, frequently upside-down from Blount's ledgers. The innkeeper had long since abandoned all resistance; out of his depth, faced with a totally unforeseen ordeal, he was now eager to gain approval.

As she worked through the ledgers, Lucinda came to the same somewhat reluctant conclusion. Blount wasn't intentionally neglectful; he hadn't meant to run the inn into the ground. He simply lacked direction and the experience to know what to do.

When, after an hour, she reached the end of her inquiries, Lucinda took off her glasses and fixed Blount with a shrewdly assessing glance. "Just so we are clear, Blount, it is up to me to make a recommendation on whether Babbacombe and Company should retain your services." She tapped her closed ledger with one arm of her glasses. "While your figures are unimpressive, I will be reporting that I can find no evidence of malpractice—all seems entirely above board.''

The burly innkeeper looked so absurdly grateful Lucinda had to sternly suppress a reassuring smile. ''I understand you were appointed to your present position on the death of the former landlord, Mr Harvey. From the books it's clear that the inn had ceased to perform well long before your tenancy.''

Blount looked lost.

''Which means that you cannot be held to blame for its poor base performance.'' Blount looked relieved. ''However,'' Lucinda continued, both tone and glance hardening, ''I have to tell you that the *current* performance, for which you must bear responsibility, is less than adequate. Babbacombe and Company expect a reasonable return on their investment, Blount.''

The innkeeper's brow furrowed. ''But Mr Scrugthorpe—he's the one as appointed me?''

''Ah, yes. Mr Scrugthorpe.''

Harry glanced at Lucinda's face; her tone had turned distinctly chilly.

''Well, Mr Scrugthorpe said as how the profit didn't matter so long as the inn paid its way.''

Lucinda blinked. ''What was your previous position, Blount?''

''I used to keep the Blackbird's Beak, up Fordham way.''

''The Blackbird's Beak?''

''A hedge-tavern, I suspect,'' Harry put in drily.

''Oh.'' Lucinda met his gaze, then looked back at Blount. ''Well, Blount, Mr Scrugthorpe is no longer Babbacombe and Company's agent, largely because of the rather odd way he thought to do business. And, I fear, if you wish to remain an employee of the company, you're going to have to learn to manage the Green Goose in a more commercial fashion. An inn in Newmarket cannot operate on the same principles as a hedge-tavern.''

Blount's forehead was deeply creased. "I don't know as how I rightly follow you, ma'am. Tap's a tap, after all."

"No, Blount. A tap is not a tap—it is the principal public room of the inn and as such should possess a clean and welcoming ambience. I do hope you won't suggest that that," she pointed in the direction of the tap, "is clean and welcoming?"

The big man shifted on his seat. "Dare say the missus could do a bit of a clean-up."

"Indeed." Lucilla nodded. "The missus and you, too, Blount. And whoever else you can get to help." She folded her hands on her ledgers and looked Blount in the eye. "In my report, I am going to suggest that, rather than dismiss you, given you've not yet had an opportunity to show the company of what you're capable, the company reserves judgement for three months and then reviews the situation."

Blount swallowed. "What exactly does that mean, ma'am?"

"It means, Blount, that I will make a list of all the improvements that will need to be done to turn this inn into one rivalling the Barbican Arms, at least in profit. There's no reason it shouldn't. Improvements such as a thorough whitewashing inside and out, all the timber polished, present bedding discarded and fresh bought, all furniture polished and crockery replaced. And the kitchen needs a range." Lucinda paused to meet Blount's eye. "Ultimately, you will employ a good cook and serve wholesome meals continuously in the tap, which will be refurbished accordingly. I've noticed that there are few places at which travellers staying in this town can obtain a superior repast. By providing the best fare, the Green Goose will attract custom away from the coaching houses which, because of their preoccupation with coaching, supply only mediocre food."

She paused but Blount only blinked at her. "I take it you are interested in keeping your position here?"

"Oh—yes, ma'am. Definitely! But...where's the blunt coming from for all that?"

"Why, from the profits, Blount." Lucinda eyed him straitly. "The profits before your wages are deducted—and before the return paid to the company. The company considers such matters as an investment in the inn's future; if you're wise, you'll consider my suggestions in light of an investment in your future."

Blount met her gaze; slowly he nodded. "Yes, ma'am."

"Good!" Lucinda rose. "I will make a copy of the improvements I'll be suggesting to the company and have my groom drop it by tomorrow." She glanced at Blount as he struggled to his feet; his expression suggested he was still reeling. "Mr Mabberly will look in on you in a month's time, to review your progress. And now, if there's nothing else, I will bid you good day, Blount."

"Yes, ma'am." Blount hurried to open the door. "Thank you, ma'am." He was clearly sincere.

Lucinda regally nodded and sailed from the room.

Reluctantly impressed, Harry followed close behind. Still inwardly amazed, he waited until they were back on the pavement, she gliding along with her nose in the air as if she had not just taken on Goliath and won, before catching her hand, neatly trapping it on his sleeve. Her fingers fluttered, then stilled. She cast him a quick glance, then studiously looked ahead. Her groom followed two paces behind, her ledgers clutched in his arms.

The young traveller who had been slouching in the tap slipped out of the inn door in their wake.

"My dear Mrs Babbacombe," Harry began in what he hoped was an even tone. "I do hope you're going to satisfy my curiosity as to why a gently reared female, however well-equipped for the task, goes about interrogating her company's employees?"

Unabashed, Lucinda met his gaze; aggravation showed clearly in the green. "Because there is no one else."

Harry held her gaze. His lips thinned. ''I find that hard to believe. What about this Mr Mabberly—your agent? Why can he not take on the challenge of such as Blount?''

Lucinda's lips quirked. ''You must admit he was a definite challenge.'' She slanted a deliberately provocative glance his way. ''I feel quite chuffed.''

Harry snorted. ''As you well know, you performed a minor miracle. That man will now work himself to the bone—which will be a distinct improvement in itself. But that,'' he continued, his tone hardening, ''is not the point.''

''But it is, you see.'' Lucinda wondered why she was allowing him to put in his oar. Perhaps because it had been a long time since anyone had tried? ''Mr Anthony Mabberly is all of twenty-three. He's an excellent man with the accounts and is scrupulously honest and fair—a far cry from Scrugthorpe.''

''Ah, yes. The undesirable Scrugthorpe.'' Harry cast her a quick glance. ''Why was he so undesirable?''

''Fraud. He was appointed by my husband just before his death—on one of his bad days, I'm afraid. After Charles's death, I by chance learned that the books as they were being presented to me did not reflect the actual figures generated by the inns.''

''What happened to Scrugthorpe?''

''I dismissed him, of course.''

Harry noted the righteous satisfaction that underlaid her tone. Clearly, Lucinda Babbacombe had not approved of Mr Scrugthorpe. ''So until recently the agent took responsibility for negotiating with your tenants?''

Lucinda lifted a haughty brow. ''Until I reorganised the company's procedures. Mr Mabberly would not know where to start with such as Blount—he's of a somewhat timid disposition. And I consider it appropriate that both Heather and myself are familiar with the inns that form our legacy.''

''Laudable though such sentiments might be, Mrs Babbacombe, I do hope—'' Harry broke off as she stopped and looked consideringly across the street. ''What is it?''

''Hmm?'' Absent-mindedly, Lucinda glanced up. ''Oh—I was just wondering if there was time left to do the Barbican Arms today.'' She glanced back at the busy inn across the street. ''But it looks rather crowded. Perhaps tomorrow morning would be better?''

Harry stared at her, an unwelcome suspicion slowly crystallising in his brain. ''Very much better,'' he averred. ''But tell me, Mrs Babbacombe—how many inns do you and your stepdaughter own?''

She looked up at him, an unlikely innocence in her powder-blue eyes. ''Fifty-four,'' she replied. Then added, as if in afterthought, ''Up and down the country.''

Harry closed his eyes and struggled to suppress a groan. Then, without another word, with no more than a single speaking glance, he escorted her into the yard of the Barbican Arms and, with heartfelt relief, handed her up to Em's gig and watched her drive away.

''SO SHE'S STAYING in Newmarket?''

Mr Earle Joliffe drew a riding crop back and forth through his fingers. A thickset man of undistinguished mien, he sat back in his chair, his pale gaze, as pale as his pasty complexion, fixed on the young roughneck he'd sent into town to track their quarry down.

''As to that, I ain't sure.'' The youngster took a swig from his tankard.

They were in a rundown cottage three miles from Newmarket, the best they'd been able to rent at short notice. Four men sat about the deal table—Joliffe, the youngster whose name was Brawn and two others—Mortimer Babbacombe and Ernest Scrugthorpe. The latter was a hulking man, rough despite the severe clothes of a clerk; he sat silently glowering into his beer. Mortimer Babbacombe, a slight figure in the attire of a would-be dandy, shifted restlessly; he clearly wished himself elsewhere.

"She got into a gig and drove out eastwards. I couldn't follow."

Scrugthorpe grunted. "See? Told you she'd go to the Green Goose. Couldn't keep away, meddling witch."

He spat contemptuously on the floor; the action made Mortimer even more uncomfortable.

"Ye-es, well." Joliffe transferred his gaze to Scrugthorpe. "Might I remind you that she should, by now, have been in our hands? That but for your lack of foresight, she would be?"

Scrugthorpe scowled. "How was I to know it were a race-week? And that gentlemen would be using that road? Everything went perfect, elsewise."

Joliffe sighed and raised his eyes heavenwards. Amateurs—they were all the same. How had he, who had spent his life thus far successfully extracting a living from the rich, descended to the company of such? Lowering his gaze, his glance fell on Mortimer Babbacombe. Joliffe's lips curled in a contemptuous sneer.

"Ought to mention," Brawn put in, surfacing from his tankard. "She was walking the street with a swell today—right chummy—looked like the same swell as wot rescued them."

Joliffe's eyes narrowed and he sat forward. "Describe this swell."

"Fair hair—like gold. Tall, looked like he'd strip to advantage. One of them bloods with a fancy cape." Brawn grimaced. "They all look the same to me."

Not so to Joliffe. "This blood—was he staying at the Barbican Arms?"

"Seemed so—the ostlers and all seemed to know him."

"Harry Lester." Joliffe tapped a pensive nail on the table. "I wonder..."

"Wonder what?" Mortimer looked at his erstwhile friend

and most urgent creditor, his expression that of a man well out of his depth. "Would this man Lester help us?"

Joliffe snorted. "Only to the hangman's noose. But his peculiar talents bear consideration." Leaning forward, Joliffe placed both elbows on the table. "It occurs to me, my dear Mortimer, that we may be involving ourselves unnecessarily here." Joliffe smiled, an empty gesture that made Mortimer shrink. "I'm sure you'd be most agreeable to any way of achieving our aim without direct involvement."

Mortimer swallowed. "But how can Lester help us—if he won't?"

"Oh—I didn't say he won't—just that we needn't ask him. He'll help us entirely for the fun of it. Harry Lester, dear Mortimer, is the rake supreme—a practitioner extraordinaire in the gentle art of seduction. If, as seems possible, he's got your uncle's widow in his sights, then I wouldn't like to bet on her chances." Joliffe's smile grew. "And, of course, once she's demonstrably no longer a virtuous widow, then you'll have all the reason you need to legally challenge her guardianship of your cousin." Joliffe's gaze grew intent. "And once your pretty cousin's legacy's in your hands, you'll be in a position to pay me, won't you, Mortimer?"

Mortimer Babbacombe swallowed—and forced himself to nod.

"So what do we do now?" Scrugthorpe drained his tankard.

Joliffe considered, then pronounced, "We sit tight and watch. If we get a chance to lay hands on the lady, we will—just like we planned."

"Aye—far as I'm concerned, that's how we should do it—no sense in leaving anything to chance."

Joliffe's lip curled. "Your animosity is showing, Scrugthorpe. Please remember that our primary aim here is to discredit Mrs Babbacombe—not satisfy your lust for revenge."

Scrugthorpe snorted.

"As I was saying," Joliffe went on. "We watch and wait. If Harry Lester succeeds—he'll have done our work for us. If not, we'll continue to pursue the lady—and Scrugthorpe here will have his chance."

At that, Scrugthorpe smiled. Lecherously.

Chapter Four

When Lucinda drove into the yard of the Barbican Arms the next morning, Harry was waiting, shoulders against the wall, arms crossed over his chest, his boot against the wall for balance. He had plenty of time to admire the artless picture of mature womanhood seated beside Grimms in his aunt's gig. Elegantly gowned in a cornflower blue carriage dress, her dark hair restrained in a severe chignon thus revealing the delicate bones of her face, Lucinda Babbacombe predictably turned the heads of those still dawdling in the yard. Thankfully, the thoroughbred races were to commence that morning; most of Harry's contemporaries were already at the track.

Grimms brought Em's gig to a neat halt in the centre of the yard. With an inward snort, Harry pushed away from the wall.

Lucinda watched him approach—his graceful stride forcefully reminded her of a prowling tiger. A very definite thrill coursed through her; she avoided smiling her delight, contenting herself with a mild expression of polite surprise. "Mr Lester." Calmly, she extended her hand. "I hadn't expected to see you this morning—I thought you were here for the races."

His brows had risen sceptically at her first remark; on her

second, his green eyes glittered. He grasped her hand—for an instant, as his eyes held hers, Lucinda wondered why she was playing with fire.

''Indeed,'' Harry replied, his habitual drawl in abeyance. He helped her from the carriage, steadying her on the cobbles. ''I own to surprise on that score myself. However, as you are my aunt's guest, and at my instigation, I feel honour-bound to ensure you come to no harm.''

Lucinda's eyes narrowed but Harry, distracted by the absence of groom or maid—Grimms had already disappeared into the stables—did not notice.

''Speaking of which, where's your groom?''

Lucinda allowed herself a small smile. ''Riding with your brother and Heather. I have to thank you for sending Gerald to us—he's entertaining company for Heather—I dare say she would otherwise grow bored. And, of course, that leaves me free to tend to business without having to worry my head over her.''

Harry didn't share her confidence—but he wasn't, at this point, concerned with her stepdaughter. His expression hardened as he looked down at her. He was still holding her hand; tucking it into his arm, he turned her towards the inn door. ''You should at least have a groom with you.''

''Nonsense, Mr Lester.'' Lucinda slanted him a curious glance. ''Surely you aren't suggesting that at my age I need a chaperon?''

Looking into her eyes, softly blue, their expression openly independent, challenging yet oddly innocent, Harry inwardly cursed. The damned woman didn't need a chaperon—she needed an armed guard. Just why he had elected himself to the post was not a point he was willing to pursue. He contented himself with repressively stating, ''In my opinion, Mrs Babbacombe, women like you should not be allowed out alone.''

Her eyes twinkled; two tiny dimples appeared in her

cheeks. "Actually, I'd like to see the stables." She turned to the archway leading from the main yard.

"The stables?"

Her gaze ranging their surroundings, Lucinda nodded. "The state of the stableyard frequently reflects the quality of the inn's management."

The state of the stables suggested the innkeeper of the Barbican Arms was a perfectionist; everything was neat, clean and in its place. Horses turned their heads to stare as Lucinda picked her way over the cobbles, still wet with dew, forced more than once to lean heavily on Harry's arm.

When they reached the earthen floor of the stables, she determinedly straightened. Regretfully withdrawing her fingers from the warmth of his sleeve, she strolled along the row of loose boxes, stopping here and there to acknowledge their curious occupants. She eventually reached the tack room and peered in.

"Excuse me, ma'am—but you shouldn't be in here." An elderly groom hurried out.

Harry stepped out of the shadows. "It's all right, Johnson. I'll see the lady safe."

"Oh!—it's you, Mr Lester." The groom touched his cap. "That's all right and tight, then. Ma'am." With another tug of his cap, the groom retreated into the tack room.

Lucinda blinked, then shot a glance at Harry. "Is it always so ordered? So..." She waved at the loose boxes, each with their half-doors shut. "So exact?"

"Yes." Harry looked down at her as she stopped beside him. "I stable my carriage horses here—you may rest assured of the quality in that respect."

"I see." Deeming all queries on the equine side of business satisfied, Lucinda turned her attention to the inn proper.

Ushered through the main door, she looked with approval on half-panelled walls, well-polished and glowing mellowly. Sunshine reflected from crisply whitewashed walls; stray beams danced across the flagged floor.

Mr Jenkins, the innkeeper, a neat, rotund person of genial mien, bustled up. Harry performed the introductions, then stood patiently by while Lucinda explained her purpose. Unlike Blount, Mr Jenkins was all gratified helpfulness.

Lucinda turned to Harry. "My business with Mr Jenkins will keep me busy for at least an hour. I wouldn't for the world impose on your kindness, Mr Lester—you've already done so much. And I can hardly come to harm within the inn."

Harry didn't blink. For her, the Arms played host to a panapoly of dangers—namely his peers. Meeting her innocent gaze with an impenetrable blandness, he waved a languid hand. "Indeed—but my horses don't run until later."

Which comment, he noted, brought a flash to her eyes. She hesitated, then, somewhat stiffly, acquiesced, inclining her head before turning back to Mr Jenkins.

Wearing patience like a halo, Harry followed his host and his aunt's guest about the old inn, through rambling passageways and storerooms, to bedchambers and even to the garrets. They were returning down an upper corridor when a man came blundering out of a room.

Lucinda, opposite the door, started; glimpsing the man from the corner of her eye, she braced herself for a collision. Instead, she was bodily set aside; the chubby young gentleman ran full tilt into a hard shoulder. He bounced off, crumpling against the door frame.

"Ouf!" Straightening, the man blinked. "Oh—hello, Lester. Slept in, don't y'know. Can't miss the first race." He blinked again, a puzzled frown forming in his eyes. "Thought you'd be at the track by now."

"Later." Harry stepped back, revealing Lucinda.

The young man blinked again. "Oh—ah, yes. Terribly sorry, ma'am—always being told I should look where I'm going. No harm done, I hope?"

Lucinda smiled at the ingenuous apology. "No—none." Thanks to her protector.

''Good-oh! I'd best be on my way, then. See you at the track, Lester.'' With an awkward bow and a cheery wave, the youthful sprig hurried off.

Harry snorted.

''Thank you for your assistance, Mr Lester.'' Lucinda slanted him a smile. ''I'm really most grateful.''

Harry took full note of the quality of her smile. Coolly, he inclined his head and waved her on in Jenkins's wake.

By the end of her tour, Lucinda was impressed. The Barbican Arms, and Mr Jenkins, were a far cry from the Green Goose and Jake Blount. The inn was spick and span throughout; she had found nothing remotely amiss. Her inspection of the books was a mere formality; Mr Mabberly had already declared the Arms a model of good finance.

She and her host spent a few minutes going over the plans for an extension to the inn. ''For we're full to overflowing during race-meets and more than half full at other times.''

Lucinda gave her general approval and left the details for Mr Mabberly.

''Thank you, Mr Jenkins,'' she declared, pulling on her gloves as they headed for the door. ''I must tell you that, having visited all but four of the fifty-four inns owned by Babbacombe and Company, I would rank the Barbican Arms as one of the best.''

Mr Jenkins preened. ''Very kind of you to say so, ma'am. We do strive to please.''

With a gracious nod, Lucinda swept out. Once in the courtyard she paused. Harry stopped beside her; she looked up at his face. ''Thank you for your escort, Mr Lester—I'm really most grateful considering the other demands on your time.''

Harry was too wise to attempt an answer to that.

Lucinda's lips twitched; she looked quickly away. ''Actually,'' she mused, ''I was considering viewing this race-meet.'' She brought her eyes back to his face. ''I've never been to one before.''

Harry looked down at her ingenuous expression. His eyes narrowed. "Newmarket race-track is no place for you."

She blinked, taken aback—Harry glimpsed real disappointment in her eyes. Then she looked away. "Oh."

The single syllable hung in the air, a potent testimony to crushed anticipation. Fleetingly, Harry closed his eyes, then opened them. "However, if you give me your word you will not stray from my side—not to admire some view, some horse or a lady's bonnet—" He looked down at her, his jaw setting. "I will engage to escort you there."

Her smile was triumphant. "Thank you. That would be very kind."

Not kind—foolish. It was, Harry was already convinced, the most stupid move he'd ever made. An ostler came running in answer to his curt gesture. "I'll have my curricle. You can tell Grimms to take Lady Hallows's gig back; I'll see Mrs Babbacombe home."

"Yessir."

Lucinda busied herself with the fit of her gloves, then meekly allowed herself to be lifted to the curricle's seat. Settling her skirts, and her quivering senses, she smiled serenely as, with a deft flick of the reins, Harry took the greys onto the street.

The race-track lay west of the town on the flat, grassy, largely tree-less heath. Harry drove directly to the stables in which his string of racers were housed, a little way from the track proper, beyond the public precincts.

Lucinda, drinking in the sights, could not miss the glances thrown their way. Stableboy and gentleman alike seemed disposed to stare; she was unexpectedly grateful when the stable walls protected her from view.

The horses were a wonder. Lifted down from the curricle, Lucinda could not resist wandering down the row of loose boxes, patting the velvet noses that came out to greet her, admiring the sleek lines and rippling muscles of what, even to her untutored eyes, had to be some of the finest horses in England.

Engaged in a brisk discussion with Hamish, Harry followed her progress, insensibly buoyed by the awed appreciation he saw in her gaze. On reaching the end of the row, she turned and saw him watching her; her nose rose an inch but she came back, strolling towards him through the sunshine.

"So all's right with entering the mare, then?"

Reluctantly, Harry shifted his gaze to Hamish's face. His head-stableman was also watching Lucinda Babbacombe, not with the appreciation she deserved but with horrified fascination. As she drew nearer, Harry extended his arm; she placed her fingertips upon it without apparent thought. "Just as long as Thistledown's fetlock's fully healed."

"Aye." Hamish bobbed respectfully at Lucinda. "Seems to be. I told the boy to just let her run—no point marshalling her resources if it's still weak. A good run's the only way to tell."

Harry nodded. "I'll stop by and speak to him myself."

Hamish nodded and effaced himself with the alacrity of a man nervous around females, at least those not equine in nature.

Suppressing a grin, Harry lifted a brow at his companion. "I thought you agreed not to be distracted by horses?"

The look she bent on him was confidently assured. "You shouldn't have brought me to see yours, then. They are truly the most distractingly beautiful specimens I've ever seen."

Harry couldn't suppress his smile. "But you haven't seen the best of them. Those on that side are two-and three-year-olds—for my money, the older ones are more gracious. Come, I'll show you."

She seemed only too ready to be led down the opposite row of boxes, dutifully admiring the geldings and mares. At the end of the row, a bay stallion reached confidently over the half-door to investigate Harry's pockets.

"This is old Cribb—a persistent devil. Still runs with the best of them though he could retire gracefully on his accumulated winnings." Leaving her patting the stallion's nose, Harry went to a barrel by the wall. "Here," he said, turning back. "Feed him these."

Lucinda took the three dried apples he offered her, giggling as Cribb delicately lipped them from her palm.

Harry glanced up—and saw Dawlish outside the tackroom, standing stock-still, staring at him. Leaving Lucinda communing with Cribb, Harry strolled over. "What's up?"

Now that he was beside him, it was clear Dawlish was staring at his companion, not him.

"*Gawd's truth*—it's happened."

Harry frowned. "Don't be ridiculous."

Dawlish turned a pitying eye on him. "Ridiculous, is it? You do realize, don't you, that that's the first female you've ever shown your horses?"

Harry lifted a supercilious brow. "She's the first female ever to have shown an interest."

"Hah! Might as well hang up your gloves, gov'nor— you're a goner."

Harry cast his eyes heavenwards. "If you must know, she's never been to a race-meet before and was curious— there's nothing more to it than that."

"Ah-hah. So *you* says." Dawlish cast a long, defeated look at the slight figure by Cribb's box. "All *I* says is that you can justify it any ways you want—the conclusions still come out the same."

With a doleful shake of his head, Dawlish retreated, muttering, back into the tack-room.

Harry wasn't sure whether to laugh or frown. He glanced back at the woman, still chatting to his favourite stallion. If it wasn't for the fact they would shortly be surrounded by crowds, he might be inclined to share his henchman's pessimism. But the race-track, in full view of the multitudes, was surely safe enough.

"If we leave now," he said, returning to her side, "we can stroll to the track in time for the first race."

She smiled her acquiescence and laid her hand on his arm. "Is that horse you were talking of—Thistledown—running in it?"

Smiling down into her blue eyes, Harry shook his head. "No—she's in the second."

Lucinda found herself trapped in the clear green of his eyes; she studied them, trying to gauge what he was thinking. His lips twitched and he looked away. Blinking as they emerged into the bright sunshine, Lucinda asked, "Your aunt mentioned you managed a stud?"

His fascinating lips curved. "Yes—the Lester stud." With ready facility, prompted by her questions, he expiated at length on the trials and successes of his enterprise. What he didn't say but Lucinda inferred, it being the logical deduction to make from his descriptions, was that the stud was both a shining achievement and the very core of his life.

They reached the tents surrounding the track as the runners for the first race were being led to the barrier. All Lucinda could see was a sea of backs as everyone concentrated on the course.

"This way—you'll see better from the stands."

A man in a striped vest was guarding a roped arena before a large wooden stand. Lucinda noted that while he insisted on seeing passes from the other latecomers ahead of them, he merely grinned and nodded at Harry and let them by. Harry helped her up the steep steps by the side of the planks serving as seats—but before they could find places a horn blew.

"They're off." Harry's words echoed from a hundred throats—about them, all the patrons craned forward.

Lucinda turned obediently and saw a line of horses thundering down the turf. From this distance, neither she nor anyone else could see all that much of the animals. It was the crowd that enthralled her—their rising excitement gripped her, making her breathe faster and concentrate on the race. When the winner flashed past the post, the jockey flourishing his whip high, she felt inordinately glad.

"Well raced." Harry's gaze was on the horses and riders as they slowed and turned back to the gates.

Lucinda grasped the moment to study him. He was intent on observation, green eyes keenly assessing, shrewdly calculating. For an instant, she saw him clearly, his features unguarded. He was a man who, despite all other distractions in his life, was totally devoted to his chosen path.

He turned his head at that moment. Their eyes met, their gazes locked. He was standing on the step below her so her eyes were almost level with his. For a moment, he said nothing, then his lips twisted wrily.

Lucinda suppressed a delicate shiver.

With a gesture, Harry indicated the crowded lawns before them. "If you truly want to experience a race-meet, then you have to promenade."

Her own lips curving, Lucinda inclined her head. "Lead on, Mr Lester—I'm entirely in your hands."

She saw his brow quirk but pretended ignorance. On his arm, she descended the steps and exited the private enclosure.

"The Jockey Club maintains the stand for the use of its members," Harry informed her when she glanced back.

Which meant he was a well-known member. Even Lucinda had heard of the pre-eminence of the Jockey Club. "I see. The races are run under their auspices, I take it?"

"Correct."

He led her on a slow perambulation through the milling crowds. Lucinda felt distinctly round-eyed—she wanted to see everything, understand the fascination that drew so many gentlemen to Newmarket.

The same fascination that drove Harry Lester.

He showed her the bookmakers, each surrounded by knots of punters eager to lay their bets. They paraded before the tents and pavilions; again and again they were stopped by some acquaintance of Harry's, keen to exchange a few words. Lucinda was prepared to be on her guard, but she encountered nothing but polite deference in the glances thrown her way; all those who stopped to talk were disarmingly correct. Nevertheless, she felt no impulse to withdraw her hand from the security of her escort's elbow, where he had tucked it, drawing her close. In the press of male bodies, it was unquestionably comforting to have Harry Lester by her side. There were, she discovered, some ladies present. "Some have a real interest in the sport—usually the older ones." Relaxed, in his milieu, Harry glanced down at her. "Some of the younger ladies have a vested interest; their families, like mine, have a long-standing connection with the turf."

Mouthing an "oh", Lucinda nodded. There were other ladies, too, whom he had not seen fit to comment upon, who, she suspected, held dubious right to the title. The racetrack, however, was an overwhelmingly male domain—every sub-category of the male population was certainly represented. Lucinda was quite sure she would have neither the courage nor the inclination to attend again—not unless Harry Lester was her escort.

"It's nearly time for the next race. I must speak to Thistledown's jockey."

Lucinda nodded, conveying with a glance her intention of staying with him.

Harry threw her a brief smile then concentrated on forging a path to the mounting yard.

"She seems very lively, sir," the jockey vouchsafed as he settled in the saddle. "But the competition's stiff—Jonquil—that mare out of Herald—is a starter. And Caught by the Scruff, too. And some of them others are experienced racers—it'll be a miracle if she wins, what with her fetlock just come good an' all."

Harry nodded. "Just let her go—let her set her own pace.

We'll consider this a trial, nothing more. Don't cram her—and no whip.''

Lucinda left his side to pat the mare's velvet muzzle; a huge, dark brown eye invited her understanding. Lucinda grinned. ''Hopeless, aren't they?'' she crooned. ''But you don't want to listen to them—men are notoriously hopeless at judging women. They should never so presume.'' From the corner of her eye, she saw Harry's lips lift; he exchanged a glance with the jockey, who grinned. ''You just go out there and win the race—then see how they react. I'll see you in the winner's circle.''

With a last pat for the mare, she turned and, with divine disregard for the expression on Harry Lester's face, allowed him to lead her back to the stands.

He secured seats in the third row, almost opposite the post. Lucinda leaned forward, eagerly scanning the horses trotting towards the barrier. She waved when Thistledown appeared.

Harry, watching her, laughed.

''She'll win—you'll see.'' With smug confidence, Lucinda sat back.

But when the horn sounded and the barrier was dropped, she leant forward again, eyes keenly searching the thundering charge for Harry's colours of green and gold. So intent was she that she didn't even notice she rose to her feet, in company with all the other spectators, as the horses rounded the bend. As they entered the straight, a gap appeared in their ranks—Thistledown shot through.

''There she is!'' Lucinda grabbed Harry's arm. Only deeply entrenched decorum kept her from jigging up and down. ''She's winning!''

Harry was too riveted to answer.

But Thistledown was indeed showing the field a clean pair of heels. Halfway down the straight, her stride lengthened even more—she appeared to be flying when she flashed past the post.

"She won! She won!" Lucinda grasped both Harry's arms and all but danced. "I *told* you she would!"

Rather more accustomed to the delights of victory, Harry looked down at her face, wreathed in smiles and lit by the same joy he still felt every time one of his horses came home first. He knew he was smiling, as delighted as she if rather more circumspect in showing it.

Lucinda turned back to locate Thistledown, now being led from the course. "Can we go and see her now?"

"Indeed we can." Harry took her hand and tucked it tightly in his arm. "You promised to meet her in the winner's circle, remember?"

Lucinda blinked as he steered her out of the crowded stand. "Is it permissible for ladies to enter the winner's circle?"

"There's no rule against it—in fact—" Harry slanted a glance at her "—I suspect the Head of the Committee will be delighted to see you." When she shot him a suspicious glance, he laughed and urged her on. Once out of the enclosure and free of those members keen to press their congratulations, a path cleared before them, leading directly to the roped arena where Thistledown, shiny coat flickering but clearly untired by her dash, waited patiently.

As soon as Lucinda emerged from the crowd, the mare pushed her head forward, dragging on the reins to get to Lucinda's side. Lucinda hurried forward, crooning her praises. Harry looked on indulgently.

"Well, Lester! Another trophy for your mantel—surprised it hasn't collapsed."

Harry turned as the President of the Jockey Club, present Head of the Race Committee, appeared at his elbow. In his hands, he held a gold-plated statuette in the shape of a lady.

"Remarkable run—truly remarkable."

Shaking hands, Harry nodded. "Particularly as she's just recovered from a strained fetlock—I wasn't sure I'd race her."

"Just as well you did." The President's eye was on the horse and the woman apparently chatting to the beast. "Nice conformation."

Harry knew very well that Lord Norwich was not referring to the mare. "Indeed." His tone was dry; Lord Norwich, who had known him from the cradle, lifted a brow at him.

Glancing at the statuette, Harry confirmed that the lady was indeed decently garbed, then nodded at Lucinda. "It was Mrs Babbacombe who delivered the inspirational address prior to the race. Perhaps she should accept the award on my behalf?"

"Excellent idea!" Beaming, Lord Norwich strode forward.

Shielded by her brimming happiness, the aftermath of fulfilled excitement, Lucinda had succeeded in blithely ignoring the avid interest of the spectators. Lord Norwich, however, was impossible to ignore. But Harry strolled forward to stand by their side, quieting her uncertainties.

Lord Norwich gave a short speech, praising the mare and Harry's stables, then gallantly presented the statuette—to her.

Surprised, Lucinda looked at Harry—he smiled and nodded.

Determined to rise to the occasion, she graciously thanked his lordship.

"Quite, quite." His lordship was quite taken. "Need to see more game fillies at the track, what?"

Lucinda blinked at him.

Harry reached for her elbow and drew her to his side. He nodded at his strapper. "Take her back to the stables."

With a last lingering look for Lucinda, Thistledown was led away. Lord Norwich and the rest of the crowd turned away, already intent on the next race.

Still conscious of the fading thrill, Lucinda looked around, then cast a glance upwards.

Harry smiled. ''And you have my heartfelt thanks, too, my dear. For whatever magic you wove.''

Lucinda met his eyes—and stopped breathing. ''There was no magic.'' She felt his fingers on hers; she watched as he raised her hand and brushed his lips across the backs of her fingers. A long shiver traced its path down her spine, leaving an odd warmth in its wake. With an effort she veiled her eyes, breaking his spell. Catching her breath, she made a bid for her usual confidence; she raised the statuette and presented it to him, defiantly meeting his eyes.

He took it in his other hand, his gaze steady on hers.

Time lost its meaning; they stood, largely forgotten, in the centre of the winner's circle. Men crowded about, jostling each other but not touching them. They stood close, so close the small ruffle on Lucinda's bodice brushed the long lapel of Harry's coat. He sensed its flutter as her breathing grew more rapid but he was lost in her eyes, in a world of misty blue. He watched them widen, darken. Her lips softened, parted. Her bodice made contact with his coat.

His head had begun its slow descent when sanity awoke—and frantically hauled on his reins.

Great heavens! They were in the winner's circle at Newmarket!

Shaken to the depths of his soul, Harry dragged in a quick breath. He tore his gaze from her face, from the consternation that was filling her eyes, and the soft blush that had started to tinge her cheeks, and looked about them. No one, thank heaven, had seen.

His heart pounding, he took a firm grip of her elbow—and took refuge in action. ''If you've seen enough of the racing, I should get you back to Em's—she'll be wondering where you are.''

Lucinda nodded—the faintly bored drawl left her no choice. She felt—she didn't know what—shaken, certainly, but regretful, and resentful, too. But she couldn't argue with his wish to be gone from here.

But they still had the gamut of well-wishers to run—they were stopped constantly, more than one gentleman wishing to make an offer for the mare.

Harry faced the hurdles with what patience he could, conscious that all he wished to do was escape. With her. But that was impossible—she was his danger, his Waterloo.

From now on, every time he looked into her face would be like looking down the barrel of a loaded gun. A weapon that could land him in painful slavery.

If he was wise, he wouldn't look too frequently.

Lucinda sensed his withdrawal although he cloaked it well. His urbane charm came to the fore—but he would not meet her eyes, her puzzled glances.

They finally escaped the crowds and walked back, in silence, to the stables. He lifted her to his curricle and swung up beside her, his expression closed.

He drove back to Hallows Hall without a word, his apparent concentration on his horses a wall Lucinda made no attempt to breach.

But when he drew up before the steps and secured the reins, then came around and lifted her down, she held her position in front of him even though his hands fell immediately from her. "Thank you for a most...instructive morning, Mr Lester."

His eyes flicked to hers; he took a step back. "A pleasure, Mrs Babbacombe." He bowed with innate grace. "And now I must bid you adieu."

Surprised, Lucinda watched as he swung up to the curricle's seat. "But won't you stay for luncheon? Your aunt would be delighted, I'm sure."

The reins in his hands, Harry drew in a deep breath—and forced himself to meet her gaze. "No."

The word hung between them—an unconditional denial. Harry saw the understanding in her eyes, sensed the sudden catch in her breathing as his rejection bit home. But it was better this way—to nip it in the bud before it could flower. Safer for her as well as for him.

But her eyes showed no comprehension of that, of the dangers he could see so clearly. Soft and luminous, they looked at him in hurt surprise.

He felt his lips twist in bitter self-mockery. "I can't."

It was all the explanation he could give. With a crack of his whip, he set his horses down the drive—and drove away.

Chapter Five

Three days later, Lucinda was still not satisfied that she understood what had happened. Seated in a wicker chair in a patch of sunlight in the conservatory, she idly plied her needle while her thoughts went round and round. Heather was out riding with Gerald, Sim in close attendance; her hostess was somewhere in the gardens, supervising the planting of a new border. She was alone, free to pursue her thoughts—little good though that seemed to be doing her.

She knew she was inexperienced in such matters, yet deep within lay an unshakeable conviction that something—something eminently to be desired—had sprung to life between herself and Harry Lester.

He had almost kissed her in the winner's circle.

The moment was etched in her memories, frustratingly incomplete, yet she could hardly fault him for drawing back. But he had then retreated, so completely it had left her feeling unexpectedly vulnerable and inwardly bruised. His parting words confounded her. She could not misconstrue the implications of that "No"—it was his "I can't" that truly baffled her.

He had not appeared since; courtesy of Gerald, who now haunted the house, she had learned he was still in Newmarket. Presumably, she was supposed to believe he was so immensely busy with his racers that he had no time for her.

With an inward snort, Lucinda jabbed her needle into the canvas. She was, she supposed, now too much the businesswoman to enjoy being shortchanged. But time was slipping away; she couldn't remain at Hallows Hall forever. Clearly, if she wanted to know just what might be possible, she was going to have to take an active hand.

But how?

Five minutes later, Em entered through the garden door, the hem of her old gardening gown liberally splattered with earth, a pair of heavy gloves in one hand.

"Phoof!" Sinking into the other armchair, separated from Lucinda's by a small matching table, Em pushed back wisps of browny-grey hair. "That's done!" She slanted a glance at her guest. "You look very industrious—quite wifely, in fact."

Lucinda smiled but did not look up.

"Tell me," Em mused, her sharp gaze belying her idle tone. "Have you ever considered remarrying?"

Lucinda's needle halted; she looked up, not at her hostess but through the long windows at the garden. "Not until recently," she eventually said. And returned to her needlework.

Em studied her downbent head, a definite glint in her eye. "Yes—well, it takes one like that. Suddenly pops into your mind—and then won't get out." With an airy wave of her gardening gloves, she continued, "Still, with your qualifications I hardly think you need worry. When you get to London you'll have a goodly selection of beaux lining up to put a ring on your finger."

Lucinda slanted her a glance. "My qualifications?"

Em's wave became a flourish. "Your breeding for one— nothing wrong with that, even if your parents were disowned. Your grandparents could hardly change the blood in their veins—as far as Society's concerned that's what counts.'' As if just struck by the fact, Em added, ''In fact, the Giffords are as well connected as the Lesters.''

''Indeed?'' Lucinda eyed her warily.

Blithely, Em continued, ''And there's your fortune, too—that legacy of yours would satisfy the most demanding. And you're hardly an antidote—you've got style, that indefinable something—noticed it straight off. Once the Bruton Street *mesdames* get a look at you they'll be vying for your custom, mark my words.''

''I am, however, twenty-eight.''

The blunt comment brought Em to a blinking halt. Turning her head, she stared at her guest. ''So?''

Lucinda grimaced and looked down at her work. ''Twenty-eight, I suspect, is somewhat long in the tooth to be attractive to town beaux.''

For an instant longer, Em stared at her, then hooted with laughter. ''*Rubbish,* my dear! The *ton*'s awash with gentlemen whose principal reason for avoiding matrimony is that they cannot stomach the bright-eyed young misses.'' She snorted. ''More hair than wit, most of them, believe me.'' She paused to study Lucinda's face, half-averted, then added, ''It's very common, my dear, for men to prefer more experienced women.''

Lucinda glanced up—and met Em's eye. A light blush slowly spread across her cheeks. ''Yes, well—that's another thing.'' Her gaze flicked to the green vistas beyond the window as she dragged in a determined breath. ''I'm not. Experienced, I mean.''

Em stared. ''Not?''

''My marriage wasn't really a marriage at all—it was a rescue.'' Lucinda frowned, her gaze dropping to her tapestry. ''You must remember I was only sixteen at the time—and Charles was nearing fifty. He was very kind—we were good friends.'' Her voice low, she added, ''Nothing more.'' Straightening her shoulders, she reached for her scissors,

"Life, I fear, has passed me by—I've been put back on the shelf without having been properly off it in the first place."

"I...see." Em blinked owlishly at the tips of her half-boots, peeking from beneath her dirtied hem. A broad smile slowly broke across her face. "You know—your...er, in-experience is not really a handicap, not in your case. In fact," she continued, her old eyes lighting, "it could well be a positive advantage."

It was Lucinda's turn to look puzzled.

"You see, you have to think of it from your prospective husband's point of view." Eyes wide, Em turned to face her. "What *he*'ll see is a mature and capable woman, one of superior sense who can manage his household and family while at the same time providing more—" she paused to gesture "—*satisfying* companionship than a young girl ever could. If you make no show of your innocence, but allow him to—" she gestured again as she groped for words "—*stumble* on it in good time, I'm sure you'll find he'll be only too delighted." With a last shrewd glance at Lucinda's face, Em added, "I'm sure Harry would be."

Lucinda's eyes narrowed. She favoured her impossible hostess with a long stare. Then, looking down to tidy her needlework, she asked, "Has he ever shown any interest in marrying?"

"Harry?" Em sat back, a smile on her lips. "Not that I ever heard. But then, he's never had need to—there's Jack before him and Gerald behind. Jack's about to marry—I just got a summons to the wedding. So Harry's thoughts are unlikely to turn to gold rings and white icing—not, that is, unless he's given an incentive to pursue the subject."

"Incentive?"

"Hmm. Often the case with gentlemen in that particular mould—won't have a bar of marriage until the benefits become so blatantly obvious that even they, with their blinkered vision, can see it." Em snorted. "It's all the fault of the light-skirts, of course. Lining up to give them anything they want—whatever their lusts desire—without any strings attached.''

"I suspect," Lucinda said, her expression guarded, Harry's "No" echoing in her ears, "that it would take a fairly...powerful incentive to make Harry actively desire to be wed.''

"Naturally—Harry's all male to his toes. He'll be as reluctant as the best of them, I don't doubt. He's lived a life of unfettered hedonism—he's hardly likely to volunteer to change." Em brought her gaze back to Lucinda's face. "Not, of course that that should deter *you*.''

Lucinda's head came up; she met Em's old eyes and saw in them a wealth of understanding. She hesitated for only a moment. "Why not?''

"Because, as I see it, you've got the most powerful weapon in your hands already—the only one that'll work.'' Em sat back and shrewdly regarded Lucinda. "Question is, are you game enough to use it?''

For a long moment, Lucinda stared at her hostess—then shifted her gaze to the gardens. Em sat patiently watching her—slim, dark-haired, fingers clasped in her lap, her expression calm and uninformative, a faraway look in her soft blue eyes.

At length, the blue eyes slowly turned back to Em. "Yes," Lucinda stated, calm and determined. "I'm game.''

Em grinned delightedly. "Good! The first thing you'll need to understand is that he'll resist for all he's worth. He'll not come to the idea meekly—you can't expect it of him.''

Lucinda frowned. "So I'll have to put up with more of this..." It was her turn to gesture as she sought for words. "This uncertainty?''

"Undoubtedly," Em averred. "But you'll have to hold firm to your purpose. And your plan.''

Lucinda blinked. "Plan?''

Em nodded. "It'll take a subtle campaign to bring Harry to his knees.''

Lucinda couldn't help but smile. "His knees?"

Em gave her a haughty look. "Of course."

Head on one side, Lucinda eyed her unpredictable host-ess. "What do you mean by 'subtle'?"

"Well." Em settled in her chair. "For instance…"

"GOOD EVENING, Fergus."

"Good evening, sir."

Harry allowed his aunt's butler to relieve him of his great-coat, then handed him his driving gloves. "Is my brother here?" Harry turned to the mirror hanging above the ormolu table.

"Master Gerald arrived half an hour ago. In his new pha-eton."

Harry's lips twitched. "Ah, yes—his latest achieve-ment." He made an almost imperceptible adjustment to the folds of his crisply white cravat.

"Your aunt will be delighted to see you, sir."

Harry met Fergus's eyes in the mirror. "No doubt." He let his lids fall, veiling his eyes. "Who else is here?"

"Sir Henry and Lady Dalrymple, Squire Moffat and Mrs Moffat, Mr Butterworth, Mr Hurst and the Misses Pinker-ton." When Harry stood stock still, green eyes hooded, his expression utterly blank, Fergus added, "And Mrs Babba-combe and Miss Babbacombe, of course."

"Of course." Regaining his equilibrium, momentarily shaken, Harry resettled the gold pin in his cravat. Then, turning, he strolled towards the drawing-room door. Fergus hurried to open it.

Announced, Harry entered.

Her eyes met his immediately—she wasn't experienced enough to cloak her spontaneous reaction. She'd been speaking with Mr Hurst, a gentleman farmer whom Em, Harry suspected, had long had in her matchmaking sights. Harry paused just inside the door.

Lucinda smiled across the room—an easy, politely welcoming smile—and turned back to Mr Hurst.

Harry hesitated, then, languidly urbane, strolled to where his aunt sat ensconced in regal purple on the end of the *chaise.* "Dear Aunt," he said, bowing elegantly over her hand.

"Wondered if you'd come." Em grinned her triumph.

Harry ignored it. He nodded to the lady sharing the *chaise.* "Mrs Moffat." He was acquainted with all those Em had deigned to invite—he simply hadn't expected her to invite them. Tonight was the last night of the race-meet; tomorrow, after the final races in the morning, all the gentlemen would head back to town. His aunt's summons to dinner was not unusual, yet he had thought long and hard before accepting. Only the certainty that Mrs Babbacombe would shortly be returning to Yorkshire, well beyond his reach, while he intended to retire to Lester Hall in Berkshire, had persuaded him to do so. That, and the desire to see her again, to look into her misty blue eyes—one last time.

He had expected to share a table with his aunt, his brother, his aunt's houseguests—and no one else. Theoretically, the current situation, with so many distractions, should have reassured him. In fact, it did the opposite.

With a nod, and a swift glance at Mrs Babbacombe's dark head, he left the *chaise,* drifting to where Sir Henry Dalrymple stood chatting with Squire Moffat. Gerald was near the windows, Heather Babbacombe beside him, both conversing easily with Lady Dalrymple. The Misses Pinkerton, determined spinsters in their thirties, chatted with Mr Butterworth, Sir Henry's secretary.

Harry's gaze lingered on Lucinda, clad in delicate blue watered silk and talking animatedly with Mr Hurst; if she felt it, she gave no sign.

"Ah, Lester—up for the races, I presume?" Sir Henry beamed a welcome.

Squire Moffat snorted good-humouredly. "Precious little else to bring you this way."

"Indeed." Harry shook hands.

"Saw that filly of yours win in the second—great run." Sir Henry's faraway gaze said he was reliving the moment. Then he abruptly refocused. "But tell me, what do you think about Grand Larrikin's chances in the Steeple?"

The ensuing discussion on the Duke of Rutland's latest acquisition took up no more than half of Harry's mind. The rest was centred on his siren, apparently oblivious on the other side of the room.

Lucinda, perfectly aware of the sideways glances he occasionally sent her way, doggedly adhered to Em's strictures and studiously ignored him, prattling on about she knew not what to the loquacious Mr Hurst. He, thankfully, seemed so taken with the sound of his voice—a soothing baritone— that he didn't notice her preoccupation.

Struggling to focus her mind on his words, Lucinda steadfastly denied the increasing compulsion to glance at Harry Lester. Since the moment he'd appeared in the doorway, clad in severe black and white, his hair gleaming guinea gold in the candlelight, every elegant, indolent line screaming his position in the *ton,* her senses had defied her.

Her heart had leapt—Em had warned her that her summons wouldn't bring him if he didn't want to come. But he had arrived; it felt like she'd won, if not the first battle, then at least the opening skirmish.

She was so excruciatingly aware of him that when he left Squire Moffat and Sir Henry to languidly stroll her way, she had to clench her fists hard to stop herself from turning to greet him.

Approaching from behind her, Harry saw the sudden tension in her shoulders, bared by her gown. Beneath his heavy lids, his green eyes glinted.

As he drew abreast of her, he ran his fingertips down her bare forearm to capture her hand. Her eyes widened, but

when she turned to smile at him there was no hint of per-
turbation in her face.

"Good evening, Mr Lester."

Harry smiled down into her eyes—and slowly raised her
hand to his lips. Her fingers quivered, then lay passive. "I
sincerely hope so, Mrs Babbacombe."

Lucinda accepted the salute with stalwart calm but withdrew her tingling fingers the instant he eased his grip. "I
believe you're acquainted with Mr Hurst?"

"Indeed. Hurst." Harry exchanged nods with Pelham
Hurst, who he privately considered a pompous ass. Hurst
was a year older than he; they'd known each other since
childhood but mixed as much as oil and water. As if to
confirm he'd changed little with the years, Hurst launched
into a recital of the improvements he had made to his fields;
Harry dimly wondered why, with a vision like Lucinda Babbacombe in the vicinity, Pelham thought he'd be interested.

But Pelham rambled on.

Harry frowned. It was wellnigh impossible to keep his
gaze on Lucinda Babbacombe's face while Hurst kept bom-
barding him with the details of crop rotation. Grasping a
rare moment when Pelham paused for breath, he turned to
Lucinda. "Mrs Babbacombe—"

Her blue eyes came his way—only to slide past him. She
smiled in welcome. "Good evening, Mr Lester. Mr Butterworth."

Harry momentarily closed his eyes, then, opening them,
forced himself to step back to allow Gerald and Nicholas
Butterworth to make their bows. Together with Heather
Babbacombe they joined their circle.

Any chance of detaching his quarry was lost.

Mentally gritting his teeth, Harry held to his position by
her side. He knew he should go and chat to the Misses
Pinkerton; he excused his lapse on the grounds that, being
what he was, he made them nervous.

The thought gave him pause.

Lucinda felt very like Daniel in the lion's den—not at all sure of her safety. When the first trickle of heat slid down her nape, she didn't immediately register its cause. But when, but moments later, she felt the skin above her breasts tingle, she shot a frowning glance sideways.

Harry met it with a blank green stare—slightly questioning, all innocence. Lucinda raised her brows and pointedly turned back to the conversation. Thereafter, she steadfastly ignored all her senses—as best she could. She greeted Fergus's arrival and his stately pronouncement that dinner was served with considerable relief.

"If you would allow me to escort you in, Mrs Babbacombe?" Pelham Hurst, ineradicably convinced of his self-worth, offered a heavily creased sleeve.

Lucinda smiled and was about to accept when a drawling voice cut off her escape.

"I'm afraid, Hurst, that I'm before you." Harry smiled at his childhood acquaintance, the gesture in no way softening the expression in his eyes. "By days."

On the words, Harry shifted his green gaze to Lucinda's face—and dared her to contradict him.

Lucinda merely threw him an equable smile. "Indeed." She gave Harry her hand and allowed him to place it on his sleeve, turning as he did so to inform Mr Hurst, "Mr Lester has been of great assistance while we've been in Newmarket. I don't know how we would have escaped our upturned carriage if he hadn't happened along."

The remark, of course, led Pelham to enquire in deeply solicitous vein as to their accident. As the Misses Pinkerton had already wandered into the dining-room eschewing all male escort, Hurst was free to stroll on Lucinda's other side as Harry guided her into the dining-room.

By the time he took his seat beside the lovely Mrs Babbacombe, Harry's temper was straining at its leash.

But there were more trials in store. Lady Dalrymple, a motherly soul who had long deplored his unmarried state, took the seat to his left. Even worse, the Pinkerton sisters settled in opposite, warily eyeing him as if he was some potentially dangerous beast.

Harry wasn't sure they were wrong.

Ignoring all distractions, he turned to his fair companion. "Dare I hope you're satisfied with the outcome of your visit to Newmarket, Mrs Babbacombe?"

Lucinda fleetingly met his eyes, confirming that the question was, indeed, loaded. "Not entirely, Mr Lester. I can't help but feel that certain interests must regrettably be classed as unfinished business." Again she met his gaze and allowed her lips to curve. "But I dare say Mr Blount will manage."

Harry blinked, breaking the intensity of his gaze.

With a gentle smile, Lucinda turned away as Mr Hurst claimed her attention. She resisted the compulsion to glance to her right until the second course was being removed. Ineffably elegant, apparently relaxed, Harry was engaged in idly entertaining Lady Dalrymple.

At that moment, Mrs Moffat called upon Lady Dalrymple to confirm some report. Harry turned his head—and met Lucinda's determinedly mild gaze.

Resigned, he lifted a brow at her. "Well, my dear— what's it to be? The weather is singularly boring, you know nothing about horses and as for what I'd prefer to discuss with you—I'm quite certain you'd rather I didn't."

Attack—with a vengeance. There was no mistaking the light in his eyes. Lucinda inwardly quivered—outwardly she smiled. "Now there you are wrong, Mr Lester." She paused for an artful second before continuing, her gaze holding his, "I'm definitely interested in hearing about Thistledown. Is she still in town?"

He sat so perfectly still Lucinda found she couldn't breathe. Then one brow slowly rose; his eyes were jewel-like, crystalline and hard, sharp and brilliant. "No—she's on her way back to my stud."

"Ah, yes—that's in Berkshire, is it not?"

Harry inclined his head, not entirely trusting himself to speak. At the edge of his vision, the Pinkertons, oddly sensitive to atmospherics, were tensing, casting glances at each other, frowning at him.

Lady Dalrymple leaned forward to speak around him. "I'm so sorry you won't be here for my little gathering next week, Mrs Babbacombe. Still, I dare say you're quite right in heading to town. So much to do, so much to see—and you're young enough to enjoy the social whirl. Will you be bringing your stepdaughter out?"

"Possibly," Lucinda answered, ignoring the sudden tension that had laid hold of the body between them. "We'll make the decision once we're in town."

"Very wise." Lady Dalrymple nodded and turned back to Em.

"London?"

The question was quiet, his tone flat.

"Why, yes." Calmly, Lucinda met his green gaze. "I have four more inns to inspect, remember?"

For a pregnant moment, Harry's eyes held hers. "Which are?"

Again his voice was soft, steel cloaked in silk. Very thin silk.

"The Argyle Arms in Hammersmith, the Carringbush in Barnet, the Three Candles in Great Dover Street and the Bells at Wanstead."

"What's that about the Bells?"

Lucinda turned her head as Pelham Hurst butted in.

"An excellent inn—I can recommend it to you, Mrs Babbacombe. Often stay there myself. Don't like to risk my cattle in town, don't y'know."

Harry ignored him completely. Luckily, as a large apple tart was placed in front of him at that moment, Pelham didn't notice. Harry grasped the opportunity as the diners sat up and looked over the dessert course to lean closer to

Lucinda. He spoke in a steely whisper. "You're out of your senses! Those are four of the busiest inns in England—they're all coaching inns on the major roads."

Lucinda reached for a jelly. "So I've been told."

Harry gritted his teeth. "My dear Mrs Babbacombe, your little act of being an inspector might work in country inns—" he broke off to thank Lady Dalrymple for passing the cream which he immediately set down "—but it'll get you nowhere in town. Aside from that, you cannot visit any of those inns alone."

"My dear Mr Lester." Lucinda turned to face him, her eyes wide. "Surely you're not trying to tell me my inns are dangerous?"

He was trying to tell her just that.

But Pelham Hurst, hearing only snippets, put in his oar. "Dangerous? Not a bit of it! Why, you'll be as safe as…as here, at the Bells. Highly recommend it, Mrs Babbacombe."

Glimpsing the goaded expression in Harry's green eyes, Lucinda kept her lips straight and made haste to assure Mr Hurst, "Indeed, sir. I'm sure that wasn't what Mr Lester meant."

"Mr Lester, as you well know, meant that you have as much experience as a green girl and rather less chance of surviving one of your 'inspections' at any of those inns without receiving at least three propositions and a *carte blanche.*" Having delivered this clarification through clenched teeth, Harry attacked the custard that had appeared before him.

"Would you care for some cream?" Lucinda, having helped herself to a generous dollop, caught a drip on her fingertip. Her eyes, innocently blue, met Harry's as she lifted her finger to her lips.

For a blind instant, as she lowered her hand, Harry could see nothing beyond her lips, ripe and luscious, begging to be kissed. He heard nothing, was blissfully unaware of the gaggle of conversation about him. Abruptly, he grabbed hold of his reins, fast disappearing. He lifted his gaze and met hers. His eyes narrowed. "No, thank you."

Lucinda simply smiled.

"It's fattening," Harry added but she only smiled more. She looked very like the cat who had found the right jug.

Stifling a curse, Harry applied himself to his dessert. It was no business of his if she insisted on swanning into danger. He'd warned her. "Why can't Mabberly do those inns? Let him earn his keep."

"As I told you before, Mr Mabberly does not have the right qualifications for conducting an inquisition." Lucinda kept her voice low, grateful that Heather had distracted Mr Hurst.

She waited for the next comment—but her neighbour merely snorted and fell silent.

His disapproval lapped about her in waves.

Harry endured the rest of the evening outwardly urbane, inwardly brooding. The gentlemen did not linger over their port, which was just as well for he was no good company. But when they repaired to the drawing room, he discovered that, rather than the general chatty atmosphere which was the norm for Em's dinners, and which he'd been determined to exploit for his own ends, tonight, they were to be entertained by the Babbacombes, Mrs and Miss.

With no good grace, Harry sat on a chair at the back of the room, unmoved by what he recognised as an exemplary performance. The tea trolley appeared as the applause died.

His temper sorely strained, he was one of the last to come forward for his cup.

"Yes, indeed," Em said as he strolled up, nodding to Lady Dalrymple. "We'll be there—I'll look for you. It's going to be such fun to go the rounds again."

Harry froze, his hand half-outstretched.

Em looked up—and frowned. "Here you are!"

Harry blinked—and took the cup, Em's frown reflected

in his eyes. "Are you contemplating going up to town, dear Aunt?"

"Not contemplating." Em threw him a belligerent glance. "I'm going. As Lucinda and Heather are set to visit there, we've decided to go together. Much the best thing. I've sent for them to open Hallows House—Fergus is going up to-morrow. It'll be wonderful, being in the swing again. I'll introduce Lucinda and Heather to the *ton*. Marvellous distraction—just what I need to give me new life."

She actually had the gall to smile at him.

Harry forced himself to utter the expected platitudes—under Lady Dalrymple's mild gaze he could hardly give his aunt the benefit of his true conclusions.

After that he beat a hasty retreat—even Squire Moffat and the intricacies of the local drainage system were preferable to farther contemplation of the web he now found himself in. The only one he could be open with was his brother.

"Em's insane. They all are," he growled as he joined Gerald by the window. Heather Babbacombe was chatting to Mrs Moffat. Harry noticed Gerald's smiling gaze rarely left the girl.

"Why? No harm in them going up to London. I'll be able to show Heather all the sights."

Harry snorted. "While London's rakes are attempting to show Mrs Babbacombe their etchings, no doubt."

Gerald grinned. "Well—you can take care of that. None of the others will come near if you hover at her shoulder."

The look Harry bent on him spoke volumes. "In case it's escaped your admittedly distracted intelligence, brother dear, I am currently the principal Lester target in the match-makers' sights. Having lost Jack to Miss Winterton, they'll redouble their efforts and turn all their guns on yours truly."

"I know." Gerald shot him an insouciant grin. "You've no idea how grateful I am that you're there for them to aim at—with any luck, they won't remember me. Good thing—I haven't a bean of your experience."

He was clearly sincere. Harry swallowed the sharp words that rose to his tongue. Lips compressed, he retired to the safety of Sir Henry's conversation, studiously avoiding any further contact with his fate. His siren. She who would lure him onto the rocks.

The guests left in concert. Harry and Gerald, as family, stood back to let the others take their leave. Em stepped onto the porch to wave farewell; Gerald and Heather were dallying by the drawing-room door. In the shadows by the front door, Harry found himself beside his temptation.

His aunt, he noticed, was in no rush to return.

"Will we see you in London, Mr Lester?"

She cast him an artless glance—Harry couldn't decide whether it was real or not. He looked down at her face, upturned to his, blue eyes wide. "I have no plans to come up again this Season."

"A pity," she said, but her lips curved. "I had thought to repay my debt to you, as we'd agreed."

It took him a moment to recall. "The waltz?"

Lucinda nodded. "Indeed. But if you will not be in town, then this is goodbye, sir."

She held out her hand; Harry took it, shook it, but didn't release it. Eyes narrowing, he studied her open expression, those eyes he would swear could not lie.

She was saying goodbye. Perhaps, after all, escape was still possible?

Then her lips curved slightly. "Rest assured I'll think of you while waltzing through the London ballrooms."

Harry's fingers closed hard about hers—and clenched even harder about his gloves. The eruption that shook him— of anger, and sheer, possessive desire—very nearly broke his control. She looked up, eyes flaring, her lips slightly parted. It was no thanks to her, and the soft, tempting look in her eyes, that he managed to mask his reaction. He forced

himself to release her hand; his face felt stiff as he bowed.
''I will bid you good night, Mrs Babbacombe.''

With that, he walked out, missing the disappointment that
clouded Lucinda's gaze.

From the top of the steps, she watched him drive away—
and prayed that Em was right.

Chapter Six

She was still praying ten days later when, flanked by Em and Heather, she strolled into Lady Haverbuck's ballroom. Her ladyship's ball was the first of the major gatherings they had attended. It had taken them four days to successfully transfer to Hallows House in Audley Street; the following days had been taken up with the necessary visits to modistes and the fashionable emporia. The previous evening, Em had hosted a select party to introduce both her guests to the *ton*. The acceptances had gratified Em; it had been many years since she had been in the capital. But there had been one who had not responded to the white, gilt-edged card.

Lucinda herself had penned it and directed it to Harry's lodgings in Half Moon Street. But she had looked in vain for his golden head.

"You'll have to let him go if you want him to come back," Em had declared. "He's like one of his horses—you can lead him to the pond but you can't make him drink."

So she had let him go—without a murmur, without the slightest hint that she wanted him.

He had yet to return.

Now, elegantly clad in shimmering blue silk the colour of cornflowers, her dark hair artfully coiffed to fall in soft curls about her brow and temples, Lucinda stood on the edge of the ballroom floor and looked about her.

They were neither early nor late; the room was already well filled but not yet crowded. Elegant gentlemen conversed with fashionable matrons; dowagers and chaperons lined the walls. Their charges, mostly young girls making their come-out, were readily identified by the pale pastel hues of their gowns. They were everywhere, the bolder ones chatting with youthful swains, others, more bashful, clinging to each other's company.

"Oh—look!" Heather clutched Lucinda's gloved arm. "There's Miss Morley and her sister." Heather glanced up at Lucinda. "May I join them?"

Lucinda smiled across the room at the cheery Misses Morley. "Certainly. But look for us when you've done."

Heather flashed her an excited smile.

Em snorted. "We'll be over there." Wielding a lorgnette, she pointed to a *chaise* by the wall.

With a bob, Heather slipped away, a vision in palest turquoise muslin, her golden curls dressed high.

"A most fetching gown—even if 'twas I who chose it," Em declared. She led the way to the *chaise*.

Lucinda followed. She was about to copy Em's descent onto the brocaded seat when young Mr Hollingsworth appeared by her elbow, an older, infinitely more elegant gentleman beside him.

"I say, Mrs Babbacombe—delighted to see you again." Mr Hollingsworth all but jigged with excitement.

Lucinda murmured a polite greeting; they had met Mr Hollingsworth at Hatchard's the day before.

"Beg you'll allow me to present my cousin, Lord Ruthven."

The elegant gentleman, dark-haired and handsome, bowed gracefully. "I am indeed honoured to make your acquaintance, Mrs Babbacombe."

Curtsying, Lucinda glanced up and met his eye; she suppressed a grimace as she recognised the speculative glint therein.

"A rose amongst so many peonies, my dear." With a languid wave, Ruthven dismissed the youthful beauties about them.

"Indeed?" Lucinda raised her brows sceptically.

Lord Ruthven was undeterred. And, as she quickly discovered, his lordship was not the only gentleman desirous of more mature company. Others, largely of similar ilk, strolled up, unhesitatingly claiming Ruthven's good offices to perform the introductions. His lordship, indolently amused, obliged. Remembering her duties, Lucinda tried to retreat, only to have Em snort—indulgently amused—and wave her away.

"I'll keep an eye on Heather. You go and enjoy yourself—that's what *ton* balls are for."

Thus adjured, and reflecting that Em knew rather more about watching over young girls at *ton* balls than she did, Lucinda inwardly shrugged and smiled on her would-be court. In a very short time, she found herself surrounded—by a collection of gentlemen she mentally categorised as Harry Lester's contemporaries. They were, one and all, ineffably charming; she could see no harm in enjoying their company.

Then the music started, lilting strains wafting over the bright heads.

"Dare I claim your first cotillion in the capital, my dear?"

Lucinda turned to find Lord Ruthven's arm before her. "Indeed, sir. I would be delighted."

A smile curved his lips. "No, my dear—it is *I* who am delighted. You will have to find another adjective."

Lucinda met his eyes. She raised her brows. "My mind is a blank, sir. What would you suggest?"

His lordship was perfectly prepared to oblige. "Devastated with joy? In alt? Over the moon with happiness?"

Lucinda laughed. As they took their places in the set, she arched a brow at him. "How about—'so impressed I am unable to find words to express it'?"

Lord Ruthven grimaced.

As the evening progressed, Lucinda found herself much in demand. As she was ranked among the matrons, she did not have a dance-card but was free to bestow her hand on whomever she chose from amongst her assiduous court. Indeed, their assiduousness triggered her innate caution; while Ruthven appeared too good-humoured and indolent to be dangerous, there were others whose eyes held a more intent gleam.

One such was Lord Craven, who strolled into the ballroom late, surveyed the field from the top of the steps, then beat a disguised but determined path to her side. Dragooning Mr Satterly into providing an introduction, his lordship was bowing over Lucinda's hand when the unmistakable strains of a waltz filled the room.

"My dear Mrs Babbacombe, dare I hope you'll take pity on a latecomer and grant me the honour of this waltz?"

Lucinda met Lord Craven's dark hooded eyes—and decided her pity would be more wisely bestowed elsewhere. She let her eyes widen and swept a questioning glance at the gentlemen surrounding her.

They instantly came to her rescue, dismissing Lord Craven's claim as outrageous, presumptuous and unfair and plying her with any number of alternatives. Laughing lightly, Lucinda withdrew her fingers from Lord Craven's clasp. "I fear you must take your chance amongst the competition, my lord."

His lordship's expression turned distinctly stiff.

"Now, let's see." Lucinda smiled at her cavaliers and was about to bestow her favour upon Mr Amberly, who, despite the appreciation in his eyes, was another more inclined to amusement than seduction, when she felt a stir beside her.

Long, strong fingers encircled her arm, sliding over the bare skin just above her glove.

"My waltz, I believe, Mrs Babbacombe."

Lucinda's breath caught. She swung to face Harry; their eyes met—his were very green, his gaze sharp, oddly intent. Elation swept Lucinda. She struggled to hide it.

Harry's lips curved, their ends lifting in a smile, which turned to a grimace, hidden as he bowed.

When he straightened, his features were impassive.

"I say, Lester! This is dashed unfair." Mr Amberly all but pouted. Others muttered in similar vein.

Harry merely lifted a supercilious brow, his now-hooded glance shifting to rest on Lucinda's face. "As I recall, my dear, you owe me a waltz. I've come to claim it."

"Indeed, sir." Savouring the sound of his deep drawl, Lucinda gave up her fight and smiled her delight. "I always pay my debts. My first waltz in the capital is yours."

Harry's lips twitched but he stilled them. With an elegant gesture he claimed her hand and settled it on his sleeve.

Lucinda slanted a quick, triumphant glance at Em, but her mentor was hidden by her court. "Gentlemen." With a sunny smile and a nod for her disappointed cavaliers, who were shooting disgruntled glances at her unexpected partner, she allowed him to lead her to the floor.

Harry held his tongue until they reached the dance floor but as soon as he had whirled them into the swirling throng, he looked down and trapped Lucinda's blue gaze. "I realise, Mrs Babbacombe, that your experience does not extend to the vagaries of the *ton*. I fear I should warn you that many of the gentlemen presently intent on your smiles should be treated with extreme caution."

More concerned with adequately following his assured lead than with her redundant court, Lucinda frowned. "That's obvious."

Harry's brows slowly rose.

Lucinda's frown grew distracted. "I'm rather more than

seven, you know. As far as I can see, there's no reason I shouldn't enjoy myself in their company—I'm hardly so green as to be taken in by their charms.''

At that, Harry snorted. For a full minute, he considered the possibility of scaring her with a more explicit warning, then mentally shook his head. She wasn't, he realised, recalling Jake Blount and the Green Goose, easily scared. But he could hardly countenance her court.

Glancing down at her face, he saw she was still frowning, but in an abstracted way. ''What's wrong?''

She started—and cast an irritated glance up at him.

''Well?''

''If you must know,'' Lucinda said. ''I'm not terribly experienced at waltzing. Charles didn't, of course. I've had lessons—but it's rather different on a crowded floor.''

Harry couldn't stop his slow grin. ''Just relax.''

The look she sent him suggested that she found his humour ill-conceived.

Harry chuckled—and drew her closer, tightening his arm about her so she could more easily sense his intentions.

Lucinda held her breath—then slowly let it out. Their new positions were just this side of decent but she felt immeasurably more secure. When Harry twirled her through a complicated set of turns as they negotiated the end of the room, she followed without faltering. Reassured, she relaxed—only to find her wits almost overwhelmed by her senses. His hard thighs brushed hers as they progressed down the room; she could feel the heat of his large body reaching for her, enveloping her, his strength effortlessly whirling her about. A strange tension gripped her, making breathing difficult. It was matched by the tension in the arm locked about her. From beneath her lashes, Lucinda glanced up. Her gaze found his lips. As she watched, they firmed into a straight line.

It was an uphill battle but Harry strove to push aside all distractions—like the enthralling curves encased in blue silk nestling in his arms, the womanly softness of those curves and the supple planes of her back, like the subtle scent of her that rose to tease his senses, and the graceful curve of her neck exposed by her new hairstyle—and remind his wandering wits just why he had returned to London. "When are you planning to visit your inns?"

Lucinda blinked, and shifted her gaze to his eyes. "Actually, I'd thought to start with the Argyle Arms at Hammersmith tomorrow."

Harry didn't bother asking if she'd arranged a suitable escort. The damned woman was so irrationally sure of herself, so ignorant of the true dangers, so determinedly wilful… His lips thinned. "I'll call for you at nine."

Lucinda's eyes opened wide.

Harry noticed—and frowned at her. "You needn't fear—we'll go in my curricle and I'll have Dawlish along. Perfectly proper, I assure you."

Lucinda swallowed her happy laugh. Em's strictures replayed in her head. She eyed him consideringly, then gracefully acquiesced. "Thank you, sir. Your company will, I'm sure, make the drive more interesting."

Harry narrowed his eyes, but could make nothing of her serene expression. Stifling a humph, he drew her a fraction closer—and set his mind to enjoying the rest of the waltz.

At its end, he strolled back with her to where her court waited, impatient and eager. Harry read the anticipation in their eyes. He stiffened. Instead of yielding his fair partner up with a flourish and an elegant bow, the prescribed procedure, he covered her hand, resting on his sleeve, with his. And remained, thus anchored, by her side.

Lucinda pretended not to notice. She chatted gaily, ignoring the intrigued glint in Lord Ruthven's perceptive eye and Mr Amberly's disapproving expression. Harry, she noted, made no attempt whatever to contribute to the conversation; she longed to look at him but standing so close, she could not. Not without making her interest obvious. She was somewhat relieved when Mrs Anabelle Burnham, a young matron ambling past on the arm of Mr Courtney, decided to join them.

"I declare, it's going to be yet another crush." Mrs Burnham fluttered her lashes at Lord Ruthven before turning her laughing brown eyes on Lucinda. "You'll grow used to them, my dear. And you have to admit these larger gatherings are...entertaining."

Another laughing glance went Lord Ruthven's way.

Lucinda struggled to keep her lips straight. "Indeed." Nothing loath, she slanted a glance up at her silent partner. "And the entertainment takes so many varied forms, too. Don't you find it so?"

Anabelle Burnham blinked, then her teasing smile brightened. "Oh, definitely, my dear Mrs Babbacombe. Definitely!"

She bestowed another arch glance on Lord Ruthven, then turned her sights on Mr Amberly.

Lucinda didn't notice—she was trapped in Harry's green gaze. The planes of his face were hard, sculpted, his expression impassive yet growing more forbidding by the second. She saw his eyes narrow slightly; his lips were a thin line. Breathing was suddenly very difficult.

The squeak of the violins saved her—she didn't know from what.

"Mrs Babbacombe—I declare you must, positively you must, bestow this quadrille on my poor self."

With a mental curse, Lucinda glanced to where Mr Amberly stood watching her, entreaty in his eyes. She blinked—and realized that he was begging her to rescue him. She couldn't help but smile.

She glanced up at Harry; gently she withdrew her hand from under his. For an instant, his fingers tensed—then he released her. "I haven't thanked you for my waltz, sir." Lucinda lifted her eyes to his. "It was most enjoyable."

His features were granite. He said nothing but bowed, effortlessly elegant in his severe black and white.

With an inclination of her head, Lucinda turned away and placed her hand on Mr Amberly's sleeve.

To her intense disappointment, Harry was no longer present when, at the conclusion of the quadrille, Mr Amberly returned her to the small group close by Em's chaise. Under cover of the conversation, Lucinda scanned the surrounding shoulders but could not find the ones she sought. She saw Heather, bright-eyed and clearly enjoying herself hugely. Her stepdaughter waved, then turned back to her set—Gerald Lester, the Morley sisters and two other young gentlemen. Feeling distinctly deflated, Lucinda forced herself to pay attention to her cavaliers. The circle around her, which had earlier thinned, now pressed in on her. She could understand why these events were labelled crushes. At least Mrs Burnham hadn't deserted her.

But her enjoyment in the evening had waned; it was an effort to conjure a bright smile and a witty response to the constant flow of repartee.

Somewhat later, the lilting strains of another waltz drifted from the musicians' dais at the other end of the room. Lucinda blinked. She had already danced with all those of her court she considered reasonably safe—she hadn't anticipated another waltz.

She glanced up—to find Lord Ruthven's eyes upon her, a curious glint in their depths. "Well, my dear?" he drawled. "Which one of us will you favour with a second dance?"

Lucinda raised her brows haughtily. And scanned those she had yet to favour at all. Three promptly pressed their claims—one, a rakish dandy a few years older than herself but infinitely more experienced, held the greatest promise. He might have impropriety on his mind but he was, Lucinda judged, manageable. With a serene smile, and a cool glance for Ruthven, she extended her hand. "Mr Ellerby?"

To give him his due, Mr Ellerby behaved with all due decorum on the dance floor. By the end of the dance, Lucinda was congratulating herself, not only on her increasing confidence in the waltz itself but on her accurate assessment of her partner, when Mr Ellerby abruptly reverted to type.

"Quite stuffy in here, don't you find, Mrs Babbacombe?"

Lucinda glanced up and smiled. "Indeed—one could hardly find it not. The room is certainly very crowded."

So crowded she could no longer see Em's *chaise*, concealed by the milling throng. The waltz had landed them at the other end of the room.

"This window leads to the terrace. And Lady Haverbuck's gardens are extensive. Perhaps a stroll through them would cool your cheeks, Mrs Babbacombe?"

Lucinda turned to stare at her erstwhile partner. The gleam in his eyes was unmistakable.

"Wouldn't want you to feel faint, would we?" Mr Ellerby leaned closer on the words, pressing her fingers meaningfully.

Lucinda stiffened. She drew a steady breath and opened her lips, fully intending to advise her importunate partner that her temper rarely induced faintness, when she was saved the necessity.

"I don't think Mrs Babbacombe needs a stroll on the terrace just now, Ellerby."

The drawled yet steely words sent a frisson of excitement through Lucinda; they turned Mr Ellerby sulky.

"Just a suggestion." He waved the point aside, then offered Lucinda his arm, all but glowering at Harry. "It's suppertime, Mrs Babbacombe."

"Indeed," came from beside her.

Lucinda glanced up and saw Harry's green gaze grow coldly challenging. His fingers feathered down her arm, then firmed about her wrist. She quelled a shiver.

Harry looked down at her. "If you wish, Mrs Babbacombe, I'll escort you in."

He lifted her hand and settled it on his sleeve. Lucinda met his eyes—then turned to coolly dismiss Mr Ellerby. "Thank you for an enjoyable waltz, sir."

Mr Ellerby looked as if he wished to argue—then he met Harry's gaze. With a grumpy air, he bowed. "My pleasure, ma'am."

"I'm sure it was," Harry muttered beneath his breath as he turned Lucinda towards the supper room.

"I beg your pardon?" Lucinda blinked up at him.

"Nothing." Harry's lips compressed. "Couldn't you chose a more suitable partner than Ellerby? You had enough real gentlemen about you—or can't you tell the difference?"

"Of course I can." Suppressing her smile, Lucinda put her nose in the air. "But I'd already danced with all of them. I didn't want to appear to be encouraging them."

Harry resisted the urge to grind his teeth. "Believe me, Mrs Babbacombe, you would do better to encourage the gentlemen and avoid the rakes altogether."

Lucinda copied one of Em's snorts. "Nonsense. I was in no danger."

She glanced up to see Harry's face turn to stone.

"Mrs Babbacombe, I have severe difficulty believing you would recognise danger if you fell over it."

Lucinda had to purse her lips to stop her smile. "Bosh!" she eventually returned.

Harry sent her a severe glance—and determinedly steered her to a table. Not one of the small, intimate tables for two in the corners of the large supper-room, but a table to accommodate a small army set close to the buffet in the room's centre. Taking the seat he held for her, Lucinda cast him a puzzled glance.

She was even more puzzled when her court tentatively descended, and Harry forbore to bite. He sat beside her, leaning back in the chair, a champagne flute in one long-fingered hand, and silently monitored the conversation. His brooding presence acted as a most efficient damper, ensuring the jocularity remained strictly within acceptable bounds. Anabelle Burnham, joining them, cast one awed glance at Harry, then caught Lucinda's eye and raised her glass in a silent toast. Lucinda risked a quick grin, then let her gaze slide to Harry's face.

He was watching her, not the others, his lips set in a line she was coming to know well, his green gaze jewel-like and impenetrable.

Lucinda quelled a shiver. Turning back to the table, she forced herself to focus on her less interesting admirers.

As HE HAD PROMISED, Harry was waiting for her in the hall of Hallows House at precisely nine o'clock the next morning.

Descending the stairs with a dark blue half-cape draped over her bluebell-hued carriage dress, Lucinda watched as his gaze skimmed knowledgeably over her. When she reached the hall and came forward, her hand extended, his gaze lifted to her face.

Harry saw the feminine smugness in her eyes—and frowned. "At least you shouldn't freeze." He took her hand and bowed over it—then considered the sight of her small, slim hand nestling in his much larger one. "Don't forget your gloves."

Lucinda lifted a brow—and drew her gloves from her reticule. "I'll be back for luncheon, Fergus." Dutifully drawing on her gloves, she glanced at Harry. "Will you join us, Mr Lester?"

"No—please convey my regrets to my aunt." Harry grasped her arm and steered her to the door. Em's house was probably safe enough but his clubs would be safer; he no longer trusted his aunt. "I have other engagements."

Lucinda stopped on the top of the steps and glanced up at him. "I do hope I'm not inconveniencing you by claiming your escort to my inns?"

Harry looked down at her, his eyes narrowing. She was an inconvenience unlike any he'd ever encountered. ''Not at all, my dear. If you recall, I wished this on myself.'' Why, he refused to consider. ''But it's time we were away.''

He led her down the steps, then lifted her to his curricle's seat. Avoiding Dawlish's eye, he retrieved the reins. He waited only until his henchman's weight tipped the carriage before giving his horses the office.

Lucinda thoroughly enjoyed her drive through the morning streets, not yet crowded. She saw orange-sellers plying their wares; she heard strawberry girls calling housewives to their doors. The city seemed different, clean and pristine beneath the morning's dew, the dust yet to be stirred by the traffic. The varied greens of the trees in the Park shifted like a kaleidoscope. Harry drove them briskly along the gravelled carriageway, then out of a distant gate. Once they were bowling along the road to Hammersmith, Lucinda turned her mind to business. Harry answered her questions on the inns they passed, occasionally referring to Dawlish. Lucinda noted that Harry's groom seemed uncommonly morose; his dour tones suggested a death in the family.

But she forgot Dawlish and his patent misery when they pulled into the yard of the Argyle Arms.

The Argyle Arms proved to have much in common with the Barbican Arms. The innkeeper, a Mr Honeywell, after one glance at Harry, deferentially escorted her over the large inn, which extended over three interconnecting wings. They were on the ground floor of one of the wings heading back towards the main entrance when Lucinda heard laughter behind a door she had assumed led to a bedchamber.

Visions of the Green Goose flitted through her mind. It had, however, been male laughter. She halted. ''What's behind that door?''

Mr Honeywell remained impassive. ''A parlour, ma'am.''

''A parlour?'' Lucinda frowned and looked about her.

"Ah, yes—this was a separate house at one time, wasn't it?"

Mr Honeywell nodded and gestured for her to proceed.

Lucinda stood stock-still and stared at the closed parlour door. "That makes four parlours—does the inn's custom necessitate so many?"

"Not directly," Mr Honeywell admitted. "But we're so near town we often rent rooms to groups for meetings."

Lucinda pursed her lips. "I would like to inspect this extra parlour, Honeywell."

Mr Honeywell's expression grew wary. "Ah—this one's currently occupied, ma'am, but there's another just like it in the other wing. If you'd like to see that?"

"Indeed." Lucinda nodded but her eyes remained on the closed door. "Who is currently using this one?"

"Er…a group of gentlemen, ma'am."

Lucinda's brows rose; she opened her mouth.

"But—" Mr Honeywell smoothly interposed his stout frame between Lucinda and the door "—I really wouldn't advise you to interrupt them, ma'am."

Taken aback, Lucinda allowed her brows to rise higher; for a silent moment, she looked down on Mr Honeywell. When she spoke, her tone was chilly. "My dear Mr Honeywell—"

"Who's in there, Honeywell?"

Lucinda blinked. It was the first time in an hour that Harry had spoken.

Mr Honeywell cast an imploring glance at him. "Just a group of young bloods, sir. You'll know the sort."

"Indeed." Harry turned to Lucinda. "You can't go in."

As frigidly imperious as any dowager, Lucinda slowly turned and met his gaze. "I beg your pardon?"

Harry's lips twisted slightly but his gaze did not waver. "Let me put it this way." His tone was peculiarly soft, silky, with an undercurrent that threatened all manner of danger. "You're not going in there."

If Lucinda had had any doubt as to the reality behind the unsubtle threat, it was laid to rest by the look in his eyes, the set of his jaw and the tension that slowly infused his large frame. Despite her rising temper, she was assailed by an instinctive urge to step back—and a totally maniacal impulse to call his bluff just to see what he would do. Ignoring the shiver that squirmed down her spine, she sent him a seething glance, then transferred her gaze, now icy, to Mr Honeywell. "Perhaps you could show me this other parlour?"

The innkeeper's sigh was almost audible.

Shown the second parlour, repeatedly assured that it was virtually identical to the other, Lucinda gave her haughty approval. Stripping off her gloves, she nodded at Honeywell. "I'll examine the books now. You may bring them in here."

Honeywell departed to fetch his ledgers.

Leaving her gloves and reticule on the table, Lucinda slowly walked down the room. Halting by the window, she drew in a steadying breath and swung to face Harry. He had followed in her wake; she watched as he drew near, stopping directly before her, one brow lifting, a challenging look in his eye.

Lucinda returned it in full measure. "It may interest you to know, Mr Lester, that I had no intention of—" she gestured dismissively "—barging into a private meeting. A fact I was about to make clear to Mr Honeywell when you chose to intervene."

The arrested, suddenly defensive expression that flickered in Harry's eyes was balm to Lucinda's temper. She immediately pressed her advantage. "I merely wished to enquire as to the bona fides of the customers using my inn—a right I'm sure even *you* will agree is mine." She waggled a finger under his nose. "Neither you nor Mr Honeywell had any justification for jumping to such a conclusion—as if I was a child unaware of the proprieties! And *you,* sir, had no right to threaten me as you did.'' Turning aside and folding her arms, Lucinda elevated her chin. ''I wish to hear an apology, sir, for your ungentlemanly behaviour.''

Silence greeted her demand. Harry studied her face, his gaze clear and steady. Then his lips twisted. ''I suggest, my dear, that you refrain from holding your breath. My behaviour throughout this morning has been gentlemanly in the extreme.''

Lucinda's eyes flew wide. *''Gentlemanly?''* Her arms dropped as she rounded on him.

Harry held up a hand. ''I'll admit that both Honeywell and I might have jumped to unwarranted conclusions.'' His eyes met hers, his expression fleetingly rueful. ''For myself, for that, I apologise unequivocally. For the rest, however…'' His face hardened. ''I fear you must excuse it on the grounds of extreme provocation.''

''Provocation?'' Lucinda stared at him. ''What provocation was that, pray tell?''

The provocation of keeping her safe, shielded, the undeniable, instinctive impulse that had him in its grip. The truth echoed in Harry's head; he struggled to shut his mind against it. He looked into her eyes; softly blue, they searched his, then widened. He dropped his gaze to her lips, full, blush red—a potent temptation. As he watched, they parted fractionally. About them, silence reigned; between them, the tension grew. Compelled, as aware of her increased breathing as he was of the deepening thud in his veins, Harry lifted a finger and, with the lightest of touches, traced her lower lip.

The shudder his touch evoked in her reverberated deep in his marrow.

His breath caught; if he met her gaze, he would be lost.

Desire welled, unexpectedly strong; he fought to shackle it. He tried to draw breath, tried to step away, and could not.

Distant footsteps drew near; in the corridor a board creaked.

Swiftly, Harry bent his head and touched his lips to hers in a caress so brief he barely registered the gentle movement of her lips beneath his.

When the door opened and Honeywell came in, he was standing by the fireplace, some yards from Lucinda. The innkeeper noticed nothing amiss; he placed the heavy ledgers on the table and looked hopefully at Lucinda.

Harry glanced her way but her back was to the window, hiding her expression.

Lucinda hesitated, just long enough to marshall her thoroughly disordered wits. Then she swept forward, plastering an expression of such haughtiness on her face that Mr Honeywell blinked. ''Just the figures for this year, I think, Mr Honeywell.''

The innkeeper hurried to do her bidding.

Immersed in figures, Lucinda struggled to soothe her tingling nerves, inflamed by that too-fleeting kiss and further abraded by Harry's lounging presence. For one instant, she had felt as if the world had spun wildly; determinedly, she put the memory aside and concentrated on Mr Honeywell's accounts. By the time she was satisfied, half an hour had passed, leaving her once more in control. Quite capable of maintaining a steady flow of artless prattle all the way back to Audley Street.

Other than bestowing on her one, long, unnervingly intent look, Harry made no particular comment, replying readily to any questions, but leaving the conversational reins in her hands. When they drew up at Em's steps, Lucinda felt she had handled them with laudable skill.

She chose the moment when Harry lifted her down to say, ''I'm really most grateful for your escort, Mr Lester.'' With what she considered commendable fortitude, she refrained from further comment.

''Indeed?'' Harry arched one brow.

Lucinda fought against a frown. "Indeed," she returned, meeting his gaze.

Harry looked down at her face, at her wonderfully blue eyes, gleaming with feminine defiance—and wondered how long he could hold her, his hands firm about her waist, before she became aware of it. "In that case, tell Fergus to inform me when you wish to inspect your next inn." She felt warm, vibrant, supple and alive between his hands.

Lucinda knew perfectly well where his hands were; she could feel his fingers burning through her gown. But that kiss, so quick it was over almost before it had begun, had been her first intimation that victory was truly possible; despite the unnerving cascade of emotions the fleeting caress had evoked, she was determined not to back down. If she had, albeit unknowingly, breached his walls once, she could do it again. Battling breathlessness, she dropped her gaze to where her fingers rested against his coat. "But I couldn't so impose on your time, Mr Lester."

Harry frowned. He could see her eyes glinting through her lashes. "Not at all." He paused, then added, native caution returning, "As I told you before, given you're my aunt's guest, at my insistence, I feel it's the least I can do."

He thought he heard a disgusted humph. Suppressing a smile, he glanced up—and met Dawlish's deeply commiserating gaze.

All expression draining from his face, Harry dropped his hands. Stepping back, he offered his aunt's guest his arm, then gallantly, in open contempt of his henchman's foreboding, escorted her up the steps.

While waiting for Fergus to open the door, Lucinda glanced up—and intercepted an exchange of glances between Harry and Dawlish. "Dawlish seems very dismal— is anything amiss?"

Harry's features hardened. "No. He's just unused to getting up so early."

Lucinda blinked. "Oh?"

''Indeed.'' The door opened; beaming, Fergus held it wide. Harry bowed. ''*Au revoir,* Mrs Babbacombe.''

Crossing the threshold, Lucinda looked over her shoulder and threw him a smile—a soft, alluring, siren's smile. Then she turned and slowly headed for the stairs. Utterly mesmerised, Harry stood and watched her go, her hips swaying gently as she crossed the tiled hall.

''Sir?''

Harry came to himself with a start. With an abrupt nod to Fergus, he turned and descended the steps. Climbing into the curricle, he fixed Dawlish with a warning glance.

Then gave his attention to his horses.

Chapter Seven

A week later, Harry sat at his desk in the small library of his lodgings. The window gave onto a leafy courtyard; outside, May bustled towards June while the *ton* worked itself into a frenzy of betrothals and weddings. Harry's lips twisted cynically; *he* was intent on other things.

A tap on the door brought his head up. The door opened; Dawlish looked in.

"Ah—there you be. Thought as how you'd want to know that they're bound for Lady Hemminghurst's this evening."

"Damn!" Harry grimaced. Amelia Hemminghurst had a soft spot for rakes—the fraternity would be well represented amongst her guests. "I suppose I'll have to attend."

"That's what I thought. You going to walk or should I bring the carriage around?"

Harry considered, then shook his head. "I'll walk." It would be twilight by then; the short stroll to Grosvenor Square would help ease the restlessness his self-imposed restrictions seemed to be creating.

With a humph and a nod, Dawlish retreated.

Idly toying with a pen, Harry reviewed his strategy. On quitting Newmarket, he had stubbornly adhered to his plans and gone home to Lester Hall. There he had found his brother Jack, along with his soon-to-be bride, Miss Sophia

Winterton and her guardians, her uncle and aunt, Mr and Mrs Webb. While he had nothing against Miss Winterton, with whom his brother was openly besotted, he had not appreciated the considering light that had lit Mrs Webb's silver blue eyes, nor the contemplative expression with which she had regarded him. Her interest had made him edgy. He had ultimately concluded that London, and the dragons he knew, might well be safer than Lester Hall.

He had arrived in town a day in advance of his aunt and her company. Knowing Em, reared in a more dangerous age, travelled nowhere without outriders, he couldn't conceive that Mrs Babbacombe might face any danger on the trip. Besides, the incident on the Newmarket road had to have been due to mere opportunism. Guarded by Em and her servants, Lucinda Babbacombe was safe enough.

Once they had settled in town, however, that had no longer been the case. He had laid low as long as he could, avoiding any unnecessary appearances, hoping thus to leave the dragons and the matchmakers in ignorance of his presence. By spending most of his days at his clubs, at Manton's or Jackson's or similar all-male venues, eschewing the Park during the fashionable hours and driving himself everywhere rather than risk strolling the pavements, a prey to dowagers and fond mamas, he had largely achieved his objective.

And with Dawlish spending most of his time in the kitchens at Hallows House, he had been able to emerge into the bright lights only when absolutely necessary.

Like tonight. He had thus far succeeded in protecting the damned woman from importunate inn-dwellers and rakes alike, to the total confusion of the *ton*. And with his appearances amongst their gilded flowers thus restricted, and so very patently centred on Lucinda Babbacombe, the dragons and matchmakers had had few opportunities to exploit.

Harry's lips twisted; he laid aside his pen. He knew better than to bask in triumph—the Season had yet to end. Rising, he frowned. He was, he hoped, as capable as the next of behaving like a gentleman until then.

He pondered the point, then grimaced. Squaring his shoulders, he went up to change.

"TELL ME, Mr Lester—are you enjoying the Season's entertainments?"

The question took Harry by surprise. He glanced down at his partner's face, composed in polite enquiry, then looked up to whirl them around the end of Lady Hemminghurst's ballroom. He had arrived to find her already surrounded—by a crop of the most eligible rakes in town. He had wasted no time in extricating her and gathering her into his arms.

"No," he answered. The realisation gave him mental pause.

"Then why are you here?" Lucinda kept her eyes on his face and hoped for a straight answer. The question had grown increasingly important as day followed day and he made not the smallest move to fix her interest. Em's likening him to a horse appeared increasingly apt—he might have followed her to London, but he seemed determined not to pursue her.

He had escorted her to all four Babbacombe inns, remaining by her side throughout her inspections, but he had thereafter shown no interest in driving her elsewhere. All comments about the Park, about the delights of Richmond or Merton, fell on studiously deaf ears. Talk of a visit to the theatre had simply made him tense.

As for his behaviour in the ballrooms, she could only describe it as dog-in-the-manger. Some, like Lord Ruthven, found the situation immensely amusing. Others, like herself, were beginning to lose patience.

Harry glanced down and met her unwavering gaze. He frowned intimidatingly.

Lucinda raised her brows. "Am I to take it you'd rather be with your horses?" she enquired sweetly.

Goaded, Harry narrowed his eyes. "Yes." A mental picture leapt to mind. "I would infinitely prefer to be at Lestershall."

"Lestershall?"

His gaze growing distant, Harry nodded. "Lestershall Manor—my stud. It's named after the village, which in turn derives its name from my family's principal estate." The old manor house was in dire need of repairs. Now he had the money, he would put it to rights. The rambling, half-timbered house had the potential to be a wonderfully comfortable home; when he married, he would live there.

When he married? Harry clenched his jaw and forced his gaze back to his partner's face.

Lucinda captured it with a challenging glance. "Why, then, aren't you there?"

Because it's empty. Incomplete. The words leapt to Harry's conscious mind before he could shut them out. Her misty blue eyes lured him to the brink; the words burned his tongue. Mentally gritting his teeth, he smiled one of his more practiced smiles. "Because I'm here, waltzing with you."

There was nothing seductive in his tone. Lucinda kept her eyes innocently wide. "Dare I hope you're enjoying it?"

Harry's lips thinned. "My dear Mrs Babbacombe, waltzing with you is one of the few compensations my current lifestyle affords."

Lucinda allowed herself a sceptical blink. "Is it such a grind, then, your current life?"

"Indeed." Harry shot her a narrow glance. "My current round is one no rake should ever be forced to endure."

Gently, her eyes on his, Lucinda raised her brows. "Then why are you enduring it?"

Harry heard the final bars of the waltz; automatically, he whirled them to a halt. Her question echoed in his ears; the answer echoed deep within him. Her eyes, softly blue, held him, beckoning, inviting—open and reassuring. It took an effort of will to draw back, to find and cling to the cynicism which had kept him safe for so long. His features hardening, he released her and offered her his arm. "Why indeed, Mrs Babbacombe? I fear we'll never know."

Lucinda refrained from gnashing her teeth. She placed her hand on his sleeve, reflecting that a single waltz, which was all he ever claimed, was never long enough to press his defences. Why he was so intent on denying what they both knew to be fact was a point that increasingly bothered her. "Your aunt was quite surprised to see you in town—she said you would be…pursued by ladies wishful to have you marry their daughters." Did he, perhaps, see marriage as a trap?

"I dare say," Harry replied. "But London during the Season has never been safe for well-born, well-heeled gentlemen." His eyes met hers. "Regardless of their reputations."

Lucinda raised her brows. "So you view the…pursuit as nothing more than a fact of life?"

"As inescapable as spring, although a dashed sight more inconvenient." Harry's lips twisted; he gestured up the room. "Come—I'll return you to Em."

"Ah…" Lucinda glanced about—and saw the gently billowing drapes hanging beside the long windows open to the terrace. Beyond lay the garden, a world of shadow and starlight. "Actually," she said, slanting a glance at him. "I feel rather warm."

The lie brought a helpful blush to her cheeks.

Harry's eyes narrowed as he studied hers. She was a hopeless liar; her eyes clouded over whenever she so much as prevaricated.

"Perhaps," Lucinda continued, trying for an airy tone, "we could stroll the terrace for a while." She pretended to peer through the windows. "There are some others out-side—perhaps we could investigate the walks?"

It was at times like this that she most felt the deficiencies of her upbringing. Being married at sixteen had ensured she had not the smallest clue how to flirt or even encourage a man. When her escort made no response, she warily peeked up at him.

Harry was waiting to capture her attention, his expression that of a deeply irate man aware of the need to remain civil. "My dear Mrs Babbacombe, it would please me immensely if you could get it fixed in your pretty head that I am here, in London, braving all manner of dangers, for one—and only one—reason."

Her eyes genuinely wide, Lucinda blinked at him. "Oh?"

"Indeed." With restrained calm, Harry turned her up the room and started to stroll. His fingers, curled about her el-bow, ensured she accompanied him. "I am here to ensure that, despite my inclinations, your inclinations and certainly despite those of your besotted court, you end this Season as you began it." He turned his head to capture her gaze. "As a virtuous widow."

Lucinda blinked again, then stiffened. "Indeed?" Look-ing forward, she lifted her chin "I wasn't aware, Mr Lester, that I had appointed you to the post of protector of my virtue."

"Ah—but you did, you see."

She glanced at him, denial on her lips—and met his green gaze.

"When you took my hand and let me pull you out of your carriage on the Newmarket road."

The moment leapt to her mind, that instant when she had knelt on the side of the carriage, locked in his arms. Lucinda quelled a shiver—and tilted her nose higher. "That's non-sense."

"On the contrary." The rake beside her appeared unper-turbed. "I recall reading somewhere that if a man rescues another, then he takes on the responsibility for that rescued life. Presumably the same holds true if the one saved is a woman.''

Lucinda frowned. ''That's an eastern philosophy. You're English to your bones.''

''Eastern?'' Harry raised his brows. ''From one of those countries where they cover their women in shrouds and keep them behind locked doors, no doubt. I've always put such eminently sensible notions down to the fact that such civilisations have apparently existed so much longer than ours.''

On the words, they reached her court. Lucinda fought the urge to grind her teeth. If she heard one more of his glib excuses for being by her side she would, she felt sure, embarrass herself and Em and everyone else by screaming in fury. She plastered a bright smile on her lips—and let the admiration of her court and their subtle compliments soothe her abraded pride.

Harry stood it for five minutes, then silently relinquished his position by her side. He prowled the room but at no great distance, exchanging a few words with a number of acquaintances before retreating to a convenient alcove from where he could keep his self-imposed burden in view.

His very presence in the room was enough to keep the dangerous blades from her skirts. Those about her were all gentlemen at heart—they wouldn't pounce without an invitation. His interest, of course, was an added deterrent; he was prepared to wager that not one soul amongst all the *ton* understood what he was about.

With a somewhat grim grin, he settled his shoulders against the wall and watched as Lucinda gave Frederick Amberly her hand.

Taking the floor in yet another waltz, an apparent fixation of Lady Hemminghurst's, Lucinda fitted her steps to Mr Amberly's strides, distinctly shorter than Harry's, and let the music take hold.

Three revolutions later, she met her partner's somewhat concerned expression—and sternly reminded herself to smile. Not a spontaneous gesture.

She was distinctly irritated.

Rakes were supposed to seduce women—widows, particularly. Was she really so hopeless she couldn't break down Harry's resistance? Not that she wished to be seduced but, given his natural flair—and her status—she had to face the fact that, for them, that might well be the most sensible first step. She prided herself on her pragmatism; there was no point in not being realistic.

He had come to London; he was dancing attendance on her. But that clearly wasn't enough. Something more was required.

They were coming up the room for the third time when Lucinda's gaze refocused on Mr Amberly. Presumably if, at her advanced age, she wanted to learn how to encourage a rake, she was going to have to arrange lessons.

The waltz, most conveniently, left them at the other end of the room. Lucinda grasped her fan, dangling by its ribbon from her wrist. Opening it, she waved it to and fro. "The room is quite warm, don't you think, Mr Amberly?"

"Indeed, dear lady."

Lucinda watched as his gaze slid to the terrace windows. Hiding a smile, she gently suggested, "There's a chair over there. If I wait there, could you fetch me a glass of lemonade?"

Her cavalier blinked and hid his disappointment. "Of course." He solicitously helped her to the chair, then, with an injunction not to move, disappeared into the crowd.

With an inward smile, Lucinda sat back, languidly waving her fan, and waited for her first lesson.

Mr Amberly duly reappeared, bearing two flutes of suspiciously tinted liquid. "Thought you'd prefer champagne."

With an inward shrug, Lucinda accepted a glass and took a delicate sip. Harry usually brought her champagne with

her supper; it didn't affect her faculties. "Thank you, sir."
She cast her escort a smile. "I was in dire need of refreshment."

"Hardly to be wondered at, my dear Mrs Babbacombe.
Yet another crush." With an idle wave, Mr Amberly indicated the throng about them. "Don't know what the hostesses see in it, myself." His gaze dropped to Lucinda's face.
"Reduces the opportunities to chat, don't y'know?"

Lucinda took due note of the gleam in Mr Amberly's eyes
and smiled again. "Indubitably, sir."

Without further encouragement, Mr Amberly chatted on,
interspersing remarks on the weather, the *ton* and events
forthcoming with gently loaded comments. Lucinda found
no difficulty in turning these aside. At the end of fifteen
minutes, having politely declined an invitation to go driving
to Richmond, she drained her glass and handed it to her
escort. He placed it on a passing footman's tray and turned
back to help her to her feet.

"I'm desolated, dear lady, that my projected excursion
fails to tempt you. Perhaps I might yet stumble on a destination that finds greater favour in your eyes?"

Lucinda's lips twitched. She stifled a giggle. "Perhaps."
Her smile felt oddly wide. She took a step, leaning heavily
on Mr Amberly's arm. Suddenly, she felt distinctly flushed.
Far warmer than she had before her drink.

"Ah…" Mr Amberly's eyes sharpened. "Perhaps, my
dear Mrs Babbacombe, a breath of fresh air might be wise?"

Lucinda turned her head to consider the long windows—
and forced herself to straighten. "I think not." She might
wish to learn a few tricks but she had no intention of damaging her reputation. Turning back, she blinked as a glass
appeared before her.

"I suggest you drink this, Mrs Babbacombe," came in
clipped accents.

The tone suggested she had better do so if she knew what
was good for her.

Obligingly, Lucinda took the glass and raised it to her lips, simultaneously raising her eyes to Harry's face. "What is it?"

"Iced water," Harry replied. He transferred his gaze to Frederick Amberly's innocent visage. "You needn't linger, Amberly. I'll escort Mrs Babbacombe back to my aunt."

Mr Amberly's brows rose, but he merely smiled gently. "If you insist, Lester." Lucinda held out her hand and he took it, bowing elegantly. "Your servant always, Mrs Babbacombe."

Lucinda bestowed a perfectly genuine smile. "Thank you for a most…delightful interlude, sir."

Mr Amberly's departing look suggested she was learning.

Then she glanced up at Harry's face. He was eyeing her narrowly.

"My dear Mrs Babbacombe, has anyone ever explained to you that remaining a virtuous widow is conditional on not encouraging rakes?"

Lucinda opened her eyes wide. "Encouraging rakes? My dear Mr Lester, whatever do you mean?"

Harry returned no answer but his lips thinned.

Lucinda grinned. "If you mean Mr Amberly," she continued ingenuously, "we were just chatting. Indeed," she went on, her smile widening again, "I have it on excellent authority that I'm *incapable* of encouraging rakes."

Harry snorted. "Rubbish." After a moment, he asked, "Who told you that?"

Lucinda's smile lit up the room. "Why, you did—don't you remember?"

Looking down into her very bright eyes, Harry inwardly groaned. And hoped Amberly hadn't noticed just how thin the lovely Mrs Babbacombe's skull was. Taking the empty glass from her fingers, he deposited it on a passing tray, then took her hand and placed it on his sleeve. "And now, Mrs Babbacombe, we are going to perambulate, very slowly, around the room."

Bright blue eyes quizzed him. "Very slowly? Why?"

Harry gritted his teeth. "So you don't stumble." Into another rake's arms.

"Ah." Lucinda nodded sagely. A delighted, distinctly satisfied smile on her lips, she let him lead her, very slowly, into the crowd.

LUCINDA'S HEAD was throbbing when she followed Em into the carriage. Heather tumbled in after them and promptly curled up on the opposite seat.

Settling her skirts, Lucinda decided that, despite her minor discomfort, her evening had been a success.

"Damned if I know what Harry's about," Em stated as soon as Heather's breathing subsided into the soft cadence of sleep. "Have you made any headway with him yet?"

Lucinda smiled into the gloom. "Actually, I think I've at last found a chink in his armour."

Em snorted. "'Bout time. The boy's too damned stubborn for his own good."

"Indeed." Lucinda settled her head against the squabs. "However, I'm unsure how long this chink might take to develop into a breach, nor yet how potentially difficult it might prove to pursue. I don't even know whether, ultimately, it will work."

Em's next snort was one of pure frustration. "Anything's worth a try."

"Hmm." Lucinda closed her eyes. "So I think."

ON MONDAY, she danced twice with Lord Ruthven.

On Tuesday, she went driving in the Park with Mr Amberly.

On Wednesday, she strolled the length of Bond Street on Mr Satterly's arm.

By Thursday, Harry was ready to wring her pretty neck.

"I suppose this campaign has your blessing?" Harry looked down at Em, settled in majestic splendour on a *chaise* in Lady Harcourt's ballroom. He made no attempt to hide his barely restrained ire.

"Campaign?" Em opened her eyes wide. "What campaign?"

Harry gave her one of her own snorts—the one that signified incredulous disbelief. "Permit me to inform you, dear Aunt, that your protégée has developed a potentially unhealthy taste for living dangerously."

Having delivered himself of that warning, he stalked away. Not, however, to join the crowd about Lucinda Babbacombe. He propped the wall nearby, far enough away so that she wasn't likely to see him, and, eyes glittering greenly, watched her.

He was thus engaged when a hearty clap on the shoulder very nearly sent him sprawling.

"There you are, brother mine! Been looking all over. Didn't think to see you here."

Resuming his languid pose, Harry studied Jack's blue eyes; he decided his brother had yet to hear of his preoccupation. "It passes the time. But why are you back in town?"

"The arrangements, of course. All set now." Jack's blue gaze, which had been idly drifting the room, returned to Harry's face. "Next Wednesday at eleven at St. George's." Jack's slow grin surfaced. "I'm counting on your support."

Harry's lips twisted in a reluctant grin. "I'll be there."

"Good. Gerald, too—I haven't found him yet."

Harry looked over the sea of heads. "He's over there— beside the blonde ringlets."

"Ah, yes. I'll catch him in a minute."

Harry noted that his brother's eyes, glowing warmly, rarely left the slender blonde dancing with Lord Harcourt. Their host appeared captivated. "How's Pater?"

"Fine. He'll live to be eighty. Or at least long enough to see us all wed."

Harry bit back his instinctive response; Jack had heard

him disparage marriage often enough. But not even his brother knew the reason for his vehemence; *that* had always remained his secret.

Following Jack's gaze, Harry studied his elder brother's chosen bride. Sophia Winterton was a charming, utterly open and honest woman whom Harry was certain Jack could trust. Harry switched his gaze to Lucinda's dark head; his lips twisted. She might serve him some tricks, as she was presently doing, but her motives would always be transparent. She was open and direct, uncommonly so; she would never seriously lie or cheat—she simply wasn't that sort of woman.

A sudden longing welled within him, followed immediately by the old uncertainty. Harry shifted his gaze, looking once more at Jack. Once he had found his particular Golden Head, Jack had moved very swiftly to claim her. As usual, his brother had been totally confident, assured in his decision. Studying Jack's smile, Harry felt an unexpected twinge of emotion—and recognized it as jealousy.

He straightened from the wall. "Have you seen Em?"

"No." Jack glanced about. "Is she here?"

Harry strolled with him through the crowd until he could point out their aunt, then left Jack to forge his way to her. Then, shackling his temper, he let his feet have their way. They took him to Lucinda's side.

From the opposite side of the large ballroom, Earle Joliffe watched Harry take his place in the select circle about Lucinda. "Odd. Very odd," was his judgement.

"What's odd?" Beside him, Mortimer Babbacombe inserted a pudgy finger beneath his neckcloth and eased the stiff folds. "Dashed warm in here."

Joliffe's glance was contemptuous. "What's odd, my dear Mortimer, is that, if there was ever a rake guaranteed to gain the entrée into your aunt-by-marriage's boudoir, it would be Harry Lester." Joliffe glanced again across the room. "But as I read it, he's holding off. That's what's odd."

After a moment, Joliffe went on, "A disappointment, Mortimer. But it seems he's disappointed her, too—she's looking over the field, no doubt about that." Joliffe's gaze grew distant. "Which means that all we have to do is wait for the first whispers—these things always percolate from under even the most tightly closed doors. Then we'll get a little hard proof—it shouldn't be too difficult. A few eye-witnesses of comings and goings. Then we'll have your sweet cousin—and her even sweeter legacy—in our hands."

It was a reassuring prospect. Joliffe was over his ears in debt, although he'd been careful to conceal his desperation from Mortimer. His erstwhile friend was reduced to a shivering jelly just knowing he owed Joliffe five thousand pounds. The fact that Joliffe had pledged the money on, with interest, and to one against whom it was never wise to default, would turn Mortimer to a quivering wreck. And Joliffe needed Mortimer, hale and hearty, sound in mind and reputation, if he was ever to save his neck.

If he failed to help Mortimer to Heather Babbacombe's legacy, he, Earle Joliffe, man about town, would end life as a beggar in the Spitalfield slums. If he was lucky.

Joliffe's gaze rested on Lucinda's dark head. Once he had seen her, he had felt a great deal more confident. She was precisely the sort of widow who attracted the most dangerous of rakes. His hard eyes lighting, Joliffe squared his shoulders and turned to Mortimer. "Mind you, Scrugthorpe will have to forgo his revenge." Joliffe's lips lifted. "But then, nothing in life is ever quite perfect. Don't you agree, Mortimer?"

"Er—ah—yes."

With a last worried glance at his aunt-by-marriage, Mortimer reluctantly followed Joliffe into the crowd.

At that moment, the opening strains of a waltz percolated through the room. Lucinda heard it; her nerves, already taut, quivered. It was the third waltz of the evening, almost certainly the last. Relief had swept her when, only moments ago, Harry had, at last, materialised by her side. She had not seen him until then although she had felt his gaze. Breath bated, she had welcomed him with a soft smile. As usual, he had not joined in the conversation but had stood, his features hard, his expression remote, beside her. She had slanted a glance up at him; he had met it with an impenetrable look. Now, a smile on her lips as she graciously acknowledged the usual clamour of offers for the dance, she waited, buoyed with anticipation, to hear Harry's softly drawled invitation.

In vain.

The still silence on her left was absolute.

A deathly moment of awkward silence ensued.

Lucinda stiffened. With considerable effort, she kept her smile unaffected. She felt hollow inside but she had her pride. She forced herself to scan those desirous of partnering her. Her gaze came to rest on Lord Craven.

He had not appeared in her circle since that first evening two weeks ago. Tonight, he had been most assiduous.

Smiling brittlely, Lucinda held out her hand. "Lord Craven?"

Craven smiled, a coolly superior gesture, and bowed elegantly. "It will be a pleasure, my dear." As he straightened, he met her eyes. "For us both."

Lucinda barely heard; automatically, she inclined her head. With a gentle smile she acknowledged those she had disappointed but by not so much as a flicker of an eyelash did she acknowledge Harry. Outwardly serene, she allowed Lord Craven to lead her to the floor.

Behind her, she left an uncomfortable silence. After a moment, Lord Ruthven, cool and suddenly as remote as Harry, with no hint of his habitual good-humoured indolence in his eyes, lifted a brow. "I do hope, Lester, that you know what you're about?"

His eyes like green ice, Harry met his lordship's challenging stare and held it, then, without a word, looked away to where Lucinda was taking the floor in Lord Craven's arms.

At first, his lordship tried to hold her too close; Lucinda frowned and he desisted. Thereafter, she paid him little heed, answering his polished sallies at random, their underlying tone barely registering. By the time the last chords sounded and his lordship whirled her to an elegant halt, her inner turmoil had calmed.

Enough to leave her prey to an enervating sense of defeat.

The emotion was not one she could approve. Straightening her shoulders and lifting her head, Lucinda reminded herself of Em's words: Harry would be no easy conquest but she had to hold firm to her plan.

So…here she was at the far end of the ballroom on Lord Craven's arm. His hand held hers trapped on his sleeve.

"Perhaps, Mrs Babbacombe, we should grasp the opportunity to become better acquainted?"

Lucinda blinked; his lordship gestured to a nearby door, set ajar.

"It's so noisy in here. Perhaps we could stroll the corridor?"

Lucinda hesitated. A corridor did not sound particularly secluded—and it was certainly crowded in the ballroom; her temples were starting to ache. She glanced up—and met Lord Craven's dark eyes and his faintly superior stare. She wasn't entirely sure of him but he was here, offering yet another potential prod to Harry's possessive nature.

She let her senses reach out, and felt the heat of Harry's gaze. He was watching over her; she cast a glance about but, in the dense crowd, could not find him.

Turning back, she met his lordship's gaze. Lucinda drew in a breath. She had told Em she was game. "Perhaps just a quick turn about the corridor, my lord."

She was quite certain her strategy was sound.

Unfortunately, this time, she had chosen the wrong rake.

Unlike Lord Ruthven, Mr Amberly and Mr Satterly, Lord Craven was not a familiar of Harry's and therefore lacked their insights into the game she was playing. They, one and all, had determined to assist her in whatever way they could, intrigued by the prospect of removing Harry from their paths. Lord Craven, however, had concluded that her flittering progress from rake to rake was merely a reflection of dissatisfaction with the distractions offered. Having seen how far the gentle touch had got his peers, he had determined on a more forceful approach.

With brisk efficiency, he whisked Lucinda through the doorway.

On the other side of the room, Harry swore, startling two dowagers gracing a nearby *chaise*. He wasted no time on apologies or speculation but started into the crowd. Aware of Craven's reputation, he had kept a close watch on his lordship and his burden but had momentarily lost them at the end of the dance, sighting them again just before Lucinda cast a glance about—then allowed Craven to lead her from the room. Harry knew very well what that glance had signified. The damned woman had been looking for him— to him—for rescue.

This time, she might need it.

The crowd, dispersing after the dance, milled aimlessly. Harry had to fight an impulse to push people out of his way. He forced himself to rein in his strides; he didn't want to focus any attention on his goal.

He finally broke free of the clinging crowd and gained the garden corridor. He didn't pause but went straight to its end where a door gave onto the terrace. Lady Harcourt had frequently bemoaned the fact that her ballroom did not open onto terrace and gardens, as was the fashionable norm. Silently, Harry stepped onto the flagstones. The terrace was deserted. His features hardening, he reined in his building rage and, hands on hips, scanned the deeply shadowed garden.

Muffled sounds drifted to his ears.

He was running when he rounded the corner of the terrace.

Craven had Lucinda backed against the wall and was trying to kiss her. She had ducked her head, frustrating his lordship's intent; her small hands on his chest, she was trying to push him away, incoherent in her distress.

Harry felt his rage claim him.

"Craven?"

The single word had Craven lifting his head and looking wildly about just as Harry caught his shoulder, spinning him into a punishing left cross that lifted his lordship from his feet and left him sprawled in an untidy heap against the stone balustrade.

Lucinda, her hand at her breast, swallowed a sob—and flung herself into Harry's arms. They closed about her; he hugged her fiercely; Lucinda felt his lips on her hair. His body was hard, rigid; she sensed the fury that possessed him. Then he shifted her to his side, keeping her within the protection of one arm. Her cheek against his coat, Lucinda glanced at Lord Craven.

Somewhat shakily, his lordship clambered to his feet. He worked his jaw, then, blinking, warily eyed Harry. When Harry made no move, Craven hesitated, then resettled his coat and straightened his cravat. His gaze shifted to Lucinda, then returned to Harry's face. His features studiously impassive, he raised his brows. "I appear to have misread the situation." He bowed to Lucinda. "My most humble apologies, Mrs Babbacombe—I pray you'll accept them."

Lucinda ducked her head, then hid her burning cheeks in Harry's coat.

Lord Craven's gaze returned to Harry's face. Something not at all civilised stared back at him. "Lester." With a curt nod, his lordship strolled carefully past and disappeared around the corner.

Leaving silence to enfold the two figures on the terrace.

Harry held himself rigid, every muscle clenched, his emotions warring within him. He could feel Lucinda trembling; the need to comfort her welled strong. He closed his eyes, willing himself to resistance, to impassivity. Every impulse he possessed impelled him to take her into his arms, to kiss her, possess her—to put an end to her silly game. A primitive male desire to brand her inescapably his rocked him to his core. Equally strong was his rage, his dislike of being so manipulated, so exposed by his own feelings, so vulnerable to hers.

Mentally cursing her for being the catalyst of such a scene, Harry struggled to suppress passions already too long denied.

The moment stretched, the tension palpable.

Trapped within it, Lucinda couldn't breathe; she couldn't move. The arm about her didn't tighten, but it felt like iron, inflexible, unyielding. Then Harry's chest swelled; he drew in an unsteady breath.

"Are you all right?"

His deep voice was flat, devoid of emotion. Lucinda forced herself to nod, then, drawing on her courage, stepped back. His arm fell from her. She drew in a deep breath and glanced up; one look at his face, at his utterly blank expression, was enough. His eyes showed evidence of some turbulent emotion, glittering in the green; what, she couldn't tell but she sensed his accusation.

Her breath tangling in her throat, she glanced away. His arm appeared before her.

"Come. You must return to the ballroom."

His face like stone, a graven façade masking turbulent feelings, Harry braced himself against the moment when her fingers settled on his sleeve.

Through the simple contact, Lucinda could sense his simmering anger, and the control that left his muscles twitching, shifting restlessly beneath her hand; for an instant, her feelings threatened to overwhelm her. She wanted him to comfort her, yearned to feel his arms about her once again. But she knew he was right—she had to reappear in the ballroom soon. Dragging in a shaking breath, she lifted her head. With the slightest of nods, she allowed him to lead her back, into the cacophany of conversation and laughter, back to the bright lights and bright smiles.

Her own smile appropriately bright if brittle, she gracefully inclined her head as, with a curt nod, Harry deposited her at the end of Em's *chaise*. He immediately turned on his heel; Lucinda watched him stride away, into the crowd.

Chapter Eight

"Good afternoon, Fergus. Is Mrs Babbacombe in?"

Harry handed his gloves and cane to his aunt's butler. His expression stonily impassive, he glanced towards the stairs.

"Mrs Babbacombe is in the upstairs parlour, sir—she uses it as her office. Her ladyship's laid down upon her bed. These late nights are greatly tiring at her age."

"I dare say." With decisive stride, Harry headed for the stairs. "I won't disturb her. You needn't announce me." His lips thinned. "I'm quite sure Mrs Babbacombe is expecting me."

"Very good, sir."

The upstairs parlour was a small room at the back of the house. Tall windows looked onto the garden at the rear; two armchairs and a *chaise* plus an assortment of side-tables graced the floral rug by the fireplace while a large daybed filled the space before the windows. An escritoire stood against one wall; Lucinda, a vision in soft blue muslin, was seated before it, pen in hand, when Harry opened the door.

She glanced around, an abstracted smile on her lips—and froze. Her smile faded, replaced by a polite mask.

Harry's expression hardened. He stepped over the threshold and closed the door.

Lucinda rose. "I didn't hear you announced."

"Probably because I wasn't." Harry paused, his hand on the doorknob, and studied her haughty expression. She was going to hear him out, come what may; he wasn't in the mood to tolerate interruptions. His fingers closed about the key; the lock slid noiselessly into place. "This isn't a social call."

"Indeed?" One brow rising, Lucinda lifted her chin. "To what, then, do I owe this honour, sir?"

Harry's smile was a warning. "Lord Craven."

As he stalked towards her, his eyes boring into hers, Lucinda had to quell a weak impulse to retreat behind her chair.

"I've come to demand an assurance from you, Mrs Babbacombe, that you will, as of this moment, cease and desist in this little game of yours."

Lucinda stiffened. "I beg your pardon?"

"As well you might," Harry growled, coming to a halt directly before her, his eyes, glittering green, holding hers. "That little scene on Lady Harcourt's terrace was entirely your own fault. This ridiculous experiment of yours, this habit you've formed of encouraging rakes, has to stop."

Lucinda summoned a haughty glance. "I don't know what you mean. I'm merely doing what many ladies, situated similarly, would do—looking for congenial company."

"Congenial?" Harry lifted a supercilious brow. "I would have thought last night would have been sufficient demonstration of how 'congenial' the company of rakes can be."

Lucinda felt a blush tinge her cheeks. She shrugged and swung aside, stepping away from the desk. "Lord Craven was clearly a mistake." She glanced back to add, "And I have to thank you most sincerely for your aid." Deliberately, she met Harry's gaze, then calmly turned and drifted towards the windows. "But I really must insist, Mr Lester, that my life is my own to live as I please. It's no business of yours should I choose to develop a..." Lucinda gestured vaguely "...a relationship with Lord Craven or anyone else."

A tense silence greeted her statement. Lucinda paused, fingers lightly trailing the high back of the daybed, her gaze fixed, unseeing, on the prospect beyond the windows.

Behind her, Harry closed his eyes. Fists clenched, his jaw rigid, he fought to shackle his response to what he knew to be deliberate provocation, to suppress the clamorous impulses her words had evoked. Behind his lids, a fleeting image took shape—of her, struggling in Lord Craven's arms. Abruptly, Harry opened his eyes.

"My dear Mrs Babbacombe." He bit the words out as he stalked after her. "It's clearly time I took a hand in your education. No rake in his right mind is interested in a relationship—other than of an extremely limited sort."

Lucinda glanced over her shoulder and saw him coming. She turned to meet him—and abruptly found herself backed against the wall.

Harry's eyes trapped hers. "Do you know what we are interested in?"

Lucinda took in his predatory smile, his glittering eyes, heard the undercurrent in his silky voice. Deliberately, she tilted her chin. "I'm not a complete innocent."

Even as the lie left her lips, her breathing seized. Harry moved closer, crowding her against the wall, stopping only when she could retreat no further, her soft skirts caressing his thighs, brushing his boots.

His lips, so fascinating, were very close. As Lucinda watched, they twisted.

"Perhaps not. But when it comes to the likes of Craven and the others—or me—you're hardly experienced, my dear."

Her expression intransigent, Lucinda met his gaze. "I'm more than capable of holding my own."

His eyes flared. "Are you?"

Harry felt barely civilised. She kept prodding the demon

within him; he felt barely sane. "Shall we put that to the test?"

He framed her face with his hands and deliberately moved one inch nearer, pressing her against the wall. He felt her draw in a quick breath; a quiver shivered through her. "Shall I show you what we *are* interested in, Lucinda?" He tilted her face to his. "Shall I show you what's on our—" his lips twisted in self-mockery "—*my* mind every time I look at you? Waltz with you?"

Lucinda didn't answer. Eyes wide, she stared into his, her breathing shallow and rapid, her pulse skittering wildly. His brows rose mockingly, inviting her comment; his eyes burned. Then his gaze dropped from hers; Lucinda watched as he focused on her lips. She couldn't suppress the impulse to run the tip of her tongue over the smooth curves.

She felt the shudder that rippled through him, heard the groan he tried to suppress.

Then his head swooped and his lips found hers.

It was the caress she had longed for, planned for, plotted to attain—yet it was like nothing she had dreamed. His lips were hard, forceful, commanding. They captured hers, then tortured them with subtle pleasures, ravishing her senses until she submitted. The kiss caught her up, conquered and willing, and skilfully swept her free of reality, into a place where only his will prevailed. He demanded—she surrendered. Completely.

When he asked, she gave, when he wanted more, she unhesitatingly yielded. She sensed his need—and wanted, deeply desired, his satisfaction. She kissed him back, thrilled to feel the surge of unleashed passion that answered her. The kiss deepened, then deepened again, until she could sense nothing beyond it and the wild longing that swelled within her.

What deep-seated alarm it was that hauled Harry to his senses he did not know. Perhaps the urgent clamouring of rampant desires and the consequent need to arrange their fulfilment? Whatever it was, he suddenly realised the danger. It took every last ounce of his strength to draw back.

When he lifted his head, he was shaking.

Searching for sanity, he stared at her face—her lids slowly rose, revealing eyes so blue, so soft, so glowing with a siren's allure that he couldn't breathe. Her lips, kiss-bruised, gleaming red, ripe and, as he could now testify, so very sweet, drew his gaze. He felt himself falling under her spell again, leaning closer, his lips hungry for hers.

He dragged in a painful breath—and lifted his gaze to her eyes.

Only to see, in the soft blue depths, an awakening intelligence, superseded by a very feminine consideration.

The sight shook him to the core.

Her gaze dropped to his lips.

Harry shuddered; fleetingly, he closed his eyes. "Don't."

It was the plea of a defeated man.

Lucinda heard and understood. But if she didn't press her advantage now, she would lose it. Em had said he'd be thrilled—but he was so stubborn, if she didn't play that card now, he might not give her another chance.

She lifted her gaze to his. Slowly, she drew her hands from between them and pushed them up over his shoulders. She saw the consternation that filled his eyes; his muscles were locked tight, paralysed. He was unable to deny her.

Harry knew it; restraining his all-but-overpowering desire took all his strength. He couldn't move, could only watch his fate draw near as her arms tightened about his neck and she stretched upwards against him.

When her lips were an inch from his, she raised her eyes and met his tortured gaze. Then her lids fell and she pressed her lips to his.

His resistance lasted all of two heartbeats, as long as it took for desire, shackled, suppressed for so long it had grown to ungovernable proportions, to sear through him, cindering every last one of his good intentions, his rational reasons, his logical excuses.

With a groan that was ripped from deep within him, he drew her into his arms and engulfed her in his embrace.

With all restraint shattered, he kissed her deeply, caressed her, let his desire ignite and set fire to them both. She kissed him back, her hands clinging, her body wantonly enticing.

Desire rose between them, wild and strong; Lucinda abandoned herself to it, to the deep surge of their passions, fervently hoping to thus disguise any false move, any too-tentative response. If he sensed her innocence, all would come to nought—of that she was sure.

His caresses were magic, the response they drew so shattering she would be shocked—if she let herself think. Luckily, coherent thought was beyond her, blocked out by heated clouds of desire. Her senses whirled. His hands on her breasts provoked an urgent, building compulsion unlike any she'd ever experienced.

When one hand dropped low and he drew her hips hard against him, moulding her to him, flagrantly demonstrating his desire, Lucinda moaned softly and pressed closer.

Burgeoning passion left them frantic, hungry for each other, so desperate Harry's head was spinning as he backed her to the daybed. He refocused his will on salvaging some modicum of his customary expertise, bringing it to bear as he divested her of her gown and petticoats, brushing her fluttering hands aside, content enough that she was too befuddled to sensibly assist. Desire urged them on, riding them both; clad only in her chemise, Lucinda flung his cravat to the floor, then fell on the buttons of his shirt with a single-mindedness as complete as his. She seemed fascinated by his chest; he had to pick her up and put her on the daybed so he could sit and tug off his boots.

Lucinda was fascinated—by him, by the sense of rightness that gripped her, by the warm desire flowing in her veins. She felt free, unrestrained by any tenets of modesty or decorum, sure that this was how it should be. He stripped and turned towards her; she wrapped her arms about him, revelling in the feel of his warm skin, burning to her touch. Their lips met; urgency welled, heating her through and through. He drew off her chemise; as their bodies met, she shivered and closed her eyes. They kissed deeply, then Harry pressed her back against the soft cushions. Caught up in the spring tide of their loving, Lucinda lay back and drew him to her.

He lay beside her and loved her but their spiralling need soon spelled an end to such play. Eyes closed, Lucinda knew nothing beyond a deep and aching emptiness, the overwhelming need he had brought to life and only he could assuage. Relief and expectation flooded her when he shifted and his weight pinned her to the bed. She tried to draw breath, to steel herself; his hand slipped beneath her hips and steadied her—with one smooth flexion of his powerful body he joined them.

Her soft gasp echoed in the room. Neither of them moved, both stunned to stillness.

Slowly, his heart thudding in his ears, Harry raised his head and looked down at her face. Her eyes were shut, a frown tangling her brows, her lower lip caught between her teeth. Even as he watched, she relaxed a little beneath him, her features easing.

He waited for his emotions to catch up with the facts. He expected to feel angry, tricked, deceived.

Instead, a shattering feeling of possessiveness, untouched by lust, driven by some far more powerful emotion, welled within him, thrusting out all regrets. The sensation grew, joyously swelling, strong and sure.

Harry didn't question it—or how it made him feel.

Lowering his head, he brushed her lips with his. "Lucinda?"

She snatched in a breath then her lips clung to his. Her fingers fluttered against his jaw.

Harry brought up a hand to gently smooth away clinging tendrils of her hair from her face.

Then, with infinite tenderness, he taught her how to love.

SOME CONSIDERABLE TIME later, when Lucinda again made contact with reality, she discovered herself wrapped in Harry's arms, her back against his chest as he half-sat, propped against the raised head of the daybed. She sighed long and lingeringly, the glory dimming yet still glowing within her.

Harry bent over her; she felt his lips at her temple.

"Tell me of your marriage."

Lucinda's brows half-rose. With one fingertip, she drew whorls in the hair on his forearm. "To understand, you need to realise that I was orphaned at fourteen. Both my parents had been disowned by their families." Using the minimum of words, she explained her past history, one hand moving slowly back and forth along Harry's arm, snug about her, all the while. "So, you see, my marriage was never consummated. Charles and I were close, but he didn't love me in that way."

Harry kept his doubts to himself, rendering silent thanks to Charles Babbacombe for keeping her safe, for loving her enough to leave her untouched. His lips in her hair, the subtle scent of her filling him, Harry made a silent vow to her late husband's shade that, as the recipient of his legacy, he would keep her safe for evermore.

"You'll have to marry me." He spoke the words as they occurred to him, thinking aloud.

Lucinda blinked. The joy that had filled her faded. After a quiet moment, she asked, "*Have* to marry you?"

She felt Harry straighten as he looked down at her.

"You were a virgin. I'm a gentleman. The prescribed outcome of our recent activity is a wedding."

His words were definite, his accents clipped. Lucinda closed her eyes; she didn't want to believe her ears. The last vestige of lingering afterglow evaporated, the promise of the long, inexpressibly tender moments they had shared vanished.

Lucinda stifled a sigh; her lips firmed into a determined line. Opening her eyes, she turned in Harry's arms and looked him straight in the eye. "You want to marry me because I was a virgin—is that correct?"

Harry frowned. "It's what's expected."

"But is it what you want?"

"It doesn't matter what I want," Harry growled, his eyes narrowing. "The matter, thank heaven, is simple enough. Society has rules—we'll follow them—to the general satisfaction of all concerned."

For a long moment, Lucinda studied him, her thoughts chaotic. It was an offer—of sorts—from the man she wanted.

But it wasn't good enough. She didn't just want him to marry her.

"No."

Stunned, Harry watched as she scrambled out of his arms and off the daybed. She found her chemise and pulled it on.

He sat up. "What do you mean—'No'?"

"No—I will not marry you." Lucinda struggled into her petticoats.

Harry stared at her. "Why not, for heaven's sake?" She started towards her gown and nearly tripped over his breeches. He heard a stifled curse as she bent to untangle her feet. Then she flung the breeches at him and continued towards her gown.

With a muttered curse of his own, Harry grabbed the breeches and hauled them on, then pulled on his boots. He stood and stalked over to where Lucinda was pushing her arms through the sleeves of her gown.

Hands on hips, he towered over her. "Damn it—I seduced you! You *have* to marry me."

Eyes ablaze, Lucinda shot him a furious glance. "*I* seduced *you*, if you recall. And I most certainly do not '*have to marry you*'!''

"What about your reputation?"

"What of it?" Lucinda tugged her gown up over her shoulders. Turning to face him, she jabbed a finger in his chest. "No one would ever believe that *Mrs* Lucinda Babbacombe, *widow,* had been a virgin until you came along. You've got no lever to use against me."

Looking up, she met his eyes.

And abruptly changed tack. "Besides," she said, looking down to do up the buttons of her bodice, "I'm sure it's not accepted practice for rakes to offer marriage to every woman they seduce."

Harry ground his teeth. "Lucinda…"

"And I have *not* made you free of my name!" Lucinda glared at him. She wouldn't let him use it—he'd whispered it, coupled with every conceivable endearment, as he'd made love to her.

Love—the emotion she knew he felt for her but was determined to deny.

It wasn't good enough—it would *never* be good enough.

She whirled on her heel and marched to the door.

Harry swore. Buttoning his shirt, he started after her. "This is crazy! I've offered for you, you demented woman! It's what you've been after ever since I hauled you out of that damned carriage!"

Lucinda had reached the door. She swung around. "If you're so adept at reading my mind, then you'll understand perfectly why I'm throwing you out!"

She gripped the doorknob, turned it and yanked. Nothing happened. She stared at the door. "Where's the key?"

Thoroughly distracted, Harry automatically reached into his breeches pocket. "Here."

Lucinda blinked, then grabbed the key and rattled it into the keyhole.

Harry watched her in disbelief. "Damn it—I've given you a proposal—what more do you want?"

Her hand on the knob, Lucinda drew herself up and turned to face him. "I *don't* want to be offered for because of some social technicality. I don't want to be rescued, or…or protected or married out of pity! What I *want*—" Abruptly, she halted and dragged in a deep breath. Then she lifted her eyes to his and deliberately stated, "What I want is to be married for love."

Harry stiffened. His face hardened. "Love is not considered an important element for marriage within our class."

Lucinda pressed her lips together, then succinctly stated, "Balderdash." She flung open the door.

"You don't know what you're talking about!" Harry ran his fingers through his hair.

"I know *very well* what I'm talking about," Lucinda averred. None better—she loved him with all her heart and soul. Glancing about, she spied his coat and cravat by the daybed. She flew across the room and pounced on them.

Harry turned to face her, blocking the doorway as she bustled back.

"There." Lucinda crammed the expensive coat and cravat into his arms. "Now get out!"

Harry drew in a steadying breath. "Lucinda—"

"*Out!*"

Without warning, Lucinda pushed hard in the middle of his chest. Harry staggered back, over the threshold.

Lucinda grabbed the door. "Goodbye, Mr Lester! Rest assured I'll bear your instructions as to the interests of your set in mind in the coming weeks!"

With that, she slammed the door and locked it.

The fury that had sustained her abruptly drained. Slumping back against the door, she covered her face with her hands.

Harry glared at the white-painted panels. He considered forcing his way back in—then he heard a stifled sob. His heart wrenched—racked by frustration, he stuffed it back behind his inner door and slammed that shut as well. His lips set in a grim line, he turned on his heel and marched down the corridor. He caught sight of himself in a mirror. Abruptly, he halted and shrugged on his coat, then draped the creased cravat about his throat.

It took him three tries before he could achieve anything remotely resembling decency. With a snort, he turned and headed for the stairs.

He had made an offer. She had refused.

The damned woman could go to hell by herself.

He was finished with being her protector.

He was finished with her.

DISCOVERED, two hours later, with dark shadows under swollen red eyes, Lucinda could hardly deny Em her confidence.

Her hostess was stunned. "I can't understand it. What the devil's wrong with him?"

Lucinda sniffed and dabbed her eyes with a lace-edged square. "I don't know." She felt like wailing. Her lips set in a mulish line. "But I *won't* have it."

"Quite right, too!" Em snorted. "Don't worry—he'll come about. Probably just took him by surprise."

Lucinda considered, then wearily shrugged.

"Seems to me that there must be something we don't know," Em mused. "Known him all his life—he's always the predictable one—always good reasons and logical arguments behind his actions—he's not an impulsive man." She grinned, her gaze distant. "Quite the opposite—Jack's impulsive. Harry's cautious." A frown slowly settled over her face. "Has been for a long time, now I think of it."

Lucinda waited, hoping for some reassuring insight, but her hostess remained sunk in thought.

Then Em snorted and shook herself, her stiff bombazine

rustling. "Whatever it is, he'll just have to come to terms with it and offer for you properly."

Lucinda swallowed and nodded. "Properly"—by which she meant he would have to tell her he loved her. After today, and all they had shared, she would settle for nothing less.

THAT EVENING, Em took charge and insisted Lucinda remain at home, there to have an early night and recover her composure and her looks.

"The last thing you want to do is show him or the *ton* a face like that."

Having thus overcome Lucinda's half-hearted resistance, Em left the redoubtable Agatha ministering with cold cucumber compresses and, with the effervescent Heather under her wing, strode forth to do battle at Lady Caldecott's ball.

She spied Harry in the throng, but was not the least surprised when her errant nephew showed no disposition to come within firing range. But it was not him she had come to see.

"Indisposed?" Lord Ruthven's cool grey eyes reflected honest concern. "I do hope it's nothing serious?"

Well—it is and it isn't." Em lifted a brow at him. "You're one who's far more awake than you appear, so I dare say you've noticed that she's been endeavouring to bring a certain recalcitrant to heel. Never an easy task, of course. A difficult road to travel—prone to find potholes in one's path. She's a bit moped at present." Em paused to glance again at his lordship. "Dare say, when she reappears tomorrow, she could do with a little encouragement, don't y'know?"

Lord Ruthven studied Harry's aunt with wary fascination. "Ah—indeed." After a moment, in which he recalled the numerous times Harry had cut him out when they'd both had the same ladybird in their sights, he said, "Pray convey my most earnest wishes for a speedy recovery to Mrs Babbacombe. I will, of course, be delighted to welcome her back to our midst—I look forward to her return with uncommon anticipation.''

Em grinned. "Dare say you do.''

With a regal wave, she dismissed him. Lord Ruthven bowed gracefully and withdrew.

Fifteen minutes later, Mr Amberly stopped by her *chaise*. The instant the formalities were over, he asked, ''Wondered if you'd be so good as to convey my regards to Mrs Babbacombe? Understand she's under the weather tonight. She's a distraction sorely missed by us poor bachelors. Wanted to assure her of my continuing support when she once again graces our halls.''

Em smiled her approval. "I'll make certain to pass your kind words on, sir.''

Mr Amberly bowed and drifted away.

To Em's satisfaction, her evening was punctuated by a succession of similar encounters as, one after another, Harry's close friends stopped by to pledge their aid in furthering Lucinda's cause.

Chapter Nine

Lady Mott's drum bade fair to being the most horrendous crush of the Season. Or so Lucinda thought as she inched through the crowd on Lord Sommerville's arm. About them, the *ton* milled *en masse;* it was difficult to see more than five feet in any direction.

"Phew!" Lord Sommerville threw her an apologetic glance. "Pity the dance landed us so far from your companions. Normally enjoy wandering the room—but not like this."

"Indeed." Lucinda tried to keep her smile bright, no mean effort when she felt like wilting. The heat was rising about them; bodies hemmed them in. "I must confess that I've yet to divine why *such* a crowd, beyond the bounds of sense, should be considered so desirable."

Lord Sommerville nodded sagely.

Lucinda hid a weak grin. His lordship was close to her own age, yet she felt immeasurably older. He was still striving for a position amongst the rakes of the *ton;* in her opinion, he had some developing yet to do before he would rival some she could name.

Harry's image rose in her mind; with an effort, she banished it. There was no point in bemoaning what was well and truly spilt milk.

Ever since she had flung his offer in his teeth, she'd been plagued by doubts—doubts she did not wish to countenance. She hadn't seen him since; he had not returned to go down on bended knee. Presumably, he had yet to see the error of his ways. Or else, despite her firm conviction—and what did she know of the matter, after all?—he did not truly love her.

She kept telling herself that if that was so, then it was all for the best—when he had forced her to put her thoughts into words, she had realised just how much a marriage built on love now meant to her. She had everything else she could want of life—except that—a loving husband with whom she could build a future. And what use was all the rest without that?

She'd been right—but her heart refused to lift, hanging like a leaden weight in her breast.

Lord Sommerville craned his neck to peer forward. "Looks like the crowd thins just ahead."

Her smile growing weaker, Lucinda nodded. The couple immediately in front of them paused to acknowledge an introduction. Trapped, they halted. Lucinda glanced to her left—directly at a gold pin in the shape of an acorn, nestling in the snowy folds of a cravat tied with mathematical precision. She knew that pin—she had pulled it free a little over twenty-four hours before.

A vice tightened about Lucinda's chest. She looked up.

Clear green eyes, the colour of a storm-tossed sea, met hers. Her heart in her mouth, Lucinda searched but could read nothing in his shadowed gaze. His expression was hard, impassive, the planes of his face an impenetrable mask. Defeated there, Lucinda looked at his lips.

Only to see them firm, thinning into a severe line.

Puzzled, she glanced up—and caught a fleeting glimpse of uncertainty in his eyes. She sensed his hesitation.

Five feet and two pairs of shoulders separated them.

His eyes returned to hers; their gazes locked. He shifted, his lips twisted, quirking up at the ends.

"Ah—there we are. At last!" Lord Sommerville turned and bowed, gesturing before them.

Distracted, Lucinda looked ahead and discovered the crowd had eased, leaving a path forward. "Ah—yes."

She glanced at Harry.

Only to see him turn aside to greet an imposing matron with a simpering young girl in tow. He acknowledged the introduction to the chit with a restrained bow.

Battling the constriction in her chest, Lucinda drew in a deep breath and turned away, forcing herself to listen to Lord Sommerville's patter with some semblance of interest.

From the corner of his eye, Harry watched her move away; he clung to the sight of her until she was swallowed up by the crowd. Only then did he give his attention to Lady Argyle.

"Just a *little* soirée—a select few only." Lady Argyle beamed. "So you younger folk can chat and get to know each other better. Not something one can readily accomplish in this crowd, is it?"

Her ladyship's protruberant eyes invited him to agree. Harry was far too old a hand to fall for the trick. His expression coldly impassive, he looked down on her from a very great distance. "I'm afraid, Lady Argyle, that I'm otherwise engaged. Indeed," he continued, languid boredom threatening, "I don't look to spend much time in the ballrooms this Season." He caught her ladyship's suspicious eye. "Pressing matters elsewhere," he murmured. With a smooth bow, he took advantage of a break in the surrounding throng to slip away, leaving Lady Argyle unsure just what, exactly, he had been telling her.

Once free, Harry hesitated, then followed in Lucinda's wake. His declaration that he was finished with her rang mockingly in his ears; he shut off the sound. After trying a number of tacks, he finally located her, at the centre of her inevitable court. Ruthven was there, as were Amberly and Satterly. Harry's eyes narrowed.

Amberly was at Lucinda's side, chatting with his usual facility; he gestured hugely and everyone laughed, Lucinda included. Then it was Satterly's turn; Hugo leaned forward and smiled, clearly retelling some *on dit* or recounting some incident. Ruthven, on Lucinda's other side, glanced down at her. He was watching her face closely. Harry's lips compressed.

Concealed by the crowd, he focused on Lucinda. She smiled at Satterly's tale yet the gesture lacked the warmth Harry knew it could hold. The conversation became general; she laughed and returned some comment but without the assured gaiety she normally displayed. The dangerous tension that had gripped him eased.

She was subdued—very possibly unhappy beneath her calm veneer.

Guilt welled; ruthlessly, Harry stifled it. Serve the damned woman right—he'd offered; she'd refused.

He'd escaped a dangerous situation. Logic suggested he remove himself from further temptation. Harry hesitated, and saw Ruthven offer Lucinda his arm.

"Might I suggest a short stroll about the terrace, m'dear?" Concerned by the wan, haunted look in Lucinda's eyes, Ruthven could think of nothing else that might bring her some ease. Her gaze, dark and shadowed, constantly roamed the crowd. "Some fresh air will help you forget this stuffy ballroom."

Lucinda smiled, aware her brightness had dimmed. "Indeed," she said, glancing around. "The atmosphere is too close for my comfort, but…" She hesitated, then glanced up at his lordship. "I'm really not sure…"

She let the words trail away, unable to put her uncertainty into words.

"Oh—don't worry about that." Mr Amberly waved expansively. "Tell you what—we'll all go." He smiled encouragingly at Lucinda. "Nothing *anyone* could make of that, what?"

Lucinda blinked—and glanced at Lord Ruthven and Mr Satterly.

"Capital notion, Amberly." His lordship again offered her his arm, this time with a gallant flourish.

"Just the ticket." Mr Satterly nodded and stepped back, waving her on.

Lucinda blinked again. Then, realising they were all watching her, waiting, genuine thoughtfulness their only motivation, she smiled gratefully, and even more gratefully relaxed. "Thank you, gentlemen, that would indeed be most kind of you."

"Only too happy," came from Mr Satterly.

"A pleasure, m'dear," from Mr Amberly.

Lucinda glanced up and found Lord Ruthven's eyes ruefully twinkling. His lips twisted in a wry smile.

"Nothing too good for a friend, you know."

More reassured than she had been all evening, Lucinda smiled back.

From the depths of the crowd, Harry watched the little cavalcade head off, Ruthven steering Lucinda in Satterly and Amberly's wake. As the realisation that Ruthven's goal was one of the long windows opening onto the terrace crystallised in his brain, tension gripped Harry anew. He took a step forward—then stopped short.

She was no longer any business of his.

Satterly and Amberly stood aside for Lucinda and Ruthven to pass through the window—then followed. Harry blinked. For an instant, he stared, eyes slowly narrowing, at the gently billowing drapes through which all four had disappeared.

Then his lips curved cynically. With such cavaliers, the lovely Mrs Babbacombe had no need of further protection.

Somewhat stiffly, he turned on his heel and headed for the cardroom.

"AURELIA WILCOX ALWAYS did give the best parties." Em rustled her silks in the dark of the carriage as it rolled down Highgate Hill. After a moment, she diffidently added, "Didn't see Harry tonight."

"He wasn't there." Lucinda heard the weariness in her voice and was glad Heather, curled on the seat opposite, wasn't awake to hear it. Her stepdaughter was thoroughly enjoying her taste of the *ton* in a wholly innocuous, innocent way. If it hadn't been for Heather's undoubted enjoyment, she would be seriously considering removing from the capital, regardless of the fact that such a move would clearly signal defeat.

She felt defeated. Tuesday night had just come and gone, with no sign of Harry. She hadn't seen him since Lady Mott's ball on Saturday evening; since then, he had not even been present at the balls and parties they had attended. His presence was not something she would miss—his gaze had always triggered a certain sensation, quite unique, within her.

A sensation she now missed—dreadfully.

"Perhaps he's already left London?" Her tone was uninflected, yet the words embodied her deepest fear. She had played her cards and lost.

"No." Em stirred on the seat beside her. "Fergus mentioned that Dawlish is still haunting the kitchens." Softly, Em snorted. "The Almighty only knows to what purpose."

After a moment, Em went on, her voice low, "It was never going to be easy, y'know. He's as stubborn as a mule—most men are over matters like this. You have to give him time to get used to the idea—to let his resistance wear itself out. He'll come around in the end—just wait and see."

Wait and see. As the carriage rattled on over the cobbles, Lucinda laid her head back against the squabs and reviewed her recent actions. No matter how she tried, she could not regret any of them—faced with the same situation, she would act as she had again. But neither dwelling on the past—nor idling through the present—was advancing her cause. But she could hardly seduce Harry again if he didn't come near her.

Worse—he was no longer concerned for her safety, even though Lord Ruthven, Mr Amberly and Mr Satterly had been particularly assiduous in their attentions. Indeed, if it hadn't been for their enthusiastic if totally platonic support, she doubted she could have held her head up over these past nights. The balls, which she had initially found fascinating, had lost their attraction. The dances were boring, the waltzes trials. As for the promenading, the incessant visiting, the constant appearances demanded by the *ton,* she increasingly saw them as a waste of time; her business persona re-emerging, no doubt. If she told true, she now viewed the time she spent in *ton*nish endeavours as a very poor investment.

It was unlikely to render her the return she sought.

Unfortunately, she had no idea what new tack to take, how to realign her strategies to bring her goal back in sight.

Her goal, in this case unfortunately not inanimate, had taken matters into his own hands—which left her with nothing to do but wait—a scenario she found intensely irksome.

Lucinda stifled a snort—Em's habit was catching.

But Em was very likely right—again. She would have to wait—she had played her cards.

It was Harry's turn now.

SOME TWELVE HOURS LATER, Harry lounged in his customary pose, propping the wall in the long ballroom of the Webb residence in Mount Street, idly watching the crowd gathered to celebrate his brother's nuptials. His father, of course, was there, sitting in his chair at the other end of the room. Beside him sat Em, resplendent in deep blue silk. Her principal houseguest had not attended.

Not, of course, that he needed to worry his head over

where she was or what she was doing. Not with the way his friends were behaving. Over the past five days, they had taken to squiring her everywhere while coolly regarding him with a pointedly critical air. Ruthven, indeed, with a sublime disregard for the cryptic, had felt moved to tell him he was "being a damned fool". Ruthven—who was six months older than Harry, but had yet to show the slightest sign of bestirring himself enough to find a wife. Ruthven—who had a title to keep in the family. Disgusted, Harry had snorted— and informed his erstwhile friend that if he was so enamoured of the lady then *he* could pay her price.

Ruthven had blinked, then had looked a trifle abashed.

Eyes hooded, Harry took a soothing sip of brandy, the glass cradled in one hand.

Only to be thumped on the shoulder at the most critical moment.

Harry choked. Recovering his breath, he swung to face his assailant. "Damn it—I hope your wife aims to teach you some manners!"

Jack laughed. "Probably—but none, I suspect, that will apply to you." Deep blue eyes twinkling, he raised his brows at Harry. "She thinks you're dangerous. In severe need of the right woman to blunt your lethal edge."

"Indeed?" Harry replied, repressively chill. He took another sip of his brandy and looked away.

Jack was undeterred. "As I live and breathe," he affirmed. "But she's of the opinion it'll take a brave woman— a Boadicea, I gather—to successfully take you on."

Harry rolled his eyes—but couldn't stop his mind supplying an image of Lucinda, half-naked, bedaubed with blue paint, driving a chariot. "Your wife is clearly blessed with a typically extravagant feminine imagination."

Jack chuckled. "I'll let you know after the honeymoon. We're off to Rawling's Cottage for a week. Nice and quiet up in Leicestershire just now."

Harry shook his head, a half-smile on his lips as he took

in his brother's bright eyes. "Just don't lose anything vital—like your wits."

Jack laughed. "I think I'll manage—just." His slow grin surfaced as his gaze found his wife at the centre of a crowd near the door. He turned to Harry and put out his hand. "Wish me luck?"

Harry met his gaze. He straightened—and took Jack's hand. "You know I do. And your Golden Head as well."

Jack grinned. "I'll tell her." Poised to leave, Jack slid Harry a sidelong glance. "Take care yourself." With a last nod, he headed for his future.

Leaving Harry to wonder just how much of his current predicament showed in his face.

Fifteen minutes later, at the top of the steps outside the Webbs' house, he watched as the carriage carrying Jack and his bride rounded the corner into South Audley Street and disappeared from view. The assembled throng turned with a sigh and shuffled back indoors. Harry hung back, avoiding Em and his father. He re-entered the hall at the rear of the crowd.

The butler had just returned with his gloves and cane when a cool, calm voice enquired, "But surely you'll stay for just a little while, Mr Lester? I feel we've hardly had a chance to become acquainted."

Harry turned to view Mrs Webb's delicate features—and her silver-blue eyes which, he was quite positive, saw far too much for his comfort. "Thank you, ma'am, but I must away." He bowed elegantly.

Only to hear her sigh as he straightened.

"I really do hope you make the *right* decision."

To Harry's intense discomfort, he found himself trapped in her silver-blue stare.

"It's quite easy, you know—no great problem, even though it always feels as if it is. One just has to decide what one wants *most* of life. Take my word for it." She patted his arm in a motherly fashion, quite at odds with her supremely elegant appearance. "It's quite easy if you put your mind to it."

For the first time in a very long while, Harry was rendered speechless.

Lucilla Webb smiled up at him, utterly ingenuous, then fluttered a delicate hand. "I must return to my guests. But do try *hard* to get it right, Mr Lester. And good luck."

With an airy wave, she glided back to the drawing-room. Harry escaped.

On reaching the pavement, he hesitated. His lodgings? Brook's? Manton's? Frowning, he shook his head and started walking.

Unsummoned, the image of Boadicea returned. Harry's frown faded; his lips twitched, then curved. A fanciful notion. But was he really such a dangerous figure that a woman needs must put on armour to deal with him?

The rake within him was not averse to the analogy; the man wasn't so sure of the compliment. He was sure, however, having had the point proved repeatedly, that Lucinda Babbacombe was not the sort of woman to *recognise* danger, much less actively consider it. She, he imagined, would simply have looked the Roman commanders in the eye and calmly pointed out that they were trespassers. Then waited, arms folded, toe tapping, for them to remove themselves from her land.

Very likely, they would have gone.

Just as he—

Abruptly, Harry shook himself free of his thoughts. Drawing in a breath, he lifted his head—and found he was nearing the end of South Audley Street. Ahead, the leafy precincts of Green Park beckoned.

Without allowing himself to consider, he strode on, then crossed Piccadilly to amble beneath the trees. There were few of the fashionable in sight—it was early yet and most would go to Hyde Park nearby. The gentle lawns about him played host to nursemaids and children, an odd couple or two strolling, like himself, aimlessly down the paths.

He strolled slowly on, letting the peace sink into him, keeping his mind purposely blank.

Until a cricket ball hit him on the side of the knee.

Harry stifled a curse. He stooped and picked up the ball, then hefted it in one palm as he looked about for its owner.

Or owners, as it happened to be.

There were three of them, one slightly older but even he was barely seven. They sidled around a tree and approached with great caution.

"I—I'm most fearfully sorry, sir," the eldest piped up. "Did it hurt terribly?"

Harry sternly quelled an impulse to laugh. "Horrendously," he replied, lending the word maximum weight. All three faces fell. "But I dare say I'll survive." They recovered—and eyed him hopefully, large eyes fringed with long lashes, faces as innocent as the dawn.

As his fingertips found the ball's seam, Harry gave up the struggle and let his lips lift. He squatted, coming down to their height, and held out the ball, spinning it so that it whizzed like a top between his fingers.

"Oh—I say!"

"How d'you do that?"

They gathered about him, polite reticence forgotten. Harry showed them the trick, a facility learned over the long summers of his childhood. They oohed and aahed and practised themselves, eagerly seeking advice.

"James! Adam? Where on earth have you got to? Mark?"

The three looked guiltily about.

"We have to go," the ringleader said. Then smiled—a smile only a young boy could master. "But thanks so much, sir."

Harry grinned. He stood and watched them hurry around

the tree and over the lawns to where a rotund nurse waited impatiently.

He was still grinning when Mrs Webb's words floated through his head. "One just has to decide what one wants *most* of life."

What he most wanted—he hadn't thought of it for years. He had once, more than ten years ago. He had been very sure, then, and had pursued his goal with what had been, at that time, his usual confident abandon. Only to find himself—and his dreams—betrayed.

So he had put them away, locked them in the deepest recess of his mind, and never let them out again.

Harry's lips twisted cynically. He turned away and resumed his stroll.

But he couldn't turn his mind from its path.

He knew very well what he most wanted of life—it was the same now as it had been then; despite the years, he hadn't changed inside.

Harry stopped and forced himself to draw in a deep breath. Behind him, he could hear the piping voices of his late companions as together with their nurse they quit the park. About him, youngsters cavorted and played under watchful eyes. Here and there, a gentleman strolled with his wife on his arm, their children ranging about them.

Harry let out the breath trapped in his chest.

Other lives were full—his remained empty.

Perhaps, after all, it was time to re-examine the possibilities. Last time had been a disaster—but was he really such a coward he couldn't face the pain again?

HE ATTENDED THE THEATRE that night. For himself, he cared little for the dramatics enacted on the stage—and even less for the histrionics played out in the corridors, the little dramas of *ton*nish life. Unfortunately, the lovely Mrs Babbacombe had voiced her wish to experience Edmund Kean; Amberly had been only too happy to oblige.

Concealed in the shadows by the wall of the pit, opposite the box Amberly had hired, Harry watched the little party settle into their seats. The bell had just rung; the whole theatre was abustle as society's blessed took their seats in the tiers of boxes, the girls and ladies ogled by the bucks in the pit, while the less favoured looked on from the galleries above.

Hugging the deep shadows cast by the boxes above him, Harry saw Amberly sit Lucinda with a flourish. She was dressed in blue as usual, tonight's gown of a delicate lavender hue, the neckline picked out with silver thread. Her dark hair was dressed high over her pale face. Settling her skirts, she looked up at Amberly and smiled.

Harry watched, a chill slowly seeping into his soul.

Amberly laughed and spoke, bending closer so she did not have to strain to hear.

Abruptly, Harry swung his gaze to the other members of the party. Satterly was chatting to Em, who had taken the seat beside Lucinda. Heather Babbacombe plumped down in the seat beyond Em; Harry spied Gerald standing behind her, his stance clearly proclaiming how he viewed his fair charge.

Momentarily taken aback, Harry frowned. Gerald's expression was easy for him to read, even at this distance. His brother looked far too intent. He was midway through making a mental note to have a quiet word in his baby brother's ear, when he pulled himself up short. Heather Babbacombe might be young but she was, to his reading, an intensely carefree and honest young girl. Who was he to speak against her?

His gaze drifted back to Lucinda. His lips twisted, more in self-mockery than in humour.

Who was he to argue with love?

What other reason could he give for being here—other than a deep need for reassurance? Even Dawlish had taken to eyeing him with something perilously close to pity. When he had, somewhat irritably, demanded, "What the devil's the matter?" his dour henchman had rubbed his chin, then opined, "It's just that you don't exactly seem to be enjoying yourself—if you know what I mean."

He had glared and stalked into the library—but he knew very well what Dawlish had meant. The last week had been sheer hell. He had thought that cutting Lucinda Babbacombe out of his life, given she had only just entered it, would be easy enough. He was, after all, a past master at leaving women behind him; avoiding relationships was part of a rake's stock-in-trade.

But putting the lovely Mrs Babbacombe out of his thoughts had proved impossible.

Which left him with only one alternative.

As Mrs Webb had so succinctly put it—what he wanted most.

But did she still want him?

Harry watched as Amberly rattled on, gesticulating elegantly. He was a wit of sorts, and a polished raconteur. The possibility that Lucinda, having rejected his proposal, might have set him aside in her heart, decided he was not worth the trouble and turned instead to someone else for comfort, was not a particularly reassuring thought.

Even less reassuring was the realisation that, if she had, he would get no second chance—had no right to demand another, nor to interfere with his friend's pursuit.

A vice closed around Harry's chest. Amberly gesticulated again and Em laughed. Lucinda looked up at him, a smile on her lips. Harry squinted, desperate to see the expression in her eyes.

But she was too far away; when she turned back to the front of the box, her lids veiled her eyes.

The fanfare sounded, erupting from the musician's pit before the stage. It was greeted with noisy catcalls from the pit and polite applause from the boxes. The house lamps were doused as the stage lamps flared. The performers in the farce made their entrance; all eyes were riveted on the stage.

All except Lucinda's.

Eyes adjusting to the darkness, Harry saw she was looking down, not at the stage, apparently staring at her hands, possibly playing with her fan. She kept her head up, so no one in the box behind her would suspect her attention was not focused on the play, as was theirs. The flickering light played over her features, calm but hauntingly sad, reserved but eloquently expressive.

Harry drew in a deep breath and straightened away from the wall. Some of the tightness in his chest melted away.

Abruptly, Lucinda lifted her head and looked around—not at the stage but at the audience, uncaring of who might notice her distraction. Harry froze as her gaze scanned the boxes above him, then shifted further along.

Even in the poor light, he could see the hope that lit her face, that invested her whole body with sudden animation.

He watched it slowly fade.

She blinked, then slowly settled back in her chair, her face composed yet inexpressibly sadder than before.

Harry's heart twisted painfully. This time, he didn't try to shut it away, to blot out the emotion. But as he turned and moved silently to the door along the wall, he acknowledged the joy that came in its wake.

He hadn't been wrong about Lucinda Babbacombe. The damned woman was so ridiculously sure of herself she hadn't even considered the danger in loving him.

Stepping out of the darkness of the pit, he smiled.

Two floors above, in the crowded gallery, Earle Joliffe was very far from smiling. In fact, he was scowling—at Lucinda, and the party in Amberly's box.

"Deuce take it! What the devil's going on?" he hissed.

Beside him, Mortimer Babbacombe returned an uncomprehending look.

Disgusted, Joliffe gestured at the box opposite. "What's

she *doing* to them? She's turned a whole gaggle of the worst wolves in London into pussycats!''

Mortimer blinked. ''Pussycats?''

Joliffe all but snarled. ''Lap-dogs, then! She *is* a damned witch—just like Scrugthorpe said.''

''Quiet there!''

''Ssh!'' came from all around them.

For a moment, Joliffe contemplated a mill with positive glee. Then sanity intruded; he forced himself to stay in his seat. But his eyes remained fixed on his sacrificial lamb— who had transmogrified into a wolf-tamer.

After a moment, Mortimer leaned closer. ''Perhaps they're softening her up—pulling the wool over her eyes. We can afford to give them a little time—it's not as if we're that desperate for the money.''

Joliffe stared at him—then sank his chin in his hands. ''Rakes don't behave as they are to your aunt-by-marriage when they're hot on a woman's trail,'' he explained through clenched teeth. His jaundiced gaze rested on Amberly and Satterly. ''They're being *nice,* for heaven's sake! Can't you see it?''

Frowning, Mortimer looked across the theatre, studying the silent tableau.

Joliffe swallowed a curse. As for not being desperate— they were—very desperate. An unexpected meeting with his creditor last night had demonstrated to him just how desperate they truly were. Joliffe quelled a shiver at the memory of the odd, disembodied voice that had floated out of the carriage, stopping him in his tracks on the mist-shrouded pavement.

''Soon, Joliffe. Very soon.'' A pause had ensued. Then, ''I'm not a patient man.''

Joliffe had heard tales enough of the man's lack of patience—and what usually transpired because of it.

He was desperate all right. But Mortimer had too weak a head to be entrusted with the news.

Joliffe concentrated on the woman seated across the darkened pit. "We'll have to do something—take an active hand." He spoke more for himself than Mortimer.

But Mortimer heard. "What?" He turned to Joliffe, a shocked, somewhat stupid expression on his face. "But... I thought we'd agreed there was no need to be openly involved—to actually *do* anything ourselves!"

His voice had risen.

"Shh!" came from all sides.

Exasperated, Joliffe grabbed Mortimer's coat and hauled him to his feet. "Let's get out of here." He sent a venomous glance across the theatre. "I've seen enough."

He pushed Mortimer ahead of him to the exit.

Immediately they gained the corridor, Mortimer turned on him, clutching his coat. "But you said we wouldn't need to kidnap her."

Jollife eyed him in disgust. "I'm not talking about kidnapping," he snapped, wrenching his coat free. He looked ahead, his features hardening. "For our purposes, there's a better way."

He glanced at Mortimer, contempt in his eyes.

"Come on—there's a certain party we need to see."

Chapter Ten

By the time Em took her seat at the breakfast table on Friday morning, she was considering visiting Harry herself. Not that it would do any good—but she felt so helpless every time she looked at Lucinda's face. Calm and pale, her guest sat toying with a piece of cold toast, her expression distant.

Em swallowed her snort. Feeling dejected herself, she poured a cup of tea.

"Are we going anywhere today?" Heather, seated further down the table, fixed big hazel eyes almost pleadingly on Em.

Em slanted a glance at Lucinda. "Perhaps we'll just have a quiet day today. A drive in the Park in the afternoon. We've Lady Halifax's ball tonight."

Lucinda's smile was perfunctory.

"Greenwich was such fun." Heather struggled to invest her words with conviction. Lord Ruthven had arranged an outing yesterday to the Observatory, hoping to lift Lucinda's spirits. He and Mr Satterly, who had made one of the party, had battled valiantly but to no avail.

Lucinda shifted in her chair. "It was very kind of Lord Ruthven to arrange it. I must send a note around to thank him."

Em doubted Ruthven would appreciate it. The poor man
had pulled out all stops but it was clear Lucinda barely saw
him. Not that she made reference to what was occupying
her mind. Her composure was faultless; those who did not
know her would detect nothing amiss. Those who did saw
the superficiality of her smiles, which no longer reached her
eyes, mistier than ever and distressingly remote. She was
naturally reserved; now, despite going amongst them, she
seemed to have withdrawn from real contact.

"Perhaps," Heather ventured, "we could go to the museum? We haven't seen Lord Elgin's marbles yet. You said
you'd like to."

Lucinda tilted her head. "Perhaps."

Helpless, Heather glanced at Em.

Em shook her head. She had originally thought Heather
too young, too immature, to sense Lucinda's silent woe.
Over the last few days, she had realised that Heather both
saw and understood, but with the confidence of youth had
imagined matters would work themselves out somehow.
Now, even Heather's confidence was flagging. She was as
concerned as Em, which worried Em all the more.

The door opened; Fergus appeared at Em's side and presented a silver salver.

"The mail, ma'am. And there's a letter just hand-
delivered for Mrs Babbacombe. The boy didn't wait for a
reply."

Em picked up the white, sealed packet, painfully aware
of the sudden tension that had gripped Lucinda. One glance
at the scrawled direction was enough to tell her it wasn't
from Harry. Helpless to do otherwise, she handed it over
without comment, trying not to watch as, the seal broken,
the expectation that had momentarily lit Lucinda's face died.

Lucinda frowned as she read the short missive, then, grimacing, laid it aside. She looked down at her toast, now
stone-cold. With a tiny sigh, she reached for the teapot.

Em was beyond social niceties. "Well?"

Lucinda glanced at her, then shrugged. "It's an invitation to some houseparty in the country."

"Whose?"

Lucinda frowned. "I can't immediately recall the lady." She sipped her tea, glancing down at the note. "Lady Martindale of Asterley Place."

"Martindale?" Em started to frown, then her face cleared. "Oh—that'll be Marguerite. She's Elmira, Lady Asterley's daughter. She must be helping out. But that's wonderful!" Em turned to Lucinda. "*Just* the thing! Some fresh air and genteel fun is precisely what you need. Elmira is one of my oldest friends although we haven't met in ages. She'll be getting on, now. When's this party to be?"

Lucinda hesitated, then grimaced. "It starts later today—but the invitation's just for me."

Em blinked. "Just for...?" Then she blinked again, her face clearing. "Ah—I see!"

Lucinda looked up. "What is it?"

Em straightened. "Just remembered. Harry's a close friend of Elmira's son—Alfred, Lord Asterley. Been thick as thieves since they were at Eton together."

She watched as Lucinda reached again for the note.

"Oh?"

"Indeed." Em's eyes glazed as she considered the possibilities. "Always hand-in-glove in mischief. Got sent down together any number of times." For a moment, she remained sunk in thought, then flicked a glance at Lucinda, busy scrutinising the invitation. "You know," Em said, sitting back in her chair, "it's probably not surprising that the invitation's just for you. I can see how it would have been—Elmira had a last-minute cancellation and asked Alfred if he could suggest someone suitable to fill the gap." Em hesitated, then added, "And Alfred and Harry *are* very close."

The more Em thought of it, the more convinced she was that Harry was behind the unexpected invitation. It would be just like him to manoeuvre to get Lucinda into the country, free of mentors, admirers and step-daughters, so he could make amends for his behaviour away from all interested eyes. Very Harry indeed.

Em snorted.

The atmosphere around the breakfast table had altered dramatically. Instead of resignation bordering on the morose, speculation now tinged the air. Varying degrees of calculation and decision were reflected in the ladies' expressions.

Pushing her plate aside, Heather put their thoughts into words. "You *have* to go."

"Absolutely," Em agreed. "Heather and I are more than capable of entertaining each other for a few days."

Lucinda, reanimated but still frowning, looked up from the invitation. "You're sure it's acceptable for me to go alone?"

"To Asterley Place? Of course!" Em dismissed the point with a wave. "It's not as if you were a young girl making her come-out. And you'll find plenty there you've already met, I don't doubt. Very fashionable, Elmira's parties."

"*Do* go." Heather leaned over the table. "I'd love to hear all about it. Maybe we'll all be invited next time."

Lucinda glanced at Heather's eager young face. Her hesitation was pure prevarication; if there was any possibility Harry had organised the invitation then she had no choice but to go.

She straightened and drew in a breath—a surge of revivifying hope came with it. "Very well. If you're sure you can manage without me?"

Em and Heather vociferously assured her they could.

AFTER LUNCHEON, Em retired to the morning room, her mood one of pleasant expectation. Sinking onto the *chaise,* she cast a contented glance about her, then relaxed against the cushions and, slipping off her slippers, swung her feet up. Propping her head on a cushion, she closed her eyes and sighed deeply.

And wondered if it was too early to feel smug.

She was deep in dreams of white tulle and confetti when the click of the door latch had her blinking awake.

What was Fergus thinking of?

Prepared to take umbrage, she turned her head—and saw Harry enter.

Em blinked again. She opened her mouth—then caught sight of the white flower in Harry's buttonhole.

He *never* wore buttonholes—except at weddings.

Harry saw her arrested expression and inwardly grimaced; he should have left the buttonhole off. But he had dressed with inordinate care—it had seemed the right touch at the time.

He was determined to do this right. If they'd had the sense to stay at home yesterday, the ordeal would be over by now. Reining in his impatience, he closed the door and turned to face his aunt just as she managed to catch her breath.

"Ah…"

"Precisely," Harry said, no trace of the languid in his tones. "If you don't mind, Aunt, I'd like to see Mrs Babbacombe." He met Em's slightly protruberant eyes. "Alone."

Em blinked. "But she's left."

"Left?" All expression drained from Harry's face. For a moment, he couldn't breathe. "Left to where?"

Em put a hand to her spinning head. "But…to Asterley, of course." Eyes widening, she sat up. "Aren't you going?"

His wits reeling, Harry stared at her. "I've got an invitation," he admitted, somewhat cautiously.

Em flopped against the cushions, a hand at her breast. "Thank heaven for that. Only reason she went." Recalling the point, she turned to glare at Harry. "Not, of course, that that'll prove any use—it's plain as a pikestaff *you* didn't organise to have her invited."

"Organise…?" Harry stared at her as if she'd run mad. "Of course I didn't!" He paused, then asked, "Why the devil did you think I did?"

Lips prim, Em shrugged. "Well, there's no reason you couldn't have—I'm quite sure Alfred could have got another name on Elmira's lists if you'd asked him."

"Elmira?"

Em waved. "I know Marguerite issued the invitations but it'll still be Elmira's party."

Fists clenched, Harry closed his eyes—and stifled the explosive anger building within him. His father was older than Em—and suffered from the same, oddly selective memory. Em clearly recalled his connection with Alfred but had totally forgotten that his mother, Elmira, had been dead some eight years.

The parties at Asterley Place were, these days, rather different from those Em recalled.

Harry drew in a deep breath and opened his eyes. "When did she leave?"

Em frowned somewhat petulantly. "About eleven." She glanced at the clock on the mantelshelf. "She'll be halfway there by now."

Grim-faced, Harry turned on his heel.

Em stared. "Where are you going?"

Harry glanced back, his hand on the knob, his expression hard and unyielding. "To rescue Boadicea from a gaggle of lecherous Romans."

With that, he departed, shutting the door behind him, leaving Em staring in bemusement at the uninformative panels.

"Boadicea?"

HARRY STRODE THROUGH the door of his lodgings, ripping the white gillyflower from his lapel and tossing it onto the hall table. "Dawlish! Where the devil are you?"

"I'm right here," came in mumbles from down the corridor. Dawlish appeared, an apron over his street clothes, silver spoons and a polishing rag in his hands. "Now what's yer trouble? I thought as how you'd gone to settle it?"

Harry ground his teeth. "I had—but apparently I should have made an appointment. The damned woman's gone off for a quiet sojourn in the country—to Asterley Place."

He had rarely seen Dawlish so dumbfounded.

"Asterley?"

"Precisely." Harry shrugged off his greatcoat. "And, no, she hasn't changed her lifestyle. The damned female has no idea what she's blithely heading into."

Dawlish's eyes grew round. "Gawd help her." He took the coat from Harry.

"I sincerely doubt he can." Harry stripped off his gloves and threw them onto the table with the gillyflower, then turned to the stairs. "Come on—stop standing there like a gawp. We'll need the greys—she's got more than a two hours' start on us."

As Harry pounded upstairs, Dawlish blinked, then shook himself. "With you fired up and the greys in their usual mood, we should be able to cut that in half easily."

Harry didn't hear. He strode into his bedroom; it was the work of a few minutes to throw a selection of clothes into a bag. Dawlish came in as he was shrugging into a bottle-green coat; he had already changed his ivory inexpressibles for buckskin breeches.

"No need to kill y'rself," Dawlish advised, picking up the bag. "We'll make it on her heels."

Frowning, Harry led the way out. "We'll get there a full hour after her," he growled.

An hour in which she, a total innocent, would have to fend for herself in a house full of wolves, all of whom would assume she was willing prey.

LUCINDA DESCENDED from her carriage before the steps of Asterley Place and looked around. The house bore a relatively recent façade, Ionic columns supporting the porch roof, classic geometric lines delineating the long windows. It stood in a large park, directly before a long sloping lawn leading down to the shores of a lake. Glimpses of gardens tantalised on both sides; the subtle scent of roses wafted over a brick wall. Wide stone steps led up to the porch; as footmen came running to assist with the baggage, Lucinda unhurriedly ascended to find her host, hostess and their major-domo waiting.

"Welcome to Asterley Place, my dear Mrs Babbacombe. Can't say how delighted I am to see you here." Lord Asterley, a gentleman of average height with a tendency to corpulence, severely restrained, bowed, then shook Lucinda's hand.

Lucinda smiled in return, recalling now that she had met his lordship during her earlier weeks in the capital. "I must thank you for your invitation, my lord. It was most… opportune—and appreciated." She couldn't suppress the hope that welled within her; anticipation lit her eyes and her smile.

Lord Asterley noticed—and was instantly smitten. "Indeed? Very pleased to hear it, m'dear." He patted her hand, then turned to the lady beside him. "Allow me to present my sister, Lady Martindale. She acts as my hostess at these little gatherings, y'know."

Lucinda turned and was engulfed in a warm smile.

Lady Martindale shook hands, a smile wreathing her pretty face. "Please call me Marguerite. Everyone else who stays does." Her ladyship was some years Lucinda's senior, a buxom blonde, as transparently good-natured as her brother. "I do hope you enjoy yourself whilst here—don't hesitate to let me know if there's anything the least amiss."

Lucinda could feel herself relaxing. "Thank you."

"The others are gathering in the conservatory—once you've had a chance to refresh yourself, do please join them." Marguerite gestured to the house, gathering Lucinda as she turned towards it. "I dare say there are others you already know but we pride ourselves on informality here." She leaned closer to add, "You may be sure there are none present who don't know *precisely* how to behave, so you need have no worries other than deciding with whom you wish to pass the time."

Lucinda returned her smile.

"Now then—we've put you in the Blue Room." Her ladyship glanced at Lucinda's cambric carriage dress. "Clearly an inspired choice. Melthorpe here will show you the way and see your maid and baggage sent up. We dine at six."

Lucinda thanked her again, then followed in the major-domo's wake. He was a small man, shrunk within his dark clothes, his long nose and hunched shoulders giving him a crow-like appearance.

As they gained the top of the wide main staircase, Lucinda caught his eye. He gestured along one corridor; she followed as he started down it. And inwardly frowned. Why on earth should Melthorpe regard her so severely? He stopped before a door at the end of the corridor, opening it and standing back so she could precede him; Lucinda took a closer look at his face as she passed.

Casting a professionally assessing glance around the room, she approved it with a nod. "Thank you, Melthorpe. If you would send my maid up immediately?"

"As you wish, ma'am."

She watched as, with a frigid air that barely avoided incivility, Melthorpe bowed and withdrew. Lucinda frowned at the door as it shut behind him.

There was little possibility she had misread his manner—she had too many years' experience of servants and underlings. The man had looked at her, treated her, as if... It was a moment before she could correctly place his behaviour. When she did, she was dumbstruck.

The door opened and Agatha appeared, a footman with

Lucinda's case immediately behind. Lucinda watched as her maid, dourly severe as only she could be, instructed the footman to place the case by the dressing-table, then closed the door behind him.

"Well!" Agatha turned to face her.

Lucinda noted the speculation in Agatha's old eyes, but did not respond. From experience, she knew she would get more information if she let Agatha deliver it in her own fashion. And she was suddenly very curious about Asterley Place.

Stripping off her gloves, she threw them on the bed—a wide four-poster with a tasselled canopy. Her bonnet followed. Then she spread her skirts and considered them. "Hmm—too crushed. I'll change into my new tea gown, just until dinner."

Agatha humphed as she bent to the case buckles. "I haven't seen much of them yet, but they do seem a stylish lot. A goodly gaggle of snooty gentlemen's gentlemen in the kitchens as I passed—and from the looks of some of the lady's maids I reckon there'll be fights over the curling tongs before nightfall. Best let me do your hair up, too."

"Later." Lucinda glanced at her reflection in the mirror over the dressing table. "There'll be time before dinner."

"Six, they said. Midway between country and town." Agatha pulled an armful of dresses from the case. "Did hear one of them mention that they have it that way so there'll be more of the evening for 'their little games', whatever that might mean."

"Games?" Perhaps the Asterley household amused themselves with the usual country house parlour games? Lucinda frowned. The vision of Lord Asterley and the buxom Marguerite presiding over such entertainments wasn't convincing. Lips firming, Lucinda stood. "Come—help me change. I want to meet the other guests before dinner."

As she'd been told, they were in the conservatory. It was an unusually large version built on at the back of the house and filled with potted palms to create a leafy grotto. There was a tiled pool at its centre; the guests were gathered about it, some in wicker chairs, others standing chatting in groups.

One glance made Lucinda very glad she had changed. They were indeed a stylish lot, confident, gaily plumed birds nestling within the greenery. She nodded to Mrs Walker, an elegant widow, and Lady Morcombe, a dashing matron, both of whom she had met in town.

"My dear Mrs Babbacombe." Marguerite rustled forward. "Pray let me introduce you to Lord Dewhurst—he's only just returned from Europe and so has yet to meet you."

Lucinda calmly returned Lord Dewhurst's greetings while inwardly gauging her companions. She could detect nothing odd to account for her flickering nerves. "Indeed," she replied to Lord Dewhurst's query. "I've quite enjoyed my time in town. But the balls are becoming a trifle…" She gestured. "Overdone—don't you find it so? So crowded one can hardly hear one's self think. And as for breathing…"

His lordship laughed, a smooth, suave sound. "Indeed, my dear. Little gatherings such as this are much more *convenable.*"

The subtle emphasis he placed on the last word had Lucinda glancing up at him. His lordship looked down at her, a warm light in his eyes.

"I'm sure you'll discover, my dear, that at Asterley Place, it's very easy to find both time and place to…think."

Lucinda stared at him. Before she could gather her wits, he took her hand and bowed low.

"Should you find yourself wishful of company, my dear, pray don't hesitate to call on me. I can be exceedingly thoughtful, I assure you."

"Ah—yes. That is," desperate, Lucinda wrestled her wits into order, "I'll bear your offer in mind, my lord." She inclined her head, somewhat stiffly.

She waited while his lordship bowed again then gracefully strolled away. Then dragged in a quick breath—and cast another, much more critical, look about her.

And wondered how she could have been so blind. Every one of the ladies present was undoubtedly that, but they were all either widowed or married, all of unquestionable breeding yet of an age when, it might be imagined, they might have a very real interest in indulging in discreet liaisons.

As for the gentlemen, they were each and every one of a type she recognised all too well.

Before she had time to think further, Lord Asterley strolled up.

"My dear Mrs Babbacombe—can't tell you how thrilled I was to learn of your interest in our little gatherings."

"My interest?" Lucinda swallowed her amazement and politely if coolly raised her brows.

Lord Asterley smiled knowingly; she half-expected him to wink and nudge her elbow. "Well—perhaps not especially in *our* gatherings, but in the type of entertainment we all find so…" his lordship gestured expansively "…fulfilling." He looked down at her. "I do hope, my dear, that, should you feel so inclined, you won't hesitate to call on me—to help enliven your stay here?"

Clinging to polite form, Lucinda inclined her head; as she could find no suitable words in which to answer his lordship, she left him to think what he would.

He beamed and bowed; to her chagrin, Lucinda found it very hard to feel indignant with one so openly cheery. She nodded and drifted to the pool. There was a seat vacant beside Mrs Allerdyne, a *ton*nish widow who, Lucinda now realised, was probably not quite as virtuous as she appeared.

Mrs Allerdyne turned as Lucinda subsided onto the wicker seat.

"Good afternoon, Mrs Babbacombe—or can I dispense with formality and call you Lucinda?"

Lucinda blinked at Henrietta Allerdyne's charmingly gentle face. "Yes, of course." Feeling as if her eyes had just been opened to yet another aspect of *ton*nish life, Lucinda, somewhat dazedly, glanced about her again.

"This is your first time here, isn't it?" Henrietta leaned closer. "Marguerite mentioned it," she explained when Lucinda switched her gaze back. "No need to feel awkward about it." Henrietta patted Lucinda's hand. "We're all friends here, of course. The very last whisper in discretion—no need to fear any comments once you're back in town." Henrietta glanced around with the air of one entirely at her ease. "It's been like that for years, ever since Harry started it."

"Harry?" Lucinda's breath stuck in her throat. "Harry Lester?"

"Mmm." Henrietta was exchanging none-too-idle glances with an elegant gentleman across the room. "As I recall, Harry was the one who thought of the idea. Alfred simply implemented it to Harry's directions."

Harry—who had sent her here.

For an instant, Lucinda felt as if she would faint—the room receded into a dark mist; a chill spread through her. She swallowed; clenching her fists in her lap, she fought back the dizziness. When she could, she murmured, "I see." Henrietta, engrossed with her gentleman, had not noticed her difficulty—nor her sudden pallor. Her cheeks felt icy; Lucinda grasped the moment to recoup, to let her senses settle. Then, with what nonchalance she could, she asked, "Does he often attend?"

"Harry?" Henrietta smilingly nodded to her gentleman and turned back. "Occasionally—he's perennially invited but one never knows if he'll show." Henrietta's smile turned affectionate. "Not one to run in anyone's harness, Harry."

"No, indeed!" Lucinda ignored the questioning look her tartness invoked. A rage unlike any she had ever experienced was rising within her.

Was her invitation here Harry's way of showing her how he now viewed her? That she had become one with these ladies, dallying with any gentleman who took their fancy? Had he sent her· here to experience the ''congenial company'' she had assured him she was seeking?

Or had he sent her here to teach her a lesson—and was planning to arrive just in time to rescue her from the consequences?

Her jaw set, her hands clenched, Lucinda abruptly stood. She felt like screaming, pacing the floor—*throwing things!*—she wasn't sure which of his possible motives enraged her the most. She dragged in a deep breath. ''I hope he comes,'' she breathed through clenched teeth.

''Lucinda?'' Henrietta leaned forward to peer up into her face. ''Are you quite well?''

Rigid, Lucinda plastered a smile on her lips. ''Perfectly, thank you.''

Henrietta didn't look convinced.

Luckily, the gong sounded, sending them to their rooms. Lucinda reined in her impatience enough to accompany Henrietta to her door—then briskly strode down the corridor to the Blue Room.

''What have you heard?'' she demanded of Agatha the instant the door shut behind her.

Agatha looked up from the navy blue silk gown she was laying out on the bed. She took one look at Lucinda's face— and answered directly. ''Not much—but nothing good. Lots of innuendo ''bout what the nobs get up to o'nights. Doors opening and closing at all hours.'' Agatha sniffed. ''An' such like.''

Lucinda sat at the dressing table and started pulling pins from her hair. She shot her maid a severe look. ''*What* else?''

Agatha shrugged. ''Seems like it's the expected thing here—not just the odd couple or so, like happens anywhere.'' The maid grimaced. ''Did hear one of the footmen liken it to a set of coaching inns—one coach pulls in as the last's pulling out.''

Lucinda sat back and stared at Agatha in the mirror. ''Great heavens,'' she finally said, somewhat weakly. Then she rallied—no matter what the general practice, she was confident that not one of the gentlemen present would force his attentions on an unwilling lady.

Her gaze fell on the navy silk gown. ''Not that one.'' Her eyes narrowed. ''The silk gauze.''

Agatha straightened, hands on her hips. ''The gauze?''

In the mirror, Lucinda raised haughty brows.

Agatha snorted. '''Tis barely decent.''

''For my purposes tonight, it'll be perfect.'' Lucinda drew out the last word to a literal purr. She wasn't the one who would learn a lesson tonight.

Grumbling beneath her breath, Agatha put away the navy silk and drew out the shimmering silk gauze, its colour a silvery sky blue. Laying it carefully on the bed, she sniffed disapprovingly, then came up and started on Lucinda's laces.

Lucinda tapped her comb on the table. ''This is a horrendous coil.'' She frowned. ''Have you asked after Lady Asterley?''

Agatha nodded. ''There isn't one. The last—her as was Lord Asterley's mother—died years ago.''

''Oh.'' Lucinda blinked, then, drawing in a breath, squared her shoulders. ''Well—tonight can't be helped—but we'll be leaving tomorrow.''

''Aye—so I thought.''

Lucinda heard the relief in Agatha's voice. She hid an affectionate grin. ''Don't worry—despite all indications to the contrary, they are entirely gentlemen at heart.''

Agatha humphed. ''So you say—but gentlemen can be very persuasive at times.''

Lucinda rose and let her gown fall to the floor. Stepping out of it, she allowed Agatha to help her into the sheath of shimmering blue silk. Only when she was finally ready to descend to the drawing-room did she deign to acknowledge Agatha's last comment.

"As I should hope you know by now," she said, fixing Agatha with a haughty glance, "I'm more than capable of managing any gentleman who might darken my horizon. So just tidy up in here—and let Joshua know that we'll be departing in the morning." Lucinda glided to the door— then paused to look back at her maid. "And don't *worry*, you old curmudgeon!"

With that, she turned and, a scintillating vision in shimmering silver blue, glided out of the door.

The drawing-room quickly filled, the guests eager for each other's company. Now sure of her footing, Lucinda found no difficulty in strolling through the crowd, acknowledging the compliments and the open admiration in the gentlemen's eyes, artfully turning aside their subtle suggestions. She was once more in control—but her nerves were taut, her whole being on edge.

The moment she'd been waiting for finally arrived.

Harry walked into the room, creating, she noticed, an immediate stir. He must have arrived while they were changing; he was dressed in his usual severe black and white, his fair hair gleaming in the candlelight. Marguerite broke off her conversation to sweep forward and greet him—with a peck on the cheek, Lucinda noted. Lord Asterley came up to wring his hand. Other gentlemen nodded and called greetings; many of the ladies prinked and preened, smiling in gracious welcome.

Abruptly finding herself the object of a piercing green stare, Lucinda didn't smile at all. Her heart stuttered, then accelerated; a vice slowly closed about her chest. Her expression studiously remote, she inclined her head fractionally and turned back to Mr Ormesby and Lady Morcombe.

And waited for him to come to her.

He didn't—nor was he about to. That much was made

plain within ten minutes. Excruciatingly aware of his gaze, dwelling on her shoulders, bare above the abbreviated neckline of her gown, and on her upper breasts, likewise revealed, Lucinda gritted her teeth and inwardly cursed. What the devil was he up to now?

Cursing her, as it happened—Harry could barely restrain the urge to cross the room, lay hold of one delicate wrist and haul her away. What the deuce did she mean by appearing in such a gown? Of the sheerest silk gauze, it shimmered and glimmered, tantalised and teased. The soft material clung wherever it touched, outlining then concealing her slender form, artfully displaying the graceful curves of hips and thighs and the smooth planes of her back. As for her breasts, they were barely concealed at all—the square neckline had been cut by a miser. Gritting his teeth, he forced his feet to remain still. As all the gentleman were openly captivated, at least he didn't need to disguise his interest.

"Harry, old chap! Didn't think to see you here. Thought you might be looking to take a leaf out of Jack's book, what?"

Harry bent a look of intense irritation on Lord Cranbourne. "Not my style, Bentley. But who have you got your eye on?"

Lord Cranbourne grinned. "Lady Morcombe. She's a ripe little plum—that old codger of a husband of hers doesn't appreciate her as he ought."

"Hmm." Harry sent another penetrating glance about the room. "Just the usual crowd, is it?"

"All except the lovely Mrs Babbacombe—but you know all about her, as I recall?"

"Indeed." Harry's gaze rested again on Lucinda. Again he quelled the urge to go to her side.

"Your interest lie that way this evening?"

Harry shot Lord Cranbourne a quick glance, but his lordship's question was clearly an idle one. "Not as you mean it."

With a nod, he strolled away—before a puzzled Lord Cranbourne could ask for clarification.

With studied nonchalance, Harry circled the room, watching, assessing. His interest was certainly centred on Lucinda—but his first concern was to determine who had placed her name on the invitation list.

He'd been halfway to Asterley before his mind had cleared enough to see the point. *He* hadn't suggested her— so who had? And why?

He prowled the room, carefully studying, not only Lucinda, but all who approached her, intent on discovering which, of his fellow rakes, felt he had first claim.

By the time dinner was announced, by Melthorpe in sepulchral vein, Lucinda had come to the conclusion that Harry was waiting for something—presumably disaster—to befall her, so that he could come to her aid and take charge of her again. Vowing it would never be so, she smiled graciously on Mr Ormesby as he offered her his arm. "Do you come here often, sir?"

Mr Ormesby gesticulated airily. "Now and then. A peaceful interlude away from the bustle of town, what?"

"Indeed." From the corner of her eye, Lucinda saw Harry frown. Then Marguerite stopped beside him and claimed his arm. Lucinda turned a bright smile on Mr Ormesby. "I will rely on you, sir, if I may, to guide me in Asterley's ways."

Mr Ormesby looked thoroughly chuffed. "A pleasure, my dear."

Lucinda blinked, and hoped she wasn't raising any false expectations. "Tell me—are the dinners very elaborate?"

Tonight's wasn't, but neither was it less than an elegant sufficiency with four full courses and two removes. The conversation, to Lucinda's relief, remained general throughout, with much exchanging of the latest gossip and *on dits,* accompanied by considerable merriment, all in the best of taste.

Indeed, if it hadn't been for the subtle undercurrent, borne on glances and the occasional whispered word, her enjoyment would have been unreserved.

"My dear Mrs Babbacombe." Lord Dewhurst, on Lucinda's left, leaned closer to claim her attention. "Have you heard of the treasure hunt Marguerite has organised for tomorrow?"

"Treasure hunt?" Aware of the growing warmth in his lordship's gaze, Lucinda dimly wondered if such an enterprise, in this company, could possibly be innocent.

"Indeed—and we play a version of Fox and Geese that will, I'm sure, delight you. Needless to say, there's no board involved." His lordship smiled. "We, ourselves, represent the pieces."

Lucinda could just imagine. But she kept her smile serene, grasping the offer of a custard to turn aside without comment. In doing so, she caught Harry's eye. He was seated across the table, some way along. Despite the distance, she could sense his simmering irritation, there in the odd tenseness that invested his apparently relaxed frame, and in the way his long fingers gripped his wine glass. Lucinda summoned a radiantly ingenuous smile—and turned it on Mr Ormesby.

Harry felt the muscle in his jaw ripple; his teeth were clenched tight. He forced his jaw to relax, turning aside as Marguerite waved at him from the end of the table.

Lucinda had hoped to catch her breath, to rest her wits and strengthen her defences, when the ladies retired to the drawing-room. But at Asterley, port was the last thing on the gentlemen's minds; they followed in the ladies' wake, not even glancing at the decanters on the sideboard.

"We generally take things quietly on the first evening," Mr Ormesby informed Lucinda as he joined her by the hearth. "Let people…get to know one another, if you take my meaning."

"Exactly!" Lord Asterley followed hard on Mr Ormesby's heels. "Tomorrow, of course, things will liven up a trifle." He rubbed his hands together and looked over the assembled company. "We'd thought to start by punting on the lake, then move on to the Treasure Hunt. Marguerite's got it all organised—to be held in the gardens, of course." He turned a perfectly innocent smile on Lucinda. "Plenty of quiet nooks to find treasure in."

"Oh?" Lucinda endeavoured to look politely vague.

"Nothing starts till after noon, of course. We generally all meet in the breakfast parlour about then. Gives everyone a chance to catch up on their sleep, don't y'know."

Lucinda nodded, making a mental note to be on the road shortly after ten. Quite how she was to excuse herself, and on what grounds, she did not know—but she'd think of something by tomorrow morning.

Lord Cranbourne and Lady Morcombe joined them; the conversation revolved about the expected entertainments of the next few days—the communal ones. As for the others, those that remained unspecified, Lucinda was increasingly aware of the speculative glances cast her way, by Mr Ormesby, Lord Asterley and Lord Dewhurst in particular.

For the first time since entering Asterley Place, she began to feel truly uneasy. Not out of fear for her virtue, but from dislike of the potentially embarrassing situations she might soon find herself in. Mr Ormesby and Lord Asterley showed no disposition to leave her side; to Lucinda's relief, they were both summoned by Marguerite to help pass the tea-cups. She grasped the opportunity to fill a vacant chair by the *chaise*. On its end sat a pretty woman much of an age with herself; Lucinda vaguely recalled being introduced at Almack's.

"Lady Coleby—Millicent." The woman smiled and nodded as she passed a teacup. ''Always a pleasure to welcome another to our circle.''

Lucinda's answering smile was a trifle weak. She hid it behind her cup. She was beginning to wonder if she should have braved the fuss and left three hours ago.

''Have you made your choice yet?'' Over the rim of her cup, Lady Coleby raised a questioning brow.

Lucinda blinked. ''Choice?''

Her ladyship gestured about her. ''From amongst the gentlemen.''

Lucinda looked blank

''Oh—I forgot. You're new.'' Lady Coleby lowered her cup and leaned closer. ''It's all very simple. One just decides which of the gentlemen one likes the best—one, two or more if your taste runs that way—then one lets them know—discreetly, of course. You don't need to do anything more; it's all miraculously well-organised.''

Faced with an unwaveringly enquiring gaze, Lucinda swallowed a mouthful of tea. ''Ah—I'm not sure.''

''Well, don't leave it too long or the best will be taken.'' Lady Coleby touched Lucinda's sleeve. ''I'm after Harry Lester, myself,'' she confided, nodding to where Harry stood on the opposite side of the room. ''He's not attended in an age—not since I've been coming anyway, which is more than a year. But all that excessive elegance, all that lethal grace—'' Lady Coleby broke off with a delicate shiver. ''Deep waters hold *dangerous* currents, so they say.'' Her gaze fixed on Harry, she took a sip of her tea. ''I never would have believed brash, impetuous Harry would turn out like that. It just goes to show. He's nothing like the fresh-faced young gentleman who offered for me all those years ago.''

Lucinda froze. Then, slowly, she set her cup back on her saucer. ''He offered for you?''

''Oh, yes! Not officially—it never came to that. Ten and more years ago it was.'' Her ladyship affected a dewy-eyed

look, then giggled. "He was most *terribly* enamoured—
well, you know how young men can be." She waved her
hand. "Utterly over the moon. Wild, impassioned declarations—it was all so thrilling for he was very handsome, even
then."

Lucinda studied Lady Coleby's face as her ladyship studied Harry, engaged in a discussion with a Mr Harding. "But
you didn't accept him?"

"Heavens, no! Poor as church mice, the Lesters. Or they
were. Mind you…" a speculative glint lit her ladyship's
brown eyes "…now that Coleby's dead and gone and the
Lesters have suffered a windfall—" Lady Coleby broke off
to state, "Positively *enormous*, my dear, so I've heard.
Well—" she turned back to survey Harry, anticipation lighting her face "—I really do believe I should renew old acquaintances."

At that moment, Harry and Mr Harding parted. Harry
directed a piercing glance across the room.

Her ladyship smiled delightedly and rose, laying aside her
teacup. "And it appears there'll be no better time. Do excuse me, my dear."

Lucinda forced herself to incline her head. Picking up
both cups, she carried them to where Marguerite sat by the
tea trolley, all the while keeping her gaze firmly fixed on
her hostess.

Harry's gaze was fixed on her. He hesitated, frowning,
his lips set in a firm line. No gentlemen had pressed her;
none had displayed any proprietary interest. Three, if not
four, were seriously enamoured; another few were watching
closely. But none seemed to consider they had first claim—
they were all vying for her favours as if she had swanned
into their orbit on her own account.

Which left him with the puzzle unsolved. With an inward
grimace, he put it aside until the morning. He was about to
cross the room, to head off what he knew would be an

embarrassing and confusing confrontation, when he felt a
touch on his sleeve.

"Harry!" Millicent, Lady Coleby, uttered the word on a
long breathy exhalation. She opened wide brown eyes at
him, her delicately tinted cheeks aglow.

Briefly, Harry nodded. "Millie." His head rose again as
he looked for Lucinda; she was still chatting to Marguerite.

"Dear Harry." Engrossed in artlessly studying his cravat,
Millie didn't notice his interest was elsewhere. "I've always
carried a torch for you—you do know that, don't you? I had
to marry Coleby—you must see that. You're so much older
now—you understand the ways of our world." Millie let a
knowing smile curve her lips. "I've heard you understand
the ways very well, Harry. Perhaps we might…travel a few
avenues together tonight?"

Millie glanced up—just as Lucinda nodded to Marguerite
and headed for the door. Harry, about to move, was forced
to focus on Millie, standing directly in front of him.

"Excuse me, Millie. I've business elsewhere."

With that, he nodded and sidestepped, then halted, his
gaze on Lucinda—and the three gentlemen who had intercepted her. Concentrating, he could just make out their
words.

"My dear Mrs Babbacombe." Alfred was the first to gain
her side. "Dare I hope you've found the evening to your
taste?"

"You've proved a most welcome addition to our ranks,
ma'am." Ormesby was close behind. "I do hope we can
entice you to spend more time with us—I, for one, can think
of little I'd like better."

Lucinda blinked; before she could answer, Lord Dewhurst
joined them.

He took her hand and bowed low. "Enchanted, my dear.
Dare I hope for some time to further our acquaintance?"

Lucinda met his lordship's calm but distinctly warm
gaze—and wished herself elsewhere. Heat tinged her

cheeks—then, from the corner of her eye, she saw Harry. Watching.

Drawing in a steadying breath, Lucinda smiled at her three would-be *cicisbei*. With what she hoped they understood as a pointed disregard for all they had hinted at, if not said, she calmly stated, ''If you'll excuse me, gentlemen, I believe I will retire early.''

With a benedictory smile, she swept them a curtsy; they immediately bowed low. Rising, Lucinda headed straight for the door. Confident she had avoided a potential quagmire, head high, she glided from the room.

Harry stared after her.

Then uttered a single, pungent expletive and spun on his heel. He exited the room by the windows to the terrace. At speed.

Millie simply stared—then lifted her shoulders in a baffled shrug—and glided after Mr Harding.

Lucinda climbed the stairs and traversed the corridors, engrossed, not with the details of her imminent departure nor yet imaginings of what she had escaped. Lady Coleby's revelations of Harry's long-ago disappointment filled her mind.

She could imagine, very clearly, how it must have been, how, with the impetuosity of youth, he had laid his love at his chosen one's feet, only to see it spurned. It must have hurt. A great deal. The fact explained many things—why he was now so cynical of love, not marriage itself, but the love needed to support it, the intensity he now harnessed, that certain something which made so many women view him as dangerous—excitingly but definitely so—and his emotionally cautious nature.

Reaching her room, Lucinda shut the door firmly behind her. She looked for a key, grimacing resignedly when she discovered there wasn't one.

Thanks to Lady Coleby, and her lack of what Lucinda felt was any proper feeling, she could now understand why

Harry was as he was. That, however, did not excuse his behaviour in engineering her present predicament.

Eyes narrowing as she considered his perfidy, Lucinda glided across the room, lit by a single candelabra on the dressing table, and gave the bell pull a definite tug.

The door opened. Her hand still clutching the embroidered pull, Lucinda turned.

To see Harry slip around the door.

He scanned the room and found her. "There's no point ringing for your maid—the house rules forbid servants the upper corridors after ten."

"What?" Lucinda stared. "But what are you doing here?"

Harry closed the door and looked around again.

Lucinda had had enough. Eyes narrowing, she sailed across the room to confront him. "However, as you *are* here, I have a bone to pick with you!"

Reassured they were alone, Harry brought his gaze to her face as she halted, slender and straight, before him. "Indeed?"

"As you well know!" Lucinda glared up at him. "How *dare* you organise to have me invited to such a gathering as this? I realise you might be somewhat irritated because I did not accept your proposal—" She broke off as the thought occurred that she, like Lady Coleby, might be said to have rejected him. "But the circumstances were nothing like those of Lady Coleby. Or whoever she was then." With an irritated wave, she dismissed Lady Coleby. "Whatever your feelings in the matter, I have to tell you that I view your behaviour in this instance as *reprehensible!* Utterly callous and without justification! It is totally inconceivable to me why you—"

"I didn't."

The steel beneath the words cut through her denunciation.

Arrested in mid-tirade, Lucinda blinked up at him. "You didn't?"

His jaw set, his lips a thin line, Harry regarded her through narrowed eyes. "For a woman of superior sense, you frequently indulge the most remarkable notions. *I* didn't arrange to have you invited. On the contrary." His tone turned conversational, his accents remained clipped; the undercurrent was positively lethal. "When I discover who did, I'm going to wring his neck."

"Oh." Lucinda backed a step as he closed the distance between them. Her eyes met his; abruptly, she stiffened and stood her ground. "That's all very well—but what are you doing here now?"

"Protecting you from your latest folly."

"Folly?" Lucinda coolly raised her brows—and her chin. "What folly?"

"The folly of the invitation you just, all unwittingly, issued." Harry glanced at the bed, then the fireplace. The fire was lit, a smallish blaze but there was plenty of wood by the hearth. An armchair sat before it.

Lucinda frowned. "What invitation?"

Harry's gaze came back to her face; he merely raised his brows at her.

Lucinda snorted. "Nonsense. You're imagining things. I issued no invitation—I did nothing of the sort."

Harry gestured to the armchair. "Let's just wait and see, shall we?"

"No—I want you out of here." Lucinda couldn't tilt her chin any higher. "Your presence is totally improper."

Harry's eyes glittered. "Naturally—that's the purpose of these parties, in case you hadn't realised." His gaze fell to her breasts. "And speaking of improper—who the devil told you that gown was decent?"

"A whole *host* of appreciative gentlemen," Lucinda informed him, belligerently planting her hands on her hips. "And I hardly need you to tell me what the purpose of this little gathering is *but,* for your information, I plan to have nothing to do with it."

''Good—we agree on that much.''

Lucinda narrowed her eyes. Harry met her gaze with a stubbornness as unwavering as her own.

A knock came on the door.

Harry smiled coldly. He pointed a finger at Lucinda's nose. ''Wait here.''

Without waiting for any agreement, he swung on his heel and retraced his steps. He opened the door. ''Yes?''

Alfred jumped. ''Oh—ah!'' He blinked wildly. ''Oh—it's you, Harry. Er—I didn't realise.''

''Obviously.''

Alfred shifted his weight from one foot to the other, then gestured vaguely. ''Right-ho! Er…I'll call later, then.''

''Don't bother—the reception will be the same.''

The words were a dire warning. Harry shut the door on his old schoolfriend's face, before he could think of doing anything else with the vacuously good-natured features.

He swung back—to find Lucinda staring at the door in utter disbelief. ''*Well!* What cheek!''

Harry smiled. ''I'm so glad you now see my point.''

Lucinda blinked, then gestured at the door. ''But he's gone now. You told him not to come back.'' When Harry merely raised his brows, she folded her arms and lifted her chin. ''There's no reason you can't leave now.''

Harry's smile turned feral. ''I can give you two very good reasons.''

They came knocking an hour or so apart.

Lucinda gave up blushing after the first.

She also stopped urging Harry to leave; this was not the sort of houseparty at which she felt comfortable.

When the hour after midnight passed and no one else came creeping to knock on the panels of her door, Lucinda finally relaxed. Curled up against the pillows on her bed, she looked across at Harry, eyes closed, head back, sprawled in the big armchair before the fire.

She didn't want him to go.

"Get into bed—I'll stay here."

He hadn't moved or opened his eyes. Lucinda could feel her heart thudding. "There?"

His lips twisted. "I'm perfectly capable of spending a night in a chair for a good cause." He shifted, stretching his legs out before him. "It's not too uncomfortable."

Lucinda considered, then nodded. His eyes looked closed. "Do you need any help with your lacings?"

She shook her head—then realised and answered, "No."

"Good." Harry relaxed. "Good night, then."

"Good night."

Lucinda watched him for a moment, then settled down amid the covers, drawing them over her. Although it was a four-poster, there were no hangings on the bed; there was no screen behind which she could change. She lay back against the pillows; when Harry made no sound, did not move, she shifted onto her side.

The soft flickering firelight touched his face, lighting the hollows, throwing the strong bone structure into relief, shading his heavy lids, etching the firm contours of his lips.

Lucinda's eyes slowly closed and she drifted into sleep.

Chapter Eleven

When she awoke the next morning, the fire had died. The chair before it was empty.

Lucinda let her lids fall and snuggled down beneath the covers. Her lips curved in a lazy smile; a deep contentment pervaded her. Idly, she searched for the cause—and remembered her dream.

The time, as she recalled, had been very late, deep in the long watches of the night. The house had been silent when she'd supposedly woken—and seen Harry sprawled in the chair before the dying fire. He had shifted restlessly and she had remembered the blanket left on a chair by the bed. She had slipped from beneath the covers, her shimmering gown slithering over her limbs. On silent feet, she had retrieved the blanket and approached the chair by the fire.

She had halted six feet away, stopped by some sixth sense. His eyes had been closed, long brown lashes gilded at the tips almost brushing his high cheekbones. She had studied his face, the angles and planes, austere in repose, the carved jaw and sculpted lips. Her gaze had travelled on, down his long, graceful body, loose-limbed in sleep, the subtle tension that normally invested it in abeyance.

A little sigh had caught in her throat.

And she had felt the touch of his gaze.

Raising her eyes, she had seen his were open, his gaze, heavy-lidded, on her face. He had studied her, not broodingly but with a gentle pensiveness that had held her still.

She had sensed his hesitation, and the instant he put it aside. Lifting one hand, he had held it out, palm upwards, to her.

Indecision had held her, poised, quivering. He said nothing; his hand hadn't moved. She had drawn in a long, deep breath—and placed her hand in his. His fingers had closed gently but firmly about hers, then he had drawn her slowly towards him.

The blanket had fallen from her grasp to lie on the floor, forgotten. He had drawn her nearer, then reached for her, pulling her gently onto his lap.

She had gone very readily, her heart soaring as she felt his heat enfold her, his thighs hard beneath hers. Then his arms had closed about her and she had raised her face for his kiss.

When they had first come together, desire had propelled them into intimacy, leaving no time for the gentler side of passion. In her dream last night they had explored that aspect fully, spending hours before the fire, wrapped in passion's web.

Beneath the covers, Lucinda closed her eyes tight; a long delicious shiver rippled through her.

In her imagination, she could feel Harry's hands upon her, the long fingers experienced, so knowing, his palms hard and calloused from frequent handling of the reins. He had opened the door to a wonderland of sensation—and conducted her through it, educating her senses until they had been filled with pleasure—and him.

He had stripped her gown from her in tantalising stages after his lips, artfully following the neckline, had made her long to rid herself of it. He had gently eased it down, revealing her breasts, on which he had lavished untold attention. In her mind, she felt again the touch of his hair, soft as silk on her heated skin.

How long she had lain, naked in his arms as he loved her, the dying firelight gilding her in bronze and gold, she couldn't recall. But it had felt like hours before he had lifted her and carried her to the bed.

He had drawn down the covers and laid her on the sheets, then rekindled the candles in the candelabra and placed it on the table by the bed. She had blushed and reached for the covers.

"No. Let me look at you."

His voice had been low, soft and deep. Deep currents, indeed, but these weren't turbulent, dangerous, but deeper still, slow, steady and infinitely strong. They had swept aside her inhibitions, leaving her with no reservations; held in his green gaze, she had lain as he had left her and watched while he undressed.

Then he had joined her on the bed and desire had flared; this time, he had held it harnessed and showed her how to manage the reins. The power was no less strong but, this time, she had appreciated it fully, felt its quality in each long-drawn moment, in each subtle movement, each lingering caress.

The end had been just as glorious but had left a deeper sense of peace, a more shattering realisation of how strong the power that held them now was.

There had been tears in her eyes when, after it was over, she had lifted her lids and looked up into his face.

And had seen therein what she had almost given up hope of ever seeing—resignation, perhaps, but acceptance, too. It had been there in his eyes, glowing beneath his heavy lids, there in the gentler cast of his features. And there most especially in his mobile lips, no longer so hard and severe, but softer, more pliable. He had met her gaze—and hadn't tried to hide his reaction, nor draw back from the reality.

Instead, he had lowered his head and kissed her, long,

deeply, lingeringly, then lifted from her and wrapped her in his arms.

A dream—nothing more, her dream, the embodiment of all her hopes, her deepest desires, the answer to her most secret needs.

Lucinda shut her eyes tight, clinging to the deep sense of peace and contentment, even if it was only illusory.

But the day had dawned; light, streaming through the open shutters, played on her lids. Reluctantly, she lifted them—and saw the blanket, half-folded still, sitting on the floor before the hearth.

Her eyes widened. Blinking, she noted the candelabra— on the table beside the bed. Slowly, hardly daring to breathe, she started to turn over. She only got halfway onto her back before she registered the chaos of the covers. Lucinda swallowed, and turned flat on her back. She slanted a glance sideways—and let out the breath she'd been holding. The bed beside her was empty. But the pillow beside hers was deeply dented.

As a final, incontrovertible piece of evidence, a sunbeam, bobbing in, highlighted two fine gold hairs, reposing on the white lawn of the pillowcase.

Lucinda groaned and shut her eyes.

The next instant, she sat bolt upright and flung the covers from her. Only then did she recall she was naked. Grabbing the covers back, she rummaged amid their confusion and discovered the nightgown Agatha had laid out the night before. Muttering curses, Lucinda struggled into it, then leapt from the bed.

She crossed the room with determined strides and yanked violently on the bell pull.

She was leaving. Now.

IN THE LIBRARY on the ground floor, Harry paced back and forth before the windows. He had dispatched an intrigued

Melthorpe to rout out his master, wherever he might be, with a message that his presence was urgently required.

The door latch clicked; Harry swung about as Alfred entered, nattily attired in a check coat over country breeches and high boots. Harry himself was dressed for travelling in his bottle-green coat and buckskins.

"There you are!" With a smile unimpaired by having been summarily summoned from someone else's bed, Alfred strolled forward. "Melthorpe didn't say what the problem was, but you look in fine fettle. Dare say your night was a great deal more exciting than mine, what? Mrs Babbacombe looks set to take the title of most delectable widow of the year—particularly if she can keep *you* entertained, happy as a grig, all night long—"

The last word ended on a strangled note as Harry's fist made contact with Alfred's face.

Harry groaned and put a hand to his brow. "Sorry—sorry." His expression openly apologetic, he extended his hand to Alfred, who was now measuring his length on the rug. "I didn't *mean* to hit you." Harry's jaw hardened. "But you'd be well advised to mute your comments on the subject of Mrs Babbacombe."

Alfred made no move to take his hand, or get up. "Oh?" He was clearly intrigued.

Disgusted with himself, Harry waved him up. "It was just instinctive. I won't hit you again."

"Ah, well." Alfred sat up and gingerly felt his left cheekbone. "I know you didn't *mean* to hit me—nothing's broken, so you must've pulled the punch. Very grateful you did, mind—but if it's all the same to you, I'll just remain here until you tell me what this is all about—just in case, with my usual babble, I inadvertently trigger any more of your instincts."

Harry grimaced. Hands on hips, he looked down at Alfred. "I think someone's been using us." He gestured about him. "The Asterley Place house-parties."

Unexpected intelligence seeped into Alfred's eyes. "How?"

Harry compressed his lips, then stated, "Lucinda Babbacombe should never have been invited. She's a thoroughly virtuous female—take it from me."

Alfred's brows rose. "I see." Then he frowned. "No, I don't."

"What I want to know is who suggested you invite her?"

Alfred sat up and draped his arms over his knees. He blinked up at Harry. "You know, I don't think I like being used. It was a chap named Joliffe—brushed up against him a couple of times at some hell or other but he's generally about town—Ernest, Earle, something like that. Ran across him on Wednesday night at that hell in Sussex Place. He happened to mention that Mrs Babbacombe was looking for a little entertainment and he'd promised he'd mention her to me."

Harry was frowning. "Joliffe?" He shook his head. "Can't say I've had the pleasure."

Alfred snorted. "Wouldn't exactly call it a pleasure. Bit of a loose fish."

Harry's gaze abruptly focused. "You took the word of a loose fish on the subject of a lady's reputation?"

"Of course not." Alfred hurriedly leaned back out of reach, his expression distinctly injured. "I checked—you know I always do."

"Who with?" Harry asked. "Em?"

"*Em?* Your aunt Em?" Alfred blinked. "What's she got to do with it? Old tartar she is—was. Used to pinch my cheeks every time she came visiting."

Harry snorted. "She'll do more than pinch your cheeks if she finds out what you invited her protégée to."

"*Her protégée?*" Alfred looked horrified.

"You obviously didn't check too hard," Harry growled, swinging away to pace once more.

Alfred squirmed. "Well, you see, time was tight. We had

this vacancy; Lady Callan's husband came back from Vienna sooner than she'd expected.''

Harry humphed. "So who *did* you check with?''

''The lady's cousin or something by marriage. Mortimer Babbacombe.''

Harry frowned and stopped pacing. The name came floating back to him from his first memories of Lucinda. "Mortimer Babbacombe?''

Alfred shrugged. "Innocuous sort, a bit weak, but can't say I've heard anything against him—other than that he's a friend of Joliffe's.''

Harry prowled over to stand directly before Alfred. "Let me get this straight—Joliffe suggested Mrs Babbacombe was looking for an invitation to the entertainment here and Mortimer Babbacombe confirmed she liked living life on the racy side?''

"Well, not in so many words. Couldn't expect him to come right out and *say* such a thing of a female relative, what? But you know how it goes—I made the suggestions and gave him plenty of time to deny them. He didn't. Seemed clear enough to me.''

Harry grimaced. Then nodded. "All right.'' He looked down at Alfred. "But she's leaving.''

"When?'' Alfred struggled to his feet.

"Now. As soon as possible. Furthermore, she's never been here.''

Alfred shrugged. "Naturally. *None* of the ladies are here.''

Harry nodded, grateful for his own past deviousness. It was his fertile mind that had devised these parties, where married ladies and widows of the *ton* could enjoy a little illicit dalliance without running the risk of any social repercussions. Total discretion was an absolute requirement— all the ladies who attended had the same secret to hide. As for the gentlemen, honour and their peers—and the likelihood of future invitations—were more than sufficient to ensure their silence.

So the damned woman, despite all, was safe—yet again.

Harry frowned.

"Come on—let's have breakfast." Alfred turned towards the door. "Might as well reap the rewards of being so early—we can snaffle two helpings of kedgeree."

Still frowning, Harry followed him to the door.

An hour later, Lucinda swept down the main staircase, Agatha, dourly protective, three steps behind. An incipient frown tangled Lucinda's brows, put there by Melthorpe, who had knocked on her door while they had been packing with a breakfast tray and a message that his lordship would hold himself in readiness to take leave of her whenever she was ready. Then, a few minutes ago, when Agatha had opened her door, it was to discover a footman patiently waiting to carry her bag to the carriage.

For the life of her, she couldn't understand how they had known she was leaving.

It was all most confusing, a situation not helped by the skittering, totally uncharacteristic panic that had laid siege to her confidence.

As she set foot on the last flight of stairs, Lord Asterley strolled out of the dining-room. Harry followed in his wake, a sight that made Lucinda inwardly curse. She switched her gaze to her gloves, tugging them on; when she lifted her face, it was set in determined lines. "Good morning, my lord. I'm afraid I must depart immediately."

"Yes, of course—I quite understand." Alfred waited by the bottom of the stairs, his most charming smile in place.

Lucinda struggled not to frown. "I'm so glad. I have enjoyed my stay, but I'm sure it's for the best if I leave this morning." She avoided looking at Harry, standing behind his host.

Alfred offered her his arm. "We're quite devastated to

have you leave, of course, but I've had your carriage brought around.''

Beginning to feel distinctly distracted, Lucinda put her hand on his sleeve. "How kind of you," she murmured. From beneath her lashes, she glanced at Harry but could make nothing of his urbane expression.

''A pleasant day for a drive—hope you reach your destination without any fuss.''

Lucinda allowed his lordship—expatiating in similar, totally inconsequential vein—to lead her down the steps.

As he had said, her carriage awaited, Joshua on the box. Lucinda paused on the last step, turning to her host as Agatha slipped past. Calmly, she held out her hand. "Thank you, my lord, for a most interesting stay—even if it was so short.''

''Delighted, m'dear, delighted.'' Alfred bowed extravagantly over her hand. "Dare say I'll see you shortly in London.'' As he straightened, his gaze met Harry's over Lucinda's shoulder. "In the ballrooms,'' he hastily added.

Lucinda blinked. Then she turned to the carriage, and discovered Agatha, her expression thoroughly disapproving, up beside Joshua on the box.

''Here—allow me.''

Before she could do anything about her maid's unexpected position, Lucinda found herself handed into the carriage. Deciding that rapid departure was undoubtedly her wisest course, she took her seat by the window and settled her skirts. She could get Agatha down once they were clear of the drive.

Lord Asterley spoke through the window. "Do hope you enjoyed your stay. We'll look to see you again next—'' Abruptly he caught himself up, a comical look on his face. ''Ah—no. Not again.''

''Quite,'' came in clipped accents from behind him.

His lordship quickly stepped back. Lucinda, features rigidly impassive, drew breath to farewell her predatory protector—only to see Harry nod to his lordship and calmly climb into the carriage.

Lucinda stared at him.

Harry smiled a touch grimly, saying, *sotto voce,* as he moved past, "Smile sweetly at Alfred—or he'll be even more confused."

Lucinda did as she was told, plastering an utterly fatuous smile on her lips. Lord Asterley stood on the steps and waved until the curve of the drive hid them from sight.

As soon as it did, Lucinda rounded on Harry. "*What* do you think you're doing? Is this another of your forcible re-patriations?"

Harry settled his shoulders against the seat. "Yes." He turned his head to look at her, brows rising arrogantly. "You aren't going to tell me you belonged at Asterley Place—are you?"

Lucinda blushed, and changed tack. "Where are we going?" She had not left Asterley Place in an unfashionable rush solely because of the activities of its guests. After last night, she had no idea how Harry now viewed her, despite what she had sensed, despite what she now hoped. Undermining her confidence was the realisation, the cast-iron certainty, that if he wanted her, she would go to him—without any marriage vows—without any vows at all. She had intended to rush back to the safety of Em's side, where her own weakness would be bolstered by Em's staunch propriety.

She had never before run from anything or anyone—but what she felt for Harry was not something she could fight.

Her heart thumping uncomfortably, she watched, eyes wide, as he sat back, laid his head against the squabs and stretched his long legs before him, crossing his booted ankles. He closed his eyes. "Lester Hall."

"Lester Hall?" Lucinda blinked—not Lestershall, his own house, but Lester Hall, his family home.

Harry nodded, settling his chin in his cravat.

"Why?"

"Because that's where you've been since yesterday. You left town in your carriage and drove there, with your maid and coachman. I followed several hours later in my curricle. Em and Heather will be following in Em's carriage this morning—Em was indisposed yesterday. That's why they didn't accompany you."

Lucinda blinked again. "Why did I go and leave them behind?"

"Because my father was expecting you last night and you didn't want to disappoint him."

"Oh." After a moment's hesitation, Lucinda asked, "*Is* he expecting me?"

Harry opened one eye, studied the delightful picture she made in her blue cambric carriage dress, her hair neatly caught in a chignon, her bonnet framing her face—the whole made distinctly more entrancing by the uncertainty he could see in her misty blue eyes and her slightly stunned expression—then closed his eye again. "He'll be delighted to see you."

Lucinda thought long and hard about that. "Where's your curricle?" she eventually asked.

"Dawlish drove it back last night with a message for Em. You needn't worry—she'll be there by the time we arrive."

There didn't seem anything more to say. Lucinda sat back—and tried to make sense of what she'd learned.

Some miles later, Harry broke the silence. "Tell me about Mortimer Babbacombe."

Hauled from deep contemplation, Lucinda frowned. "Why do you want to know about him?"

"Is he a cousin of your late husband's?"

"No—he's Charles's nephew. He inherited the Grange and the entailed estate when Charles died."

Eyes still closed, Harry frowned. "Tell me about the Grange."

Lucinda shrugged. "It's a small property as such things

go. Just the house and enough fields to support it. Charles's wealth derived from the Babbacombe Inns, which he'd bought with the fortune he'd inherited from his maternal grandfather.''

Half a mile had passed before Harry asked, "Was Mortimer Babbacombe familiar with the Grange?''

"No.'' Lucinda let her gaze wander over the lush fields through which they were passing. "It was one of the things I found particularly strange—that having barely set foot in the place—I believe he had visited for a day the year before Charles and I married—he was so very keen to take up residence.''

Another long silence ensued; again, Harry broke it. "Do you know if Mortimer was aware of Charles's wealth?''

Lucinda frowned. It was some moments before she answered. "If you mean did he know Charles was personally wealthy, then yes, I think he must have known. Although he didn't visit while I lived at the Grange, he did appeal to Charles for financial relief. Basically on an annual basis. Charles used to look on it as a pension for his heir, but the sums were often quite large. The last two were for two and three thousand pounds. However...'' Lucinda paused to draw breath. She glanced at Harry. His eyes were now open, narrowed and fixed on the carriage seat opposite as he pondered her words. "If you mean did Mortimer know the details of Charles's fortune, then I can't be sure he did. Certainly, in the past ten years, Charles made no effort to communicate such matters.'' She shrugged. "They were, after all, none of Mortimer's business.''

"So he might not have known that Charles's money did not derive from the estate itself?''

Lucinda humphed. "I would have thought any fool could have seen that the Grange could not possibly generate anything like the amounts Charles regularly sent to Mortimer.''

Not from London. And they had no guarantee that Mortimer Babbacombe was not, in fact, just such a fool. But

Harry kept such observations to himself. He closed his eyes and listened to the rumble of the wheels as his mind juggled the facts. Someone, he was now convinced, was taking an unwarranted interest in Lucinda's affairs—but to what end he couldn't fathom. Mischief, pure and simple, was impossible to rule out, yet instinct warned him that alone was insufficient reason. On the face of it, Mortimer Babbacombe seemed the most likely candidate, but it was impossible to ignore the fact that he was not Lucinda's heir—her aunt in Yorkshire stood nearest in line. And anyway, why send her to Asterley?

Who could possibly benefit by her enjoying a discreet liaison?

Harry inwardly shook his head—and let the matter slide. Time enough to bend his mind to it when they headed back to London. Until then, she was going to be under his eye every minute of the day—and very close, and safe, every minute of the night. Lester Hall and its surrounding acres were the safest place on earth for a Lester bride.

Her eyes on the greenery sliding past the windows, Lucinda decided that she should feel reassured, not only by Harry's manner, but by his efforts to protect her name. She cast a sideways glance at him; he appeared to be asleep. Recalling how he had spent the night, she could hardly feel surprise. She was physically tired herself but too keyed up to relax.

But as the wheels went around and the miles rumbled past and she had more time to dwell on their state, it occurred to her that she had no guarantee Harry had actually altered his stance.

The carriage hit a rut; a strong arm shot out and saved her from falling to the floor.

Lucinda righted herself; Harry's hand fell away. She turned to him—and glared at his still shut eyes. "Lady Coleby was speaking to me yesterday."

Languidly, his brows rose. "Oh?"

Despite his tone, he had tensed. Lucinda pressed her lips together and forged on. "She told me you had once been in love with her."

She could feel her heart thudding in her chest, in her throat.

Harry opened his eyes. Slowly, he turned his head until his eyes, very green, met hers. "I didn't—then—know what love was."

His eyes held hers for a long moment, then he turned forward and closed them again.

The wheels rolled on; Lucinda stared at him. Then, slowly, she drew in a deep breath. A smile—of relief, of welling hope—broke across her face. Her lips still curved, she settled her head against the squabs—and followed Harry's example.

Chapter Twelve

Three days later, Harry sat in a garden chair under the spreading branches of the oak at the bottom of the Lester Hall lawn, squinting through the early afternoon sunshine at the blue-clad figure who had just emerged onto the terrace.

She saw him; she raised her hand, then descended the steps and headed his way. Harry smiled.

And watched his intended stroll towards him.

Her gown of cerulean blue muslin clung to her figure as she walked. Her face was shaded by a villager hat, three blue daisies decorating its band. He had put them there himself, first thing this morning, when their petals had still sparkled with dew.

Harry's smile deepened; contentment swept through him. *This* was what he wanted—what he was determined to have.

A shout, greeted by gay laughter, drew his attention to the lake. Gerald was punting Heather Babbacombe about. Face alight, Heather was laughing up at Gerald, smiling down at her from his place in the stern.

Harry raised his brows, resigned to what he strongly suspected was the inevitable. But Heather was still very young, as was Gerald; it would be some years yet before they realised just what this Season had begun.

He hadn't been at all surprised to see his younger brother

drive up to the Hall a bare hour after he and Lucinda had arrived. As he had foreseen, Em and Heather had reached the Hall before them; Em had already had the household in hand.

Other than casting him a curious, almost wary look, Em had forborne to comment on his arrangements. To his considerable satisfaction, after the debacle of Asterley Place, it appeared his aunt was content to run in his harness.

Just as his intended, albeit suspiciously, was doing.

Harry rose as she approached, his smile openly welcoming.

Returning his smile, Lucinda put a hand to her hat as a gentle breeze whipped her skirts about her. "It's such a lovely afternoon, I'd thought to stroll the grounds."

"An excellent idea." The breeze died; Harry claimed her hand and with a calmly proprietorial air, tucked it in his arm. "You haven't explored the grotto at the end of the lake, have you?"

Lucinda dutifully admitted ignorance and allowed him to steer her onto the path skirting the lake's edge. Heather saw them and waved; Gerald hallooed. Lucinda smiled and waved back, then let silence fall.

And waited.

As she'd been waiting for the past three days.

Her sojourn at Lester Hall was proving far more pleasant than her projected stay at Asterley Place could ever have been. From the moment Harry had led her into the drawing-room and introduced her to his father, his intentions had been plain. Everything—every glance, every touch, every little gesture, every single word and thought that had passed between them since—had underscored the simple fact. But not once during their twilight strolls on the terrace, throughout their ambling rides through woods and fields, through all the hours they had spent together out of the past seventy-two, had he said one single word to the point.

He hadn't kissed her either—a fact which was fuelling

her impatience. Yet she could hardly fault his behaviour—
it was gentlemanly in the extreme. The suspicion that he
was wooing her—traditionally, according to all the accepted
precepts, with all the subtle elegance only one of his experience could command—had taken firm root in her mind.

Which was all very well, but...

With one hand on the crown of her hat, Lucinda tipped
her head up and studied the sky. "The sunshine's been so
constant one forgets the days are winging past. I fear we
should return to London soon."

"I'll escort you back to town tomorrow afternoon."

Lucinda blinked. "Tomorrow afternoon?"

Harry raised his brows. "As I recall, we're all promised
to Lady Mickleham on the following evening. Em, I suspect,
will need the rest."

"Yes, indeed." Lucinda had forgotten Lady Mickleham's
ball entirely. After a moment's hesitation, she continued, "I
sometimes wonder if Em is overtiring herself in our cause.
Heather and I would never forgive ourselves if she ran herself aground because of us."

Harry's lips twisted in a reluctant grin. "Fear not. She's
a seasoned campaigner; she knows how to pace herself.
Moreover, I can assure you the prospect of playing hostess
to you both for the rest of the Season is currently providing
her with expectations of untold enjoyment." That, he knew,
was the unvarnished truth.

Lucinda shot him a glance from beneath her lashes, then
looked ahead. "I'm relieved you think so, for I must confess
I'm looking forward to rejoining the throng. It seems an age
since I was swirling around a ballroom, held in a gentleman's arms."

The look Harry sent her was distinctly dry. "Indeed—
I'm quite looking forward to your return to the ballrooms
myself."

"Oh?" Lucinda bestowed on him a smiling glance. "I
hadn't thought you so enamoured of the balls."

"I'm not."

Wide-eyed, Lucinda looked up at him. "What, then, lures you there?"

A siren. Harry looked down into her soft blue eyes—and raised his brows. "I dare say you'll understand once we're part of the crush again."

Lucinda's answering smile was weak. She looked forward—and concentrated on not gnashing her teeth. It was all of a piece—she wondered if he was actually trying to drive her to some rash act. Like visiting his room late tonight.

It was a measure of her frustration that she actually considered the idea before, regretfully, setting it aside. The initiative was no longer hers; he had claimed it when he'd brought her here. She wasn't at all sure how to wrest it from him—and even less certain that he would let it go.

"Here we are."

Harry gestured ahead to where the path apparently disappeared into a hedge of greenery. They approached; he put out a hand and held aside a curtain of vines and creepers—blooming honeysuckle among them—to reveal white marble steps leading upward into a cool, dimly lit cave.

Enchanted, Lucinda ducked under his arm and went ahead, climbing the steps to emerge onto the tassellated floor of a mock-temple, formed by four marble pillars separating a rockface on one quadrant, with the lake on the other three. The pillars supported a domed ceiling, covered in blue and green tiles, highly glazed, reflecting the sunshine glancing in off the lake in myriad hues from turquoise to deep green. Leafy vines and the apricot blooms of honeysuckle wreathed the arches looking onto the lake, the gentle breeze stirring their shadows.

The temple was built out over the water, the central arch giving onto steps which led down to a small stone jetty. Wide-eyed, Lucinda halted in the very centre of the temple—and discovered one of its secrets. Each of the three open arches gave onto a different vista. The one to her right led the eye over a short stretch of lake then straight down a glade thick with ferns and shrubs. To her left lay a view over a long arm of the lake to a distant shore lined with willows and beech. Straight ahead lay the most charming vista of all—Lester Hall itself lay perfectly framed within the arch, glinting water in the foreground, manicured lawns leading up to the imposing façade, flanked by the shrubbery and wilderness to the left, the rose garden, just coming into bloom, and the formal gardens on the right.

"It's beautiful." Lucinda went to stand by one of the pillars to better appreciate the view.

Harry hung back in the shadows, content to watch the play of sunlight across her face. When she leaned back against the pillar and sighed contentedly, he strolled forward to stand beside her. After a moment, he asked, "Have you enjoyed your Season? Do you look to become a devotee— enamoured of the *ton* in all its glory, the crushes, the never-ending carousel of balls, parties and yet more balls?"

Lucinda half turned to look into his face. She searched his eyes, but neither they nor his expression gave any hint of his feelings. She considered, then answered, "By and large, I find the *ton* and its entertainments amusing." Her lips curved in a self-deprecating smile, her eyes reluctantly twinkling. "But you will have to remember that this is my first exposure to 'the carousel'—I'm still enjoying the novelty." Her expression growing serious, she put her head on one side the better to study him. "But the *ton* is your milieu—have you not enjoyed the balls this Season?"

Harry's gaze touched hers, then he looked down. He took one of her hands in his. Small, slender, her hand nestled in his much larger palm, confidently trusting. Harry closed his fingers about hers, his lips twisting. "There have been… compensations."

His lids rose; he met Lucinda's gaze.

Slowly, she raised her brows. "Indeed?" When he offered nothing more but simply looked away across the lake, she followed his gaze to Lester Hall, basking in the afternoon sun. As at Hallows Hall, Lucinda felt the tug of old memories. She sighed. "However, to answer your question, despite my fascination, I seriously doubt I could stomach a never-ending round of *ton*nish life. I fear I would need a steady diet of country peace to enable me to brave the Season on a regular basis." She slanted a glance at Harry and found him watching her. Her lips quirked. "My parents lived very retired in a rambling old house in Hampshire. When they died, I removed to the Yorkshire moors, which, of course, is as retired as it's possible to be."

Harry's features relaxed, subtly but definitely. "So you're a country miss at heart?" He lifted one brow. Slowly, his eyes on hers, he raised her hand. "Naïve?" He brushed his lips across her fingertips, then turned her hand in his. "Innocent?" His lids fell as he pressed a kiss to her palm.

Lucinda shuddered; she made no effort to hide it. She couldn't breathe, could barely think as Harry's lids rose and his eyes, green and direct, met hers.

His lips twisted; he hesitated, then shifted closer and bent his head to hers.

"And mine?"

He breathed the question against her lips, then captured them in a long, commanding kiss.

Lucinda answered in the only way she could—she turned to him, sliding her arms up and wrapping them about his neck, then kissed him back with a fervour to match his own.

Instinct prompted Harry to edge back, drawing her around the pillar to where the shadows shielded them from inadvertent eyes.

Silence filled the small pavilion. The breeze idly played with the honeysuckle, wafting perfume through the air; a drake hooted from some distant reed-fringed shore. The shadows shifted gently over the figures entwined in the pillar's lee. Spring had blossomed; summer stood in the wings, eager for its day.

"Oh! How lovely—a Grecian temple! Can we go and see?"

Heather's high-pitched tones carried easily across the water, hauling Harry and Lucinda back to their senses. Harry's chest swelled as he drew in a deep breath—then looked down. Lucinda's eyes slowly filled with comprehension; Harry felt his lips firm as he saw his frustration mirrored in misty blue.

Muttering a curse, he bent his head to taste her lips one last time, then drew his hand from her breast and quickly, expertly, rearranged her bodice, doing up the tiny buttons with a dexterity equal to that with which he had undone them.

Blinking, struggling to subdue her harried breathing, Lucinda straightened his collar and brushed back the heavy lock of hair she'd disarranged. She had shifted his cravat; her hands fluttered uncertainly.

Harry abruptly stepped back, long fingers reaching for the starched folds. "Your skirts."

Lucinda looked down—and swallowed a gasp. She shot an indignant glare at Harry, which he met with an arrogantly raised brow, then shook the clinging muslin down, smoothing the folds so that the skirts once more hung free. She spied her hat lying on the floor; she swiped it up and set it in place, tangling the ties in her haste.

"Here—let me." Harry deftly separated the ribbons, then tied them in a neat bow.

Putting up a hand to check on his efforts, Lucinda threw him a haughty glance. "Your talents are quite astonishing."

Harry's smile was a touch grim. "And extremely useful, you'll admit."

Lucinda tilted her chin, then, turning, plastered a bright smile on her lips as Gerald's voice floated up from the bottom of the steps.

"Take care! Wait till I make fast."

Lucinda strolled forward into the sunshine at the top of the steps. "Hello—did you have a pleasant time on the lake?"

Gerald looked up at her and blinked. When Harry appeared from the shadows behind her, Gerald's expression turned wary.

But Harry only smiled, albeit a touch coolly. "Just in time, Gerald. Now we can take the punt and you can show Miss Babbacombe around the temple then stroll back."

"Oh, yes! Let's do that." Heather could barely wait for Gerald to assist her from the bobbing craft. "It's such a lovely spot—so secluded."

"Usually," Harry murmured, so low only Lucinda heard.

She shot him a warning glance but her smile didn't waver. "The tiles on the ceiling are quite splendid."

"Oh?" Heather trod up the steps and into the temple without further encouragement.

Gerald, meanwhile, was staring, mesmerised, at Harry's gold acorn pin, the one his excessively precise brother used to anchor his cravat. The pin was askew. Blinking in bemusement, Gerald raised his eyes to Harry's, only to be met by a languid, distinctly bored green gaze—which he knew very well meant he'd be well advised to quit his brother's presence forthwith. "Ah—yes. We'll walk back."

His expression studiously blank, Gerald nodded to Lucinda and hurried after Heather.

"Mrs Babbacombe?"

Lucinda turned to find Harry, the long pole in one hand, steadying the boat, as he held his other hand out to her. She put her fingers in his; he helped her into the punt. Once she had settled her skirts on the cushions in the prow, he stepped into the stern and poled off.

The dark water glided past the hull; reclining against the cushions, Lucinda trailed her fingertips in the lake—and filled her sight with Harry. He avoided her gaze, concentrating, to all appearances, on their surroundings.

With a small, disbelieving sniff, Lucinda switched her gaze to the shores slipping past.

The ends of Harry's lips lifted; his gaze, falling to her profile, was unusually soft but cynical, too. Hands on the pole, he propelled them through the water; not even the most inveterate rake could seduce a woman while poling a punt. He hadn't planned their recent close brush with intimacy—for once, he was truly grateful for his younger brother's interruption. He had reason enough to marry his siren, and too many excuses he had yet to convince her he no longer needed. Their night at Asterley had only added to the list, lending weight to the social pressures she might imagine had influenced him. Social pressures he himself had foolishly raised in order to hide the truth.

Harry lifted his gaze to the vista before them—the façade of Lester Hall—Jack's home now, no longer his. His gaze grew distant; his jaw firmed.

She had made it plain that it was important for her to know the truth of why he wished to wed her; during the past days, he had realised it was important to him to know that she did. So before they were done, before he again asked her to be his bride, they would have it all clear between them.

His siren would know the truth—and believe it.

LUCINDA OPENED HER EYES the next morning to discover a dusky pink rose unfurling on her pillow. Enchanted, she took the delicate bloom into her hand, cradling it gently. The dew on the petals fractured the sunshine.

Her smile wondering, delighted, she sat up and pushed the covers back. Every morning she had spent at Lester Hall, she had woken to find just such a tribute waiting somewhere in her room.

But on her pillow…?

Still smiling, she rose.

Fifteen minutes later, her expression serene, she glided through the breakfast parlour doors, the rose between her fingers. As usual, Harry's father was not present—he was a semi-invalid and did not stir before noon; Em adhered to town hours so would not rise until eleven. As for Heather and Gerald, they had the night before announced their intention of riding to a distant folly; they would, Lucinda judged, be well on their way by now. Which left Harry alone, seated at the table's head, long legs stretched out before him, his fingers crooked about the handle of a cup.

Lucinda felt his gaze as she entered; with every appearance of unconsciousness, she considered her lover's token, then, with a softly distant smile, tucked it lovingly into her cleavage, making great show of nestling the velvet petals against the curves of her breasts.

She looked up to see Harry transfixed. His fingers had tightened about the handle of his cup, a stillness, like that of a predator about to pounce, had settled over his long frame. His gaze was riveted on the rose.

"Good morning." Lucinda smiled sunnily and went forward to take the seat the butler held for her.

Harry tried to speak, then had to clear his throat. "Good morning." He forced his gaze to Lucinda's; it sharpened as he read her expression. He shifted in his seat. "I'd thought to visit the stud before we head back to town. I wondered if you'd care to accompany me—and perhaps renew your acquaintance with Thistledown."

Lucinda reached for the teapot. "Thistledown's here?"

Harry nodded and took a long sip of coffee.

"Is it far?"

"Only a few miles." He watched as Lucinda spread a muffin with jam. She leant both elbows on the table, the muffin held with both hands, and took a bite; a minute later, the tip of her tongue went the rounds of her lips. Harry blinked.

"Will we ride?" Lucinda didn't think to voice her agreement formally; he had known from the first she would go.

Harry stared at the rose nestling between her breasts. "No—we'll take the gig."

Lucinda smiled at her muffin—and took another bite.

Twenty minutes later, still clad in her lilac walking dress, the dusky pink rose in pride of place, she sat beside Harry as he tooled the gig down a narrow lane. "So you don't spend much time in London?"

Harry raised his brows, his attention on the bay between the shafts. "As little as possible." He grimaced. "But with a venture like the stud, it's necessary to remain visible amongst the *cognescenti,* which is to say, the gentlemen of the *ton.*"

"Ah—I see." Lucinda nodded sagely, the wide brim of her villager hat framing her face. "Contrary to all appearances, you care nothing for the balls, the routs, the parties— and less for the good opinion of the feminine half of the *ton.* Indeed—" she opened her eyes wide "—I cannot understand how you have come by the reputation you bear. Unless—" She broke off to look enquiringly up at him. "Perhaps it's all a hum?"

Harry's attention had left the bay gelding; it was focused on Lucinda, the light in his eyes enough to make her shiver. "My reputation, my dear, was not gained in the *ballrooms.*"

Lucinda kept her gaze wide. "Oh?"

"No," Harry stated—more in answer to the hopeful expression in her eyes than her question. His expression severely reproving, he clicked the reins, setting the horse to a trot.

Lucinda grinned.

The stud was soon reached. Harry tossed the reins of the gig to a groom, then lifted Lucinda down. "I need to talk to my head-stableman, Hamish MacDowell," he said as they strolled towards the stable complex. "Thistledown should be in her box. It's in the second yard."

Lucinda nodded. "I'll wait for you there." The stables were a massive conglomerate of buildings—stables proper, as well as tackrooms and barns housing training gigs as well as what appeared to be quite enormous quantities of fodder. "Did you start it up—or was it already in existence?"

"My father established the stud in his youth. I took over after his accident—about eight years ago." Harry's gaze swept over the stud—the neat, cobbled yards and stone buildings before them, the fenced fields on either side. "Whenever I'm home I offer to drive him over—but he never comes." He looked down, then added, "I think seeing it all—the horses—reminds him of his inability. He was a bruising rider until a fall put him in that chair of his."

"So you're the son who takes after him most in the matter of horses?"

Harry's lips twitched. "In that regard—and, some might argue, his other most consuming passion."

Lucinda glanced at him, then away. "I see," she replied, her tone repressive. "So is this now all yours?" Her gesture took in the whole complex. "Or is it a family concern?"

She looked up at Harry, light colour in her cheeks, but made no attempt to excuse the question.

Harry smiled. "Legally, it's still my father's. Effectively—" He halted, lifting his head to sweep his surroundings, before looking down to meet her gaze. "I'm master of all I survey."

Slowly, Lucinda raised her brows. "Indeed?" If he was her master, did that make her his mistress? But no—she knew very well that was not his aim. "I believe you said Thistledown was in the second yard?" When Harry nodded, she inclined her head regally. "I'll await you there."

Nose in the air, she headed through the archway into the second yard. Inwardly, she humphed dejectedly. What *was* his reason for delay?

She located Thistledown by the simple expedient of

standing in the middle of the square yard and looking about until an excitedly bobbing head caught her eye.

The mare seemed overjoyed to see her, pushing her nose against her skirts. Lucinda hunted in her pockets and located the sugar lumps she'd stolen from the breakfast table; her offering was accepted with every evidence of equine pleasure.

Folding her arms on the top of the stall door, Lucinda watched as the mare lapped water from a bucket. "Can it really be so very difficult to simply ask me again?"

Thistledown rolled a dark eye enquiringly.

Lucinda gestured. "Women are notoriously changeable—in all the novels *I've* ever read, the heroines always said no when first asked."

Thistledown harrumphed and came to nudge her shoulder.

"Precisely." Lucinda nodded and absent-mindedly stroked the mare's nose. "I'm entitled to a chance to change my mind." After a moment, she wrinkled her nose. "Well—at least revise my decision in the light of fresh developments."

For she very definitely hadn't changed her mind. She knew what she knew—and Harry knew it, too. It was simply a matter of the damned man admitting it.

Lucinda humphed; Thistledown whinnied softly.

From the shadows by the tack room, Harry watched the mare shake her head and nudge Lucinda. He smiled to himself—then turned as Dawlish came lumbering up.

"Seen Hamish, have you?"

"I have. That colt of Warlock's looks promising, I agree."

"Aye—he'll win a pot before he's done, I reckon." Dawlish followed Harry's gaze to Lucinda. He nodded in her direction. "P'raps you should introduce the lady to him—get her to have a little chat to him like she did with the mare?"

In mock surprise, Harry stared at his henchman. "Is that approval I detect? From you—the arch-misogynist?"

Dawlish frowned. "Don't know as how I know what a misogynist is, rightly, but at least you've had the sense to find one as the horses like—and who might actually come in handy to boot." Dawlish snorted. "What I wants to know is why you can't get a move on—so's we can all get back to knowing where we are?"

Harry's gaze clouded. "There are a few loose ends I'm presently tying up."

"Is that what you calls them these days?"

"Apropos of which," Harry continued imperturbably, "Did you get that message to Lord Ruthven?"

"Aye—his lordship said as he'd see to it."

"Good." Harry's gaze had returned to Lucinda. "We'll leave about two. I'll take the curricle—you can go with Em."

He didn't wait for Dawlish's grumbling grunt but sauntered after Lucinda. She had left the mare and wandered along the loose boxes to stop at the end where a grey head had come out to greet her.

She looked around as Harry drew near. "Did he win at Newmarket?"

Harry grinned and stroked Cribb's nose. "He did." The horse nudged his pockets but Harry shook his head. "No apples today, I'm afraid."

"When's he racing next?"

"Not this year." Harry took Lucinda's arm and steered her towards the gate. "The Newmarket win took him to the top of his class; I've decided to retire him at his peak, so to speak. He'll stand for the rest of this season. I might give him a run next year, but if the present interest in him as a stud continues, I'd be a fool to let him waste his energies on the track."

Lucinda's lips quirked; she struggled to suppress her grin. Harry noticed. "What is it?"

Colouring slightly, Lucinda shot him a glance from beneath her lids.

Harry raised his brows higher.

Lucinda grimaced. "If you must know," she said, switching her gaze to the horizon. "I was simply struck by the fact that managing a stud is a peculiarly apt enterprise for... er, one with your qualifications."

Harry laughed, an entirely spontaneous sound Lucinda realised she had not before heard.

"My dear Mrs Babbacombe!" His green eyes quizzed her. "What a thoroughly shocking observation to make."

Lucinda glared, then put her nose in the air.

Harry chuckled. Ignoring her blushes, he drew her closer. "Strangely enough," he said, his lips distinctly curved, "you're the first to ever put it into words."

Lucinda fell back on one of Em's snorts—the one that signified deep disapproval. Disapproval gave way to hope when she realised Harry was not leading her back to the gig but towards a small wood bordering the nearest field. A path led between the trees, cut back to permit easy strolling.

Perhaps...? She never finished the thought, distracted by the discovery that the wood was in reality no more than a windbreak. Beyond it, the path was paved as it ambled about a small pond where water lilies battled with reeds. "That needs clearing."

Harry glanced at the pond. "We'll get to it eventually."

Lucinda looked up and followed his gaze—to the house. Large, rambling, with old-fashioned gables, it was made of local stone with a good slate roof. On the ground floor, bow windows stood open to the summer air. A rose crept up one wall to nod pale yellow blooms before one of the upstairs windows. Two large, leafy oaks stood one to each side, casting cool shade over the gravelled drive which wound from some gateway out of sight down a long avenue to end in a sweep before the front door.

She glanced at Harry. "Lestershall?"

He nodded, his eyes on the manor house. "My house."
Briefly, his lips twisted. "My home." With a languid wave,
he gestured ahead. "Shall we?"

Suddenly breathless, Lucinda inclined her head.

They strolled on to where their path debouched onto the
lawn, then crossed the grassy expanse and ducked beneath
the low branches of one of the oaks to join the drive. As
they approached the shallow stone steps, Lucinda noticed
the front door stood ajar.

"I've never really lived here." Harry steadied her as they
scrunched across the gravel. "It had fallen into disrepair, so
I've had a small army through to set it to rights."

A burly individual in a carpenter's leather apron appeared
in the doorway as they set foot on the steps.

"Mornin', Mr Lester." The man ducked his head, his
cheery face lit by a smile. "It's all coming together nicely—
as I think you'll find. Not much more to do."

"Good morning, Catchbrick. This is Mrs Babbacombe. If
it won't inconvenience you and your men, I'd like to show
her around."

"No inconvenience at all, sir." Catchbrick bowed to Lucinda, bright eyes curious. "Won't be no trouble—like I
said, we're nearly done."

So saying, he stood back and waved them on into the
hall.

Lucinda crossed the threshold into a long and surprisingly
spacious rectangular hall. Half-panelling in warm oak was
surmounted by plastered walls, presently bare. A mound
draped in dust covers in the centre of the floor clearly contained a round table and a large hall stand. Light streamed
in from the large circular fanlight. Stairs, also in oak with
an ornately carved balustrade, led upwards, the half-landing
sporting a long window which, Lucinda suspected, looked
out over the rear gardens. Two corridors flanked the stairs,
the left ending in a green baize door.

"The drawing-room's this way."

Lucinda turned to find Harry standing by a set of hand-some doors, presently set wide; a boy was polishing the panels industriously.

The drawing-room proved to be of generous proportions, although on far smaller a scale than at the Hall. It boasted a deep bow window complete with window seat and a long low fireplace topped by a wide mantel. The dining-room, now shaping to be an elegant apartment, had, as had the drawing-room, a large mound of furniture swathed in dust cloths in its midst. Lucinda couldn't resist lifting one corner of the cloth.

"Some pieces will need to be replaced but most of the furniture seems sound enough." Harry's gaze remained on her face.

"Sound enough?" Lucinda threw back the cover to re-veal the heavy top of an old oak sideboard. "It's rather more than that. This is a very fine piece—and someone's had the sense to keep it well-polished."

"Mrs Simpkins. She's the housekeeper," Harry supplied in answer to Lucinda's raised brows. "You'll meet her in a moment."

Dropping the dustsheet, Lucinda went to one of the pair of long windows, presently propped open, and looked out. The windows gave onto a terrace which ran down the side of the house and disappeared around the corner to run be-neath the windows of the parlour, which itself gave off the dining-room, as she next discovered.

Standing before the parlour windows, looking out across the rolling lawns, ringed by flowerbeds, presently a colour-ful riot of spring and early summer blooms, Lucinda felt a deep sense of certainty, of belonging, as if she was putting down roots where she stood. This, she knew, was a place she could live and grow and blossom.

"These three reception-rooms open one into the other." Harry waved at the hinged panels separating the parlour from the dining room "The result's quite large enough to host a hunt ball."

Lucinda blinked at him. "Indeed?"

His features impassive, Harry nodded and waved her on. "The breakfast parlour's this way."

So was the morning room. As he led her through the bright, presently empty and echoing rooms, lit by the sunshine streaming in through the diamond-paned windows, Lucinda noted the dry plaster walls waiting to be papered, the woodwork and panelling already polished and gleaming.

All the furniture she saw was old but lovingly polished, warm oak, most of it.

"There's only the decorating left to do," Harry informed her as he led her down a short corridor running beside the large room he had described as his study-cum-library. There, the bookshelves had been emptied and polished to within an inch of their lives; piles of tomes stood ready to be returned to their places once the decorating was done. "But the firm I've hired won't be in for a few weeks yet—time enough to make the necessary decisions."

Lucinda eyed him narrowly—but before she could think of any probing comment, she was distracted by what lay beyond the door at the end of the corridor. An elegantly proportioned room, it overlooked the side garden; roses nodded at the wide windows, framing green vistas.

Harry glanced about. "I haven't yet decided what this room should be used for."

Looking around, Lucinda found no pile of shrouded furniture. Instead, her gaze was drawn to new shelves, lining one wall. They were wide and open, just right for stacking ledgers. She glanced about; the windows let in good light, an essential for doing accounts and dealing with correspondence.

Her heart beating in a very odd cadence, Lucinda turned to look at Harry. "Indeed?"

"Hmm." His expression considering, he gestured to the door. "Come—I'll introduce you to the Simpkins."

Suppressing a snort of pure impatience, Lucinda allowed him to steer her back down the corridor and through the baize-covered door. Here she came upon the first evidence of established life. The kitchens were scrupulously clean, the pots gleaming on their hooks on the wall, a modern range residing in the centre of the wide fireplace.

A middle-aged couple were seated at the deal table; they quickly got to their feet, consternation in their faces as they gazed at Lucinda.

"Simpkins here acts as general factotum—keeping an eye on the place generally. His uncle is butler at the Hall. Mrs Babbacombe, Simpkins."

"Ma'am." Simpkins bowed low.

"And this is Mrs Simpkins, cook and housekeeper—without whom the furniture would never have survived."

Mrs Simpkins, a buxom, rosy-cheeked matron of imposing girth, bobbed a curtsy to Lucinda but fixed Harry with a baleful eye. "Aye—and if you had only thought to warn me, Master Harry, I would have had tea and scones ready and waiting."

"As you might guess," Harry put in smoothly, "Mrs Simpkins was once an undernurse at the Hall."

"Aye—and I can remember you in short coats quite clearly, young master." Mrs Simpkins frowned at him. "Now you just take the lady for a stroll and I'll pop a pot on. By the time you come back I'll have your tea laid ready in the garden."

"I wouldn't want to put you to—"

Harry's pained sigh cut across Lucinda's disclaimer. "I hesitate to break it to you, my dear, but Martha Simpkins is a tyrant. It's best to just yield gracefully." So saying, he took her hand and led her towards the door. "I'll just show Mrs Babbacombe the upstairs rooms, Martha."

Lucinda turned her head to throw a smile back at Mrs Simpkins, who beamed delightedly in reply.

The stairs led to a short gallery.

"No family portraits, I'm afraid," Harry said. "Those are all at the Hall."

"Is there one of you?" Lucinda looked up at him.

"Yes—but it's hardly a good likeness. It was done when I was eighteen."

Lucinda raised her brows but, recalling Lady Coleby's words, made no comment.

"This is the master suite." Harry threw open a pair of panelled doors at the end of the gallery. The room beyond was large, half-panelled, the warm patina of wood extending to the surrounds of the bow window and its seat. A carved mantel framed the fireplace, unusually large; a very large structure stood in the centre of the floor, screened by the inevitable dustcovers. Lucinda glanced at it curiously, but obediently turned as Harry, a hand at her back, conducted her through the adjoining dressing-rooms.

"I'm afraid," he said, as they returned to the main chamber, "that Lestershall doesn't run to separate bedrooms for husband and wife." Lucinda glanced up at him. "Not, of course," he continued imperturbably, "that that should concern you."

Lucinda watched as he leaned a shoulder against the window frame. When he merely returned her expectant look with one of the blandest innocence, she humphed and turned her attention to the large, shrouded mound.

"It's a four-poster," she decided. She crossed to lift a corner of the dustcover and peer under. A dark cave lay before her. With thick, barley-sugar posts, the bed was fully canopied and draped with matching brocades. "It's enormous."

"Indeed." Harry watched her absorption. "And has quite a history, too, if the tales one hears are true."

Lucinda looked up from her study. "What tales?"

"Rumour has it the bed dates from Elizabethan times, as does the house. Apparently, all the brides brought back to the house have used it."

Lucinda wrinkled her nose. "That's hardly surprising." She dropped the covers and dusted her hands.

Harry's lips slowly curved. "Not in itself, perhaps." He pushed away from the window and strolled to where Lucinda stood waiting. "But there are brass rings set into the headboard." His brows rose; his expression turned pensive. "They quite excite the imagination." Taking Lucinda's arm, he turned her towards the door. "I must remember to show them to you sometime."

Lucinda opened her mouth, then abruptly closed it. She allowed him to lead her back into the corridor. She was still considering the brass rings when they reached the end of the hall, having looked in on a set of unremarkable bedchambers along the way.

"These stairs lead to the attics. The nursery is there, as well as the Simpkins's rooms."

The nursery proved to take up one entire side of the commodious space beneath the rafters. The dormer windows were set low, just right for youngsters. The suite comprised five interconnecting rooms.

"Bedrooms for the head nurse and tutor on either end, bedrooms for their charges, male and female and this, of course, is the schoolroom." Harry stood in the centre of the large room and looked around, a certain pride showing in his expression.

Lucinda eyed it consideringly. "These rooms are even larger, relatively speaking, than your bed."

Harry raised his brows. "I had rather thought they would have need to be. I'm planning on having a large family."

Lucinda stared into his clear green eyes—and wondered how he dared. "A large family?" she queried, refusing to retreat in disorder. "Taking after your father in that respect, too?" She held his gaze for an instant longer, then strolled to look out of a window. "Three boys, I assume, is your goal?"

Harry's gaze followed her. "And three girls. To preserve a reasonable balance," he added in reply to Lucinda's surprised glance.

Annoyed at her reaction, and the fluttery feeling that had laid siege to her stomach, Lucinda snorted. And glanced about again. "Even with six, there's room enough to spare."

She had thought that would be the end of that particular conversation but the reprobate teasing her hadn't finished.

"Ah—but I'd thought to leave sufficient space for the odd few who might not come in the correct order, if you take my meaning. Begetting boy or girl is such a random event, after all."

Lucinda stared into impassive green eyes—and longed to ask if he was joking. But there was something in the subtle tension that held him that left the distinct impression he wasn't.

Feeling a quiver—no longer odd but decidedly familiar—ripple through her, Lucinda decided she'd had enough. If he could talk about their children then he could put his mind to the first of the points that came before. She straightened and lifted her head, her gaze holding his.

"Harry—"

He shifted, turning to look out of the window. "Mrs Simpkins has our tea and scones waiting. Come—we can't disappoint her." With an innocent smile, he took Lucinda's arm and turned her towards the door. "It's nearly noon, too—I suspect we should get back immediately after our impromptu feast. We don't want to be late getting on the road this afternoon."

Lucinda stared at him in disbelief.

Harry smiled. "I know how much you're looking forward to getting back to town—and waltzing in gentlemen's arms."

Frustration filled Lucinda, so intense it made her giddy.

When Harry merely raised his brows, all mild and innocent, she narrowed her eyes and glared.

Harry's lips twitched; he gestured to the door.

Lucinda drew in a deep, steadying breath. If she wasn't a lady...

Setting her teeth against the urge to grind them, she slid her hand into the crook of his arm. Lips set in a thoroughly disapproving, not to say disgruntled line, she allowed him to lead her downstairs.

Chapter Thirteen

"So—do you have it clear?" Seated behind the desk in his library, Harry drew an unnibbed pen back and forth between his fingers, his gaze, very green, trained on the individual in the chair before him.

Plain brown eyes regarded him from an unremarkable countenance; the man's attire proclaimed him not of the *ton* but his occupation could not be discerned from the drab garments. Phineas Salter could have been anything—almost anyone—which was precisely what made him so successful at his trade.

The ex-Bow Street Runner nodded. "Aye, sir. I'm to check up on the gentlemen—Mr Earle Joliffe and Mr Mortimer Babbacombe—with a view to uncovering any reason they might have to wish a Mrs Lucinda Babbacombe—the said Mortimer's aunt-by-marriage—ill."

"*And* you're to do it without raising a dust." Harry's gaze became acute.

Salter inclined his head. "Naturally, sir. If the gentlemen are up to anything, we wouldn't want to tip them the wink. Not before we're ready."

Harry grimaced. "Quite. But I should also stress that we do not wish, at any time, for Mrs Babbacombe herself to become aware of our suspicions. Or, indeed, that there might be any reason for investigation at all.''

Salter frowned. ''Without disrespect, sir, do you think that's wise? From what you've told me, these villains aren't above drastic action. Wouldn't it be better if the lady's forewarned?''

''If it were any other lady, one who would be predictably shocked and content thereafter to leave the matter in our hands, I'd unhesitatingly agree. However, Mrs Babbacombe is not one such.'' Harry studied his newest employee; when he spoke his tone was instructive. ''I'd be willing to wager that, if she were to learn of Babbacombe's apparent involvement with her recent adventures, Mrs Babbacombe would order her carriage around and have herself driven to his lodgings, intent on demanding an explanation. Alone.''

Salter's expression blanked. ''Ah.'' He blinked. ''A bit naïve, is she?''

''No.'' Harry's tone hardened. ''Not particularly. She's merely incapable of recognising her own vulnerability but, conversely, has infinite confidence in her ability to prevail.'' The planes of his face shifted, his expression now mirroring his tone. ''In this case, I would rather not have her put it to the test.''

''No, indeed.'' Salter nodded. ''From what little I've heard tell, this Joliffe's not the sort for a lady to tangle with.''

''Precisely.'' Harry rose; Salter rose, too. The ex-Runner was a stocky man, broad and heavy. Harry nodded. ''Report back to me as soon as you have any word.''

''I will that, sir. You may depend on me.''

Harry shook Salter's hand. Dawlish, who, at Harry's intimation, had silently witnessed the interview, straightened from his position by the door and showed Salter out. Turning to the windows, Harry stood idly flicking the pen between his fingers, gazing unseeing at the courtyard beyond.

Salter was well-known to the intimates of Jackson's saloon and Cribb's parlour. A boxer of some skill, he was one of the few not of the *ton* with a ready entrée to those *ton*nish precincts. But it was his other skills that had led Harry to call him in. Salter's fame as a Runner had been considerable but clouded; the magistrates had not approved of his habit of, quite literally, using thieves to catch thieves. His successes had not ameliorated their disapproval and he had parted company from the London constabulary by mutual accord. Since then, however, he had established a reputation among certain of the *ton*'s gentlemen as a reliable man whenever matters of questionable, possibly illegal, behaviour needed to be investigated with absolute discretion.

Such a matter, in Harry's opinion, was Mortimer Babbacombe's apparent interest in Lucinda's well-being.

He would have handled the matter himself but was at a loss to understand Mortimer's motives. He could hardly let the matter rest and, given his conviction that it was linked with the incident on the Newmarket road, he had opted for caution, to whit, the discretion and skill for which Salter was renown.

"Well, then!" Dawlish returned and shut the door. "A fine broiling, altogether." He slanted a glance at Harry. "You want me to keep an eye on her?"

Slowly, Harry raised his brows. "It's an idea." He paused, then asked, "How do you think her coachman—Joshua, isn't it?—would take the news?"

"Right concerned, he'd be."

Harry's eyes narrowed. "And her maid, the redoubtable Agatha?"

"Even more so, unless I miss my guess. Right protective, she is—after you took them away from Asterley and organised to cover the lady's tracks, she's revised her opinion of you."

Harry's lips twitched. "Good. Then recruit her as well. I have a feeling we should keep as many eyes on Mrs Babbacombe as possible—just in case."

"Aye—no sense in taking any risks." Dawlish headed for the door. "Not after all your hard work."

Harry's brows flew up. He turned—but Dawlish had escaped.

Hard work? Harry's lips firmed into a line. His expression resigned, he turned back to the greenery outside. The truly hard part was yet to come but he had charted his course and was determined to stick to it.

When next he proposed to his siren, he wanted no arguments about love.

"Oh!" Dawlish's head popped back around the door. "Just remembered—it's Lady Mickleham's tonight. Want me to organise the carriages and all when I see Joshua?"

Harry nodded. The skies outside were a beautiful blue. "Before you go, have the greys put to."

"You going for a drive?"

"Yes." Harry's expression turned grim. "In the Park."

Fergus opened his aunt's door to him fifteen minutes later. Harry handed him his gloves and shrugged off his greatcoat. "I assume my aunt is resting?"

"Indeed, sir. She's been laid down this hour and past."

"I won't disturb her—it's Mrs Babbacombe I wish to see."

"Ah." Fergus blinked, his expression blanking. "I fear Mrs Babbacombe is engaged, sir."

Harry slowly turned his head until his gaze rested on Fergus's impassive countenance. "Indeed?"

He waited; Fergus, to his relief, deigned to answer his unvoiced question without insisting on an embarrassing prompt.

"She's in the back parlour—her office—with a Mr Mabberly. A well-spoken young gentleman—he's her agent, I understand."

"I see." Harry hesitated, then, quite sure Fergus understood only too well, dismissed him with a nod. "No need to announce me." With that, he mounted the stairs, reining in his impatience enough to make the ascent at least appear idle. But when he gained the upper corridor, his strides lengthened. He paused with his hand on the parlour door-knob; he could hear muted voices within.

His expression distinctly hard, he opened the door.

Lucinda was seated on the *chaise,* an open ledger on her lap. She looked up—and broke off in mid-sentence to stare at him.

A youngish gentleman, precise and soberly dressed, was hovering by her shoulder, leaning over to look at the figures to which she was pointing.

"I wasn't expecting you," Lucinda said, shaking her wits into order.

"Good afternoon," Harry replied.

"Indeed." Lucinda's glance held a definite warning. "I believe I've mentioned Mr Mabberly to you—he's my agent. He assists me with the inns. Mr Mabberly—Mr Lester."

Mr Mabberly somewhat hesitantly put out his hand. Harry regarded it for an instant, then shook it briefly. And immediately turned to Lucinda. "Will you be long?"

Lucinda looked him in the eye. "At least another half-hour."

Mr Mabberly shifted, casting a nervous glance from Lucinda to Harry and back again. "Er…perhaps—"

"We have yet to do the Edinburgh accounts," Lucinda declared, shutting the heavy ledger and lifting it from her lap. Mr Mabberly hastened to relieve her of it. "It's that book there—the third one." As Mr Mabberly hurried across the room to retrieve the required tome, Lucinda raised limpid eyes to Harry's face. "Perhaps, Mr Lester—"

"I'll wait." Harry turned, walked two paces to the nearest chair, and sat down.

Lucinda watched him impassively—she didn't dare smile. Then Anthony Mabberly was back and she turned her attention to her three Edinburgh inns.

As Lucinda checked figures and tallies and rates, comparing the present quarter with the last and that of the year before, Harry studied Mr Mabberly. Within five minutes, he had seen enough to reassure him; Mr Mabberly might regard his employer as something of a goddess, but Harry was left with the distinct impression that his admiration was occasioned more by her business acumen than by her person. Indeed, inside of ten minutes, he was ready to swear that Mr Mabberly's regard was entirely intellectual.

Relaxing, Harry stretched out his legs—and allowed his gaze to settle on his principal concern.

Lucinda sensed the easing of his tension—not a difficult feat as it had reached her in waves—with a measure of relief. If he refused to accept she would need to deal with such as Anthony Mabberly, that regardless of all else she had a business to run, then they would face serious hurdles all too soon. But all appeared serene. While waiting for Mr Mabberly to fetch the last ledger, she glanced at Harry to find him regarding her with nothing more unnerving than very definite boredom in his eyes.

He lifted a brow at her but offered no word.

Lucinda turned back to her work—and quickly completed it.

Mr Mabberly did not dally but neither did he run. He very correctly took his leave of Lucinda, then bowed punctiliously to Harry before departing, promising to carry out Lucinda's commissions and report as usual the next week.

"Humph!" Harry remained standing, watching the door close behind Mabberly.

After one glance at his face, Lucinda remarked, "I do hope you're not about to tell me there is any impropriety in my seeing my agent alone?"

Harry bit his tongue; he swung to face her, his gaze distinctly cool. As he watched Lucinda's gaze shifted, going past him.

"After all," she continued, "he could hardly be considered a danger."

Harry followed her gaze to the daybed before the windows. He looked back at her, and surprised an expression of uncertainty, mixed with a readily identifiable longing. They were, once again, very much alone; his inclinations, he knew, matched hers. Harry cleared his throat. "I came to persuade you to a drive in the Park."

"The Park?" Surprised, Lucinda looked up at him. Em had told her Harry rarely drove in the Park during the hours of the fashionable promenades. "Why?"

"Why?" Harry looked down at her, his expression momentarily blank. Then he frowned. "What sort of a ridiculous question is that?" When Lucinda's gaze turned suspicious, he waved a languid hand. "I merely thought you might be bored and could do with the fresh air. Lady Mickleham's balls are notoriously crowded."

"Oh." Lucinda slowly rose, her eyes searching his face but with no success. "Perhaps a drive would be a good idea."

"Indubitably." Harry waved her to the door. "I'll wait downstairs while you get your coat and bonnet."

Ten minutes later, Lucinda allowed him to lift her into his curricle, still not at all sure she understood. But he was here—she could see no reason to deny herself his company. Reflecting that after yesterday, when he had driven her all the way from Lester Hall to Audley Street in his curricle, she should have had a surfeit of his dry comments, she blithely settled her skirts and looked forward to a few more.

He didn't disappoint her.

As they passed through the heavy wrought-iron gates and on into the Park, bowling along the shaded drive, Harry slanted her a glance. "I regret, my dear, that as my horses are very fresh, we won't be stopping to chat—you'll have to make do with waves and smiling glances."

Engaged in looking about her, Lucinda raised her brows. "Indeed? But if we aren't to chat, why are we here?"

"To see and be seen, of course." Again Harry diverted his attention from his leader, who was indeed very skittish, to glance her way. "That, I have always understood, is the purpose of the fashionable promenades."

"Ah." Lucinda smiled sunnily back at him, not the least perturbed. She was quite content to sit beside him in the sun and watch him tool about the gravel drives, long fingers managing the reins.

He met her gaze, then looked back at his horses. Still smiling, Lucinda looked ahead to where the drive was lined by the barouches and landaus of the matrons of the *ton*. The afternoon was well advanced; there were many who had reached the Park before them. Harry was forced to rein in his horses as the traffic increased, curricles and phaetons of all descriptions wending their way between the carriages drawn up by the verge. Lady Sefton, holding court in her barouche, waved and nodded; Lucinda noticed that she appeared somewhat startled.

Lady Somercote and Mrs Wyncham likewise greeted her, then Countess Lieven favoured them with a long, dark-eyed stare before inclining her head graciously.

Harry humphed. "She's so stiff-necked I keep waiting to hear the crack."

Lucinda smothered a giggle as, rounding the next curve, they came upon Princess Esterhazy. The Princess's large eyes opened wide, then she beamed and nodded delightedly.

Lucinda smiled back; inwardly, she frowned. After a moment, she asked, "Do you frequently drive ladies in the Park?"

Harry clicked his reins; the curricle shot through a gap between a swan-necked phaeton and another curricle, leaving both the other owners gasping. "Not recently."

Lucinda narrowed her eyes. "*How* recently?"

Harry merely shrugged, his gaze fixed on his horses' ears.

Lucinda regarded him closely. When he offered not a word, she ventured, "Not since Lady Coleby?"

He looked at her then, his green glance filled with dire warning, his lips a severe line. Then he looked back at his horses. After a moment, he said, his tone exceedingly grudging, "She was Millicent Pane then."

Harry's memory flitted back through the years; "Millicent Lester" was what he'd been thinking then. His lips twisted wrily; he should have noticed that didn't sound right. He glanced down at the woman beside him, in blue, as usual, her dark hair framing her pale face in soft curls, the whole enchanting picture framed by the rim of her modish bonnet. "Lucinda Lester" had a certain balance, a certain ring.

His lips curved but, her gaze abstracted, she didn't see. She was, he noted, looking decidedly pensive.

The drive ahead cleared as they left the area favoured by the *ton*. Harry reined in and joined the line of carriages waiting to turn back. "Once more through the gauntlet, then I'll take you home."

Lucinda shot him a puzzled glance but said nothing, straightening and summoning a smile as they headed back into the fray.

This time, heading in the opposite direction, they saw different faces—many, Lucinda noted, looked surprised. But they were constantly moving; she got no chance to analyse the reactions the sight of them seemed to be provoking. Lady Jersey's reaction, however, needed no analysis.

Her ladyship was in her barouche, languidly draped over the cushions, when her gimlet gaze fell on Harry's curricle, approaching at a sedate walk. She promptly sat bolt upright.

"Merciful heavens!" she declared, her strident tones dramatic. "I never thought to see the day!"

Harry shot her a malevolent glance but deigned to incline his head. "I believe you are acquainted with Mrs Babbacombe?"

"Indeed!" Lady Jersey waved a hand at Lucinda. "I'll catch up with you next Wednesday, my dear."

Her ladyship's glance promised she would. Lucinda kept her smile gracious but was relieved when they passed on.

She slanted a glance at Harry to discover his face set in uncompromising lines. As soon as the traffic thinned, he clicked the reins.

"That was a very short drive," Lucinda murmured as the gates of the Park hove in sight.

"Short, perhaps, but quite long enough for our purposes."

The words were clipped, his accents unencouraging. Lucinda's inner frown deepened. "Our purposes". What, precisely, were they?

SHE WAS STILL WONDERING when, gowned in hyacinth-blue watered silk, she descended the stairs that evening, ready for Lady Mickleham's ball. Being in constant expectation of an offer was slowly sapping her patience; there was no doubt in her mind that Harry intended making her another, but the when and the why of his reticence were matters that increasingly worried her. She descended most of the stairs in an abstracted daze, glancing up only as she neared their foot. To have her gaze lock with one of clear green.

Eyes widening, Lucinda blinked. "What are you doing here?"

Her astonished gaze took in his severely, almost austerely cut evening clothes, black and stark white as always. The gold acorn pin in his cravat winked wickedly.

She watched his lips twist in a wry grimace.

"I'm here," Harry informed her, his accents severely restrained, "to escort you—and Em and Heather—to Lady Mickleham's ball." He strolled to the end of the stairs and held out a commanding hand.

Lucinda looked at it, a light blush staining her cheeks. She was glad there were no servants about to witness this exchange. As her fingers, of their own volition, slid into his, she raised her eyes to his face. "I wasn't aware you considered it necessary to escort us to such affairs."

His features remained impassive, his eyes hooded, as he drew her down to stand before him.

The door at the end of the hall swung open; Agatha strode through, Lucinda's evening cloak over her arm. She checked when she saw Harry, then merely nodded at him, severe as ever but with less hostility than was her wont, and came on. Harry held out a hand; Agatha readily surrendered the cloak, then turned on her heel and retraced her steps.

Lucinda turned; Harry placed the velvet cloak about her shoulders. Raising her head, she met his gaze in the mirror on the wall. In the corridor above a door opened and shut; Heather's voice drifted down, calling to Em.

If she clung to polite phrases, he would fence and win. Lucinda drew in a quick breath. "Why?"

For a moment, his gaze remained on hers, then dropped to her throat. She saw his lips quirk, in smile or grimace she couldn't tell.

"Circumstances," he began, his voice low, "have changed." He raised his head and his eyes met hers. His brows rose, faintly challenging. "Haven't they?"

Lucinda stared into his eyes and said nothing at all; she wasn't about to gainsay him. But had things truly changed? She was no longer so sure of that.

Heather came skipping down the stairs, followed, more circumspectly, by Em. Amid the bustle of finding cloaks and gloves, Lucinda had no further chance to question Harry's new tack. The short trip to Mickleham House in Berkeley Square was filled with Heather's bright prattle and Em's reminiscences. Lucinda remained silent; Harry sat in the shadows opposite, equally quiet.

The ordeal of the crowded stairway left no opportunity for private converse. Lucinda smiled and nodded to those about them, aware of the curious glances thrown their escort. For his part, Harry remained impassively urbane but as they neared their host and hostess, he bent his head to murmur, very softly, in her ear, "I'll take the supper waltz—and I'll escort you into supper."

Her lips setting, Lucinda shot him a speaking glance. *Take* the supper waltz, indeed! She inwardly humphed, then turned to greet Lady Mickleham.

As Harry had foretold, her ladyship's rooms were full to overflowing.

"This is ridiculous," Lucinda muttered as they forged a path towards one side of the ballroom, hoping to find a *chaise* for Em.

"It's always this bad at the end of the Season," Em returned. "As if building to a frenzy before summer sends everyone home to the country."

Lucinda stifled a sigh as thoughts of the country—the grotto by the Lester Hall lake, the peace and serenity of Lestershall Manor—returned to her.

"Well—there's only a few weeks left to go," put in Heather. "So I suppose we should make the most of them." She glanced at Lucinda. "Have you decided where we'll spend the summer?"

Lucinda blinked. "Ah…"

"I dare say your stepmother feels such decisions are a trifle premature," Harry drawled.

Heather's lips formed an innocent "O"—she seemed perfectly content to accept the uninformative statement.

Lucinda let out a slow breath.

Em found a place on a *chaise* with Lady Sherringbourne; the two ladies promptly fell to exchanging revelations on the alliances forged that year.

Lucinda turned—to find herself all but engulfed by her court, who, as she was rapidly informed, had been awaiting her reappearance with bated breath.

"A whole week you've been away, m'dear. Quite desolate, we've been." Mr Amberly smiled benignly.

"Not that I can't understand it," Mr Satterly remarked. "The crushes are becoming far too real for my liking. Drive anyone away." His gaze rose to Harry's face, his expression utterly bland. "Don't you think so, Lester?"

"Indeed," Harry replied, casting a steely glance about them. With him on one side and Ruthven, equally large, on the other, Lucinda was at least assured of space enough to breathe. The rest of her court gathered before them, creating an enclosure of relative sanity for which, he was sure, they were all rendering silent thanks.

"And where did you go to recoup, my dear Mrs Babbacombe? The country or the seaside?"

It was, predictably, Lord Ruthven who voiced the inevitable question. He smiled encouragingly down at Lucinda; she sensed the subtle teasing behind his smile.

"The country," she vouchsafed. Then, prompted by some inner devil, released, she knew, by the repressive presence on her left, she added, "My stepdaughter and I accompanied Lady Hallows on a visit to Lester Hall."

Ruthven blinked his eyes wide. "Lester Hall?" Slowly, he lifted his gaze to Harry's face. Entirely straightfaced, his lordship raised his brows. "Noticed you were absent from town this week, Harry. Took some time from the frantic whirl to recuperate?"

"Naturally," Harry drawled, clinging to his usual imperturbability, "I escorted my aunt and her guests on their visit."

"Oh, naturally," Ruthven agreed. He turned to Lucinda. "Did Harry show you the grotto by the lake?"

Lucinda regarded his lordship with as bland an expression as she could manage. "Indeed—and the folly on the hill. The views were quite lovely."

"The views?" Lord Ruthven looked stunned. "Ah, yes. The views."

Harry ground his teeth but was too wise to react—at least not verbally. But his glance promised retribution—only

Ruthven, one of his oldest friends, was prepared to ignore it.

To Lucinda's relief, his lordship's teasing, although in no way openly indelicate, was cut short by the musicians. It took a moment or two before it became clear that Lady Mickleham had decided to open her ball with a waltz.

The realisation brought the usual clamour of offers. Lucinda smiled graciously—and hesitated. The room was very crowded, the dance floor would be worse. In cotillion or quadrille, with sets and steps fixed, demanding a certain space, there was little chance of unexpected intimacy. But the waltz? In such cramped conditions?

The thought brought in its wake a certainty that her circumstances had indeed changed. She did not wish to waltz close with anyone but Harry. Her senses reached for him; he was standing, very stiff, intensely contained, beside her.

Harry saw her glance up, unconscious appeal in her eyes. His reaction was immediate and quite impossible to restrain. His hand closed over hers; he lifted it to place her fingers on his sleeve. "My waltz, I believe, my dear."

Relief flooded Lucinda; she remembered to incline her head, and smile fleetingly at her court as Harry led her from their midst.

On the ballroom floor, she relaxed into Harry's arms, allowing him to draw her close with no attempt at dissimulation. She glanced up at him as they started to slowly twirl; his eyes met hers, his expression still aloof but somehow softer. Their gazes held; they communicated without words as they slowly revolved down the room.

Then Lucinda lowered her lashes; Harry's arm tightened about her.

As she had foreseen, the floor was crowded, the dancers cramped. Harry kept her safe within the circle of his arms; she was very aware that if anything threatened, she had only to step closer and he would protect her. His hard body was no threat—she had never seen it as such. He was her guard-

ian in the oldest sense of the word—he to whom she had
entrusted her life.

The waltz ended too soon; Lucinda blinked as Harry's
arms fell from her. Reluctantly, she stepped away and
placed her hand on his arm, then let him steer her back
through the throng.

Harry glanced at her face, his features impassive, concern
in his eyes. As they neared her court, he leaned closer to
murmur, "If you don't care to waltz, simply plead fatigue."
Lucinda glanced up at him; he felt his lips twist. "It's the
latest fashionable ploy."

She nodded—and straightened her shoulders as they re-
joined her court.

Lucinda was inexpressibly grateful for that piece of advice—her supposed fatigue was accepted without a blink;
as the evening wore on, she began to suspect that her earnest
court were no more enamoured of dancing in such cramped
surrounds than she.

Immovable, repressively silent, Harry remained by her
side throughout the long evening. Lucinda greeted the supper waltz with a certain measure of relief. "I understand Mr
Amberly, Mr Satterly and Lord Ruthven are particular
friends of yours?"

Harry glanced fleetingly down at her. "Of a sorts," he
reluctantly conceded.

"I would never have guessed." Lucinda met his sharp
glance with wide eyes. Harry studied her innocent expression, then humphed and drew her closer.

At the end of the waltz, he led her directly to the supper
room. Before she could gather her wits, Lucinda found herself installed at a secluded table for two, shaded from much
of the room by two potted palms. A glass of champagne
and a plate piled high with delicacies appeared before her;
Harry lounged gracefully in the seat opposite.

His eyes on hers, he took a bite of a lobster patty. "Did
you notice Lady Waldron's wig?"

Lucinda giggled. "It nearly fell off." She took a sip of champagne, her eyes sparkling. "Mr Anstey had to catch it and jiggle it back into place."

To Lucinda's delight, Harry spent the entire half-hour regaling her with anecdotes, *on dits* and the occasional dry observation. It was the first time she had had him to herself in such a mood; she gave herself up to enjoying the interlude.

Only when it ended and he led her back to the ballroom did it occur to her to wonder what had brought it on.

Or, more specifically, why he had put himself out to so captivate her.

"Still here, Ruthven?" Harry's drawl hauled her back to the present. He was eyeing his friend with a certain, challenging gleam in his eye. "Nothing else here to interest you?"

"Nothing, I fear." Lord Ruthven put his hand over his heart and quizzed Lucinda. "Nothing as compares with the joys of conversing with Mrs Babbacombe."

Lucinda had to laugh. Harry, of course, did not. His drawl very much in evidence, he took charge of the conversation. As the languid, distinctly bored accents fell on her ear, Lucinda realised that he never, normally, drawled at her. Nor Em. When he spoke to them, his accents were clipped. Apparently, he reserved the fashionable affectation for those he kept at a distance.

With Harry holding the reins, the conversation predictably remained in stultifyingly correct vein. Lucinda, smothering a yawn, considered an option that might, conceivably, assist her cause while at the same time rescuing her poor court.

"It's getting rather warm, don't you find it so?" she murmured, her hand heavy on Harry's arm.

He glanced down at her, then lifted his brows. "Indeed. I suspect it's time we left."

As he lifted his head to locate Em and Heather, Lucinda

allowed herself one, very small, very frustrated snort. She had intended him to take her onto the terrace. Peering through the crowd, she saw Em deep in discussion with a dowager; Heather was engaged with a party of her friends. "Ah…perhaps I could manage for another half-hour if I had a glass of water?"

Mr Satterly immediately offered to procure one and ploughed into the crowd.

Harry looked down at her, a faint question in his eyes. "Are you sure?"

Lucinda's smile was weak. "Positive."

He continued to behave with dogged correctness—which, Lucinda belatedly realised, as the crowds gradually thinned and she became aware of the curious, speculative glances cast their way, was not, in his case, the same as behaving circumspectly.

The observation brought a frown to her eyes.

It had deepened by the time they were safely in Em's carriage, rolling home through the now quiet streets. From her position opposite, Lucinda studied Harry's face, lit by the moonlight and the intermittent flares of the streetlamps.

His eyes were closed, sealed away behind their heavy lids. His features were not so much relaxed as wiped clean of expression, his lips compressed into a firm, straight line. Seen thus, it was a face that kept its secrets, the face of a man who was essentially private, who revealed his emotions rarely if ever.

Lucinda felt her heart catch; a dull ache blossomed within.

The *ton* was his milieu—he knew every nuance of behaviour, how every little gesture would be interpreted. He was at home here, in the crowded ballrooms, as she was not. As at Lester Hall, here, he was in control.

Lucinda shifted in her seat. Propping her chin in her palm, she stared at the sleeping houses, a frown drawing down her fine brows.

Free of her scrutiny, Harry opened his eyes. He studied her profile, clear in the moonlight. His lips curved in the slightest of smiles. Pressing his head back against the squabs, he closed his eyes.

AT THAT MOMENT, in Mortimer Babbacombe's lodgings in Great Portland Street, a meeting was getting underway.

"Well—did you learn anything to the point?" Joliffe, no longer the nattily attired gentleman who had first befriended Mortimer, snarled the question the instant Brawn ambled through the door. Heavy-eyed from lack of sleep, his colour high from the liquor he had consumed to calm his nerves, Joliffe fixed his most junior accomplice with a dangerous stare.

Brawn was too young to heed it. Dropping into a chair at the parlour table about which Joliffe, Mortimer and Scrugthorpe were already seated, he grinned. "Aye—I learned a bit. Chatted up the young maid—no mor'n a bit of a thing. She told me a few things before that groom—yeller-haired lot—came and fetched her orf. Heard him giving her what for "bout talking to strangers, so I don't think I'll get any more by that road." Brawn grinned. "Pity—wouldn't ha' minded—"

"Damn you—get on!" Joliffe roared, his fist connecting with the table with enough force to set the tankards jumping. *"What the devil happened?"*

Brawn shot him a look more puzzled than frightened. "Well—the lady did go orf to the country that day—just like you'd planned. But seemingly she went to some other house—a place called Lester Hall. The whole household went up the next day—the maid said as she thought it'd been planned."

"Damn!" Joliffe swilled back a mouthful of porter. "No wonder I couldn't get any of the crew who'd gone up to Asterley to say they'd seen her. I thought they must've been

practising discretion—but the damned woman hadn't gone!''

''Seems not.'' Brawn shrugged. ''So what now?''

''Now we stop playing and kidnap her.'' Scrugthorpe lifted his face from his tankard. ''Like I said from the first. It's the only way of being sure—all this trying to get the rakes to do our job for us has got us precisely *nowhere*.'' He spat the last word, his contempt bordering on the open.

Joliffe held his eye; eventually, Scrugthorpe looked back at his mug.

''That's what I say, anyway,'' Scrugthorpe mumbled as he took another swallow.

''Hmm.'' Joliffe grimaced. ''I'm beginning to agree with you. It looks like we'll have to take an active hand ourselves.''

''But…I thought…'' Mortimer's first contribution to the conversation died away as both Joliffe and Scrugthorpe turned to look at him.

''Ye-es?'' Joliffe prompted.

Mortimer's colour rose. He put a finger to his cravat, tugging at the floppy folds. ''It's just that…well—if we do do anything direct—well—won't she know?''

Joliffe's lip curled. ''Of *course* she will—but that's not to say she'll be in any hurry to denounce us—not after Scrugthorpe here has his revenge.''

''Aye.'' Scrugthorpe's black eyes gleamed. ''Jus' leave her to me. I'll make sure she ain't in no hurry to talk about it.'' He nodded and went back to his beer.

Mortimer regarded him with mounting horror. He opened his mouth, then caught Joliffe's eye. He visibly shrank, but muttered, ''There must be another way.''

''Very likely.'' Joliffe drained his tankard and reached for the jug. ''But we don't have time for any more convoluted schemes.''

''Time?'' Mortimer looked confused.

''Yes, *time!*'' Snarling, Joliffe turned on Mortimer. Mortimer paled, his eyes starting like a frightened rabbit's. With an effort, Joliffe reined in his temper. He smiled, all teeth. "But don't you worry your head over it. Just leave everything to Scrugthorpe and me. You do your bit when asked— and everything will work out just fine."

"Aye." Brawn unexpectedly chipped in. "I was thinking as you'd better get a different plan. From what the maid told me, seems like the lady's in expectation of 'receivin' an offer,' as they says. I don't know as I understand these things rightly, but seems pretty useless making her out to be a whore if she's going to marry a swell."

"What?" Joliffe's exclamation had all of them starting. They stared at their leader as he stared—in total stupefication—at Brawn. "She's about to *marry?*"

Warily, Brawn nodded. "So the maid said."

"Whom?"

"Some swell name of Lester."

"Harry Lester?" Joliffe calmed. Frowning heavily, he eyed Brawn. "You sure this maid got it right? Harry Lester's not the marrying kind."

Brawn shrugged. "Wouldn't know about that." After a moment, he added, "The girl said as this Lester chap had called this afternoon to take the lady for a drive in the Park."

Joliffe stared at Brawn, all his certainties fading. "The Park," he repeated dully.

Brawn merely nodded and cautiously sipped his beer.

When Joliffe next spoke, his voice was hoarse. "We've got to move soon."

"Soon?" Scrugthorpe looked up. "How soon?"

"Before she's married—preferably before she even accepts an offer. We don't need any legal complications."

Mortimer was frowning. "Complications?"

"Yes, damn you!" Joliffe struggled to mute his snarl. "If the damned woman marries, the guardianship of her stepdaughter passes into her husband's hands. If Harry Lester takes the reins, we can forget getting a farthing out of your lovely cousin's estate.''

Mortimer's eyes widened. "Oh."

"Yes—oh! And while we're on the subject, I've a little news for you—just to strengthen your backbone." Joliffe fixed his eyes on Mortimer's wan countenance. "You owe me five thousand on a note of hand. I passed that vowel on, with one of my own, to a man who charges interest by the day. Together, we now owe him a cool twenty thousand, Mortimer—and if we don't pay up soon, he's going to take every pound out of our hides." He paused, then leaned forward to ask, "Is that clear enough for you, Mortimer?"

His face a deathly white, his eyes round and starting, Mortimer was so petrified he could not even nod.

"Well, then!" Scrugthorpe pushed his empty tankard away. "Seems like we'd best make some plans."

Joliffe had sobered dramatically. He tapped the tabletop with one fingernail. "We'll need information on her movements." He looked at Brawn but the boy shook his head.

"No good. The maid won't talk to me again, not after the roasting that groom gave her. And there's no one else."

Joliffe's eyes narrowed. "What about the other women?"

Brawn's snort was eloquent. "There's a few o'them all right—but they're all as sour as green grapes. Take even you till next year to chat 'em up—and they'd likely refuse to talk even then."

"Damn!" Joliffe absentmindedly took a sip of his porter. "All right." He set the tankard down with a snap. "If that's the only way then that's the way we'll do it."

"How's that?" Scrugthorpe asked.

"We watch her—all the time, day and night. We make our arrangements and keep all in readiness to grab her the instant fate gives us a chance."

Scrugthorpe nodded. "Right. But how're we going to go about it?"

Joliffe sent an intimidating glance at Mortimer.

Mortimer swallowed and shrank in his chair.

With a contemptuous snort, Joliffe turned back to Scrugthorpe "Just listen "

Chapter Fourteen

Five nights later, Mortimer Babbacombe stood in the shadows of a doorway in King Street and watched his aunt-by-marriage climb the shallow steps to Almack's unprepossessing entrance.

"Well." Heaving a sigh—of relief or disappointment he was not quite sure—he turned to his companion. "She's gone in—no point in watching further."

"Oh, yes, there is." The words came in a cold hiss. In the past five days, Joliffe's polite veneer had peeled from him. "You're going to go in there, Mortimer, and keep a careful eye on your aunt. I want to know everything—who she dances with, who brings her lemonade—*everything!*" Joliffe's piercing gaze swung to fix on Mortimer's face. "Is that clear?"

Mortimer hugged the doorframe, his relief rapidly fading. Glowering glumly, he nodded. "Can't think what good it'll do," he grumbled.

"Don't think, Mortimer—just do as I bid you." In the shadows, Joliffe studied Mortimer's face, plain and round, the face of a man easily led—and, as was often the case with such, prone to unhelpful stubbornness. Joliffe's lip curled. "Do try to recapture a little of your earlier enthusiasm, Mortimer. Remember—your uncle overlooking your claim to be your cousin's guardian and appointing a young woman like your aunt instead is an insult to your manhood.''

Mortimer shifted, pulling at his fleshy lower lip. ''Yes, it is.''

''Indeed. Who is Lucinda Babbacombe, anyway, other than a pretty face smart enough to take your uncle in?''

''Quite true.'' Mortimer nodded. ''And, mind, it's not as if I've any bone to pick with her—but anyone would have to admit it was dashed unfair of Uncle Charles to leave all the ready to her—and just the useless land to me.''

Joliffe smiled into the night. ''Quite. You're merely seeking redress for the unfair actions of your uncle. Remember that, Mortimer.'' He clapped Mortimer on the shoulder and waved towards Almack's. ''I'll wait at your lodgings for your news.''

Mortimer nodded. Straightening his rounded shoulders, he headed for the sacred portal.

Deep within the hallowed halls, Lucinda nodded and smiled, responding to the chatter with confident ease while her mind trod an endless trail of conjecture and fact. Harry had driven her in the Park on the past five afternoons, albeit briefly. He had appeared every evening, unheralded, simply there, waiting when she descended the stairs to escort them to the balls and parties, remaining by her side throughout but saying not a word as to his purpose.

She had gone beyond impatience, even beyond chagrin—she was now in the grip of a deadening sense of the inevitable.

Lucinda summoned a smile and gave her hand to Mr Drumcott, a not-so-young gentleman who had recently become betrothed to a young lady in her first Season.

''I beg you'll do me the honour of dancing this quadrille with my poor self, Mrs Babbacombe.''

Lucinda acquiesced with a smile but as they took their places she caught herself scanning the crowd—and inwardly sighed. She should, of course, be glad Harry had not arrived this evening to escort them here—that, she was convinced, would have been the last straw.

That he intended making her his bride was patently clear—his likely motive in underscoring that fact publicly was what was dragging her heart down. The memory of his first proposal—and her refusal—haunted her. She hadn't known, then, of Lady Coleby and her earlier rejection of Harry's love. Her own refusal had been driven by the simple belief that he loved her and would, if pushed, acknowledge that love. To hear the words on his lips was something she craved, something she needed. But not, she was increasingly certain, something Harry needed.

She couldn't rid herself of the idea that he was painting her into a corner, that his present behaviour was designed to render a second rejection impossible. If, after all his studied performances, she refused him again, she would be labelled cruel-hearted, or, more likely, as Sim would put it, "dicked in the nob".

Lucinda grimaced—and had to hurriedly cover the expression with a smile. As they embarked on the final figures of the quadrille, Mr Drumcott blinked at her in concern; she forced another smile—a travesty considering her true state. If Harry kept on as he was, when next he proposed, she would have to accept him, regardless of whether he offered his heart along with his hand.

The quadrille ended; Lucinda sank into the final, elaborate curtsy. Rising, she straightened her shoulders and determinedly thanked Mr Drumcott. She was not, she told herself, going to dwell on Harry's motives any longer. There must be some other explanation—if only she could think what it was.

At that precise moment, the object of her thoughts sat at the desk in his library attired in long-tailed black evening coat and black knee-breeches, garments he considered outmoded in the extreme.

"What have you learned?" Harry leaned both arms on the blotter and pinned Salter with a steady green gaze.

"Enough to make my nose quiver." Salter settled himself in the chair before the desk. Dawlish, who had shown him in, closed the door; folding his arms, he leaned back against it. Salter pulled out a notebook. "First—this Joliffe chap is more of a bad egg than I'd thought. A real sharp—specialises in 'befriending' flats, preferably those who come fresh on the town, gullible and usually young, though, these days, as he's no spring chicken himself, his victims also tend to be older. Quite a history—but nothing, ever, that could be made to stick. Lately, however, quite aside from his usual activities, Joliffe's taken to deep play—and not in the hells either. Word has it he's heavily in debt—not to his opponents—he's paid them off—but the total sum amounts to a fortune. All evidence points to Joliffe being in the clutches of a real bloodsucker—a certain individual who works out of the docks. Don't have any information on him except that he's not one to keep dangling too long. A mistake that often turns fatal, if you take my meaning."

He lifted his gaze to Harry's face; his expression grim, Harry nodded.

"Right then—next up is Mortimer Babbacombe. A hopeless case—if Joliffe hadn't picked him up one of the other Captain Sharps would have. Born a flat. Joliffe took him under his wing and underwrote his losses—that's the usual way these things start. Then, when the flat gets his hands on whatever loot is coming his way, the sharps take the major cut. So when Mortimer came into his inheritance, Joliffe was sitting on his coattails. From then, however, things went wrong."

Salter consulted his notebook. "Like Mrs Babbacombe told you, it seems Mortimer had no real understanding of his inheritance—but Charles Babbacombe had paid off his debts annually, to the tune of three thousand at the last. Seems certain Mortimer assumed the money came from his uncle's estate and the estate was therefore worth much more than it is. My people checked—the place can't make much more than expenses. It's apparently common knowledge up that way that Charles Babbacombe's money came from Babbacombe and Company.''

Shutting his book, Salter grimaced. ''That's all right and tight—and a nasty surprise it must have been for Joliffe. But what I can't see is why he's gone after Mrs Babbacombe—knocking her on the head isn't going to benefit them. Joliffe's more than experienced enough to work that out—some old aunt of hers is her nearest kin. Yet they're keeping constant watch on Mrs Babbacombe—and not as if they've got anything cordial on their minds.''

Harry stiffened. ''They're watching her?''

''And my people are watching them. Very closely.''

Harry relaxed. A little. He frowned. ''We're missing something.''

''Precisely my thought.'' Salter shook his head. ''Operators like Joliffe don't make too many mistakes—after his first disappointment with Mortimer, he wouldn't have hung around unless there's a chance of some really rich pickings in the wind.''

''There's money all right,'' Harry mused. ''But it's in the business. As you know, Charles Babbacombe willed that to his widow and his daughter.''

Salter frowned. ''Ah, yes—this daughter. A young chit, barely seventeen.'' His frown deepened. ''From all I've seen, Mrs Babbacombe's no easy mark—why pick on her rather than the daughter?''

Harry blinked, somewhat owlishly, at Salter. ''Heather,'' he said, his tone oddly flat. After a moment, he drew in a long breath and straightened. ''That must be it.''

''What?''

Harry's lips twisted. ''I've often been told that I've a devious mind—perhaps, for once, it can be of real use. Just hear me out.'' His gaze grew distant; absent-mindedly, he reached for his pen. "Heather is the one they *could* use to milk the business of cash—*but*—what if Lucinda is Heather's guardian, as well as Heather's mentor? In either role, Joliffe and company would have to *get rid* of Lucinda to get to Heather."

Slowly, Salter nodded. "That's possible—but why try that ramshackle business of sending Mrs Babbacombe to that fancy orgy palace, then?"

Harry hoped Alfred never heard of his ancestral home referred to in such vein. He tapped the blotter with the pen. "That's what makes me so certain Heather's guardianship must be the key—because in order to get rid of Lucinda for such purposes, showing her as unfit to be guardian of a young girl would be sufficient for Mortimer, who is Heather's next of kin, to apply to overturn Lucinda's guardianship in favour of himself. Once that's done, they could simply cut all contact between Heather and Lucinda—and use Heather to draw funds from her half of the investment."

Gazing into space, Salter nodded. "You're right—that must be it. Roundabout but it makes sense."

"And now they've failed to paint the lady scarlet," put in Dawlish, "they're planning to snatch her up and do away with her."

"True enough," agreed Salter. "But my people know what to do."

Harry refrained from asking just who Salter's "people" were.

"Even so," Dawlish continued, "they can't keep a-watching her forever. And seems to me this Joliffe character's one as should be behind bars."

Salter nodded. "You're right. There's been a few unexplained 'suicides' in Joliffe's past that the magistrates were never convinced about."

Harry repressed a shudder. The thought of Lucinda mixed up with such characters was not to be borne. "At this instant, Mrs Babbacombe is safe enough—but we need to make sure our conjecture's true. If it's not, we could be following the wrong scent—with potentially serious consequences. It strikes me that there might well be a second guardian, which would render our hypothesis unlikely.''

Salter lifted a brow. ''If you know the lady's legal man, I could make some discreet inquiries.''

''I don't. And he's very likely in Yorkshire.'' Harry thought—then looked at Dawlish. ''Mrs Babbacombe's maid and coachman have been with the family for years. They might know.''

Dawlish straightened from the door. ''I'll ask.''

''Couldn't you just ask the lady herself?'' Salter asked.

''No.'' Harry's reply was unequivocal. His lips twisted in a grimace. ''At the moment, the very last thing I want to do is ask Mrs Babbacombe about her legal affairs. The question of Heather's guardianship can't be all that hard to answer.''

''No. And I'll tip my people the wink to yell the instant they sniff any shift in the wind.'' Salter got to his feet. ''As soon as we know for sure what these jackals are about, we'll devise a way to trip them up nicely.''

Harry didn't reply. He shook hands with Salter, the thought in his mind that if tripping up Joliffe involved placing Lucinda in any danger at all, it simply wouldn't happen.

When Dawlish returned from showing the ex-Runner out, Harry was standing in the centre of the room, strapping his gloves on his palm.

''Well!'' Dawlish opened his eyes wide. ''There you be—all tricked out and not at the party. Best I drive you there, then.''

Harry looked down, casting a long-suffering glance at breeches he had long ago sworn never again to don. His expression grimly resigned, he nodded. ''Best you do.''

His knock on Almack's door very nearly prostrated old Willis, the porter. ''*Never* did I think to see *you* here again, sir!'' Willis raised his shaggy brows. ''Something in the wind?''

''You, Willis, are as fervent a gossip as any of your mistresses.''

Unrepentant, Willis grinned. Harry gave him his gloves and cloak and sauntered into the ballroom.

To say his entrance caused a stir would be a gross understatement. It caused a flutter, a ruffling of feathers, and, in some, a mild panic akin to hysteria, all fuelled by the intense speculation that rose in feminine breasts as he strolled, gracefully but entirely purposefully, across the room.

Her emotions aswirl, Lucinda watched his approach with unwilling fascination. Her heart started to soar, her lips lifted—then her earlier thoughts engulfed her. A tightness gripped her lungs, squeezing slowly. Candlelight gleamed on his golden hair; in the old-fashioned attire, he looked less suave and debonair but, if anything, even more the rake than before. As she felt the touch of a hundred eyes, her lips firmed. He was exploiting them all, manipulating the whole *ton*—shamelessly.

As he neared, she held out her hand, knowing he would simply take it if she didn't. ''Good evening, Mr Lester. How very surprising to see you here.''

Her gentle sarcasm did not escape Harry; he raised his brows as he raised her fingers to his lips and gently brushed a kiss across their tips.

He had done it so often Lucinda had forgotten it was no longer the accepted mode of greeting. The collective gasp that seemed to fill the ballroom reminded her of the fact. Her smile remained in place but her eyes flashed.

The reprobate before her merely smiled. And tucked her hand in his arm. ''Come, my dear, I rather think we should stroll.'' With a nod, he excused them from the two gentlemen who had been passing the time by Lucinda's side. ''Gibson. Holloway.''

They had barely taken two steps before Lady Jersey appeared in their path. Harry promptly bowed, so elaborately it was almost a joke, so gracefully it was impossible to take offense.

Sally Jersey humphed. "I had meant to ask Mrs Babbacombe for news of you," she informed Harry without a blink. "But now you're here, I need hardly enquire."

"Indeed," Harry drawled. "I'm positively touched, Sally dear, that you should think to take an interest in my poor self."

"Your self isn't so poor anymore, if you recall."

"Ah, yes. A twist of fate."

"One which has brought you once more within the sights of the ladies here. Take care, my friend, else you slip and get tangled in their nets." Lady Jersey's eyes twinkled. She turned to Lucinda. "I would congratulate you, my dear— but I fear he's quite incorrigible—utterly irreclaimable. But if you seek revenge, all you have to do is take him to the furthest point from the door and cut him loose—then watch him flounder."

Her expression serene, Lucinda raised her brows. "I'll bear the point in mind, ma'am."

With a regal nod, Sally Jersey swept on.

"Don't you dare," Harry murmured as they strolled on, his drawl instantly evaporating. His hand rose to cover hers where it lay on his sleeve. "You couldn't be so hard-hearted."

Again Lucinda lifted her brows; her eyes, no longer laughing, met his. "No?"

Harry's eyes searched hers; Lucinda saw them narrow slightly.

Suddenly breathless, she squeezed his arm and forced a smile to her lips. "But you hardly need me to protect you."

Determinedly, she looked ahead, still smiling, her expression as serene as before.

A short silence ensued, then Harry's voice sounded in her

ear, low and completely expressionless, "You're wrong, my dear. I need you—very much."

Lucinda couldn't risk looking at him; she blinked rapidly and nodded to Lady Cowper, beaming from a nearby *chaise*. Were they talking of protection from the matchmaking mamas—or something else?

She got no chance to clarify the point—the mamas, the matrons and the dragons of the *ton* descended *en masse*.

To Harry's irritation, his evening at Almack's proved even more trying than he had imagined. His transparent obsession with the woman on his arm, which he had been at such pains to advertise, had, as he had known it would, doused all hope that he might be struck by lightning and forget himself enough to smile on one of the matrons' young darlings. They had got the point; unfortunately, they had all taken it into their heads to be first with their congratulations.

The very first of these thinly veiled felicitations came from the indefatigable Lady Argyle, her pale, plain daughter still in tow. "I can't say how pleased I've been to see you at our little entertainments again, Mr Lester." She bestowed an arch glance before turning her gimlet gaze on Lucinda. "You must make sure he continues, my dear." She tapped Lucinda's arm with her fan. "*Such* a loss when the most handsome gentlemen cling to their clubs. Don't let him backslide."

With another arch glance and a flutter of her fingers, her ladyship departed, silent daughter in her wake. Harry idly wondered if the girl actually spoke.

Then he glanced down—and saw Lucinda's face. No one else would have noticed anything amiss, but he was now too used to seeing her relaxed, happy. She was neither, now, her features tense, her lips without the full softness they normally displayed.

They sustained two more delighted outpourings in rapid succession, then Lady Cowper caught them. Her ladyship was her usual, kind-hearted self, quite impossible to curtail.

Harry bore her soft smiles and gentle words—but as soon as she released them, he took a firm grip on Lucinda's arm and steered her towards the refreshment-room. "Come—I'll get you a glass of champagne."

Lucinda glanced up at him. "This is Almack's—they don't serve champagne."

Harry looked his disgust. "I'd forgotten. Lemonade, then." He looked down at her. "You must be parched."

She didn't deny it or make any demur when he handed her a glass. But even in the refreshment-room the avalanche of felicitations he'd unwittingly triggered continued. There was, Harry quickly discovered, no escape.

By the time the next dance, a waltz, the only one of the evening, let them seek refuge on the floor, he had realised his error. He grasped the moment as he drew Lucinda into his arms to apologise. "I'm afraid I miscalculated." He smiled down into her eyes—and wished he could see in. They were more than misty, they were cloudy. The sight worried him. "I'd forgotten just how competitive the matrons are." He couldn't think of any acceptable way to explain that, when it came to a prize such as he now was, the matrons would rather accept someone like Lucinda, an outsider albeit one of their class, than see an archrival triumph.

Lucinda smiled, apparently at ease, but her eyes did not lighten. Harry drew her closer and wished they were alone.

When the dance ended, he looked down at her face, making no attempt to hide the frown in his eyes. "If you like we'll go and find Em. I dare say she'll have had enough of this."

Lucinda acquiesced with a nod, her expression rigidly serene.

Harry's prediction proved true—Em had also been besieged. She was very ready to depart.

"A bit like running under fire," she grumpily informed Lucinda as Harry handed her into the carriage. "But it's a dashed sight too much when they start angling for invitations to the wedding.'' Her snort was eloquent.

Harry glanced at Lucinda, already seated in the carriage; a shaft of light from the doorway illuminated her face. Her eyes were huge, her cheeks pale. She looked tired, worn down—almost defeated. Harry felt his heart lurch—and felt a pain more intense than any Millicent Pane had ever caused.

''Now don't forget!'' Em tapped him on the sleeve. ''Dinner's at seven tomorrow—we'll look to see you before that.''

''Ah. Yes.'' Harry blinked. ''Of course.'' With a last glance at Lucinda, he stepped back and closed the door. ''I'll be there.''

He watched the carriage roll away, then, frowning, turned towards his club, just a few steps around the corner. But when he reached the lighted door he paused, then, still frowning, continued on to his rooms.

An hour later, sunk in her feather mattress, Lucinda stared up at the canopy of her bed. Tonight had clarified matters— unequivocally, incontrovertibly. She'd been wrong—no other explanation existed for Harry's actions, other than the obvious. The only thing *she* now needed to decide was what she was going to do about it.

She watched the moonbeams cross her ceiling; it was dawn before she slept.

HARRY DIDN'T LEAVE his rooms the next morning, alerted by a message from Salter and disappointing information from Dawlish.

''They don't know,'' Dawlish repeated for Salter's benefit when they gathered in Harry's library at eleven. ''Both are sure Mrs Babbacombe's Miss Heather's guardian but whether there's another they can't say either way.''

''Hmm.'' Salter frowned. He looked at Harry. ''Word came in from some of my people. Joliffe's hired a carriage with four strong horses. No particular destination and he didn't hire any boys with it—paid a goodly deposit to take it without.''

Harry's fingers tightened about his pen. ''I think we can conclude that Mrs Babbacombe is in danger.''

Salter grimaced. ''Perhaps—but I've been thinking about what your man here said. You can't go watching them for forever—and if they don't take one, they might take the other. The stepdaughter's still their ultimate goal.''

It was Harry's turn to grimace. ''True.'' He stood poised to remove Lucinda from all danger but it was undoubtedly true that, if Joliffe was desperate enough, such a move would expose Heather as Joliffe's next target.

''I've been thinking,'' Salter continued, ''that this matter of the carriage is probably for the best. It means he's planning a move soon. We're alerted—something Joliffe doesn't know. If we can sort out the facts about this guardianship, meanwhile keeping a close watch on Joliffe and his crew, then before they can make their move, we can tie them up with a warrant. My sources are sure Mortimer Babbacombe will talk readily enough. Seems he's in over his head.''

Harry drew his pen back and forth through his fingers, his gaze distant as he considered the next twenty-four hours. ''If you need the information about the guardianship to obtain a warrant, then we'll have to investigate further.'' His gaze shifted to Dawlish. ''Go and see Fergus—ask if he knows where to contact a Mr Mabberly of Babbacombe Inns.''

''Ah—no need.'' Salter held up a large finger. ''Leave that to me. But what shall I tell Mr Mabberly?''

Harry's lips compressed. ''He's Mrs Babbacombe's agent—she trusts him, I gather—so you may tell him whatever you must. But he'll very likely know the answer. Or at least know who does.''

''Still no thoughts of just asking the lady?''

Slowly, Harry shook his head. "But if we haven't got the answer by tomorrow evening, I'll ask her."

Salter accepted the deadline without comment. "Need any help keeping an eye on the pair of them?"

Again Harry shook his head. "They won't be leaving Hallows House today or tonight." He looked at Salter, his expression resigned. "My aunt is holding a soirée."

IT WAS THE BIGGEST SOIRÉE Em had held in years and she was determined to enjoy it to the full.

Lucinda said as much as, side by side, she and Harry ascended the stairs to the ballroom. "She's positively wound tight. You could almost believe it was she making her come-out."

Harry grinned. The exceedingly select dinner Em had organised to precede her "little entertainment" had been a decided success; the company had been such as to gratify the most ambitious hostess. "She's enjoyed herself tremendously these last few months. Ever since you and Heather joined her."

Lucinda met his eyes briefly. "She's been very good to us."

"And you've been very good for her," Harry murmured as they reached the head of the staircase.

Em was already there, taking up her position to greet the first of the guests who were even now milling in the hall.

"Don't forget to compliment her on the décor," Lucinda whispered. "It's all her own effort."

Harry nodded. When Em waved insistently, summoning Lucinda to her side, he bowed and strolled on into the ballroom. It was indeed a sight—garlanded with purple and gold—Em's favourite colours—lightened here and there with a touch of blue. Cornflowers stood in urns on tables by the side of the room; blue bows tied back the curtains about the long windows. Harry smiled and paused to glance back at the trio at the door—Em in heavy purple silk,

Heather in pale gold muslin with a hint of blue at neckline and hem, and Lucinda—his siren—stunning in a gown of sapphire silk trimmed with fine golden ribbons.

Harry decided that sincerely complimenting his aunt would, in this instance, be easy. He strolled the room, chatting with acquaintances, even steeling himself to converse with the few ageing relatives Em had seen fit to invite. But he did not lose sight of the welcoming party; when Em finally quit her position, he was already at Lucinda's side.

She smiled up at him, unaffectedly open, the gesture warm yet with a lingering sense of…Harry gazed down into her softly blue eyes, even softer now, and realised with a jolt that what he could sense was melancholy.

"If the crowds keep rolling in as they are, Em's soirée will be declared the very *worst* crush of the Season." Lucinda placed her hand on his arm and laughed up at him. "I might very well have to plead fatigue from the first."

Harry returned her smile but his gaze remained acute. "Lady Herscult is one of Em's oldest friends; she's charged me most straitly to bring you directly to her."

With a serene smile and an inclination of her head, Lucinda allowed him to lead her into the growing crowd.

As they passed through the throng, people stopped them to chat, all beaming. They discovered Lady Herscult on a *chaise;* she twitted Harry and Lucinda both before letting them escape. Throughout, Harry watched Lucinda carefully; with unshakeable serenity, she turned aside any questions too probing, her smile calmly assured.

The first waltz interrupted their meanderings—Em had chosen to enliven her soirée with three dances, all waltzes.

As, without seeking any permission, Harry drew Lucinda, unresisting, into his arms, he arched a brow. "A novel arrangement."

A gurgle of laughter came to his ears.

"She said," Lucinda explained, "that she could see no

point in wasting time with quadrilles and cotillions when what everyone really wanted was waltzes.''

Harry grinned. ''Very Em.''

Lucinda smiled as he whirled her through the turn, her ease on the dance floor a far cry from her first excursion. She felt supple in his arms, fluidly matching her steps to his, following effortlessly, not, he suspected, even conscious that he held her so close. She would probably notice if he didn't.

His lips curved; she noticed.

''Now why are you smiling?''

Harry couldn't stop his slow smile from breaking. His eyes caught hers—he felt he could lose himself in the blue. ''I was just thinking what a good job I've made of teaching you to waltz.''

Lucinda raised her brows. ''Indeed? Can I not claim some small achievement for myself?''

Harry's smile went crooked. He drew her a fraction closer, his eyes a brilliant green. ''You've achieved a great deal, my dear. On the floor—and off.''

Her brows rose higher. She held his gaze, her expression serene, her smile soft, her lips eminently kissable. Then she lowered her lids and looked away, leaning her head fleetingly against his shoulder.

When they weren't playing waltzes, the musicians had been instructed to entertain Em's guests with gentle airs and sonatas, all pleasing to the ear. As they wandered the crowds, engaging in the usual banter and occasional repartee, without question or, indeed, thought, remaining by each other's side, Harry realised that his siren was indeed calmer, more her usual self than she had been at Almack's the night before.

His relief was telling; he had, he realised, been harbouring a deep concern. Presumably, last night, it had merely been the unexpected gush of semi-congratulations that had shaken her; tonight, she seemed at ease, assured, typically confident.

If he could only discover the cause of the strange hint of sorrow that lay, deep but present, beneath her serene veneer—and eradicate it—he'd be happier than any man, he felt, had any right to be.

She was perfect, she was his—as he had always sensed she could be. All he wanted of life was here, with her, within his grasp; time was all that now stood in his path.

But tomorrow would come—it wasn't what he'd originally planned but he wasn't going to wait any longer. He had completed all the important acts—she would simply have to believe him.

The supper waltz came and went, as did supper itself, an array of delicacies Em's old cook had, Lucinda assured him, been up the past three nights producing. Filled with laughter and repartee, the hours fled past until, at the last, the musicians laid bow to string once more and the strains of the last waltz rose above the sea of glittering heads.

The third waltz.

Close by the edge of the floor, Harry and Ruthven were deep in discussions of a distinctly equine nature while beside them Mr Amberly and Lucinda pursued a shared interest in landscapes. As the music swelled, Harry turned to Lucinda—just as she turned to him. Their gazes locked; after a moment, Harry's lips twisted wryly.

His eyes on hers, he offered her, not his arm but his hand.

Lucinda glanced at it, then looked into his green eyes. Her heart accelerated, pulsing in her throat.

Harry's brows slowly rose. ''Well, my dear?''

Her gaze steady on his, Lucinda drew in a breath. Her smile soft and oddly fragile, she placed her hand in his.

Harry's fingers closed tight over hers. He bowed elegantly; Lucinda's smile grew—she sank into a curtsy. Harry raised her, a light in his eyes she had not before seen. He drew her into his arms, then, with consummate skill, whirled them onto the floor.

Lucinda let herself flow with his stride. His strength surrounded her; he was protection and support, lover and master, helpmate and friend. She searched the hard planes of his face, chiselled, austere; with him, she could be what she wished—what she wanted to be. Her gaze softened, as did her lips. He noticed; his gaze fell to her lips, then rose again to capture hers, a subtle shift in the green raising a slow heat beneath her skin, a warmth that owed nothing to the crowds and everything to what lay between them.

With inherent grace, they swirled down the long room, seeing no one, aware of nothing beyond their shared existence, trapped by the waltz and the promise in each other's eyes.

Lord Ruthven and Mr Amberly looked on, smugly satisfied smiles on their faces.

"Well—I think we can congratulate ourselves, Amberly." Lord Ruthven turned and held out his hand.

"Indeed." Mr Amberly beamed and shook it. "A job well done!" His eyes lifted to the couple circling the floor. His smile grew broader. "No doubt about it."

Lord Ruthven followed his gaze—and grinned. "Not a one."

As she leaned back against Harry's arm and let the magic of the moment take her, Lucinda knew that was true. Even while a small part of her sorrowed, she felt elation sweep her. He would ask her very soon—and she knew how she would answer. She loved him too much to deny him again, even should he deny her. Deep inside, her conviction that he loved her had never waned—it never would, she was sure. She could draw on that for strength as she had hoped to draw on his acknowledgement of his love. If it was not to be, it wasn't; she was too prosaic a creature to rail against a much-desired fate.

With the last ringing chord of the waltz, the evening was declared over.

As family, Harry hung back, allowing the other guests to depart. Gerald finally headed downstairs, leaving Harry with Lucinda at their head. His hand found hers in the folds of her gown; twining his fingers through hers, he drew her to face him. Ignoring Em leaning against the balustrade on Lucinda's other side, Harry raised Lucinda's hand to brush a kiss across her knuckles, then shifting his hold, his gaze steady on hers, he tipped her fingers back to place a kiss on her inner wrist.

Lucinda, trapped in his gaze, suppressed a delicious shiver.

Harry smiled—and traced her cheek with one long finger. "We'll talk tomorrow."

The words were soft, low—they went straight to Lucinda's heart. She smiled softly; Harry bowed, first to her, then to Em. Then, without a backward glance, he descended the stairs—to the very last, the very picture of the elegant rake.

Outside Hallows House, lurking in the shadows on the opposite side of the street, unremarkable amid the small gathering of urchins and inveterate watchers who congregated outside any ball or party, Scrugthorpe kept his eyes fixed on the lighted doorway and muttered beneath his breath.

"Just wait till I get my hands on you, bitch. Once I'm done with you, no high-stickler of a gentleman will want to sully himself with you. Damaged goods, you'll be—well and truly damaged." He cackled softly, gleefully and rubbed his hands. In the shadows, his eyes gleamed.

A link-boy, waiting to pick up any likely trade, strolled past, casting Scrugthorpe an incurious glance. A few paces on, the boy passed a street-sweeper, leaning on his broom, his face obscured by an ancient floppy hat. The link-boy grinned at the sweeper, then ambled on to prop against a nearby lamppost.

Scrugthorpe missed the exchange, intent on the last stragglers emerging from Hallows House.

"You'll be mine very soon," he leered. "Then I'll teach you not to give a man lip. Too hoity by half." His grin turned feral. "I'll bring you back to earth right quick."

A thin, tuneful whistle floated across Scrugthorpe's senses, distracting him from his plotting. The tune continued—a popular air; Scrugthorpe stiffened. Alert, he scanned the shadows for the whistler. His gaze settled on the linkboy. The tune continued; Scrugthrope knew it well, even down to the curious lilting catch the whistler put at the end of each verse.

Scrugthorpe cast a last glance at the empty doorway across the road, then, with every evidence of unconcern, headed off down the street.

The sweeper and link-boy watched him go. Then the link-boy nodded to the sweeper and slipped into the shadows in Scrugthorpe's wake.

Chapter Fifteen

The next morning, Harry was flat on his stomach deep in dreams, his arms wrapped about his pillow, when a large hand descended on his bare shoulder.

His response was instantaneous—half-rising, eyes wide, muscles tensed, fists clenching.

"Now, now!" Dawlish had wisely backed out of reach. "I wish as you'd get out of that habit—there ain't no angry husbands 'round here."

Eyes glittering, Harry hauled in a breath then expelled it irritably. Propping himself on one arm, he raked his hair out of his eyes. "What the devil's the time?"

"Nine," Dawlish replied, already at the wardrobe. "But you've got visitors."

"At *nine?*" Harry turned over and sat up.

"Salter—and he's brought that agent of the missus's—Mr Mabberly."

Harry blinked. Draping his arms over his knees, he stared at Dawlish. "I haven't married the damned woman yet."

"Just getting in some practice, like." Dawlish turned from the robe with a grey coat over his arm. "This do?"

Ten minutes later, Harry descended the narrow staircase, wondering if Lucinda would prefer a grander place when they stayed in town. He hoped she wouldn't—he'd been renting these rooms for the past ten years; they felt comfortable, like a well-worn coat.

He opened the door to his study and beheld his visitors, Salter standing by the desk, Mabberly, looking thoroughly uncomfortable, perched on the chair before it.

At sight of him, Mabberly rose.

"Good morning, Mabberly." Harry nodded and shut the door. "Salter."

Salter returned his nod but refrained from comment, his lips compressed as if holding the words back.

Stiff as a poker, Mr Mabberly inclined his head fractionally. "Mr Lester. I hope you'll forgive this intrusion but this gentleman—" he glanced at Salter "—is most insistent that I provide answers to questions regarding Mrs Babbacombe's affairs that I can only describe as highly confidential." Decidedly prim, Mr Mabberly brought his gaze back to Harry's face. "He tells me he's working for you."

"Indeed." Harry waved Mr Mabberly back to his chair and took his own behind the desk. "I'm afraid we are in pressing need of the information Mr Salter has requested of you, in a matter pertaining to Mrs Babbacombe's safety." As Harry had expected, the mention of Lucinda's safety stopped Mr Mabberly in his tracks. "That is," Harry smoothly continued, "assuming you do, in fact, know the answers?"

Mr Mabberly shifted, eyeing Harry somewhat warily. "As it happens, I do—it's necessary for one in my position, acting as the company's representative, to be absolutely certain just whose interests I'm representing." He shot a glance at Salter, then brought his gaze back to Harry. "But you mentioned Mrs Babbacombe's safety. How can the information you requested be important?"

Succinctly, Harry told him, detailing no more than the bare bones of the presumptive plot; Mr Mabberly was businessman enough to readily follow their hypothesis. As the

tale unfolded, his open features reflected shock, outrage—
and, eventually, a dogged determination.

"The cads!" Slightly flushed, he glanced at Harry. "You
say you intend taking out a warrant against them?"

Salter answered. "We've cause enough for a warrant *provided* we can find evidence on this guardianship business—
without that, their motive's uncertain."

"So." Harry fixed Mr Mabberly with a flat green gaze.
"The question is will you help us?"

"I'll do anything I can," Mr Mabberly vowed, his voice
ringing with fervour. Even he heard it. A trifle shocked, he
hurried to excuse it. "Mrs Babbacombe's been very good
to me, you understand—there aren't many who would appoint someone as relatively young as myself to such an important position."

"Of course." Harry smiled, endeavouring to make the
gesture as unthreatening as he could at that hour of the
morning. "And, as a loyal employee of Babbacombe and
Company, you would naturally be anxious to assist in ensuring your principals' personal safety."

"Indeed." Obviously more comfortable, Mr Mabberly sat
back. "Mrs Babbacombe is indeed Miss Babbacombe's sole
legal guardian." Again, a slight flush rose in his cheeks.
"I'm perfectly sure because, when I first took up my position, I was uncertain as to the point—so I asked. Mrs Babbacombe's always a model of business etiquette—she insisted I see the guardianship deed."

Salter straightened, his expression lightening. "So—not
only do you *know* she's the sole guardian—you can swear
to it?"

Mr Mabberly nodded, swivelling to look at Salter. "Certainly. I naturally felt obliged to read the document and
verify the seal. It was unquestionably genuine."

"Excellent!" Harry looked at Salter—the big man's face
was alight, his frame suddenly thrumming with harnessed
energy. "So we can get that warrant without further delay?"

"If Mr Mabberly here will come with me to the magistrate and swear to Mrs Babbacombe's status, I can't see anything that'll stop us. I've already got friends in the force standing by—they'll do the actual arrest but I, for one, definitely want to be there when they take Joliffe into custody."

"I'm prepared to come with you immediately, sir." Mr Mabberly stood. "From the sounds of it, the sooner this Joliffe person is a guest of His Majesty's government the better."

"I couldn't agree more." Harry stood and offered Mr Mabberly his hand. "And while you two are tying up Joliffe and his crew, I'll keep Mrs Babbacombe under my eye."

"Aye—that'd be wise." Salter shook hands with Harry and they all turned to the door. "Joliffe's got the makings of a fairly desperate character. It wouldn't hurt to keep the lady close—just until we've got him safely stowed. I'll send word the instant we've got the blackguards in custody, sir."

"Send word to me at Hallows House," Harry told him.

After seeing his guests to the hall, Harry returned to the study and quickly glanced through his letters. He looked up as Dawlish entered with a cup of coffee. "Here you are." Dawlish set the cup down on the blotter. "So—what's the sum of it, then?"

Harry told him.

"Hmm—so that clerk fellow's not so useless after all?"

Harry took a sip of his coffee. "I never said he was useless. Gormless. And I'm willing to accept that I might have misjudged him."

Dawlish nodded. "Good! Last day of this ramshackle business, then. Can't say I'm sad."

Harry snorted. "Nor I."

"I'll get breakfast on the table." Dawlish glanced at the long-case clock in the corner. "We've still an hour to go before we're due at Hallows House."

Harry set down his cup. "We'd best use the time to get

all tidy here—I expect to leave for Lester Hall later this evening.''

Dawlish looked back from the door, brows flying. ''Oh-ho! Finally going to take the plunge, are you? 'Bout time, if you ask me. Mind—wouldn't have thought you'd choose a family picnic to do it at—but it's your funeral.''

Harry lifted his head and glared but the door had already closed.

LATER THAT AFTERNOON, Harry recalled Dawlish's observation with grim resignation. Not in his wildest dreams had he imagined playing the most important scene of his life on such a stage.

They were seated on colourful coach rugs on a long grassy slope leading down to the gently rippling River Lea. Some miles north of Islington, not far from Stamford Hill, the woods and meadows close by the river provided a pleasant spot for young families and those seeking a draught of country peace. Although some way down the low escarpment, their position afforded them an uninterrupted view over the river valley, meadows giving way to marshland, water glinting in the sun. Roads meandered through the marshes, leading to Walthamstow, just beyond the valley. Oaks and beeches at their backs shielded them from the sun; the haze of a glorious afternoon surrounded them. Bees buzzed, flitting from fieldflower to hedgerow bloom; doves cooed overhead.

Harry drew in a deep breath—and shot a considering glance at Lucinda, stretched out beside him. Beyond her reclined Em, her hat over her face. On a neighbouring rug sat Heather and Gerald, engrossed in animated discourse. Beyond them, at a suitable distance, perched on and about a collection of fallen logs, sat Agatha and Em's even more severe dresser, together with Em's coachman, Dawlish, Joshua, Sim and the little maid Amy. In their dark clothes, they looked like so many crows.

Harry grimaced and looked away. Fate had chosen a fine moment to turn fickle.

The instant he had realised that it was Heather's guardian-ship that was Joliffe and Mortimer Babbacombe's goal, he had determined to come between them and Lucinda with all possible speed. By marrying her, he would assume legal responsibility in all such matters—automatically, without question. It was the one, absolutely guaranteed way of pro-tecting her, of shielding her from their machinations.

But her yesterday had been filled with preparations for the soirée; the household had been at sixes and sevens. He hadn't liked his prospects of finding a quiet moment, let alone a quiet corner to propose.

As for today, they had organised this outing a week ago as a quiet relaxation away from the *ton* after the excitement of the soirée. They had come in two carriages, Em's and Lucinda's, the menservants riding atop; Agatha and Amy had shared Lucinda's carriage with their mistress and him-self. They had lunched surrounded by sunshine and peace. Now Em looked set for her postprandial nap; it would prob-ably be at least an hour before hunger again prodded Heather and Gerald to a more general awareness.

So, since learning of her danger, this was his first chance to remove her from it. Hiding his determination behind an easy expression, Harry got to his feet. Lucinda looked up, putting up her hand to shield her eyes. Harry smiled reas-suringly down at her before lifting his gaze to her drab watchdogs. With a slight movement of his head, he sum-moned Dawlish, then strolled back towards the trees. When he was out of earshot of his intended and his aunt, he stopped and waited for Dawlish to reach him.

"Something wrong?"

Harry smiled politely. "No. I just thought I'd let it be known that, when I take Mrs Babbacombe for a stroll in a few moments, we won't need an escort." When Dawlish screwed up his eyes, as if considering arguing, Harry continued, his tone growing steely, ''She'll be perfectly safe with me.''

Dawlish humphed. ''Can't say as I blame you. Cramp anyone's style, it would, having to go down on your knees before an audience.''

Harry raised his eyes heavenwards in a mute gesture of appeal.

''I'll tell the others.''

Harry hurriedly lowered his gaze but Dawlish was already stomping back through the trees. Muttering a curse, Harry did the same, returning to the rugs on the grass.

''Come for a walk.''

Lucinda glanced up at the soft words—which cloaked what sounded like a command. Beside her, Em was gently snoring; Heather and Gerald were in a world of their own. She met Harry's eyes, very green; he raised a brow and held out his hand. Lucinda studied it for an instant, savouring the thrill of anticipation that shot through her, then, with studied calm, laid her fingers in his.

Harry drew her to her feet. Tucking her hand in his arm, he turned her towards the leafy woods.

The woods were not extensive, merely stands of trees separating fields and meadows. They strolled without words, leaving the others behind, until they came to a large field left fallow. The meadow grasses and flowers had taken over; the ground was carpeted in a shifting sea of small bright blooms.

Lucinda sighed. ''How lovely.'' She smiled up at Harry.

Engaged in scanning their surroundings, he glanced back at her in time to return her smile. The trees screened them from their companions and any others strolling the river banks; they were not isolated but as private as, in the circumstances, it was probably wise to be. He gestured ahead; by unvoiced agreement, they strolled to the centre of the field where a large rock, weathered to smoothness, created a natural seat.

With a swirl of her blue muslin skirts, Lucinda sat. Harry noticed that her gown matched the cornflowers scattered through the grass. She had worn a new bonnet but had let it fall to dangle by its ribbons on her back, leaving her face unshadowed. She lifted her head and her gaze met his.

Stillness held them, then her delicate brows arched slightly, in query, in invitation.

Harry scanned her face, then drew in a deep breath.

"Ah-hem!"

They both turned to see Dawlish striding across the field. Harry bit back a curse. "What *now?*"

Dawlish cast him a sympathetic glance. "There's a messenger come—'bout that business this morning."

Harry groaned. "Now?"

Dawlish met his eye. "Thought as how you might think it better to get that matter all tied and tight—before you get…distracted, like."

Harry grimaced—Dawlish had a point.

"Set on seeing you specifically, this messenger—said as that was his orders." Dawlish nodded back at the trees. "Said he'd wait by the stile yonder."

Swallowing his irritation, Harry shot a considering glance at Lucinda; she met it with an affectionate smile. Spending five minutes to acknowledge the end of Joliffe's threat would leave him free to concentrate on her—wholly, fully, without reservation. Without further interruption. Harry looked at Dawlish. "Which stile?"

"It's along the fence a little way."

"We didn't pass a fence."

Dawlish frowned and surveyed the woods through which he'd come. "It's that way—and around to the left, I think." He scratched his head. "Or is it the right?"

"Why don't you just show Mr Lester the way?"

Harry turned at Lucinda's words. She had plucked some blooms and started to plait them. He frowned. "I'll find the stile. Dawlish will stay here with you."

Lucinda snorted. "Nonsense! You'll take twice as long." She picked a cornflower from her lap, then tilted her face to look up at him, one brow arching. "The sooner you get there, the sooner you'll be back."

Harry hesitated, then shook his head. Joliffe might be behind bars but his protective instincts still ran strong. "No. I'll—"

"Don't be absurd! I'm perfectly capable of sitting on a rock in the sunshine for a few minutes alone." Lucinda lifted both arms to gesture about her. "What *do* you imagine could happen in such a sylvan setting?"

Harry glared, briefly, aware she would very likely be perfectly safe. Hands on hips, he scanned the surrounding trees. There was open space all around her; no one could creep up and surprise her. She was a mature and sensible woman; she would scream if anything untoward occurred. And they were all close enough to hear.

And the sooner he met with Salter's messenger, the sooner he could concentrate on her, on them, on their future.

"Very well." His expression hard, he pointed a finger at her. "But stay there and don't move!"

Her answering smile was fondly condescending.

Harry turned and strode quickly across the field; the damned woman's confidence in herself was catching.

Like many countrymen, Dawlish could retrace his steps to anywhere but could never describe the way. He took the lead; within a matter of minutes, they found the fence line. They followed it to a small clearing in which stood the stile—surrounded by a small army of people.

Harry halted. "What the devil…?"

Salter pushed through the crowd. Harry caught sight of Mabberley and three representatives of Bow Street among a motley crew of ostlers, grooms and stablelads, link-boys, jarveys, street urchins, sweepers—basically any likely looking scruffs to be found on the streets of London. Obviously Salter's "people".

Then Salter stood before him, his face decidedly grim. "We got the warrant but when we went to serve it, Joliffe and his crew had done a bunk."

Harry stiffened. "I thought you were watching them?"

"We were." Salter's expression grew bleaker. "But someone must have tripped up somewhere—we found our two watchers coshed over the head this morning—and no sign of our pigeons anywhere."

Harry's mind raced; chill fingers clutched his gut. "Have they taken the coach?"

"Yep," came from one of the ostlers. "Seems like they left 'bout ten—just afore the captain here came with his bill."

Mr Mabberly stepped forward. "We thought we should warn you to keep an especially close eye on Mrs Babbacombe—until we can get this villain behind bars."

Harry barely heard him. His expression had blanked. *"Oh, my God!"*

He whirled and raced back the way he'd come, Dawlish on his heels. The rest, galvanised by Harry's fear, followed.

Harry broke from the trees and scanned the field—then came to a skidding halt.

Before him the meadow grasses swayed in the breeze. All was peaceful and serene, the field luxuriating in the heat. The sun beat down on the rock in its centre—now empty.

Harry stared. Then he strode forward, his expression like flint. A short chain of blue cornflowers had been left on the rock—laid down gently, not flung or mauled.

Breathing rapidly, Harry, hands on hips, lifted his head and looked about. "Lucinda?"

His call faded into the trees—no one answered.

Harry swore. "They've got her." The words burned his throat.

"They can't have got far." Salter gestured to his people. "It's the lady we're after—tallish, dark-haired—most of you've seen her. Name of Mrs Babbacombe."

Within seconds, they were quartering the area, quickly, efficiently, calling her name, threshing through undergrowth. Harry headed towards the river, Dawlish beside him. His throat was already hoarse. His imagination was a handicap—he could conjure visions far too well. He had to find her—he simply had to.

LEFT IN THE PEACE of the meadow, Lucinda smiled to herself, then settled to convert the cornflowers growing in abundance around the base of the rock into a blue garland. Beneath her calm, she was impatient enough, yet quite confident Harry would shortly be back.

Her smile deepened. She reached for a bright dandelion to lend contrast to her string.

"Mrs Babbacombe! Er—Aunt Lucinda?"

Blinking, Lucinda turned. She searched the shadows beneath the trees and saw a slight, shortish gentleman waving and beckoning.

"Good lord! Whatever does *he* want?" Laying aside her garland, she crossed to the trees. "Mortimer?" She ducked under a branch and stepped into the cool shade. "What are you doing here?"

"A-waiting for you, bitch," came in a growling grating voice.

Lucinda jumped; a huge paw wrapped about her arm. Her eyes widened in incredulous amazement as she took in its owner. "*Scrugthorpe!* What the devil do you think you're doing?"

"Grabbing you." Scrugthorpe leered, then started to drag her deeper into the trees. "Come on—the carriage's waiting."

"What carriage? Oh, for goodness' sake!" Lucinda was about to struggle in earnest when Mortimer took her other elbow.

"This is all most distressing—but if you'll only listen— it's really nothing to do with you, you know—simply a mat-

ter of righting a wrong—fixing a slight—that sort of thing.''
He wasn't so much helping to drag her along as clinging to
her arm; his eyes, a weak washy blue, implored her understanding.

Lucinda frowned. "What on earth is all this about?"

Mortimer told her—in disjointed phrases, bits and pieces,
dribs and drabs. Totally engrossed in trying to follow his
tale, Lucinda largely ignored Scrugthorpe and his dogged
march forward, absent-mindedly letting him pull her along,
shifting her attention only enough to lift her skirts over a
log.

"Damned hoity female!" Scrugthorpe kicked at her
skirts. "When I get you alone, I'm going to—"

"And then, you see, there was the money owed to Joliffe—must pay, y'know—play and pay—honour and all
that—"

"And after that, I'll tie you up good—"

"So it turned out to be rather a lot—not impossible but—
had to find it, you see—thought I'd be right after Uncle
Charles died—but then it wasn't there—the money, I
mean—but I'd already spent it—owed it—had to raise the
wind somehow—"

"Oh, I'll make you pay for your sharp tongue, I will.
After I've done, you'll—"

Lucinda shut her ears to Scrugthrope's ravings and concentrated on Mortimer's babblings. Her jaw dropped when
he revealed their ultimate goal; their plan to reach it was
even more astonishing. Mortimer finally concluded with,
"So, you see—all simple enough. If you'll just make the
guardianship over to me, it'll all be right and tight—you do
see that, don't you?"

They had reached the edge of the river; a narrow foot-
bridge lay ahead. Abruptly, Lucinda hauled back against
Scrugthorpe's tow and stood her ground. Her gaze, positively scathing, fixed on Mortimer.

"You ass!" Her tone said it all. "Do you really believe

that, just because you're so weak and stupid as to get…?'' Words momentarily failed her; she wrenched her elbow from Mortimer's grasp and gestured wildly. ''Gulled by a sharp.'' Eyes flashing, she transfixed Mortimer; he stood rooted to the spot, his mouth silently opening and shutting, his expression that of a terrified rabbit facing the ultimate fury. ''That I will meekly hand over to you my stepdaughter's fortune so you can line the pockets of some cunning, immoral, inconsiderate, rapacious, fly-by-night excuse for a man?'' Her voice had risen, gaining in commanding volume. ''You've got *rocks* in your head, sir!''

''Now see here.'' Scrugthorpe, somewhat dazed by her vehemence, shook her arm. ''That's enough of that.''

Mortimer was exceedingly pale. ''But Uncle Charles owed me—''

''Nonsense! Charles owed you *nothing!* Indeed, you got more than you deserved. What you have to do, Mortimer,'' Lucinda jabbed him in the chest, ''is get back to Yorkshire and get your affairs in order. Talk to Mr Wilson in Scarborough—he'll know how to help. Stand on your own feet, Mortimer—believe me, it's the only way.'' Struck by a thought, Lucinda asked, ''Incidentally, how is Mrs Finnigan, the cook? When we left she had ulcers, poor thing—is she better?''

Mortimer simply stared at her.

''*Enough*, woman!'' Scrugthorpe, his face mottling, swung Lucinda about. Opting for action rather than words, he grabbed her by the shoulders and pulled her to him. Lucinda uttered a small shriek and ducked her head—just in time to avoid Scrugthorpe's fleshy lips. He grunted; she felt his fingers grip her shoulders tightly, bruising her soft flesh. She struggled, rocking to keep him off balance. Her gaze directed downwards, she saw his feet, clad in soft leather shoes, shuffling to gain greater stability. Lucinda lifted her knee, inadvertently striking Scrugthorpe in the groin. She heard his sharp intake of breath—and brought her boot heel down with all the force she could muster, directly onto his left instep.

"*Ow!* You *bitch!*" His voice was crazed with pain.

Lucinda jerked her head up—her crown connected with Scrugthorpe's chin with a most satisfying crack. Scrugthorpe yowled. He put one hand to his foot and the other to his chin—Lucinda was free. She whisked herself away—and Mortimer grabbed her.

Furious, she beat at his hands, his face; he was no Scrugthorpe—she broke free easily enough, pushing Mortimer into a bush in the process. Gasping, dragging much needed air into her lungs, Lucinda picked up her skirts and fled onto the bridge. Behind her, Scrugthorpe, swearing foully, hobbled in pursuit.

Lucinda cast a quick glance behind—and ran faster.

She looked ahead and saw a gentleman striding onto the other end of the bridge. He was dressed neatly in riding breeches and top coat and wore Hessians. Lucinda thanked her stars and waved. "Sir!" Here, surely, was one who would aid her.

To her surprise, he stopped, standing with his feet apart, blocking the exit to the bridge. Lucinda blinked, and slowed. She halted in the centre of the bridge.

The man had a pistol in his hand.

It was, Lucinda thought, as she slowly watched it rise, one of those long-barrelled affairs gentlemen were said to use when duelling. The sun struck its silver mountings, making them gleam. Beneath her, the river gurgled onwards to the sea; in the wide sky above, the larks swooped and trilled. Distantly, she heard her name called but the cries were too weak to break the web that held her.

A chill spread over her skin.

Slowly, the pistol rose, until the barrel was level with her chest.

Her mouth dry, her heart pounding in her ears, Lucinda

looked into the man's face. It was blank, expressionless. She saw his fingers shift and heard a telltale click.

A hundred yards downstream, Harry broke through the woods and gained the river path. Panting, he looked around—then glanced up at the bridge. He froze.

Two heartbeats passed as he watched his future, his life, his love—all he had ever wanted—face certain death. Salter and some of his men were on the opposite bank, closing fast, but they would never reach Joliffe in time. Still others were rushing for this end of the bridge. Harry saw the pistol level—saw the slight upward adjustment necessary to bring the aim to true.

"Lucinda!"

The cry was wrenched from him, filled with despair and rage—and something more powerful than both. It sliced through the mesmeric daze that held Lucinda.

She turned, her hand on the wooden rail—and saw Harry on the nearby shore. Lucinda blinked. Safety lay with Harry. The rail was a simple one, a single wooden top-rail supported by intermittent posts. Before her, the area below the rail was empty, open. She put both hands on the rail and let herself drop through.

She plummeted to the river as the shot rang out.

Harry watched her fall. He had no idea whether she'd been hit or not. She entered the river with a splash; when it cleared, there was no sign of her.

Cursing, Harry raced forward, scanning the river. Could she swim? He reached the bank just short of the bridge and sat down. He was tugging off one boot when Lucinda surfaced. Pushing her hair out of her eyes, she looked about and saw him. She waved, then, as if she went swimming in rivers every day, calmly stroked for shore.

Harry stared. Then, his expression hardening, he slammed his foot back in his boot. He rose and strode to the river's edge. His emotions clashing wildly, swinging from elation to rage with sufficient intensity to make him dizzy, he stood on the bank and waited for her to reach him.

He had lost Dawlish somewhere in the woods; those of Salter's people who had been near, seeing him waiting, wisely left him to it. He was distantly aware of the commotions engulfing both ends of the bridge but he didn't even spare them a glance. Later, they learned that Mr Mabberly had distinguished himself by laying Mortimer Babbacombe low while Dawlish had taken great pleasure in scientifically darkening the daylights of the iniquitous Scrugthorpe.

Gaining the shallows, Lucinda stood and glanced back at the bridge. Satisfied that her attackers were being dealt with as they deserved, she reached behind her and caught hold of her dripping hat. Tugging the wet ribbons from about her neck, she stared in dismay at the limp creation. "It's ruined!" she wailed.

Then she looked down. "And my dress!"

Harry couldn't take anymore. The damned woman had nearly got killed and all she was concerned with was the fate of her hat. He strode into the shallow water to stand towering by her side.

Still mourning her headgear, Lucinda gestured at it. "It's beyond resurrection." She looked up at him—in time to see his eyes flare.

Harry slapped her wet bottom—hard enough to leave his palm stinging.

Lucinda jumped and yelped. "Ow!" She stared at him in stunned surprise.

"The next time I tell you to stay where I leave you and *not* to move you will do precisely *that*—do I make myself clear?" Harry glared down at her, into eyes that, even now, held a hint of mutinous determination. Then his gaze fell to her breasts. He blinked. "Good lord! Your dress!" Immediately, he shrugged off his coat.

Lucinda sniffed. "Precisely what I said." With injured dignity, she accepted the coat he placed about her shoulders—she even allowed him to do up the buttons, closing it loosely about her.

"Come—I'm taking you home immediately." Harry took her elbow and helped her onto the bank. "You're soaked—the last thing I need is for you to take a chill."

Lucinda tried to look back at the bridge. "That was Mortimer back there, you know."

"Yes, I know." Harry drew her into the woods.

"You do?" Lucinda blinked. "He had some strange idea that Charles had done him out of his rightful inheritance, you know, that—"

Harry let her fill his ears with an account of Mortimer's justification of his deeds as he steered her through the woods. It was infinitely reassuring to hear her voice. His fear that she might suffer from delayed shock receded, lulled by her calm and logical recital, her unflustered observations. She was, he had to grudgingly, somewhat astonishingly concede, totally unaffected by her ordeal. *He* was a nervous wreck. He led her directly to the carriages.

Lucinda blinked when they appeared before them. "But what about the others?"

Harry hauled open the door of her carriage as Joshua and Dawlish hurried up. "We can leave a message for Em and Heather—Mabberly can explain."

"Mr Mabberly?" Lucinda was astonished. "Is he here?"

Harry cursed his loose tongue. "Yes. Now get in." He didn't wait for her to do so—he picked her up and put her in. Joshua was already climbing to the box; Harry turned to Dawlish. "Go back and explain everything to Em and Miss Babbacombe—assure them Mrs Babbacombe's taken no hurt other than a soaking."

From inside the carriage came a definite sniff. Harry's palm tingled. He put a foot on the carriage step. "I'm taking her back to Hallows House—we'll wait for them there."

Dawlish nodded. "All the rest's taken care of."

Harry nodded. He turned back to the carriage, remembering to grab his greatcoat, left on the rack atop, before he ducked through the door. Dawlish shut it behind him and slapped the coach's side. It lurched into motion; heaving a heavy sigh, Harry subsided onto the seat and shut his eyes.

He remained thus for a full minute; Lucinda watched him somewhat warily. Then he opened his eyes, tossed his greatcoat onto the opposite seat, and reached out and systematically let down all the blinds. The sun still penetrated the thin leather, suffusing the interior with a golden glow.

"Ah…" Before Lucinda could decide what to say, Harry sat back, reached for her and hauled her onto his lap.

Lucinda opened her lips on a token protest—he captured them in a long, searing kiss, his lips hard on hers, demanding, commanding, ravishing her senses until her thoughts melted away and took her wits with them. She kissed him back with equal fervour, perfectly willing to take all he offered.

When he finally consented to raise his head, she lay against his chest, dazedly blinking up at him, with not two thoughts to her name.

The sight filled Harry with a certain satisfaction. With an approving grunt, he closed his eyes and let his head fall back against the squabs. "If you ever do anything like that again, you'd better be prepared to eat standing up for the following week. At least."

Lucinda threw him a darkling glance and reached a hand to her abused posterior. "It still hurts."

Harry's lips lifted. He raised his lids enough to look down at her. "Perhaps I should kiss it better?"

Her eyes flew wide—then she looked intrigued.

Harry caught his breath. "Perhaps we'd better leave that until later."

Lucinda raised a brow. She held his gaze, then shrugged and snuggled closer. "I didn't plan to be set upon, you know. And who were all those people?"

"Never mind." Harry juggled her around so she was sitting on his knees facing him. ''There's something I want to say—and I'm only going to say it once.'' His eyes met hers. ''Are you listening?''

Lucinda drew in a breath—and couldn't let it out. Her heart in her mouth, she nodded.

''I love you.''

Lucinda's face lit up. She leaned towards him, her lips parting—Harry held up a restraining hand.

''No—wait. I haven't finished.'' He held her with his eyes. Then his lips twisted. ''Such words from a man such as I can hardly be convincing. You know I've said them before—in reams. And they weren't true—not then.'' His hand found hers where it rested on his chest; he raised her fingers to his lips. ''Before you came along, I didn't know what the words meant—now I do. But I couldn't expect you to find the words convincing, when I wouldn't myself. So I've given you all the proof that I can—I've taken you to visit with my father, shown you my ancestral home.'' Lucinda blinked—Harry continued with his list. ''You've seen the stud and I've shown you the house that I hope we'll make our home.'' He paused, eyes glinting, lips lifting at the ends as he met Lucinda's gaze. ''And I *was* joking about the six children—four will do nicely.''

Breathless, dazed, giddy with happiness, Lucinda opened her eyes wide. ''Only four?'' She let her lids fall. ''You disappoint me, sir.''

Harry shifted. ''Perhaps we can settle on four to begin with? I wouldn't, after all, wish to disappoint you.''

Lucinda's rare dimple appeared in her cheek.

Harry frowned. ''Now where was I? Ah, yes—the proofs of my devotion. I accompanied you back to London and drove you in the Park, I danced attendance on you in every conceivable way—I even braved the dangers of Almack's.'' His eyes held hers. ''All for you.''

''Is *that* why you did it—to convince me you loved me?''

Lucinda felt as if her heart would burst. She had only to look into his eyes to know the truth.

Harry's lips twisted in a self-deprecatory grin. "Why else?" He gestured expansively. "What else could move me to prostrate myself at your feet?" He glanced at them—and frowned. "Which, incidentally, are very wet." He reached down and eased off her sodden boots. That done, he pushed up her wet skirts and started on her garters.

Lucinda smiled. "And you danced three waltzes with me—remember?"

"How could I forget?" Harry returned, busy rolling down her stockings. "A more public declaration I cannot imagine."

Lucinda giggled and wriggled her chilled toes.

Harry straightened and met her eyes. "So, Mrs Lucinda Babbacombe—after all my sterling efforts—do you believe me when I say I love you?"

Lucinda's smile lit her eyes. She reached up both hands to frame his face. "Silly man—you had only to say." Gently, she touched her lips to his.

When she drew back, Harry snorted disbelievingly. "And you'd have believed me? Even after my *faux pas* that afternoon you seduced me?"

Lucinda's smile was soft. "Oh, yes." Her dimple came back. "Even then."

Harry decided to leave it at that. "So you agree to marry me without further fuss?"

Lucinda nodded once, decisively.

"Thank heaven for that." Harry closed his arms about her. "We're getting married in two days at Lester Hall—it's all arranged. I've got the licence in my pocket." He glanced down and saw the damp patches on his coat, close about her. He frowned and lifted her back so she was once more sitting upright on his knee. "I hope you haven't got it wet enough for the ink to run." He undid the coat buttons and lifted the garment from her.

Lucinda laughed, so delirious with happiness she couldn't contain it. She reached out and drew his head to hers and kissed him longingly. The kiss deepened, then Harry disengaged.

"You're very wet. We should get you out of these things."

Siren-like, Lucinda raised her brows, then obediently turned so he could undo her laces. He eased her from her gown, dropping it to the floor where it landed with a soft splat.

Her chemise, drenched and all but transparent, clung like a second skin. A soft blush rose beneath it; Lucinda let her lids veil her eyes, watching Harry's hands from beneath her lashes as, gently yet deliberately, he peeled the delicate material from her.

Harry sensed the heat rising within her, heard the sudden shallow intake of her breath as he drew the last shred of concealment from her. She shivered—but he didn't think it was due to being cold. Drawing in a deep breath, she raised her eyes to his.

Lucinda looked into eyes brilliantly green, screened by heavy lids; nothing could hide the desire that burned in their peridot depths.

She sat naked on his lap. His hands moved gently over her, over her back, over her arms, languidly stroking, caressing. He leaned forward and pressed kisses to the bruises Scrugthorpe had left on her shoulders. Lucinda shuddered. Unbidden, entirely unexpected, a long-forgotten conversation drifted through her mind. Eyes agleam, she chuckled softly.

Harry stared at her hungrily, the siren who had lured him to his doom. Clinging to sanity, he raised a brow in the nearest he could get to languid enquiry.

Lucinda laughed. She caught his eyes with hers, then, leaning closer, let her lids screen her eyes. "Em once said," she murmured, "that I should aim to get you on your knees.'' Fleetingly, she lifted her eyes to his, her lips gently curved. ''I don't think she meant it in quite this way.''

The body beneath her was hard, rigid, powerful but harnessed.

''Ah, yes. An eminently wise old lady, my aunt.'' Gently, Harry lifted Lucinda, settling her so she was straddling his knees, her knees on the seat on either side of his hips. ''But she tends to forget that—sometimes—it's very hard for a rake to—er—change his spots.''

Lucinda wasn't at all sure about her change in position. ''Ah, Harry?''

''Hmm?'' Harry wasn't interested in further conversation.

Lucinda realised as much when he urged her towards him and his lips closed gently about one tightly furled nipple. Her breath caught. ''Harry—we're in a carriage.''

Her protest was breathless. His lips left her; he put out his tongue and rasped her sensitised flesh. Lucinda shuddered and closed her eyes; his hands on her hips held her steady—every time she caught her breath, he stole it away. ''You can't be serious,'' she eventually managed to gasp. She paused—then sucked in a quick breath. ''Not here? In a moving carriage?''

His answering chuckle sounded devilish. ''Perfectly possible, I assure you.'' His hands shifted. ''The rocking's part of the fun—you'll see.''

Lucinda struggled to draw her mind from the sensual web he had so skilfully woven. ''Yes, but—'' Abruptly, her eyes flew open. ''*Dear heaven!*'' After a stunned moment, her lids fell. She whispered, a soft catch in her voice, ''Harry?''

A long moment of breathy silence ensued, then Lucinda sighed—deeply. ''Oh, *Harry!*''

AN HOUR LATER, as the carriage slowly rolled into the leafy streets of Mayfair, Harry looked down at the woman in his lap. She was curled snugly in his greatcoat, dry and warm—he was prepared to swear no chill could have survived the fire that had recently claimed them. Her clothes lay in a sodden heap on the floor; his coat and breeches would keep Dawlish occupied for hours. Harry didn't care—he had all he most wanted of life.

He glanced down—and dropped a kiss on her curls.

He'd been a most unwilling conquest but he was ready to admit he was well and truly conquered.

Tipping his head, he looked into his siren's face, blissful in repose.

She stirred, then snuggled closer against him, one hand on his chest, over his heart.

Harry smiled, closed his eyes—and closed his arms about her.

A Comfortable Wife

Chapter One

"Thirty-Four, my dear Hugo, is a decidedly sobering age."

"Heh?" Startled from somnolence, Hugo Satterly opened one cautious eye and studied the long-limbed figure gracefully lounging on the opposite carriage seat. "Why's that?"

Philip Augustus Marlowe, seventh Baron Ruthven, did not deign to answer—not directly. Instead, his gaze on the summer scenery slipping past the carriage window, he remarked, "I would never have thought to see Jack and Harry Lester competing over who would provide the first of the next generation of Lesters."

Hugo straightened. "Tricky prediction, that. Jack suggested laying odds but Lucinda heard of it." Hugo grimaced. "That was the end of it, of course. Said she wasn't about to have us all watching her and Sophie, counting the days. Pity."

A fleeting smile touched Philip's lips. "An uncommonly sensible woman, Lucinda." After a moment he added, more to himself than to his friend, "And Jack was lucky with his Sophie, too."

They were returning from a week's house party at Lester Hall; the festivities had been presided over by Sophie, Mrs Jack Lester, ably seconded by Lucinda, now Harry Lester's bride. Both recent additions to the Lester family tree were discreetly but definitely *enceinte,* and radiant with it. The unabashed happiness that had filled the rambling old house had infected everyone.

But the week had drawn to its inevitable close; Philip was conscious that, despite the calm and orderly ambiance of his ancestral home, there would be no such warmth, no promise for the future, awaiting him there. The idea that he had invited Hugo, a friend of many years, confirmed bachelor and infrequent rake, to join him solely as a distraction, to turn his thoughts from the depressing path he saw opening before him, floated through his mind. He tried to ignore it.

He shifted in his seat, listening to the regular pounding of his carriage horses' hooves, firmly fixing his attention on the ripening fields—only to have Hugo ruthlessly haul his problem into the light.

"Well—I suppose you'll be next." Hugo settled his shoulders against the squabs and gazed at the fields with unruffled calm. "Dare say that's what's making you glum."

Narrowing his eyes, Philip fixed them on Hugo's innocent visage. "Surrendering to the bonds of matrimony, walking *knowingly* into parson's mousetrap, is hardly a pleasant thought."

"Don't think of it at all myself."

Philip's expression turned decidedly sour. A gentleman of independent means and nought but distant family, Hugo had no need to wed. Philip's case was very different.

"Don't see why you need make such a mountain of it, though." Hugo glanced across the carriage. "Imagine your stepmother'll be only too happy to line up the young ladies—all you need do is look 'em over and make your selection."

"Being no less female than the rest of them, I'm certain Henrietta would be only too glad to assist. However," Philip continued, his tone tending steely, "should she be mistaken in one of her candidates, 'tis *I,* not she, who will pay the price. For life. No, I thank you. If mistakes capable of wrecking my life are to be made, I'd rather make them myself.''

Hugo shrugged. ''If that's the case, you'll have to make your own list. Go through the debs, check their backgrounds, make sure they can actually speak and not just giggle and that they won't simper over the breakfast cups.'' He wrinkled his nose. ''Dull work.''

''Depressing work.'' Philip shifted his gaze once more to the scenery.

''Pity there aren't more like Sophie or Lucinda about.''

''Indeed.'' Philip delivered the word tersely; to his relief, Hugo took the hint and shut up, settling back to doze.

The carriage rattled on.

Reluctantly, Philip allowed his likely future to take shape in his mind, envisioning his life with one of society's belles by his side. His visions were unappealing. Disgusted, he banished them and determinedly set his mind to formulating a list of all the qualities he would insist on in his wife.

Loyalty, reasonable wit, beauty to an acceptable degree— all these were easy to define. But there was a nebulous something he knew Jack and Harry Lester had found which he could find no words to describe.

That vital ingredient was yet proving elusive when the carriage turned through tall gateposts and rumbled down the drive to Ruthven Manor. Tucked neatly into a dip of the Sussex Downs, the manor was an elegant Georgian residence built on the remains of earlier halls. The sun, still high, sent gilded fingers to caress the pale stone; stray sunbeams, striking through the surrounding trees, glinted on long, plain windows and highlighted the creepers softening the austere lines.

His home. The thought resonated in Philip's head as he descended from the carriage, the gravel of the forecourt crunching beneath his boots. With a glance behind to confirm that Hugo had awoken and was, in fact, alighting, he led the way up the steps.

As he approached, the front doors were set wide; Fenton, butler at the Manor since Philip had been in short-coats, waited, straight as a poker but smiling, beside them.

"Welcome home, my lord." Deftly, Fenton relieved his master of his hat and gloves.

"Thank you, Fenton." Philip gestured as Hugo strolled in. "Mr Satterly will be staying for a few days." Unencumbered by ancestral acres, Hugo was a frequent visitor to the Manor.

Fenton bowed, then reached for Hugo's hat. "I'll have your usual room made ready, sir."

Hugo smiled in easy acquiescence.

Completing a brief scan of his hall, Philip turned back to Fenton. "And how is her ladyship?"

On the floor above, poised at the top of the grand staircase, her head cocked to listen, Antonia Mannering decided that his voice was deeper than she remembered it. His question, however, was quite obviously her cue.

Drawing in a deep breath, she closed her eyes in fleeting supplication, then opened them and started down. In a hurry. Not so precipitously as to be labelled hoydenish but rapidly enough to appear unconscious of the arrivals presently in the hall. She cleared the landing and started down the last flight, her eyes on the treads, one hand lightly skimming the balustrade. "Fenton, her ladyship wishes Trant to be sent up as soon as may be." Only then did she allow herself to glance up.

"Oh!" Her exclamation was perfectly gauged, containing just the right combination of surprise and fluster; she had practised for hours. Antonia slowed, then halted, her gaze transfixed. As it transpired, she needed no guile to make her eyes widen, her lips part in surprise.

The scene before her was not as she had pictured it—not exactly. Philip was there, of course, turning from Fenton to view her, his strongly arched brows lifting, his eyes, grey, as she knew, reflecting nothing more than polite surprise.

Swiftly, she scanned his features: the wide brow, heavy-lidded eyes and strongly patrician nose, the finely drawn lips above a firm and resolute chin. There was nothing in his expression, mildly distant, to cause her heart to beat wildly. Nevertheless, her pulse started to gallop; her breathing slowly seized. Panic of a wholly unprecedented nature fluttered to life within her.

His gaze dropped from her face; snatching in a breath, Antonia grabbed a dizzying moment to take in his broad-shouldered frame. Freed by a smooth shrug, a many-caped greatcoat slid into Fenton's waiting arms; the coat thus revealed was an unremarkable grey but so distinguished by line and form that not even she could doubt its origins. Brown hair waved in elegant disorder; his cravat was a collage of precise folds secured by a winking gold pin. Buckskin breeches clung to his long legs, outlining the powerful muscles of his thighs before disappearing into highly polished Hessians.

Dragging in a second breath, Antonia hauled her gaze back to his face. In the same instant, his eyes lifted and met hers.

He held her gaze, a frown in his eyes. His gaze shifted, focused on her hair, then dropped to her face. His frown dissolved into undisguised amazement.

"Antonia?"

Philip heard astonishment echo in his voice. Mentally cursing, he struggled to recapture his habitually indolent air, a task not aided by the fleeting smile Antonia Mannering cast him before gathering her skirts and descending the last stairs.

He stood anchored to the tiles as she glided towards him. His mind reeled, juggling memories, trying to reconcile them with the slender goddess crossing his hall, calm serenity in her heart-shaped face, a gown of sprig muslin cloaking a figure he unhesitatingly classed as exemplary.

The last time he had seen her she'd been only sixteen, thin and coltish but even then graceful. Now she moved like a sylph, as if her feet barely touched solid earth. He remembered her as a breath of fresh air, bringing ready laughter, open smiles and an unquenchable if imperious friendliness every summer she had visited. Her lips now bore an easy smile, yet the expression in her eyes, as she neared, was guarded.

As he watched, the curve of her lips deepened and she held out her hand.

"Indeed, my lord. It is some years since last we met. Pray excuse me." With an airy wave, Antonia indicated her descent from above. "I hadn't realized you'd arrived." Smiling serenely, she met his eyes. "Welcome home."

Feeling as if Harry Lester had scored a direct hit to his jaw, Philip reached out and took her fingers in his. They quivered; instinctively, he tightened his grip. His gaze dropped to her lips, drawn irresistibly to the delectable curves; he forced his eyes upward, only to become lost in a haze of gold and green. Dragging himself free, he lifted his gaze to her lustrous golden curls.

"You've cut your hair." His tone reflected his dazed state as clearly as it did his disappointment.

Antonia blinked. One hand still trapped in his, she hesitantly put the other to the curls bouncing above one ear. "No. It's all still there…just…twisted up."

Philip's lips formed a silent "Oh".

The odd look Antonia threw him, and Hugo's urgent cough, hauled him back to earth with a thump. Thrusting aside the impulse to pull a few pins and reassure himself that her golden mane was indeed as he recalled, he drew in a definite breath and released her. "Allow me to present Mr Satterly, a close friend. Hugo—Miss Mannering. My stepmother's niece."

Hugo's suave greeting and Antonia's unaffected reply gave Philip time to repair his defences. When Antonia turned back, he smiled urbanely. "I take it you finally succumbed to Henrietta's pleas?"

Her expression open, Antonia met his gaze. "Our year of mourning was behind us. The time seemed ripe to visit."

Resisting an unexpected urge to grin delightedly, Philip contented himself with, "My humble house is honoured—it's a pleasure to see you within its walls again. I hope you've planned an extended stay—having you by will greatly ease Henrietta's mind."

A subtle smile curved Antonia's lips. "Indeed? But there are many factors which might influence how long we remain." She held Philip's gaze for an instant longer, then turned to smile at Hugo. "But I'm keeping you standing. My aunt is presently resting." Antonia glanced at Philip. "Do you wish to take tea in the drawing-room?"

Beyond her, Philip glimpsed Hugo's appalled expression. "Ah…perhaps not." He smiled lazily down at Antonia. "I fear Hugo is in need of more robust refreshment."

Brows rising, Antonia met his gaze. Then her lips curved; an irrepressible dimple appeared at the corner of her mouth. "Ale in the library?"

Philip's lips twitched. His eyes on hers, he inclined his head. "Your wits, dear Antonia, have obviously not dulled with age."

One delicate brow arched but her eyes continued to smile. "I fear not, my lord." She nodded to Fenton. "Ale in the library for his lordship and Mr Satterly, Fenton."

"Yes, miss." Fenton bowed and moved away.

Returning her gaze to Philip's face, Antonia smiled calmly. "I'll let Aunt Henrietta know you've arrived. She's just woken from her nap—I'm sure she'll be delighted to receive you in half an hour or so. And now, if you'll excuse me…?"

Philip inclined his head.

Hugo bowed elegantly. "Look forward to seeing you at dinner, Miss Mannering."

Philip shot him a sharp glance; Hugo was too busy returning Antonia's smile to notice.

Forsaking Hugo, Philip fleetingly met Antonia's eyes before she turned away. He watched her cross the hall, then climb the stairs, her hips gently swaying.

Hugo cleared his throat. "What happened to that ale?"

Philip started. With a quick frown, he gestured towards the library.

By the time she reached her bedchamber door, Antonia had succeeded in regaining her breath. She had not imagined her little charade would require such an effort. Her stomach was still tied in knots; her heart had yet to find its customary rhythm. Nervousness was not a reaction to which she was normally susceptible.

A frown knitting her brows, she opened the door. The windows were set wide; the curtains billowed in a gentle breeze. The scents of summer filled the airy chamber—green grass and roses with a hint of lavender from the borders in the Italian garden. Shutting the door, Antonia crossed the room. Placing both palms on the window sill, she leaned forward, breathing deeply.

"Well, I declare! That's your best new muslin."

Whirling, Antonia discovered her maid, Nell, standing before the open wardrobe. Thin and angular, her grey hair pulled tight in an unbecoming bun, Nell was busy replacing chemises and petticoats in their appointed places. Task complete, she turned, hands going to her hips as she surveyed Antonia. "I thought you was keeping that for a special occasion?"

A secretive smile tugged at Antonia's lips; shrugging, she turned back to the view. "I decided to wear it today."

"Indeed?" Nell's eyes narrowed. She picked up a pile of

kerchiefs and started to sort them. "Was that the master who arrived just now?"

"Yes. Ruthven." Antonia leaned against the window frame. "He's brought a friend—a Mr Satterly."

"Just the one?"

Nell's tone had turned suspicious. Antonia smiled. "Yes. They'll be at dinner. I'll have to decide what to wear."

Nell snorted. "Shouldn't take you long. If you're to sit down with gentlemen from London, it's either the pink taffeta or the jonquil silk."

"The jonquil silk, then. And I'll want you to do my hair."

"Naturally." Nell closed the wardrobe doors. "I'd best give a hand downstairs but I'll be back to pretty you up."

"Hmm." Antonia leaned her head against the window-frame.

Nell swallowed her snort and headed for the door. Hand on the knob, she paused, eyeing the slim figure by the window with open affection. Antonia did not move; Nell's eyes narrowed, then her features relaxed. "Should I warn Master Geoffrey to come to the table prepared to be civil?"

The question jerked Antonia from her reverie. "Heavens, yes! I forgot about Geoffrey."

"That's a first," Nell muttered.

Frowning at the bedpost, Antonia didn't hear. "Be sure to warn him *not* to come to table with his nose in a book."

"Aye. I'll make the matter plain." With a grim nod, Nell departed.

As the door clicked shut, Antonia turned back to the garden, letting her senses slide into the sylvan beauty. She loved Ruthven Manor. Coming back had felt like coming home; at some instinctive level she had always belonged, not at Mannering Park, but here—amid the gentle rolls of the Downs, surrounded by trees so old they stood like massive sentinels all around the house. Those feelings and her affection for Henrietta had both influenced her decision.

Given Geoffrey was soon to enter the world, it was time

for her to do the same. At twenty-four, her prospects were few; prosaic consideration had brought her here.

Philip, Lord Ruthven, had yet to take a wife.

Antonia grimaced, her unprecedented nervousness very fresh in her mind. But there was no place in her scheme for faintheartedness; this afternoon, she'd taken the first step. Playing out her part was now inevitable—aside from anything else, she would never forgive herself if she didn't at least *try*. If Philip didn't see her in that light, so be it.

Recalling her promise to warn her aunt of his arrival, she shook herself. Glancing in the mirror, she fluffed her curls, her fingers stilling as she recalled Philip's fixation. Her lips quirked. Almost as if he'd been bowled over—in the circumstances, a definitely heartening thought.

Holding tight to that prop to her confidence, she headed for her aunt's rooms.

Downstairs in the library, duly fortified by a tankard of superlative ale, Hugo turned his thoughts to satisfying his curiosity. "Mannering, Mannering," he mused, then cocked a brow at Philip. "Can't quite place the family."

Jerked from contemplation of the most beguiling lips he'd ever seen, Philip set aside his empty tankard. "Yorkshire."

"Ah—that explains it." Hugo nodded sagely. "The wilds to the north."

"It's not as bad as that." Philip settled back. "Mannering Park, so I understand, is an estate of some significance."

"So what's the darling of it doing here?"

"She's Henrietta's niece—her father was Henrietta's only brother. He and Lady Mannering used to visit every summer." Philip felt the years roll back, saw again a young girl with long thick plaits astride his father's favourite hunter. "They'd leave Antonia here while they went the rounds through summer. She was always about." Laughing, chattering but, somehow, never irritating. He was ten years her senior, but that had never stopped her—he'd never been able to retreat behind any superior social façade, not with Antonia. He'd watched her change from a delightfully precocious brat to an engagingly quick-witted young girl; he had yet to come to terms with her most recent transformation.

"Their visits stopped when her father died." Philip paused, calculating. "Eight years ago now. I understand Lady Mannering declared she was too weary to face the social round thereafter. Henrietta was—is—very fond of Antonia. She issued a standing invitation but apparently Lady Mannering could never spare her daughter."

Hugo raised his brows. "So at long last Miss Mannering's escaped the maternal clutches?"

Philip shook his head. "Lady Mannering died about a year ago. Henrietta renewed her entreaties with a vengeance but, if I recall Henrietta's ramblings aright, Antonia was adamant on remaining at Mannering Park to care for her brother—he's much younger than she." Philip frowned. "I can't remember how old he'd be now—I can't even remember his name."

"Whatever, it looks like she's changed her mind."

"Knowing Antonia, that's unlikely. Not unless she's altered dramatically." After a moment, Philip added, "Perhaps her brother's gone up to Oxford?"

Studying his friend's distant expression, Hugo sighed. "I hate to be obvious but there's a mystery here, in case you haven't noticed."

Philip glanced at him. "Mystery?"

"You've seen the lady!" Hugo sat up, gesticulating freely. "There she is—beautiful as be damned. Not a giddy girl, nor yet too long in the tooth but the sort to stop a charge of *chasseurs* in their tracks. *And,* to all appearances, she's unwed." Sinking back in his chair, Hugo shook his head. "Doesn't make sense. If she's as well-born and well-connected as you say, she'd have been snapped up years ago." As an afterthought, he asked, "They do have gentlemen up north, don't they?"

Philip's brows slowly rose. "I'm sure they do—and they can't all be blind." A long moment passed while they both considered a situation that, in their experience, constituted a conundrum. "A mystery indeed," Philip eventually mused. "Given the facts you've so eloquently expounded, I can only conclude that you and I, dear Hugo, might be the first to catch sight of Miss Mannering in many a long year."

Hugo's eyes slowly widened. "You're not suggesting her mama kept her locked up?"

"Not locked up, but possibly very close. Mannering Park *is* isolated and, I gather, Lady Mannering became something of a recluse." Uncrossing his legs, Philip stood, his expression unreadable. Settling his sleeves, he glanced at Hugo. "I rather think I should pay my anticipated visit to Henrietta. As to Miss Mannering's state, I strongly suspect we'll discover that to be a direct consequence of her mother's malaise."

Henrietta, Lady Ruthven, put it rather more forcefully.

"A damned shame, if you ask me. No!" She held up one hand, pink chins quivering with indignation. "I know one is not supposed to speak ill of the dead but Araminta Mannering's neglect of poor Antonia was nothing short of *wicked!*"

They were in Henrietta's sitting-room, a cosy apartment made bright with flowers and floral embroideries. Henrietta occupied her favourite armchair beside the hearth; Philip stood before her, one arm negligently extended along the mantelpiece. At the back of the room, Henrietta's dresser, Trant, sat stitching industriously, head bent, ears flapping.

Lifting eyes of faded blue presently lit by her ire to Philip's face, Henrietta went on, "Indeed, if it hadn't been for the good offices of the other local ladies, that poor child would have grown to womanhood with not the first *inkling* of the social graces." Her expression mulish, she fluffed up her shawls. "And as for contracting a suitable alliance—it pains me to say it but I'm *quite sure* that that was the furthest thought from Araminta's mind!''

With her frown as near as it ever came to forbidding, she looked like an irate owl; Philip set himself to soothe her. "I met Antonia as we came in. She seemed wholly confident, quite in her customary mould.''

"Of course!'' Henrietta threw him a scornful glance. "The girl's no namby-pamby chit full of die-away airs! Araminta left the running of that huge old house entirely on Antonia's shoulders. Naturally she knows how to greet visitors and act the hostess—she's been doing it for years. Not only that, she had to manage the estate and take complete care of Geoffrey, too. It's a wonder she hasn't become bowed down beneath the weight of all the accumulated responsibilities.''

Philip raised one brow. "Her shoulders—indeed, her carriage—seem to have held up admirably under the strain.''

"Humph!'' Henrietta shot him a glance, then settled deeper into her armchair. "Be that as it may, it's not right! The poor child should have been brought out years ago.'' She fell silent, idly toying with a fringe, then she looked up at Philip. "I don't know if you were aware of it but we offered to sponsor her—take her to London and introduce her to the *ton*. Puff her off with all the trimmings. Your father insisted—you know Horace always had a soft spot for Antonia.''

Philip nodded, aware that was the truth. Even when, as a scrawny twelve-year-old, Antonia had blithely put a saddle on his father's favourite hunter and taken the ferocious beast on a long amble about the lanes, his sire, stunned as they all had been, had praised her bottom rather than spanked it. His sire had never disguised the admiration he felt for Antonia's particular brand of straightforward confidence, an admiration Philip was well aware he shared.

"We argued and even pleaded but Araminta wouldn't hear of it.'' Henrietta's gaze grew cold. "It was perfectly plain she considered Antonia's place was to act as her nurse-maid and chatelaine; she was determined the girl would have no chance at any other role.''

Philip said nothing, his expression remote.

''Anyway,'' Henrietta said, her tone that of one who would brook no denial, ''I'm determined, now that she has come to me, to see Antonia right.'' Lifting her head, she fixed Philip with a challenging stare. ''I intend taking her to London for the Little Season.''

For one instant Philip felt shaken, but by what force he couldn't comprehend. Holding fast to his customary imper-turbability, he raised his brows. ''Indeed?''

Henrietta nodded, the action an eloquent testimony to the strength of her resolution.

A pause ensued, which Philip, somewhat diffidently, broke. ''Might I enquire as to whether you have any…'' he gestured languidly ''…further scheme in mind?''

A beatific smile lit Henrietta's lined face. ''I intend find-ing her a husband, of course.''

For an instant, Philip remained perfectly still, his expres-sion utterly impassive. Then his lids fell, veiling his eyes. ''Of course.'' Gracefully, he bowed; when he straightened, his expression was as bland as his tone. ''Hugo Satterly's downstairs—I should return to him. If you'll excuse me?''

Only when the door had closed behind him and she had listened to his footsteps retreat along the corridor did Hen-rietta allow herself a gleeful cackle. ''Not a bad start, if I do say so myself.''

Trant came forward to plump the cushions at her back and straighten her myriad shawls. ''Seems like they've al-ready met.''

''Indeed—nothing could be more fortunate!'' Henrietta beamed. ''So like dear Antonia to remember to summon you to make sure I didn't oversleep. I detect fate's blessing in Philip arriving at just that moment.''

''Maybe so, but he didn't seem all that taken. You don't

want to get your hopes too high.'' Trant had been with her mistress ever since her marriage to the late Lord Ruthven. She had seen young ladies aspiring to the role of her mistress's successor come and go with sufficient frequency to entertain serious reservations as to the present Lord Ruthven's susceptibility. ''I don't want you getting moped if it don't come off.''

''Nonsense, Trant!'' Henrietta turned to view her henchwoman. ''If there's one thing I've learned after sixteen years of observing Philip, it's that one should never place any reliance on how he reacts. His nerves, I'm persuaded, have become so deadened by fashionable disinterest that even should he suffer a…a *coup de coeur,* he would merely raise a brow and make some mildly polite comment. No impassioned speeches or wild declarations from Philip, of that you may be sure. Nevertheless, I'm determined, Trant.''

''So I see.''

''*Determined* to see that languidly uninterested stepson of mine legshackled to Antonia Mannering.'' Henrietta thumped her chair arm for emphasis, then swivelled to look at Trant who had retreated to the windowseat. ''You have to admit she's everything he needs.''

Without raising her eyes from her stitchery, Trant nodded. ''She's that and more—you'll get no argument from me on that score. We've watched her grow and know her background—good bones, good breeding and all the graces you could want.''

''Precisely.'' Henrietta's eyes gleamed. ''She's just what Philip needs. All we have to do is ensure he realizes it. Shouldn't be too difficult—he's not at all dull-witted.''

''That's what worries me, if you want to know.'' Trant snipped a thread and reached into her basket. ''Despite that sleepy air of his, he's wide awake enough on most suits. If he gets wind of your plans, he might just slip his leash. Not so much a case of not liking the girl as of not liking the persuading, if you take my meaning.''

Henrietta grimaced. "I do indeed. I haven't forgotten what happened when I invited Miss Locksby and her family for a week and promised them Philip would be here—remember?" She shuddered. "He took one look, not at Miss Locksby but at her mother, then recalled a prior engagement at Belvoir. *Such* a coil—I spent the entire week trying to make amends." Henrietta sighed. "The worst of it was that after that week I couldn't help but feel grateful he wouldn't marry Miss Locksby—I could never have borne Mrs Locksby as a relative."

A sound suspiciously like a smothered snort came from Trant.

"Yes, well." Henrietta fluffed her shawls. "You may be sure that I understand that we must go carefully in this—and not just because of Ruthven. I warn you, Trant, if Antonia gets any inkling of my active interest, she's likely to...to...well, at the very least, she's likely to become uncooperative."

Trant nodded. "Aye. She likes running in harness no more'n he."

"Exactly. But whether they like it or not, I see this as my duty, Trant. As I've said before, I don't believe it's my place to criticize Ruthven, but in this particular area I feel he's allowing his natural indolence to lead him to neglect his obligations to his name and to the family. He must marry and set up his nursery—he's thirty-four years gone and has shown no signs whatever of succumbing to Cupid's darts."

"Mind you," Henrietta declared, warming to her theme, "I freely admit that susceptibility on his part would be the most desirable avenue to pursue, but we cannot base our plans on improbabilities. No! We must do what we can to, very tactfully, promote a match between them. Antonia is now *my* responsibility, whatever she may think. And as for Ruthven—" Henrietta paused to lay a hand on her ample bosom "—I consider it my sacred duty to his sainted father to see him comfortably established."

Chapter Two

At precisely six o'clock, Philip stood before the mirror above the mantelpiece in the drawing-room, idly checking his cravat. It was the household's habit to gather there during the half-hour preceding dinner; Henrietta, however, rarely made it down much in advance of Fenton's appearance.

Focusing on his reflection, Philip grimaced. Dropping his hands, he surveyed the room. When no distraction offered, he fell to pacing.

The latch clicked. Philip halted, straightening, conscious of a surge of expectation—which remained unfulfilled. A boy—or was it a young man?—came diffidently into the room. He stopped when he saw him.

"Er…who are you?"

"I believe that's my line." Philip took in the wide hazel eyes and the thick thatch of wavy blonde hair. "Antonia's brother?"

The youth blushed. "You must be Ruthven." He blushed even more when Philip inclined his head. "I'm sorry—that is, yes, I'm Geoffrey Mannering. I'm staying here, you know." The boy stuck out his hand, then, in a paroxysm of uncertainty, very nearly pulled it back.

Philip solved the problem by grasping it firmly. "I didn't

know," he said, releasing Geoffrey's hand. "But had I considered the matter, I should, undoubtedly, have guessed." Studying the boy's open face, he raised a brow. "I presume your sister felt she needed to keep you under her wing?"

Geoffrey grimaced. "Exactly." His eyes met Philip's and he promptly blushed again. "Not that she's not probably right, of course. I dare say it would have been dev—" he caught himself up "—*deuced* slow staying at Mannering by myself."

Rapidly revising his estimates of Geoffrey's age downwards and his intelligence upwards, Philip inclined his head. The boy had the same ivory skin Antonia possessed, likewise untouched by the sun—strange in one of his years. "Are you down for the summer?"

Geoffrey flushed yet again, but this time with gratification. "I haven't actually gone up yet. Next term."

"You've gained entrance?"

Geoffrey nodded proudly. "Yes. Quite a stir it was, actually. I'm only just sixteen, you see."

Philip's lips curved. "No more than I would expect of a Mannering." He had years of experience of Antonia's swift wits on which to base that judgement.

Engaged in an entirely unaffected scrutiny of Philip's coat, Geoffrey nodded absentmindedly. "Dare say you don't remember me, but I *was* here, years ago, when the parents used to leave Antonia and me with Henrietta. But I was mostly in the nursery—and when I wasn't I was with Henrietta. She used to be very…well, *motherly,* you know."

Draping an arm along the mantelpiece, Philip's smile wry. "I do, as it happens. You've no idea how grateful I was, first to Antonia, then to you, for giving Henrietta an outlet for her maternal enthusiasms. I'm extremely fond of her, but I seriously doubt our relationship would be quite so cordial had she been forced to exercise her talents on me in lieu of other, more suitable targets."

Geoffrey regarded Philip measuringly. "But you must

have been quite…that is, almost an adult when Henrietta married your father.''

''Not quite a greybeard—only eighteen. And if you think you've outgrown Henrietta's mothering just because you've reached sixteen, I suggest you think again.''

''I already know that!'' With a disgusted grimace, Geoffrey turned aside, picking up a figurine and turning it in his hands. ''Sometimes,'' he said, his voice low, ''I think I'll always be a child in their eyes.''

Philip flicked a fleck of lint from his sleeve. ''I shouldn't let it bother you.'' His tone was even, man to man. ''You've only so many weeks to go before they'll be forced to cut the apron strings.''

Geoffrey's expressive features contorted. ''That's just it—I can't believe they actually will. They've never let me go before.'' His brow clouded. ''Mama wouldn't hear of me going to school—I've had all my learning from tutors.''

The door opened, cutting short their *tête à tête*. Philip straightened as Antonia came into the room. Geoffrey noted the movement. Replacing the figurine, he unobtrusively followed suit.

''Good evening, Antonia.'' Philip watched as she approached, a picture in soft yellow silk, the sheening fabric draping her curves, clinging, then hanging free, concealing then revealing in tantalizing glimpses. Her guinea-gold curls rioted in prolific confusion about her neat head; her expression was open, her hazel gaze, as always, direct.

''My lord.'' Graciously, Antonia inclined her head, her eyes going to her brother. ''Geoffrey.'' Her serene smile faded slightly. ''I see you two have met.'' Inwardly, Antonia prayed Geoffrey hadn't developed one of his instant dislikes—something he was distressingly prone to do when confronted with gentlemen.

Philip returned her smile. ''We've been discussing Geoffrey's impending adventure in joining the academic establishment.''

"Adventure?" Antonia blinked, her gaze shifting to Geoffrey, then back to Philip.

"Adventure indeed," Philip assured her. "Or so it was when I went up. I doubt it's changed. High drama, high jinks, life in all its varied forms. All the experience necessary to set a young gentleman's feet on the road to worldly confidence."

Antonia's eyes widened. "Worldly confidence?"

"*Savoir faire,* the ability to be at home in any company, the knowledge with which to face the world." Philip gestured broadly; his grey eyes quizzed her. "How else do you imagine gentlemen such as I learned to be as we are, my dear?"

The words were on the tip of Antonia's tongue—she only just managed to swallow them. "I dare say," she replied, in as repressive a tone as she could. The teasing light in Philip's eyes was doing the most uncomfortable things to her stomach. A swift glance at Geoffrey confirmed that her precocious brother was not ignorant of the purport of their host's sallies. Tilting her chin, she caught Philip's eye. "I'm sure Geoffrey will find the *academic* pursuits all absorbing."

Whether Philip would have capped her comment she was destined never to know; the door opened again, this time admitting Henrietta, closely followed by Hugo.

As she turned to her aunt, Antonia surprised a fleeting look of chagrin on Philip's face. It was there and then gone so rapidly she was not, in truth, entirely certain she had interpreted his expression correctly. Before she could ponder the point, Fenton entered to make his announcement.

"My honour, I believe?"

Antonia turned to find Philip's arm before her. Glancing across, she saw Henrietta being supported by Mr Satterly, the pair already deep in conversation. With a regally acquiescent glance, Antonia placed her hand on Philip's sleeve. "If you will, my lord."

Philip sighed. "Ah, what it is to be master in one's own house."

Antonia's lips twitched but she made no reply. Together, they led the way to the dining-room. They were five, leaving Philip at the head of the table and Henrietta at the foot with Hugo Satterly on one side and Geoffrey on the other. With a subtle smile, Philip delivered Antonia to the chair next to Geoffrey, the one closest to his own.

The conversation was at first general, with Hugo relating a succession of *on dits*. Having heard them all before, Philip bided his time until Henrietta, eager for gossip, predictably buttonholed Hugo, demanding further details. Equally eager to learn of the world he had yet to join, Geoffrey drank in Hugo's entertaining replies.

With a faint smile, Philip shifted in his chair, bringing Antonia directly under his gaze. "I understand, from what Henrietta let fall, that you've lived the last eight years very quietly."

Antonia met his gaze directly, her expression serious and, he thought, a touch sombre. She shrugged lightly. "Mama was unwell. There was little time for frivolities. Naturally, once I was of an age, the ladies about invited me to join their parties." She looked away as Fenton removed her soup plate. "To the Assemblies at Harrogate."

"Harrogate." Philip kept his expression impassive. She might as well have been buried alive. He waited until Fenton laid the next course before venturing, "But your mother must have entertained to some degree?"

Sampling a morsel of turbot cloaked in rich sweetbread sauce, Antonia shook her head. "Not after Papa's death. We received, of course, but more often than not, when the ladies arrived, Mama was too ill to come down."

"I see."

The quiet comment drew a quick glance from Antonia. "You must not imagine I've been pining away, dreaming of a gay life." Reaching for a dish of morels, she offered them to Philip. "I had more than enough to occupy myself, what with running the household and the estate. Mama was never well enough to tend to such matters. And there was Geoffrey, of course. Mama was always in a fret that he was sickly, which, of course, he never was. But she was sure he had inherited her constitution. Nothing would convince her otherwise."

Philip looked past Antonia; Geoffrey was wholly immersed in the conversation at the other end of the table. "Speaking of Geoffrey, how did you manage to find tutors to keep up with him? He must have been quite a handful."

Instantly, he realised he'd discovered the key to Antonia's confidence. Her eyes fairly glowed. "He certainly was. Why, by the time he was nine, he had outstripped the curate."

There followed an animated catalogue of Geoffrey's successes, liberally sprinkled with tales of misdeeds, catastrophes and simple country pleasures. In between the highlights of Geoffrey's life, Philip heard enough to gauge what manner of existence had been Antonia's lot. What encouragement was needed to keep her revelations flowing, he artfully supplied. As her history unfolded, he realised the unnamed curate was featuring remarkably often.

Laying aside his fork, he reached for his wineglass. "This curate of yours seems to have taken his duties very seriously."

Antonia's smile was fond. "Indeed. Mr Smothingham was always a great support. He really is a true knight—a most chivalrous soul." With a small sigh, she gave her attention to the gooseberry fool Fenton had placed before her.

Leaving Philip to wonder how he could possibly feel so aggressive towards a probably perfectly innocent curate whom he had never met. He cleared his throat. "Henrietta mentioned she was thinking of going up to town for the Little Season."

"Indeed." Savouring the tartness of the gooseberry treat,

Antonia slanted him a glance. "She's invited me to accompany her. I hope you don't disapprove?"

"Disapprove?" Philip forced his eyes wide. "Not at all." Picking up his spoon, he attacked the frothy concoction before him. "In fact, I'll be relieved to know she'll have your company."

Antonia smiled and gave her attention to her dessert.

Philip rejected his, reaching instead for his wineglass. He took a long sip, his gaze on Antonia. "Am I to understand you're looking forward to taking the *ton* by storm?"

She met his gaze with another of her disconcertingly direct looks. "I don't know." Her brows rose; her lips curved lightly. "Do you think I would find it diverting?"

Beyond his will, Philip's gaze was drawn to her lips, to the rich fullness of the ripe curves. He watched as the tip of her tongue traced their contours, leaving them sheening. His expression rigidly impassive, Philip drew in a deep breath. Slowly, he lifted his eyes and met Antonia's steady gaze. "As to that, my dear, I would not dare hazard a guess."

He had only questioned her intentions in London to assure himself she was a willing partner in Henrietta's schemes. His motives, Philip assured himself, were entirely altruistic. Henrietta could be a battleship when she was so moved. Unless he had misread the signs, when it came to Antonia's future, Henrietta was definitely moved.

"I'm not in the mood for billiards." Tossing back the last of his port, he stood and settled his coat. "Let's join the ladies, shall we?"

Geoffrey, for the first time elevated to the rank of gentleman to the extent of remaining to pass the port, saw nothing odd in the suggestion.

Hugo was not so innocent. He turned a face of amazed incomprehension on Philip.

Philip ignored it, leading the way to the drawing-room without further comment.

If Henrietta was surprised by his unheralded break with long established habit, she gave no sign. Seated on the *chaise,* she looked up from her needlework to smile benignly. "Wonderful—just what we need. Geoffrey, do go and sing a duet with Antonia."

Henrietta waved towards the pianoforte, which stood before the long windows, presently open to the terrace. Antonia sat at the instrument, her fingers on the keys. A gentle, elusive air hung faint in the evening breeze.

With an obedient nod, Geoffrey headed for his sister. Antonia smiled a welcome, breaking off her playing to reach for the pile of music sheets resting on the piano's edge. With his customary lazy grace, Philip strolled in Geoffrey's wake. Left standing by the *chaise,* Hugo studied the small procession, then shrugged and brought up the rear.

"Let's try this, shall we?" Antonia placed a sheet on the stand.

Geoffrey scanned the lines, then nodded.

Philip took up a position by the side of the grand piano from where he could watch Antonia's face. As her fingers ranged the keys and the first chords of an old ballad filled the room, she looked up and met his gaze. A slight smile touched her lips; for an instant, their gazes held. Then she looked down and the music swept on.

She and Geoffrey sang in unison, Geoffrey's pure tenor weaving in and about her fuller tones. For one stanza, she sang alone; Philip briefly closed his eyes, listening, not to the song, but to the music of her voice. It was not the light voice of the girl he remembered but richer, a warm contralto with an undercurrent of huskiness.

As Geoffrey's voice blended once more with hers, Philip opened his eyes. He saw Antonia glance encouragingly up at Geoffrey, then they launched into the last verse. As the final chords died, he, Henrietta and Hugo burst into spontaneous applause.

Almost squirming, Geoffrey blushed and disclaimed. Her expression one of affectionate exasperation, Antonia turned and deliberately met Philip's gaze. Lips curving, she arched a delicate brow. "Are you game, my lord?"

Philip detected at least two meanings in her challenge; he was uncertain if there was a third. Languidly, he inclined his head and straightened, responding to the more obvious of her prompts. Coming around the piano, he dropped a hand on Geoffrey's shoulder. "After that masterful effort, I fear my poor talents will be a disappointment to you all, but if you can find a *simple* ballad, I'll endeavour to do my poor best." He took up his stance behind Antonia's shoulder; Hugo took his place by the side of the piano.

With an approving smile, Antonia obliged with a rolling country ballad; Philip's strong baritone managed the changing cadences with ease. Unexpectedly caught up in the simple entertainment, Hugo consented to favour them with a rollicking shanty with a repeating refrain; Antonia made the performance even more humourous by consistently lengthening the long note at the end of the second last line of the reprieve. The shanty had a full twenty verses. First Geoffrey, then Philip, joined in, assisting Hugo through the increasingly jocular song. By the end of it, they were all laughing, very much out of breath.

A smile wreathing her face, Henrietta applauded vigorously, then summoned them to take tea.

Laughter lighting her eyes, Antonia swivelled on the stool to find Philip beside her. Deliberately, she looked up and met his eyes. Despite his easy expression, the grey orbs were veiled. Calmly, she raised a brow, then watched as the chiselled line of his lips lengthened into a definite smile.

He held out his hand. "Tea, my dear?"

"Indeed, my lord." Tilting her chin, Antonia laid her fingers in his palm and felt his hand close about them. A peculiar shiver shot up her arm, then slithered slowly down her spine. Ignoring it, she rose; side by side, they crossed the room to where Henrietta was dispensing the tea.

With studied calm, Antonia accepted her cup but made no move to quit her aunt's side. A host of unfamiliar sensations flickered along her nerves; her heart was thudding distractingly. Such unexpected susceptibility was not, to her mind, a helpful development. She had never before been so afflicted—she hoped the effect would fade quickly.

To her relief, Henrietta kept up a steady spate of inconsequentialities, abetted by Hugo Satterly. Geoffrey, having gulped his tea, wandered back to the piano. Sipping slowly, Antonia concentrated on settling her nerves.

From behind his languid mask, Philip watched her.

"Actually, Ruthven—" Henrietta turned from Hugo "—I had meant to consult you as soon as you appeared about holding some entertainment for the neighbours. We haven't done anything in years. Now Antonia's here to help me, I really feel I should grasp the nettle with both hands."

Philip raised a brow. "Indeed?" None who heard those two syllables could doubt his reluctance.

Henrietta nodded imperiously. "It's one's duty, after all. I had been thinking of a grand ball—musicians, dancing, all the trimmings."

"Oh?" Philip's tone grew steadily more distant. He exchanged a glance with Hugo.

"Yes." Henrietta frowned, then grimaced. "But Antonia pointed out that, after all this time, we should really do something for our tenants as well."

Philip glanced at Antonia; she was sipping her tea, her eyes demurely cast down. He swallowed a disbelieving "humph".

"All things considered—and I really do not feel I can let this opportunity slide, Ruthven—I do believe dear Antonia's suggestion is the best." Folding her hands in her lap, Henrietta nodded decisively.

"And what," Philip asked, his tone deliberately even "*is* dear Antonia's suggestion?"

"Why, a *fête-champêtre*—didn't I say?" Henrietta regarded him wide-eyed. "A positively *inspired* idea, as I'm sure even you will allow. We can set everything up on the lawns. Battledore and shuttlecock, races, bobbing for apples, archery, a play for the children—you know how these things go. We can have the food and ale set up on trestles for the tenants and entertain our neighbours on the terrace, overlooking all the fun."

Henrietta gestured grandly. "A whole afternoon in which everyone can enjoy themselves. I rather think we should hold it in the next week or so, before the weather turns, but naturally you'd have to be present. Shall we say next Saturday—a week from now?"

Philip held her enquiring gaze, his expression as informative as a blank wall. A garden party was infinitely preferable to a local ball—but at what price? A vision of hordes of farmers and their wives tramping across his lawns swam through his mind; in his imagination he could hear the high-pitched shrieks of multitudes of children and the screams as some, inevitably, fell in the lake. But worse than all that, he could clearly see the bevy of simpering, silly, local young misses to whom he would, perforce, have to be civil.

"Naturally, I'll assist in any way I can."

Antonia's soft words cut across Philip's thoughts. He glanced her way, then, one brow slowly rising, turned back to Henrietta. "I admit to reservations that acting as hostess at such a large and varied gathering will overly tire you."

Henrietta's grin was triumphant. "No need to worry over me. Antonia can stand in my stead for the most part—I'm looking forward to sitting on the terrace with the other dowagers, keeping an eye on it all from a suitable elevation."

"I can imagine," Philip returned drily. He shifted his gaze to Antonia. "Yet your 'most part' is not precisely a light load."

Antonia's chin came up; she shot him a distinctly haughty glance. "I think you'll discover, my lord, that I'm more than up to snuff. I've managed such gatherings at Mannering for years—I anticipate no great difficulty in overseeing my aunt's entertainment."

Philip ensured his expression held just enough scepticism to make her eyes flash. "I see."

"Good." Henrietta thumped the floor with her cane. "So it's Saturday. We'll send out the invitations tomorrow."

Philip blinked. Hugo, he noticed, looked vaguely stunned. Henrietta, of course, was beaming happily up at him. Drawing in a deep breath, he hesitated, then inclined his head. "Very well."

As he straightened, he deliberately caught Antonia's eye. Her expression was innocent but her eyes, tapestries of green and gold, were infinitely harder to read. She raised her brows slightly, then reached for his empty cup.

Eyes narrowing, Philip surrendered it. "I intend to hold you to your offer."

She treated him to a sunny, utterly confident smile, then moved away to straighten the tea trolley.

Suppressing a snort, Philip turned to find Hugo beside him.

"Think I'll go join Geoffrey." Hugo wriggled his shoulders. "In case you haven't noticed, there's an aura about here that's addling wits."

The dew was still on the grass when Antonia headed for the stables the next morning. Early morning rides had been a long-ago treat; Philip's return had resurrected pleasant memories.

Entering the long stable, she paused, allowing her eyes to adjust to the dimmer light. Rising on her toes, she looked along the glossy backs, trying to ascertain whether the chestnut gelding the headgroom, Martin, had told her was Philip's favourite, was still in his box.

"Still an intrepid horsewoman, I see."

Antonia smothered her gasp and swung about. The velvet skirts of her habit swirled, brushing Philip's boots. He was so close, she had to tilt her head up to meet his eyes, one hand on her riding hat to keep it in place.

"I didn't hear you." The words were breathless; inwardly, Antonia cursed.

"I noticed. You seemed absorbed in some search." Philip's eyes held hers. "What were you looking for?"

For an instant, Antonia's mind went blank; prodded by sheer irritation, she replied, "I was looking for Martin." She turned to survey the empty stable, then slanted a glance at Philip. "I wanted him to saddle a horse for me."

Philip's jaw firmed. He hesitated, then asked, "Which of my nags have you been using?"

"I haven't been out yet." Picking up her skirts, Antonia strolled down the aisle, knowledgeably gauging the tall hunters and hacks.

Philip followed. "Take your pick," he said, knowing very well she would.

"Thank you." Antonia stopped before a stall housing a long-tailed roan, a raking, raw-boned stallion Philip privately considered had a chip on his shoulder—he was perennially in a bad mood. "This one, I think."

With any other woman, Philip's veto would have been automatic. Instead, he simply snorted and strode on to the tack room. Returning with a side-saddle, bridle and reins, he found Antonia crooning sweet nothings to the giant horse. The stallion appeared as docile as the most matronly mare.

Swallowing another "humph", Philip swung the stall door wide. Quickly and efficiently, he saddled the stallion, glancing now and then at Antonia, standing at the horse's head communing with the beast. He knew perfectly well she could have saddled the horse herself; she was the one woman in all the millions he would trust to do so.

But it would have been churlish to suggest she wrestle with the saddle, not when she made such a delightful picture, her habit of topaz-coloured velvet a deeper gold than her hair, the tightly fitting bodice outlining the womanly curves of her breasts, nipping in to emphasize her small waist before flaring over her hips. As if sensing his regard, she looked up; Philip jabbed an elbow into the roan's side and cinched the girth. "Wait while I saddle Pegasus."

Antonia nodded. "I'll walk him in the yard."

Philip watched as she led the stallion out, then returned to the tack room. He was on his way back, his arms full of his own tack, when ringing footsteps sounded on the cobbles of the yard. Frowning, Philip set his saddle on the stall door. Hugo, he knew, would still be sound asleep. So who…?

"Hello! Sorry I'm a bit late." Geoffrey waved and headed for the tack room. As he passed, he flung Philip a grin. "I guessed you'd ride early. I won't keep you." With that, he disappeared into the tack room.

Philip smothered a groan and dropped his head against his horse's glossy flank. When he straightened and turned, he found himself eye to eye with Pegasus. "At least you can't laugh," he muttered savagely.

By the time he emerged from the stable, Antonia had discovered the mounting block and was perched atop the roan, a slim slender figure incomprehensibly controlling the great beast as she walked him around the yard.

Gritting his teeth, Philip swung up to the saddle; in less than a minute, Geoffrey joined them, leading a grey hunter.

"All right?" he asked, looking first to Philip and then to Antonia.

Philip nodded. "Fine. Let's get going."

They did—the brisk ride, flying as fast as the breeze, did much to restore his temper. He led the way but was unsurprised to see the roan's head keeping station on his right. Geoffrey followed on his heels. It had been years—at least eight—since Philip had enjoyed that sort of ride—fast, unrestrained, with company that could handle the going as well as he. One glance as they cleared a fence was enough to reassure him that Antonia had not lost her skill; Geoffrey was almost as good as she.

In perfect amity with their mounts, they fled before the wind, finally drawing rein on an open hillock miles from the Manor. Philip wheeled, dragging in a deep breath. His eyes met Antonia's; their smiles were mirror images. Exhilaration coursed through his veins; he watched as she tipped her head up and laughed at the sky.

"That was *so good!*" she said, smiling still as her eyes lowered and again met his.

They milled, catching their breaths, letting their mounts settle. Philip scanned the surrounding fields, using the moment to refresh his memory. Antonia, he noticed, was doing the same.

"That copse," she said, pointing to a small wood to their left, "had only just been planted last time I rode this way."

The trees, birches for the most part, were at least twenty feet tall, reaching their fingers to the sky. The undergrowth at their bases, home to badgers or fox, was densely intertwined.

"This brute's still fresh." Geoffrey wheeled the grey tightly. "There looks to be some ruins over that way." He nodded to the east. "Think I'll just shake the fidgets with a quick gallop." He glanced at Philip and lifted a brow.

Philip nodded. "We'll go back by way of the ford. You can join us on the other side."

Geoffrey located the stream and the ford, nodded agreement, and left.

Antonia watched him cross the fields, an affectionate smile on her lips. Then she sighed and turned to Philip, her eyes holding an expression he could not immediately place. "I can't tell you how relieved I am to see he hasn't lost the knack."

Leading the way off the knoll, Philip raised his brows. "Of riding neck or nothing? Why should he?"

Keeping pace beside him, Antonia's lips twisted; she gave a light shrug. "Eight years is a long time."

Philip blinked. A long moment passed before he asked, "Haven't you—and Geoffrey—been riding regularly?"

Antonia looked up, surprised. "I thought you knew." When Philip threw her a blank look, she explained, "Papa died in a hunting accident. Virtually immediately Mama sold his stable. She only kept two carriage horses—she said that's all we'd need."

Philip kept his eyes fixed ahead; his face felt like stone. His tone was careful even when he asked, "So, essentially since you were last here, you've been unable to ride?"

Simply voicing the idea made him blackly furious. She had always found immense joy in riding, delighting in her special affinity with the equine species. What sort of parent would deny her that? His opinion of the late Lady Mannering, never high, spiralled downwards.

Her attention on the roan, Antonia shook her head. "For me, it didn't really matter, but for Geoffrey—well, you know how important such skills are to young gentlemen."

Philip forced himself to let her answer pass unchallenged; he had no wish to reopen old wounds. As they gained the flat, he tried for a lighter note. "Geoffrey has, after all, had excellent teachers. Your father and yourself."

He was rewarded with a swift smile.

"Many would say that I'm hardly a good example, riding as I do."

"Only because they're jealous."

She laughed at that, a warm, husky, rippling sound Philip was certain he'd never heard before. His eyes locked on her lips, on the column of her white throat; his gelding pranced.

Instinctively, he tightened his reins. "Come, let's ride. Or Geoffrey will tire of waiting."

They rode side by side, fast but not furiously, chestnut

and roan flowing effortlessly over the turf. Geoffrey joined them at the ford; they wheeled and rode on, ultimately clattering into the stableyard a short hour after they had left it.

The two men swung down from their saddles; Philip tossed his reins to Geoffrey, who led both grey and chestnut away.

Before Antonia had well caught her breath, she lost it again. Philip's hands closed, strong and sure, about her waist. He lifted her, as if she weighed no more than a child, lowering her slowly until her feet touched the ground.

Antonia felt a blush tinge her cheeks; it was all she could do to meet his gaze fleetingly. "Thank you, my lord." Her heart was galloping faster than any horse.

Philip looked down at her. "The pleasure, my dear, is entirely mine." He hesitated, then released her. "But do you think you could possibly stop 'my lording' me?" His tone, slightly acid, softened. "You used to call me Philip."

Still breathless, but at least now free of his paralysing touch, Antonia wrestled her wits into order. Frowning, she looked up and met his grey gaze. "That was before you came into the title." Considering, she tilted her head. "Now that you have, I'll have to call you Ruthven—like everyone else."

His eyes, cloudy grey, held hers; for an instant, she thought he would argue. Then the ends of his long lips twisted, in grimace or self-deprecation she couldn't say. His lids fell; he inclined his head in apparent acquiescence.

"Breakfast awaits." With a graceful flourish, Philip offered her his arm. "Shall we? Before Geoffrey devours all the herrings."

Chapter Three

"Ah—I wondered who was attacking my rose bushes."

Startled in the act of lopping off a developing rose-hip with a buccaneer-like swipe, Antonia jumped. Half-turning, she glanced reprovingly at Philip as he descended the steps to the walk. "Your rose bushes, my lord, are running to seed. Not at all the thing." With a decisive click, she removed another deadhead.

She had spent the morning inscribing invitations for the *fête-champêtre*. In the silence of the afternoon, with Henrietta napping, she had taken to the gardens. After their ride that morning, she hadn't expected to see Philip before dinner.

Smiling lazily, Philip strolled towards her. "Henrietta mentioned you were easing her burden by taking things in hand around the house. Am I to take it you intend to personally deal with anything you discover running to seed around here?"

Poised to pluck a half-opened rose, the delicate bloom cradled in her hand, Antonia froze. Philip had halted a bare foot away; she could feel his gently teasing gaze on her half-averted face. Catching her breath, surreptitiously, she hoped, she looked up and met his eyes. "As to my personal interest, I rather suspect it depends on the subject. However,'' she said, turning back and carefully snipping the rose, ''as far as the garden is concerned, I intend speaking with your head gardener immediately.'' She laid the bloom in the basket on her arm, then looked up. ''I take it you don't disapprove of my...'' she gestured gracefully ''...impertinence?''

Philip's smile deepened. ''My dear Antonia, if acting as chatelaine can be termed impertinent, you may be as impertinent as you please. Indeed,'' he continued, one brow rising, his gaze sweeping her face, ''I find it distinctly reassuring to see you thus employed.''

For an instant, Antonia met his gaze, then, with the slightest inclination of her head, turned and glided along the path. Reassuring? Because, as she hoped, he saw such actions as evidence of her wifely skills? Or because she might, conceivably, make his unfettered existence more comfortable?

''The design of your gardens is unusual,'' she said, glancing back to find him strolling in her wake like a predator on her trail. ''I've studied both contemporary and classical landscapes—yours seems a combination of both.''

Philip nodded. ''The fact that the lake and stream are so distant from the house rendered the usual water features ineligible. Capability Brown saw it as a challenge.'' His eyes met Antonia's. ''One he couldn't resist.''

''Indeed?'' Inwardly cursing the breathlessness that seemed to afflict her whenever he was near, Antonia halted beside a clump of cleomes. ''To my mind, he's succeeded in moulding the raw ingredients into a veritable triumph. The vistas are quite enchanting.'' Setting aside her basket, she bent over the clump of soft white flowers, selecting and snipping two stems for her collection.

Beside her, Philip stood transfixed, his gaze on an unexpected but thoroughly enchanting vista. Antonia shifted, then straightened; Philip quickly lifted his gaze to the neat row of conifers bordering the sunken garden. "Yes," was all he could think of to say.

Antonia threw him a swift, slightly suspicious look; he promptly smiled charmingly down at her. "Have you been through the peony walk?"

"Not for a few days."

"Come, walk with me there—it's always a pleasant route."

Antonia hesitated, then acquiesced. Together, they climbed the steps from the sunken garden, then turned into the narrow hedged walk where peonies of every description filled beds on either side of the flags. Although past their best, the plants were still blooming, displaying splashes of white and all shades of maroon against glossy green leaves. The path had been laid like a stream, gently twisting; here and there, small specimen trees grew, no longer in blossom but adding interest with their foliage.

They strolled in companionable silence, stopping intermittently to admire the extravagant displays. Antonia paused to examine the blooms carried on one long stem; Philip watched the subtle play of her thoughts rippling through her expression.

She was, on the one hand, so very familiar; on the other, so startlingly different.

He had almost grown accustomed to the change in her voice, to the husky undertone he found so alluring. Her eyes, a complex medley of greens and golds, had not altered but her gaze, although still direct, seemed more deeply assured. As for the rest of her, that had certainly changed. There was poise, now, where before had been youthful hedonism; elegant grace had replaced a young girl's haste.

His gaze caressed her hair, glinting golden in the sunlight; he was prepared to accept that it was still as long and thick as he recalled. The curves that filled her muslin gown were, however, an entirely new development—a thoroughly distracting development.

Her head used to barely reach his shoulder yet when she turned, Philip found his lips level with her forehead.

Bare inches away.

His gaze dropped and met hers, wide and, he realised, somewhat startled. Her scent wafted about him, rose, honeysuckle and some essence he could not name.

Her gaze trapped in his, Antonia caught her breath, only to find she could not release it. Unable to move, unable to speak, unable to tear her eyes from the darkening grey of his, she stood before him, feeling like a canary staring at a cat.

Smoothly, Philip stepped back. "It's nearly time for luncheon. Perhaps we should return?" His lids veiled his eyes; languidly, he waved to a cross-path that would lead them back to the house.

Slowly exhaling, Antonia glanced up at the sky. Her heart was racing. "Indeed." In search of a topic—any topic—she asked, "What was it that brought you to the garden?"

Philip's gaze ranged ahead, his expression bland as he considered and rejected the truth. In the distance, he saw Geoffrey returning from the stables. "I wanted to ask if Geoffrey had had any experience of driving. After what you told me of your last years, I imagine he's lacked male guidance. Would you like me to teach him?"

Looking down, he caught the peculiar expression that flitted, very briefly, across Antonia's features.

"Oh, yes," she said, throwing him a grateful glance. "If you would, you would earn his undying gratitude. And mine."

"I'll take him out then."

Antonia nodded, her eyes downcast. Side by side, they walked towards the house. Puzzling over her strange look, Philip shot her a shrewd glance, then slowly smiled. Schooling his features to an expression of deep consideration, he said, "Actually, I have to confess I've no experience of teaching striplings. Perhaps, as you are, unquestionably, a

superior horsewoman and *in loco parentis,* as it were, I
should practise my tutoring skills on you?''

Antonia's head came up; she fixed him with a clear, very
direct glance. ''You'll teach me to drive?''

Philip managed to keep the smile from his face. ''If you
would care for it.''

''I didn't think—'' Antonia frowned. ''That is, I'd understood that it was no longer particularly fashionable for
ladies of the *ton* to drive themselves.''

''Only in certain circumstances and only—pray God—
when they can actually manage the reins.'' Halting at the
bottom of the terrace steps, Philip turned to face her. ''It's
entirely acceptable for a lady to drive a gig or a phaeton in
the country.''

Antonia raised a brow. ''And in town?''

Both Philip's brows rose. ''My dear Antonia, if you imagine I'll let you tool my horses in the Park, you're misguided,
my child.''

Antonia's eyes flashed; she lifted her chin. ''What carriage do you drive in London?''

''A high-perch phaeton. Forget it,'' Philip tersely advised.
''I'll permit you to drive my curricle, but only here.''

Brows rising haughtily, Antonia started up the steps.
''But when we get to London—''

''Who knows?'' Philip mused. ''You might turn out to
be ham-fisted.''

''*Ham—!*'' Antonia rounded on him—or tried to, only to
feel his fingers close about her elbow. Effortlessly, he propelled her over the threshold into the morning-room where
Henrietta sat tatting.

''One step at a time, my dear.'' His words were a murmur
in her ear. ''Let's see how well you can handle the reins
before you reach for the whip.''

That comment, of course, ensured she was on her mettle
when, the following afternoon, Philip lifted her to the box-

seat of his curricle. Determined that nothing—not even he—would distract her from her lesson, Antonia thrust her ridiculous sensitivity to the back of her mind and carefully gathered the reins.

"Not like that." Philip climbed up beside her, settling on the seat alongside. Deftly plucking the reins from her fingers, he demonstrated the correct hold, then laid the leather ribbons in her palms, tracing their prescribed path through her fingers with his. Despite her gloves, Antonia had to lock her jaw against the sensation of his touch. She frowned.

Philip noticed. He sat back, resting one arm along the back of the seat. "Today, we'll go no faster than a sedate trot. Not having second thoughts, are you?"

Antonia shot him a haughty look. "Of course not. What now?"

"Give 'em the office."

Antonia clicked the reins; the horses, a pair of perfectly matched greys, lunged.

Her shriek lodged in her throat. Philip's arm locked about her; his other hand descended over hers as she grappled with the reins. The curricle rattled down the drive, not yet fast but with the greys lengthening their stride. The next seconds passed in total confusion—by the time she had the horses under control and pacing, restless but aware of her authority at the other end of the ribbons, Antonia was more rattled than she had ever been in her life before.

She shot Philip a fiery glance but could not—dared not—take exception to the steely arm anchoring her safely to his side. And despite the urge to tell him just what she thought of his tactics, she felt ridiculously grateful that he had not, in fact, taken control, but had let her wrestle with his thoroughbreds, entrusting their soft mouths to her skill, untutored though he knew that to be.

It took several, pulse-pounding minutes before she had herself sufficiently in hand to turn her head and meet his improbably bland gaze with one of equal impassivity. "And now?"

She saw his lips twitch.

"Just follow the drive. We'll stay in the lanes until you feel more confident."

Antonia put her nose in the air and gave her attention to his horses. She had, as she had earlier informed him, some experience of driving a gig. Managing a dull-witted carriage horse was not in the same league as guiding a pair of high-couraged thoroughbreds. At first, the task took all her concentration; Philip spoke only when necessary, giving instructions in clear and precise terms. Only when she was convinced she had mastered the "feel", the response of the horses to her commands, did she permit herself to relax enough to take stock.

Only then did the full import of her situation strike her.

Philip's arm had loosened yet still lay protectively about her. Although still watchful, he sat back beside her, his gaze idly scanning the fields. They were in a lane, bordered by hedges, meandering along a rolling ridge. Glimpses of distant woods beyond emerald fields, of orchards and of willows lining streams, beckoned; Antonia saw none of them, too distracted by the sensation of the solid masculine thigh pressed alongside hers.

She drew in a deep breath and felt her breasts swell, impossibly sensitive against her fine chemise. If she'd been wearing stays, she would have been sure they were laced too tight. That left only one reason for her giddiness—the same ridiculous sensitivity that had assailed her from the first, from the moment she had met Philip in the hall. She had put it down to simple nervousness—if not that, then merely a dim shadow of the infatuation she had felt for years.

An infatuation she had convinced herself would fade when confronted with reality.

Instead, reality had taken her infatuation and turned it into—what?

A shiver threatened—Antonia struggled to suppress it.

She didn't, in fact, succeed.

Through the arm about her, Philip felt the telltale reaction. Lazily, he studied her, his gaze shrewd and penetrating. Her attention was locked on his leader's ears. "I've been thinking—about Geoffrey."

"Oh?"

"I was wondering if, considering his age, it might not be advisable to temporarily delay his departure for Oxford. He hasn't seen much of the world—a few weeks in London might be for the best. It would certainly put him on a more even footing with his peers."

Her gaze on the road, Antonia frowned. After neatly if absentmindedly taking the next corner, she replied, "For myself, I agree." She grimaced and glanced fleetingly at Philip. "But I'm not sure he will—he's very attached to his books. And how can we argue, if the time wasted will put him behind?"

Philip's lips curved. "Don't worry your head about convincing him—you may leave that to me."

Antonia shot him a glance, clearly not sure whether to encourage him or not.

Philip pretended not to notice. "As for his studies, his academic performance is, I'm sure, sufficiently strong for him to catch up a few weeks without difficulty. Where's he going?"

"Trinity."

"I know the Master." Philip smiled to himself. "If you like, I'll write and ask permission to keep him down until the end of the Little Season."

Antonia slowed the greys in order to turn and study him. "You know the Master?"

Philip lifted a haughty brow. "Your family is not the only one with a connection to the college."

Antonia's eyes narrowed. "You went there?"

Philip nodded, his expression impassive as he watched her struggle with her uncertainty.

In the end, convinced there was no subtle way in which to frame her question, Antonia drew in a deep breath and asked, "And what, do you think, will be the Master's response to such a request—from you?"

Philip met her gaze with bland incomprehension. "My dear Antonia, whatever do you mean?"

She shot him a fulminating glance, then turned back to the horses. "I mean—as you very well know—that such a request from one whose reputation is such as yours can be construed in a number of ways, not all of which the Master is likely to approve."

Philip's deep rumbling laughter had her setting her teeth.

"Oh, well done!" he eventually said. "I couldn't have put it better myself."

Antonia glared at him, then clicked the reins, setting the horses to a definite trot.

Philip straightened his lips. "Rest assured that my standing with the Master is sufficient that such a request will be interpreted in the most favourable light."

The glance Antonia threw him held enough lingering suspicion to make him narrow his eyes. "I do not, dear Antonia, have any reputation for corrupting the innocent."

She had, he noted, sufficient grace to blush.

"Very well." Antonia nodded but kept her gaze locked on the leader. "I'll mention the matter to Geoffrey."

"No—leave that to me. He'll be more receptive to the idea if I suggest it."

Antonia knew her brother well enough not to argue. Head high, she turned the horses for home, determinedly disregarding the inward flutter Philip had managed to evoke.

After studying her profile, Philip said no more until she pulled the horses up before the front steps. Descending, he strolled leisurely around to come up beside her, meeting her watchful, slightly wary gaze with open appreciation. "A commendable first outing. To my mind, you're still holding them a little tight in the curves but that judgement will come with practice."

Before she could reply, he twitched the reins from her hands and tossed them to the groom who had come running from the stables. While the movement had her distracted, he closed his hands about her waist, well aware of the tension that gripped her as he lifted her down.

"You'll be pleased to know," he glibly stated, holding her before him and gazing down into suddenly wide eyes, "that I'm completely satisfied that your peculiar ability to communicate with the equine species operates even when you're not perched upon their backs."

Antonia continued to stare at him blankly. Reluctantly, Philip released her.

"You—" Antonia blinked wildly. It was an effort to summon not only her voice but the indignation she felt sure she should feel. Breathless, she continued, "Do you mean to say that today was a…a *test?*"

Philip smiled condescendingly. "My dear Antonia, I know of your talents—it seemed rational to test them. Now I know they're sound, there seems little doubt you'll prove a star pupil."

Antonia blinked again—and wished there was some phrase in his speech to which she could take exception. In the end, she drew herself up and fixed him with a direct and openly challenging stare. "I assume, my lord, that when we go out tomorrow, you'll permit me to get above a trot?"

The subtle smile that played about his lips did quite peculiar things to her nerves. "I wouldn't suggest you reach for the whip just yet, my dear."

"Well! That seemed a most successful outing." Henrietta turned from the window high above the drive, having watched her stepson and niece until they'd disappeared into the hall below.

"That's as may be." Trant continued to fold linens, laying them neatly on the bed. "But I'd reserve judgement if I was you. Early days yet to read anything into things like simple drives in the countryside."

"Phooh!" Henrietta waved the objection aside. "Ruthven rarely drives ladies—let alone lets them drive *him*. Of *course* it means something."

Trant merely sniffed.

"It means," Henrietta went on, "that our plan has real promise. We must ensure they spend as much time in each other's company as possible—with as little distraction as we can manage."

"You're planning on encouraging them to be alone?" Trant voiced her query with a suitably hesitant air.

Henrietta snorted. "Antonia is twenty-four, after all—hardly a green girl. And whatever Ruthven's reputation, he has never, to my certain knowledge, been accused of seducing innocents."

Trant shrugged, unwilling to risk further comment.

Henrietta frowned, then shifted her shawls. "I'm convinced, in this case, that strict adherence to society's dictates is not necessary. Aside from anything else, Ruthven will not—would not—seduce any lady residing under his own roof under my protection. We must put our minds to making sure they spend at least some part of every day together. I'm a great believer in propinquity, Trant—if Ruthven is to see what a gem Antonia is, we'll need to keep her before him long enough for him to do so."

Three days later, Antonia climbed the stairs and entered her bedchamber. She had spent all morning going over the plans for the *fête,* to be held, as Henrietta had decreed, two days hence; it was now mid-afternoon and Henrietta was napping. As usual, the garden was her destination but she had fallen into the habit of checking her appearance whenever she ventured forth. Crossing to the dressing-table, she smiled absentmindedly at Nell, seated by the window, a pile of darning beside her. "Don't strain your eyes. I'm sure some of the younger maids could lend a hand with that."

"Aye—no doubt. But I've little confidence in their stitches—I'd rather see to it myself."

Picking up her brush, Antonia carefully burnished the curls falling in artful disorder from the knot on the top of her head.

Nell threw her a swift glance. "Seems you've been seeing a lot of his lordship lately."

Antonia's hand stilled, then she shrugged. "I wouldn't say a lot. We ride in the mornings, of course. Geoffrey, too." She did not think it necessary to mention that for at least half the time she spent on horseback, she and Philip were alone; Geoffrey, encouraged to try the paces of his mount, was rarely within hailing distance. "Other than that, and the three occasions he's let me drive his curricle, Ruthven only seeks me out if he has some matter to discuss."

"That so?" Nell remarked.

"Indeed." Antonia tried to keep the irritation from her voice. Although Philip often sought her company during the day, spending half an hour or more by her side, he invariably had some reason for doing so. She sank the brush into one curl. "He's a busy man, after all—a serious landowner. He spends hours with his agent and baliff. Like any sensible gentleman, he puts effort into ensuring his estate runs smoothly."

"Strange—it's not what I'd have thought." Nell shook out a chemise. "He seems so...well, lazy."

Antonia shook her head. "He's not lazy at all—that's just an image, a fashionable affectation. Ruthven's never been truly lazy in his life—not over anything that matters."

Nell shrugged. "Ah, well—you know him better than most."

Antonia swallowed a "humph" and continued to tend her curls.

Five minutes later, she was descending the steps from the terrace when she heard her name called. Looking about, she saw Geoffrey striding up from the stables. One glance at his face was enough to tell her her brother was in alt.

"A great day, Sis! I had them trotting sweetly from the first. Who knows—next time our teacher might let me take out his greys."

Antonia grinned, sharing his delight. "Bravo—but I wouldn't get your hopes too high." While Ruthven had entrusted his greys to her, he had started Geoffrey with a pair of match chestnuts, by any standards a well-bred pair but not in the same league with his peerless Irish greys. "In fact," Antonia said, linking her arm in Geoffrey's, "I'd rather you didn't suggest it—he's really been very generous in helping you take the reins."

"I wasn't about to," Geoffrey replied, fondly condescending. "That was just talk." Obediently, he fell in beside her as she strolled the gravel path. "Ruthven's been far more encouraging than I'd ever looked to see. He's a great gun—one of the best!"

Antonia heard the fervour in his tone; glancing up, she saw it reflected in his face.

Unconscious of her scrutiny, Geoffrey went on, "I assume you know he's suggested I should accompany you to London? I wasn't too sure at first—but he explained how it would set yours and Henrietta's minds at ease—if you could see me in society a bit, build your confidence in me, that sort of thing."

"Oh?" When Geoffrey glanced her way, Antonia hurriedly changed her tone. "I mean—yes, that's right." After a moment, she added, "Ruthven's very good at thinking of such things."

"He said that's one of the traits that distinguishes a man

from a boy—that a man thinks of his actions in the wider context, not just in terms of himself.''

Despite her inclination, Antonia felt a surge of gratitude towards Philip; his subtle mentoring would help to fill the large gap their father's death had left in Geoffrey's life. Any lingering reservations she had regarding Geoffrey's visit to London evaporated. ''I think you would be very wise to take Ruthven's hints to heart. I'm certain you can have every confidence in his experience.''

''Oh, I have!'' Geoffrey strode along beside her, then recalled he should match his steps to hers. ''You know—when you decided to come here, I thought I'd be—well, the odd man out. I didn't think Philip would still be friendly, like he was to you all those years ago. But it's just the same, isn't it? He might be a swell and a gentleman about town and all that, but he still treats us as friends.''

''Indeed.'' Antonia hid a glum grimace. ''We're very fortunate to have his regard.''

Grinning, Geoffrey disengaged. ''Think I'll take a fowling piece out for the rest of the afternoon.''

Antonia nodded absentmindedly. Alone, she let her feet follow the gravel walks, her mind treading other paths. Geoffrey, unfortunately, was right. While Philip could be counted on to tease and twit her, in all their hours together, whether strolling the gardens or driving his greys, she had never detected anything in his manner to suggest he saw her other than as a friend. An old friend, admittedly—one on whom he need not stand on terms—but nothing more than an agreeable companion.

It was not what she wanted.

Looking back, analysing all their interactions, the only change the years had wrought was what she termed her ''ridiculous sensitivity''—the leaping, fluttering feeling that afflicted her whenever he was close, the tension that immobilized her limbs, the distraction that did the same to her wits, the vice that made breathing so difficult every time he touched her, every time he lifted her down and held her between his strong hands, every time he took her hand in his to help her up a step or over some obstacle.

As for the times his fingers had inadvertently brushed the back of her hand—they were undoubtedly the worst. But all that came from her, not him. It was simply her reaction to his presence, a reaction that was becoming harder and harder to hide.

Halting, she looked around and discovered she'd reached the Italian garden. Neat hedges of lavender bordered a long, raised rectangular pool on which white water lillies floated. Gravelled walks surrounded the pool, themselves flanked by cypress and box, neatly clipped. It was a formal, quite austere setting—one which matched her mood. Frowning, Antonia strolled beside the pool, trailing her fingers in the dark water.

Her ''ridiculous sensitivity'' was the least of her problems. Philip still saw her as a young girl and the *fête* was looming; soon after, they would leave for London. If she wanted to succeed in her aim, she would have to *do* something. Something to readjust his vision of her—to make him see her as a woman, a lady—as a potential wife. And whatever she was going to do, she would have to do it soon!

''Well, my lady of the lake—are my goldfish nibbling your fingers?''

Antonia whirled and saw the object of her thoughts strolling towards her. He was wearing a flowing ivory shirt, topped with a shooting jacket, a scarf loosely knotted about his tanned throat. His long thighs were clad in buckskin breeches, his feet in highly polished top-boots. One brow rising in gentle raillery, his hair tousled by the breeze, he looked every inch the well-heeled landowner—and a great deal more dangerous than the average country gentleman.

Calmly, Antonia lifted her wet fingers and studied them. ''Not noticeably, my lord. I suspect your fish are too well fed to be tempted.''

Philip halted directly before her; Antonia nearly jumped when his fingers slid about her wrist. Lifting her hand, he examined her damp fingers. "Fish, I understand, are not particularly intelligent."

His heavy lids lifted; his gaze, sky grey with clouds gathering, met hers.

Antonia's heart lurched, her stomach knotted; familiarity didn't make the sensations any easier to bear. His fingers felt strong and steely, his grip on her wrist warm and firm. Her diaphragm seized; she waited, breathless, trapped by his gaze.

Philip hesitated, then the ends of his lips lifted lightly. Glancing down, he reached into a pocket and drew out a white handkerchief. And proceeded to wipe each finger dry.

Her heart pounding, Antonia tried to speak. She had to clear her throat before she could. "Ah—did you wish to speak to me about something?"

Philip's smile deepened. She always asked. On principle, he never prepared an answer; inventing one on the spot kept him on his toes. "I wanted to ask if there was anything you needed for the *fête*. Do you have all you require?"

Antonia managed to nod. His stroking of her fingers, even with his touch muted by the fine lawn handkerchief, was sending skittering sensations up her arm. "Everything's under control," she eventually managed.

"Really?"

There was just enough amused scepticism in Philip's tone to make her stiffen. She lifted her fingers from his slackened grasp and met his gaze. "Indeed. Your staff have thrown themselves into the spirit of the thing—and I must thank you for the services of your steward and baliff. They've been most helpful."

"I hope they have." With a gesture, Philip invited her to walk beside him. "I'm sure the entertainments will be a credit to you all."

Haughtily, Antonia inclined her head and fell into step beside him. Slowly, they paced beside the narrow pool.

Philip glanced at her face. "What brings you here? You seem…pensive."

Antonia drew in a deep breath and held it. "I was thinking," she said, tossing back her curls, "of what it would be like when we're in London."

"London?"

"Hmm." Looking ahead, she airily explained, "As you know, I've not much experience of society. I understand poetry is much in vogue. I've heard it's common practice for *ton*nish gentlemen to use poetry, or at least, poetic phrases, to compliment ladies." She slanted an innocent look upwards. "Is that so?"

Philip's mind raced. "In some circles." He glanced down; Antonia's expression was open, enquiring. "In fact, in certain company it's *de rigueur* for the ladies to answer in similar vein."

"It is?" Antonia's surprise was unfeigned.

"Indeed." Smoothly, Philip captured her hand and placed it on his sleeve. "Perhaps, as you'll shortly be joining the throng, we ought to sharpen your rhymes?"

"Ah—" Her hand trapped beneath his warm palm, Antonia struggled to think. His suggestion was a considerable extrapolation of her plan.

"Here." Philip stopped by a wrought-iron seat placed to look over the pool. "Let's sit and try our wits."

Not at all certain just what she had started, Antonia subsided. Philip sat beside her, half-turning, resting one arm along the back of the seat. "Now—where to start?" His gaze roamed her face. "Perhaps we should stick to mere phrases—considering your inexperience?"

Antonia shifted to face him. "That would undoubtedly be wise."

Only years of experience allowed Philip to keep the smile from his lips. "And perhaps I'd better start the ball rolling.

How about—'Your hair shines like Caesear's gold, for which battalions gave their lives'?''

Wide-eyed, Antonia stared at him.

"Your turn," Philip prompted.

"Ah…'' Antonia bludgeoned her wits then lifted her gaze to his hair. She dragged in a breath. '''Your hair glows like chestnuts, burnished by the sun'?''

"Bravo!'' Philip smiled. "But that was purely a visual description—I think I win that round.''

"It's a competition?''

Philip's eyes gleamed. "Let's consider it one. My turn. 'Your brow is white as a snow martin's breast, smooth as his flight through the sky.'''

On her mettle, Antonia narrowed her eyes, studying the wide sweep of his brow. Then she smiled. '''Your brow is as noble a Leo's ever was, your might not less than his.'''

Philip's smile deepened. '''Emerald your eyes, set in gold, precious jewels their value untold.'''

'''Grey clouds and steel, mists and fog, stormy seas and lightning, mix in the depths of your gaze.'''

Brows rising, Philip inclined his head. "I'd forgotten what a quick learner you are. But onward! Let's see…'' Slowly, he raised his hand and gently, very gently, brushed her cheek with the back of one finger. '''Your cheeks glow soft, ivory silk over rose.''' His voice had deepened.

For a long instant, Antonia sat as one stunned, wide-eyed, barely breathing. The only thought in her head was that her stratagem was working. The effects of his touch slowly dissipated; her wits filtered back. She swallowed, then frowned and met his gaze. "It should have been my turn to lead. So—'''Firm of chin and fair of face, your movements marked by languid grace.'''

Philip laughed. "Mercy!—how can I hope to counter that?''

Antonia's smug glance turned superior.

Philip studied her face. "All right. But—'' Glancing

down, he saw her hands, lightly clasped in her lap. "Ah, yes." Shifting, he reached out and circled her wrist once more, gently tugging one hand free. Under his fingers, he felt her pulse leap.

She didn't resist as he lifted her hand, turning it as though examining her slim fingers. Fleetingly, he let his gaze meet hers. Then, still holding her captive, he trailed the fingers of his other hand against her sensitive palm.

The swift intake of her breath sounded sharp to Antonia's ears. Philip's eyes flicked up to hers; a smile unlike any she'd yet seen slowly curved his lips. His fingers shifted, so that his fingertips supported hers.

"'Delicate bones, sensitive skin, awaiting a lover's caress.'"

His voice was deep and low, the cadence striking chords deep within her. Antonia watched, trapped by his gaze, by his touch, as he slowly lifted her hand and, one by one, touched his lips to her fingertips.

The quivers that ran through her shook her to her core.

"Ah…" Desperation flayed her wits to action. "I've just remembered." Her voice was a hoarse whisper. She coughed and cleared her throat. "A message I promised to deliver for my aunt—I shouldn't have forgotten—I should go straight away." Retreat, disorderly or otherwise, seemed imperative yet, despite all, she couldn't bring herself to tug her hand free.

Philip's eyes held hers, steady, unyielding, an expression in the grey that she did not recognize. "A message?"

For one long moment, he studied her eyes, then the planes of his face relaxed. "About the *fête?*"

Numb, Antonia nodded.

Philip's lips quirked; ruthlessly, he stilled them. "One you have to deliver immediately?"

"Yes." Abruptly, Antonia stood; she felt immeasurably grateful when Philip, more languidly, rose too. He still hadn't let go of her hand. In an agony of near panic, she waited.

"Come—I'll escort you back."

With that, Philip tucked her hand into the crook of his elbow and turned her to the house. All but quivering, Antonia had perforce to acquiesce; to her relief, he strolled in companionable silence, making no reference by word or deed to their game by the pool.

He halted by the steps to the terrace and lifted her hand from his sleeve, holding it and her gaze for an instant before releasing her. "I'll see you at dinner." With a gentle smile and a nod, he strode away.

Antonia watched him go. Slowly, a warm flush of triumph permeated her being, driving out the skittering panic of moments before.

She had achieved her object. However Philip now viewed her, it was not as a young friend of the family.

"Goodnight, then." With a nod and a smile, Geoffrey left the billiard room to his host and Hugo, having unexpectedly taken revenge on Hugo for an earlier defeat.

"Quick learner," Hugo muttered in defense of his skills.

"Mannerings are," Philip replied, chalking a cue. The rest of the household had retired, Antonia somewhat breathlessly assuring him that she intended getting an early start on the preparations for the *fête*. A smile in his eyes, Philip waited while Hugo racked the balls, then he broke.

"Actually," Hugo said, as he watched Philip move about the table, "I've been trying to catch you for a quiet word all day."

"Oh?" Philip glanced up from his shot. "What about?"

Hugo waited until he had pocketed the ball before answering. "I've decided to return to town tomorrow."

Philip straightened, his question in his eyes.

Hugo grimaced and pulled at his ear. "This *fête*, y'know. All very well for you in the circumstances—you'll have

Miss Mannering to hide behind. But who's to shield me?''
Palms raised in appeal, Hugo shuddered. ''All these earnest
young misses—your step mama's been listing their best features. Having succeeded with you, I rather think she's considering fixing her sights on me. Which definitely won't
do.''

Philip stilled. ''Succeeded?''

''Well,'' Hugo said, ''it was pretty obvious from the start.
Particularly the way her ladyship always clung to yours
truly. I was almost in danger of thinking myself a wit until
the penny dropped. Perfectly understandable, of course—
what with Miss Mannering being an old family friend and
you being thirty-four and the last in line and so on.''

Slowly, Philip leaned over the table and lined up his next
shot. ''Indeed.''

''Mind,'' Hugo added. ''If I couldn't *see* your reasoning—Miss Mannering being well in the way of being a
peach—I wouldn't have thought you'd stand it—being
hunted in your own house.''

Sighting along his cue, Philip smelt again the teasing
scent of lavender, heard the scrunch of gravel beneath slip-
pered feet, saw again Antonia's airily innocent expression
as she ingenuously led him along the garden path.

His shot went awry. Expression impassive, he straightened and stepped back.

Hugo studied the table. ''Odd of you to miss that.''

''Indeed.'' Philip's gaze was unfocused. ''I was distracted.''

Chapter Four

The next morning, Antonia awoke with the larks. By nine o'clock, she had already spoken with the cook and Mrs Hobbs, the housekeeper, and seen the head-gardener, old Mr Potts, about flowers for the morrow. She was turning away from a conference with Fenton on which of the indoor tables should be used on the terrace when Philip strode into the hall.

He saw Antonia and immediately changed course, his heels ringing on the black and white tiles. He halted directly before her.

"You didn't come riding."

Staring up into storm-clouded eyes, Antonia felt her own widen. "I did mention that there was a great deal to do."

His jaw firming, Philip cast a jaundiced eye over the figures scurrying about his hall. "Ah yes." His quirt struck the white top of one boot. "The *fête*."

"Indeed. We're going to be terribly busy all day."

He swung back to Antonia, his gaze intent. "*All* day?"

Antonia lifted her chin. "All day," she reiterated. "And all tomorrow, too, until the festivities begin. And then we'll be even more busy."

Beneath his breath, Philip swore.

Antonia stiffened. Her expression aloof, she waved to the

dining-room. ''I believe you'll find breakfast still available—if you hurry.''

The look Philip cast her could only be called black. Without a word, he swung on his heel and headed for the dining-room.

A frown in her eyes, Antonia watched him go—then realized what seemed so strange. He was striding. Briskly.

''Excuse me, miss, but should I put this chair with those for the terrace?''

''Ah…'' Antonia swung around to see a footman struggling with a wing-chair. ''Oh, yes. The dowagers will need all of those that we can find. They'll want to doze in the sun.''

As she laboured through the morning, Antonia kept her mind firmly fixed on her aim. The *fête* had to be a success—a complete, unqualified *tour de force*. It was a perfect opportunity to demonstrate to Philip that she was, at least at a county level, fully qualified to be his bride.

Summoning two maids, she led them to the Italian garden and pointed out the lavender. ''You need to cut not just the flower but the stem as well—as long as you can. We'll need them to freshen the withdrawing-rooms.''

Watching the maids as they set to work, Antonia found her gaze drawn to the seat at the end of the pool. The look in Philip's eyes as he'd kissed her fingers returned, crystal clear, to her mind. A smile tugged at her lips. Despite her panic, she had made definite progress there. Unbidden, the memory of his odd behaviour in the hall rose to taunt her. A frown chased the smile from her eyes.

''This right, miss?''

Jerked back to reality, Antonia examined the spike held up for her approval. ''Perfect.'' The little maid glowed. ''Be sure to collect two handfuls each—take them up to Mrs Hobbs as soon as you're done.'' Ruthlessly banishing Philip from her mind, Antonia stalked back to the house, determined more than ever to focus on the job at hand.

*   *   *

He would have taken refuge in the library or the billiard room but she had commandeered those as well. In a mood close to perilous, Philip abandoned his search for peace and quiet to wander through the throngs of his servitors, all furiously engaged in executing Antonia's commands.

He wondered if he should tell her her assertiveness was showing. He knew it of old—her tendency to take charge, to organise, to get things done. His lawns looked like chaos run mad, but even he could see, beneath the hectic bustle, that it was effective, organised activity. Pausing to watch two of his farm labourers struggle to erect a stall, he mused on Antonia's very real talent for getting people to work for her, often for no more direct reward than her smile and a brief word of approbation. Even now, he could see her at the far end of the lawn, where a narrow arm of the distant lake lipped a reed-fringed shore, exhorting the undergardeners to get all the punts cleaned and launched.

"Watch it there, Joe! Easy now, lad—just let me see if we've got this thing straight."

Refocusing on the action more immediately before him, Philip saw the younger of the two labourers trying to balance the front beam of the stall while simultaneously holding one of the side walls erect. The older man, a hammer and wooden strut in his hands, had backed, trying to gauge if the beam and wall were at the right angle. Joe, however, had no hope of keeping both pieces still.

Philip hesitated, then stepped forward and clapped the older man on the shoulder. "Give Joe a hand, McGill—I'll direct you."

McGill touched his cap. "If you would, m'lord, we'll get on a dashed sight faster."

Joe simply looked grateful.

Before they were done, Philip had his coat off and was helping to hammer in nails. That was how Antonia found him when she did her rounds, checking on progress.

She couldn't keep the surprise from her face.

Philip looked up—and read her expression. It didn't improve his mood. Nor did the instant urge he felt to call her to him—or go to her. Instead, he held her gaze, his own, he knew, dark and moody. Half of him wanted to speak to her, the other half wasn't at all sure it was a good idea—not yet. He hadn't yet decided how he felt about anything—about her, about what he inwardly labelled her machinations. Looking away, he grimly hammered in another nail. He hadn't felt this uncertain in years; pounding metal into wood was a comforting occupation.

Released from his mesmerising stare, Antonia couldn't resist a swift survey of his shoulders and back, muscles flexing beneath his fine shirt as he worked, his hands, long-fingered but strong, gripped about nail and handle. When she moved on, her mouth was dry, her heartbeat not entirely even. Oblivious of the activity about her, she reviewed their recent meetings. He was usually so even-tempered, too indolent to be moved to any excess of emotion—his aggravated mood was a mystery.

She glanced back—he had paused, shoulders propped against the side of the stall. He was watching her, his gaze brooding and intent.

"Miss—do you want the doilies put out now or tomorrow?"

"Ah…" Whirling, Antonia blinked at the young maid. "Tomorrow. Leave them in the morning-room until then."

The maid bobbed and scurried away. Drawing in a deep breath, Antonia followed more gracefully in her wake.

Philip watched her go, hips gently swaying as she climbed the slope, then pushed away from the wall and reached for another handful of nails.

An hour later, lunch was served—huge plates of sandwiches and mugs of ale laid out on the trestles already up and waiting. Exhorted by Antonia, no one stood on ceremony; as he helped himself to a sandwich stuffed full of ham, Philip noticed Geoffrey's fair head among the crowd. The boy waved and pushed through to him.

"Antonia's put me in charge of the Punch and Judy. Fenton's helping me—one of the footmen is going to do Punch but I think I'll have to do Judy. None of the maids will stop giggling long enough to say the lines."

Philip uttered a short laugh. Geoffrey's eyes were alight.

"We've got the booth up, but the stage is going to take some work."

Philip clapped him on the shoulder. "If you can keep the children out of the lake, I'll be forever in your debt."

Geoffrey grinned. "I might take you up on that once we get to London."

"Just as long as it's not my greys you're after."

Geoffrey laughed and shook his head. Still grinning, he moved away.

Sipping his ale, Philip saw his steward and baliff, both ostensibly lending a hand. Normally, both men considered themselves above such activities; Philip wondered whether it was his presence that had changed their minds—or Antonia's confident imperiousness.

His eye ranging the throng, he saw one of the maids— Emma was the name that came to mind—artfully jog Joe's elbow. Joe was a likely lad, well grown and easy-mannered, barely twenty. As he watched Emma apologise profusely, smiling ingenuously up at Joe, Philip felt cynicism raise its mocking head. Joe smiled down at her, truly ingenuous. The little scene was played out in predictable vein; Philip moodily wondered if it might not be his duty to warn Joe that, despite the common assumption that man was the hunter, there were times when he might prove to be the prey.

As he himself had found.

He could see it now—now that Hugo had ripped the scales from his eyes. Henrietta's behaviour should have triggered his innate alarms—instead, as he'd admitted, he'd been distracted. Not by the usual flirtatious encouragements—they wouldn't have worked. But Antonia had not sought to attract him in the usual way—she'd used other wiles—more sophisticated wiles—wiles more likely to succeed with an experienced and recalcitrant gentleman rake who had seen it all before.

She'd used their old friendship.

With a grimace, Philip set aside his empty tankard and hefted the hammer he'd been using. He was still not sure how he felt—how he should feel. He had thought Antonia was different from the rest. Instead, she'd simply been using different tactics.

His expression still grim, he headed back to help McGill and Joe put up the rest of the refreshment stalls. They were banging the supports into place on the last of the stalls when a sound to his left had him turning his head. Antonia stood three feet away.

She met his gaze, then, with a slight smile, gestured to the tray she had placed on the counter of the next stall. "Ale—I thought it might be more acceptable than tea."

Philip glanced about and saw the womenfolk bearing trays and mugs to the men. Most of the small workforce had completed their tasks; the refreshment was welcomed by one and all.

Looking back, Philip met Antonia's calmly questioning gaze, then turned and, with one heavy blow, drove his last nail home. Laying the hammer aside, he called Joe's and McGill's attention to the ale. Antonia stepped back, hands clasped before her. Turning, Philip picked up a mug—and took the two strides necessary to trap her between the stall and himself.

Scanning his lawns, he took a long draught of ale. "Is there much more to do?"

Distracted from watching his lean throat work as he downed the ale, Antonia blinked and quickly looked about. "No—I think most of what we can do we've done." She reviewed her mental lists. "The only thing remaining is for the barrels to be brought out. We decided to leave them under tarpaulins for the night.''

Still not looking at her, Philip nodded. ''Good. That leaves us time to talk before dinner.''

''Talk?'' Antonia stared at him. ''What about?''

Philip turned his head and met her gaze. ''I'll tell you when we meet.''

Antonia studied his eyes, what she could see of them before he looked away. ''If it's about the *fête*—?''

''It's not.''

The finality in his tone declared he was not about to explain. Inwardly, Antonia frowned; outwardly, she inclined her head gracefully. ''In that case, I'll just—''

Her words were cut off by shouts and yells and a muffled rumbling. Antonia turned—as did everyone else—to see an ale barrel come rolling down the lawn.

''Stop it!'' someone yelled.

''Heavens!'' Antonia picked up her skirts and hurried forward.

For one stunned instant, Philip watched her rush towards the barrel. Then, with a comprehensive oath, he flung aside his tankard and went after her.

She slowed as she drew in line with the oncoming barrel, deaf to the cries of warning. Close on her heels, Philip wrapped one arm about her waist and swung her out of harm's way, pulling her hard against him.

''Wha—!''

Her strangled exclamation was music to his ears.

''Philip!'' Antonia eventually got out, all in a breathless rush. ''Put me *down!* The barrel—!''

''Weighs at least three times as much as you and would have flattened you into the ground.'' Philip heard it rumble past them.

His terse words came from directly behind Antonia's right ear. Horrified, she waggled her toes but couldn't touch the grass. He had scooped her up, holding her with her back against his chest, one large hand splayed across her middle, easily supporting her weight. He made no move to obey her injunction. She considered struggling—and blushed. The realisation of her predicament sent shock waves to merge with the odd heat spiralling through her.

Men had rushed from all around to slow the rolling barrel. Antonia watched as they brought it under control, then turned it and rolled it towards the stall which would serve the ale.

Only then did Philip consent to set her feet back on solid earth.

Antonia immediately drew in a deep breath. She drew in another before she turned around.

Philip got in first. "You would never have stopped it."

Antonia put her nose in the air. "I hadn't intended to try—I would merely have slowed it until the men reached it—then they could have managed it as they did."

Philip narrowed his eyes. "After it had rolled right over you."

Antonia eyed his set chin, then lifted her eyes to his. Her jaw slowly set. "In that case," she said, determinedly gracious although she spoke through clenched teeth. "I suspect I must thank you, my lord."

"Indeed. You can thank me by coming for a ride."

"A ride?"

Philip caught her hand. Lifting his head, he scanned the scene. "Everything's finished here, isn't it?"

Casting about for relief, Antonia found none. "Perhaps the Punch and Judy—"

"Geoffrey's got that in hand. I don't think it would be wise for you to undermine his authority."

Antonia's jaw dropped. "I *wouldn't*—" she began hotly.

"Good. Let's go." Philip started for the booth where he'd left his coat, towing her along, not caring who saw. His jaw set, he swiped up his coat but didn't stop, tugging Antonia up so he could trap her hand in the crook of his elbow.

Stunned, Antonia blinked free of the masculine web that held her. Her eyes narrowed. "I believe you've forgotten one point, my lord."

Philip glanced frowningly down at her. "What?"

Antonia smiled sweetly. "I can't ride in this dress."

She shut her ears against his muttered curse. He abruptly changed direction; in seconds, they were through the side door and into the hall.

Philip halted at the foot of the stairs. "You've got five minutes," he said, releasing her. "I'll wait here."

Antonia sent him a furiously disbelieving look. And watched his eyes slowly narrow.

With an exaggerated sniff, she tossed her head and headed up the stairs.

It took longer than five minutes to scramble into her habit but Philip was still waiting, pacing at the foot of the stairs, when she came down. He looked up, nodded, then waved her on.

Her chin defiantly high, Antonia sailed ahead.

The grooms had their horses ready; Philip must have sent word. He gripped her waist and tossed her up, then swung up to his chestnut's back. He wheeled; Antonia fell in beside him. As usual, they rode before the wind, streaking across his fields.

Philip had decided where to stage their talk. Somewhere they would be assured of being pavate. Hardly in line with accepted precepts, but he was beyond such considerations. He led her deep into the Manor woods, to a cool glade where a stream widened into a pool.

He swung down and tethered Pegasus to a low-hanging branch. A jay shrilled. Sunshine dappled the grass, growing thick and lush by the water's edge. Enclosed by old oaks, the glade was still and silent—entirely theirs.

Antonia frowned as Philip lifted her down; the catch in her breath, the need to still her heart, no longer even registered. Her hand in his, he strode away from the horses, towards the pool. He was moving far too fast for her liking.

"What is it?" she asked, hurrying to keep up with his long strides. She glanced up at his face. "Is something amiss?"

Abruptly, Philip halted. Jaw clenched, he swung to face her. "As to that, I'm not sure."

His eyes, Antonia saw, were patterns of roiling grey. Throughout the day, his abrupt movements, his clipped accents, had undermined her confidence—now he was talking in riddles. Taking advantage of his slackened grasp, she pulled her hand from his. Standing her ground, she lifted her chin. "There's something bothering you—that much is plain."

"There is indeed," he replied, his hands rising to his hips, his eyes boring into hers.

When she simply continued to stare at him, waiting, open challenge in her gaze, Philip muttered a curse. Tense as a bowstring, he glanced away, then abruptly turned back. Capturing her gaze, he caught her hand; he lifted it, deftly turned it and placed a kiss on her wrist, on the pulse point exposed by her glove.

And felt her reaction, the quick shiver she tried to suppress, stiffening against it. Her eyes widened but not with amazement. The rise and fall of the lace ruffle at her breast increased.

Philip's eyes narrowed. "Tell me, Antonia. Am I seducing you—or are you seducing me?"

For an instant, Antonia was sure the world had spun. She blinked. "Seducing...?" Stunned, she stared at him.

"Seducing." Ruthlessly, Philip held her gaze. "As in capitalising on the age-old attraction that sometimes flares between a man and a woman."

Antonia strangled the impulse to repeat the word attraction—she could hardly deny its existence. She could feel it shimmering between them. Dazed, she blinked again. What was he suggesting? "I…?"

"Don't know what I'm talking about?" Philip supplied, catching her chin in one hand.

The cynicism in his tone stung. Antonia's eyes flashed. "I wouldn't know how to *begin* seducing you!"

"Know?" Philip pretended to consider the point while the tension that had held him all day wound tight. "I don't suppose you would actually need to know how—you could do it by instinct alone." Looking down at her, at her wide green-gold eyes, her softly curved lips, he felt the tumult inside him swell. The urge to surrender to it waxed strong— he who never permitted himself to be driven, compelled, coerced, frustrated, aggravated or obsessed.

"Whatever," he said, his voice deepening, darkening. "You've succeeded." If he took what was offered, would he know peace again? On the thought, he bent his head and set his lips to hers.

And felt, as he had known he would, her instantaneous response. It rose to his touch, to his caress, easily overriding her equally instinctive stiffening. Her unfettered reaction was balm to his bruised ego—at least she was, at this level, as helpless as he. Her lips softened; at his subtle urging, hesitant, beguiling, they parted under his.

Antonia felt the whirlpool rise and snatch her up, so strong she could only ride its tide. Her wits scattered, her senses stretched, heightened by excitement, eager, clamouring for experience. She felt his arms slide around her; as her limbs softened, they tightened and locked, crushing her to him.

Wanting more of his caress, she tilted her head and felt his lips firm. Driven, she pressed closer. The magic of his kiss had her firmly in thrall; tentatively, she returned it, revelling in the shocking intimacy, marvelling at the sensations crowding her mind. The seductive hardness of the muscles surrounding her, the tempting heat of his large body—all were new discoveries; the slow crescendo building within her, the swelling tempo of her heart, were fascinating, novel perceptions.

His strength surrounded her, his kiss intoxicated her. The feel of him, the taste of him, overwhelmed and excited her. Dragging her hands from where they had been trapped against his chest, she wound them about his neck, returning his kiss with an ardent fervour she hadn't known she possessed.

Philip groaned and crushed her even more tightly to him, her breasts firm and swollen against his chest. He let one hand roam over her hips, urging her against him, moulding her to him.

The whirlpool had caught him, too.

He was too experienced to let it pull them down. Nevertheless, dragging them both free of its turbulent power took all the strength he possessed. When he finally managed to raise his head, soothing her hungry lips with a gentle brush of his, they were both breathing raggedly.

Tense, his muscles locked tight, he waited for common sense to return and save them. Very slowly, Antonia's lids rose. Mesmerised, he watched as her eyes were revealed, the gold flecks blazing, the green more deeply jewel-like than he had ever seen. Then darkness swam in, dulling the brilliance. Her breath caught; she caught her lower lip between her teeth, her eyes widening with what could only be alarm.

She stiffened in his arms.

Philip felt the panic grip her. "Don't," he said, in the instant before she started struggling.

To his relief, she stilled, a frightened bird locked in the cage of his arms, tense and quivering.

Holding her gaze, Philip dragged in a deep breath, his chest swelling, making him unwillingly aware of the softness pressed against it—and took a firm grip on the reins. "I'm not about to ravish you."

She was an innocent; he had frightened her.

The expression in her wide, shadowed eyes was not one he could read but he thought he detected a hint of scepticism. Exasperation drove him to say, "Oh, I'm thinking about it." Pressed to him as she was from shoulders to knees, she could hardly miss the evidence of his desire. "But I'm not about to do it—all right?"

His jaw ached, as did the rest of him; experience was not enough to hide his frustration. He concentrated on keeping still—he had no intention of moving until the dangerous moment had passed, until the compulsion driving them both had faded.

Antonia had no breath with which to answer. Her heart was still thudding in her ears. For a long moment, she simply held his gaze, wondering dazedly how much he could see. Had he noticed how unrestrained her ardour had been— how wantonly she had kissed him? Was the aching need still pulsing within her visible in her eyes?

She could only pray it wasn't.

Stunned, staggered, shocked beyond measure, she felt heat rise to her cheeks. When he raised one brow, she recalled his question and forced herself to nod. Then blushed even more.

"We've got to go back." Once more in control, Philip forced his arms from her and caught her hand.

"Back?" Before she could say more, Antonia found herself towed unceremoniously back to her horse. Recollections returning, her mind was awhirl. "But—"

With a muted snarl, Philip rounded on her, trapping her with her back against her horse. He towered over her, muscles locked, jaw clenched, his eyes a steely grey. "Antonia—do you *want* to be ravished here and now?"

She actively considered the question—then caught herself and blushed furiously. She felt like sinking. The effort it took to make herself shake her head was even more damning.

"Then we go back," Philip said through clenched teeth. "Immediately." He grasped her waist and tossed her up to her saddle, then pulled her reins free and threw them up to her. In seconds, he had Pegasus free and was mounting.

Without further words, he led the way back to the Manor.

As the miles sped past, Antonia's memory cleared; by the time they reached the Manor, her cheeks were flushed, her eyes glittering.

They pulled up in the stableyard, but no one came running. Philip glanced about, then remembered he had given the stablehands permission to visit the local inn in compensation for their sterling efforts in organising another of Antonia's entertainments—pony rides for the younger children, with a series of low jumps in the nearest paddock for the older children to attempt. Smothering an oath, he dismounted. "We'll have to take care of the horses ourselves."

Her lips compressed, Antonia kicked free of her stirrups, slid down from her perch—and rounded on him.

"After accusing me of attempting to seduce you, you *expect* me to—?" Words failed her; her eyes blazed. With a smothered scream, she flung her reins at his head, swung on her heel and marched out of the yard.

Chapter Five

Seducing him? As if that was possible.

Smothering a snort, Antonia dragged her brush through her thick wavy hair. Sunshine streamed in through her bed-chamber window; the morning breeze came with it, bringing the crisp tang of grass and dew-washed greenery. The day of the *fête* had dawned bright and clear; unable to sleep, she had risen and donned her sprig muslin, then sat down to tend her curls.

And consider how best to deal with her host.

She might have tried to make him notice her, she might have tried to make him see her as a potential wife. But to accuse her of *seducing* him?

"Hah!" Frowning direfully at the mirror, she gritted her teeth and ruthlessly dealt with a tangle. She was *not* such a scheming female!

The very notion that a lady such as she, of severely re-stricted experience, *could* seduce a gentleman of his vast and, she had no doubt, *varied background,* was ludicrous. None of the seducing that had been done to date could be laid at *her* door.

She knew very well who had been seducing whom.

Those moments in the woods had opened her eyes; until then she had been too distracted by her reactions, too caught up with suppressing them, to focus on what drew them forth. Now she knew.

The Lord only knew what she was going to do about it.

The hand holding her brush stilled; Antonia studied the face that looked back at her from her mirror, the trim figure displayed therein. It had never occurred to her that Philip, with all the accommodating ladies of the *ton* from whom to choose, would fix any real part of his interest on her

She had thought to be his wife but had envisaged he would feel nothing beyond mere affection for her—that and the lingering warmth of long-standing friendship. That was what she had expected, what she had steeled herself to accept—the position of a conventional wife.

His actions in the woods suggested she had miscalculated. He wanted her—*desired* her. A delicious thrill ran through her. For an instant, she savoured it, then, frowning again, resumed her brushing. A serious problem had surfaced with his ardour—namely, hers. Or, more specifically, how, given a gentleman's expectations of his wife, she was supposed to keep her feelings hidden or, at the very least, acceptably disguised.

The door opened; Nell walked in, stopping in amazement at the sight of her.

"Great heavens! And here I'd thought to wake you."

Antonia brushed more vigorously. "There's still a lot to do—I don't wish to be rushed at the last."

Nell snorted and came to take the brush. "Seemingly you're not the only one. I just saw his lordship downstairs. Thought he must be going riding, but then I noticed he wasn't in top boots. Very natty, he looked, I must say."

"Indeed." Clasping her hands in her lap, Antonia infused the word with the utmost disinterest. Philip had tried to speak with her last night, first in the drawing-room before dinner, when Geoffrey's enthusiasm had saved her, then later, when she was pouring the tea. She had affected deafness to his low-voiced ''Antonia?'' and handed him a brimming cup.

She was not about to forgive him, to let him close again, not until the panicky feelings inside subsided, not until she was again confident of carrying off their interaction with the assurance expected of a prospective wife.

''Dare say you'll have your hands full today, acting as hostess in her ladyship's stead.'' Nell deftly wound the golden mass of Antonia's hair into a tight bun, teasing tendrils free to wreathe about her ears and nape. ''She told Trant she intends going no further than the terrace.''

Antonia shifted on the stool. ''She's getting too old to stand up to the crowds—I'm only glad I can help her in this way.''

''Aye—and his lordship, too. Can't think that he'd appreciate having to face it all by himself.''

Antonia glanced searchingly at Nell but there was no evidence of intent in her maid's homely features. ''Naturally I'll be on hand to aid his lordship in any way I can.''

A role she could hardly escape, having worked so diligently to earn it. Being at odds with Philip on today of all days was going to be simply impossible. They would have to make their peace before the guests arrived.

As soon as Nell pronounced her fit to face the day, Antonia headed downstairs. As she descended the last flight, her nemesis strolled into the hall. Looking up, he stopped at the foot of the stairs—and waited. Antonia paused, meeting his gaze. In the hall above, a door opened then slowly closed. Drawing in a steadying breath, Antonia continued her descent, her expression determinedly aloof.

Philip turned to face her, effectively blocking her way. As Nell had intimated, he was precise to a pin in a grey morning coat, his cravat tied in a simple but elegant knot. A subdued waistcoat, form-fitting breeches and glossy Hessians completed the outfit—perfect for a wealthy gentleman about to greet his neighbours. His movements, Antonia noted, were once again lazy; his habitual air of languid indolence hung like a cloak about him. She stopped on the last step, her eyes level with his. "Good morning, my lord." She kept her tone coolly polite.

Only his eyes, his grey gaze sharply intent as it met hers, gave evidence of yesterday's turmoil.

"Good morning, Antonia." Holding her gaze, Philip raised a brow. "Pax?"

Antonia narrowed her eyes. "You accused me of seducing you."

"A momentary aberration." Philip kept his eyes on hers. "I know you didn't." He had managed that all by himself.

She was, after all, an innocent; regardless of any scheme she and Henrietta had concocted, what had flared between them was more his doing than hers.

Antonia hesitated, studying his bland countenance.

Despite his determination to remain distant, Philip felt his lips twist. He reached for her hand. "Antonia—"

The sound of a heavy footstep had them both looking up.

"Henrietta." Lips tightening, Philip caught Antonia's gaze. "I need you as my hostess, Antonia." His fingers tightened about hers. "I want you by my side."

It took a moment for Antonia to subdue her response to his touch, his plea. Stiffly, she inclined her head; behind her, she could hear Henrietta on the landing. "You may count on me, my lord." She kept her voice low. "I won't let you down."

Philip held her gaze. "And *I* won't let *you* down." For an instant, he held still, then, eyes glinting, swiftly raised her fingers to his lips. "I'll even promise not to bite."

As the day progressed, Antonia found herself grateful for the reassurance. Henrietta had elected to greet her visitors at the bottom of the terrace steps; Fenton was stationed at the front of the house, directing all arrivals around the corner to the south lawn.

After settling Henrietta by the balustrade, Antonia, her eye on Mrs Mimms, approaching like a galleon under full sail, two anaemic daughters in tow, murmured, "I'll just go the rounds and check—"

"Nonsense, my dear." Closing her crabbed fingers about Antonia's wrist, Henrietta smiled up at her. "Your place is beside me."

Antonia frowned. "There's no need—"

"What say you, Ruthven?" Henrietta glanced at Philip, standing behind her, his gaze fixed on Mrs Mimms. "Don't you think Antonia should stand by us?"

"Indubitably," Philip stated. He shifted his gaze to Antonia, subtle challenge in his eyes. "How else, my dear, will we cope with Mrs Mimms—let alone the rest of them?"

She had, of course, to acquiesce; the result was predictable. Introduced by a beaming Henrietta as "My very dear niece—dare say you remember her—spent many summers here with us all. Don't know how we could have managed this without her", she found herself transfixed by Mrs Mimms' basilisk stare.

"Indeed? Helping out?" Mrs Mimms cast a knowledgeable eye over the tables and booths scattered over the lawns and terrace. Her lips thinned as her gaze fell on Philip, already greeting the next guests. "I see."

Those two bare words effectively summarized Mrs Mimms' reading of the situation. Determined not to let it, or anything else, rattle her, Antonia smiled serenely. "I do hope you enjoy yourself." With a gentle nod, she allowed her gaze to shift to Horatia and Honoria Mimms, both of whom had yet to drag their attention from Philip. Their protuberant eyes were fixed on his face in cloying adoration. "And your daughters, too, of course."

Mrs Mimms glanced sharply at her offspring. "Come along, girls!" She frowned intimidatingly. "Stop dilly-dallying!" With a swirl of her skirts, she led the way up the terrace steps.

Mrs Mimms was not alone among the local ladies in having seen in the Manor's invitation a chance to press their daughters' claims. That much was made clear as the guests flooded in. Antonia found herself the object of quite a few disconcerted stares. Many recalled her from her earlier visits; while most greeted her warmly, the matrons with unmarried daughters in tow were distinctly more reserved.

Lady Archibald was characteristically forthright in her surprise. "Damnation! Thought you'd disappeared. Or at least were safely wed!"

Antonia struggled to hide her grin. It was impossible to take offence; her ladyship, while hardly the soul of tact, possessed an indefatigably kind heart. She watched as her ladyship, frowning, looked down on the mousy young lady hugging her shadow, her gaze, like all the other young ladies' gazes seemed to be, fixed on Philip. Lady Archibald humphed. "Come along, Emily. No point in making sheep's eyes in *that* direction."

Antonia made a point of shaking hands with Emily, to soften that trenchant remark. But the girl appeared not to have heeded it, continuing to cast shy but glowing glances at Philip.

After directing her ladyship and Emily to the terrace, Antonia turned to greet the next guest, in doing so, she met Philip's eye.

She had never before seen such an expression of aggravated exasperation on his face. It was a fight to keep her lips in the prescribed gentle smile; her jaw ached for a full five minutes. Thereafter, she studiously avoided his gaze whenever smitten young ladies stood before them.

The novelty of the event had ensured a large turnout. All their neighbours had accepted, rolling up the drive in chaises and carriages, many open so the occupants could bask in the bright sunshine. Philip's tenants came in carts or on foot, lifting their caps or dropping shy curtsies as they passed the reception line on their way to join the congregation on the lawn.

Amongst the last to arrive was the party from the Grange, some miles beyond the village. Sir Miles and Lady Castleton were new to the district since Antonia's last visit; she studied them as they approached, her ladyship strolling in the lead, an aloof expression on her lovely face, a slim, dark-haired young lady in her wake.

"My dear Ruthven!" With a dramatic gesture, Lady Castleton presented her hand. A statuesque brunette, fashionably pale, she was elegantly gowned in figured muslin, her face set in lines of studied boredom. "What a novel—quite *exhausting*—idea!" A cloud of heady perfume engulfed the reception party. Her ladyship's gaze shifted to Henrietta. "I don't know how you could bear to handle all this, my dear. You must be positively prostrated. So naughty of Ruthven to expect it of you."

"Nonsense, Selina!" Henrietta frowned and straightened her shoulders. "If you must know, having a major gathering was *my* idea—Ruthven was merely good enough to humour me."

"Indeed," Philip drawled, releasing her ladyship's hand after the most perfunctory shake. He turned to Sir Miles. "I can confirm that it was not my will that gave rise to today's entertainment."

Sir Miles, bluffly genial, was a stark contrast to his wife. Chuckling, he pumped Philip's hand. "No need to tell me that! Not a man here doesn't know what it's like."

"As you say." Philip's smile remained easy as he nodded to the girl who stood between Sir Miles and his wife. "Miss Castleton."

"Good afternoon, my lord." Boldly, Miss Castleton presented her hand with the same dramatic flair as her mother. She accompanied it with an openly inviting, distinctly brazen look. Not as tall as Antonia, she was possessed of a full figure, more revealed than concealed by her fine muslin gown.

Philip glanced at her hand as if mildly surprised to find it hanging before him. He clasped it but fleetingly, his gaze, blank, shifting to Lady Castleton, then Antonia as he half-turned.

"Haven't introduced you to my niece." Henrietta gestured to Antonia, adroitly deflecting attention from Miss Castleton, who promptly pouted. "Miss Mannering."

With a calm smile, Antonia held out her hand.

Lady Castleton's sharp, black-eyed gaze travelled over her; an arrested expression flitted over her pale face. "Ah," she said, smiling but not with her eyes. Briefly touching Antonia's fingers, she looked down at Henrietta. "It's reassuring to see that you've found someone to act as companion at last."

"Companion?" Henrietta blinked; Antonia noted her aunt's straight back but could not fault her guileless expression as she exclaimed, "Oh—I keep forgetting you're *newcomers!*" Henrietta smiled, all confiding condescension. "No, no—Antonia's often visited here. Been her second home for years. Now her mama's passed on, she's naturally come to stay with me." Turning, Henrietta squeezed Antonia's arm. "But you're right in part—it's a great relief to have someone capable of organising all this sort of thing—exhausting at my age but, as you must know, *quite* one's duty."

Antonia took her cue, smiling fondly at Henrietta. "Indeed, but I assure you, aunt, I haven't found it exhausting at all." Glancing up, still smiling, she met Lady Castleton's hard gaze. "I'm quite used to organising such affairs—all part of a young lady's education, as my mama was wont to say."

Lady Castleton's eyes narrowed. "Indeed?"

"Be that as it may," Philip said, deftly coming between Antonia and Henrietta, "I believe it's time we adjourned to the terrace.'' Capturing Antonia's hand, he tucked it into one elbow, then held his other arm rigid as Henrietta leaned heavily upon it. "Sir Miles?"

"Indeed, m'lord.'' Before Lady Castleton could reclaim the initiative, Sir Miles drew her arm through his, then offered his other arm to his daughter. "Couldn't agree more. Let's go, what?"

Without a backward glance, Sir Miles ushered his ladies up the steps.

Philip waited until they were out of earshot, then glanced pointedly down at the ladies on his arms. "Might I suggest, my dears, that we get this exhausting, exceedingly well-organised event underway?"

They saw Henrietta settled in her seat at one end of the long table, then Philip escorted Antonia to her chosen position halfway down the board. "I never thought to say it, but thank heaven for Ladies Archibald and Hammond."

As she sat, Antonia glanced at the head of the table where the two ladies in question, imposing matrons both, flanked Philip's empty chair. Settling her skirts, she cast a questioning glance up at him.

Philip bent close. "They take precedence over Lady Castleton." With a glint of a smile and a lifted brow, he straightened and moved away.

Antonia disguised her grin as a cheery smile; she hunted for Lady Castleton and found her seated on the opposite side, some places away, her exquisite features marred by an expression of disaffected boredom. Her ladyship's disdain, however, was not evinced by others; as the food, laboured over by Mrs Hobbs, Cook and a small battalion of helpers, appeared on the crisp damask cloth, genial conversation rose on all sides. As Fenton and his minions filled goblets and glasses, the festive atmosphere grew.

Philip proposed a toast to the company, then bade them enjoy the day. When he sat, the feast began.

From the corner of her eye, Antonia kept watch over the

steady stream of maids carrying platters to the lower tables. To her mind, Philip's tenants were, in this instance, as important if not more so than his neighbours. Neighbours would be invited on other occasions; this was one of the few when tenants partook of their landlord's largesse. Trestles groaned as trays loaded with mouth-watering pastries, succulent savouries and roasted meats, together with breads, cheeses and pitchers of ale, were placed upon them. The company seemed in fine fettle; she could detect nothing but unfettered gaiety around the tables on the lawn.

She had wondered whether the noise from the lower tables would prove overwhelming. As she returned her attention to the conversations about her, she dismissed the thought; those on the terrace were more than capable of holding their own.

The long meal passed without incident, bar an altercation which arose at the table set aside for the tenants' children, which their fathers promptly quashed. When the fruit platters were all but empty, the boards were drawn; the dowagers and others ill-inclined to the games, contests and feats of skill slated to fill the afternoon, settled in their chairs on the terrace to enjoy a comfortable cose and possibly a nap in the warm sunshine.

The more robust of the guests adjourned to the lawns.

Straightening from having a last word with Henrietta, Antonia found Philip by her side.

When she looked her surprise, he raised a brow. "You didn't seriously imagine I'd brave the dangers of the lawns without you to protect me?"

"Protect…?" Antonia temporarily lost her track when he drew her close, trapping her hand in the crook of his elbow. He was very large—and very hard; she was not yet accustomed to his nearness. "What am I supposed to protect you against?" She managed what she felt was a creditably sceptical look.

Her nemesis merely smiled. "Piranhas."

"Piranhas?" Antonia cudgelled her brains as, with an elegant nod for the dowagers, Philip led her down the steps. "I thought they were fish," she said once they gained the lawns.

"Precisely. Social but carnivorous and definitely cold-blooded."

"On your lawns?"

"Indeed. Here comes a young one, now."

Antonia looked up to see Miss Castleton bearing down upon them, arm linked with Honoria Mimms.

"Ah—Miss Mannering, is it not?" Miss Castleton came to a halt directly before them. "Poor Honoria seems to have ripped her flounce."

Looking thoroughly puzzled, Honoria was twisting about, trying to see her trailing flounce. "I don't know how it happened," she said. "I felt it rip but when I turned around there was nothing for it to catch on. Luckily, Calliope was standing close by and told me how bad it was."

"Perhaps, if you would be so good, Miss Mannering," Calliope Castleton glibly broke in, "you might take poor Honoria up to the house and help her to pin up her lace?"

Honoria blushed beet-red. "Oh, I *couldn't*—! I mean, you have all your other guests…"

"Exactly," Philip calmly interjected. "As you've been such a good friend to Miss Mimms, Miss Castleton, I know you won't mind helping her to the terrace and asking one of the maids for assistance." He bestowed a smile of calculated charm on Honoria Mimms. "I'm afraid, my dear, that I have great need of Miss Mannering's talents at present."

Miss Mimms was dazzled. "*Naturally*, my lord." Her eyes were wide and shining. "I wouldn't *dream* of…of *discommoding* you."

"Thank you, my dear." Philip took her hand and bowed over it, his grateful smile enough to turn any young girl's head. "I am in your debt."

Honoria Mimms looked as if she would burst. Her round face alight, she grabbed Miss Castleton's arm. "Come on, Calliope—I'm sure we can take care of this ourselves."

Beaming, Miss Mimms towed Miss Castleton towards the terrace. The sound of Miss Castleton's protests died behind them.

Antonia opened her eyes wide. "Miss Castleton didn't seem all that taken with your suggestion, my lord."

"I dare say. Miss Castleton, as you will have noticed, is somewhat enamoured of her own path."

Antonia's eyes lit; her lips quirked.

Philip noticed. "Now what is there in that to make you laugh?" Mentally replaying the conversation, he could see nothing to account for the laughter he sensed welling within her. He lifted one brow interrogatively. "Well?"

Antonia's smile broke. "I was considering, my lord," she said, shifting her gaze to the crowds before them, "whether your last comment might not be an example of the pot calling the kettle black?"

She glanced up at him; he trapped her gaze, both brows rising. For a long moment, he held her mesmerised; Antonia felt a shiver start deep inside, spreading through her until it quivered just beneath her skin.

Only when awareness blossomed in her eyes did Philip glance away. "You, my dear, are hardly one to talk." After a moment, he added, his tone less dark, "I suspect that we should mingle. When are the archery contests scheduled to start?"

The hours passed swiftly, filled with conversations. They strolled the lawns, stopping every few feet to chat with their guests. Antonia was of the firm opinion that Philip should spend at least five minutes with each of his tenants; it transpired he was of similar mind; she was not called on to steer him their way. A fact for which she gave due thanks.

Her control of the *fête* and its associated events might be absolute; it did not extend to him.

To her surprise, he held by her side, even waiting patiently while she exchanged recipes with one of his farmers' wives. Despite the years, the majority of his tenants were still known to her; they were keen to renew their acquaintance as well as catch up with their landlord. After every encounter, Philip drew her close before moving on.

Exactly as if she did indeed provide the protection he claimed.

While most of the mamas had read the signs aright and consequently made no effort to put their darlings in his way, their darlings proved less perceptive. Miss Abercrombie and Miss Harris, greatly daring, accosted them as they strolled.

"Such a frightfully warm day, don't you think, my lord?" Miss Abercrombie's gaze was certainly sultry. She fanned herself with her hand, the action drawing attention to the ample charms revealed by her deeply scooped neckline.

"Quite positively *enervating*, I think." Miss Harris, not to be outdone, fluttered her lashes and cast Philip a languishing look.

Antonia felt him stiffen; his expression was shuttered, remote.

"Before you find yourselves prostrated, ladies, might I suggest you repair to the drawing-room?" Philip's tone alone lowered the temperature ten degrees. "I believe there are cold drinks laid out there." With a distant nod, he changed tack, steering Antonia away from the budding courtesans.

After one glance at the rigid set of his lips, Antonia amused herself looking over the stalls. She could have told all the young misses that gushing declarations and fluttering lashes were definitely the wrong way to approach their host. He disliked all show of emotion, preferring the correct, properly restrained modes of interaction. He was a conventional man—she strongly suspected most gentlemen were.

They paused to allow Philip to discuss crop rotation with one of his tenant farmers. Covertly studying him, Antonia smiled wrily. His languid indolence was very much to the fore, at least in his projected image.

The girls watching could not hear his brisk words on ploughing and the optimum depth of furrows. As handsome as any, with that subtle aura of restrained power which derived, she suspected, from that affected indolence, while strolling the lawns with smoothly elegant stride, every movement polished and assured, he was a natural target for the sighing, die-away looks of the massed host of young girls.

Quelling an unhelpful shiver, Antonia looked around. Horatia Mimms and two of the girls from the vicarage stood in a knot nearby, giggling and whispering. Feeling immeasurably older, she let her gaze pass over them.

Concluding his discussion, Philip placed his hand over hers and turned towards the archery butts. "Looks like the contests are well underway." He glanced down at her. "I'm not at all sure you shouldn't be the one to present the ribbon to the winner."

Antonia shook her head. "*You* are their master—to the youngsters you're an idol. Of course they want you to award the prize."

She shifted as she spoke, swinging slightly forward to glance into his eyes. Unfortunately, that placed her in Horatia Mimms's path. In a balletic manoeuvre, Horatia flew forward, her trajectory calculated to land her, gracefully tripping, in Philip's arms. Instead, she cannoned into Antonia's back.

With a stifled cry, Antonia catapulted forward, coming up hard against Philip's chest. His arms closed around her, steel bands crushing her to him as he lifted her free of the wild tangle that was Horatia, now sprawled on the grass.

"Are you all right?" Easing his hold, Philip looked down at her.

Antonia nodded, struggling to find her voice. "Just a

bump—'' She couldn't help a wince as she tried to pull back.

Philip steadied her, his hands firming on her back, gently kneading. His gaze shifted to the scene before them, where a winded Horatia was being helped to her feet by her two supporters from the vicarage.

Philip's eyes blazed. "That was the most *inconsiderate* piece of witless behaviour it has ever been my misfortune to witness!"

Helpless in his arms, unable to stop her senses luxuriating in the feel of his warm hands massaging her back, her forehead resting, for one weak moment, against his chest, Antonia stifled a hysterical giggle. From his tone, from the tension holding him, she knew his temper was on a very short leash. Luckily, they were halfway between the stalls and the crowds watching the archery; there were few witnesses to the scene.

"I cannot believe your parents—" Philip's gaze coldly swept all three girls "—will find your antics at all acceptable." His icy words cut like a lash. "I intend to make plain to them—"

Antonia pushed hard against his chest, forcing him to loosen his hold. As she struggled free of his arms, she wasn't at all surprised to glimpse three white faces, stricken with alarm. "I'm perfectly all right." One glance at Philip was enough to confirm he wasn't mollified by her assurance. His face remained stony, his expression chilling. Antonia felt like grimacing at him; she contented herself with narrowing her eyes warningly before facing the girls. "Miss Mimms—I hope you sustained no injury?"

White as a sheet, Horatio Mimms blinked, then dazedly looked down. A long grass stain marred the pink of her muslin skirts. "My best dress!" she moaned. "It's ruined!"

Philip snorted. "You may consider yourself—"

Antonia stepped back—onto his foot. Philip broke off and frowned down at her.

"Perhaps, Miss Carmichael, Miss Jayne, you could accompany Miss Mimms into the house and see if the stain will shift?"

The vicar's daughters nodded, quickly taking Horatia's arms. But Horatia unexpectedly stood her ground, her cheeks slowly turning an unfortunate shade of red. She looked helplessly at Antonia. "I'm most extremely sorry, Miss Mannering. I didn't mean to—" She broke off and bit her lip, her gaze dropping to the ground.

Antonia took pity on her. "An unfortunate occurrence— we'll say no more about it."

The relief that flooded all three faces was almost comical. With quick bobs, the three took themselves off, moving out of Philip's orbit as fast as they could.

"An unfortunate occurrence, my foot!" Philip glowered after them. "The little wretches—"

"Were only behaving as young girls often do." Antonia slanted him a glance. "Particularly when presented with such provocation as is present here today."

Philip's eyes narrowed. "I do not appreciate being the butt of their silly fancies."

Antonia smiled. "Never mind." She patted his arm soothingly. "Come and present the archery prizes—from the whoops, I think the contests must be over."

Philip sent her a darkling glance but allowed her to steer him to the area by the lake where the archery contest had been held.

He might not appreciate the adoration of young girls, but he clearly had no difficulty coping with the same emotion in youthful cubs. Antonia watched as they danced about him while he gave an impromptu speech congratulating the winners of the three competitions. With the prizes awarded, he returned to her side.

They adjourned to the terrace for tea. Despite numerous invitations to do otherwise, Philip held trenchantly to her

side. Then it was time to cross to where the junior equestrians had been kept busy for most of the afternoon.

They regained the lawns, only to discover Lady Castleton
in their path. Her daughter walked beside her on the arm of
Mr Gerald Moresby, a younger son of Moresby Hall.

"There you are, Ruthven." Lady Castleton placed one
manicured hand firmly on Philip's sleeve. "You've been
positively hiding yourself away amongst the farmers, sir—
quite ignoring those who would, one might imagine, have
far greater claim to your attention."

One glance convinced Antonia that her ladyship saw
nothing outrageous in her statement. Philip, she noticed,
looked bored.

Oblivious, Lady Castleton rolled on. "So you've driven
us to make our wishes plain, my lord. Calliope has con-
ceived a great wish to view your rose garden but unfortunately Gerald cannot abide the flowers—they make him
sneeze."

"Quite right." Gerald Moresby grinned. "Can't abide the
smell, y'know."

"So," Lady Castleton concluded, "as Miss Mannering is
apparently acting as hostess in her aunt's stead, I suggest
she takes Mr Moresby on an amble about the lake while
you, my lord, can lend me your arm and escort myself and
Calliope through your rose garden."

Gerald rubbed his hands together, his gaze on Antonia.
"Capital idea, what?"

Antonia did not think so. Eight years ago, Gerald had
been a most untrustworthy character. Judging by the expression in his pale blue eyes and the way his weak mouth
shifted, he had not improved with the years.

Sensing sudden tension beside her, she glanced up to find
Philip's gaze fixed on Gerald's face, his lips curved in a
smile that was not entirely pleasant.

"I'm afraid, dear lady," Philip smoothly said, shifting his
gaze from Gerald Moresby's lecherous countenance, thereby

denying a sudden urge to rearrange it, "that as Miss Mannering and I are sharing the honours in entertaining my tenants, our time is not our own. I'm sure you understand the situation," he sauvely continued, "being yourself the chatelaine of an estate."

He was well aware of Lady Castleton's background; it did not encompass any great experience of "lady of the manor" duties.

Which was why, stumped by his comment, unable to contradict it, her ladyship resorted to a cold-eyed stare.

"I knew you'd understand." Philip inclined his head, his hand trapping Antonia's where it rested on his sleeve. "But I'm afraid you'll have to excuse us—the junior equestrians await." He included Lady Castleton and her daughter in his benedictory smile; it didn't stretch as far as Gerald Moresby.

As they passed out of earshot, Antonia drew a deep breath. "How positively…" She paused, hunting for words.

"Brilliant?" Philip suggested. "Glib? Artful?"

"I was thinking of ruthless." She cast him a reproving glance.

The look he bent upon her was less readable. "You *wanted* to wander by the lake with Gerald Moresby?"

"Of course not." Antonia quelled a shudder. "He's a positive toad."

Philip humphed. "Well, Miss Castleton's a piranha, so they're well matched—and we're well rid of them."

Antonia had no wish to argue.

They arrived at the edge of the roped-off area in time to watch the final rounds of the low jumps. Johnny Smidgins, the headgroom's son, won by a whisker. His sister, little Emily, a tiny tot barely big enough to hold the reins, guided a fat pony through the course to take the girls' prize.

Everybody made much of them both. Ruthven gravely shook Johnny's hand and presented him with a blue ribbon. Antonia couldn't resist picking up little Emily and giving her a quick kiss before pinning her blue rosette to her dress.

Sheer pride struck the little girl dumb; Philip patted her curls and left well alone.

After that, only the last event remained—the Punch and Judy show. Virtually everyone, even some of the dowagers, crowded before the stage erected in front of the green wall of the shrubbery.

The children sat on the grass, their elders standing behind them. Among the last to join the throng, just as the make-shift curtain arose to whoops, claps and expectant shrieks, Antonia and Philip found themselves at the very back of the crowd. Philip could see; despite ducking and peering, Antonia could not.

"Here." Philip drew her aside to where a low retaining wall held back a section of lawn. "Stand on this." Gathering her skirts, Antonia took his proffered hand and let him help her up. The stone was not high but narrow on top.

"Put your hand on my shoulder."

She had to to keep her balance. He stood beside her and they both turned to watch the stage.

Geoffrey's script was hilarious, the puppets inspired. Some of the props, including such diverse items as the cook's favourite ladle and a motheaten tiger's head from the billiard room, were both novel and inventively used. By the time the curtain finally dropped—literally—Antonia was leaning heavily on Philip's shoulder, her other hand pressed to the stitch in her side.

"Oh, my!" she said, blinking away tears of laughter. "I never knew my brother had such a solid grasp of *double entendres*."

Philip threw her a cynical look. "I suspect there's a few things you don't know about your brother."

Antonia raised a brow. She straightened, about to lift her hand from his shoulder. And sucked in a breath as her bruised back protested.

Instantly, Philip's arm came around her.

"You *are* hurt."

The words, forced out, sounded almost like an accusation. Leaning into the support of his arm, Antonia looked at him in surprise. Courtesy of the stone wall, their eyes were level; when his lids lifted and his gaze met hers, she had a clear view of the stormy depths, the emotions clouding his grey eyes.

Their gazes locked; for an instant, his sharpened, became clearer, then he blinked and the expression was gone. Her heart thudding, Antonia dropped her gaze and let him lift her gently down. She stretched and shifted, trying to ease the spot between her shoulder blades where Horatia Mimms's elbow had connected. She wished he would massage it again.

He remained, rigid, beside her, his hands fisted by his sides. Antonia glanced up through her lashes; his face was unreadable. "It's only a bit stiff," she said, in response to the tension in the air.

"That witless female—!"

"Philip—I'm perfectly all right." Antonia nodded at the people streaming across the lawns. "Come—we must bid your guests farewell."

They did, standing by the drive and waving each carriage, each family of tenants, goodbye. Needless to say, Horatia Mimms was treated to an unnerving stare; Antonia held herself ready throughout the Mimms's effusive leave-taking to quell, by force if necessary, any outburst on Philip's part.

But all passed smoothly; even the Castletons eventually left.

When all had departed, Antonia returned to the lawns to supervise the clearing. Philip strolled beside her, watching the late afternoon sun strike gold gleams from her hair.

"I'm really very impressed with Geoffrey," he eventually said. "He took on the responsibility of staging the Punch and Judy and saw it through."

Antonia smiled. "And very well, too. The children were enthralled."

''Mmm. As far as I know, none fell in the lake, either—for which he has my heartfelt thanks.'' Philip glanced down at her. ''But I think some part of his glory is owed to you.'' They had almost reached the nearest shore of the lake. Brows rising in question, Antonia stopped on a small rise; meeting her gaze, Philip halted beside her. ''You must have had a hard time bringing him up, essentially alone.''

Antonia shrugged and looked away across the lake. ''I never regretted having the care of him. In its way, it's been very rewarding.''

''Perhaps—but there are many who would say it was not your responsibility—not while your mother still lived.''

Antonia's lips twisted. ''True, but after my father died, I'm not entirely certain my mother did live, you see.''

There was a pause, then Philip answered, ''No. I don't.''

Antonia glanced at him, then turned and headed back towards the house. Philip kept pace beside her. They were halfway to the terrace before she spoke again. ''My mother was devoted to my father. Totally caught up with him and his life. When that ended unexpectedly, she was lost. Her interest in me and Geoffrey sprang from the fact we were his children—when he died, she lost interest in us.''

Philip's jaw set. ''Hardly a motherly sort.''

''You mustn't misjudge her—she was never intentionally negligent. But she didn't see things in the light you might expect—nothing was important after my father had gone.''

Together, they climbed the rising lawns towards the terrace. As they neared the house, Antonia paused and looked up, putting up a hand to shade her eyes so she could admire the elegant façade. ''It took a long time for me to understand—to realise what it was to love so completely—to love like that. So that nothing else mattered anymore.''

For long moments, they stood silently side by side, then Antonia lowered her hand. She glanced briefly at Philip then accepted his proffered arm.

On the terrace, they turned, surveying the lawns, neat again but marked by the tramp of many feet.

Philip's lips twisted. "Remind me not to repeat this exercise any time soon."

He turned—and read the expression in Antonia's eyes. "*Not* that it wasn't a roaring success," he hastened to reassure her. "However, I doubt my temper will bear the strain of a repeat performance too soon."

The obvious riposte flashed through Antonia's mind so forcefully it was all she could do to keep the words from her lips.

Philip read them in her eyes, in the shifting shades of green and gold. The planes of his face hardened. "Indeed," he said, his tone dry. "When I marry, the problem will disappear."

Antonia stiffened but did not look away. Their gazes locked; for a moment, all was still.

Then Philip reached for her hand. He raised it; with cool deliberation, he brushed a lingering kiss across her fingertips, savouring the response that rippled through her, the response she could not hide.

Defiantly, her eyes still on his, Antonia lifted her chin.

Philip held her challenging gaze, one brow slowly rising. "A successful day—in all respects."

With languid grace, he gestured towards the morning room windows. Together, they went inside.

"Ah, me!" Geoffrey yawned hugely. "I'm done in. Wrung out like a rag. I think I'll go up."

Setting the billiard cues back in their rack, Philip nodded. "I'd rather you did—before you pass out and I have to haul you up."

Geoffrey grinned. "I wouldn't want to put you to the trouble. G'night, then." With a nod, he went out, closing the door behind him.

Philip shut the cue case; turning, his wandering gaze fell

on the tantalus set against the opposite wall. Strolling across, he poured himself a large brandy. Cradling the glass, he opened the long windows and went out, thrusting his free hand into his pocket as he slowly paced the terrace.

All was still and silent—his home, his estate, rested under the blanket of night. Stars glimmered through a light cloud; stillness stretched, comforting and familiar, about him. Everyone had retired, to recoup after the hectic day. He felt as wrung out as Geoffrey but too restless to seek his bed.

The emotions the day had stirred still whirled and clashed within him, too novel to be easily dismissed, too strong to simply ignore. Protectiveness, jealousy, concern—he was hardly a stranger to such feelings but never before had he felt them so acutely nor in so focused a fashion.

Superimposed over all was a frustrated irritation, a dislike of being compelled even though the compulsion sprang from within him.

In its way, it was all new to him.

He took a long sip of his brandy and stared into the night.

It was impossible to pretend that he didn't understand. He knew, unequivocally, that if it had been any other woman, he would have found some excuse, some fashionable reason, for being elsewhere, far distant, entirely out of reach.

Instead, he was still here.

Philip drained his glass and felt the fumes wreathe through his head. Presumably this was part of being thirty-four.

Chapter Six

Two days later, Philip stood at the library windows, looking out over the sun-washed gardens. The business that had kept him inside on such a glorious day was concluded; behind him, Banks, his steward, shuffled his papers.

"I'll take the offer in to Mrs Mortingdale's man then, m'lord, though heaven knows if she'll accept it." Banks' tone turned peevish. "Smiggins has been doing his best to persuade her to it but she just can't seem to come at putting her signature to the deed."

Philip's gaze roamed the gardens; he wondered where Antonia was hiding today. "She'll sign in the end—she just needs time to decide." At Banks's snort, he swung about. "Patience, Banks. Lower Farm isn't going anywhere—and all but surrounded by my land as it is, there'll be precious few others willing to make an offer, let alone one to match mine."

"Aye—I know," Banks grumbled. "If you want the truth it's that that sticks. It's nothing but senseless female shilly-shallying that's holding us up."

Philip's brows rose. "Shilly-shallying, unfortunately, is what one must endure when dealing with females."

With a disapproving grunt, Banks took himself off.

After a long, assessing glance at his gardens, Philip followed him out.

She wasn't in the rose garden, the formal garden was empty. Deserted, the peony walk slumbered beneath the afternoon sun. The shrubbery was cool and inviting but disappointingly uninhabited. Eyes narrowed, Philip paused in the shadow of a hedge and considered the known characteristics of his quarry. Then, with a grunt to rival Banks's, he strode towards the house.

He ran her to earth in the still-room.

Antonia looked up, blinking in surprise as he strolled into the dimly lit room. "Hello." Hands stilling, she hesitated, her gaze shifting to the shelves of bottles and jars ranged along the walls. "Were you after something?"

"As it happens, I was." Philip leaned against the bench at which she was working. "You."

Antonia's eyes widened. She looked down at the herbs she was snipping. "I—"

"I missed you this morning." Philip lifted a brow as her head came up; he trapped her gaze with his. "Can it be you've grown tired of riding?"

"No—of course not." Antonia blinked, then looked down. "I was merely worn out by the *fête*."

"Not still stiff after your collision with Miss Mimms?"

"Indeed not. That was barely a bruise." Gathering up her chopped herbs, she dumped them into a bowl. "It's entirely gone, now."

"I'm glad to hear it. I finished with Banks earlier than I'd expected—I wondered if you were wishful of chancing your skill with my greys?"

Brushing her hands on her apron, Antonia considered the prospect. It was definitely enticing. And she'd have to take the first step some time—chancing her skill in an entirely new arena.

"If you can hold them in style," Philip mused, "perhaps

I could demonstrate the basics of handling a whip?'' Brows lifting, he met her gaze.

Antonia did not miss the subtle challenge in his eyes. Just how much he truly saw she did not know, but the only way of testing her developing defences was to risk some time in his company. ''Very well.'' She nodded briskly, then stretched on tiptoe to peer through the high windows.

Philip straightened. ''It's a beautiful day—you'll just need your hat.'' Capturing her hand, he drew her to the door. ''I'll have the horses put to while you fetch it.''

Before she could blink, Antonia found herself by the stairs. Released, she threw a speaking look at her would-be instructor before, determinedly regal, she went up to find her hat.

Ten minutes later, they were bowling down the gravelled sweep, the greys pacing in prime style. The drive, through leafy lanes to the nearby village of Fernhurst, was uneventful; despite her stretched nerves, Antonia could detect not the slightest hint of intent in the figure lounging gracefully by her side. He appeared at ease with the world, without a thought beyond the lazy warmth of the bright sunshine and the anticipation of an excellent dinner.

Quelling an unhelpful spurt of disappointment, she lifted her chin. ''As I've taken you this far without landing you in a ditch, perhaps you'd consent to instruct me on handling the whip?''

''Ah, yes.'' Philip straightened. ''Put the reins in your left hand, then take the whip in your right. You need to loop the lash through your fingers.'' After she had fumbled for a minute, he held out a hand. ''Here—let me show you.''

The rest of the drive passed with the horses pacing steadily, equally oblivious to Philip's expert and intentionally undistracting wielding of the lash and her less-than-successful attempts to direct them with a flick to their ears.

Indeed, by the time they reached the Manor drive, she would have given a considerable sum just to be able to flick their ears. Philip's stylish expertise with the long whip, sending the lash reaching out to just tickle a leaf then twitching it back so it hissed up the handle, back to his waiting fingers, was not at all easy to emulate.

She was frowning when he lifted her down.

"Never mind—like many skills, it's one that comes with practice."

Antonia looked up—and wondered where he'd left his mask. His eyes had taken on the darker hue she had first recognized in the glade, his hands were firm about her waist, long fingers flexing gently. Cambric was thicker than muslin but even combined with her chemise, the fabric was insufficient to protect her from the heat of his touch.

He held her before him, his gaze on hers; she felt intensely vulnerable, deliciously so. Her wits were drifting, her breath slowly seizing.

His gaze sharpened, the grey darkening even more.

For one pounding heartbeat, Antonia was convinced he was going to kiss her—there, in the middle of his forecourt. Then the planes of his face, until then hard and angular, shifted. His lips curved lightly, gently mocking. He reached for her hand, his fingers twining with hers. His eyes still on hers, he raised her hand and pressed a kiss to her knuckles.

Philip's smile was wry. "Another accomplishment requiring practice, I fear."

The sound of hurrying footsteps heralded the arrival of a stable lad, apologetic and breathless. Philip benignly waved aside the lad's stuttered excuses; as the carriage was removed, he settled Antonia's hand on his sleeve. She glanced up, suspicion and uncertainty warring in her eyes.

One brow rising in unconscious arrogance, Philip turned her towards the house. "We've made definite progress, my dear, don't you think?"

"*That*'s better!" Perched at her window high above the forecourt, Henrietta heaved a sigh and turned back into the room. "I tell you, Trant, I was beginning to get seriously worried."

"I know." Trant's gaze was sharp as she scanned her mistress's features.

"After the *fête—well!*—you have to admit no prospect *could* have looked brighter. Ruthven was so pointedly attentive, so *insistent* on remaining by Antonia's side, no matter the lures thrown at his head."

Trant sniffed. "I never heard it said he had bad taste. Seemed to me those 'lures' would more rightly send him in the opposite direction. Miss Antonia, no doubt, seemed a veritable haven."

Henrietta humphed. "To you and me, Trant, Miss Castleton and her ilk may appear quite impossibly ill-bred *but,* while I have nothing but the highest regard for Ruthven's intelligence, there's no question that gentlemen see such matters in a different light. All too prone to overlook substance in favour of the obvious—and you have to admit Miss Castleton had a great deal of the obvious on view. I must say I was greatly relieved that Ruthven appeared unimpressed."

Busy mending, Trant couldn't suppress a snort. "Unimpressed? More properly a case of being distracted."

"Distracted?" Henrietta stared at her maid. "Whatever do you mean?"

Trant stabbed her needle into her work. "Miss Antonia's not precisely unendowed, even if she isn't one as flaunts her wares. Looked to me like the master's eye was already fixed." Trant glanced up from beneath her heavy brows, watching to see how her mistress reacted to that suggestion.

Henrietta's considering expression slowly dissolved into one of smug content. "Well," she said, reaching for her cane. "They're together again, no doubt of that, and if Philip's inclination is engaged, so much the better. I've been worrying that something had gone amiss—Antonia's been on edge, positively skulking about the house." Her eyes narrowed. "I dare say that might be nerves on her part—and Philip, of course, is simply taking things at his usual pace."

Snorting, Henrietta stood, a martial light in her eyes. "Time to shake the reins. I believe, Trant, that it's high time we planned our removal to London."

Parting from Philip in the hall, Antonia sought her chamber. Nell was elsewhere; Antonia sent her hat skimming to land on the bed, then crossed to the window. Leaning on the wide sill, she breathed in the warm scented air.

She'd survived.

More importantly, despite the unnerving sensation that, within the landscape of their relationship, she had yet to gain a proper footing, that she might stumble at any step and was not certain he would catch her if she did, there seemed little doubt that she and Philip were intent on walking the same path.

Thankfully, he plainly understood her need for time—time to develop her defences, to develop a proper, wifely demeanour, to learn how not to embarrass him and herself with any excess of emotion. How else could she interpret his words? Sinking onto the window-seat, Antonia propped an elbow on the sill and rested her chin in her palm.

A cloud drifted over the sun; sudden coolness touched her. An echo dark with warning, her mother's voice replayed in her head. *"If you're wise, my girl, you won't look for love. Believe me, it's not worth the pain."*

Subduing a shiver, Antonia grimaced. Her mother had uttered those words on her deathbed, a conclusion drawn from experience, from a badly broken if selfish heart. In pursuing her present course, was she risking all her mother had lost?

Being Philip's wife was what she wanted to be, had always wanted to be; she had not come to Ruthven Manor seeking love.

But what if love found her?

Ten minutes' wary pondering brought no answer.

With a disgruntled grimace, Antonia banished her uncertainty—and focused her mind on her immediate goal.

Before they went to London, she was determined to be sufficiently accustomed to Philip's attentions to have the confidence to appear with him in public. The accumulated wisdom on which she had to rely—the few strictures her mother had deigned to bestow plus the snippets of advice gleaned from the Yorkshire ladies—was scant and very likely provincial; she would, however, learn quickly. Philip himself was an excellent model, coolly sophisticated, always in control. Parading through the *ton* on his arm would, she felt sure, be the ultimate test.

Once she had conquered her reactions and demonstrated her ability to be the charming, polished, coolly serene lady he required as his wife, then he would ask for her hand.

The road before her was straight—as Philip had intimated, it was simply a matter of learning to handle the reins.

Lips lifting, confidence welling, she rose and crossed to the bellpull.

She slept in the next morning; she was almost running when she rushed into the stableyard, her skirts over one arm, her crop clutched in one hand, the other holding on to her hat. Only to see Philip leading out both Pegasus and her mount, the tall roan, Raker. Both horses were saddled. Halting precipitously, Antonia stared. Philip saw her and raised a brow; lowering her hand from her hat, Antonia lifted her chin and calmly walked to Raker's side.

Philip came to lift her up; she turned towards him, raising her hands to his shoulders as she felt his slide, then firm, about her waist. Wide-eyed, she met his gaze—and saw his brows lift, a quizzical expression in his eyes.

She opened her mouth—and realized how he would answer her question. She clamped her lips shut, debating the wisdom of a glare.

Philip's lips twitched. "I saw no reason why you wouldn't." With that, he lifted her to her saddle.

Antonia made a production of arranging her skirts. By the time she was ready, Geoffrey had joined them; with a nod, Philip led the way out.

A three-mile gallop was precisely what she needed to shake her wits into place. Riding never failed to soothe her; atop a fine horse, she could fly over the fields, beyond the touch of time, beyond the present. It was an escape she had sorely missed over the past eight years; she knew very well no man alive bar Philip would permit her to ride in such a way.

She glanced at him, to her left a half-length in advance, his body flowing easily with the big gelding's stride. Man and horse were both strong; combined they presented a picture of harnessed power.

Quelling a shiver, Antonia looked ahead.

They pulled up on a knoll overlooking green meadows; they had not previously ridden this way. A stone cottage sat in the midst of a small garden, a narrow lane leading to its gate.

"Who lives there?" Antonia leaned forward to pat Raker's sleek neck. "This is still your land, isn't it?"

Philip nodded. "But that patch—" with his crop, he transcribed the boundaries of what Antonia estimated was a twenty-acre block "—belongs to a recently bereaved widow, a Mrs Mortingdale."

Wheeling slowly, Antonia checked her bearings. "Wouldn't it be sensible for you to purchase it—incorporate it with your holdings? She couldn't be getting much return on such a small piece."

"Yes and no in that order. I've made her an offer but she's yet to come to terms with selling up. I've told Banks to increase the offer slightly and let it stand. She has family elsewhere; she'll come around in time.''

Geoffrey was eager to investigate a nearby ridge; Philip nodded and he left with a whoop.

Antonia clicked her reins and set Raker to ford the narrow stream by which they'd paused. ''You seem very busy of late.'' He had spent most of the last two days with Banks. ''Surely the estate doesn't normally take so much of your time?''

''No.'' Slanting her a glance, Philip brought Pegasus alongside. ''But it seemed a propitious time to get the books to order.''

Antonia frowned. ''I would have thought after harvest would be more useful. That's when I did the tallies at Mannering.''

Philip's lips quirked; he forced them straight. ''Indeed? I rather think, however, that the exigencies I presently face are somewhat different to those you encountered at Mannering.''

Puzzled, Antonia glanced at him. ''I'm sure they are—I didn't mean to criticise.''

Philip's answering glance was distinctly wry. ''For which forbearance, my dear, I am truly grateful.''

Antonia straightened. ''You're talking in riddles.''

''Not intentionally.'' Meeting her sceptical gaze, Philip raised a languid brow. ''What do you think of Henrietta's plans for London?''

Antonia hesitated, then shrugged and obediently turned her mind to her aunt's projections. ''Leaving in a week seems wise. I would certainly appreciate a little time to accustom myself to the pace before the balls begin—and there's Geoffrey, too.'' Her brow clouded. ''Once the parties start, I doubt I'll have much time to spend with him.''

Philip's gaze was on Geoffrey, heading back at a gallop. ''Once he finds his way about, I doubt you'll need worry your head over him. I can't see him as a slow-top.'' Glancing at Antonia, he saw the concern in her eyes. "Of course, given he'll be under my roof, I will, naturally, be keeping an eye on him."

Antonia shot him a surprised look as Geoffrey thundered up. "Oh?"

"Indeed." Wheeling to head home, Philip met her gaze. "The least I can do. In the circumstances."

Antonia blinked. With a brisk nod for Geoffrey, Philip tapped his heels to Pegasus's sides; the chestnut surged. Raker followed. By the time they regained the stables, Antonia had thought better of enquiring as to precisely what circumstances he referred—she wasn't, she decided, ready to deal with his likely answer.

London and the *ton*—her proving ground—was, after all, still before her.

Philip decided to precede his stepmother and her guests to town, ostensibly to ensure Ruthven House was ready to receive them, in reality to take a quick look-in at his clubs and test the waters of the *ton* before permitting Antonia or Geoffrey to take a dip in society's sea. Departing one day before them would be enough; leaving early and driving his curricle, he would reach Grosvenor Square by midday, giving him two full days in which to gauge the tide before they arrived on the scene.

He did not, however, intend to leave the Manor before settling one significant point with his stepmother's niece. Time and place were crucial to his cause; he waited until the night before he was to leave, until tea had been taken and the cups stacked on the tray.

Antonia set the tray on the trolley then, turning, headed for the bellpull. Standing before the fireplace, Philip reached out as she passed him, capturing her hand before she reached her objective. Ignoring her surprised look, he spoke to Geoffrey, yawning by the *chaise*. "I left that book you wanted on the desk in the library."

Geoffrey's eyes brightened. "Oh, good! I'll take it up to bed."

He was already turning to the door. Philip raised a resigned brow—and raised his voice. "Perhaps, when you cross the hall, you could send Fenton in?"

Without turning, Geoffrey waved. "I will." He paused in the doorway to beam a belated smile at them all. "Good night."

As the door clicked shut, Philip glanced briefly at Antonia, then shifted his gaze to Henrietta, comfortably ensconced on the *chaise*. "I had thought to show your niece the beauties of the sunset. I believe I've heard you extoll its splendours when viewed from the terrace at this time of year?"

Transfixed by a gaze far too sharp for her comfort, Henrietta shifted. "Ah—yes." When Philip's gaze remained pointedly upon her, she shook her wits into order. "Yes, indeed! The effect can be quite..." she gestured airily "...breathtaking."

Philip smiled. Approvingly. Any doubt in Henrietta's mind that he had divined her secret purpose was firmly laid to rest.

"I believe you intend retiring early?"

Caution and curiosity warred in Henrietta's breast. Caution won. "Indeed," she said. Affecting a die-away air, she reclined against the cushions and waved listlessly. "If you'll ring for Trant, I think I'll go up immediately."

"An excellent notion." Philip crossed to the bellpull and tugged it twice. "You wouldn't want to overdo things."

Henrietta did not risk a reply. With a mildly affectionate smile, she waved dismissal to them both.

Intrigued, Antonia bobbed a respectful curtsy. Philip bowed with his customary grace, then, taking Antonia's arm, turned her towards the long windows which stood open to the terrace. "Come—give me your opinion."

Guided irresistibly through the gently billowing curtains,

Antonia dutifully lifted her eyes to the western sky. "On the sunset?"

"Among other things."

Philip's tone, clipped and dry, had her shifting her gaze to his face.

Looking down into her wide eyes, he saw speculation leap into being, only to be replaced by a certain wariness. He halted by the balustrade, his gaze locked on hers. "I believe, my dear, that it's time for a little plain speaking."

Antonia felt giddy. Searching his eyes, she asked, "On what subject?"

"On the subject of the future. Specifically, ours." In an endeavour to disguise the tension that had, somewhat unexpectedly, gripped him, Philip sat on the stone balustrade. Meeting Antonia's gaze levelly, he raised an impatient brow. "It can hardly come as a surprise to you that I hope you will consent to be my wife?"

"No." The word was out before she had considered it; Antonia blushed furiously and tried to erase the admission with a wave. "That is…"

The look on Philip's face halted her.

"*Plain* speaking I believe I said?"

Antonia lifted her chin. "I had *hoped*—"

"You and Henrietta *planned*."

"Henrietta?" Utterly bemused, Antonia stared at him. "What has Henrietta to do with it?" She blinked. "What plans?"

Faced with her patent bewilderment, Philip had to accept his error. "Never mind."

Antonia stiffened; her eyes flared. "But I *do* mind! You thought—"

"I *didn't* think!" Philip made the admission through clenched teeth, belatedly realizing the truth. Antonia, wilful, stubborn Antonia, was no more likely to be a party to Henrietta's machinations than he. "I *assumed*— incorrectly, I admit. However, that subject is now entirely beside the point—I no longer particularly care how we reached our present pass.'' Much to his amazement, that statement, too, held the undeniable ring of truth. ''What concerns me now—what we need to discuss—is what comes next.''

Forcing himself to remain seated, Philip caught Antonia's glittering gaze and held it. ''We both know what we want—don't we?''

Antonia studied his expression, grey eyes clear, filled with undisguised, unmistakable purpose. Holding his gaze, she drew in a slow breath, then nodded.

''Good—at least we agree on that much.'' Philip linked his fingers, laying them on one thigh, the better to resist a distracting urge to catch hold of her. ''My affairs are currently in order; the matter of settlements can be decided at any time.''

Antonia's eyes widened. ''Your discussions with Banks…''

''Indeed.'' Philip couldn't resist a superior glance.

Antonia sniffed. ''If we're speaking of planning—''

''Which thankfully we aren't.'' Ignoring her haughty glance, Philip continued, ''Henrietta is your nearest adult relative. I don't see much point in asking her permission to pay my addresses—she's going to be unbearably smug as it is. As for Geoffrey, I doubt he'll object.''

''Given he's halfway to idolising you,'' Antonia retorted. ''I sincerely doubt it, too.''

Philip's brows rose. ''Do you mind?''

Antonia met his gaze; inherently truthful, she shook her head. A species of dizzying panic was gathering momentum inside her. Consternation threatened. This was all happening much too soon.

''Which leaves only your inclination in question.'' His tone deepening, Philip held out his hand. ''So—will you, dear Antonia, agree to be my wife?''

The world was definitely spinning. Her heart raced—Antonia could feel it beating wildly in her throat. Disregarding the fact, her gaze trapped in the grey of his, she laid her hand in Philip's palm. "Yes, of course. Eventually."

Philip's fingers closed about hers, then convulsively tightened. His features, about to relax into lines of arrogant satisfaction, froze; his expression wavered between shock and incredulity. "Eventually?"

Antonia gestured vaguely. "Afterwards."

"Afterwards *when?*"

She frowned. "After we return from London was what I had imagined."

"Well, imagine again." Abruptly, Philip stood. "If you *imagined* I'd consent to letting you swan through London's ballrooms without the protection of a betrothal, free as a bird, attracting God-knows-what attention, you are, my dear, fair and far out. We'll announce our betrothal tomorrow— I'll place a notice in the *Gazette* when I reach town."

"Tomorrow?" Antonia stared at him. "But that's impossible!"

"Impossible?" Philip towered over her, his expression growing more intimidating by the second.

Lifting her chin, Antonia met his gaze squarely. "Impossible," she reiterated—and watched his eyes darken, felt his fingers tighten about hers. "I thought you understood," she said, as the familiar vice tightened about her chest. Frowning, she dropped her gaze to his cravat. "You *do* understand—of course you do." Raising her head, she looked directly into his eyes. "So why can't you see it?"

For one, long instant, Philip closed his eyes. Then, opening them, he drew in a deep, steadying breath, and forced himself to release her hand. "I fear, my dear, that despite your conviction, I must claim temporary mental obfuscation. I have no idea what it is that I'm supposed to be able to see, much less why or how it, whatever it might be, comes to render my proposal ineligible."

Antonia blinked at him. "I didn't say your proposal was

ineligible—just that it's impossible to announce our betrothal before we return from London.''

Philip frowned at her; the tension locking his muscles slowly dissipated. ''Let's see if I've got this straight. You agree to marry me as long as we don't announce our betrothal until *after* we return from London.'' He held Antonia's gaze. ''Is that right?''

Antonia coloured. ''If…I mean…'' hands clasped before her, she lifted her chin ''…presuming you still want me as your wife.''

''*That*, thank heavens, is not in question.'' Eyeing her uptilted face, Philip had to fight the urge to take advantage of it. He fell to pacing, two steps away, then two steps back. ''Kindly get it fixed in your head that I wish to marry you— if I had my way, immediately. Society and the laws, however, require a certain interval between proposal and execution. I had therefore planned…'' he paused to throw Antonia a narrow-eyed glance ''…in light of our apparent similarity of purpose, to announce our betrothal immediately so that we may be married on our return from town. Now you inform me that that's not possible!''

Antonia stood her ground. ''It may be theoretically possible, but it's a great deal too soon.''

''Too *soon?*''

Shutting her ears to his disbelief, Antonia nodded. ''Too soon for me. You must see that, Philip. You know what… that is…'' She frowned, searching for words to delicately allude to the effect he had on her. ''You know how I react— I don't yet know how to go on in *ton*nish society. I need to learn the knack—and I can't do that if we're betrothed.''

''Why not?'' Philip frowned back. He kept pacing. ''What difference does it make if we're betrothed, married or merely acquaintances?''

Antonia lifted her chin. ''As you very well know, if we were married or betrothed, people—certainly all the ladies—would expect me to know how things were done, how to behave in all circumstances. They would expect the lady you had chosen as your bride to be accomplished in such matters.''

Seeking his face, she fixed her eyes on his. ''As you also know, I don't have any experience of society at large— nothing more than a limited exposure to selected entertainments in Yorkshire. That's hardly sufficient basis on which to, as you phrased it, swan through the *ton*. I'd fall at the first hurdle.'' Her lips twisted wrily. ''You know I would. In that particular arena, I've no experience in the saddle, and even less confidence in my ability to clear the hedges.''

Philip slowed, then stopped. His frown had deepened.

Calmly, Antonia held his gaze. ''You told me I needed to practice my skills before I tried handling the whip. The same is true here—I need to learn how to go on, how to behave as your wife, *before* we marry.''

Philip grimaced then glanced away. To his mind, she needed no instruction in how to behave socially; her innate breeding, her natural directness, her honest openness, would stand her in good stead. Her performance on the day of the *fête* had been exemplary, but she clearly did not see that success as equivalent to facing the *ton*, a point he could hardly argue.

An uncertain, less-than-confident Antonia was a being he had little experience of, yet he felt a pressing need to reassure her, to accede to her plans. He scowled at his lawns. ''Everyone will know that having hailed from Yorkshire, you might be feeling your way.''

''Exactly.'' Antonia nodded. ''And should our betrothal have been announced, they'll be watching like hawks, taking note of any and all mistakes I make. If I am merely your stepmother's niece being introduced to the *ton*, beyond natural curiosity no great attention will focus on me. I'll be able to study how ladies go on without giving rise to any adverse comment.''

Philip remained silent; sensing victory, Antonia pressed her point. "You know that's true. In the eyes of the *ton,* a deficient upbringing is no excuse for gauche behaviour."

"You couldn't be gauche if you tried."

Antonia smiled. "Unintentionally, perhaps." She sobered, studying his profile, the rigid line of his shoulders. Straightening her own, metaphorically girding her loins, she drew in a deep breath. "I comprehend…that is, I imagine your expectations of your wife are that she will manage your households, act as your hostess both here and in town, and…and…" Dragging in another breath, she rattled on, "In short, that she will fulfill all the usual functions and roles ascribed by society."

"I would want your friendship, Antonia." That and a great deal more. Philip kept his gaze on the gardens, unwilling to let her glimpse the emotions visible in his eyes.

Heartened by his statement, Antonia replied, "I, too, would hope our friendship would continue." She waited; when he said no more, she prompted, "I do want to marry you, Philip, but you do see, don't you, why we can't be betrothed until after our return?"

Philip turned, his jaw set, his gaze sharp and penetrating. For a long moment, he studied her eyes, and the conviction therein. She was asking for four, possibly five weeks of grace. Curtly, he nodded. "Very well—no—*announcement* of our betrothal. There is, however, no reason whatever why we cannot be betrothed, but keep the fact a secret."

Antonia met his gaze with one of her very direct looks. "Henrietta."

Philip swore beneath his breath. Hands rising to his hips, he swung away, facing the lawns again. Henrietta! His fond stepmama would never be able to keep the news to herself. And a legal betrothal was impossible without her knowledge.

It was an effort not to grind his teeth. He drew in a very deep breath, then slowly let it out. "Antonia, I am not about to let you waltz through the ballrooms of London without some agreement.'' He turned on the words, shifting to stand directly before her, trapping her with his gaze. ''I will agree—*grudgingly,* make no mistake—not to press you for a formal betrothal, secret or otherwise, until we return to the Manor—which we will do immediately you've gained sufficient experience of the *ton.*''

Holding hard to his reins, acutely conscious of the debilitating effects of frustration, Philip reached for her hands. Lifting them, he held them, palm to palm, between his and looked down into her eyes. ''Antonia, I want you as my wife. If we cannot be betrothed formally, then I ask that we be betrothed privately—an agreement between the two of us.''

Briefly, Philip glanced up at the sickle moon, riding high in the softly tinted sky, then looked down to recapture Antonia's green-gold gaze. ''I ask that we plight our troth witnessed only by the moon—to consider ourselves promised, you to me and me to you, from now until we return to the Manor, after which we will wed as soon as custom permits.''

He felt her fingers flutter between his, sensed the catch in her breath. For a long moment, he held her gaze, then, slowly, he separated her hands and carried one to his lips. ''Do you agree, Antonia?'' He brushed a kiss across her knuckles, then lifted her other hand, his eyes all the while on hers. ''To be mine?''

His words were so deep, so velvety dark, Antonia barely heard them. She sensed them deep inside her, and felt a compulsion she couldn't deny. His lips grazed her fingers and she shivered. ''Yes.'' She had always been his.

His eyes still held her trapped; slowly, he drew her hands up and out. When he let them go, they fell to his shoulders; his shifted to her waist, spanning it, then firming as he drew her close.

Antonia felt a quake ripple through her. ''Philip?''

The question was the merest whisper. Philip heard and understood "All troths must be sealed with a kiss, sweet-heart."

Her heart blocking her throat, Antonia felt her bodice brush his coat. She watched his head lower; her lids fell.

His lips found hers; warm and persuasive, their pressure soothed and reassured. Antonia relaxed, then stiffened as he gathered her into his arms, locking her in his embrace. Yet his hold remained gentle; his hands stroked her back.

Again she relaxed, again the kiss took hold, sweeping her into some magical realm of mystery, of sensation. His lips firmed; hesitantly, she parted hers, a flicker of nervousness distracting her momentarily, called forth by recollections of their encounter in the woods. But this time there was only warmth and pleasure, enticing, beckoning caresses that made her hungry—for what she didn't know. No unbridled passions arose to confront her, to elicit the wanton craving she was convinced she had to hide.

Reassured, she drifted deeper, giving herself up to gentle pleasure.

It took all of Philip's skill to keep the kiss, if not light, then at least non-conflagrationary. He was acutely aware of her untutored responses, of the way her body slowly softened in his arms, accepting his embrace in the same way her lips accepted his kiss. As in all things, she was deliciously direct, unambiguously open, totally innocent of intrigue. For one of his ilk, the novelty was as heady as summer wine.

He forced himself to draw back, to gradually bring the kiss to an end, despite the ravenous hunger eating him. He was familiar with that demon; while it might make his life hell, he was its master.

When he eventually lifted his head, it was to the pleasure of watching Antonia's eyes, heavy-lidded, slowly open. She blinked at him, then made an obvious effort to compose herself.

"Ah…" Gently, Antonia tried to draw back, only to feel his arms firm.

"Not yet." Prodded by his demon, Philip lowered his head and stole another kiss, then another, before she could catch her breath.

"Philip!" Antonia barely got the word out; this time she insisted on pulling back.

Reluctantly, Philip dropped his arms but kept hold of one of her hands. "You're mine, Antonia." Possessiveness surged; he shackled it, unaware of the deep resonance of his voice, of the dark glitter in his gaze, of the way his fingers tightened about hers. Raising her hand, he pressed a kiss to her fingertips, then turned her hand and pressed a warm kiss to her palm. "Never forget it."

Antonia shivered as he released her hand.

Holding her with no more than his gaze, Philip lowered his head one last time, barely touching his lips to hers. "Sleep well, my dear. I'll see you next in London."

She drew back, wide-eyed and, he thought, wondering. Then she inclined her head and slowly turned away. He let her go, watching as she retreated into his house, to spend the night under his roof, as she would from now on.

The smile on his lips slowly fading, Philip turned back to the lawns. After a moment, he grimaced feelingly, then descended the steps; hands in his pockets, he strode into the cool night.

Chapter Seven

"There's a message arrived for you, m'lord. Up from the Manor."

Seated in a wing-chair in his library, Philip waved Carring, his major-domo, forward. After spending an afternoon about town, calling in at his club and spending an hour at Manton's, he had retreated to his library secure in the knowledge that few of his peers had yet quit their summer hunting grounds. The continuing fine weather gave little incentive for returning to town before the round of balls and parties that made up the Little Season. Which meant Antonia would have a relatively quiet few weeks in which to gain her balance.

The silver salver Carring presented held a note addressed in Banks's finicky script. Frowning, Philip picked it up and unfolded it. He read Banks's few lines, then swore. "The damned woman's finally made up her mind!"

"Is that good news or bad news, m'lord?" Carring held himself correctly by his master's side, his lugubrious tone absolving his query of any hint of impertinence.

Philip considered the point, eyeing Banks's missive with distaste. "Both," he eventually replied. "It means that at long last we'll be able to close the sale of Lower Farm. Unfortunately, Mrs Mortingdale wants to see me in person over the matter of certain unspecified assurances." Exasperated, he sighed. "I'll have to go back." He glanced at the clock. "Not tonight. Tell Hamwell to have the greys ready at first light—wake me before then."

If he took the Brighton road, he could reach the Manor by midday; if luck was with him, he might be free of the vacillating widow in time to make the trip back that evening.

"Very good, m'lord." Carring, ponderously round and suited all in black, unhurriedly headed for the door. There, he turned, his hand on the knob. "Am I to take it, my lord, that her ladyship and her visitors will still be arriving tomorrow?"

"They will." Philip's tones were clipped. "Make sure all is ready."

Carring's brows rose fractionally as he turned away. "Naturally, m'lord."

Contrary to his plans, it was early afternoon two days hence before Philip returned to Grosvenor Square.

Carring helped him out of his greatcoat. "I take it the business of Lower Farm was successfully completed, m'lord?"

"Finally." Resettling his coat, Philip turned to the hall mirror to check his cravat. "Her ladyship and the Mannerings arrived yesterday?"

"Indeed, m'lord. I comprehend their journey passed without incident."

"No highwaymen—not even a scheming landlord to chouse us over the reckoning."

Turning, Philip beheld Antonia, a vision in soft turquoise muslin floating down the stairs. A stray sunbeam lancing through the fanlight struck golden gleams from her hair. "I should hope not," he said, moving forward to meet her. Taking her hand, he raised it to his lips, brushing a kiss across her fingers. "I presume my coachman and grooms took good care of you?"

Antonia raised a brow. "Of all of us. But what of you? Did the widow eventually weaken?"

"She finally came to her senses." Tucking her hand in his arm, Philip turned her down the corridor. "However, nothing would do for it but that she had to see me in person so that I could give her an assurance—word of a gentleman—that I would keep her farm labourers on."

As he opened the door to the back parlour and handed her through, Antonia mused, "Actually, that seems rather wise—and kind of her, too."

Philip hesitated, then reluctantly nodded. "But I would have kept them on anyway. As it was, her summons meant I wasn't here to greet you. It appears I'm fated to return to my house to find you gracing my hall."

He shut the door behind them. Antonia slanted him a questioning glance as he came to stand beside her. "Do you find that so disturbing?"

Philip looked down into her green-gold eyes. "Disturbing?" For all his experience, he felt his senses slide. Taking firm hold of his wits, he clasped his hands behind his back. "On the contrary." His lips curved in a deliberately provocative smile. "That's precisely the result I'm aiming for. In this particular case, however, I had looked forward to welcoming you on your first evening in London."

Antonia smiled back. "We would hardly have been scintillating company." Calmly, she strolled to the *chaise* before the windows. "Henrietta retired immediately. Geoffrey and I had an early dinner and followed her upstairs." With a swish of her skirts, she settled on the flowered chintz.

"And this morning?" Gracefully, Philip sat beside her, neither overly close nor yet greatly distant. "I have difficulty believing you slept until noon."

"No, indeed." Antonia's smile grew gently teasing. "Geoffrey and I did discuss riding in the Park—he was sure you wouldn't mind if we raided your stable. But I convinced him to wait for your return."

Philip's expression blanked as he imagined what might have been.

Antonia shifted to face him. "What is it?"

Philip grimaced. "There's something I should explain—to you both." He focused on Antonia's face. "About riding in town."

Antonia frowned. "I had thought it was acceptable to ride in the Park."

"It is. It's the definition of the term 'riding' wherein the *ton* and the Mannerings differ."

"Oh?" Antonia looked her question.

Philip pulled a face. "For ladies, the prescribed activity known as 'riding in the Park' involves a slow walk for much of the time, with at the most a short canter. Galloping, at least as you know it, is not just frowned upon—for you, it's utterly out of the question."

Antonia sat back, her expression a study of disgust and dismay. "Good heavens!"

One of her curls fell in a golden coil over one ear; Philip put out a hand and wound the curl about one finger, then, letting it slowly slip free, he gently brushed his finger against her cheek.

Her eyes flicked to his; Philip felt the familiar tension tighten. He let it hold for one discreet moment, then smoothly retrieved his hand.

"Ah...I don't think I'd actually want to ride if I had to restrain myself to a walk or a canter." Forcing in a breath, Antonia shook her head. "I don't think I could."

"An unquestionably wise decision." Philip shifted slightly. "But we'll only be in town for four weeks or so—you'll be able to ride to your heart's content once we return to the Manor."

"Well, then." Antonia gestured resignedly. "I'll just have to consider it a sacrifice made in pursuit of a greater goal."

Lips lifting, Philip inclined his head. When he looked up, his smile had faded. "Unfortunately, that's not all."

Antonia transfixed him with one of her direct looks. "What?"

"Driving in the Park." His eyes on hers, Philip grimaced. "I know I mentioned I might consent to let you drive yourself but I had, at that time, imagined myself on the box beside you."

Antonia frowned. "So?"

"So, my dear, given we are *not* about to announce our betrothal, the sight of *you* driving *me* behind my greys in the Park would lead to instant and quite rabid speculation—something I take it you are keen to avoid."

"Oh." The single syllable accurately conveyed Antonia's feelings.

"Despite such restrictions," Philip continued, his tone deliberately light, "London is generally considered a haven of entertainment." Catching Antonia's eye, he lifted a brow. "What have you planned for this afternoon?"

Shaking aside her disappointment, a childish response, she told herself, Antonia straightened. "Henrietta thought a visit to the modistes in Bruton Street to decide which to choose." Colouring slightly, she met Philip's gaze. "I'm afraid my wardrobe is hardly up to town standards."

"Having only just escaped from Yorkshire?" Reaching out, Philip took her hand. "I fear I'm not surprised."

Reassured by his touch rather than his cynical tone, Antonia continued, "Then we thought to stroll Bond Street to look in on the milliners, followed perhaps by a quick turn through the Park."

Idly playing with her fingers, noting the contrast between her slim digits and his much larger hands, Philip considered, then nodded. He glanced up at the clock on the mantelshelf. "Henrietta should be stirring from her nap. Why don't you go and tell her I've arrived?" Turning his head, he met Antonia's slightly surprised gaze. And smiled. "Give me ten minutes to change and I'll accompany you.'' Rising, he drew her to her feet, then lifted her hand to his lips. ''On your first outing in town.''

Twenty minutes later, as she settled into a corner of the Ruthven town carriage, Henrietta and her shawls beside her, Philip directly opposite, Antonia was still in the grip of what she told herself was quite uncalled-for gratification. Despite her trenchant lecturing, her happiness swelled. She had never imagined Philip would join them.

The carriage rattled over the cobbles and rounded a corner. Swaying with the movement, Antonia met Philip's eye; she smiled, then let her gaze drift to the window. She had started allowing herself to think of him as her husband; she was, after all, going to be his wife.

That thought, unfortunately, focused her mind on the anxiety nagging quietly in the back of her mind. Philip's proposal had made success in London even more imperative; the *ton* was her last hurdle—she could not, must not, falter here.

Luckily, the drive to Bruton Street was too short for her to dwell too deeply on her prospects; the carriage pulled up outside a plain wooden door. Philip jumped down, then turned to assist her to the pavement.

As she straightened the skirts of her simple gown, Antonia's gaze fell on the creation displayed in the window beside the door, a breathtakingly simple robe of blue silk crêpe. It was, to her eyes, the epitome of stylish elegance, combining simplicity of line with the richness of expensive fabric. An all-but-overwhelming desire to have a such gown rose within her.

''*Not* in blue,'' came Philip's voice in her ear.

Antonia jumped, then shot him a frown, which he met with a raised brow and an all-too-knowing smile. Offering her his arm, he gestured to the door through which the footman was assisting Henrietta. ''Come and meet Madame Lafarge.''

Guided up a narrow stair and into a salon draped in silk, Antonia felt her eyes widen. Small knots of ladies, young and old, were scattered about the apartment, grouped on chairs, each with an attendant hovering, offering samples of cloths. Murmured discussions, intent and purposeful, hummed in the air.

Philip was not the only gentleman present; others were freely giving their opinions on colours and styles. Quite a few turned to look at her; one groped for his quizzing glass, half-raising it to his eye before apparently thinking better of it. An assistant hurried up; Philip spoke quietly and she scurried away, disappearing through a curtained doorway.

Five seconds later, the curtain was thrown back; a small, black-clad figure glided into the room, pausing for a dramatic instant before heading towards them.

"My lord. My lady." The woman, black-eyed and black-haired, spoke with a pronounced accent. She bowed, then, straightening, lifted her hands palms up as she said, "My poor talents are entirely at your disposal."

"Madame." Philip inclined his head. He introduced Henrietta, then stood back and let her take charge. Turning his head, he caught Antonia's eye.

Confused, she lifted a brow at him but was distracted by Henrietta's introduction.

Nodding in acknowledgement of Antonia's greeting, Madame Lafarge walked slowly around her, then gestured down the room. "Walk for me, *mademoiselle*—to the windows and back, if you please."

Antonia glanced at Philip; he smiled reassuringly. She strolled down the long room, drawing covert glances from the modiste's other patrons with miffed looks from some of the younger ladies. By the time she returned to Philip's side, Henrietta and Madame had their heads together, whispering avidly.

"Excellent." Nodding, Henrietta straightened. "We'll return for a private session tomorrow at ten."

"*Bien.* I will have all ready. Until tomorrow, my lady. My lord. *Mademoiselle.*" Madame Lafarge bowed deeply, then gestured to an underling to see them to the door.

Gaining the pavement in advance of Henrietta, slowly descending the steep flight on the arm of her footman, Antonia let her gaze travel the short street, taking in the numerous signs indicating the establishments of modistes and the odd tailor. Turning to Philip, standing patiently by her side, she raised a determined brow. "Why here?"

Philip raised a brow back. "Because she's the best—at least for style and, in my humble opinion, for that indefinable something that gives rise to true elegance."

Glancing again at the blue gown in the window, Antonia nodded. "But it was you who had the entrée—not Henrietta."

When, turning, she fixed an openly enquiring gaze upon him, Philip wished her understanding was not quite so acute. He considered a white lie, but she had already noted his hesitation.

Again her brow rose, her expression half playful, half distant. "Or is that one of those matters into which young ladies should not enquire too closely?"

It was; for the first time in his lengthy career, the fact made Philip uncomfortable. Inwardly frowning, he kept his expression impassive. "Suffice to say that I have had call to make use of Madame's expertise in the past."

"For which," Henrietta said, puffing slightly as she came up with them, "we are both duly grateful." She fixed Philip with an approving stare. "Wondered why you had John Coachman stop here." Turning to Antonia, she explained, "*Horrendously* difficult to interest personally, Madame. But if you can catch her eye, then your wardrobe, you may be assured, will be enough to set the tabbies on their tails." Straightening, Henrietta waved to her coachman, "You may wait for us at the end of Bond Street, John." Then she gestured her footman forward. "Come, Jem, give me your arm. We can stroll from here."

Philip offered Antonia his arm. She hesitated only fractionally before placing her hand on his sleeve. Head high, a distant smile on her lips, she strolled by his side as they followed Henrietta into Bond Street.

Her joy in his company, in his introducing her to Madame Lafarge, had been quite effectively depressed.

Their foray up and down the fashionable thoroughfare was punctuated by frequent halts before the windows of milliners and glovers, haberdasherers and bootmakers.

"No sense in deciding on anything until we've consulted with Lafarge tomorrow," Henrietta opined. "Elsewise, we'll end with the wrong colour or style."

Dragging her gaze from a quite hideous chip bonnet sprouting a border of fake daisies, Antonia nodded absentmindedly. One of their last halts was before the windows of Aspreys, the jewellers. Necklaces and rings, baubles of every conceivable hue, glittered and winked behind the glass.

Her gaze locked on the display, Henrietta pursed her lips. "If memory serves, your mama was never one for jewellery."

Antonia, still wrestling with unwelcome realization, shook her head. "She always said she didn't need much. But I have her pearls."

"Hmm." Henrietta squinted at a necklace and drop-earrings set on a velvet bed towards the back of the display. "Those topazes would suit you."

"Where?" Blinking, Antonia summoned enough interest to follow her aunt's gaze.

"Not topazes."

Philip spoke from behind them; it was the first utterance he had made since they'd gained Bond Street. Both Antonia and Henrietta turned in surprise.

Endeavouring to retain his habitually impassive mien,

Philip reached past them to point to the items arrayed on a bed of black silk in pride of place in the centre of the window. "Those."

"Those" were emeralds. Eyeing the exquisite green gems, set, not in the usual heavily ornate settings, but with an almost Grecian restraint in simple gold, Antonia felt her eyes grow round. Just like the gown in Lafarge's window, the delicate necklace with pendant attached, matching earrings and matching bracelets exerted a charm all their own. She would love to have them—but that was impossible. Even she could tell they were worth the proverbial king's ransom. They were, she suspected, the sorts of gifts a gentleman might give to his mistress, especially were she one of those beings referred to in hushed whispers as "high-flyers"—the sort who might qualify for peignoirs from Madame Lafarge. She stifled a sigh. "They're certainly beautiful." Determinedly, she turned away. "There's John."

The carriage was waiting just up from the corner. His face expressionless, Philip stepped back. Without comment, he gave Antonia his arm across the street then handed his stepmother, then her niece into the carriage.

Henrietta leaned forward. "I'd thought to go for a quick turn about the Park—just to let Antonia get a feel for the place. Will you join us?"

Philip hesitated. He shot a glance at Antonia; the shadows of the carriage hid her eyes. She made no move to encourage him. Gracefully, he stepped back. "I think not." Feeling his jaw tighten, he forced his face to impassivity. "I believe I'll look in on my clubs." He executed a neat bow, then shut the door and gave John Coachman the office.

Philip rose late the next day, having spent the evening idly gaming with Hugo Satterly, whom he had opportunely sighted late in the afternoon napping behind a newsheet in White's. After a leisurely dinner, they had moved on to Brooks and settled in for the evening, a sequence of events so common they had not even bothered to discuss their intent.

Determined to cling to such comfortable routines, he descended his stairs at noon, carefully pulling on his gloves. As he set foot in his hall, the library door opened and Geoffrey looked out.

"Ah—there you are." Grinning engagingly, Geoffrey came forward.

Instantly suspicious, Philip raised one brow. "Yes?"

Geoffrey's grin turned ingenuous. "I wondered if you recalled your promise that you'd help me in town if I kept all of the children out of the lake during the *fête?*"

"Ah, yes," Philip mused. "As I recall, no one got wet."

"Exactly." All but bouncing on his toes, Geoffrey nodded. "I wondered if you'd consider sponsoring me at Manton's—in return for my sterling efforts?"

His smile was infectious; briefly, Philip returned it. Manton's was, in fact, one of the safer venues for one of Geoffrey's years. "I'll have to speak with Manton himself—he doesn't normally encourage youngsters."

Geoffrey's face fell. "Oh."

"Don't get your hopes too high," Philip advised, turning to accept his cane from Carring who had silently approached. "But he may make an exception." Turning to Geoffrey, he raised his brows. "Provided, that is, that you can handle a pistol?"

"Of course I can! What sort of countryman can't?"

"As to that, I can't say." Extracting a card from his case, Philip handed it to Geoffrey. "If you get caught anywhere, use that. If not, meet me outside Manton's at two."

"Capital!" Eyes glowing, Geoffrey scanned the card, then put it in his pocket. "I'll be there." With a nod, he turned to go, then turned back. "Oh, I say—Antonia mentioned about the riding."

"Ah, yes." Philip waved away the hat Carring offered.

"Would it be a problem if I took one of your horses out

in the mornings? I was speaking with your grooms—they seemed to think it was all right—that is, permissible—for me to ride early, say about nine.''

''Indeed.'' Philip nodded. ''And yes, before you ask, you can gallop down the tan—as long as you remain on the track. The keepers don't appreciate having their lawns cut to pieces.''

''Oh, good!'' Geoffrey's face glowed. ''Antonia explained how she can't gallop but I thought that might just be one of those feminine things.''

''Precisely,'' Philip replied. With a wave, he headed for the door.

One of those feminine things.

The words returned to haunt Philip as he idly strolled the clipped lawns bordering the carriageway in the Park, his gaze scanning the landaus and barouches wending their way along the fashionable avenue. He had dined well with friends at a select eatery in Jermyn Street, then met Geoffrey at Manton's.

After prevailing on the proprietor to overlook Geoffrey's age, an argument greatly assisted by his protégé's undeniable skill with a pistol, he had left Geoffrey happily culping wafers and repaired to Gentleman Jackson's Boxing Salon. Declining an invitation to don a pair of gloves and spar with the great man himself, an acquaintance of many years, he had strolled the rooms, catching up with cronies and identifying the notables already in town. What gossip there was he had gleaned, then, with no pressing engagement, he had let his feet wander where they would.

They had brought him here. He wasn't sure whether he approved or not.

On the thought, he spied the Ruthven barouche, rolling slowly around the circuit. He raised his arm; his coachman saw him and drew the carriage into the verge. He strolled up as John was explaining his actions.

''Oh, it's you.'' Turning, Henrietta fixed him with one of her more intimidatory stares ''Perfect. You can take Antonia for a stroll on the lawns.''

Philip's answering glance held a definite hint of steel. ''Precisely my intention, ma'am.''

Henrietta fluffed her shawls and sank back against the cushions. ''I'll wait here.''

His lips compressed, Philip opened the door and held out his hand commandingly—before pulling himself up. His gaze flew to Antonia's face; the blank look in her eyes struck him like a blow. He drew in a quick breath. ''That is, if you would like to take the air, my dear?'' Where on earth had his years of experience gone? He had never acted so insensitively in his life.

Bundling an uncharacteristic spurt of temper, and a less well-defined hurt, aside, Antonia forced herself to nod. Outwardly serene, she placed her fingers in his. She did not meet his gaze as he assisted her out of the carriage, even though she could feel it on her face.

Settling her hand on his sleeve, Philip drew in a deep breath. And set himself to regain the ground he'd lost.

About them, the lawns were merely dotted with other couples, not crowded as they would be in a few weeks' time. ''The company, I'm afraid, is somewhat thin at the moment.'' Glancing down at Antonia's face, he smiled. ''As soon as the weather turns, the *ton* will flood back and then the entertainments will start with a vengeance.''

Determined to hold her own, Antonia lifted her chin. ''I've heard that there's no place on earth to rival London for all manner of diversions.''

''Quite true.'' Philip succeeded in catching her eye. ''Are you looking forward to being diverted?''

Shifting her gaze forward, Antonia raised her brows. ''I suppose I am. Henrietta seems quite caught up with it all. She was certainly in her element at Lafarge's this morning.''

''Ah, yes. How did your session with Madame go?''

Antonia shrugged lightly. "I have to admit I'm very impressed by her designs. She's sending the first of the gowns tomorrow." Glancing down at her cambric skirts, she pulled a face. "Not a moment too soon, I suspect." Her gaze rose to take in the stylish toilettes of two ladies strolling by.

"After tomorrow, my dear, you'll take the shine out of all the London belles."

Despite her determination to remain aloof, Antonia's lips twitched. She shot Philip a glance—which he was waiting to catch.

He laid a hand on his heart. "Nothing more than the truth, I swear."

She had to laugh; to her surprise, it cleared the air, allowing her to respond more easily.

"The smaller, less formal parties will be starting soon, I imagine."

"Indeed," she replied evenly. "Henrietta already has a small stack of invitations."

"And then will come the crushes as the major hostesses return to the fray."

"Hmm." She hid a frown.

Philip glanced down at her. "I thought you were looking forward to experiencing the *ton* in all its glory?"

Fleetingly, Antonia met his gaze. "I certainly expect my time here to be an experience—an undertaking necessary to extend my understanding of society and its ways. As for enjoyment—" She shrugged. "I don't know enough to anticipate it."

Philip studied her face, open and honest as always; his expression softened. "Strange to tell, there's more to London than *ton* parties."

Antonia looked up, brows lifting.

"There's the theatre and opera, of course—but you know of them. Then there's Astley's and Vauxhall across the river, both worth a visit if it's simple pleasures you seek." Looking down, Philip met her gaze. "And I own to surprise that neither you nor Geoffrey has yet developed a yearning to see the museum.''

Without waiting for her comment, he continued, blithely extolling the virtues of the capital, detailing sights and possible excursions, gently twitting her on her ignorance until, with a laugh, she conceded, ''Very well—I will own that I might, indeed, enjoy my stay in London. I hadn't realized there was so much we—'' Abruptly, Antonia caught herself up. She drew in a steadying breath. ''So much to see,'' she amended.

Trying but failing to trap her gaze, Philip inwardly frowned. ''Having been interred in the wilds of Yorkshire as you have, that's hardly surprising. We must make an effort to take in some of the sights at least, before the season gets into full swing.''

Antonia glanced up and met his gaze. ''That would be very…pleasant.''

Philip smiled. ''We'll have to see what we can squeeze in.''

They had reached the barouche; opening the door, he handed her in. ''Until later,'' he said, his eyes on hers.

Antonia nodded, regally assured. Henrietta humphed and tapped John Coachman on the shoulder. Philip watched the carriage draw away; a frown slowly formed in his eyes. An odd constraint seemed to have sprung up between them— he couldn't for the life of him see why.

At six o'clock that evening, Antonia started up the stairs. The dinner gong had just sounded; it was time to change her gown. Nearing the landing, she heard footsteps above. Looking up, she met Philip's gaze. She stopped on the landing, watching as he descended.

He was wearing a stylish coat of Bath superfine over ivory inexpressibles; an intricately tied cravat, tasselled Hessians and a waistcoat of amber silk completed the outfit. His hair looked freshly brushed, waving gently about his head.

In one hand, he carried a pair of gloves, flicking them gently against one thigh.

His lips curving, he stopped directly before her.

"I had wondered, my dear, if you are free tomorrow afternoon, whether you might care to drive to Richmond? We could take tea at the Star and Garter and return in good time for dinner."

The poor light on the stairs hid the flash of happiness that lit Antonia's eyes. It also hid the faint blush that succeeded it. "I..." Lifting her chin, she clasped her hands before her. "I wouldn't wish to disrupt your normal routine, my lord— I'm sure there are other claims on your time."

"None that can't wait." Philip hid his frown. "Are you free?"

She met his gaze but he could read nothing in her eyes. "I can't recall any other engagement."

Philip tightened his grip on his gloves. "In that case, I'll meet you in the hall at...shall we say half past one?"

Gracious but determinedly distant, Antonia inclined her head. "I'll look forward to the outing, my lord."

What, Philip wondered, had happened to his name? "Antonia—"

"Will you be dining with us this evening?" It took all Antonia's courage to ask the question; she waited, breath bated, for the answer, dismally aware she was only making a rod for her own back.

Philip hesitated, then forced himself to shake his head. "I'm dining with friends." He was, at Limmer's. As if from a distance, he heard himself say, "I often do." The shadows hid her eyes, too well for him to be sure of her expression. Few men of his age, married or not, dined frequently at their own board; it was a fact of fashionable life, not a situation of his own choosing.

"Indeed?" Determinedly bright, Antonia flashed him a brittle smile. "I'd better go up or I'll be late. I wish you a good night, my lord." With another fleeting smile and a nod, she went past him and on up the stairs. She was, she sternly lectured herself, being foolish beyond permission. To feel rejection when none was intended, to feel downhearted just because he was behaving as he usually did. This was, after all, what she had come to London to learn—how she would fit into his life.

She reached the upper gallery and all but ran to her room.

Philip listened to her footsteps fade. Slowly, he resumed his descent. By the time he reached the hall, the planes of his face had hardened. She had said not a word out of place, said nothing to make him suspect she was wishful of his company. Not once had she made the mistake of trying to make him feel guilty; she had made no demands of him whatever.

Why, then, did he feel so dissatisfied? So certain something was, if not precisely wrong, then very definitely not right?

Chapter Eight

At half past one the following afternoon, Philip stood in his hall and watched Antonia descend the stairs. She was wearing a new carriage dress delivered that morning from Madame Lafarge's workshop, a creation in leaf-green twill that emphasized her slender shape and set off the gold of her hair. The bodice and skirt were edged with forest green ribbon, the same shade as the parasol Philip held furled in one hand.

It, too, had come from Madame Lafarge, expressly chosen on his instructions and delivered by one of Madame's lackeys at precisely one o'clock.

The parasol held behind his back, Philip strolled forward, taking Antonia's hand to help her down the last steps. "You look positively enchanting."

Buoyed by the confidence stemming from her first London gown, Antonia returned his smile. When Philip's gaze dropped, shrewdly judging, she obligingly twirled, her skirts flaring about her. "Madame's skill is beyond question."

"True." Philip recaptured her hand. "But as I am sure she would tell you, perfection can only be attained when one works with the very best of raw materials."

His eyes met Antonia's; her heart skittered alarmingly.

She lowered her gaze and bobbed a curtsy. "I fear you flatter me, my lord."

A frown fleetingly crossed Philip's face. "Philip." He held up the parasol, then presented it with a flourish.

Antonia put out a hand to the carved wooden handle, her expression a study in surprise. "For me?" Taking it, she held the parasol as if it were glass. Mesmerised, she stared, then threw Philip a wavering smile. "Thank you." Her voice was husky. "I'm sorry—you must think me a fool." Blinking rapidly, she looked down. "It's been a long time since anyone gave me anything like this—for no real reason."

Philip's mask slipped. It took effort to wrestle it back into place, to hide his reaction to her words. "I would gladly give you more, Antonia—but until we make our relationship public, I'm reduced to such trumpery to win your smiles."

She gave a shaky laugh, then held the parasol against her gown. "It's a perfect match."

"Indeed." Philip smiled. "Obviously an inspired choice."

Antonia's expression immediately turned suspicious. Philip laughed. Taking her arm, he guided her to the door.

Once in his curricle, bowling along behind his greys, the awkwardness Antonia found herself all too often a prey to evaporated. Unfurling the parasol, she deployed it to protect her complexion, then hit upon the notion of asking Philip's advice on how to most elegantly dispose it. His suggestions were half serious, half teasing. She enjoyed the drive, and his company, relaxing enough to let her pleasure show.

The outing passed off without a hitch; Philip returned well content.

Thereafter, he made a point of spending some part of every day by Antonia's side, trying with all the skill at his command to ease the reticence he sensed behind her smiles. He escorted both Mannerings to Astley's Amphitheatre, spending most of the performance in pleasant contemplation of the emotions flickering across Antonia's face. The following afternoon, he yielded to their entreaties and took them on a tour of St Paul's and the city, surprising himself with how much he remembered of the history of the town.

Throughout, Antonia appeared serenely content, yet her underlying hesitancy disturbed him. Aside from anything else, she frequently reverted to addressing him as "my lord", something, he had noticed, she only did when trying to keep him at a distance.

Then came the first of the informal parties.

Philip had already changed for the evening but had yet to quit the house. He was in the library, idly flicking through the stack of invitations on his desk when he heard voices in the hall. Lifting his head, he identified Geoffrey's voice raised in a bantering tone; Antonia answered with a laugh, gayer than any he'd heard in a long while.

Intrigued, he strolled to the door.

The sight that met his eyes as he paused in the doorway locked the breath in his chest. Antonia stood in the centre of his hall, her hair burnished guinea gold by the chandelier above. Bright curls clustered in artful disarray on the top of her head; a few gilded wisps wreathed about her delicate ears and nape, drawing attention to her slender neck. Her shoulders, warmly tinted ivory, were quite bare, entirely revealed by a stunningly elegant gown of the palest green. Lafarge's hand was easily discerned in the long, flattering lines, in the smooth sweeps of the skirt, in the subtle way the bodice emphasized the contours beneath. Tiny puffed sleeves were set well off the shoulders, so small they in no way distracted from the long, graceful curves of Antonia's arms.

Her face was uptilted; as he watched, she laughed, responding to Geoffrey, out of sight up the stairs. Deep inside, Philip felt something tighten, harden, clarifying and coalescing into one, crystal-clear emotion. Antonia's cheeks were delicately flushed, her eyes alight; her lips, rose tinted, parted as she smiled, raising her hands, not yet covered by the regulation long gloves, palms upward.

"I assure you I am very definitely your sister—if you come down here I'll demonstrate that my unique technique for boxing your ears is very much intact."

Geoffrey answered; Philip didn't register his words. Compelled, he moved slowly forward, out of the shadows that had thus far hidden him.

Antonia heard him; she turned and her eyes met his. His gaze held her as she held his attention, absolutely, completely.

He sensed the swift intake of her breath, saw her eyes widen then darken. Her arms slowly drifted together, as if to fold about her, responding to some age-old instinct to protect her body from his gaze. Moving with slow deliberation, Philip reached for her hands, taking them in his to hold them wide. Then, slowly, he raised one to his lips.

He felt his chest swell against the vice clamped so powerfully about it. "You are beauty personified, Antonia."

His voice was deep, darkly enticing; Antonia felt it reverberate through her, felt its seductive quality sink to her marrow. Still moving like one in a dream, he raised one of her arms high; obediently, she twirled, compelled to turn her head to keep her eyes on his. The normally shimmering grey was dark with storm clouds, harbingers of passion. She couldn't tear her gaze from them, from the promise in their depths.

He moved with her; for a moment, it was as if they were dancing, twirling about each other, gazes locked. Then he stopped; her silk skirts shushed softly about her legs, then settled as she halted, facing him.

An age seemed to pass as, eyes locked, they stood, tensed, quivering, as if balanced on the edge of some invisible precipice. Antonia couldn't breathe, dared not blink.

Geoffrey's clattering footsteps as he came down the stairs broke the spell.

"Don't think you *can* reach my ears anymore." Grinning widely, he strode towards them.

Smoothly, Philip released Antonia's hand; turning, he noted Geoffrey's dark coat and neat but simple cravat. "From your sartorial elegance, I take it you're to make one of the party tonight?"

Geoffrey pulled a face. "Aunt Henrietta thought that seeing I was here, I might as well broaden my horizons."

"It's just an informal gathering of family and friends at the Mountfords in Brook Street." Still breathless, Antonia struggled to keep her tone even. "Nothing too elaborate. According to Henrietta it'll be mostly genteel conversation with some country dances to help the less experienced ladies get accustomed to *ton*nish ways."

Philip had heard of such mild affairs. "I believe it's the regulation way one commences one's first season." He glanced at Antonia; excitement glowed in her eyes. "Tell me, do you dine in Brook Street or here?"

"Here." Antonia gestured. "I was just on my way to the drawing-room."

"And I was following, intending to get in a little practice." Frowning, Geoffrey shook his head. "Cotillions and quadrilles are all the same to me."

"Nonsense." Antonia linked her arm through his. "If you think to slide out of standing up with such comments you'll have to think again." Glancing at Philip, she smiled. Politely. "But you were on your way out—we're holding you up."

"No," Philip lied. "I'm dining in tonight."

"Oh?" Antonia blinked in surprise.

"Indeed. Why don't you make a start putting your brother through his paces? I'll join you in a moment and adjudicate."

The smile Antonia flashed him was as bright as the sun.

Inventively grumbling, Geoffrey allowed her to drag him away.

Amused, Philip watched. When the drawing-room door shut behind them, he turned towards the library. Only then did he see his major-domo standing in the shadows of the stairs. Philip's expression blanked. "Carring." He wondered how much Carring had seen. "Just the one I want."

In the library, Philip crossed to his desk. He scrawled a note to Hugo, informing him that he had been unexpectedly detained but would join him later. Sealing the missive, he directed it then handed it to Carring. "Have that delivered to Brooks."

"Immediately, m'lord. And shall I instruct Cook you've changed your mind?"

Ten full seconds of silence ensued. "Yes. And I expect you should also instruct a footman to lay an extra place at table." Philip eyed his henchman straitly. "Was there anything else?"

"No, indeed, m'lord," Carring's expression was smugly benign. "As far as I can tell, all's well with the world." On that cryptic utterance, he departed, Philip's note in hand.

Philip wasted no more than a moment glowering at Carring's black back before rising and heading for the drawing-room.

When, fifteen minutes later, Henrietta entered the drawing-room, she discovered her stepson dancing a cotillion with her niece. Geoffrey was perched on a nearby chair, grinning delightedly.

The gathering at the Mountfords' was much as Antonia had imagined it.

"So glad to see you again, my dear." Lady Mountford greeted Henrietta fondly; she acknowledged Antonia's curtsy and Geoffrey's bow with a matronly nod. "You'll find there's no need to stand on ceremony tonight. My girls are about—you've already met, but introduce yourselves and chat as you please. Getting to know your peers is what the night's for—the musicians won't arrive until later.'' Her ladyship waved them into a spacious salon already well-filled with young ladies and, in the main, equally young gentlemen.

"You can help me over there." With her cane, Henrietta indicated a large grouping of comfortable chairs at one end of the salon. "Plenty of old friends there for me to catch up with while you two learn the ropes."

Geoffrey assisted her to a chair in the middle of the group. Antonia helped settle her shawls, then, when Henrietta waved them away, turned back into the room.

"Well!" she murmured, anticipation in her voice. "Where to start?"

"Where indeed?" Geoffrey had already scanned the room. "Here—take my arm." Antonia threw him a surprised look. He grimaced. "It'll make me less conspicuous."

Smiling affectionately, Antonia did as he asked. "You don't look conspicuous at all." With his Mannering height and Mannering build, set off by his relatively restrained attire, Geoffrey looked, if anything, a few years older than some of the young sprigs currently gracing her ladyship's floor. Some, indeed, decked out in the height of fashion, looked far younger than they doubtless wished.

"Hmm." Geoffrey's gaze was fixed on a gentleman to their left. "Just look at that silly bounder over there. His collar's so high he can't turn his head."

Antonia raised her brows. "You being such an expert on fashion?"

"Not me," Geoffrey answered, busy scanning the crowd for further spectacles. "But Philip said no true gentleman would be caught dead sporting such extreme affectations—restrained elegance is the hallmark of the out-and-outers."

"The out-and-outers?"

Geoffrey glanced at her. "Top o' the trees. The Corinthians. You know."

Antonia hid a grin. "No—but I suspect I can imagine. Am I to take it you aspire to such heady heights?"

Geoffrey considered, then shrugged. "I can't say I'd mind being top o' the trees some day, but I've decided to concentrate on getting a working notion of this *ton* business for now—I'll be going up in a few weeks after all."

Antonia nodded. "A wise idea, I'm sure."

"Philip thought so, too." Geoffrey was looking over the room. "What's say we do as we were bid and go introduce ourselves to some fellow sufferers?"

"Just as long as you refrain from informing them of their status." When he looked expectantly down at her, Antonia raised a brow. "I'm on your arm, remember? You're supposed to lead."

"Oh, good!" Geoffrey grinned and lifted his head. "That means I get to choose."

Predictably, he chose the group gathered about the prettiest girl in the room. Luckily, this included Cecily Mountford who, mindful of her mama's strictures, promptly introduced them to the three ladies and four gentlemen loosely grouped before the fireplace. None were more than twenty. Geoffrey was immediately included as one of the group; Antonia, her age declared not only by her innate poise but also by the elegant lines of Lafarge's creation, stood on its outskirts, metaphorically if not literally. Not that any attempted to exclude her—indeed, they treated her so deferentially she felt quite ancient. The young gentlemen blushed, stuttered and bowed while the young ladies leaned forward to shake hands, casting glances of muted envy at her gown.

It rapidly became apparent that their hostess's injunction to set formal restraint aside had been enthusiastically embraced; with the customary facility of youth, the company quickly got down to brass tacks.

The beauty, a sweet-faced young miss in a pale blue gown with dark ringlets bobbing on her shoulders, proved to be a Miss Catriona Dalling, an orphan from east Yorkshire who was in town under the aegis of her aunt, the Countess of Ticehurst.

"She's a dragon," Miss Dalling informed the company, her big blue eyes huge, her distinctly squared little chin jutting aggressively. "No! I tell a lie—she's worse than that, she's a *gorgon!*"

"Is she truly insisting on marrying you to the highest bidder?" Cecily Mountford was no more bashful than her guests.

Lovely lips set in a line, Miss Dalling nodded. "What's more, she's set her heart on poor Ambrose here." Dramatically, she put a hand on the bright green embossed silk sleeve of the young gentleman on her right and squeezed meaningfully. "So now we're *both* being persecuted!"

Ambrose, who gloried in the title of the Marquess of Hammersley, was a pale, obviously nervous young gentleman, short and slightly stocky; he blushed and muttered, and tried to smooth the creases Miss Dalling's strong little fingers had left in his sleeve.

Geoffrey frowned. "Can't you both just say no?"

The comment earned him a host of pitying looks.

"You don't understand," Miss Dalling said. "My aunt is set on me marrying Ambrose because he's a *marquess* and we haven't had one of those in the family before and a marquess is better than an earl, so she sees it as advancing the family's cause. And *Ambrose*'s mama is pushing the match because of my inheritance, because his estates are not bringing in enough to dower all his sisters. *And,*" she added, with a darkling look, "because I'm so young she thinks I'll be easy to manage."

Antonia couldn't help but wonder if the Marquess's mama was blind.

"It's all arranged for consequence and money," Miss

Dalling continued with undisguised contempt. "But it won't do! I've decided to marry for love or not at all!"

Her dramatic declaration drew approving nods from all around, particularly from the Marquess. Antonia inwardly frowned, wondering if they were all really so young, so untutored in society's ways—or if they were merely headstrong, trying their wings in vocal but not active rebellion.

Miss Dalling's championship of the gentle passion provoked argument on all sides, most, Antonia noted, thoroughly supportive of the heiress's position while openly condemning her aunt's.

Her spirits clearly unimpaired by the browbeating she had assured the company she had endured *en route* to Brook Street, Catriona Dalling flashed her an engagingly confiding smile. "I understand you're in town for the first time, as indeed we all are, but you have doubtless more experience than we in searching for your one and only love. I do hope you'll forgive me for speaking so plainly and rattling on so, but I dare say you can see things have reached a pretty pass. Ambrose and I will have to make a stand, don't you think?"

Arguments raged about them, revolving about how to spike Lady Ticehurst's ambitions; Geoffrey, Antonia could hear, was urging the participants to check with their men of affairs. Looking into Miss Dalling's unquestionably innocent eyes, she felt the weight of her years.

"While I would certainly not condone your being coerced into marriage, Miss Dalling, the fact remains that most marriages within our class are arranged, at one level or another. Some, perhaps, are underpinned by affection or longstanding acquaintance, but others are promoted on the basis of what I admit sound cold-blooded reasons. However, in the absence of either party's affections being fixed elsewhere, don't you think there's the possibility that your aunt's suggestion might, in the end, bear fruit?" In making the suggestion, Antonia's gaze touched the Marquess; she felt an immediate pang of uncertainty.

"There is that, of course." Miss Dalling nodded sagely. "But you see, I *have* found my only true love, so the argument does not hold."

"You have?" Antonia could not help eyeing her in concern. The heiress looked barely older than Geoffrey. "Forgive my impertinence, Miss Dalling, but are you sure?"

"Oh, yes. Absolutely sure." Catriona Dalling's decisive nod set her ringlets bouncing. "Henry and I have known each other since we were children and we're quite sure we want to marry. We had thought to wait for a few years—until Henry has proved himself in running his father's farms, you see—but Aunt Ticehurst stepped in."

"I see." The heiress's straightforwardness rang truer than any impassioned declarations. Antonia frowned. "Have you explained your attachment to your aunt?"

"My aunt does not believe in love, Miss Mannering." The militant gleam was back in Catriona Dalling's eye. "She might be more amenable were Henry a marquess too, only unfortunately he's simply a squire's son, so she's not disposed to acquiescence."

"I had not realized," Antonia admitted "that your situation was quite so…awkward. To be urged to turn your back on love, given the connection is not ineligible and your attachment has proved constant, must be distressing."

Catriona gave another of her decisive nods. "It would be, if I had the slightest intention of giving in to the pressure. As it is, I'm determined to stand firm. Not only would marrying Ambrose ruin my life and Henry's, it would undeniably ruin Ambrose's as well."

Viewing the determined cast of Miss Dalling's fair features, and seeing the Marquess, weak-chinned and timid, in earnest conversation with Geoffrey beyond, Antonia could only concur.

"One way or another, I'm determined to win out. It's not as though love matches are all that rare these days." Catriona gestured grandly. "Even in days gone by, such affairs were known. My very own aunt—not Ticehurst, of course, but my other aunt, her sister, now Lady Copely—she defied the family and married Sir Edmund, a gentleman of sufficient but not extravagant means. They've lived very happily for years and years—their household is one of the most comfortable I know. If I could have as much by marrying for love, I would be entirely satisfied.'' She paused only for breath. ''And only last year, my cousin Amelia—my Aunt Copely's eldest daughter—she married her sweetheart, Mr Gerard Moggs.'' She broke off to point out a young couple across the room. ''They're over there—you can see for yourself how happy they are.''

Antonia looked, effectively distracted from Miss Dalling's concerns. This was, after all, what she had come to London to see—married ladies consorting in public with their spouses.

What she saw was a young gentleman of twenty-five or six, standing by a *chaise* on which a pretty young lady was seated, angled around and looking up to meet her husband's gaze. Mr Moggs made some comment; his wife laughed up at him. She laid a hand on his sleeve, squeezing lightly, affectionately. Mr Moggs responded with an openly adoring look. Reaching out, he touched a finger to his wife's cheek, then bent and whispered in her ear before straightening and, with a nod, leaving her.

Antonia noted he went no further than the refreshment table, returning with two glasses.

''Miss Mannering, is it not?''

With a start, Antonia turned to find a gentleman of much her own age bowing before her. He was neatly if fashionably dressed, having avoided the excesses to which the younger generation had fallen prey.

''Mr Hemming, my dear Miss Mannering.'' As he straightened, Antonia looked into mild brown eyes set under wavy brown hair. ''I hope you'll excuse my impertinence, but Lady Mountford tipped me the wink that the musicians are about to start up. Can I prevail on you to honour me with the first cotillion?''

The invitation was accompanied by an engaging smile; Antonia responded spontaneously, graciously extending her hand. ''Indeed, Mr Hemming. I would be pleased to stand up with you.''

She was well-versed in the cotillion, more adept, as it transpired, than Mr Hemming. Despite his pleasant disposition, he was forced to give his attention to the figures, leaving Antonia free to pursue her principal purpose. As she twirled and swirled, it was easy to examine those not dancing for couples who might be husband and wife. Other than the Moggs, she found no likely candidates. As for the Moggs, they, she felt certain, were hardly representative specimens.

It would, she felt sure, be unwise to use their behaviour as a guide to how she might behave with Philip. For a start, Philip was a good deal older than Mr Moggs. As, hand held high, she pirouetted, Antonia scanned the room. Indeed, she couldn't imagine Philip at such a gathering—there were no gentlemen like him present.

The age difference was telling in another way. She could not, by any fanciful stretch of her imagination, imagine Philip casting adoring glances at her, in public or otherwise. Likewise, she was quite certain any affectionate squeezes would result in a frown and a reprimand for damaging his suiting.

Gentlemen, her mother and all Yorkshire ladies had assured her, were made uncomfortable by any public show of fondness; ladies must never, so she had been taught, wear their hearts on their sleeves. While Miss Dalling and her family, one branch at least, as well as the youth of the *ton,* might freely acknowledge the softer emotions, Antonia could not believe that gentlemen of Philip's age and temperament had been won over.

The dance ended and she sank into the prescribed curtsy.

Mr Hemming, beaming, raised her. "An excellent measure, Miss Mannering." Gallantly, he offered her his arm. "I take it you'll be attending the coming balls and parties?"

"I expect we'll attend our fair share." Antonia accepted his arm; he very correctly escorted her back towards the fireplace.

"Have you seen Lord Elgin's marbles? Quite worth a visit, in my humble estimation."

Antonia was about to reply when they were joined by an acquaintance of Mr Hemming's, a Mr Carruthers. Introduced, Mr Carruthers bowed extravagantly. Within minutes, two others had joined them, Sir Frederick Smallwood and a Mr Riley. Before Antonia could blink, she found herself at the centre of a small circle of gentlemen. They chatted amiably, pleasantly; she danced the quadrille with Sir Frederick and the last cotillion with Mr Carruthers. Mr Riley begged to be remembered when next they met.

Then the party started to break up. Geoffrey appeared by her elbow with the information that Henrietta was ready to depart; Antonia excused herself to her cavaliers and politely withdrew.

Once she had settled Henrietta in the carriage, draping extra shawls about her shoulders, Antonia sat back and pondered all she had seen. "Aunt," she eventually asked, as the carriage rocked into motion, "is it common for married gentlemen to accompany their wives to such entertainments?"

Henrietta snorted. "Noticed the Moggs, did you? Hardly surprising—they attracted quite a bit of interest, that pair of lovebirds." Her tone suggested the matrons had not been impressed. "But to answer your question—no, it's not general practice, but not only is Gerard Moggs quite openly besotted with his wife, she's also in an interesting condition, so I expect we'll have to excuse him."

Antonia nodded; she now had the Moggs in their proper perspective.

"Quite a fine line, actually—just how much husbandly attention is allowable." Henrietta spoke into the darkness, her voice only just audible over the rattle of the carriage wheels. "Not, of course, that the question arises in many cases—gentlemen being what they are. Only too glad to keep to their clubs and their dinners. Most put in an appearance at the best balls and parties, enough to nod to their wives in passing, but the consensus has always been that, in town at least, husbands and wives follow essentially separate social calendars." She fluffed her shawls. "That, of course, limits the opportunities for the sort of exhibition you witnessed tonight."

Any doubts as to her aunt's opinion of the Moggs' behaviour was laid to rest. Antonia shifted in her seat. "I had thought gentlemen often escorted ladies to the various entertainments?"

"Indeed." Henrietta yawned. "But, in the main, such escort duties fall to the unmarried males, the confirmed bachelors or the yet-to-be-snared. Only occasionally would a married lady expect her husband to act as her escort, and then only if he was wishful of attending the same function."

The shadows hid Antonia's frown. Her enjoyment of the outings Philip had organised, the laughter they had shared, the undeniable pleasure she found in his company—would all that change once they were wed? Be relegated to history, never to be experienced again? What, she wondered, was the point of being married—of having a firm friendship with one's husband—if being married prohibited him from spending time in your company?

The carriage swayed around a corner then rumbled on into Grosvenor Square; Geoffrey shifted in his corner. As they drew up outside Ruthven House, he jumped down, smothering a yawn. Between them, Antonia and he helped Henrietta up the steps; Carring stood at the top, holding the door wide.

Behind him, in the glow of the hall chandelier, Antonia

spied Philip. He strolled forward as Carring shut the door. "A pleasant evening?"

The question was addressed to her but Geoffrey answered it.

"Dull work," he said, around another yawn. "Nothing of any substance except for the heiress's dragon of an aunt. She really did look like a gorgon."

"Indeed?" Philip raised an amused brow.

"Absolutely," Geoffrey assured him. "But I'm for bed."

"In that case," Henrietta said, poking him in the ribs, "you can give me your arm up the stairs." She glanced over her shoulder. "Send Trant up at once, please, Carring."

Carring bowed deeply. "Immediately, m'lady."

Antonia stood by Philip's side, watching until her brother and her aunt gained the upper landing.

"Come into the library." Philip's words and his hand at her elbow had her turning in that direction. "Was there much dancing?"

He had gone out after they had left, stifling a ludicrous wish that he could join them, instead meeting Hugo and a small coterie of friends at Brooks. Together, they'd gone on to Boodles, then to a select establishment in Pall Mall, but he'd been too restless to settle to the play. In the end, he'd cried off and returned home to idly pace the library floor.

"Two cotillions and a quadrille." Antonia yielded to his persuasion. They entered the library; Philip shut the door behind them.

"And you danced them all?"

"Indeed."

Philip stopped by one of the wing chairs flanking the fireplace, filled with a cheery blaze. Antonia sat, her skirts sighing about her. Philip paused, studying her. "Would you like a nightcap?"

Antonia looked up, her expression arrested, then smiled and shook her head.

Philip was not deceived. "What?"

Her smile reminded him forcefully of the irrepressible girl she had been. "Actually," she said, her eyes dancing, "I would dearly love a glass of warm milk but I cannot imagine how Carring would react to such a request."

"Can you not?" Philip's brows slowly rose. Turning, he crossed to the bellpull.

"Philip!" Antonia sat up.

Philip waved her back. "No—I have a score to settle—hush!" He returned to take the chair opposite hers.

Carring entered, ponderously solemn. "You rang, m'lord?"

"Indeed." Philip's expression was utterly bland. "Miss Mannering would like a nightcap, Carring. A glass of warm milk."

Carring's eyes flickered, then he bowed. "Will that be for two, m'lord?"

It took Philip a moment to master his tone. "No—you may pour me a brandy when you return."

"Very good, m'lord." Bowing, Carring withdrew.

As soon as the door closed, Antonia succumbed. "The thought of you drinking warm milk," she eventually got out, hugging her aching ribs.

Despite himself, Philip's lips curved upward. "One day, I keep telling myself, I'll have the last word."

He was not destined to succeed that night. Carring reappeared bearing a glass of perfectly warmed milk on a silver tray. He deposited it on the table by Antonia's side with the same care he would have taken had it been aged port, then crossed to the cabinet and poured Philip's brandy, leaving the large glass by his master's elbow.

"Thank you, Carring. You may lock up."

"M'lord." With his usual deep obeisance, the major-domo withdrew.

Reaching for the brandy glass, Philip discovered it was half-full. A subtle hint, he supposed, of Carring's estimation of his state. Taking a sip, he smiled at Antonia. "With whom did you dance?"

Cradling her glass in her hand, she settled back in the chair. "Most of those present were more Geoffrey's age than mine but there were a few older gentlemen present— Mr Riley, Mr Hemming, Sir Frederick Smallwood and a Mr Carruthers."

"Indeed?" Philip did not recognize the names, which gave him some idea of their station. He fixed her with a mildly enquiring gaze. "And did you, like Geoffrey, find it dull work?"

Antonia smiled. "While it certainly did not rival Astley's, it was not totally without interest."

"Oh?"

It was more to the light in his eyes and his tone that she responded, relating her observations on all she had seen as she slowly sipped her milk.

Philip watched the firelight strike gleams from her hair; the play of the fire-glow over her pale face, over her lips, sheened by the milk, held him in thrall. The cadence of her voice rose and fell; he sipped his brandy and listened as she painted a picture he had seen many times—through her eyes, it held an innocence, a sparkling freshness he had long grown too jaded to see.

She concluded with a thumbnail sketch of the major protagonists in what promised to be one of the season's more entertaining imbroglios.

"Indeed," Antonia said, setting aside her empty glass. "The situation of Miss Dalling and the Marquess does seem to be of some urgency—but how much of that derives from Miss Dalling's undeniable sense of the dramatic I could not say. Whatever, I'm certain Miss Dalling will prevail, gorgon aunt or no." She looked across at Philip, smiling, inviting him to share her amusement.

To her surprise, his face remained expressionless.

Abruptly, he stood, setting his glass on the table beside him. "Come. It's time you went upstairs."

There was a note in his voice she could not place. Bemused, Antonia gave him her hands and let him draw her to her feet. Only then, as she stood directly before him, feeling the warmth of the fire strike through her thin gown did he meet her gaze. In the flickering firelight, his eyes were dark, slate-grey and stormy. Antonia felt her breath catch; she hesitated, then, calmly, her lips gently curving, she inclined her head. "Good night, Philip."

She was not going to retreat in disorder this time, nor take refuge in distance.

Stiffly, Philip returned her nod. He tensed to step back, to let her go—his fingers twined with hers and held tight. He hesitated, his gaze on her face, then slowly, gently, he drew her towards him until her bodice brushed his coat. His fingers slid from hers; he lifted both hands to frame her face.

Antonia held his gaze, her breath tangled in her chest, her heart pulsing in her throat. She saw his lids lower, his head angle over hers, then slowly descend. Her hand rose to his shoulder as she stretched upward, her lips slightly parted.

He kissed her, not forcefully but confidently, as one sure of his welcome. His lips firmed, his tongue teased and tantalised, tracing the ripe curves of her lips. She parted them fully, inviting him to taste; he did, sampling her softness, laying claim to all she offered with a possessive, consummate skill.

The fire burned; the flames leapt. For long minutes, a gentle magic held sway.

Then, very slowly, very deliberately, Philip drew back. His lips bare inches from Antonia's, he waited until her lids fluttered opened. He studied her eyes, burnished gold in emerald green. When they focused, he straightened. Holding tight to his reins, he released her.

"Good night, Antonia." His smile held a wry quality he doubted she'd understand. "Sweet dreams."

She blinked; her eyes searched his, neither frightened nor puzzled, but with an intensity he could not place. Then her lips curved. "Good night."

The soft whisper reached him as she turned away. He watched her go, saw her glance back, once, at the door, then slip through it, shutting it softly behind her.

Drawing in a deep breath, Philip turned towards the fire. Bracing one arm against the mantelpiece, he gazed into the flames. Wonderingly, he ran the tip of his tongue over his lips—and fought to quell a shudder.

He had never imagined milk could taste erotic.

Chapter Nine

At noon the next day, Philip returned to his home after breakfasting with friends at a coffee house in Jermyn Street. His expression unruffled, his disposition one of calm expectation, he entered the cool dimness of his hall.

Carring rolled forward to relieve him of his greatcoat and cane.

Philip resettled his sleeves. "Is Miss Mannering about?"

"Indeed, m'lord." Carring fixed his gaze on the wall beyond Philip's right shoulder. "Miss Mannering is presently in the ballroom receiving instruction from the dancing master. *Maestro* Vincente."

Philip studied his major-domo's eloquently blank expression. "The ballroom?"

Carring inclined his head.

The ballroom lay beyond the drawing-room. The familiar chords of a waltz reached Philip's ears as he neared the door. Like all his doors, it opened noiselessly; crossing the threshold, he swiftly scanned the room.

The curtains had been drawn back along one side; sunlight spilled in wide beams across the floor. Geoffrey sat at the piano at the far end, industriously providing the music, frowning as he squinted at the music sheets. In the centre of the polished parquetry, Antonia, distinctly stiff, revolved awkwardly in the arms of a middle-aged man Philip unhesitatingly classed as an ageing roué.

Maestro Vincente showed little evidence of Italian blood. Short and rotund, he sported a florid, suspiciously English complexion. He was wearing a brown tie-wig and a bottle-green coat of similarly ancient vintage; his spindle shanks were clad in knitted hose. Most damning of all, Maestro Vincente possessed a distinctly lecherous eye.

Philip strode forward, letting his boot-heels ring on the boards. The music abruptly halted. Antonia looked up; Philip saw the relief in her eyes. His jaw hardened. "I fear there has been a misunderstanding."

Maestro Vincente's eyes started. He hurriedly released Antonia. "A misunderstanding?" His high-pitched voice rendered the exclamation a squeak. "No, no. I was hired, dear sir, I assure you."

Halting by Antonia's side, Philip looked down on the hapless maestro. "In that case, I regret to inform you that your services are no longer required." Without looking at the door, he raised his voice. "Carring?"

"M'lord?"

"Maestro Vincente is leaving."

"Indeed, m'lord."

"But…really! I must insist…!" Hands outspread, Maestro Vincente appealed to Philip.

Philip ignored him; gripping Antonia's elbow, he guided her down the room.

"If you'll just come this way, *sir?*" Carring's heavy tones left no room for argument. As always, he had the final word, efficiently ushering the deflated maestro out of the room.

The door shut; Antonia stared at Philip. "Why did you do that?"

Halting by the piano, Philip raised a supercilious brow. "He was hardly a proper person to instruct you in anything."

"Precisely what I said," Geoffrey interjected.

Antonia ignored her brother. She fixed Philip with an exasperated look. "Be that as it may, how, pray tell, am I now supposed to learn to waltz? In case it's escaped your notice, these days, every young lady *must* be able to waltz. The *ton* will expect it of—" Abruptly, she broke off. She glanced at Geoffrey, then continued, "Of me."

Philip nodded. "Indeed. So, having dismissed your appointed instructor, it would seem only fair that I take his place."

Antonia's eyes widened. "But—"

Exuberant chords drowned out her protest. Before she could marshal her wits, they were effectively scattered as Philip drew her into his arms.

"I assure you I'm every bit as competent as Maestro Vincente."

Antonia threw him a speaking look.

Philip met it with an improbably humble expression. "I've been waltzing around the *ton*'s ballrooms for…let me see." He frowned, then raised his brows. "More years than I can recall."

Antonia humphed and straightened her spine. As usual, she felt breathless; as he effortlessly steered her into the first gliding steps, a definite giddiness took hold. She wasn't at all sure this was a good idea but the challenge in his grey eyes made demurring unthinkable. Tilting her chin, she tried to concentrate on where he was headed.

"Relax." Philip looked down at her. "Stop thinking and you'll follow my lead easily enough." When she looked her uncertainty, he raised one brow. "I'll even forgive you should you scuff my Hessians."

Antonia widened her eyes at him. "Given you've just high-handedly dismissed my dancing master, who came with quite remarkable recommendations I'll have you know, then I should think you must accept whatever consequences follow." As she capped the haughty comment with a toss of her curls, Antonia was struck by the oddity of the situation. Philip's intervention had been an impulsive, spur-of-the-moment reaction, unquestionably out of character. She cast a glance up at him—he was frowning.

He caught her eye. "Who recommended Maestro Vincente?"

Antonia grimaced. "Lady Castleton and Miss Castleton. They were full of his praises, so Henrietta said."

Philip's expression turned cynical. "The Castleton ladies appear to have a definite predilection for toads. Sir Miles has my sympathy."

Antonia wrinkled her nose. "I did wonder how they had stood him." She shuddered expressively. "He was decidedly slimy."

Philip's smile was fleeting, quickly superseded by a frown. He glanced at Geoffrey, busy with the keys, then captured Antonia's eye. "Kindly understand you have no cause whatever, henceforth, to have any dealings with toads, fish, or any other amphibian or reptilian species." He held her gaze steadily. "Do I make myself clear?"

Antonia stared at him. "But what if—?"

"There are no circumstances I can imagine that would make acquaintance nor even contact with such persons necessary." His gaze fixed on her face, Philip steered them through a turn. "Henceforth, should you be approached by any such persons, I would take it kindly if you referred them to me." He paused, his imagination playing with the possibilities. "No—let me rephrase that." His jaw hardened; again he trapped Antonia's gaze. "Should any such approach you, I will *expect* you to refer them to me."

"Indeed?"

"Indeed. In fact," Philip continued, spurred on by memories of her wilful confidence, "if you do *not* call any such incidents to my notice, I will not be held accountable for my reactions."

"Philip—he was only a dancing master."

He frowned at her, noting the affectionate laughter lurking in her eyes. The sight soothed the aggressive compulsion gripping him. "It's not the dancing master I'm worried about," he acidly informed her. "Incidentally, you're waltzing quite creditably."

Antonia's eyes flew wide; she nearly missed her step but Philip's arm tightened, holding her steady. "So I am," she said, distinctly breathless. She lowered her gaze to his shoulder. Distracted by his conversation, she had not been directing her limbs at all. Of their own volition, they had followed his assured lead; as the music flowed, they continued to do so. Freed, her mind opened to the sensations of the dance, to the subtle play of her skirts about her legs, to the hardness of his thighs as they brushed hers through the turns.

The seductive swirl of the music was mirrored in their movements; the smooth swoop and sway was a sensual delight. Philip's hand at her waist was firm, his touch confident as he guided her where he willed. Tentatively, she shifted the fingers of her right hand and felt his clasp tighten possessively.

Quelling a shiver of pure awareness, Antonia had a fleeting, distinctly scarifying vision of waltzing like this, held captive in Philip's arms, under the long noses of the *ton*. How on earth would she manage with every nerve-ending afire? Appalled, she banished the vision—she did not need to deal with that potential calamity today. Today, she was here, waltzing with Philip, with none—not even Geoffrey, too busy at the piano—to watch. Today, she could enjoy herself.

Unexpectedly, she felt a sense of warmth and triumph steal through her. A soft smile curved her lips. Raising her head, she let her gaze touch Philip's. "I have to admit that your...technique is a great improvement over Maestro Vincente's."

Philip humphed.

"That aside," she smoothly continued, "I had meant to thank you for your gift—the reticule." Today's gift—the latest in a long line. Ever since he had given her the parasol, no day had passed without some small token appearing in her room—a pair of gloves to match the parasol, a big bunch of satin ribbon in the same shade, a fashionable new bonnet, a pair of exquisite half-boots. This morning, a small beaded reticule she had admired in a Bond Street window had found its way to her dresser. "It goes perfectly with my new gold silk—I'll carry it tonight to the Quartermains."

Philip studied her smile, pleased yet exasperated, too. "Mere trumpery, as I said, but if it finds favour in your eyes, then I'll rest content." For now. He was irritatingly aware that, could he behave as he wished, he would shower her with jewels, furs and all manner of expensive tokens of an affection he was prepared to admit was very real. But while she wished their liaison to remain unacknowledged, trumpery was all he could afford. He was finding the restriction unexpectedly irksome.

The piece they had been waltzing to drew to its conclusion. "That's it!" Geoffrey declared. "All very well for you," he said, as both Antonia and Philip glanced his way. "But my fingers are cramping."

Philip grinned. Reluctantly releasing Antonia, he caught her hand, drawing her with him as he strolled towards the pianoforte. "What time did you start? Half past eleven?"

Flexing his fingers, Geoffrey nodded.

"Very well—we'll meet again tomorrow at the same time."

Geoffrey nodded again; it was Antonia who protested. "Tomorrow?"

Turning, Philip raised her hand and placed a quick, proprietorial kiss on her knuckles. "Indeed." He raised a brow at her. "You can hardly imagine you're an expert already?"

"No-oo." Looking up into his eyes, Antonia hesitated. Here in his ballroom, they'd be essentially alone; she was increasingly confident of behaving appropriately while they were private. And practice was surely needed to strengthen her defences against the evening when she would waltz with him in public, in a crowded ballroom under the glare of the chandeliers. Drawing in a deep breath, she nodded. "No doubt you're right."

The look Philip sent her made her arch her brows haughtily.

Antonia lifted her chin. "Until tomorrow at eleven-thirty, my lord."

Later that afternoon, Antonia with Geoffrey in tow again crossed the path of Catriona Dalling and the Marquess of Hammersley.

Together with Henrietta, they had taken advantage of the bright autumnal sunshine and driven forth in the Ruthven barouche to see and be seen in the Park. Tempted by the clemency of the weather, they had left Henrietta in the barouche, chatting to Lady Osbaldestone, and descended to join the numerous couples fashionably strolling the lawns. They were halfway down the Serpentine Walk when they came upon Miss Dalling and the Marquess.

Heads together, voices lowered, the pair broke off what appeared to be frantic plotting to greet Antonia and Geoffrey. Shaking hands, Miss Dalling declared, "Fate has clearly sent you to us, for we stand greatly in need of support."

"Oh?" Geoffrey's eyes lit.

"Why do you need support, Miss Dalling?" Antonia felt rather more reticent over leaping to Miss Dalling's conclusions.

"Please call me Catriona," Miss Dalling said, smiling radiantly. "I truly believe we were meant to be friends."

Antonia could not help responding with a smile. "Very well—and you must call me Antonia. But why do you need aid?"

"My mama." Ambrose, who had already exchanged names with Geoffrey, looked dejected. "She's arrived in town, deadly keen to see the knot tied."

"More than *keen*," Catriona decried. "Positively insistent! What with Aunt Ticehurst on one side and the Marchioness on the other, we're being *hounded* into marriage! We were just deciding what to do when you came up."

"Nothing too drastic, I hope. You would not wish to bring any scandal down upon your head."

"Indeed not." Catriona shook her head so vigorously her dark ringlets danced. "Any breath of scandal would avail us nought, for they would simply use that to force our hands. No—whatever we do must be done in such a way that there's no possibility Aunt Ticehurst and Ambrose's mama can use it against us."

"So what do you plan to do?" Geoffrey asked.

Catriona's brow clouded. "I don't know." For an instant, her lips quivered, then she blinked and lifted her chin. "That's why I've decided to send for Henry."

"Henry?"

"Henry Fortescue, my intended." Catriona's lips firmed. "*He*'ll know what to do."

"A capital idea, I think." Ambrose looked hopefully at Geoffrey.

"But there's one problem." Catriona frowned. "I cannot write a letter to Henry for Aunt Ticehurst keeps a very close watch on me. We're not even out of her sight here—she's in her brougham, watching from the carriageway. I was just telling Ambrose he'll have to write for me."

"Ah…" Ambrose shifted his weight from one foot to the other. "No one more eager than I to be free of this coil." He looked pleadingly at Catriona. "But you can see, can't you, that it's not really the thing? Me writing to your intended telling him to come and see you?"

Catriona's expression turned mulish. "I don't see—"

"By Jove, yes!" Geoffrey looked horror-struck. "Dashed awkward."

"Precisely." Ambrose nodded rapidly. "Won't do—the poor fellow won't know what's afoot."

Antonia managed to keep her lips straight. "Indeed, Catriona, I do feel that any note would be better coming from you."

Catriona sighed. "But *that*'s the problem—how can we manage it?"

No one had an answer. At Antonia's suggestion, they strolled the path, all racking their brains for a solution.

"The museum!" Geoffrey halted; the others swung to face him. Eyes alight, he grinned at them. "I read somewhere that they have desks at the museum for scholars—you bring paper and pen and they provide the desk and inkwell for a small fee."

Catriona beamed. "We can go there tomorrow—" She broke off; her smile faded. "No, we can't. Aunt Ticehurst would insist on coming too."

Geoffrey glanced at Antonia. "Perhaps...?"

Antonia read his look and inwardly sighed. Shifting her gaze to the scenery, she considered. "Not tomorrow—that would appear too precipitous. But perhaps we could arrange to make a party to visit the museum the day after tomorrow? I understand Lord Elgin's marbles are a sight not to be missed."

She looked at Catriona in time to be dazzled by the transformation her words had wrought. Smiling, Catriona was the most radiantly beautiful girl.

"Oh, Miss Mannering—I mean, Antonia!" Catriona caught Antonia's hand and clasped it warmly. "I will be your dearest friend for life! That's a brilliant suggestion."

Geoffrey humphed.

"If we present the thing right," Ambrose mused. "They'll be sure to approve." He turned to Catriona. "If we make it sound like I invited you and then asked Miss

Mannering and Geoffrey to make up the party, it will allay their suspicions.''

''Indeed, yes! Nothing could be better.'' Buoyed with purpose, Catriona flashed both Antonia and Geoffrey another stunning smile. ''As I said, fate clearly intended us to meet. Nothing could have been more *fortuitous!*''

Two days later, Philip strolled across Grosvenor Square, basking in the afternoon sunshine. Swinging his cane as he walked, he noted that the leaves still clinging to the trees were golden and brown. They had completely changed colour since his return to London, their altered hue a record of the passage of time. To his mind, somewhat unexpectedly, that time had been well spent.

Their first days, admittedly, had been a trifle strained, but once Antonia had found her feet, their interactions had run smoothly. The Little Season would commence tomorrow evening; the round of balls and parties would fill the coming weeks. Given Antonia would be introduced as Henrietta's niece, no one would remark on his presence by her side. No eyebrows would be raised when he waltzed with her. A subtle smile curved his lips. Even more to his liking was what would happen every night when they returned to Ruthven House. He had been at pains to establish their nightly routine. At the end of every day, they would repair to his library, comfortable and at ease, she to drink her milk and favour him with her observations, he to sip his brandy and watch the firelight gild her face.

As he climbed the steep steps to his door, Philip realised he was smiling unrestrainedly. Abruptly sobering, he schooled his features to their usual impassive mien. Carring opened the door, bowing deeply before relieving him of his gloves and cane.

Philip glanced at the hall mirror, then frowned and straightened one fold of his cravat. Satisfied, he opened his lips.

"I believe Miss Mannering and Master Geoffrey have gone to the museum, m'lord."

Philip shut his lips. Turning, he shot Carring a narrow-eyed glance, then headed for the library.

The museum? Philip wandered about the library, ultimately halting before his desk to idly flip through his mail. He glanced at the stack of invitations piled on the desk but felt no burning desire to examine them. What to do with the afternoon? He could go to Manton's and hunt up some congenial company. Grimacing, he remained where he was. Long minutes passed as he stared unseeing out of the window, fingers tapping on the polished mahogany. Then his jaw firmed. Turning on his heel, he headed back into the hall.

Carring was waiting by the front door, Philip's gloves and cane held ready in his hands.

Philip cast him a withering look, accepted both gloves and cane, then strode out.

He reached the museum to find it unexpectedly crowded; it took him some time to locate his stepmother's niece. It was Geoffrey he found first, deep in examination of a group of artifacts purported to be Stone Age relics. Geoffrey's absorption was so intense Philip had to clap him on the shoulder to get his attention.

Blinking, Geoffrey focused on Philip's face, then smiled absentmindedly. "Didn't expect to see you here. Antonia's over there." He pointed to the next room, a large alcove beyond one of the display cases, then promptly returned to the relics.

Exasperation growing, Philip left him to them and pushed through into the next room.

Only to discover his stepmother's niece surrounded by no fewer than five gentlemen.

Antonia looked up to see Philip bearing down upon her. She smiled warmly. "Good day, my lord."

"Good afternoon, my dear."

As his fingers closed, tightly, about hers, Antonia registered the change from languid indolence to clipped abruptness. Rapidly whipping her wits to order, she turned a suddenly wary gaze on her companions. "Ah—I believe I have mentioned Sir Frederick Smallwood, my lord."

Philip nodded stiffly in reply to Sir Frederick's bow. "Smallwood."

Disregarding the menace underlying his tone, Antonia doggedly introduced every last one of her court. "Mr Carruthers was about to favour us with the tale of the discovery of the stone implements displayed over there." Antonia smiled encouragingly at Mr Carruthers.

A student of antiquities, Mr Carruthers promptly launched into his dissertation. As his tale unfolded, encompassing numerous tangents, all described in glowing detail, Antonia felt Philip shift impatiently. When Mr Dashwood asked a question, which led to a lively discussion involving all the other gentlemen, Philip leaned closer and whispered in her ear, "You can't be so bored you consider *this* amusement?"

Antonia threw him a warning glance. "It's an improvement over staring at the relics."

"The trick is to keep strolling." Philip caught her hand and placed it on his sleeve. "That way, you don't end up collecting so much extraneous baggage."

His hand closed over hers, his intention plain; Antonia held firm. "No!" she hissed. "I can't leave here—I'm waiting for someone."

Philip's eyes locked on hers. The arrested look in them made Antonia's heart skip a beat. "Oh?" he said. One brown brow slowly arched. "Who?"

Antonia cast a distracted glance at her companions; their discussion was slowly winding down. "I'll explain it all later—but we have to stay here." With that, she gave her attention to Sir Frederick.

"Tell me, my dear Miss Mannering." Sir Frederick smiled engagingly. "What do you say to the age of these gold cups?'' He gestured to a large display in the centre of the room. ''Are we really to believe such workmanship dates from before Christ?''

Philip raised his eyes to the ceiling. Resisting the urge to simply haul Antonia away, he clenched his jaw and endured fifteen minutes of the most utterly inane discussions. Having very little to do with younger gentlemen, he had never before suffered any similar experience. By the time Antonia abruptly straightened, he was ready to admit that young ladies of the *ton* might have a cross to bear he had not hitherto appreciated.

Scanning the room, his gaze passed over a stunningly pretty girl strolling forward on the arm of a pasty-faced youth. Failing to discover any likely candidate for Antonia's attention he was rescanning their surroundings when Antonia broke off her conversation. ''Ah—here's Miss Dalling.''

Miss Dalling and her companion were well known to the other gentlemen; introduced, Philip exchanged greetings. He did not need Antonia's swift glance to realize it was Miss Dalling and the Marquess for whom she'd been waiting. Her reasons, however, remained a mystery.

Miss Dalling turned wide lavender-blue eyes upon the assembled company. ''All these old things are quite fascinating, are they not?''

While Catriona chattered animatedly, Antonia, somewhat distractedly, considered her court. When she had planned this excursion, she had imagined strolling quietly about the displays on Geoffrey's arm while Catriona with Ambrose in attendance composed her missive. But no sooner had she set foot in the museum than gentlemen had appeared as if sprouting from the woodwork, all intent on passing the time by her side. Luckily, Mr Broadside and Sir Eric Malley had had previous engagements which had forced them to leave; that still left her with five unexpected cavaliers to dismiss.

She had not the first idea how to accomplish the deed.

"Perhaps," she said, smiling meaningfully at Catriona, "we should stroll about the rooms?"

"Oh, yes! I expect I should take particular note of some of the displays." Eyes twinkling, Catriona took Ambrose's arm. Antonia surmised the summons to Henry Fortescue had been successfully inscribed and handed into Ambrose's care.

Her hand on Philip's sleeve, Antonia smiled upon her court. "Gentlemen, I thank you for your company. Perchance we'll meet tonight?"

"Yes, indeed—but no need to break up the party." Sir Frederick gestured expansively.

"No—indeed no," came from Mr Dashwood. "Haven't actually *looked* at anything in the museum for years—only too pleased to take a squint around."

"I'll come too—just in case you need some information on the artifacts." Mr Carruthers nodded benignly.

Antonia's answering smile was weak. When they strolled from the room, all five gentlemen ambled in their wake. As they wended their way between the display cases, she bit her lip—then slanted a glance up at Philip. He met it with an expression she was coming to know well—pure cynicism combined with insufferable male superiority. He arched a distinctly supercilious brow at her. Antonia narrowed her eyes at him, then, head high, shifted her gaze forward.

Philip hid his smile. He saw Geoffrey and shot him a glance sharp enough to bring him to heel. When they reached the centre of the main room, he halted and pulled out his watch. Consulting it, he grimaced. "I'm afraid, my dear, that we've run out of time. If you want your surprise, we'll have to leave now."

Antonia stared at him, her lips forming a silent "Oh".

"Surprise?" Geoffrey asked.

"The surprise I promised you all," Philip glibly replied. "Remember?"

Geoffrey met his gaze. "Oh! That surprise."

"Indeed." Smoothly turning to Antonia's trailing court, Philip raised a languid brow. "I'm afraid, gentlemen, that you'll have to excuse us."

"Oh—yes. Naturally!"

"Until next time, Miss Mannering. Miss Dalling."

To Antonia's inward disgust, amid a host of similar phrases, her five encumbrances obediently took themselves off. As the last bowed and withdrew, she glanced up at Philip, only to see his jaw firm.

"I suggest we get moving immediately." Before any of them could question his intent, he had them all outside, Catriona and Ambrose included. A hackney was waiting at the kerb; Philip hailed it and bundled Catriona, Ambrose and Geoffrey aboard. Shutting the door on them, he slapped the side. "Gunters."

The jarvey nodded and clicked his reins. The old coach lumbered away.

Left standing on the pavement, distinctly bemused, Antonia stared at Philip. "What about us?"

Exasperated, he looked down at her. "Do we have to follow?"

Antonia stiffened. "Yes!"

Philip narrowed his eyes at her but she refused to retreat. Heaving a long-suffering sigh, he called up another hackney.

"Now," he said, the instant the hackney's door shut upon them. "You can explain what Miss Dalling and the Marquess are about."

Antonia was perfectly willing to do so; by the time the hackney drew up outside Gunters, Philip was considering retreating himself. Unfortunately, the sight that met his eyes as he glanced out of the hackney window rendered that course of action impossible.

"Good God!" he said, sitting forward and reaching for the handle. "The silly clunches are standing outside."

Predictably, Catriona Dalling had started to attract an audience. Gritting his teeth, Philip handed Antonia down, then deftly extricated Miss Dalling and, feeling very like a sheep-dog with his sheep, ushered his little group into the shop.

It was hardly a venue at which he was well known. Nevertheless, the waitress took one look at him and immediately found a discreet booth big enough to accommodate the whole party. By the time he sank onto the bench beside Antonia, Philip found he was actually looking forward to an ice.

The waitress took their orders; the ices arrived before they had well caught their breaths. Catriona, Ambrose and Geoffrey attacked theirs in style; Philip and Antonia were rather more circumspect.

Catriona finished first and patted her lips with her napkin. ''Ambrose will post my letter tomorrow,'' she informed the table at large. ''I know Henry will come post-haste to the rescue—just like the true knight he is.'' She clasped her napkin to her bosom and affected a romantically distant gaze. Then she sighed. ''He'll know exactly what to do for the best. Everything will be right as a trivet once he arrives.''

When she and Ambrose fell to discussing their respective guardians' likely plans, Philip caught Antonia's eye. ''I can only hope,'' he murmured, ''that Mr Fortescue is up to handling Miss Dalling's dramatic flights. Don't ever think I'm not grateful for your lack of histrionic tendencies.''

Antonia blinked, then smiled and looked down at her ice. As she took another mouthful, her smile grew. She had wondered if Philip would prove at all susceptible to Catriona's undeniable beauty. Apparently not. His comment, indeed, suggested quite otherwise; she couldn't help feeling pleased.

Watching her, Philip narrowed his eyes, astute enough to guess what lay behind her smug smile. He attacked his ice, inwardly humphing at the implied slight to his taste. To any with experience, certainly any of his ilk, Miss Dalling's mere prettiness could not hold a candle to Antonia's mature beauty. The heiress might be a handful in her own way but she was very definitely not the same sort of handful his bride-to-be obviously was. He glanced at Antonia, then, all but automatically, scanned the room.

Four gentlemen rapidly averted their eyes. Philip's expression hardened. At the museum, all five gentlemen had had Antonia in their sights, a fact that had not escaped him.

Shifting in his seat, Philip let his gaze rest on her face.

She felt it; turning, she briefly studied his eyes, then lifted a brow. "I think perhaps it's time we left. We have Lady Griswald's musical soirée this evening."

As they left the shop, Philip found himself wondering who would be at Lady Griswald's tonight. Antonia shook his arm.

"Catriona and Ambrose are leaving."

Philip duly took his leave of the pair, who intended visiting Hatchard's before returning to Ticehurst House. With Antonia on his arm and Geoffrey ambling behind, Philip headed in the opposite direction. Absorbed with thoroughly unwelcome considerations, he stared, unseeing, straight ahead.

Antonia cast a puzzled glance up at him. She opened her lips to comment on his brown study, simultaneously following his gaze. Her words froze on her lips.

Ten yards ahead stood two ladies, both exquisitely gowned and coiffed. Both were ogling Philip shamelessly.

She might have been raised in Yorkshire but Antonia knew immediately exactly what sort of ladies the two were. She stiffened; her eyes flashed. She was about to bestow a chillingly haughty glance when she caught herself up—and glanced at Philip.

In the same instant, Philip refocused and saw the two Cyprians. Absentminded still, he idly took stock of their wares, then felt Antonia's gaze. He glanced down at her, just in time to see her lids veil her eyes. She stiffened and pointedly looked away, every line infused with haughty condemnation.

Philip opened his mouth—eyes narrowing, he bit back his words. He had, he reminded himself, no need to excuse himself over something she should not, by rights, even have noticed. He halted. "We'll take a cab."

He hailed a passing hackney. The three of them climbed in; Antonia sat beside him, cloaked in chilly dignity. Philip stared out of the window, his lips a thin line. He had had to put up with her being ogled all afternoon, let alone what might happen tonight. She had no right to take umbrage just because two ladybirds had cast their eyes his way.

By the time the hackney turned into Grosvenor Square, he had, somewhat grudgingly, calmed. Her sensitivity might irritate but her intelligence was, to him, one of her attractions. It was, he supposed, unreasonable to expect her to be ignorant on specific topics—such as his past history or potential inclinations.

The hackney pulled up; he let Geoffrey jump down, then descended leisurely and helped Antonia to the pavement, affecting indifference when she refused to meet his eyes. He tossed a half-crown to the jarvey then, studiously urbane, escorted her in, pausing in the hall to hand his cane to Carring.

"So," he said, coming up with her as she removed her bonnet. "You're bound for Lady Griswald's tonight?"

Still avoiding his gaze, Antonia nodded. "A musical soirée, as I said. Hordes of innocently reticent young ladies pressed to entertain the company with their musical talents." Looking down, she unbuttoned her gloves. "Not, I believe, your cup of tea."

Her words stung; ruthlessly, Philip clamped down on his reaction, shocked by its strength. His polite mask firmly in place, he waited, patiently, beside her—and let the silence stretch.

Eventually, she glanced up at him, haughty wariness in her eyes.

Trapping her gaze, he smiled—charmingly. ''I hope you enjoy yourself, my dear.''

Briefly, her eyes scanned his, then, stiffly, she inclined her head. ''I hope your evening is equally enjoyable, my lord.''

With that she glided away; regally erect, she climbed the stairs.

Philip watched her ascend, then turned to his library, his smile converting to a wry grimace. He was too old a hand to try to melt her ice; he'd wait for the thaw.

Chapter Ten

Three nights later, the atmosphere was still sub-zero.

Following Henrietta and Geoffrey up Lady Caldecott's stairs, Antonia on his arm, Philip cast a jaundiced glance over the crowd about them. Their first two evenings of the Little Season had been spent at mere parties, relatively quiet affairs at which the guests had concentrated on catching up with the summer's developments rather than actively embarking on any new intrigues. Lady Caldecott's Grand Ball marked the end of such simple entertainments.

They had yet to gain the ballroom door, but at least three of his peers had already taken due note of Antonia, serenely beautiful if somewhat tense by his side. Even at a distance, he could detect the gleam in their eyes. He didn't need to look to know she presented a stunning spectacle, garbed in another of Lafarge's creations, a shimmering sheath of pale gold silk trimmed at neckline and hem with delicate lace edged with tiny pearls. Despite his intentions, his eyes were drawn to where her mother's pearls lay about her throat, their priceless sheen matched by her ivory skin.

She glanced up, cool distance in her gaze. "It's dreadfully crowded. I hope Henrietta will manage."

Philip's gaze flicked forward to where Henrietta doggedly stumped upwards, leaning heavily on Geoffrey's arm. "I think you'll discover she's made of stern stuff. She won't wilt in this climate.''

Antonia hoped he was right. The crowd was dense, the press of bodies up the stairs disconcerting. It was her first experience of this degree of enthusiasm. ''Is this what they term a 'crush'?'' Glancing up, she surprised an arrogant, almost aggressive look on Philip's face. It disappeared as he looked down at her.

''Indeed.'' Philip shackled the urge to draw her closer. ''The epitome of every hostess's ambitions. That said, I suspect Lady Caldecott has overstepped her mark. Her ballroom, I hesitate to inform you, is not this,'' he gestured at the crowd surging about them, ''large.''

The accuracy of his prediction was confirmed when, fifteen cramped minutes later, they passed down the receiving line and gained the ballroom.

Henrietta, too short to see beyond the shoulders surrounding them, jabbed Geoffrey in the arm. ''There should be a group of three or four *chaises* somewhere about. Where?''

Geoffrey lifted his head.

''To the left,'' Philip said.

''Good! That's where my set will gather. You,'' Henrietta poked Geoffrey again, ''can escort me there and then you may take yourself off. As for you two—'' she cast a glance at Philip and Antonia ''—you'll have to take care of yourselves.'' Henrietta smiled, decidedly smug. ''In this crush, we'll never find each other—you can fetch me when it's time to leave.''

Philip's brows rose but he made no demur. He bowed gracefully. ''As you wish, ma'am.''

Antonia bobbed a curtsy. Henrietta shuffled into the crowd and was immediately lost to sight. As Philip resettled her hand on his sleeve, Antonia looked about, taking stock of her first Grand Ball. Silks and satins, ribbons and lace, paraded before her. A hundred voices were raised in avid chatter; perfumes drifted and mingled into a heady haze, wafting as bejeweled ladies nodded and curtsied. Elegant gentlemen in superbly cut evening coats inclined their heads; comforted by the hardness of Philip's arm beneath her hand, Antonia smiled coolly back.

"Before we go any further," Philip said, interrupting her reconnaissance, "I would be greatly obliged if you would write my name in your card against the first waltz." A number of gentlemen were headed their way.

Antonia looked up at him. "The first waltz?"

Philip nodded. "Your first waltz." There had been only cotillions, quadrilles and country dances over the past two nights; he was determined her first waltz in the capital would be his.

Reading as much in his eyes, Antonia resigned herself to the inevitable. Lips compressed, she opened the small card Lady Caldecott had handed her. The first waltz was the third dance; under Philip's watchful eye, she duly inscribed his name in the space beside it—then showed him the card.

He actually read it before nodding. Antonia set her teeth. She would have caught his eye and glared—she was distracted by Hugo Satterly who appeared through the ranks before them.

"A great pleasure to welcome you to town, Miss Mannering." Hugo bowed with ready grace, his pleasant smile creasing his face.

He was but the first to express that sentiment. To Antonia's surprise, they were rapidly surrounded by a select group of elegant gentlemen, none of whom bore any relation to her relatively innocuous, easy-to-manage cavaliers of the past weeks. These gentlemen were all contemporaries of Philip's, many his friends, smoothly claiming his offices in making the introductions. At first, she wondered if it was he rather than she with whom they had stopped to chat. They were, however, assiduous in claiming the blank spaces in her dance card; long before the first cotillion, her card was gratifyingly full.

Surrounded by broad shoulders, she waited for the musicians to start up, not entirely sure if she was relieved or otherwise when her circle of gentlemen plainly set themselves to entertain her. Philip, however, large and relatively silent by her side, gave her no hint he saw anything remarkable in their attentions; lifting her chin, Antonia smiled graciously on her would-be cavaliers.

A lull in the conversation brought Hugo Satterley's voice to her ears; he was standing beyond Philip—a quick glance confirmed it was to Philip he spoke.

"Meant to thank you for coming out that night—dashed awkward, but it saved my hide."

Philip's eyes narrowed. "If I'd known it was simply a matter of making a fourth at whist I wouldn't have set foot beyond my door. From your note, I'd imagined some life-threatening situation."

Hugo opened his eyes wide. "If you think engaging oneself to entertain the Bishop of Worcester and then finding oneself one short for the table isn't life-threatening, you know nothing of the Bishop. Can't tell you how grateful I was to be saved from excommunication."

Philip's snort was drowned by the summoning of the violins.

"Ah!" Eyes brightening, Hugo turned to Antonia. "My dance, I believe, Miss Mannering?"

Antonia smiled and gave him her hand. Hugo deftly cleared a path onto the dance floor; while they waited for the rest of the company to find places in the sets, Antonia turned to him. "I overheard your comment on the Bishop of Worcester. Was it recently you entertained His Grace?"

"Just the other night." Hugo grimaced. "Deuced awkward, but I had to do it—he's m'godfather, you know. He'd received a summons from his sister, Lady Griswald, to some musical affair. Old man's tone deaf—virtually ordered me to rescue him."

Antonia's eyes widened. "I see." She managed a weak

smile. She'd returned from Lady Griswald's to find Philip absent; that night had been the first on which she'd declined her nightcap.

"At last!" Hugo held out his hand as the music for the cotillion began.

Antonia had danced countless cotillions in recent weeks; habit, she was certain, was all that kept her twirling in the right direction. A horrible suspicion had taken root in her mind; as it grew, a sinking sensation swelled inside her. She was relieved when, at the cotillion's end, Hugo returned her to Philip's side. Unfortunately, a gavotte with Lord Dewhurst followed virtually immediately. Raising her from her final curtsy, his lordship guided her around the room. After passing some time in idle, on her part disjointed, conversation, they finally came up with Philip; her heart sank when she saw the steely look in his eyes.

Reclaiming Antonia's hand, Philip settled it on his sleeve then caught Lord Dewhurst's eye. "I believe, Dewhurst, that our hostess is searching for you."

"Heh?" Jerked from contemplation of Antonia's smile, Lord Dewhurst focused on Philip's face. His expression turned to one of dismay. "Don't say that. Dash it all—this is what comes of letting on I'm on the look-out for a wife." Openly chagrined, he confided to Antonia, "If her ladyship's after me, it'll mean she's got some protégée that she wants me to look over. I'll have to take refuge in the card-room."

His features impassive, Philip scanned the crowds. "If her ladyship's on the prowl, I wouldn't waste any time."

Lord Dewhurst sighed and bowed over Antonia's hand. "Dashed shame. But no doubt we'll meet at the next ball, Miss Mannering." With a hopeful smile, he straightened. "I'll look forward to furthering our acquaintance."

Antonia smiled with what grace she could muster; his lordship turned away, his eyes on her to the last. Lord Marbury stepped in, keen to engage her attention.

Philip gritted his teeth.

Tonight, strolling the rooms, his favoured method for disposing of unwanted encumbrances, was out of the question; Lady Caldecott had outdone herself with a vengeance. There was barely room to stand; the dance floor would be impossibly crowded.

Not that the idea of waltzing with Antonia at excusably close quarters was bothering him. Quite the opposite. But the crowding left him with few options to thin out her court.

He was contemplating a few novel possibilities when the musicians returned and set bow to string. Sternly suppressing a surge of anticipation, he turned to Antonia. "The first waltz. My dance, I believe, my dear."

"Indeed, my lord." Straightening her spine, Antonia inwardly cursed the fluster that threatened. Her smile overbright, she gave Philip her hand. "I rely on you to lead me through this maze."

With the merest inclination of his head, he led her to where couples were jostling for space on the floor. Tense as she was, the overcrowding claimed all of Antonia's attention; it was only when they were precessing freely, albeit in distinctly circumscribed circles, that she relaxed enough to think. Only to have her senses rush in; a most peculiar panic gripped her.

Philip was holding her very close, a fact necessitated by the proximity of the surrounding couples. As realization sank in, Antonia felt her breath catch, felt the familiar vice close about her chest. Held against him, the shift and sway of their bodies as they revolved through the dance was a dizzying distraction, a potent inducement to set her wits free and let her senses slide into a world of sensation. Her gaze wide, unseeing, she stiffened, struggling to shackle her wits, to keep her face, her posture, free of any hint of the drugging effect of the dance, of her awareness of Philip.

She felt him glance down at her. She looked up, only to

discover his lips mere inches away; her gaze, beyond her control, focused on them. They twisted wryly.

"Relax. You're stiff as a poker."

The comment, spoken in a tone that was clearly private, only made her stiffen further. Forcing her gaze upwards, she met his gaze. She watched a frown gather in his eyes. "I—"

She had no idea how to explain, how to describe the panic mushrooming within her. This was the first waltz of the Little Season, her first public waltz with him—and any second she was going to stumble.

Instinctively, Philip gathered her closer, his hand at her waist reassuringly caressing her spine as he guided her into a turn.

Like a brand, the heat of his hand seared Antonia, exciting skin not accustomed to his touch. At the same moment, his thigh parted hers in the turn, hard muscle impressing itself against her softer flesh.

Her breath caught on a stifled gasp; her feet missed a step.

Philip caught her to him, preventing her stumble. Frowning, very aware of her distress, he deftly stepped clear of the circle of dancers rounding the end of the room. Smoothly releasing Antonia, he took her hand and ushered her before him towards the doors standing open to the terrace, his shoulders effectively screening her from any interested stares. Pale, she cast a wide-eyed glance up at him; he met it with a superficial smile. "This crowd is impossible—a little fresh air will clear your head."

Antonia hoped it would. She felt dreadful; her head had started to throb. She felt immeasurably grateful when Philip propelled her irresistibly out of the door.

The cool night air hit her like a slap; she stopped dead. "Wait! We can't—"

"There's nothing the least improper in our being out here." Philip's accents, warningly clipped, came from directly behind her. "We are, after all, hardly private."

Glancing about, Antonia discovered he was right. The terrace was a wide, stone-flagged extension of the ballroom floor; other couples, like them, had sought refuge on its uncluttered expanse. There were sufficient others present, strolling and chatting in groups, to nullify any question of impropriety. None, however, were close enough to overhear their conversation.

"Now." Capturing Antonia's attention by the simple expedient of putting one finger under her chin and turning her face to him, Philip raised a commanding brow. "What's wrong?"

Antonia met his gaze, then lifted her chin free of his finger. Her stomach had knotted tight. "I...simply had trouble with the waltz."

Philip couldn't help himself. "Strange. I was under the impression you considered yourself something of an expert—certainly in no need of further lessons." The morning after Lady Griswald's musical soirée, she had failed to appear in the ballroom. Geoffrey, too, had not shown; when questioned in suitably nonchalant vein, Geoffrey had let fall that his sister had somewhat waspishly informed him that she had learned quite enough.

Antonia risked a glance from beneath her lashes, then, tilting her chin, fixed her gaze on the gardens. "I did not feel it right to take so much of your time. You've been very generous—I did not wish you to feel duty-bound."

Philip managed not to growl. "I never saw teaching you to waltz as a duty." A pleasant distraction, yes—one he had missed. "And it's quite obvious you need further lessons." The startled glance she threw him was some small consolation. "We'll start again tomorrow. But aside from all that, I'm a great deal more than seven, you know."

Startled by the change in his tone, Antonia glanced up; Philip trapped her gaze. "I've taught you well enough and you learn like a sponge—it wasn't the steps of the waltz that brought you undone.'' His gaze sharpened. ''What was it? Has anyone done anything to upset you?''

His second question and the tension behind it convinced Antonia prevarication would not be wise. She hesitated, then drew in a strengthening breath and, her gaze unfocused, admitted, ''I find I have great difficulty keeping a proper distance.''

Philip frowned. ''The distance between us was perfectly proper. I'm far too old a hand to step over the line during the first waltz of the season.''

Antonia threw him an exasperated look. ''*That*'s not what I meant.''

Philip looked down at her. ''Then what *did* you mean?''

Antonia glared. ''You know perfectly well what I mean. And it's not at all helpful to tease me about it.'' Her voice caught; swinging around, she quickly crossed to the balustrade.

Eyes narrowing, Philip watched her, then followed at a more leisurely pace. When he stopped beside her, she was staring into the darkness, her hands clasped tightly before her. ''I vaguely recall having this conversation before. While I'm naturally flattered that you persist in thinking me omniscient, I must confess that what you apparently find obvious is very frequently far from obvious to me.''

She hesitated, then slowly turned to face him.

Antonia met his gaze with one of her very direct looks. What she saw in his eyes reassured her. ''I—'' She broke off, frowning, then, lifting her head, swung to face the gardens. ''I find the…sensations of waltzing with you so distracting that I. . . In short, I cannot be sure I will not commit some indiscretion.''

Tilting his head, Philip studied her face. ''While waltzing?''

Her gaze on the shadows, Antonia nodded.

A slow smile broke across Philip's face. Then he recalled that he did not always read her aright. ''I take it,'' he said, carefully composing his features, "that you would not feel…compelled to indiscretion while waltzing with anyone else?"

Antonia frowned at him. "Of course not." She studied his face. "I had thought I could cope but…" She gestured vaguely.

Philip caught her hand; he waited until she met his eyes before raising it to his lips. He paused, studying her wide eyes, aware of the slim fingers resting in his, aware of the demon too close to his surface. "Geoffrey said you had told him he could trust my advice unreservedly." He raised a brow. "Will you, too, place your trust in me?"

Uncertainty darkened her eyes; Philip allowed his impatience to show. "I have, as I believe you know, been waltzing through the *ton*'s ballrooms for rather many years."

"I know." Antonia felt breathless. They were, she was perfectly certain, no longer talking about mere waltzing. "But…"

Philip held her gaze; again he lifted her hand, gently brushing his lips across her fingertips, well aware of the reaction she struggled to hide. "Believe me." His voice deepened. "I won't let you falter." He waited, watching her, willing her, then lifted one brow. "Trust me?"

The moment that followed stretched, fragile as spun glass, timeless as eternity. Antonia felt each beat of her heart, felt the shallowness of each breath. "You know I do."

"Then close your eyes. It's time for your next lesson."

Antonia hesitated, then complied.

"Imagine we're in the ballroom at Ruthven House."

She felt Philip's arm slide about her, felt his hold on her fingers shift.

"Geoffrey is supplying the music."

She frowned. "I can hear violins."

"He's brought some friends to help him."

The clipped accents made her lips twitch. Philip raised her hand; his arm tightened about her.

Antonia baulked. "Philip—!"

"Trust me."

A second later she was waltzing.

"Keep your eyes closed. Remember, we're in Ruthven House—there's no one else about."

Antonia knew very well where they were; the cool night air shifted over her bare shoulders, a light breeze played with her skirts. But Philip's arm held her steady; with her eyes closed, she had no alternative but to relax and follow his strong lead. She heard muted chatter and laughter, the musicians were still scraping away. He held her close; as they whirled and twirled, the sensations that had earlier assailed her rose up, heightened by her earlier sensitivity. Detached, distanced from worry, she could not find it in her to fight them; instead, her senses stretched, luxuriating in the moment.

Watching her face, Philip saw her lips lift; his own curved knowingly. He drank in the sight of her face, then said, "Open your eyes."

Antonia did, blinking as her eyes adjusted. She took in Philip's arrogantly satisfied expression, then glanced past his shoulder—and gasped.

They were no longer the only ones waltzing on the terrace. As they revolved, she turned her head this way and that, amazed at the collection of fashionable couples now whirling in the starlight.

"It appears we've started a new trend."

"Indeed."

Seconds later, the music slowed. Philip whirled them to a flourishing halt, touching Antonia's hand to his lips. "Believe me—there's nothing in your behaviour to give you cause to blush."

Antonia met his gaze; a frown slowly gathered in her eyes. "While I concede that your experience might be extensive, I'm not at all certain you're an appropriate judge of such matters."

Philip narrowed his eyes. "Antonia, which of us has been buried in the wilds to the north for the last eight years?"

Antonia's eyes flashed. "And which of us, my lord, has any previous experience of our current relationship?"

Philip held her gaze steadily. "Rest assured, my dear, that should you commit any indiscretion, however minor, I will be the first to bring it to your notice."

Antonia raised a haughty brow. "Unfortunately, it's your definition of 'indiscretion' that I question."

"Indeed? Then you'll undoubtedly be relieved to know that to be a fully-fledged member of the fraternity to which I belong, an exquisitely detailed understanding of indiscretions, in all their varied forms, is mandatory." Philip placed her hand on his sleeve, then calmly raised his brows at her.

Stumped, Antonia cast him a distinctly mulish glance.

With a pointed smile, Philip turned her towards the ballroom. "You may trust me to guide you through the shoals of the *ton*, Antonia."

She glanced at his face, her gaze familiar and open. As they neared the ballroom, she regally inclined her head. "Very well. I will place my reliance on you, my lord."

His satisfaction hidden behind his usual impassive mask, Philip steered her into the throng.

At eleven o'clock the next morning, Philip descended the stairs, very definitely in charity with the world. It was an effort to keep from whistling; he had to keep his mind from dwelling on their interlude in the library the night before in order to keep a smug smile from his face.

Carring appeared from the nether regions; Philip had often wondered if his major-domo possessed some peculiar facility which alerted him to his impending appearance in the hall.

"I'm lunching at Limmer's, then I expect we'll go on to Brooks."

"And then to the Park?"

Philip shot Carring a severe glance. "Possibly." He paused to check his cravat in the hall mirror; a fragment of the past night's activities, when Antonia's fingers had become entangled in the starched folds about his throat, drifted through his mind. "Incidentally, where did the *chaise* that matches the chairs in the library go?"

"If you recall, my lord, we removed it to the back parlour after you declared that it cluttered up the library to no good purpose."

"Ah, yes." Satisfied with the drape of the linen folds about his neck, Philip resettled his collar. "You may move it back to the library."

"You require more comfortable seating, my lord?"

Philip glanced up and located Carring's face in the mirror. Unless he was grossly mistaken, his major-domo was struggling to hide a grin. Philip narrowed his eyes. "Just move the damned *chaise*, Carring."

"Immediately, my lord."

Philip did not glance back as he went out of his door, positive that if he did, he would see Carring grinning knowingly.

Just to prove Carring wrong, he returned to Ruthven House later in the afternoon—but only to pick up his phaeton.

Antonia was strolling in the Park with Geoffrey, Catriona and Ambrose, when they heard Geoffrey hailed from the carriageway. Turning, she saw Philip waving from the box-seat of the most elegant high-perch phaeton she had yet set eyes upon. Both Geoffrey and Ambrose needed no urging to cross the lawns to the carriageway.

"I say! What a bang-up set of blood and bone!" Ambrose eyed Philip's greys with fervid admiration.

Geoffrey turned big eyes on his mentor. "I don't suppose there's any chance you'll let me take this rig out, even without the greys?"

Philip, who had been gazing at Antonia, a picture in soft sprigged muslin, her face shaded by the brim of the bonnet he had bought her, shifted his gaze briefly to Geoffrey's face. "None."

Geoffrey grimaced. "That's what I thought."

"Did you want Geoffrey for some reason?" Antonia had spared only a passing glance for Philip's carriage; his horses she knew well.

"Actually," Philip said, his gaze once more on her face, "It was you I came to see. I wondered if you'd care for a turn about the Park?"

Antonia's heart leapt; the subtle challenge in his eyes gave her pause. High-perches were notoriously unstable, safe only in the hands of experienced drivers. She had no concern on that score but gaining the seat, a full six feet above the carriageway, was a different matter.

"What a positively *thrilling* invitation." Standing beside Antonia, Catriona looked glowingly up at Philip, her gaze innocent yet knowing. "You'll be the envy of every lady present."

Antonia looked up at Philip. "I would gladly go with you, my lord. Yet I greatly fear…" She gestured at the high step.

"A problem very easily solved." Philip tied off the reins. "Geoffrey—hold their heads."

Geoffrey hurried to the greys' heads; Ambrose followed. Before Antonia fully grasped his intent, Philip jumped down, drew her forward, then lifted her high.

Antonia bit back a squeal—and frantically clung to the side of the high seat. His expression mild, his eyes laughing, Philip followed her up; Antonia quickly but carefully shuffled along the precariously tilting seat. To her relief, Philip's weight once he sat seemed to stabilise the flimsy contraption.

"Relax." He flicked her a glance as he took up the reins. "I seem to be advising you to do that rather often these days.'' He sent her another teasing glance. ''I wonder why?''

''Because,'' Antonia tersely replied, ''you are forever giving me cause to panic.''

Philip laughed as he set the greys in motion. ''Never fear—I give you my word I won't upend you in the middle of the Park. Aside from any other consideration, just think of the damage it would do to my reputation.''

''I'm fast coming to think,'' Antonia returned, holding fast to the railings edging the seat, ''that this reputation of yours is all a hum, invented by you as a convenient excuse.''

That riposte earned her a distinctly unnerving look.

Before he could think of a comment to go with it, she asked, ''Are you sure I'm not breaking any rules in being driven in such a dangerous equipage?''

''Quite sure,'' Philip replied, his tones distinctly dry. ''If anyone is breaking any rules here, 'tis I.''

Antonia widened her eyes at him. ''You?''

''Indeed. And seeing I have bent my heretofore inviolable rules and taken you up in the Park, I think it's only fair that *you* should entertain *me,* thus leaving me free to devote all my skills to keeping us upright.''

Hiding a smile, Antonia put her nose in the air. ''I'm not at all sure it's proper for me to run on, like some ill-bred gabblemonger.''

''Heaven forbid!'' Philip dispensed with his town drawl entirely. ''Just put my mind at rest and tell me what you four were planning.''

Giving up the fight to contain her delight, Antonia smiled dazzlingly, startling a youthful gentleman driving in the opposite direction.

''Cow-handed clunch!'' Philip deftly avoided the ensuing mêlée. ''Now cut line. Remember, I've made myself responsible for your brother.''

''Very well.'' Settling more comfortably beside him, shielded from the light wind by his shoulder, Antonia related the latest developments. ''Mr Fortescue has not yet shown his face, but as I gather he must come up from Somerset, I don't believe we can hold that against him.''

Philip shook his head. ''He may be a true knight but he obviously lacks a ghostly steed. Or should that be an errant charger?''

''Mr Fortescue, I gather, is a model of decorum.''

''Good lord!'' Philip shot her a disbelieving glance. ''And Miss Dalling wishes to marry him?''

''Most definitely.'' Antonia paused, then diffidently added, ''Actually, while I originally thought some of Miss Dalling's tales might owe more to her imagination than to fact, the latest involve Ambrose as well and he is undeniably not given to flights of fancy.''

''By which you mean he's a slow-top.'' Philip glanced down at her. ''But what are these latest exploits?''

''Not so much exploits as experiences. It seems the Countess of Ticehurst and the Marchioness have taken to engineering interludes when Catriona and Ambrose are left alone.''

Philip raised his brows. ''I see.''

''Catriona and Ambrose are both trying quite desperately to ensure there's nothing improper that can be used to force their consent, but the situation is daily becoming more difficult.''

Philip was silent for some minutes, then said, ''It's hard to see what they can do, short of Mr Fortescue coming to the rescue. Even then, given Miss Dalling is under age, the situation's likely to be messy.''

''Indeed. I raised that very point, but Catriona's convinced all will be well once Mr Fortescue arrives.''

Philip raised his brows. ''Which event, I suppose, we should all devoutly pray for.'' He cast a glance at Antonia's pensive face. ''Having dispensed with that subject, perhaps we can move to some more interesting topic?''

Antonia opened her eyes wide. "That depends on what you consider *interesting,* my lord."

For one pregnant instant, Philip held her gaze; when she coloured, he smiled and looked ahead. "How about your observations on town life and the Little Season? I dare say I would find those quite fascinating."

"Indeed?" Antonia stifled the urge to fan her face. "Very well." On her mettle, she cast about for inspiration. She found it in a pair of strutting Macaronis, so gaily garbed they resembled walking pansies. "The strongest impression I have of the *ton* is of things being other than they seem. There is, to my mind, a great deal of obfuscation and round-aboutation—a great deal of hiding the truth."

The brief look Philip cast her held a gratifying degree of surprise. Then a curve forced him to give his attention to his greys. Antonia saw his lips firm, then twist in a wry, self-deprecatory smile.

"Remind me, my dear, not to ask such a question of you again."

"Why not?" Tilting her head, she studied his face. "I didn't find it impertinent."

"No—but I'd forgotten your intelligence. Your answers go too deep." Philip shot her a quick glance. "The trick with flirtatious repartee is to keep the tone light."

Antonia blinked. "Flirtatious repartee?"

"Indeed. What else? Now concentrate. Are you intending to grace Lady Gisborne's ballroom tonight?"

"What-ho, Miss Mannering! Dare I claim this cotillion?"

Antonia turned and, laughing, gave her hand to Hugo Satterly. "Indeed, sir. I had begun to wonder if you had forgotten me."

"Never." Straightening from his bow, Hugo placed a hand over his heart. "After all the trouble I went to to get my name in your card? Fie, my dear—I'm not such a slow-top."

"You are, however, a rattlepate," Philip put in from beside Antonia. "If you don't make a move soon, you'll miss out on the sets."

"Don't mind him." Hugo tucked Antonia's hand into his arm and turned her towards the floor. "He's just jealous."

Antonia responded with an ingenuous look and a confident smile. She felt entirely at ease with Hugo; he was the perfect companion, always charming, never one to take offence or become difficult over some imagined slight. Like all Philip's set, he was an excellent dancer and could be counted on to fill her ears with the latest *on dits*.

As they took their places in the nearest set forming on the floor of Lady Gisborne's ballroom, Hugo winked at her. "Hope you don't mind me trying for a rise out of Ruthven? All innocent fun, y'know."

Antonia smiled and sank into the first curtsy. "I don't mind at all." Rising, she gave Hugo her hand. "I dare say being twitted is good for him."

Hugo grinned back as the dance parted them.

As she dipped and swayed through the measure, Antonia considered his words. He was one of Philip's closest friends; thus far, he was the only one she had encountered who accurately understood Philip's interest in her. Certainly no one would guess it from Philip's behaviour; while he was always by her side, he made no effort to monopolise her company, either in the ballrooms or the supper rooms where, admittedly under his watchful eye, her entire court would adjourn to refresh themselves.

His behaviour, overtly aloof with but the subtlest undercurrent of possessiveness, was, she decided, intended to be instructive. Presumably, this was how she was to comport herself after they were wed. He would be about, but she was not to rely on him for her entertainment nor her male company. Her court, comprised of gentlemen of whom he approved, would provide that.

Discovering her gaze scanning the surrounding crowd,

searching for Philip's chestnut locks, Antonia sternly refocused on Hugo, currently on the opposite side of the set. If overtly aloof was the correct image to project, then it was past time she started practising.

"What the devil's the matter? Is my cravat askew or what?"

Philip's words, delivered in a growled mutter, succeeded in hauling Antonia's gaze to his face.

Wide-eyed, she blinked up at him, oblivious of the other dancers about them. "What on earth do you mean? Your cravat's perfect—as it always is. The Oriental, isn't it?"

"The Mathematical—and don't try to change the subject."

Astounded, she stared at him. "I wasn't!" She blinked, then added, "I don't even know what the subject is."

Exceedingly irritated, even more so because his rational mind could find no reasonable cause, Philip whirled her into a complex series of turns, supposedly to negotiate the end of Lady Gisborne's ballroom, in reality purely as an excuse to hold her tighter. "The subject is," he said through clenched teeth, "why it is you suddenly seem to find me invisible. You've hardly glanced my way all night. I'm beginning to feel like a ghost."

Antonia felt dizzy and wondered if it was the waltz. He was certainly whirling her around with rather more concerted force than was his custom. "I thought that was what you wanted me to do—that I shouldn't…" To her annoyance, she felt a blush steal into her cheeks.

Philip studied the evidence of her confusion and felt his own grow. "That you shouldn't look at me?"

Antonia flicked him an exasperated glance, then fixed her gaze over his right shoulder. "That I should not display any overt awareness of your presence. As I understand it, such behaviour is construed as wearing one's heart on one's sleeve. I would not wish to embarrass you." She paused, then added, "Your own behaviour is very correct—I naturally took my lead from you."

Philip frowned down at her. "Yes—well." He hesitated, not quite certain which way to step. Then his lips firmed. "Might I suggest that there's a viable path between, on the one hand, clinging to my arm and making sheep's eyes at me, and, on the other, behaving as if I was literally not there?"

Antonia's gaze slid sideways, meeting his. "You know perfectly well I always know you're there."

Looking down into her eyes, Philip felt the dark cloud that had enshrouded him all evening melt away. He held her gaze, then his lips twisted wryly. "A few of your smiles and a few lingering glances wouldn't go astray."

For an instant longer, Antonia studied his eyes—then she smiled up at him. "If you wish it, my lord."

Philip tightened his hold as they went into the turn. "I do."

Two days later, Philip, strolling the broad verges in the Park, happened upon the Ruthven barouche. Languidly coming abreast of it, he discovered Henrietta deep in discussion with two other ladies, *grande dames* both.

"Ah, Ruthven! *Just* the one we need." Catching sight of him, Henrietta beamed him a smile. "I was just saying to the Countess here, that what we need is a reliable gentleman, one who knows the ropes, to keep an eye on our little party."

"Indeed?" Raising his brows, Philip let his tone convey his utter antipathy to the idea that he might be such a specimen.

"But I don't believe you've met the Countess of Ticehurst?" Blithely oblivious, Henrietta indicated the lady beside her. "And, of course, the Dowager Marchioness of Hammersley."

His expression fashionably distant, Philip bowed gracefully, inwardly conceding that both the Countess, with her sharply angular features and frizzed red curls, and the Dowager Marchioness, heavy and portly with three chins to her credit, bade fair to living up to the varied descriptions he had had of them.

"Indeed, Ruthven, nothing could be more fortunate than your appearance here. The Countess and I haven't seen each other for years—we're keen to have a comfortable coze but her ladyship is uneasy over her niece." Raising her head, Henrietta looked out over the lawns. "She's over there somewhere," she said, waving one plump hand in the general direction of the flower walks. "She's walking with Antonia and Geoffrey. And the Marquess, of course." Apparently realizing that this last needed further clarification, Henrietta exchanged quick glances with the other two ladies, then leaned to the side of the carriage. Lowering her voice, she fixed Philip with a sapient eye. "There's an understanding between the Marquess and Miss Dalling, the Countess's niece, but there seems to be some slight hitch in the works. Nothing serious but you know how these things go." Assured that all was now crystal clear, Henrietta sat back and waved a dismissal. "Sure you'll want to join them."

Philip hesitated, then bowed. "Indeed, ma'am. Ladies." They let him go with thin smiles and magisterial nods. As he strode across the lawns, Philip found himself sympathizing with Miss Dalling and the Marquess.

He discovered Antonia strolling arm in arm with Catriona. The heiress's eyes were alight, her cheeks glowing; it was almost as if Antonia was physically restraining her but from what action Philip could not tell.

Antonia looked up as he approached; she smiled warmly and held out her hand. "Good afternoon, my lord."

Philip took her hand; unable to deny the compulsion, he raised it to his lips, his eyes quizzing her as he said, his voice too deep for even Catriona to hear, "My lady." Antonia blushed delightfully; Philip switched his gaze to Catriona, who bobbed a curtsy then flashed him one of her dazzling smiles. Philip smiled back. "I fear I should warn you that I've been dispatched as an envoy to keep an eye on you all."

Catriona's eyes widened. "How…? Who…?"

"As I understand it," Philip said, smoothly claiming Antonia's arm, thus separating her from Catriona, "my stepmother and your aunt are long-standing bosom-bows. At the moment, they're in Henrietta's barouche, exchanging their recent histories, with Ambrose's fond mama looking on."

"Indeed?" Catriona was hanging on his words. "And they sent you to watch over us?"

"Precisely."

"Behold—the hand of fate!" Hands clasped to her bosom, Catriona pirouetted dramatically. Halting, she fixed glowing eyes on Philip. "*Nothing* could be more fortunate!"

The declaration set Philip's teeth on edge. "I do hope," he said, "that you'll allow me to be the judge of that. Why the transports?"

Noting the absence of his drawl, Antonia quickly explained, "Mr Fortescue has arrived. He's arranged to join us here, but we were worried the Countess would interfere."

Glancing back over the lawns to the distant carriage, Philip humphed. "Not much chance of that at this point." He looked back at Catriona. "But where's this beau of yours?"

He was not about to assist in any havey-cavey affair.

But Henry Fortescue proved to be a great relief. Philip's hackles settled the instant he laid eyes on him, striding along between Geoffrey and Ambrose. Antonia had hurriedly explained their plan—they had sent Ambrose and Geoffrey to fetch Mr Fortescue so as to make it appear he was one of Ambrose's or Geoffrey's acquaintances. Quite what Mr Fortescue had thought of the arrangement Philip found himself dying to know.

Introduced, he shook hands.

In his early twenties, of middle height and powerful build, Henry Fortescue was readily identifiable as a scion of the noble family of that name; he bashfully acknowledged Philip's supposition. "Distant cousin of m'father's."

Catriona, clinging to his arm, declared, "We must be very careful, Henry, or Aunt Ticehurst will descend like the dragon she is and tear us apart."

Henry glanced down at her and frowned. "Nonsense." He took the sting from the comment by patting her hand. "You always were one to overdramatise, Catriona. What on earth do you imagine your aunt will do? It's not as if I'm some caper-merchant with no fortune and less prospects. Given I had your father's permission to address you, it's not as if there was any reason for her to shove in her oar."

"But she will!" Catriona looked horrified. "Ask Ambrose."

Ambrose dutifully nodded. "Terribly set on us marrying, y'know. That's why we sent for you."

"You can't talk to Aunt Ticehurst." Catriona clung to Henry's arm. "She'll banish you. I know she will."

Henry's jaw firmed. "I've no intention of speaking to your aunt—I'll speak to the Earl, as is proper."

Philip held Antonia back, letting the youthful foursome go ahead. Once they were out of earshot, he murmured, "I can't tell you how relieved I am to make Mr Fortescue's acquaintance."

"He does seem very steady." Antonia studied Catriona and her intended. "And he seems to know how to handle Catriona's flights."

"He's just what she needs—an anchor." Ambling in the youthful foursome's wake, Philip idly scanned the lawns. Abruptly, he halted. "Great heavens!"

Antonia followed his riveted gaze to a couple strolling towards them on an intersecting path. The gentleman she recognized immediately; Frederick Amberly was one of

Philip's friends. He had not, however, spent much time in her circle, usually drifting into the crowd after the customary exchange of greetings. The young lady presently on his arm, a pretty miss in pink spotted muslin, was unknown to Antonia. From the warm appreciation readily apparent in Mr Amberly's expression, she surmised the lady might well be the cause of Mr Amberly's frequent preoccupation.

"Good afternoon, Amberly."

At the sound of Philip's voice, Frederick Amberly started. "What? Oh—it's you, Ruthven." Consternation showed fleetingly in his eyes. "Didn't expect to meet you here."

"So I perceive." Philip smiled charmingly at the young lady, now clinging wide-eyed to Mr Amberly's arm.

"Beg to make you known to my friends, m'dear." Mr Amberly patted her hand reassuringly. "Miss Mannering and Lord Ruthven—Miss Hitchin."

Miss Hitchin smiled sweetly and gave Antonia her hand; Antonia returned her smile encouragingly and pressed her fingers. Philip bowed, then looked at Frederick Amberly. "Just strolling?"

"I thought the flowers looked so very pretty," Miss Hitchin volunteered somewhat breathlessly. "Mr Amberly very kindly offered to escort me to see them at closer range."

"They really are very lovely," Antonia agreed.

"I had heard there was a rhododendron walk further on." Miss Hitchin looked appealingly at Mr Amberly.

"Ah, yes." Mr Amberly smiled down at her. "We'd best get on if we're to see the bushes then get back to your mama's carriage in good time." He nodded to Antonia. "Your servant, Miss Mannering. Ruthven."

Philip watched them hurry away. "Who would have thought it—a miss just out of the schoolroom, barely old enough to put up her hair?" He shook his head. "Poor Amberly."

"Why 'poor'?" Antonia asked as they started to stroll again.

"Because," Philip explained, "being caught strolling in the Park with a young lady on your arm ostensibly viewing the flowers is tantamount to declaring oneself irretrievably smitten."

They strolled on a few steps before Antonia said, her tone carefully neutral, "You're strolling by the flower-beds with me."

"True—but there's nothing surprising in a man's being smitten with you. But a chit just out of the schoolroom?" Again, Philip shook his head. "Poor Amberly."

Chapter Eleven

"Well, my dear? Were you impressed with Hugo's flourishes?" Philip extended his arm as Antonia, cheeks flushed, eyes sparkling, joined him by the side of Lady Darcy-d'Lisle's ballroom.

"Indeed!" Placing her fingertips on his sleeve, Antonia slanted a playful glance at Hugo. "I cannot recall a more *enthusiastic* gavotte in all the past weeks."

Hugo's grin turned to a grimace. "Sssh!" Theatrically, he looked about him. "I declare—you'll give me a bad name. Not a rake in London wants to be known as *enthusiastic.*"

His expression had Antonia laughing aloud.

Philip savoured the silvery sound. In the last week, Antonia's confidence had steadily grown; his pride and satisfaction had kept pace, swelling at moments like this, feeding his impatience. Suavely, his expression discreetly restrained, he covered her hand with his. "Come. The ball is ended." Her eyes met his. "It's time to go home."

To his house, his library—and their regular nightcap.

To his delight, she blushed delicately, then lifted her head to look across the room. "It appears we'll have to pry Aunt Henrietta from Lady Ticehurst's side."

"Indeed." Philip followed her gaze to where his stepmother was talking animatedly to the Countess. "I'm not at all certain I approve of the connection."

As they started across the floor, Antonia threw him a puzzled look. Philip saw it. He waited until Hugo had taken leave of them before saying, "To my experienced eye, Henrietta is showing alarming signs of involving herself in your youthful friend's affair."

His supposition proved correct; as they strolled up, the Countess was in full flight, declaiming on the wisdom of young ladies allowing their elders to be their matrimonial guides. "For mark my words, it's substance that counts, as my dear niece will be forced to admit." She capped this grim pronouncement with a severe nod, directing a basilisk stare around the ballroom as if searching for dissenters.

Henrietta dutifully nodded, although her expression suggested her opinion was somewhat less trenchantly set.

Antonia watched as Philip applied his not-inconsiderable charm to disengaging Henrietta from her ladyship's side. That accomplished, they found Geoffrey waiting by the door. With smiles and nods, they took leave of their hosts, then descended to their carriage.

As he handed Antonia in, Philip heard his name called.

Turning, he saw Sally Jersey tripping down to her carriage, a distinctly arch look on her face. He replied with a repressive nod. Her ladyship had not been alone in shooting speculative glances his way. Climbing into the carriage, Philip inwardly shrugged. In a few weeks, possibly less, they'd be back at the Manor; thereafter, the rabid interest of the *ton* would be a matter of no importance, certainly not something he need consider every time he smiled at Antonia. The prospect grew daily more alluring.

Screened by the dark, he settled back against the carriage seat.

Facing him, Antonia sat similarly shrouded by shadows, her thoughts, like Philip's, very much on themselves. Like him, she felt smugly satisfied. She now knew how to act, how to behave as his wife, whilst under the *ton*'s chande-liers. She had paraded before the hostesses' censorious eyes and had not stumbled. No more need she fear to put a foot wrong, to bring opprobrium down on her head through some gauche and unforgivable act—to shame Philip by her lack of sophisticated knowledge.

Under his tutelage, her knowledge, her understanding, had grown in leaps and bounds.

Her eyes sought his face, then scanned his frame, large and impressively elegant in the shadows opposite. Her attention was caught by the diamond pin in his cravat, shimmering in the weak light.

She was now confident she could be his wife—the wife he wanted, the wife he needed, the wife he deserved. His support had been steadfast, underlaid by past affection. In every word and deed, his attitude was evident, a subtle fondness that never overstepped the bounds of propriety.

At least not in public.

Her gaze fixed on his diamond pin, Antonia shifted. His private behaviour had not fitted within her mental framework of a conventional relationship—not until she had admitted the existence of desire. It was not an emotion she had had previous experience of, yet it was there, staring back at her every time they were alone and she looked into his eyes. She had finally accepted that it was an integral part of how he viewed her—she was no longer a girl, after all, but a woman grown.

The thought sent a long shiver slithering down her spine. Abruptly, she straightened and switched her gaze to the passing streetscape.

Despite her sudden breathlessness, despite her leaping heart, she was not foolish enough to confuse desire with love. Philip's comment in the Park three days before, so easy, so open, so very off-hand, had placed the matter firmly in perspective. Not the most ardent of young ladies—not even Catriona—could have mistaken those few words, his

roundabout admission he was smitten with her, as a declaration. It had been no more than a simple restating of his
fondness for her, an acknowledgement of his clear prefer-
ence for her company.

That, admittedly, had surprised her. From beneath her
lashes, Antonia viewed the still figure opposite. She had
imagined, in light of his freely acknowledged reputation,
that other women, perhaps even ladies, would feature rather
more significantly in his life.

Perhaps he was reforming?

How would it feel to know that she had been responsible
for such a transformation?

A yearning rose within her, deep and strong. Swallowing
a contemptuous "humph", she straightened her shoulders
and ruthlessly quashed it. *That* was no part of the bargain
between them; *that* was no part of a conventional marriage.
That was none of her business.

A part of her mind jeered—Antonia ignored it. She was,
she sternly reminded herself, aiming to be a very comfortable wife, one who did not create ructions over matters beyond her jurisdiction.

With that objective firmly in view, she swept into the hall
of Ruthven House. Henrietta and Geoffrey were already on
the stairs, deep in conversation. With a smile for Carring,
Antonia glided into the library.

As she settled in her usual chair, her gaze fell on the
chaise, set directly opposite the hearth. It had appeared
nearly a week before; every night since, Philip had inveigled
her onto it—and thence, into his arms. Sternly repressing
her memories, she reminded herself there was nothing remarkable in a betrothed couple sharing kisses.

Grey eyes dark with desire swam through her mind. A
shiver threatened.

Philip had paused at the door; she heard him speak to
Carring, then shut the door. He strolled forward, his gaze
meeting hers.

''You seem quite at home in the *ton* these days. I always did think you learned quickly.'' Gracefully crouching, he built up the fire. The flames transformed his chestnut hair to bronze, each lock burnished bright.

Smiling serenely, Antonia leaned back. ''Ah, but I've had an excellent teacher, have I not? I doubt I would have found it half so easy had I had to brave the dragons alone.''

Philip straightened, one brow rising. ''Flattery, my dear?''

A knock on the door heralded Carring, bearing her glass of milk. Antonia took it with a smile. Carring fetched Philip his brandy then withdrew, leaving them both sipping.

With his usual grace, Philip sank into the chair across the hearth. Silence settled; Antonia relaxed, feeling the warmth of the milk drive the chill from her shoulders. Her lips curved; as peace slowly enfolded her, she lowered her lids.

Cradling his glass in his hands, Philip studied her, his gaze skimming her shoulders, bare above the abbreviated bodice of her evening dress, a confection in pale green silk that had caused any number of ladies to turn greener still. She had not worn her pearls, leaving her throat and the expanse of creamy skin exposed above the low neckline tantalizingly bare. Unadorned, it had drawn more eyes than Lady Darcy-d'Lisle's diamonds. There was an untouched innocence in the gentle swell of her breasts that had halted any number of male conversations.

His eyes on the delicate curves, Philip shifted restlessly.

Antonia blinked. ''What's the matter?''

Philip slowly raised a brow. ''I was at the point, as it happens, of concluding that women endowed as you are should be forbidden to appear in public without the distraction of jewellery.''

As his gaze dropped from hers on the words, Antonia had no difficulty divining his meaning. The warmth that touched her skin owed nothing to the fire. ''Indeed?'' Determined not to fluster, she sipped her milk.

"Definitely." Abruptly, Philip set aside his glass. Standing, he crossed to his desk; a moment later, he returned, a flat velvet box in his hand.

Placing her glass on a sidetable, Antonia raised wide eyes from the box to his face. "What—?"

"Come—stand before the mirror." Philip caught her hand and drew her to her feet.

Excitement gripping her, Antonia did as he asked.

"No peeking," he said when she tried to glance over her shoulder.

The next instant, he dropped the box on the *chaise* and held his hands high over her head, a strand of sparkling stones strung between them.

Antonia looked up and caught her breath. "The emeralds from Aspreys!" Her words came in a whisper. "I wondered who had bought them."

"'Twas I." Philip lowered the necklace, setting it about her throat. He bent his head to fasten the catch at her nape. "They were obviously made for you—it was only right that you have them."

Her eyes on their reflection, Antonia raised fluttering fingers to the gems. "I. . .I don't know what to say." She sought Philip's gaze in the mirror; her dazed smile faded. "Philip—I can't wear them. Not yet."

"I know." Grimacing, he placed his hands on her shoulders, squeezing gently. "Keep them until we get back to the Manor. You can wear them at our betrothal ball—my gift to you on the occasion."

For a moment longer, Antonia held his gaze, then she turned. "Thank you." Reaching up, she twined her arms about his neck and, stretching up on tiptoe, set her lips to his.

For a fractional instant, Philip hesitated, then his hands slid around her silk encased form, smoothly gathering her into his arms. For a single minute, he savoured the freshness of her untutored caress, then desire welled; he parted her lips, confident of his welcome, eager for the taste of her sweetness. She responded as she always did, with simple, unrestrained passion, warm and enticing.

Antonia gave herself up to his kiss, swept up, as she always was, by the warm tide he so effortlessly called forth. When Philip gathered her closer, his head slanting over hers, she tightened her arms about his neck. Her senses drifted; beyond coherent thought, she yielded to the compulsion to press against him.

His hands shifted to her back, tracing the long lines, then dropped to her hips, firming gently, encouragingly. Unable to deny the urging of her senses, she responded, letting her softness sink against his hardness, thrilled, seduced by the unfamiliar excitement that welled within her. The kiss went on; the novel sensation swelled and grew until it filled her entirely.

An indescribable longing swept her.

Philip's hand at her breast felt just right; his gentle fondling eased the odd throbbing ache that had developed there. Then his fingers stroked and her knees went weak; Antonia clung to his shoulders, relieved when his arm tightened about her waist.

Then he was lowering her to the *chaise,* easing her down to the brocaded cushions without breaking their kiss. Unwilling to leave her realm of delight, Antonia clung to the caress, one arm about his neck. Her other hand fluttered along his jaw in pleading supplication.

Philip felt her tentative touch; accurately interpreting it, he devoted one part of his mind to appeasing her innocent hunger with gentle, lingering kisses while his fingers dealt with the tiny buttons of her bodice. As the closures yielded one by one, he tightened his hold on his passions, ruthlessly harnessing them. Step by step, point by slow point, he had been leading her down the road to seduction by the longest route he could devise. He knew precisely how far he would lead her tonight; that far and no further.

It was a point he made very clear to his surging, restless passions before the last button gave and he slid one hand beneath the fine seagreen silk.

Her breast swelled to his touch; her skin, soft as satin, smoother than the silk he brushed aside, burned him. As he gently closed his fingers about one firm mound, he felt her breath catch, felt tension grow then dissolve into desire. Her lips clung to his, urgent, entreating. She shifted beneath him, flagrantly wanton, deliciously divine.

Philip drank from her lips, fulfilling her needs even as his own raged. It was he who eventually drew back, raising his head to catch his breath.

Her skin flushed and aglow, Antonia lay relaxed against the cushions, her lids too heavy to lift, her lips throbbing and tender yet still hungry for his. She floated on a sea of dreams, cocooned by passion, her desire-drenched mind suborned by sensation.

Blissfully content, she sighed.

Philip's hand shifted; long fingers stroked her breast.

Antonia's eyes flew wide. *"Oh!"* Jerked back to reality, her stunned mind registered her position, reclining on the chaise with Philip beside her, one hand cupping her breast. "I..." She faltered to a stop, her dazed wits struggling to recall just what had transpired. What had she said? Done? "Oh, *heavens!*" Sunk in embarrassment, Antonia closed her eyes. Mortification swept her. "I'm so *sorry,* Philip."

Bemused, Philip nuzzled her ear. "Why sorry?" Bending his head, he touched his lips to the pulse beating wildly in her throat. "If anyone should be making apologies, it is I." He looked down to where her breast filled his hand. "But I've no intention of doing so. I wouldn't hold your breath in expectation of the event."

Antonia promptly drew in a deep breath; lips lifting, Philip bent his head.

"Philip!" Antonia's eyes flew open again; this time she was even more shocked. Her indrawn breath was trapped in

her chest; her fingers tangled in Philip's hair as he continued his shocking caress. She was suddenly very glad of the *chaise;* if they'd been standing, she was quite sure she would have swooned. As his lips, his tongue, continued their play, her wits whirled. *"Good God."*

Hearing the weakness in her voice, Philip drew back, softly chuckling. "There's no need to be so shocked." He considered the evidence of her agitation, the rapid rise and fall of her bare breasts, with a certain masculine satisfaction. Looking up, he met her befuddled gaze. "We are, after all, going to be married shortly. Thereafter, we'll be doing precisely this rather often."

Antonia's lips formed a silent "O".

Philip felt the tremor that rippled through her. Puzzled, he looked into her eyes, only to discover the most peculiar expression—surely it couldn't be anguish?—darkening the hazel depths. He frowned. "What is it?"

She didn't reply. Instead, her eyes glazed as, of their own volition, his fingers caressed the rosy nipple that had been the focus of his attentions thus far. He forced his fingers to stillness but could not bring himself to withdraw his hand from the soft fullness of her breast. Bending his head, he touched his lips to her temple. "You trust me, remember? So tell me."

Her gaze slowly focusing, Antonia blinked up at him. She parted her lips, then had to moisten them before she could speak. Speech, explanations, were imperative—before events got completely out of hand. "I… That is…" With an effort, she drew in a deep breath. "When you kiss me passionately—" She broke off, blushing vividly.

Philip felt the heat spread through the skin beneath his fingers; he fought to keep them still.

Antonia swallowed, battling the vice about her chest, struggling to steady her voice. "When you touch me." Her hand rose flutteringly to touch his. She looked down, then abruptly hauled her gaze up and dragged in a shattering breath. "I can't control how I respond," she rushed on. "I feel…" Her eyes darkening, she sought his; briefly, her tongue touched her lips. "Quite wanton."

Desire surged; Philip fought to shackle it. Before he could respond, Antonia continued, her eyes locked on his, "Such unseemly behaviour will give you a disgust of me." Her gaze fell. "I know it's no way for a lady to behave."

The agonised sincerity in her eyes, in her voice, slew any impulse to levity. Philip recognized the dictum to which she alluded, to which she apparently expected to be forced to subscribe. He had long ago concluded that that particular stricture was primarily responsible for making so many married ladies such easy prey for rakes—men who encouraged rather than suppressed their passions. That his wife might, through such reasoning, fall victim to his peers was not a situation he was prepared to countenance. His lips thinned. "At the risk of shocking you further, I've a confession to make."

Dazed hazel eyes met his.

Reluctantly, Philip withdrew his hand from its warm haven and let the halves of her bodice fall shut. "Naturally, I hesitate to make a point of the matter, but I would hardly bear the reputation I do if women's passions—or passionate women—disgusted me." Gazing into her eyes, he added, "Indeed, I can assure you the very opposite is the case."

She continued to look uncertain. His eyes on hers, Philip raised a worldly brow. "It's a well-known fact gentlemen such as I tend to marry late. We wait, hoping to find a lady who responds in the ways we've learned to value—one whose passions are honest and direct, whose delight is natural and unfeigned." He hesitated, then went on, his voice deepening, "You know what I am, what I've been—I see no purpose in any fashionable deceit. Given that background, can you possibly imagine I would be satisfied with mild passions—with the tepid response of a merely complaisant wife—when I know of the fire that flows through your veins?''

His eyes were dark, clouded grey; Antonia struggled to suppress the shudder of awareness his words provoked. Befuddled, uncertain as to whether she should be scandalised or in alt, she shook her head.

Ignoring the tension building within him, Philip continued, ''I want you to be wild and wanton, at least in private.'' His lips twisted into a provocative smile. ''I happen to like you that way.'' Antonia stiffened; he quickly added, his tone tending acerbic, ''And I assure you it's perfectly acceptable for a wife to be wild and wanton with her husband.''

Antonia threw him a sceptical look.

Philip lifted one hand and tapped her nose with one finger. ''I promise I'm not bamming you for my own, nefarious ends.'' He fought to lighten his tone. ''Within the *ton,* there are two sides to any successful marriage—the social and the private. Given the evidence of their Graces of Eversleigh, as well as Jack and Sophie Lester, not to mention Harry and Lucinda—all of whom you have yet to meet but whose marriages I, for one, envy—there's no gainsaying the fact that—'' He paused, caught by the tide of his own eloquence. ''Marriages based on…'' Philip hesitated, then continued, ''Deep mutual attraction have a great deal to recommend them.''

He looked down and met Antonia's searching gaze.

''I thought you wanted a comfortable wife—one who would not make any…'' Antonia blushed again. Irritated, she lifted her chin. ''Any demands on your time.''

Philip smiled, the gesture strained. ''You mean one who would *not* be a constant distraction?'' With one tug, he pulled the ribbon from her hair. The heavy mass cascaded down, scattering pins on the cushions. His smile tightened as he plunged one hand into the golden wave. ''Who would *not* leave me daydreaming of how she will look, how she will feel, when I have her naked beneath my hands?'' His eyes on the golden curls, he spread his fingers, then drew them through the thick mane, laying it across Antonia's shoulder. Then he trapped her gaze in his. "Is that what you thought I wanted?"

Wide-eyed, barely able to breathe, Antonia nodded.

Philip's gaze dropped, fastening on her lips. "Then you were wrong."

His head lowered, his lips found hers. He kissed her and kept kissing her, whirling her back into the mesmerising world of desire and delight, commanding her senses and her responses, murmuring encouragements in gravelly tones whenever her preconceived notions threatened to intrude.

The logs he had earlier placed on the fire were glowing embers when he finally lifted his head. Satisfied with Antonia's regretful sigh, he drew back.

Wits still adrift, her senses swimming, Antonia heard him murmur, "Lady *mine.*"

"I hadn't thought to see so many here today." One hand on her bonnet, anchoring it against the stiff breeze, Antonia looked ahead to where the usual congestion of carriages constricted the main avenue of the Park.

Beside her on the box-seat of his phaeton, Philip smothered a snort. "Nothing less than a deluge will serve to keep them away. Mere threats—" his glance took in the lowering clouds scudding across the leaden sky "—have no power to intimidate the *grande dames* of the *ton.*"

"Obviously." Sinking her fingers into the swansdown lining of her new muff, Antonia returned the gracious nods of the matrons they passed, her smile serenely confident. Inwardly, she remained amazed at her assurance, at the steady, unruffled beat of her heart.

After last night, and their interlude following Lady Darcy-d'Lisle's ball, she had expected to feel distinctly ruffled when next she set eyes on Philip. Instead, unexpectedly meeting over the breakfast table, they had fallen into their

usual friendly banter; there had been nothing in their interaction to unnerve her. Not even the gleam that occasionally
lit his eyes, and the understanding she detected behind it,
had served to disrupt the deep happiness that had laid hold
of her.

Her fingers gently flexed; Antonia glanced down at her
muff. Philip's latest present. She eyed it consideringly, then
slanted him a glance. "I've noticed, my lord, that any item
I admire has a tendency to become mine. Parasols, bonnets,
even emeralds."

Engrossed with managing his greys, Philip merely arched
a brow.

"Will it work if I admire a high-perch phaeton?"

She had quickly lost her fear of the lightweight carriage,
she now revelled in its power and speed.

"No." Philip's answer was unequivocal. Stealing a moment from his cattle, he frowned at Antonia. "I will never
consent to letting you risk your neck—don't even *think* it."

Antonia opened her eyes wide.

Philip humphed and turned back to his horses. His tone
marginally less severe, he added, "If you behave yourself
and don't tease me, you can have a pair of high-steppers
for your carriage. I'll speak to Harry when next I see him."

The comment diverted Antonia. "Harry?" He had mentioned a Harry before.

Philip nodded. "Harry Lester—brother of Jack." After a
second's pause, he added, "Both good friends of mine."

"Ah." Antonia knew what she was supposed to make of
that. "Does this Harry have horses to sell?"

"Possibly." Philip glanced at her, a smile in his eyes.
"Harry Lester is the owner of one of the country's foremost
studs. That stallion you claimed at the Manor—Raker—is a
colt of one of his champions. When it comes to quality
horseflesh, you can't go past Harry."

"I see." As they slowed to join the line of carriages waiting to turn and retrace their route along the avenue, Antonia asked, "Is this the same Harry who married a Lucinda?"

Philip nodded. "Lucinda—Mrs Babbacombe that was. They married a few months ago, towards the end of the Season."

"Is there some reason they aren't in London?"

"Knowing Harry," Philip replied, wheeling his horses, "I assume they're too busy amusing themselves at home."

Antonia slanted him a glance. "Amusing themselves?"

Setting his horses to a trot, Philip turned to meet her gaze. "Strange to tell, there's one attraction guaranteed to hold greater allure for rakes than the *ton* in all its glory."

Antonia opened her eyes wide. "What?"

"Their wives in all their glory."

Blushing furiously, she threw him a speaking look, then switched her attention to the approaching carriages.

Hiding a grin, Philip looked to his horses. Antonia blushing was a sight very much to his liking; the response was not one to which she had previously been particularly susceptible. He was becoming adept at making her blush—yet another talent that improved with practice.

He waited until they passed the last of the stationary carriages before glancing her way again. "With the weather turning, the ranks will start to thin soon. There's really only a week more of the Little Season to go."

Antonia met his gaze, her own open and direct. "And then?"

Philip felt a fierce tension close like a fist about his heart. He kept all hint of the compelling force within him from his expression, from his eyes. "If you're agreeable, we'll return to the Manor. And then—" He broke off, quickly glancing at his horses. When he looked back, his expression was mild. "And then, my dear, we'll proceed as planned."

Antonia's gaze remained steady. She searched his eyes, then, her smile serene, inclined her head. "As we agreed, my lord."

* * *

Two nights later, Philip stood by the side of Lady Carstairs's ballroom and wondered if there was any way he could make the Little Season end sooner. There were still five full nights of balls and parties to be endured; he wasn't sure his patience was up to it—up to the challenge of toeing the line he had drawn, the line beyond which he would not step. Given they were to wed and wed soon, he was not particularly averse to seducing Antonia. Seducing her while she resided under his roof, essentially under his protection, was another matter entirely, one which impinged on his honour, rather than simply his morals.

Swallowing a disgusted "humph", he resisted the urge to cross his arms and glower at the delightful picture she made, swirling down the room in the Roger de Clovely. Lord Ashby, one of his peers, was her partner; despite that, Philip felt no qualms. The fact gave him pause.

He was, now he thought of it, totally, unshakeably, sure of Antonia—sure of her affection, sure of her loyalty, sure of her wish to marry him. Why, then, was he torturing himself by standing here, watching over her?

None who saw her could doubt her assurance. If she should need any help, Henrietta was there, gossiping avidly with her intimates. Geoffrey, too, was somewhere in the throng, almost certainly with the Marquess, Miss Dalling and Mr Fortescue.

As the music swirled towards its conclusion, Philip cast one last glance about. There was no reason he couldn't do as husbands did and leave the room. Antonia didn't need him; he, however, could use the time to consider an urgent problem—what additional steps he could introduce, what byways they could explore, to lengthen her road to seduction.

Given the unexpected violence of his feelings, and her passionate response, that was an increasingly pertinent requirement.

As she rose from her final curtsy, Antonia laughed gaily

at Lord Ashby, then automatically scanned the room. She saw Philip's back as he passed through the main door; smiling, she assumed he had gone to get some air.

Confident, buoyed by content, she chatted with Lord Ashby and the others who gathered around. Ten minutes of artless, on her part distracted, prattle convinced her that her thoughts had gone with Philip. Idly glancing around, she decided there was really no reason she, too, couldn't slip out to get some air. The blustery weather outside had meant the terrace doors were firmly shut; the temperature in the ballroom was steadily rising.

Smiling sweetly, she turned to Lord Ashby. "If you'll excuse me, my lord, I believe I must have a word with my aunt."

Given Henrietta was ensconced in the heart of the Dowager Marchioness of Hammersley's circle, Antonia was not the least surprised when none of the gentlemen present insisted on accompanying her. Slipping through the crowd, initially towards her aunt, she then changed tack and headed for the ballroom door.

In the library, otherwise deserted, Philip paced slowly before the hearth, his mind engrossed with Antonia and the latest unforeseen problem she had managed to present him. He did not hear the door ease open, then quietly close. It was the soft rustle of silk skirts, a very familiar sound, that brought him alert.

He turned, his heart lifting spontaneously, only to find it was not Antonia who stood artfully poised by the end of the *chaise*.

"Good evening, my lord."

Any thought that Lady Ardale had innocently happened upon him was laid to rest by her tone—pure unadulterated adulteress. A stunningly handsome woman, her voluptuous curves were encased in silk so fine it was clear she wore little beneath. Her skirts rustled again, a softly seductive sound, as, her dark gaze on his, she came slowly towards him.

Despite himself, Philip felt a certain fascination—the sort anyone would feel on observing a sight one had heard tell of but had never before encountered. He had certainly heard tell of Lady Ardale. She was one of those he would unhesitatingly label a piranha—in her case, she ate up rakes and spat out their bones. Rumour had it she was impossible to satisfy; attempting that feat that had literally brought some of the fraternity to their knees. As Lord Ardale was still strong enough to insist on discretion, her ladyship limited her prey to those already safely wed. Until now, Philip had thought himself safe.

Her ladyship's next words banished the illusion.

"You've been exceedingly clever, Ruthven." Halting directly before him, Lady Ardale smiled knowingly. Lifting one long-nailed finger, she traced a fold of his cravat. "Finding a friend of the family, a young lady of breeding but no knowledge of the *ton*—a sweet, innocent miss to be your bride." Archly, Lady Ardale lifted one brow. "Very clever indeed."

Almost imperceptibly, Philip stiffened.

"Indeed, my lord, such cleverness fairly begs a reward." Lady Ardale swayed closer; automatically, Philip put out one arm to steady her; his hand came to rest on one curvaceous hip. Lady Ardale drifted closer still, settling her curves against him. "I expect," she said, her words breathy but definite, "that your plans to marry the chit are well advanced. Might I suggest that, rather than waste the next three weeks at your estate, you join me and my guests at Ardale Place? A convivial little gathering." Lady Ardale's rouged lips curved. Her dark eyes on Philip's face, she caught his free hand and, unblushingly, guided it to her breast, trapping his fingers against the ripe swell. "I can assure you you'll get plenty of opportunity to partake of your just desserts. After all your careful planning, you won't want to deny yourself.''

The intensity of the revulsion that swept him, the appallingly strong impulse to fling Lady Ardale from him, forced Philip to pause, to draw a slow, steady breath before declining, with what civility he could muster, her ladyship's salacious invitation. The idea that he would prefer her overripe, tawdry charms to those of Antonia struck him as an insult to his intelligence; her pronouncements on Antonia only raised his hackles further.

Lady Ardale misread his stillness; with a siren-like smile, she reached up, intending to draw his head to hers.

Philip's expression hardened. The hand at her hip firmed; his other hand, freed, moved to grip her shoulder.

What made him look up he did not know, but he did—and saw Antonia, a wraith in the shadows, standing just inside the door. Philip froze.

Lady Ardale plastered herself to him.

The sob that escaped Antonia broke the web of horror, of utter disbelief, that held her. Philip heard it, a small, broken plaint. She pressed her hand to her lips, suppressing the sound, then whirled and fled the room.

The next thing Lady Ardale knew she lay sprawled upon the *chaise*—in precisely the position she had intended to assume, with one notable correction. Philip was supposed to have been with her, not striding to the door.

"Ruthven!"

Her ladyship's strident outrage brought Philip up short. Swinging about, he transfixed her with his gaze, cold contempt in his eyes. ''Madam,'' he said, biting off the words, ''I suggest that in future you exercise greater discretion in selecting your paramours. You are greatly mistaken if you believe that *I* would wish to join their ranks.''

With that, he swung on his heel and strode after Antonia.

Entering the ballroom, he paused by the wall and scanned the company. He eventually located his bride-to-be, dancing the cotillion with some youthful sprig. To any casual observer, her carefree expression would have passed unremarked. Philip saw through it, saw the effort she put into every smile, every lighthearted gesture, saw the pain behind her disguise. He fought the overwhelming urge to go to her, to gather her into his arms and tell her the truth of what she had seen, what she had overheard—only his sure knowledge of the *ton*'s reaction to such an act prevented him from committing it.

Tense, impatient, he waited until the cotillion ended, then strolled purposefully across the ballroom to claim his usual place by her side. She did not look up as he did so, but merely inclined her head.

Philip drew in a calming breath—and waited. When a heated discussion of the rival sporting merits of pheasant over grouse claimed the attention of her attendant swains, he leaned closer. "Antonia, we must talk. Come, stroll with me."

She gave a brittle laugh, drawing attention back to them. "I greatly fear, my lord, that my dance card is full." On pretext of displaying her card, she slipped her right wrist from his hold. "See?" Without looking at him, she held the card up for his perusal, then she beamed upon her court. "Indeed, I couldn't disappoint so many earnest cavaliers."

Her court immediately came to her rescue, decrying his right to take her from them. Gritting his teeth, Philip was forced to acquiesce with a semblance of grace. He had waltzed with her earlier; as usual, she had no further dances free.

With that avenue blocked, he remained by her side, increasingly aware of how tenuous, how flimsy, her blithely gay façade truly was. The knowledge stayed his hand from any further attempt to gain time alone with her; after all her hard work, after all her trepidations, to push her to the brink of some hysterical outburst here, in a *ton* ballroom, would be the act of a cad. The same consideration kept him where he was; if she did stumble and fall, he was one of the few he would trust to catch her.

And, after all, they would shortly be home; the library fire would already be lit.

With that objective in mind, he escorted her smoothly from the ballroom at the close of the evening, shielding her as best he could from any too-observant eyes. Helpfully, Henrietta proved greatly distracted by Miss Dalling's prospects; Geoffrey, drawn into the discussion, filled the gap Antonia left.

She followed Henrietta from the carriage, leaving him to descend in her wake. But Henrietta's slow progress up the steps held her back; coming up beside Antonia, Philip caught her hand and trapped it on his sleeve. She started at his touch, then acquiesced, allowing him to lead her to the door.

Henrietta, still demanding to know more of Miss Dalling, stumped up the stairs on Geoffrey's arm. From the hall, Antonia fast by his side, Philip watched until the pair gained the landing.

"My lord?"

Carring stood waiting to take his evening cloak. Releasing Antonia, Philip untied the loose ribands and shrugged the cloak from his shoulders. Turning back, he discovered Antonia halfway to the stairs.

"I greatly fear, my lord," she said, one hand rising to her brow, "that I have quite the most hideous headache. If you'll excuse me?"

With a swirling bob by way of farewell, she turned and sailed on up the stairs, not once meeting his gaze.

Philip's eyes narrowed as he watched her ascend; his expression hardened with every step she took.

When Antonia had passed from sight, Carring coughed, then murmured, "No nightcaps tonight, my lord?"

His expression like flint, Philip growled, "As you know

damned well, I can pour my own brandy. You may lock up.''

With that, he strode into the library, shutting the door firmly behind him.

Upstairs, Antonia reached her chamber only to discover she had to ring for Nell, who had grown used to her interludes in the library. Tense as a bowstring, she waited until Nell appeared, then, resigned, submitted to the maid's ministrations, excusing her departure from the norm with, ''I'm merely feeling a bit peaked. A good night's sleep will no doubt see me right.''

Busy with her buttons, Nell shot her a searching glance. ''Sure you don't want me to mix up a Blue Powder? Or I could fetch you up the jar of Dr Radcliffe's Restorative Pork Jelly. A spoonful of that does strengthen one.''

She could certainly use some strength. ''No, thank you.'' Antonia held herself stiffly, restraining her thoughts, her emotions, by main force. ''Just help me into my nightgown—I'll do my hair.''

Mumbling, grumbling, citing the benefits of Dr Radcliffe's Jelly to the last, Nell eventually took herself off.

Alone, Antonia drew in a deep, difficult breath, then, her brush in her hand, sank onto the stool before her dressing-table. Like one in a dream, she fell to brushing out her thick curls, her gaze fixed on her image in the mirror. The candelabra to her right threw steady light over her face; briefly, she focused on her image, then reached for the snuffer. Only when the candles were doused, leaving the room wreathed in shadows with the only light coming from the single candle by her bed, did she look back at the mirror.

She had no need to see the misery in her eyes to know of the misery in her heart.

For which she had only herself to blame.

She had let her heart rule her head, let love lead her to believe in miracles. Her mother had warned her—she had warned herself—but she hadn't listened. Seduced by love, she'd thought herself safe from its pain. Tonight, she had discovered she was not.

The hold she had maintained over her emotions abruptly shredded; love hit her like a blow, as it had in Lady Carstairs's library, when concealed by shadows, she had watched Philip respond to some sophisticated harlot. As before, the impact left her reeling; pain speared through her, a vice squeezed her heart. A dull ache filled her, a miasma spreading insidiously through her, swallowing all hope.

Dully, Antonia blinked at the mirror, then laid aside her brush. She had always been strong, always able to cope. She would cope with this, too, and she *would not cry*—not even when her mother had sold her mare, the last gift her father had given her, had she given way to tears. Slowly, she straightened her shoulders and determinedly stared at her reflection, all but hidden by the flickering shadows.

Her hurt, her anguish, was entirely her own fault. Philip had never said he loved her—she had no cause to reproach him. The truth was as it had always been; she had been foolish to imagine otherwise. Her feelings, her unspoken, unacknowledged hopes, were irrelevant. Ruthlessly, she bundled them together, then buried them deep—and spent the next hour sternly repeating all the strictures, the strictures necessary to play the part of Philip's wife, unexpectedly finding strength in the clear-cut, unemotional edicts. Only when she had regained her sense of purpose did she allow herself to think of other things.

The rest of the night went in a fruitless endeavour, a futile attempt to mend her broken heart.

Chapter Twelve

"**C**an I fetch you anything, my lord?"

Seated behind his desk in the library, Philip looked up. Carring stood in the open doorway. Philip frowned. "No. Not at the moment."

Carring bowed and backed, reaching for the doorknob.

"And you may leave the door open."

Carring bowed again. "Of course, my lord."

Smothering a growl, Philip refocused on the *Gazette*. The weak rays of the midday sun intermittently pierced the clouds, throwing fitful beams across the page.

The weather was not the only thing to have suddenly turned uncertain.

Antonia had given him no chance to explain, no chance to set the record straight. He trusted her implicitly; despite her agreement to do so, she obviously didn't trust him. Admittedly, he carried a certain reputation, one he'd made no effort to hide, but they were friends and had been for years. He had thought that would count for rather more than it had. To his mind, the matter was clear. She should have known better—known him better.

Rather than believe the evidence of her eyes. And her ears.

Philip grimaced. His gaze, fixed unseeing on the page, grew more deeply abstracted.

A faint creak sounded from beyond the library door.

Instantly, he was out of his chair and rounding the desk. By the time Antonia started down the last flight of stairs, he was waiting to greet her.

"Good morning, my dear. I missed you at breakfast."

The rest of his carefully rehearsed speech, his "I trust you slept well?" followed by a pointed request for a moment of her time, went winging from his head the instant he saw her face.

Antonia hesitated, one hand clutching the balustrade, her gaze deliberately unfocused. "I'm afraid…" Dragging in a breath, she lifted her head. "That is, I slept in." She felt chilled to the marrow, very close to shivering, but if she wished to be his comfortable wife, she had to comport herself appropriately, even at moments like this.

Stiffly poised, she continued her descent, concentrating on her carriage. Behind her, Nell's heavier footfalls followed down the stairs. Defiantly, she kept her head high; Nell had ministered with cucumber water and Denmark Lotion; she assumed the worst was disguised. Reaching the last step, she bestowed an unfocused glance on her husband-to-be. "I trust you are well, my lord?"

"Tolerably," came the brief answer. Then, after a fractional hesitation, "I wonder, my dear, whether you can spare me a moment of your time?"

Surprised, not only by the request but by the gentler tone of his voice, Antonia blinked; unintentionally, she focused on Philip's face. The concern in his eyes had her turning her head away; she disguised the movement by flicking out her skirts. "As it happens, my lord, I was on my way to the back parlour to write letters. I regret to confess I've been greatly remiss in my correspondence; there are many ladies in Yorkshire to whom I owe a degree of thanks."

She was determined to make no fuss, but the idea of being

alone with him just now was simply too much. Her gaze fixed on his cravat, she continued, "I've put the matter off unconscionably long. I understand that if I complete my letters by two, Carring will be able to post them."

"Carring," Philip said, acutely aware of his major-domo hovering behind him, "may put them on my desk. I'll frank them."

Antonia inclined her head. "Thank you, my lord. If you'll excuse me, I'll begin them immediately." She made to turn away.

"Perhaps we could take the air later—a stroll around the square once your correspondence is dealt with?"

Antonia hesitated. The idea of a walk in the fresh breeze was tempting but the vision her mind supplied—of them, stiff and silent, circumnavigating the square—was more than enough to dissuade her. "Ah—I believe Henrietta and I are due to take tea with Lady Cathie, and then we had thought to look in on Mrs Melcombe's at-home."

The lame excuse hung in the air; Antonia stiffened, her brittle façade tightening. Tension swelled and stretched, holding them all frozen, then Philip bowed with his usual fluid grace.

"In that case, I'll see you this evening, my dear."

Unnerved by the undercurrent she detected in his tone, Antonia cried off from their evening's engagements. She did not even risk dinner, requesting a tray in her room on the grounds of an incipient headache.

Ensconced in lonely splendour at the head of the dining-table, Philip sat sunk in thought, his gaze fixed on the empty seat beside him. At the table's end, Henrietta and Geoffrey were deep in machinations.

"I have to say that I'm not a great believer in newfangled notions, yet I cannot see my way clear, in this instance, to agree with Meredith Ticehurst." Henrietta pushed away her soup plate. "There's nothing the least—well, *questionable* about Mr Fortescue, is there?"

"Questionable?" Geoffrey frowned. "Not that I know of. Capital fellow from all I can make out. Drives a neat curricle with a nicely matched pair."

Henrietta returned his frown. "That's not what I meant." Raising her head, she looked up the table. "Do you know anything against Mr Fortescue, Ruthven?"

The sound of his name shook Philip from his thoughts. "Fortescue?"

Henrietta threw him a disgusted look. "Mr Henry Fortescue—Miss Dalling's would-be suitor. I have to tell you, Philip, that I am not at all happy in my mind about the tack Meredith Ticehurst is taking with her niece. No—and not with the Marquess either, although he is, after all, a man and, one would suppose, capable of taking care of himself."

Recalling the Marchioness of Hammersley, Philip considered that last far from certain. "I know nothing against Mr Fortescue—indeed, what I do know would suggest he is an eminently eligible, even desirable, *parti*."

Having delivered himself of that pronouncement, Philip reached for his wine glass. As he sipped, Henrietta's suppositions and concerns, and Geoffrey's predictably straightforward views, drifted past his ears. Their tacit alliance and their half-formed plans to overturn the Countess's applecart did not even register.

Then the meal was at an end; Philip could not even recall if he had eaten. He did not particularly care; he had lost his appetite, among other things.

But when they gathered in the hall preparatory to quitting the house, destined for Lady Arbuthnot's drum, his gaze sharpened. He glanced at Henrietta, his expression bland. "No doubt you'll wish to check on Antonia before we leave."

"Antonia?" Henrietta looked up in surprise. "Whatever for? She's not seriously ill, y'know."

"I had thought," Philip returned, steel glimmering in his tone, "that you might wish to reassure yourself that her indisposition is indeed merely that, and not something more alarming. She is, after all, in your care."

"Phooh!" Henrietta waved her hand dismissively. "It's doubtless merely an upset brought on by going at it too hard." Slanting him a glance, she added, "Have to remember she's a country girl at heart. She might have adapted well to town life but we've been racketing about in grand style these past weeks. She's entitled to some time to recuperate." Henrietta patted his arm in a motherly way then, beckoning Geoffrey, stumped towards the front door.

His expression stony, Philip hesitated, then reluctantly followed.

They returned from Lady Arbuthnot's drum at midnight; to Philip's relief, Henrietta had shown no interest in attending any other of the parties around town. Heads together, thick as thieves, she and Geoffrey negotiated the stairs; frowning, Philip headed for the library. From the corner of his eye, he caught Carring's expression; he shut the door with a decided click.

He hesitated, then crossed to the sideboard and poured out a large brandy. Cradling the glass, he returned to sink into his chair, the one on the left of the hearth. Slowly, he sipped the fine brandy, his gaze broodingly fixed on the empty chair opposite.

Last night he had paced the hearth rug, glowering, possessed by an impotent and thoroughly uncharacteristic anger. Tonight, the anger was still there but tempered by growing concern.

Antonia was avoiding him; now Carring was regarding him with chilly disapproval.

Philip directed a steely glare at the empty chair. *He* wasn't at fault. Antonia should have been more trusting— ladies were supposed to trust their husbands-to-be. She loved him—

Philip stopped.

For one instant, his world wavered—then he snorted impatiently.

He knew, beyond all doubt, beyond any possibility of error, that Antonia loved him. He had known it for more than eight years. Her love was there in her eyes, a certain wistfully warm expression glowing in the hazel depths. He had not responded to it years ago but he had recognised it nonetheless. It had been there even then.

Philip let the thought warm him. He took a long sip of his brandy then frowned at the smouldering fire.

If she loved him, she should have trusted him. She should have had more confidence in him. She should have had the courage of her convictions.

Again his thoughts faltered and halted; Antonia possessed abundant courage. The courage needed to fearlessly manage high-couraged horses, the courage to face with equanimity eight long years of seclusion and deprivation she had never been raised to expect. Her reservoir of courage could not be questioned; why, then, would she not face him over this? Why had she so readily accepted the obvious and retreated, rather than confronting him and letting him explain?

Why hadn't she had the confidence in him that he had in her?

Philip slowly blinked, then grimaced and took another sip from his glass.

He had told her he was smitten, that they shared a deep mutual attraction—she knew he desired her. Surely it was reasonable to expect a lady of her intelligence to make the appropriate deduction?

His frown deepening, he shifted restlessly.

The clock in the corner ticked relentlessly on; when it struck one, he drained his glass. Grimacing, he stood.

They couldn't go on like this. The pain he had seen in her face that morning was etched in his mind; her misery lay like a lead weight around his heart. If she needed some more formidable declaration, then she would have it.

He would talk to her privately—and sort the matter out.

He had forgotten what a quick learner she was.

Despite his best endeavours, his next opportunity to speak with Antonia privately occurred the next evening when they took to the floor in the first waltz at Lady Harris's ball. As he drew her into his arms, Philip felt a distinct tremor ripple through her. Drawing her closer still, he deftly swung them into the swirling throng.

"Antonia—"

"Lady Harris's décor is positively inspired, don't you think, my lord? Whoever would have thought of a fairy grotto lined with miniature cannon?"

Philip's lips thinned. "Lord Harris was a naval man—something to do with Ordinance. But I wanted to—"

"Do they fire, do you suppose?" Her features animated, Antonia raised her brows. "I wouldn't think that would be too wise, what with young sprigs like Geoffrey about."

"I doubt anyone else has considered the matter. Antonia—"

"Now there I am sure you are wrong, my lord. I'm perfectly certain the idea of firing one would have occurred to Geoffrey by now."

Philip drew in a slow, steady breath. "Antonia, I want to explain—"

"There is, my lord, absolutely no reason you should." Resolutely, Antonia lifted her chin, her gaze fixed beyond Philip's right shoulder. "There is nothing you have to explain—it is I who should beg your pardon. I assure you such an incident will not occur again. I'm fully conscious of my indiscretion; I assure you there's no reason we need discuss the matter further."

Metaphorically girding her loins, she let her gaze fleetingly touch Philip's face. His expression was hard and distinctly stern.

"Antonia, that's—"

She missed the beat and stumbled.

Philip caught her, steadying her. For an instant, he wondered if she had stumbled on purpose; the startled, darting glances she sent this way and that assured him she had not. "Nobody saw—it was nothing remarkable." He eased his hold once they were circling freely again. "Now—"

"If it is all the same to you, my lord, I suspect I should concentrate on my steps."

Inwardly, Philip swore. The tremor in her voice was entirely genuine. Reining in his impatience, he guided them on through the couples crowding the floor. When next he spoke, his voice was carefully urbane. "I wish to see you privately, Antonia."

She glanced up fleetingly, then looked away. He could feel the quivering tension that held her.

Antonia took a full minute to gather her defences, to ensure her voice was steady when she said, "I believe, my lord, that it would be wisest for us henceforth to follow the conventional paths. In light of our yet-to-be formalised relationship, I would respectfully suggest we should not meet privately until such meetings are customary."

It took every ounce of Philip's *savoir-faire* to smother his response to that suggestion. To quell the primitive urge that threatened to shatter his social veneer. "Antonia," he said, his voice deadly calm. "If you imagine—"

"Have you seen Lady Hatchcock's new quizzing glass? Hugo said it made her eye big beyond belief."

"I have not the slightest interest in Lady Hatchcock's quizzing glass."

"No?" Antonia opened her eyes wide. "Then perhaps you have heard of the latest *on dit*. It seems…" She babbled on, barely pausing for breath.

Philip heard the brittleness in her voice; he noted her wide eyes and too-rapid breathing. Frustration mounting, he desisted, only to be forced to listen to her run on without pause until he handed her back into the bosom of her court.

Breathlessly, she thanked him. Philip bestowed upon her a look she should have felt all the way to her bones, then turned on his heel and headed for the cardroom.

He ran her to earth the following afternoon; she had taken refuge in the back parlour, her maid in close attendance.

Antonia looked up as he entered. She was seated at the round table in the centre of the room; thick papers and board, swatches of brocade and silk, ribbons, braids, silk cords and fringes lay scattered across its surface. Her fingers plying a large needle, she was engaged in fastening a circle of brocade over a piece of thick paper.

"Good afternoon, my lord." Blinking in surprise, Antonia succumbed to the temptation to drink in his elegance— then she noticed the gloves he was carrying. "Are you going driving?"

"Indeed." Determinedly languid, Philip halted before the table. "I had wondered, my dear, whether you might care to accompany me? You seem to have been hiding yourself away of late—some fresh air will do you good."

Her gaze fixed safely on his cravat, Antonia blinked again, then looked down. "Unfortunately, my lord, you catch me at an inopportune moment." With a wave of her hand, she indicated the materials spread before her. "I broke my reticule last evening and needs must fashion another to match my gown before Lady Hemminghurst's ball tonight."

"How unfortunate." Philip's polite smile did not waver. "Particularly as I had thought that, perhaps, the day being remarkably calm, I might hand the ribbons to you for a short spell."

Antonia's fingers stilled. Slowly she raised her head until her eyes met Philip's.

Philip hid his triumph; it was the first time since Lady

Ardale's unwelcome intrusion into their lives that she had gifted him with one of her wonderfully direct glances.

Then he saw the reproach in her gaze.

"In your phaeton?" she asked.

Philip hesitated, then nodded.

Antonia sighed and looked down. "I have to confess, my lord, that I'm not feeling quite the thing this afternoon—just a mite queasy—I suspect Lady Harris's salmon patties are to blame. So difficult, these days, to be certain of one's salmon." Laying out a piece of silk fringe, she airily continued, "So I'm afraid I must decline your kind—indeed, your very *tempting* invitation. I really could not trust myself to the rocking of a phaeton." Her face artfully brightening, she glanced upwards, not quite meeting Philip's eyes. "Perhaps if we went in your curricle?"

Philip felt his mask harden, he fought not to narrow his eyes. It was a moment before he replied, his tone determinedly even, "I regret to say I left my curricle at the Manor." A fact he was certain she knew.

Regretfully, Antonia sighed. "In that case, my lord, I fear I must decline your offer." Directing a sweet smile his way, she added, "Do convey my respects to Mr Satterly, should you see him."

Philip looked but she would not meet his eyes again. After a moment's uncomfortable silence, he said, his tone flat, "In that case, my dear, I will bid you a good afternoon." He bowed, the action lacking his customary grace, then swiftly strode from the room.

When, two nights later, Philip took refuge in his library, alone yet again, he was ready to freely curse Antonia's quick wits.

Every move he made, she blocked. Every tried and true strategy ever devised for getting a young lady alone, she, an innocent from the wilds of the north, had somehow developed a counter for.

She never went anywhere within the house without her maid; she never went anywhere outside except on social engagements and, while in society, was always either surrounded by her court or anchored by Miss Dalling's side. Short of creating an almighty scene in some *grande dame*'s ballroom, he had to acknowledge himself stymied. And, given Antonia knew he would not create a public fuss, he couldn't even use that as a threat!

He didn't bother with a brandy, but fell to pacing before the hearth.

What could he do? Enact a melodrama in the middle of his hall with Carring and her po-faced maid as audience? The thought made him grind his teeth. He'd be dammed if he'd fall so low. To his knees if need be—but no further.

Overhead, a beam creaked. Pausing, Philip glanced up. His gaze lingered on the ceiling; his irate expression slowly turned considering. Then he frowned and resumed his pacing.

That particular avenue remained open but taking their quarrel—it now figured as such in his mind—to her bedchamber would qualify, he felt sure, as an act of outright lunacy. The potential, not to say likely ramifications, even should she prove willing to listen, were altogether too damning.

However, the alternative—of returning to the Manor, present situation intact and ongoing—was too bleak to contemplate. She had withdrawn from him in a way he could never have foreseen—he'd had no idea that the simple absence of the warmth behind her smiles would affect him so deeply.

Halting, he drew in a breath, battling the now permanent constriction about his chest. Closing his eyes, he focused on his problem. Society had long ago labelled him hedonistic—even now, he knew what he wanted.

He wanted to put the brightness back in Antonia's eyes, wanted to experience again the teasing glances they used to share. He wanted to make her blush again. More than anything else, he wanted her to look at him as she always had before—openly, directly, honestly—with her love shining in her eyes.

Abruptly, Philip opened his eyes. A log settled in the grate—he frowned at it. His lady love was too clever for her own good—and for his—but there was one front on which he had never approached her—in deference to her innocence and some deeply ingrained chivalrous instinct.

The time for chivalry had passed.

Slowly, his expression considering, Philip sank into his usual chair. As always, his gaze settled on its mate, this time with clear calculation in his eyes.

He had never pursued Antonia.

Next morning, seated beside Henrietta at the breakfast table, Antonia attacked a poached pear with single-minded ruthlessness. The same relentless, dogged destruction she would like to visit upon a certain overblown harlot who made a habit of appearing in public in too-tight silk gowns. Indeed, if Lady Ardale—she had learned the woman's name the very next evening—stood anywhere near a duckpond, the outcome would be beyond doubt.

And the only guilt she would feel was for the startled ducks.

Crunching a mouthful of toast, Antonia mulled on the possibilities of a horse trough.

"No—I'm more than convinced!" Beside Antonia, Henrietta nodded pugnaciously. "My dears, we simply *cannot* let this happen."

"Seems a thoroughly rum set-up," Geoffrey opined, reaching for the marmalade. "The way the gorgon's been talking, if Catriona and Ambrose don't toe the line, they'll be left with no choice. Stuck away in the country with only those two old tartars and a bunch of servants—well, any fool can see how the thing'll be done."

"Hmm." Henrietta frowned. "Such a pity the Earl is so…" She grimaced. "Well—*ineffectual.*"

"According to Henry," Geoffrey said, "the poor old toper's been living under the cat's paw for so long he daren't sneeze without permission."

"Yes, well—he never was a forceful character." Leaning one elbow on the table, Henrietta gestured with her butter knife. "Which is all the more reason we must accept this invitation. If there's any chance of deflecting Ticehurst's intentions, I really feel we owe it to those two poor young things to do our best."

"No doubt about it," Geoffrey concurred. "Got to spike her guns somehow."

"Precisely." Henrietta turned to Antonia. "What say you, my dear?"

"Hmm?" Antonia blinked, then nodded. "Yes, of course."

Her expression resolute, Henrietta turned back to Geoffrey; Antonia turned back to her plate—and her thoughts. On a superficial level, she had remained abreast of the developments in Catriona's drama. The majority of her reflections, however, revolved about her own.

When she had decided how she should respond to what she mentally termed Philip's unfortunate tendency, when she had initially set out to be his comfortable wife, she had been under the impression her emotions would be content to be ruled by her intellect, rather than the other way about.

The reality, consequently, was requiring a degree of adjustment. Indeed, she wasn't sure she would not need to completely rescript her role.

Given the anger that welled within her every time she even thought of Lady Ardale, given the almost overwhelming impulse to march into Philip's library and demand an explanation in a more flagrantly histrionic style than Catriona could even imagine, given that, combined with the determination that had sprung from nowhere, the determination to insist that he was hers and hers alone, the absolute conviction that she could, if she dared, reform even such a rake as he, she was no longer at all sure she was cut out to be a comfortable wife.

She frowned at her plate—then reached for a boiled egg.

The door opened and Philip entered. In keeping with her recent habit, Antonia allowed her gaze to rise only as far as the diamond pin in his cravat. It was an effort not to scowl at it. The smile she did manage was decidedly tight.

"Ah, good morning, Ruthven. I trust you slept well?"

Philip shifted his gaze from Antonia to Henrietta; his stepmother's fond smile fed the instant suspicion her words had evoked. "Tolerably well, thank you." Taking his seat at the table's head, Philip nodded to Carring, proffering the coffee pot. "I had intended, ma'am, to ask when you intended to remove to the country."

"Indeed—and that's precisely the point I wish to discuss with you, my lord." Henrietta sat back in her chair. "We have all received an invitation to a houseparty—three or four days in Sussex, just the thing to round off the season."

Philip's hand, carrying his coffee cup, halted in mid-air. "Sussex?"

"Sussex," Henrietta confirmed. "You're included in the invitation, naturally."

"Naturally?" Philip met his stepmother's eye. "Do I know our hosts, by any chance?"

Slightly flustered, Henrietta fluffed her shawls. "You've met the Countess. The party's at Ticehurst Place." She looked up, prepared to be belligerent, fully expecting to have to do battle to gain her ends.

Philip's slowly raised brows, his unexpectedly considering expression, held her silent.

"Ticehurst Place?" Settling back in his chair, Philip sipped his coffee, and cast a quick glance at Antonia's bent head. Her attention appeared wholly focused on a boiled egg, which she was decapitating with military precision. Philip's gaze sharpened. "Three days, I believe you said?"

"Three—possibly four. Starting tomorrow." Henrietta regarded him a trifle warily. "I understand it's to be a smallish gathering."

Philip's gaze flicked her way. "How small?"

Henrietta waved dismissively. "Just the four of us—and the Hammersleys, of course."

"Of course."

When Philip said nothing more, his gaze resting thoughtfully on Antonia, who remained apparently oblivious, Henrietta humphed. "I dare say, if you don't wish to go, we can get along without you."

"On the contrary." Abruptly, Philip sat forward. Setting his cup down, he reached for the platter of ham. "I confess to being somewhat at a loose end. I see no reason I cannot accompany you to Sussex, if you wish it."

Henrietta blinked in amazement; she quickly grabbed the offer. "Indeed—nothing would please me more. I won't conceal from you, my lord, that affairs might become rather touchy—it would be a great relief to me if you were by."

"Consider it settled, then." As he helped himself to three slices of ham, Philip was conscious of Antonia's swift, appraising, distinctly suspicious glance. He resisted the urge to smile wolfishly at her. Time enough for that once he had her at Ticehurst Place—at a houseparty without the party, in what would doubtless prove to be a huge rambling mansion, mostly empty, with large grounds likewise free of unwanted spectators—all of it glorying in one significant advantage.

None of it would be his.

He had spent half the night and all the morning considering the constraints his honour dictated while Antonia remained under his roof, on his lands.

Ticehurst Place was neither. Not his roof, not his grounds.

Open season.

He slanted a quick glance at Antonia, engrossed in slicing a piece of ham to ribbons. Returning his gaze to his plate, Philip allowed himself a smug smile.

At last, at long last, fate had dealt him an ace.

Chapter Thirteen

Late the next morning, Antonia descended the stairs, Henrietta in her wake. Both she and her aunt were ready to depart for Ticehurst Place; they had both elected to breakfast in their bedchambers, Henrietta due to her slow preparations, Antonia due to a sudden conviction that facing Philip over the breakfast table with only Geoffrey for protection was not a sensible undertaking.

There'd been something in his demeanour, a certain intentness in his manner during their previous evening's parade through the ballrooms that had set her senses on edge. She had no real idea what it was she detected—she was not about to hazard a guess.

As they started down the last flight, Antonia keeping a watchful eye on Henrietta's ponderous progress, the front door opened. Geoffrey strode in, his tall form enveloped in a white drab driving coat sporting quite as many capes as Philip's.

Antonia halted on the last step. "Where on earth did you get that?"

Geoffrey grinned. "Philip introduced me to his tailor. Quite a dab hand at his trade, don't you think?" He whirled, setting the capes fluttering.

When he stopped and looked pointedly at her, Antonia

nodded. "It's certainly…" She hesitated, then, beguiled by Geoffrey's obvious delight, smiled. "Something like."

Geoffrey glowed with pride. "Philip suggested arriving at Oxford in such togs wouldn't hurt. And, of course, it's the perfect garb for today."

Joining them, Henrietta humphed. "The sun's decided to remember us—you'll be too hot in the carriage in that."

"Indeed."

Antonia quickly turned as Philip strolled into the hall. His gaze met hers fleetingly, then he glanced down, lips firming as he pulled on his driving gloves. "So it's as well he's not travelling in the carriage."

"Oh?" Henrietta asked the question, much to Antonia's relief, allowing her to keep her lips shut and her expression satisfyingly distant.

"I'm taking my phaeton." Philip glanced at Antonia. "Geoffrey may as well come with me."

It was an effort not to meet his gaze. Determinedly cool, Antonia nodded. "An exceedingly good notion." Tilting her chin, she added, "It will leave us more space in which to be comfortable."

For an instant, Philip's gaze rested on her face, then he smiled—a slow predatory smile. "It would, perhaps, be wise to gain what rest you might. I suspect you'll discover this houseparty unexpectedly exhausting."

Antonia flicked him a suspicious glance but his expression as he moved forward to help Henrietta down the last steps was bland and uninformative.

The front door bell pealed; Carring came hurrying from the nether regions. He looked out, then set the front door wide. "Your phaeton and the carriage, my lord."

Between them, Philip and Geoffrey helped Henrietta down the front steps. Marshalling his footmen, Carring saw to the stowing of the luggage, assisted by acid comments from both Trant and Nell. Resembling a pair of black crows, the maids between them got Henrietta settled against the padded cushions, protected by a veritable mountain of shawls. Left on the pavement, Antonia glanced about. Geoffrey was already on the box-seat of the phaeton, the reins in his hands as he helped restrain the restive horses.

The sight stiffened her spine. Unbidden, her memory replayed the three, separate excuses she had spent the small hours devising, one for every possible tack Philip might have taken to inveigle her into sharing the phaeton's box-seat on the long drive to Ticehurst Place.

Excuses she had not needed.

Suppressing a disaffected sniff, Antonia turned, one hand raising her skirts to climb the carriage steps. Philip's hand appeared before her. For an instant, she regarded it, the long strong fingers and narrow palm. Reminding herself of her role, she lifted her chin and placed her hand in his.

Philip smoothly raised her fingers to his lips, artfully, lingeringly, caressing her fingertips.

Antonia froze, her breathing suspended. She glanced up through her lashes; Philip trapped her gaze in his.

"Enjoy the drive. I'll be waiting at the other end—to greet you."

Eyes widening, Antonia took in the hard planes of his face, the subtle aggression in the line of his jaw—and the clear intent that stared at her from the depths of his grey eyes. A skittering sensation shivered over her skin. Ignoring it, she set one foot on the carriage step. "I dare say there'll be many distractions at Ticehurst Place."

She'd intended the comment as a dismissal of his avowed intention; she expected it to be the conclusion of their exchange. Instead, as he handed her up, Philip's voice reached her, wickedly low. "You may count on that, my dear."

The promise in his words distracted her all the way to Ticehurst Place.

Although her gaze remained fixed on the scenery, she did not notice the sunshine beaming down from between fluffy clouds, did not feel the soft touch of the unexpectedly mild breeze. Summer's last stand had enveloped the country, a final burst of golden weather that had set the doves to cooing again in the trees along the way.

Lulled by the sound, Antonia found her mind treading a circuitous path, forever leaving her facing one, unanswerable question: Just what was her prospective husband about?

She had reached no conclusion when the carriage rocked to a stop on the gravel sweep before Ticehurst Place. As soon as the door was opened and the steps let down, Trant and Nell descended. Two footmen came hurrying down the long flight of steps leading up to the front door; together with the maids, they endeavoured to ease Henrietta from the carriage.

Antonia glanced out of the window—and saw Philip descending the steps, his pace relaxed and leisurely, his expression mild and urbane. Longing to escape the close confines of the carriage, aware of the dull headache its stuffiness had evoked, she gave vent to a disgusted sniff—and struggled to keep her mind from dwelling on how pleasant the drive in his phaeton must have been.

''Heh-me!'' Henrietta exclaimed as her feet touched the ground. ''My old bones are cramping my style.'' Grimacing, she leant heavily on the footmen's arms and slowly started up the steps.

Her head haughtily high, Antonia shifted along the seat, then moved to the carriage door.

As he had promised, Philip was there to assist her to the gravel. Alighting, her hand in his, Antonia glanced up—only to see him grimace.

''Much as it goes against the grain, I fear I must plead Miss Dalling's cause. Her situation is more serious than I'd imagined.''

Antonia looked her question.

Drawing her hand through his arm, Philip turned her towards the steps. ''To use Geoffrey's description, it appears the gorgon has entirely fallen off her perch. On arrival, we were treated to what I can only describe as a supremely distasteful scene in which her ladyship endeavoured to impress upon me that her niece has all but accepted the Marquess.''

Outwardly nonchalant, they climbed the broad steps. Philip lifted his gaze to the small knot of people waiting on the porch. ''It appears that dramatic flights are a Dalling family trait. The upshot was that Miss Dalling, for whom I must reluctantly concede a certain sympathy, has implored our help in avoiding a marriage by *force majeure*.''

''Great heavens!'' Antonia followed Philip's lead in schooling her features to the semblance of polite conversation. ''Is Catriona in a fury?''

''Worse. She's in a blue funk.''

''Catriona?'' Antonia looked up at him, her gaze direct. ''You're bamming me.''

Philip's brows rose. ''Not at all—but see for yourself.'' With a nod, he indicated the reception party now a short way before them.

Antonia followed his gaze. A moment later, they reached the porch—and she discovered he'd spoken no less than the truth. The Catriona who stood mute by her aunt's side was a far cry from the defiantly confident young girl who had first come on the town. Eyes still huge but now filled with die-away despair fastened upon her. As she turned from acknowledging the Countess's somewhat strident greeting, Catriona stepped forward to clasp her hand.

''I'm so glad you've come.'' Her accents were hushed, fervent. ''Come—I'll show you to your room.'' A quick glance revealed that Henrietta was the focus of the Countess's attention. ''I have to unburden myself to someone who understands—I do not know *what* I would have done if you hadn't taken pity and travelled thus, into the lion's den.''

Stifling an impulse to suggest that that last should be the ''gorgon's den'', Antonia allowed herself to be drawn inside. Only to have her nonsensical vision take on real shape. The hall was dark and gloomy; its ceiling was so high it could only be described as cavernous. Panelled in dark wood, the walls were hung with old wooden shields and dark-hued tapestries. A fire smoked and smouldered in a huge stone fireplace; a heavy wooden table stood on the dark flags. The chamber exuded a pervading sense of being the anteroom of some dangerous animal's lair.

Pulling back against Catriona's tug, Antonia halted in the centre of the room to stare at the huge, ornately carved staircase filling the end of the hall. Its wide treads led upward into the shadows of what she assumed was a gallery.

"Welcome to the delights of Ticehurst Place."

The deep, softly menacing words, uttered from just behind her ear, made her jump. Antonia threw a frowning glance over her shoulder; Philip had followed them in; he stood close behind her, his gaze roving the shadowed walls.

"It possesses a certain cachet, don't you think?" His eyes lowered to meet hers.

Catriona, apparently inured to the décor, gently tugged Antonia forward. Antonia did not move, anchored by Philip's hand at her waist.

"Don't leave her," he murmured, his eyes holding hers. "Not even when you're dressing."

Fleetingly, Antonia searched his eyes, then nodded and yielded to Catriona's insistent urging. Drawing closer, she tucked her arm in Catriona's. Together, they climbed the stairs, ascending into the shadows.

Philip watched them go, a frown gathering in his eyes.

With no attempt at her usual chatter, Catriona led Antonia to a large chamber, roomy but somehow oppressive. Nell was there, unpacking Antonia's bags. Eyeing the maid warily, Catriona towed Antonia to the window seat, pressing her to sit. "My room's just along the corridor," she said, her voice close to a whisper. Sinking onto the brocaded cushion beside Antonia, she grimaced. "So is Ambrose's."

Antonia blinked. "Ah." That was not, to her understanding, the habit when accommodating young people. "I see."

"I haven't told you the half of it yet." In suitably dramatic style, Catriona proceeded to do so, inevitably embellishing her account.

But no amount of dramatic description could detract from the impact of the basic facts; appraised of the full story of how Ambrose, on arriving late the previous evening, had been shown to Catriona's room, ostensibly by mistake, Antonia had no doubt of the appropriateness of her sympathies.

"If it hadn't been for the fact that I'd asked for more coal and the girl was late bringing it up, Ambrose and I could have been…" Catriona's eyes glazed. "Why—we could have ended sharing a bed." Her voice faded; Antonia did not think her undisguised horror owed much to her histrionic tendencies.

"Luckily," she said, leaning forward to pat Catriona's hand bracingly, "that eventuality was averted. I take it you had not yet gone to sleep and as the girl was there, Ambrose got no further than the threshold?"

Catriona nodded. "But you can see, can't you, how hopeless it all is? Unless Henry can find some way to rescue me from my aunt's talons, I'll be *forced* to the altar."

"Along with Ambrose." Antonia frowned. "What does he say to this?"

Catriona sighed. "He was horrified, of course. But his mother is truly overpowering—she has him well under her thumb. He simply cannot stand up to her, no matter how hard he tries."

"Hmm." Recalling Philip's words, Antonia stood and shook out her skirts. "Come—help me choose what to wear. Once I've changed, we must see what we can do to brighten you up a trifle." When this projected endeavour raised no gleam of response, Antonia added, "I should warn you that Ruthven is something of an authority on the subject of feminine attire. If I were you and wished to retain my standing in his eyes, I would not appear at dinner less than well presented.''

Catriona frowned. ''He does seem well disposed.''

''Indeed. And if anyone can assist you and Henry, it is he.'' As she sailed across the chamber, Antonia added, somewhat acidly, ''I can attest that his experience in arranging clandestine meetings is beyond compare.''

As it transpired, that was to be her one and only allusion to what lay between herself and Philip. Absorbed in reinflating Catriona's confidence while simultaneously considering all possible avenues the Countess might attempt to gain her ends, she had no time to dwell on her husband-to-be's unfortunate tendencies.

When she met him in the drawing-room two hours later, she made not the slightest demur when he possessed himself of her hand, kissed it, then settled it on his sleeve. The drawing-room was a cold and sombre chamber, designed on the same grandiose scale as the hall, its walls hung with a dark, heavily embossed paper, the ornately carved furniture upholstered in thick black-brown velvet. A small fire in an enormous grate struggled unsuccessfully to dispel the gloom.

Quelling a shiver, Antonia drew closer to Philip, conscious of the aura of safety emanating from his large, familiar frame. Catriona, who had entered with her, reluctantly responded to an imperious summons; haltingly, she made her way to the Countess's side, to where Ambrose, looking pale and uncomfortable, stood beside his mama.

Leaning towards Philip, Antonia murmured, ''Catriona told me what occurred last night.''

Glancing down, Philip frowned. ''Last night?''

Antonia blinked, then briefly outlined Catriona's tale. ''It's no wonder, after that, that she appears so moped. I believe she feels helpless.'' Looking up, she saw Philip's jaw firm, his gaze fixed on the unconvincing tableau the Countess had assembled by the *chaise*.

"If I wasn't convinced Miss Dalling deserved our support, I would have you—and Henrietta—out of here within the hour."

His clipped accents left little doubt as to his temper. Antonia studied his stern profile. "What should we do?"

Philip met her gaze, then grimaced. "Stall. Place hurdles in the gorgon's path." He looked again at the group about the *chaise*. "At the moment, that's the only thing we can do. Until we see our way clear, I would suggest the less time Miss Dalling spends in the Marquess's orbit, the better."

Antonia nodded. "Apparently Mr Fortescue remained in town with the intention of making a last push at securing the Earl's support. I understand he believes that it must be the Earl, not the Countess, who is her legal guardian."

"That's very likely." Glancing down, Philip met her gaze. "But from what I know of the Earl, that legal nicety will have precious little practical significance."

"You don't believe he'll consent to come to Catriona's aid?"

"I don't believe he'll stir one step from the safety of his club." Looking again at the Countess, resplendent in bronzed bombazine, a turban of gold cloth perched atop her frizzed curls, her eagle eye cold and openly calculating, Philip grimaced. "Entirely understandable, unfortunately."

The butler, Scalewether, entered on the words. Tall and ungainly, possessed of a distressingly sallow complexion, in his regulation black he resembled an undertaker without the hat. "Dinner is served, m'lady."

At the Countess's urging, Ambrose, all but squirming, led the way, Catriona a martyr on his arm. With suave grace, Philip followed, leading Antonia. He guided her into the echoing dining room, a chamber so immense the walls remained in shadow.

To Antonia's relief, the table had had most of its leaves removed, leaving space for only twelve. The Countess, sweeping all before her, took her seat at its head; the Marchioness haughtily claimed the foot. Henrietta was graciously waved to a seat beside the Countess. Having claimed Geoffrey's arm from the drawing-room, the Marchioness kept hold of him, placing him to her right. Which left Ambrose and Catriona on one side of the table; Antonia felt an undeniable surge of relief when Philip took his seat beside her.

The meal had little to recommend it, the conversation even less. Dominated by the Countess, aided and abetted by the Marchioness, it remained in stultifyingly boring vein. As her hostess droned on, Antonia studied the servitors who, under the direction of the cadaverous Scalewether, silently set the dishes before them.

She had rarely seen such a crew of shifty-eyed, soft-footed men. Crafty, watchful eyes followed every move made by their mistress's guests. As she attacked a custard, unpalatably tough, Antonia told herself she was being fanciful—that their constant surveillance was simply the outward sign of conscientious staff trying to anticipate their masters' needs.

From under her lashes, she watched Scalewether watching Catriona and Ambrose. There was patience and persistence in his unemotional gaze. Antonia felt her skin crawl.

"I must say, Ruthven, that I had thought you would hold a much stricter line in shouldering your new responsibilities." The Countess fixed Philip with a steely eye. "I believe, my lord, that the university term is well advanced."

Languid urbanity to the fore, Philip briefly touched his napkin to his lips, then, sitting back in his chair, regarded the Countess blandly. "Indeed, ma'am. But as the Master of Trinity acknowledged in his most recent communication, we must make allowance for the natural talents of a Mannering." Philip bestowed a swift glance on Geoffrey before turning back to the Countess. "It's my belief the Master thinks to restore the *status quo* by having Geoffrey start later than most.''

Geoffrey grinned.

The Countess humphed discouragingly. ''That's all very well, but I cannot say I am at all in favour of letting young people go idle. It's tempting providence and all manner of mischief. While I say nothing to your belief that the boy should gain experience of the *ton,* I profess myself astonished to find him here, amongst us still.'' Her bosom swelling as she drew in a portentous breath. ''Not, of course, that we are not perfectly happy to have him here. But I am nevertheless at a loss to account for your laxity, Ruthven.''

Antonia glanced at Philip. He was reclining gracefully in his chair, long fingers stroking the stem of his wine glass. His expression was a mask of polite affability. His gaze was as hard as stone.

''Indeed, ma'am?''

For a defined instant, the soft question hung in the air. The Countess shifted, suddenly wary yet unquenchably belligerent.

Philip smiled. ''In that case, it's perhaps as well you won't be called upon to do so.''

Antonia held her breath; across the table, she caught Geoffrey's decidedly militant eye. Almost imperceptibly, she shook her head at him.

Stricken silence had engulfed the table; the Countess broke it, setting down her spoon with a decided click. ''It's time we ladies retired to the drawing-room.'' Majestically, her expression haughtily severe, she rose, fixing Philip with a baleful eye. ''We will leave you gentlemen to your port.'' With a regal swish of her skirts, she led the way.

As she rose to follow, Antonia caught Philip's eye. He raised a brow at her. Quelling a smile, Antonia followed in their hostess's wake.

In the drawing-room, Catriona was banished to the pianoforte with instructions to demonstrate her skill. Visibly tired, Henrietta reluctantly summoned Trant; with polite smiles and nods—and one very direct glance for Antonia—she retired. Reduced to the role of unnecessary cypher, Antonia duly sat mum and counted the minutes.

She had lost count and Catriona was flagging before the gentlemen reappeared. They were led by Philip, who strolled into the room as if it was his own. With a glib smile, he appropriated her as if she, too, was his.

Antonia told herself she bore it only because she was all but bored witless. "What now?" she asked *sotto voce,* watching as, beneath the cool glare of his mother's eye, Ambrose dragged his feet to the piano.

Philip took the scene in one comprehensive glance. "Speculation."

Stunned, Antonia stared. "You can't be serious?"

He was—before her astonished eyes, he overrode all resistance, somehow inducing Scalewether to produce a pack of cards and counters to serve as betting chips. Ambrose, grasping at straws, hurried to set up a small table and chairs. Within ten minutes, the five of them were seated around the table, leaving the two older ladies isolated by the fireplace.

One glance at the Countess was enough for Antonia; thereafter, she studiously avoided their hostess's basilisk stare.

"Five to me."

Philip's demand focused her attention on the game. "Five?" Antonia studied the cards laid on the table, then sniffed. She doled out the required counters, then reached for the pack. She won three back, but her stack of counters was steadily eroded, falling prey to Philip's ruthless machinations. He was, apparently, a past master at this pastime, too.

Reaching for the pack, Antonia cast him a disapproving glance. "I admit I had not thought to find you so expert at this game, my lord."

The smile he turned on her made her toes curl.

''I dare say you'll be amazed, my dear, by just how many games I can play.''

Unexpectedly trapped in his gaze, by what she could read in the grey, Antonia froze, her hand, outstretched, hovering above the pack.

''C'mon, Sis—you going to forfeit your turn?''

Geoffrey's words broke the spell. Glancing around, Antonia drew in a quick breath.

''Not,'' Geoffrey continued, ''something I'd advise—if we don't take care, Ruthven's going to wipe us out. We'll have to use our wits if we're to counter his predatory incursions.''

Antonia studied the situation afresh—and discovered he was right. ''Nonsense,'' she declared, straightening and picking up the pack. ''We'll come about.'' She dealt, settled the question of trumps, then turned up her first card; it was the ace of trumps. Smiling, she lifted her chin and glanced Philip's way. ''When opponents believe they're invincible, they're sure to be defeated.''

She received a very direct, definitely challenging look in reply.

Thereafter, the fight was on. Their attention fully engaged, Antonia and Geoffrey combined to counter Philip's steady accumulation of chips, draining his pile at every opportunity. Philip struck back, catching Geoffrey more frequently than Antonia, who, very much on her mettle, took care to cover her back.

Fifteen minutes later, Ambrose edged his chair from the table and somewhat ruefully declared, ''That's my last three counters.''

''I've only got one left,'' Catriona said.

Their comments halted play. Three heads came up; Antonia exchanged a glance with Philip. He grimaced, catching Geoffrey's eye as he pulled out his watch. ''Too early,'' was his verdict.

''Right then.'' Geoffrey seized the pack and dealt.

During the following fifteen minutes, the three endeavoured to lose as many counters as they had earlier won, amidst a great deal of unexpected hilarity.

"Your pile is still a great deal too high, my lord." Magnanimously, Antonia handed six counters to Catriona. "It's my belief you're not trying hard enough."

Removing the pack from her fingers, his hand closing briefly about hers, Philip caught her eye. "Put it down to my having to fight against deeply ingrained habit."

Antonia opened her eyes wide. "Oh?"

"Indeed." Philip held her gaze. "None of my ilk like to lose."

Antonia's eyes widened even more; with an effort, she directed them to the table, to the cards he negligently dealt. "See?" Righteously, she nodded. "A knave. You will have to do better, my lord."

"Once this present distraction is passed, I will endeavour to do so, my dear."

The promise in those words sent a delicious shiver down Antonia's spine. Determined to ignore it, and the breathlessness it evoked, she fought to keep her attention on the cards, aware that Philip's too-perceptive gaze remained on her face.

Salvation came from an unlikely source; the doors opened and Scalewether rolled in the tea-trolley. Summoned to take their cups, they abandoned their game; by unspoken accord, they all remained together, standing in a loose group as they sipped.

Under the direction of her aunt, Catriona dutifully extolled the attractions to be found within the grounds. "The folly is probably the most interesting," she concluded. "It stands by the lake and is quite pretty when it's sunny."

Her tone suggested Newgate would be more appealing.

Antonia caught Philip's eye. "Actually, I'm rather tired." Delicately, she smothered a yawn.

"Doubtless the effects of the drive down." Smoothly,

Philip relieved her of her cup; together with his, he laid it aside. "So enervating," he murmured solicitously as, turning, he met Antonia's gaze. "Travelling in a carriage."

Brows rising haughtily, Antonia turned to Catriona, raising her voice for the benefit of the ladies nearby. "I believe I should retire—perhaps, Miss Dalling, you would care to accompany me?"

"Yes, indeed." Catriona set down her cup.

"Not deserting us yet, are you, miss?" The Countess's gimlet gaze fastened on Catriona's face. "Why, what will the Marquess think of you, leaving him to entertain himself like this?"

"Indeed," the Marchioness of Hammersley opined. "I suspect my son, like any other young gentleman, would be very grateful for your company, Miss Dalling." With a commanding wave, she continued, "The night is quite mild. I dare say a turn on the terrace in the moonlight is just what you young people would like."

"Ah—no. That is..." Aghast, Ambrose goggled at his mother. "Mean to say—"

The Marchioness transfixed him with a penetrating stare. "Yes, Hammersley?" When Ambrose just stared at her, rabbit-like, she enquired, her tone sugar-sweet, "Do you find something objectionable about the notion of strolling her ladyship's terrace?"

"Nothing to say against her ladyship's terrace," Ambrose blurted out. His hand strayed to his neckcloth. "But—"

Philip cut in, his tones dripping with fashionable languor. "Perhaps I should explain, Lady Ticehurst, that Miss Mannering, hailing as she does from Yorkshire, is unaccustomed to finding her way about such..." his graceful gesture encompassed the house about them "...*grand* establishments as your own. I beg you'll allow Miss Dalling to act as her guide. Indeed," he continued, his gaze shifting to Antonia's face, "I must admit the idea of Miss Mannering wandering lost through your corridors quite exercises my imagination.

Dare I hope you'll take pity on her poor sense of direction and allow your niece to accompany her?''

Frowning, the countess shifted on the *chaise*. ''Well…''

''As for Hammersley,'' Philip smoothly continued, ''there's no need to concern yourself over his entertainment. He and I had thought to adjourn to the billiard room.'' Turning, he bestowed an elegantly condescending look on the Marchioness. ''I understand that, due to the late Marquess's early demise, Hammersley has lacked the opportunity to polish his talents in such manly arts as billiards. I had thought, perhaps, to be of some use to him while here.''

The Marchioness's expression blanked. ''Yes, of course. How very kind…'' Her frown grew as her words trailed away.

''So—if you'll excuse us?'' With a supremely graceful bow, Philip turned from the *chaise*. Avoiding Antonia's eye, he captured her hand and placed it on his sleeve. ''Come, Hammersley—let's escort these young ladies to the stairs. Mannering?''

With that, he led the way; in less than a minute, the drawing-room door was shut upon the twin harpies, leaving the rest of them safe in the hall. Pausing at the foot of the stairs to wait for Catriona, Antonia glanced at Philip. ''Quite a *tour de force,* my lord.''

Philip met her gaze; he smiled, deliberately, with the full force of his intent. ''As I told you, my dear, I'm not one who generally loses.'' Raising her hand, he kissed each fingertip, his eyes on hers all the while. ''I suspect you'll be amazed by what forces I can, when moved, bring to bear.''

The ripple of awareness that shivered through Antonia and the soft blush that tinged her cheeks stayed with him long after she retreated up the stairs.

At eight the following morning, Antonia slipped from the lowering bulk of Ticehurst Place and headed for the stables. The sun again ruled the sky; as she entered the low-ceilinged stables, she paused, blinking rapidly. As her vision adjusted, she saw a cap bobbing in a nearby loose box. She hurried forward.

"I'd like a horse, please. As quick as you can." Rounding the end of the open box, Antonia cast a swift glance over the bay the stableman was bridling. "This one will do nicely."

The aged retainer blinked owlishly at her. "Beggin' your pardon, miss." He broke off to tug at his cap. "But this one's for the gentleman."

"Gentleman?" On the instant, Antonia felt her senses shiver. She swung around—to find herself breast to chest with her nemesis. She took a step back, and hauled in a quick breath. "I didn't see you there, my lord."

"Obviously." Philip studied the tinge of colour highlighting her cheekbones, then let his gaze meet hers. "And where are you headed?"

Inwardly, Antonia cursed. She hesitated, then, recognizing the hint of steel beneath the soft grey of his eyes, capitulated. "I was going for a ride."

Philip's brows rose. "Indeed? Then I'll ride with you." Reaching forward, he took hold of her arm and drew her closer, clear of the bay the stableman was turning. "So much more suitable," he murmured, "than a young lady riding alone."

Suppressing a snort, Antonia swallowed the rebuke with what grace she could muster.

"Here you be, sir." The groom came up, leading the bay. He handed the reins to Philip, then turned to Antonia. "Now, miss. I've a nice steady mare that would suit you. Not one as gets overly frisky, so you won't have to panic."

He turned away on the words, heading for the row of boxes across the stables, leaving Philip as the only witness to Antonia's stunned reaction. Horror and outrage mixed freely in her expression, dazed disbelief filled her eyes. Then her jaw firmed.

Philip swallowed his laughter and called to the stableman. "I fear you mistake Miss Mannering's abilities. She's perfectly capable of managing one of your master's hunters. By the look of them, they could do with the exercise."

Frowning, the stableman shuffled back. "I don't rightly know as how I should, sir. Wondrous powerful, the master's hunters."

"Miss Mannering can handle them." Philip felt his face harden. "She's a dab hand at reining in all manner of untamed beasts." Conscious of Antonia's swift glance, he lifted his head and scanned the hunters shifting restlessly in their boxes. "That one." He pointed to a glossy black, every bit as powerful as the bay he had chosen. "Put a side saddle on—I'll take all responsibility."

With a resigned shrug, the stableman headed for the tackroom.

"Come—let's wait in the yard." Taking Antonia's arm, Philip steered her out of the stable, the bay following eagerly.

Antonia glanced about. "I'd thought Geoffrey or Ambrose would be about."

"According to the stableman, they've already gone out. Or should that be 'escaped'?"

Antonia grimaced. "You'll have to admit Ambrose has just cause."

Walking the restive bay, Philip spoke over his shoulder. "You may console yourself with the thought that your brother is doing an excellent job of putting their ladyships' collective noses out of joint."

"Geoffrey?" Antonia frowned. "How?"

"By sticking with Ambrose." When she continued to look bemused, Philip smiled wryly. "I fear Geoffrey is very much the fly in their ladyships' ointment. In case you haven't yet realized, this so-called 'houseparty' was very carefully designed. We each have specific roles: Henrietta, you and me to lend countenance—imagining, of course, that

Henrietta is a like-minded soul who shares their ladyships' proclivities and that you and I will be too involved with each other to notice anything else. Geoffrey's presence, however, has thrown a definite spanner into the works. Although she extended the invitation, the Countess had imagined he'd go up to Oxford after the last of the parties.''

Antonia narrowed her eyes. ''The Countess is a very manipulative woman.''

''Indeed.'' Philip's tone hardened. ''And I do not appreciate being manipulated.''

Antonia shot him a glance, then elevated her chin. ''Nor do I.''

It was Philip's turn to glance suspiciously but Antonia had turned away to greet the sleek black hunter the stableman led forth. Under her direction, the stableman held the horse by the mounting block. Philip inwardly snorted and swung up to the bay's saddle. The instant Antonia had settled her skirts, he turned the bay's head for the fields.

He held back only long enough to ensure Antonia was secure and in command, then loosened his reins, letting the bay's stride eat the distance to the trees on the first hill. They drew into the shade of the outliers of the wood and Philip drew rein. He waited until Antonia brought the restive black up alongside, then fixed her with a distinctly strait look. ''Now—where are you going?''

Inwardly, Antonia grimaced; outwardly, she lifted her chin. ''To meet Mr Fortescue—should he be there to meet.''

''Fortescue?''

''Catriona arranged to meet him at the end of the ride through the woods. He said he'd come to tell her how he'd got on with the Earl. She was to keep watch every day but at present, she's convinced herself no one can save her from the Countess's machinations.''

Annoyance crept into Antonia's voice as she recalled the hours she had spent trying valiantly to raise Catriona's spirits. ''From my previous experience of her, I would not have believed she would give up so easily. I've been telling her she must make a push to secure what she wants from life— that if one really wants something, one has to be prepared to fight for it.''

The bay jibbed; Philip tightened his reins. His eyes, fixed on Antonia, narrowed. ''Indeed.'' He might have said more had another, more immediate realisation not intruded. ''You were on your way to meet a gentleman alone.''

Antonia shot him a frowning glance. ''Only Mr Fortescue.''

''Who happens to be a perfectly personable gentleman some years your senior.''

''Who happens to be all but betrothed to a young lady I regard as a good friend.'' Chin high, Antonia gathered her reins.

Philip held her with his eyes. ''I have to inform you, my dear, that meeting personable gentlemen alone is not the behaviour I expect of Lady Ruthven.''

Antonia held his gaze, her own eyes slowly narrowing, golden glints appearing in the green. Then she hauled on the reins, pulling the black about. ''I am not,'' she replied, decidedly tart, ''Lady Ruthven *yet*.''

With that, she touched her heels to the black's sides and took off through the woods.

Philip watched her go, his eyes slitted, his gaze as sharp as honed steel. Suddenly, he recalled he rode much heavier than she—he couldn't let her get too far ahead. With a curse, he set out in pursuit.

Despite his best efforts, Antonia was still in the lead when the end of the ride hove in sight. It led up to a small knoll at the back of the woods; cresting the rise, Antonia saw a single horseman waiting patiently. Recognizing his square frame, she waved; moments later, she drew up alongside Henry Fortescue.

He returned her greeting punctiliously, nodding as Philip

joined them, then, somewhat glumly, turned to Antonia. "From your presence, I take it all is lost?"

Antonia blinked at him. "Heavens, no! Catriona is too well watched for it to be safe for her to ride out to meet you—Ruthven and I came in her stead."

Ignoring Philip's glance, she smiled brightly and was rewarded with a smile in return.

"Well, that's a relief." Henry's smile faded. "Not that my news holds out any hope."

Philip brought his bay up beside Antonia. "What did the Earl say?"

Henry grimaced. "Unfortunately, things weren't as we thought. There was no legal guardianship established, so the Earl has no real rights in the matter. The Countess assumed Catriona's guardianship by custom, so there's no gainsaying her. Not, at least, until Catriona comes of age—but that's years from now."

"Oh." Despite her earlier optimism, Antonia felt her spirits sink.

"Not that we wouldn't be prepared to wait," Henry went on. "If that was the only way. But the problem is, the Countess has her own row to hoe. And she's not one to let up."

Antonia grimaced. "Indeed not."

Henry drew a deep breath. "I don't know what Catriona will say—or do—when she hears the truth."

Antonia didn't bother to answer; Henry's gloom was contagious.

"Then before we tell her, I suggest we establish the facts ourselves."

Antonia stared at Philip. "What do you mean?"

"I mean that I suspect we have not yet reached the truth." Hands folded over his pommel, Philip raised a brow at her. "I took refuge in the library last night—a little habit of mine, you might recall."

Antonia narrowed her eyes. "So?"

"So, while idly pacing, not having any other distraction to hand, I noticed a family bible on a lectern in one corner. It's a handsome volume. Out of sheer curiosity, I looked at the fly-leaf. It doesn't, as I had imagined, belong to the Earl's family but to the Dallings. Indeed, I imagine it might belong to Catriona as it was certainly her father's before."

Henry frowned. "But what has that to say to oversetting the Countess's schemes?"

"Nothing in itself," Philip acknowledged. "But the information the bible contains bears consideration. Inscribed on the fly-leaf are the recent generations of the Dalling family. The history clearly shows the Countess is one of twins—her only sister is her twin. As is often the case with twin females, there's no distinction made between them—no record of who was born first—that fact is stated explicitly in the bible. So, by my reckoning, Catriona's other aunt would have equal right to act as her guardian by custom."

"Lady Copely!" Henry sat his horse as one stunned. "She's always been Catriona's favourite but she couldn't come to Catriona's father's funeral because one of her children came down with whooping cough. Instead, the Countess arrived and swept Catriona up as if she had the right to do so. Naturally, we all assumed she had."

Philip raised a hand in warning. "We do not, at this stage, know if the Countess acted with Lady Copely's assent. Do you know if Lady Copely would be willing to aid Miss Dalling in marrying as she wishes?"

Henry frowned. "I don't know."

"I do." Eyes bright, Antonia looked at Philip. "I saw Lady Copely's daughter and her husband in town. Catriona told me they had married for love." Blushing lightly, she transferred her gaze to Henry. "Indeed, she told me Lady Copely herself had married for affection, rather than status. From all she said, her ladyship sounds the perfect sponsor for yours and Catriona's future."

"If that's so," Henry mused, "then perhaps Catriona could claim her ladyship's protection?"

Philip nodded. "It seems a likely possibility."

"Well, then!" Fired with newfound zeal, Henry straightened in his saddle. "All that remains is to discover her ladyship's direction and I'll apply to her directly." He looked hopefully at Antonia.

Antonia shook her head. "Catriona never mentioned where Lady Copely lives."

Henry grimaced.

"I suggest," Philip said, "that as Catriona may have information on how best to approach Lady Copely, it would be wise for you to meet with Catriona prior to hunting up her ladyship."

Henry nodded. "I confess I would like to do so. But if she's truly kept close, how will we manage it?"

Dismissively, Philip waved one elegant hand. "A little forethought, a spot of strategic planning and the thing's done. There's a small field, part of an old orchard, at the back of the shrubbery. If you leave your horse in the woods on that side, you should be able to reach it easily. Be there at three this afternoon. The older ladies will be snoozing. I'll arrange for Catriona to be there."

Henry's eagerness was tempered by caution. "But if the Countess keeps watch on her—Catriona said even the servants spy on her—then what hope has she of winning free?"

"You may leave all to me." Philip smiled and gathered his reins. "I assure you the Countess herself will speed her on her way."

Henry managed to look doubtful and grateful simultaneously.

Philip laughed and clapped him on the shoulder. "Three—don't be late."

"I won't be." Henry met Philip's gaze. "And thank you, sir. I can't think why you should put yourself out for us like this, but I'm extremely grateful for your help."

"Not at all." Philip wheeled his mount, collecting Antonia with his gaze. "It's the obvious solution."

With a nod, he clicked his reins; with a wave to Henry, Antonia fell in beside him. Together, they cantered back towards the woods. As they neared the entrance to the ride, Philip slowed and glanced at Antonia's face. She was frowning. "What now?"

From beneath her lashes, she shot him a suspicious glance.

Philip met it, and pointedly raised his brows.

Antonia pulled a face at him. "If you must know," she declared, her accents repressive, "I was recalling telling Catriona that you were a past master at arranging clandestine meetings." With that, she tossed her head, setting her curls dancing, then flicked her reins and entered the ride.

Following on her horse's heels, Philip smiled. Wolfishly.

Chapter Fourteen

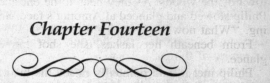

Operating under strict instructions, Antonia said nothing to Catriona regarding her impending salvation. "Her dramatic talents hardly lend themselves to concealment," Philip had drily observed. "The Countess will take one look at her and our goose will be cooked."

Hence, when she took her seat at the luncheon table, Catriona was still in the grip of morose despair. Slipping into the chair beside Philip's, Antonia shot him a reproving glance.

He met it with bland imperturbability, then, turning, addressed the Countess.

The meal passed much as its predecessor, with one notable exception. The previous evening, the conversation had been dominated by the Countess and the Marchioness. Today, Philip set himself to engage, then artfully divert their attention. Applying herself to her meal, Antonia wondered if their ladyships would see the danger therein.

"Indeed." Philip leaned back in his chair, gesturing languidly in response to a comment by the Marchioness on the immaturity of young gentlemen. "It's my contention that until the age of thirty-four, gentlemen understand very little of the real forces extant in the *ton*—the forces, indeed, that will shape their lives."

Antonia choked; glancing up, she caught Henrietta's eye—they both quickly looked elsewhere.

"Quite so." The Countess nodded grimly, her gaze on Ambrose. "Until they have reached the age of wisdom, it behoves them to take all heed of the advice of their elders."

"Indubitably." Across the table, Philip met Henrietta's gaze. He smiled urbanely, a smile his stepmother was unlikely to misconstrue. "So helpful, when others point out the reality of things."

"I can only say I wish more gentlemen had your insight, Ruthven." With that, the Marchioness embarked on a succession of anecdotes illustrating the varied horrors that had befallen young gentlemen lacking such discernment.

By the time the platters were empty, Ambrose was sulking while Catriona had sunk even deeper into gloom. Only Geoffrey, Antonia noticed, appeared oblivious of Philip's defection. She concluded her brother was either too fly to the time of day to believe any such thing, or was already appraised of Philip's plan.

The latter seemed most likely when the Countess leaned forward to demand, "Now—what are your plans for the afternoon?"

"Mr Mannering," Philip replied, "is for his books, I believe?" His gaze rested on Geoffrey, who nodded equably. Philip turned to the Countess. "We discussed the point you made regarding his presence here, rather than at Oxford, and concluded a few hours study each day would be a sound investment against the time when he goes up."

The Countess glowed. "I'm very glad you saw fit to take my advice."

Philip inclined his head. "As for the rest, Miss Mannering and I are for the gardens. They appear quite extensive—a pity to waste this weather indoors. I wondered if the Marquess and Miss Dalling would like to accompany us?"

"I'm sure they would." The Marchioness nodded approvingly, her compelling gaze fixed on her hapless son.

Ambrose hid a grimace, then glanced at Catriona, mute, beside him. "Perhaps…"

"Of course! *Just* the thing!" The Countess weighed in to stamp her seal on the plan. "Catriona will be thrilled to accompany you."

When everyone looked her way, Catriona nodded dully.

Ten minutes later, they left the house by the morning-room windows and headed into the rose gardens. Strolling on Philip's arm, Antonia studied Catriona and Ambrose, drifting aimlessly ahead, feet trailing, shoulders slumped.

"So—what did you think of my superlative strategy?"

Glancing up, she met Philip's eye. "It was, quite definitely, the most sickeningly cloying exhibition of humbug I have ever witnessed."

Philip looked ahead. "There were a few grains of truth concealed amidst the dross."

Antonia snorted. "Flummery, pure flummery, from start to finish. I'm surprised it didn't stick in your throat."

"I have to admit the whole was rather too sweet for my liking, but their ladyships lapped it up, which was, after all, my purpose."

"Ah, yes—your purpose." Antonia longed to ask, point-blank, what that was. It was not, after all, Catriona and Ambrose's problem which had brought him here.

The thought focused her mind on what lay, ignored yet unresolved, between them. As they strolled in the sunlight, largely without words, she had ample time to consider the possibilities and the actualities—and whether she could convert the former to the latter.

Beneath her fingers, she could feel the strength in Philip's arm; as their shoulders brushed, awareness of him enveloped her. Like a well-remembered scent laid down in her memories, he was part of her at some deep, uncomprehended level. And just like such a scent, she longed to capture and hold him, his attention, his affection, precisely as laid down in her mind.

"There you are!"

They halted; turning, they saw Geoffrey striding towards them. "You've been with your books barely an hour," Antonia exclaimed.

"Time enough." Grinning, Geoffrey joined them in the middle of the formal garden. "The three *grande dames* are snoring fit to shake the rafters."

"Good." Philip shifted his gaze to Catriona as she and Ambrose, alerted by Geoffrey's appearance, joined them. "It's time, I believe, that we headed for the shrubbery."

"The shrubbery?" Ambrose frowned. "Why there?"

"So that Miss Dalling can meet with Mr Fortescue and help him with his plan to apply to Lady Copely for aid."

"Henry?" Catriona's eyes blazed. "He's here?" Her die-away dismals dropped from her like a cloak; eyes sparkling, colour flowing into her cheeks, she positively vibrated with suppressed energy. "Where?"

Gesturing towards the shrubbery, Philip raised a cynical brow. "We'll meet him shortly. However, remembering your aunt's servitors—namely the gardener over there—" with a nonchalant wave he indicated a man on a ladder clipping a weeping cherry "—I suggest you restrain your transports until we're in more shielded surrounds."

Catriona, all but dancing with impatience, led the way.

Following more sedately on Philip's arm, Antonia humphed. "You would be hard-pressed to believe that only this morning she was on the brink of a decline."

Entering the shrubbery, screened from prying eyes by the high clipped hedges, Catriona stopped and waited. Philip shooed her on, consenting to halt and explain only when they were well within the protection of the walks.

"The field at the back of the shrubbery," he eventually deigned to inform her. "He'll be there at three." Pulling his watch from his pocket, he consulted it. "Which is now."

With a squeal of delight, Catriona whirled.

"But—" Philip waited until she looked back at him. "Ambrose and Geoffrey will naturally go with you."

That, of course, presented no problem to Catriona. "Come on!" Lifting her skirts, she ran off.

With a laugh, Geoffrey loped in pursuit; dazed, Ambrose hurried after them.

"Just a minute!" Antonia looked at Philip. "Catriona needs a chaperon. She and Ambrose should not be alone at any time—especially now."

Philip took her elbow. "Geoffrey is gooseberry enough. Our appointment lies elsewhere."

"Appointment?" Antonia looked up to see his mask fall away, revealing features hard and uncompromising. His fingers were a steel vice about her elbow. As he guided her inexorably into the maze, she narrowed her eyes. "*This* was what you were planning all along! Not Catriona's meeting, but ours."

Philip shot her a glance. "I'm surprised it took you so long to work that out. While I'm sympathetic enough to Catriona and even Ambrose, though for my money he'd do well to develop a bit more gumption, I have and always have had only *one* purpose in crossing the Countess's benighted threshold."

That declaration and the promise it held—the idea of their impending, very private interview—crystallised Antonia's thoughts and gave strength to her decision—the decision she had only that instant made. They reached the centre of the maze in a suspiciously short space of time. Impelled by a sense of certainty, she barely glanced at the neat lawns of the central square, at the small dolphin gracing the marble fountain at its heart. Determined to have her say—to retain control of the situation long enough to do so—she abruptly halted. Pulling back against Philip's hold, she waited until he turned to face her, brows rising impatiently. Lifting her chin, she declared, "As it happens, I'm very glad of this chance to speak with you alone, for I have to inform you that I've suffered a change of heart."

She looked up—and saw his face drain of all expression. His fingers fell from her elbow. He stilled; she sensed in his immobility the energy of some turbulent force severely restrained.

One of his brows slowly rose. "Indeed?"

Decisively, Antonia nodded. "I would remind you of the agreement we made—"

"I'm relieved you haven't forgotten it."

His flinty accents made her frown. "Of course I haven't. At that time, if you recall, we discussed the role you wished me to fulfil—in essence, the role of a conventional wife."

"A role you agreed to take on."

His voice had deepened; his expression was starkly aggressive. Her lips firming, Antonia stiffly inclined her head. "Precisely. I have also to acknowledge your chivalrous behaviour in allowing me to come to London without formalising or making known our agreement." Gliding towards the fountain, she clasped her hands and turned. Raising her head, she met Philip's gaze, now opaque and impenetrable, squarely. "As it happens, that was likely very wise."

Mute, Philip looked into her wide eyes—and knew what he thought of that earlier decision. He should have kept her at the Manor—acted the tyrant and married her regardless—anything to have avoided this. He could hardly think—he certainly didn't trust himself to speak. He couldn't, in fact, believe what she was saying; his mind refused to take it in. His emotions, however, were already on the rampage.

"Very wise," Antonia affirmed. "For I have to tell you, my lord—"

"Philip."

She hesitated, then stiffly inclined her head. "Philip—that on greater acquaintance with the mores of the *ton,* I have come to the conclusion that I am fundamentally ill-suited to be your wife—at least along the lines we agreed."

That last, thoroughly confusing phrase was, Philip was convinced, the only thing that allowed him to retain any semblance of reason. "What the devil do you mean?" Hands rising to his hips, he glowered at her. "What other lines are there?"

Lifting her chin, Antonia gave him back stare for hard stare. "As I was *about* to explain, I have discovered there are certain...criteria—essential prerequisites, if you will—for carrying off the position of a *ton*nishly comfortable wife. In short, I do not possess them, nor, I have decided, am I willing to develop them. No." Eyes glinting, she defiantly concluded, "Indeed, on the subject of marriage I find I have my *own* criteria—criteria I would require to be fulfilled *absolutely*."

Philip's eyes had not left hers. "Which are?"

Antonia didn't blink. "First," she declared, raising one hand to tick off her points on her fingers. "The gentleman I marry *must* love me—*without reservation*."

Philip blinked. He hesitated, his eyes searching her face, chest swelling as he drew in a slow breath. Then he frowned. "Second?"

Antonia tapped her next finger. "He will *not* have any mistresses."

"Ever?"

She hesitated. "After we are wed," she eventually conceded.

The tension in Philip's shoulders eased. "Third?"

"He cannot waltz with *any other lady*."

Philip's lips twitched; he fought to straighten them. "Not at all?"

"*Never.*" There was no doubt in Antonia's mind on that point. "And last but not least, he should *never* seek to be private with any other lady. *Ever.*" Eyes narrowed, she looked up and met Philip's gaze challengingly, indeed belligerently. "Those are my criteria—if you do not feel you can meet them, then I will, of course, understand."

Abruptly, the reality of that alternative struck home; Antonia caught her breath; pain unexpectedly speared through her.

She looked away, disguising her faltering as a gracious nod. Swinging about to gaze at the fountain, she concluded, her voice suddenly tight, "Just as long as you understand that if such is the case, then I cannot marry you."

Philip had never felt so giddy in his life. Relief so strong it left him weak clashed with a possessiveness he had never thought to feel. Emotions rose and fell like surging waves within him, all dwarfed, subsumed, by one steadfast, rock-like reality. The reality that, despite his understanding, still shook him to the core. Recollection of his customary imperturbability, of the unshakeable impassivity that had, until now—until Antonia—been his hallmark, drifted mockingly through his mind.

Drawing in a steadying breath, he studied her half-averted face. "You were going to marry me regardless. What changed your mind?"

She hesitated so long he thought she would not answer. Then she turned her head and met his gaze openly—directly. "You."

Philip felt his lips twist, and recalled his earlier resolution never to ask such questions of her again; she would always floor him with her honesty. He drew in another deep breath—and recalled his purpose—his one and only purpose in engineering this meeting, in coming to Ticehurst Place. "Before I deal with your criteria—your demands of a prospective husband—there's one pertinent point I wish to make crystal clear."

His features hardening, he caught Antonia's gaze. "Lady Ardale's performance was no fault of mine. I did not encourage her in any way, by any look, word or gesture."

A frown slowly formed in her eyes. "She was in your arms."

"No." Philip held her gaze steadily. "She pressed herself against me—I had to take hold of her to set her away."

A slow blush stained Antonia's cheeks. She looked away. "Your hand was on her breast."

Fleetingly, Philip grimaced. "Not by inclination, I assure you."

His tone held sufficient disgust to have her glancing his way again. Her shocked expression tried his control.

"She…?" Confounded, Antonia gestured.

"Indeed." Philip's lips thinned. "Strange to tell, some ladies are exceedingly forward—and not a little predatory. If you'd remained a moment longer, you would have witnessed her come-uppance."

Antonia's eyes widened. "What happened?"

"She landed on the *chaise*."

Philip saw her lips twitch, saw the beguiling glint of laughter in her eyes. The stiffness that had, until then, afflicted him, eased; he held out his hand. "And now, if you'll come here, I'll endeavour to address the criteria you enumerated so clearly."

Antonia studied his face, uncertain of the undertone in his voice. Slowly, she shook her head—and stepped closer to the fountain. "I would much prefer that we discussed this matter in a business-like way."

Philip opened his eyes at her—and took a strolling step forward. "I intend to be exceedingly business-like. In this case, by my reckoning, that requires having you in my arms."

"There's no sense in that—I can't think while in your arms—as you very well know!" Frowning as disapprovingly as she could, Antonia circled to put the fountain between them; his intent apparent in every graceful stride, Philip followed. Antonia could not miss the devilish gleam in his eyes. Despite her irritation, she still felt a thrill all the way to her toes. "This is ridiculous," she muttered, feeling her heartbeat accelerate, feeling breathlessness slowly claim her. "Philip—stop!" Imperiously, she halted and held up a hand.

Philip took no notice. In two strides he had rounded the fountain.

Antonia's eyes widened. With a smothered squeal, she grabbed up her skirts and ran.

Unfortunately, she was on the wrong side of the fountain to escape the maze.

And Philip was far too fast. He caught her halfway to the hedge, easily lifting her from her feet. He juggled her in his arms, then carried her, struggling furiously in a froth of muslin, to a weathered stone seat with an ample thyme cushion.

He was grateful for that last when he half-sat, half-fell onto it, Antonia squirming on his lap. He could hear her muttering a string of curses; he was so gripped by the urge to laugh triumphantly that he didn't dare try to speak. Instead, he caught her chin in one hand and turned her face to his.

Her eyes met his, green spitting golden chips. In that instant, awareness struck—he saw it catch, felt the sudden hitch in her breathing, saw her eyes widen, her lips soften and part. She stilled, her breasts rising and falling, her gaze trapped in his. The same awareness reached for him, effortlessly drawing him under its spell, even while some remnant of sanity frantically fought to remind him where they were, who they were, and how inappropriate was the spectacle they were about to create. As his head slowly lowered, Philip groaned. "God—I must be as besotted as Amberly."

The realization did not stop him from kissing her, from parting her lips and drinking in her sweetness. Like a man parched, he filled his senses with the taste of her, the feel of her, the heady, dizzying scent of her. Experience stopped him from releasing her curls, from running his hands through her hair. But nothing could stop him from laying her breasts bare, from experiencing again the thrill of her reaction as he caressed her.

Trapped in his arms, caught up in the tide, it took all

Antonia's remaining strength to complain, "You haven't told me your response to my criteria."

"Do you still need telling?"

His fingers shifted; her mind melted. It was some moments before she could muster enough breath to explain, "I did intend to be a comfortable wife for you but I don't think—" Her breathing suspended wholly; weakly, she rushed on, "That I can manage it."

She arched gently in his arms; Philip groaned again. His lips sought hers, then he drew back enough to murmur against their soft fullness, "I never wanted you as a 'comfortable' wife—that was your idea." The words focused his attention on what he was trying very hard to overlook. "As God is my witness, the word 'comfortable' is the very last word I would associate with you. I've been wretchedly *uncomfortable* ever since I walked into the hall at the Manor and saw you come floating down the stairs, the embodiment of my need, the answer to my prayers."

She was, Antonia decided, adapting to his lovemaking; she could actually think enough to take in his words. "Why uncomfortable?"

Philip gave up groaning; he took her hand and showed her.

"Oh." Antonia considered, then glanced at his face. "Is that really uncomfortable?"

"Yes!" Gritting his teeth, Philip caught her hand. "Now shut up and let me kiss you." He did, delighting in her response, setting aside his rehearsed periods until he had recouped all he had missed through the past week of enforced abstinence.

"I saw them go in—they must be at the centre."

Geoffrey's voice came clearly over the hedges.

Philip raised his head, blinking dazedly. Antonia's eyes opened, then flew wide as she took in her state.

Her *"Great heavens!"* was weak with shock.

Philip wasted no time in curses; with practised speed, he

stood, setting Antonia on her feet, steadying her when she swayed. When her hands fluttered over the halves of her open bodice, he swatted them away. "No time—let me. They're only three turns away."

Her head still spinning, Antonia watched in bemused fascination as he did up her buttons with a speed that would have left Nell stunned, then straightened her skirts and settled the lace about her neckline.

Philip barely had time to settle his coat before Catriona rushed into the square, Geoffrey and Ambrose on her heels.

"He was there! Henry told me of your suggestion—Aunt Copely will help, I *know* she will." Eyes gleaming, smile beaming, Catriona was again the stunning beauty of the early weeks of their acquaintance. "It's so wonderful, I could cry!" With that unnerving declaration, she flung her arms about Antonia and hugged her wildly.

"At the risk of appearing a wet blanket, I suggest you restrain your transports, my child." Suavely, Philip settled his cuffs. "If you float into the house at your present elevation, the Countess is likely to puncture your hopes."

"Oh, don't worry." Exuberant, Catriona let go of Antonia to clutch Philip's hand and press it between her own. "I can take care of her—when we go back to the house, I'll be so down in the mouth she'll never suspect we're hatching a plot."

Smiling, pleased to see Catriona so restored, Antonia glanced at Geoffrey, only to discover a quizzical, somewhat speculative look in his eye. As she watched, a slow, oddly knowing smile curved his lips.

To her intense mortification, Antonia felt a blush steal into her cheeks. She shifted her gaze to Catriona. "So, is Mr Fortescue off to plead your case to Lady Copely?"

"Yes!" Catriona beamed delightedly. "And—"

"All's right and tight," Geoffrey remarked. "But we shouldn't discuss anything here—one of the gardeners might overhear. And it's getting on for tea-time. If we don't want to be caught conspiring by one of those odious footmen, we'd better get back to the house.''

"Indeed." There was enough frustrated resignation in Philip's tone to draw a glance from both Mannerings. Philip offered Antonia his arm. "I greatly fear your brother is right." As they all turned towards the exit from the maze, Catriona going ahead with Ambrose, practising her die-away airs, Philip murmured for Antonia's ears alone, "We'll continue our interrupted discussion later."

Exchanging glances, neither he nor Antonia noticed Geoffrey hanging back in their shadow, his gaze, shrewdly pensive, on them.

By the time they regained the front hall, Philip had re-evaluated the amenities of Ticehurst Place. While the others continued into the drawing-room where the Countess was regally dispensing tea and cakes, he held Antonia back long enough to whisper, "The library—after they've all settled for the night."

Antonia glanced up at him, meeting his gaze squarely. She read the promise in his eyes. Her heart swelled; letting her lids veil her eyes, she inclined her head. "In the library tonight."

Chapter Fifteen

Night fell. In her chamber, Antonia paced impatiently, waiting for the great house to fall silent, waiting for the last of the servitors to retreat to their quarters and leave the mansion to its ghosts. She felt certain there'd be some lost souls haunting the gorgon's lair; the thought did not trouble her. Philip had yet to reply to her criteria; nothing—not even a ghost—was going to prevent her from hearing his response, from hearing the words she longed to hear.

After their interlude in the shrubbery, she was perfectly confident of the substance of his reply. Confidence, however, was no substitute for direct experience.

Kicking her skirts about, she turned, then paused. A door along the corridor creaked open, then shut. Ears straining, she made out the heavy, measured tread of Trant's footsteps retreating to the servants' stair; Henrietta had, at last, settled for the night. Soon, she could risk going down.

Deciding another ten minutes' wait would be wise, she crossed to the window seat. Catriona's histrionic talents had risen to the challenge of gulling both the Marchioness and the Countess. Neither eagle-eyed lady had batted an eyelid; neither had seen anything in Catriona's drooping stance, in her lacklustre gaze, to alert them.

Crossing her arms on the sill and resting her chin upon

them, Antonia gazed out at the moon-silvered gardens. If Catriona could keep up her charade, then Henry would have time to mobilise Lady Copely. Doubtless, if all was as Catriona had said, Lady Copeley would visit and rescue her from the Countess's talons.

Finding a certain delight in that prospect, Antonia smiled. Catriona's problems would soon be at an end; for herself, resolution was at hand. Love, despite her doubts, would reign triumphant. Her gaze on the shifting shadows, her lips curving gently, she let her mind slide into pleasurable anticipation.

The clip-clop of horses' hooves jerked her back to reality. Straightening, she leaned forward and peered out, just in time to glimpse a gig being driven down the drive at a brisk trot. There were two figures on the seat; as she watched, the smaller, the passenger, a large package clasped in her arms, turned and gazed back at the house. Catriona's heart-shaped face was instantly recognisable.

Stunned, Antonia looked again; the second figure was wearing a white drab driving coat. "*Merciful heavens!* What *are* they up to?"

For five full seconds, she sat transfixed, listening to the hoofbeats grow fainter. Then, with a muttered curse, she grabbed a cloak from the wardrobe, pausing only to swing it about her shoulders before quietly opening her door.

She paid not the slightest attention to the deep shadows, to the gloom that pervaded the darkened house. Not even the suit of armour, shrouded in Stygian shadow on the landing, had the power to make her pause. Hurrying as fast as she dared, she reached the bottom of the stairs; her evening slippers skidded on the polished hall tiles. With a valiantly smothered shriek, Antonia grabbed the newel post just long enough to right herself, then, in a flurry of silk skirts, she dashed down the corridor.

Pacing before the fire in the library dutifully rehearsing his lines, Philip heard the scratch and slide of Antonia's feet on the tiles. The odd sound she made had him heading for the door. He opened it in time to see her pale skirts, visible beneath the hem of her cloak, disappear around a distant corner.

Mystified, he followed.

The turning she had taken led to the garden hall; when he reached it, the door to the gardens stood wide. Frowning, wondering if, by some mischance, she had thought to meet him in the maze, Philip stepped into the night. The gardens were a mass of moonlight and shadow, the gentle breeze creating a fantastical landscape of shifting shapes. Antonia was nowhere to be seen. His frown deepening, Philip strode towards the shrubbery.

He'd reached the centre of the maze when the sound of hoofbeats and the rattle of carriage wheels reached him. For one incredulous instant, he stood stock-still, then he swore.

And ran for the stables.

Skidding to a halt in the stableyard, he caught a glimpse of his greys drawing his phaeton—his *high-perch* phaeton— disappearing at a rattling clip down the drive. Of the identity of the figure holding the reins he had not the slightest doubt.

Cursing fluently, Philip plunged into the dark stables.

By the time he'd saddled the chestnut he'd ridden the previous day, Antonia had a good start on him. Halting at the end of the drive, he scanned the fields—and caught sight of her, tooling his horses at a spanking pace along a straight stretch of lane hugging an already distant ridge. Jaw clenched, his face like stone, Philip set off in pursuit.

Feathering the next corner, Antonia checked the skittish greys. The road ahead was deeply shadowed; she couldn't see if there were potholes. Grimacing, she kept the reins tight as she guided the greys on, inwardly praying the horses, occasionally as devilish as their master, would behave.

Always eager, they had let her pole them up without fuss; luckily, the phaeton was so light she'd been able to manoeuvre it easily. Harnessing had taken longer but she'd forced herself to do it carefully, comforting herself with the reflection that Philip's horses would easily overtake the single beast Geoffrey had put to the gig.

It was only then, as she tightened the final buckles, that she remembered Philip, waiting for her in the library. Focused on protecting Catriona and Geoffrey, used to acting on her own, she had not, until then, considered the possibility of throwing herself on her husband-to-be's chest and demanding he fix things. Grimacing, she hesitated, only to decide she couldn't afford the time to retrace her steps and tell Philip what she'd seen. She couldn't risk Geoffrey getting too far ahead; she was certain Philip had no more idea of what was afoot than she.

Her memory replayed Geoffrey's words in the maze, the odd glance he, Catriona and Ambrose had shared as they'd prepared to retire. She had a strong suspicion her brother had guessed what was in the wind between herself and Philip—and had decided to leave them undisturbed while he and Catriona brought off whatever mad scheme they'd hatched.

Emerging from the shadowed stretch, Antonia set the greys up a long hill. Looking up, she glimpsed the gig, Geoffrey and Catriona in silhouette as they topped the rise ahead. They sank from view; with a muttered curse, Antonia clicked the reins. The gig was more stable than the phaeton; Geoffrey was not having to be as cautious as she. Despite the greys' superiority, the distance between them and the gig had not decreased.

Driving as fast as she dared, she sent the phaeton rushing up the hill. There were lanes aplenty—she had no idea which way they were headed. The thought of the likely outcome if their plans, whatever they might be, went awry, and Geoffrey and Catriona ended spending the night essentially alone, spurred her on, the spectre of the Countess as a relative-by-marriage at her back.

Pushing the greys to the limit of safety, she topped the rise, then rattled on down the slope.

Labouring in her wake, Philip had run through his repertoire of curses. While he presumed his intended had a reason for rushing off into the night, he did not, he had decided, actually care what it was. What he did care about was her safety and the sublime disregard for his tender sensibilities she was presently displaying. Gritting his teeth, he urged the chestnut on. Catching up with his greys was out of the question; all he could hope for was to keep Antonia in sight until she reached her destination.

Once he caught up with her, the rest, he felt sure, would follow naturally.

He quite clearly recalled telling her he would never consent to her risking her neck; he quite clearly recalled warning her not to even *think* of so doing. She had evidently not believed him.

He would make the matter plain—along with a few other points.

"All I want is to tell the damn woman that I love her!"

The wind whipped away the growled words. Gripped by frustration, Philip set the chestnut up the hill.

He pulled up at the top, briefly scanning the valley below. He saw Antonia in his phaeton—and for the first time glimpsed the carriage she was following.

"What the devil…?" Philip frowned. He was too far away to make out the figures in the gig but he could guess who they were. Shaking the reins, he took to the fields, shaving a little off Antonia's lead in the descent from the ridge. But once they gained the flat, not knowing which way they would turn, he was forced to keep to the roads.

Ahead of him, Antonia had managed to draw closer to the gig, but it was still too far distant for her to hail it. Given the state of the country lanes, she'd given up hope of catching Geoffrey this side of a main road. Having assumed his intention was to deliver Catriona to Lady Copely, she was surprised to see him check, then turn the gig under the gateway of what appeared to be an inn.

The small town the inn served lay beyond it, nestled in a hollow, its residents no doubt slumbering soundly. Perched halfway down the slope overlooking the town, the inn looked to be substantial, a solid structure in stone with a good slate roof.

Filled with relief, Antonia whipped up the greys and forged on, drawing rein only to enter the innyard.

A sleepy, middle-aged ostler was leading away the gig. His eyes widened, whether in alarm or understandable surprise Antonia had no time to wonder as she wrestled the greys to a snorting halt.

"Here—take them." She flung the reins at the ostler, grateful when he caught them. Scrambling down from the box-seat with what decorum she could, she added, "And...er...do whatever needs to be done. They're quite valuable."

"Aye, mum." Stupefied, the ostler nodded.

Waiting for no more, Antonia hurried into the inn. The door was unlatched; there was no sign of the host but a lighted candle stood on a wooden table at the back of the hall. Her attention caught by wavering light from above, Antonia glanced up the dark stairwell in time to see shadows, thrown by candlelight, flung up against a wall. The shadows disappeared as their owners continued down one of the upstairs corridors.

Antonia grabbed the candle from the table and followed.

When she gained the head of the stairs, there was no one in sight. Following the corridor she was sure Geoffrey and Catriona had taken, she paused outside each door to place her ear against the panel. She heard nothing more than snores and snorts until she came to the last door, right at the end of the corridor.

Gruff voices rose and fell; others spoke but she could not make out their words. Antonia frowned—then glanced at the door to her right. Ear against the panel, she listened carefully but no sound came from within. Holding her breath, she gently eased the latch free. Pushing the door open, she warily raised her candle.

The room was empty. With a sigh of relief, she whisked herself in and shut the door firmly. Glancing about, she saw another door, set into the wall shared with the last room—the one on which she wished to eavesdrop. Thanking her stars, she set the candle down on a tallboy and gently eased the door open.

Beyond lay a small space, the space between the thick walls, bound by another door. As the voices beyond reached her easily, Antonia surmised this last door opened directly into the room at the end of the corridor.

"I knows as how that was what you asked for, but, like Josh here said, it ain't what you're getting."

The owner of the gruff voice sounded the opposite of refined. He also sounded smugly threatening. Antonia heard Geoffrey answer but her brother's accents were too measured, too controlled, for her to catch what he said. Grimacing, she carefully gripped the knob of the door; breath bated, she turned it until she felt the latch give, then eased the door open the merest fraction.

"Ain't no point arguing no more," came a second, very deep, distinctly menacing voice. "The whelp over there got us here—you've heard our price. T'my way of thinkin', it's take it or leave it."

A whispered conference was the result. Carefully releasing the knob, Antonia leaned as close as she dared to the open door, her senses straining to pick up her brother's and Catriona's words.

A hand came over her shoulder, fastening over her mouth; an arm slid about her waist, hauling her back, locking her against a very large, very hard, definitely masculine body.

Eyes starting from her head, Antonia went rigid.

Then relaxed—and tugged at the hand over her lips.

Philip eased his hold, bending his head to growl directly into her ear, *"What the devil are you doing here?"*

Antonia ignored his tone—and all it promised. Pressing her head back into his shoulder, she managed to catch his eye—she decided to ignore the fury she saw there, too. With her own eyes, she indicated the room beyond the door. "Listen," she mouthed.

"My friend here hired you—you agreed on a sum to take us to London."

Antonia's eyes widened. She tugged again at Philip's hand. "That was Mr Fortescue."

Philip flicked her a warning glance. "Shh."

"Aye, that we did," came in gloating tones. "But that was afore we realized there'd be a young miss making one of your party. The way we figures it, now we knows the score, is that it's got to be worth a great deal more to you to make the trip to Lunnon. What with the pretty young miss an' all."

"Mind," came in the other, even more disturbing voice. "If'n you're pressed for the ready, there's likely other ways we'd agree to take our cut."

Antonia suppressed a shiver.

The suggestion gave rise to a muted discussion centred on the far end of the room.

A long-suffering sigh distracted Antonia. Glancing up and back, she saw Philip close his eyes fleetingly. When he opened them, Antonia saw his jaw firm. Before she could speak, he lifted her bodily and set her back against the narrow side wall of the tiny space they shared.

"Stay there." His eyes boring into hers, Philip put all the dire warning he could into his necessarily muted tones. "Do not move."

"What—?"

"And be *quiet!*"

Suppressing the urge to sniff disdainfully, Antonia did as he said.

Settling his coat with a deft flexing of his shoulders, Philip grasped the door knob and calmly walked into the room.

As he had surmised, the two hulking coachmen had their backs to him; beyond, a quartet of surprised faces stared at him, thoroughly stunned. The door had been well-oiled; no squeak had given him away. The room was furnished with a large square rug, muting the sound of his footsteps. The villainous coachmen had not heard him.

Predictably, Geoffrey was the first to find his wits. Shifting his gaze back to the coachmen, he glibly stated, "Actually, I don't think you've quite taken our measure. We have powerful backers you might not care to cross."

"Ho! That's a good one," the larger of the coachmen jeered. "Very likely, that is, with you three and the young miss making your getaway in the dead of night."

"Indeed, I fear I must agree with our friend here," Philip remarked in his finest Bond Street drawl. "I must admit the point mystifies me—you'll really have to explain to me, Geoffrey, why you saw fit to haul your sister out in the dead of night."

Both coachmen froze—they exchanged sideways glances, then the heavier of the two swung about, huge fists rising. He never saw the clip that caught him on the jaw and laid him out upon the rug. The second coachman came in, arms flailing. Philip ducked, caught his assailant with hip and shoulder and threw him across the room. He landed with a resounding thud against one wall, then slid slowly down to slump on the floor.

Philip waited, but neither villain was in any condition for further argument.

"Great heavens! I never knew you boxed."

Straightening, automatically resetting his coat, Philip glanced over his shoulder; Antonia stood a mere foot behind him, a heavy candlestick in one upraised hand. Lips compressed, he reached out and took the candlestick. "I told you to stay put."

She met his gaze openly. "If you'd told me you boxed, I would have."

"My boxing prowess had not previously figured in my mind as an inducement to wifely obedience," Philip heard himself say—he had to fight an urge to close his eyes and groan.

Catriona arrived to fling herself into Antonia's arms; in the same instant, a furious pounding came on the door.

"Open up in there! This is a respectable inn, I'll have you know."

"The landlord," Geoffrey somewhat unnecessarily remarked.

Philip directed a feeling look at the ceiling. "Why me?" He didn't wait for an answer but strode to the door, indicating with one long finger that Geoffrey and Henry should pick up one comatose coachman.

As they struggled to lift their burden, Philip opened the door. "Good evening. I'm Ruthven. You, I take it, are the landlord?"

With glowing approval, Antonia listened as Philip glibly explained how his wards, never specified, and their friends had decided to return to town rather than remain at a nearby houseparty and had, for reasons he did not deign to clarify, decided to meet with the coachmen they had hired at the inn, rather than at the residence they had visited, only to be grossly deceived in the character of their hired help.

Under Philip's artful direction, the innkeeper professed all sympathy, agreeing, as they all did, that it was exceedingly fortunate that, responding to the note his wards had sent him, Philip had arrived in the nick of time to rout the villains.

By this time, the villains had been hauled out of the inn and left groaning in the ditch. Catriona, truly rattled, had been soothed.

Having arranged to hire the inn's own coach and the services of a groom and coachman, both of whom needed to be roused from their slumbers at a nearby farm, Philip repaired to the inn's parlour, where, at his suggestion, his party now waited. Shutting the door firmly on the reassured innkeeper, he swept the gathering with a jaundiced eye. "Would one of you care to explain precisely what is going on?"

As intrigued as he, Antonia glanced at the younger members of the party.

Catriona's expression instantly turned mulish. Ambrose squirmed, looking even more gormless than usual. Henry Fortescue reddened, then cleared his throat.

Geoffrey spoke first. "It's straightforward enough—or at least, our plan was. Catriona's sure Lady Copely will take her in and support her in marrying Henry."

"I remembered that Aunt Copely came to visit," Catriona put in. "Quite early on, just after I'd joined Aunt Ticehurst's household. I was banished to my room throughout but I overheard the maids saying that there'd been the most awful row. Aunt Copely must have wanted to see me—if I'd known Aunt Ticehurst didn't have any legal right to insist I stay with her, I'd have gone to Aunt Copely long ago."

"Given that," Geoffrey continued, "there didn't seem much point in going to inform Lady Copely *then* returning to Ticehurst Place to rescue Catriona, particularly if the gorgon was going to keep on trying to marry her to Ambrose."

"We decided that if we four all went up to town together, there'd be no question of impropriety," Henry explained. He glanced at Ambrose. "Hammersley did not wish to remain at Ticehurst Place—particularly not after their ladyships discover Catriona's disappearance. He volunteered to hire the coachmen—unfortunately, they turned out to be less than honest."

Ambrose grimaced. "Didn't want to go to any of the local

places—they might have got back to Lady Ticehurst. Found a hedge-tavern—those two were the best I could find.''

Philip raised a long-suffering brow.

''Never mind—as it fell out, there was no real harm done.'' Antonia smiled reassuringly. ''Thanks to Ruthven,'' she added as Philip turned his gaze on her.

''Indeed, my dear—but I have yet to hear *your* reasons for mounting such a dangerous pursuit.''

The comment focused all eyes on Antonia; realizing that none other than Philip knew she had taken his horses and phaeton, she kept her expression serenely assured. ''I caught sight of Geoffrey and Catriona leaving in the gig. Naturally, not knowing their plan, I hurried after them.''

Philip pondered that ''naturally''. ''You didn't, perchance, consider informing me?''

His tone was mild, perfectly polite; Antonia sensed the steel behind it. ''I did consider the matter,'' she felt forced to admit. ''But by the time the thought occurred, the gig was too far ahead to risk further dallying.''

''I see.'' Philip's gaze, narrowing, remained locked on hers.

''I remembered the bible.''

Catriona's comment distracted them both. They turned to see her hefting a brown paper-wrapped package from the table. ''It *was* Papa's; if it contains the proof of Aunt Copley's right to act as my guardian, I thought I should keep it by me.''

Philip nodded approvingly. ''A wise move.'' He hesitated, then grimaced. ''Very well—we'll continue with your plan. I agree that if all four of you travel together, there'll be no hint of impropriety. And I can sympathise with Hammersley not wanting to be about when the Countess and his mother discover their applecart has been ditched. Apropos of which, might I ask how you were proposing to convey that news?''

Four blank faces stared at him.

"We hadn't imagined informing them specifically," Geoffrey finally said. He caught Philip's eye. "We thought you'd be there—and you'd guess what was up if we all went missing."

For a long moment, Philip held Geoffrey's gaze, his own distinctly jaundiced, then his expression turned resigned. "Very well—I suppose I can settle that matter, too."

The relief in the parlour was palpable.

Twenty minutes later, Philip watched the four young people climb into the inn's carriage. Geoffrey was the last.

"Here's a note for Carring." Philip handed over a folded missive. "He'll pay the carriage off and see you to the coaching station. Write once you've settled in—we'll be at the Manor."

"Oh?" Waving a last farewell to Antonia, standing back in the inn porch, Geoffrey looked again at Philip, a question in his eyes.

Philip raised a languid brow. "*And,* given you're the senior male in the Mannering line, I suspect you'd better hold yourself ready to make a dash down—just for a day or two, considering how much of the term you've already missed. I'll send up to the Master."

Geoffrey's grin broke into a huge smile. "Thought so." He clapped Philip on the shoulder, then mounted the steps. Philip shut the carriage door; Geoffrey leaned out of the window to add, insouciantly irreverent to the end, "Don't let her get her hands on your reins."

"Not bloody likely," was Philip's terse reply.

The carriage rumbled out of the yard. Philip turned and strode back to the inn. The innkeeper was waiting just behind Antonia, his keys in his hand.

Taking Antonia's elbow, Philip guided her into the inn. "You may lock up, Fellwell. Her ladyship and I can find our way up."

Antonia's eyes flew wide; Fellwell, yawning as he bowed, did not notice. Steered inexorably up the stairs, she heard the heavy inn door close, heard the bolts shoot home. Her heart started to pound. By the time they reached the door to the inn's main guest chamber, she felt quite giddy.

Opening the door, Philip guided her through, then followed, shutting the door behind him. His face was all hard angles and planes; no hint of his social mask remained.

"Ah...does Mr Fellwell believe we're married?"

"I sincerely hope so." Shifting his grip to her hand, Philip strolled forward, surveying the room. "I told him you were Lady Ruthven." Satisfied with their accommodation, he stopped before the fireplace, turning to meet Antonia's wide gaze. "I couldn't think of any other way to acceptably explain your presence here—alone—with me." He cocked a brow at her. "Can you?"

Antonia was sure she couldn't; breathless, she shook her head.

"If we're agreed on that," Philip said, shifting to stand directly before her, "before anything *else* can happen to distract us, I suggest that I give you my responses to your stipulations on your future husband's behaviour."

Releasing her hand, he raised both of his to frame her face, tilting it up until her eyes locked with his. "Lastly but by no means least, you required that the man you married should not seek to be private with any other lady." He raised a brow. "Why would I wish to be alone with another, if I could, instead, have you by my side?"

Eyes wide, Antonia searched his grey gaze; it was calm, clear, unclouded, as incisive as tempered steel.

"And as for not waltzing with any other lady—if you were there to waltz with me, why would I wish to dance with another?"

Inwardly, Antonia frowned.

"And as for mistresses—" Philip raised a suggestive brow. "If I had you to warm my bed, to satisfy my needs, would I want—or, indeed, have time for—a mistress?"

Disregarding the blush that warmed her cheeks, Antonia

raised a brow back. ''Your responses are questions, not answers.''

Philip's lips twisted. ''Imponderable questions, my love. For which the answers lie, all encompassed, in my response to your first criterion.''

Antonia felt his strength reach for her, even though his hands remained about her face. His head lowered slightly, his lips hovering tantalisingly above hers. Lifting her gaze from them, she studied his eyes, watched as desire slowly pushed aside the curtain of steel, darkening his gaze. Her ''My first criterion?'' came on a breathless whisper.

Philip smiled; the gesture did not soften his expression. ''I hoped you would know without needing to be told.'' His eyes held hers; his chest swelled as he drew in a steadying breath. ''God—and half the *ton*— know I love you.'' He searched her eyes, then added, his voice deepening, ''Unreservedly, without restraint, far more completely, deeply, *madly* than I suspect is at all wise.''

Antonia stared back at him, the words ringing in her ears, in her head, in her heart. Her welling joy showed in her eyes; Philip bent his head and kissed her, the caress direct and deeply intimate.

When he raised his head, she had to fight for breath. ''Wise?''

She watched the steel flow back into his eyes, clashing with turbulent desire. He raised one brow slowly, his jaw firming ominously.

''Indeed.'' His tones were suddenly clipped. ''Which brings us to your escapade tonight.'' His hands fell from Antonia's face, only to slip about her waist.

She blinked. ''That was Geoffrey's and Catriona's escapade, not mine.''

Philip's eyes narrowed. ''No more Mannering logic—I've heard quite enough for one night.''

A log crashed in the grate, sending up a shower of sparks; with a muttered curse, Philip reluctantly released Antonia and bent to resettle the logs. Antonia glided a few steps away, out of his immediate reach. He straightened and set aside the firetongs; his eyes narrowed when he saw where she was. "I was referring to your appropriation of my phaeton."

Antonia took due note of the glint in his eye. "You did offer to let me drive it." An armchair stood conveniently before the hearth; she drifted around it.

"I offered to let you take the reins in town, on a Macadamised surface, with me on the box-seat beside you—*not* on a deserted country lane in the dead of night with the road obscured by shadows!" Philip stalked after her; catching her wide gaze, he transfixed her with a distinctly strait look. "See what I mean about wise?" He made the comment through set teeth. "*This* is what loving you does to me. I used to be calm, collected, the embodiment of gentlemanly *savoir-faire,* unruffled, unflappable—*always* in control!"

With one shove, he sent the chair sliding from between them. Eyes flaring wide, Antonia took a step back—Philip caught her by the elbows and pulled her hard against him. "*This* is what loving you does to me."

On the words, he kissed her—parting her lips, possessing her senses, demanding, commanding, letting passion have its say. He felt her sink against him, felt her surrender to the power that held them both, held them fast in its silken web, a web stronger than any man would willingly admit. Drawing back, he spoke against her lips. "Damn it—you could have been *killed.* I would have gone mad."

"Would you?" The words came on a breathy whisper.

Philip groaned. "Completely." He kissed her again, revelling in the feel of her as she pressed against him, soft warm curves fitting snugly against his much harder form, promising all manner of prospective delights. He felt desire, warm and unrestrained, rise strongly within her. Satisfied, he drew back, unable to resist dropping kisses on her eyelids and forehead.

"You're lucky the others were here when I caught up with you." His voice had deepened to a raspy growl. "I spent the last two miles thinking about putting you over my knee and ensuring you wouldn't sit any box-seat for at least the next month."

Adrift on a sea of happiness with no horizon in sight, Antonia sighed happily. "You wouldn't."

"Probably not," Philip temporised. "But it was a comforting thought at the time."

A gentle smile on her lips, Antonia drew his head back to hers and kissed him. "I promise to behave in future. I take leave to remind you this outing wasn't my idea."

"Hmm." Lifting his head, Philip studied her face. "Be that as it may, I plan on using this transgression of yours— your flight into the night—to call an abrupt halt to this peculiar hiatus of ours."

"Oh?"

"Indeed." His lips curved. "I've something of a reputation for extracting the greatest benefit from unexpected situations."

Antonia looked her question.

Philip wondered if she knew how innocent she looked. His smile twisted then fled; gently taking her face between his hands, he gazed deeply into her gold-green eyes. "I need you, my love. Despite the fact you'll turn me—my life, my emotions—upside down, I want no other." He smiled faintly. "You imagined yourself as my comfortable wife— that was impossible from the outset and I knew it." His lips twisted wryly. "It simply took me a while to acknowledge the inevitable."

His expression sobering, he held her gaze steadily. He spoke slowly, intently, his voice deep and low. "But all that's behind us—our future together starts here, now. We're already married in our hearts—married in all ways bar two. I propose we rectify that situation forthwith. We'll spend the night here—" Philip's hands shook slightly; he willed them still, unaware his gaze had darkened dramatically. The planes of his face hardened as he searched Antonia's eyes. "Don't ask me to let you go tonight. I've waited for weeks to make you mine."

He was confounded by her smile, a bewitching, beguiling, very gentle siren's smile. "I've been waiting—" Antonia declared, her voice soft, serene, her eyes meeting his directly. "I think for years—for you to do just that."

Desire bucked; Philip dragged in a shuddering breath. Very conscious of his limitations, he directed a warning glance at her. "If you could refrain from doing anything *too* encouraging, I'd be grateful."

She shot him a mischievous glance—Philip saw the teasing glint he loved in her eyes. The sight made him groan—just the thought of what it might mean if she brought her usual, questing mind to bear in that arena too, threatened his already overtried control.

Antonia stretched up; shifting his hands to her waist, Philip held her back. "We'll go directly to town tomorrow, given we have my phaeton. We'll stop at Ruthven House so you can change and pick up anything you want, then go straight on to the Manor. We can be married in a few days." He paused to draw breath, then forced himself to add, "Or wait the usual three weeks—whichever you prefer."

Antonia studied his face, his eyes, then raised one brow in open speculation. "I think I'll reserve my decision—until tomorrow." She smiled, and pressed closer. "Tonight, after all, might influence my conclusion."

Philip closed his eyes and groaned. "Is that an invitation or a threat?"

"Both."

Antonia reached up, twining her arms about his neck, stretching up to kiss him, letting her lips, her body, make her promises, purposely inviting, then inciting him to take all she had—all she was.

He did, kissing her until she was breathless, witless, filled with an unnameable longing, before tumbling her into the billows of the bed. Slowly, leisurely, he divested her of her clothes. Passion burned freely within her; she felt neither the chill of the air nor any lingering restraint.

Inevitable, he had termed it; as she lay back against the pillows and waited for him to join her, Antonia felt the rightness, the unquestionable truth, of his words. This had been destined to be. From the first.

Then he returned to her, taking her in his arms, wrapping her in a cocoon of warm desire, sating her senses with delight. The night spun about them, a wild kaleidoscope of stars and suns set spinning by passion's hand.

He held her tight, guiding her through the whirling of their senses, holding her steady, safe in his arms. He conducted her through a landscape she had never known existed, guiding her unerringly through each deepening layer of intimacy until they came together, as it was always meant to be, the ease of old friendship and long-standing love investing each caress with a significance far greater than its physical form.

Later, wrapped in the warm haven of his arms, settled against the heat of him, delicious languor in every limb, she felt his lips at her temple. The words he murmured were so low, she only just caught them.

"Tonight, tomorrow—and forever."

The note of finality in his voice set the seal on her happiness. Buoyed on its swell, Antonia slept.

Philip woke the next morning to the distracting sensation of a warm, curvaceous, silk-encased form snuggled into his side. As the silk in question was his wife-to-be's skin, his reaction was instantaneous. He glanced at her—but all he could see was a mass of golden curls fanned out on the pillow. Raising his brows, he considered his next move— and recalled a few loose ends. Carefully, he eased from the bed.

Dressing quickly, he left Antonia slumbering while he went downstairs.

He returned twenty minutes later, having dispatched the Countess's gig along with various missives, some rather longer than others, back to Ticehurst Place, only to discover Antonia still hidden beneath the covers. With a rakish grin, Philip shrugged out of his coat.

He was pulling off his shirt when he heard rustling from the bed. Looking up, he watched as Antonia blinked awake. She saw him; her lips curved in a sleepy, sated, gloriously happy smile.

Philip felt his lips curve in automatic response. Dropping the shirt on a chair, he walked to the side of the bed, his hands at his waistband.

It took a moment for Antonia's mind to clear enough to realise his clothes were coming off, rather than going on. "What are you doing?" With an effort, she tugged her gaze all the way up to his face.

His smile made her toes curl. "I thought," he said, raising a brow in the way only he could, "that I should attend to our unfinished business without delay."

Her mind still dimmed by the aftereffects of the long night, Antonia could not divine what he meant. "I thought," she said, trying to frown as he lifted the covers and slid in beside her, "that we'd concluded things quite satisfactorily." Nagging uncertainty made her add, "Didn't we?"

His laugh was as devilish as his look.

"Indubitably." Philip rolled her into his arms, settling her against him. "However, as we have a little time, I thought it might be wise to grasp the opportunity to…" His lips trailed down her throat. "Get in a little extra persuasion—just to help you make up your mind."

"My mind?" Antonia wasn't sure it was functioning at all. "On what matter?" Her memory tended to stall, fixed on certain memorable moments of the previous evening, all the rest merging into a less interesting background haze.

"On whether we should marry sooner—" Philip bent his head to place a kiss on one pert nipple "—or later." He transferred his attention to its twin, hiding a smug grin when Antonia shifted restlessly against him.

"Ah…" Antonia tried very hard to think. "I don't believe I've yet made up my mind." As his hands fastened on her soft flesh, she was suddenly very sure of her answer. Moistening her lips, she glanced down and found Philip's eyes. "Maybe you'd better persuade me a bit more?"

Philip's eyes gleamed. "That, my love, is precisely my intention."

They returned to Ruthven House late that afternoon. Carring opened the door; Philip smiled, openly smug, when he saw his major-domo blink. A blink from Carring was the equivalent of an openmouthed stare from less controlled mortals.

With a laughing smile, Antonia hurried upstairs, as eager as he to be on their way home—to the Manor, where they both belonged. Her smile hadn't faded all morning—he'd enjoyed every minute of the time he had invested putting it on her face.

His own smile reflected his satisfaction as he stood in his hall and watched her disappear up the stairs.

"And the wedding, my lord—if I might make so bold as to enquire?"

Philip glanced at Carring. "Miss Mannering and I have reached a mutual understanding. We'll be married as soon as can be arranged."

Carring's smile held a reciprocating smugness Philip wasn't at all sure he understood.

"Very good, my lord," Carring intoned. "Might I request to be apprised of the date on which the nuptials will be celebrated?"

Philip fought a frown. "Why?"

"With your permission, my lord, I'd like to close the

house on that day—so the staff can travel to the Manor to be on hand to tender their wishes to you and your lady.''

Philip raised his brows. ''If they wish it, by all means.''

''Rest assured, my lord, we will certainly be there.'' Magisterially ponderous, Carring headed for the baize door. ''Indeed, I have long looked forward to throwing rice at your wedding.''

The baize door swung closed before Philip could think of a suitable reply. Eyes narrowed, he glared at the door—and wondered how good Carring's aim might be.

Antonia's breathless return distracted him; he forgot the matter entirely—until the moment, three days hence, when, with Antonia radiant on his arm, he left the safety of the door of the local church to brave a positive hail of rice.

One particular handful hit him on the back of his head; the grains quickly slid down beneath the folds of his cravat.

Philip swore beneath his breath. He wriggled his shoulders to no avail. Glancing back, he searched the crowd—and located Carring, a wide grin on his face.

An answering grin transformed Philip's face. The carriage, bedecked with flowers, stood before them. He pulled Antonia to him; to the cheers of their well-wishers, he kissed her soundly, then lifted her up to the carriage.

Carring, as always, had had the last word; as he followed his wife into the carriage, Philip decided he didn't care in the least.

He glanced at Antonia, gloriously happy as she waved to their friends.

She was the wife he wanted, the wife he needed—not the comfortable wife she had thought to be but one to keep him on his toes.

Smiling proudly, Philip settled back against the squabs, his gaze firmly fixed on his wife.

His thirty-fifth year would be one he'd remember; he was, he discovered, looking forward, not just to the next, but to all the rest of his life.

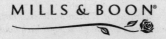

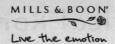

PENNINGTON

BOOK TWELVE

Available from 4th June 2004

*Available at most branches of WHSmith, Tesco, Martins, Borders,
Eason, Sainsbury's and most good paperback bookshops.*